Where Wolves Dream

A Novel

Armand Nassery

Where Wolves Dream

A Novel

By
Armand Nassery

Copyright © 2010 Armand Nassery

ISBN: 0984833609

ISBN-13: 978-0984833603

LCCN: 2010918095

DEDICATION

To my daughter, Sara. The color of her eyes and

the perfume of her hair keep me living and dreaming.

To all the women in my life,

who loved me and never needed to.

To my mother, as she is an eternal victim...

To my talented Wolves brothers who dreamed...

To my friends who had the privilege of facing a firing squad.

To Iraq.

To America.

And all the souls within.

ACKNOWLEDGMENTS

My gratitude goes to my brilliant and loving brother Dr. Ashraf,

as he is the Theo to my Van Gogh.

To Jeannie Mussa,

as she is and always will be my true friend through thick and thin.

To Dawn Bergom,

who kept me going through days of despair.

My thanks to my talented editor Lindsay Welbers who worked
Tirelessly to finish this novel.

CONTENTS

BALLURIA

Balluria existed long before the world was created.

Balluria was born from the seeds of the prehistoric lust of dying kings who were infatuated by exuberant colors of life spreading their shades on the young Arab women's cheeks. And by the temptations of hidden desires in their eyes, the inviting moves of their hips, and the distinctive yet mysterious perfumes of their long clips of deceiving black hair with ends that traveled to a place far beyond where the senses of men ended and surrendered.

Balluria was a lonesome tree watered by the drops of pouring manhood from the rugged men of the Arabian Sahara. Men who willingly traveled the dimensions of being, searching for the mirage shores of true love and manhood satisfaction.

Balluria is a lonesome tree that withstood time, watered by the pearly drops of sweat of its beautiful young women as they lay in the long hot nights of the Arabian Sahara, yearning for the touch of a true lover that probably would never come.

Balluria was a vision that infatuated many braves, who wasted their lives in chasing that vision only to find it was just a dream of an old Gypsy witch who lived in the white palace that stands on a chicken leg.

Balluria was born at the intersection of the dustiest roads in the history of the universe, where dust blew for eternity. Magnificent dust that covered not only faces and eyelashes, but also prevented the truth from being revealed. The persistent and everlasting dust calmly settled in the miniature mud mountains by the roots of palm trees and the mud empires of ants and the falling dates.

Balluria blossomed in tales of love, poetry, pain, sadness, and despair.

Balluria survived on the endless journeys of its sons to the other places in the world. And as far as they've gone, they've always come back, wounded and spent, asking for forgiveness and redemption and a peaceful death and a quiet burial in the cemetery of all mankind.

Balluria is the peak of manhood and the stench of adulthood streamed from the sweaty veins of hard labor and unbearable livelihood.

Balluria is feminism at its flimsiest state of self-ratification and the ravenous hunger for human touch manifested in unique dancing of its daughters as they reveal their true identities as mixtures of women, snakes, and female wolves.

Balluria is a river, and its water is the unmistakable contrast of a light blue mixture created by the dark soil of the Euphrates and magnificent red oozing from the internal wounds of its sons. They are the soldiers of eternal deceptions and the bloody unfortunate revolutions.

Balluria is an artwork and architectural masterpiece built by all the greedy and sinful ancient empires, the houses painted in a color that is unknown to mankind.

Balluria drank the blood of the Romans, Persians, Mongols, Turks, English, and Americans, and it drank from rivers of the blood of its own natives, but it was never satisfied.

Balluria is the ancient town of ultimate mirages that deceived all of those who passed through these parts in their eternal search for the true fountains of youth, desire, and wealth.

Balluria is a crossroad. All of those searching for the invisible line of ancestry shared the ultimate grandfather, the divine breeder.

Balluria was divinely born on the steps of the ancient ruins of the temple of one true prophet who was willing to sacrifice his own son for the satisfaction of the true, invisible God.

No one will ever understand the remarkable patience, the ability of Balluria and its inhabitants to wait lifetime after lifetime without knowing if they would ever stop coming to Balluria.

All the passersby had carried something with them from Balluria, something that will last a lifetime and will be passed to their offspring.

Was it a dream? A sin? Love?

Or a mere emotional artifact?

Since the beginning of time all passersby left Balluria with no regrets, no feelings of victory or defeat. Finally they accepted, cherished, and loved the idea of wasting their lifetimes in Balluria.

Because deep in their hearts, they all knew that they had been deceived. They had been lied for and lied to, in the long and endless wait for the ultimate truth.

The only truth they will ever find is that it is fate to be deceived by Balluria. For all passersby, it is fate to love Balluria. It is fate to hate Balluria. And it is fate to believe what has been written on thousands of ancient stones and secret books and translated to the curvy lines of henna painted on the delicate hands of Gypsy dancers willingly cheated out of a lifetime just like all the inhabitants of Balluria since the beginning of time

The Book of the Gypsy Witches

Chicago–Balluria

1

Deep inside her heart, Emily was looking for approval from her family. Even though she had no doubt that her love and commitment for her husband were true and genuine, she asked herself many times about the matter and tested her feelings. After so many years, she still felt the delicious tingle in her toes whenever she kissed him or he kissed her. She always thought of him as a dreamer with a heart of gold. As for her family, only her father showed his unlimited support and approval. Her relationship with Salam created a problem of discomfort and chatter among her family members and the circle of family friends. When she met him, he was unemployed. He had just finished his Master's degree in art history, a degree that looked more like a felony than an achievement on the header of a resume. Though he had been painting diligently for years, not one of his paintings had sold for more than five hundred dollars. Other than self-portraits and murals that had kept him afloat when Emily met him, Salam was almost penniless all the time. Yet, he had a charming personality and lacked the Middle Eastern inescapable sarcasm and the "know it all" demeanor. Also, Salam rarely talked about politics or Arab-Israeli issues. He hated politics and conflicts, as he knew they were lost causes. They depressed him and seemed a waste of time since they were never resolved.

They had begun dating shortly after meeting five years earlier. The start of their relationship was rocky and undirected, but slowly Emily became Salam's most steadfast supporter and confidante, and he found it difficult to be without Emily in his life. They dated exclusively for a year when one day he asked her hypothetically if she would marry him if he were to ask her to.

"Are you going to ask me?" she prodded.

"I am just asking...what if?"

He was sure that he wanted to marry her, he was sure that he loved her somehow. Although he knew that he was not in love with her, he knew that his feelings toward Emily were not pure love; they were mixed emotions of love, need, and yearning—yearning that he could not shake off whenever she was not there with him. He yearned for her smell and her presence next to him, he felt complete and secure whenever she held his arm as they walked together on Michigan Avenue and he felt a delicious sense of warmth whenever she laid her head on his shoulder when they watched movies in the Piper's Alley Theatre on North Avenue. He never questioned her beauty as a woman; she was tall, slender with fair and clear skin, and had a dirty blond hair that went down lower than her shoulders, but he loved her eyes the most. They were green with a mysterious dark black circle around the pupils. He always looked at them and in them.

He stared at them longer than usual one time, and she asked, "Babe, why are you always looking in my eyes?"

"Just want to look at the mixture of green and black colors in them," he replied, justifying his stares with his abnormal infatuation with colors, and then he added, "I was looking for me in them." That was the truth; he was looking for himself in her eyes. Moreover, he was looking for a home in them; he had always searched for one since he left his family home when he was seventeen.

One cold February night, as the snow was falling outside, he put his face on her chest and slept, smelling the mixture of her natural scent and the vanilla-scented lotion she used on her skin. He felt at peace. He left the window open to let the oxygen in and watched the moon as he fell asleep.

Later he wrote in a notebook that she inspires him to keep painting.

"February was cold in Chicago, but the moon was bright and complete. It looked like the moon in the desert, and the cool breeze from the window felt like it was coming from another world. Last night I knew that I loved Emily. Last night Emily introduced me to the vanilla scent."

He wanted to use the way he felt as the subject for a painting that he would give to her one day to show her how he felt about her, but he never did. The feeling of incomplete, perfect true love prevented him from doing so.

After that brief and incomplete talk about the marriage proposal, the two were lost in the eternal abyss of Western society's endless search for hidden simple pleasures and rightful arrangements. One night, at the bar they frequented on Clark Street, they initiated their ultra-righteous partnership, as he always referred to their marriage. A few days before that he asked David, his only friend, whom he met at an anarchist party in a basement of a run-down bar on Milwaukee Avenue, what he thought was the best way to propose marriage to a woman.

David, with his own proclaimed school of life philosophy, claimed that marriage was overrated. "It's like an open-door prison with a lot of paperwork, and why do you want to enter a prison of your own free will? I will be single forever," he concluded.

David was not stingy with his strange ideas, or his assistance, when he was asked to do something. With his hippie-like appearance and beliefs, undirected train of thought, and enjoyable personality, David was not the ideal consoler to his friend Salam. David never gave him one answer that made sense, and this lack of coherence made Salam ask him the same questions many times over.

"Are you sure you are American? I mean do you have any Middle Eastern blood in you?" Salam asked.

"If you think Jewish is Middle Eastern," David replied.

Despite their many differences, the two men had become close friends since they met with common ideals and beliefs in socialism, self-acceptance, and love for art and alcohol, which made them the only close friends of each other. Although David smoked marijuana like he smoked cigarettes and Salam did not, the two always managed to get along. Regardless of his endless inhaling of hemp and his extraordinary love for beer, David could be surprisingly sober and sharp with answers and comments when he wanted to be. It was a Thursday evening as the two men sat in the Lebanese diner on Lincoln Avenue, David's favorite place to satisfy what he called "ultimate munchies." Salam was waiting for ideas of an appropriate marriage proposal from David, who was chain-smoking his cigarettes and started coaching his friend about the best way to propose to a woman.

"Listen, man, you know what I think I would do if Amy might accept my marriage proposal, if I ever actually considered getting married?" David said, as he ate hastily.

"What?" Salam asked.

"First I would get high and take her to Joliet, Illinois. They have skydiving joint there, and we would both jump. In different parachutes, with me controlling both parachutes or the release or whatever they call it, and we would be connected by radio or a walkie-talkie. Then I would propose to her there in the sky, as we faced death in the sky...she would say yes. Guaranteed. What do you think?" David asked.

"David, I am terrified of heights, and I don't think Emily would go skydiving. Besides, I think you are a very manipulative person, and what if Amy said no?" Salam asked.

"I would just open the parachute for myself and let her free fall...hahaha," David laughed and concluded, "And with the weight of her ass, it would be a very fast free fall."

"You are sick," Salam replied with a frustrated smile.

"Oh, come on, man...think about it...I mean that's like so romantic. That's like Romeo and Juliet...and it will be in Joliet, Illinois...hahahaha." David continued laughing with his deep and scratchy voice.

"OK, Romeo...another idea?" Salam asked.

"You are the artist, man. I mean you can come up with something creative, plus Emily is not like any other woman. At least she is not like all the airheads I hang out with. So, I don't think she would like any of my ideas of a proposal," David said as he downed his entire glass of Guinness.

Later that evening, they linked up with Emily, Amy, Julia, and Julia's boyfriend Russell. Salam waited until the annoying live band was between songs at the John Barleycorn Pub in Lakeview, and he quietly asked Emily, "Emily, how would you like me to propose to you?"

Emily, with her irresistible charm, smiled and said, "You are a dork...just ask me..." Then with a devilish gleam, "Or, you know what," she said.

"What?" Salam asked.

"You have to kneel with flowers and an expensive ring in your hand...a twenty-carat diamond ring."

Salam thought that she was serious, so he said he had to go to the men's room and signaled to David to follow him because he wanted to ask him about how big a twenty-carat ring was and how much it would cost, but David was too wasted to notice or to understand the signal and sat nodding in apparent acknowledgement. As Salam waited impatiently for David in the men's room, Julia asked Emily what Salam said to her before unceremoniously rushing off. Emily told her. Julia had no patience with waiting for a gentle resolution, so with her ferocious ways of settling things, especially after a few drinks, she climbed to where the band was getting ready to play the next song and snatched the microphone from the lead singer before he could sing a note. Into the microphone she said, "Excuse me, everyone, we have something special for you." Not everyone in the bar paid attention, but most of the patrons tilted their heads, looking for an exciting announcement.

"Two people here are just about to be hitched...I mean get married, but the man, just like any man, does not know how he should propose, so I will do the honors because he is just like all men, a chicken," Julia said.

Woo hoos and boos began rising from all corners of the bar...

Salam realized that something was happening outside the bathroom door as he heard Julia's voice on the microphone, but he was more intrigued with all of the classified ads and phone numbers written on the bathroom door, all of the straight and gay sex invitations and political and philosophical statements, which were written with a strange perseverance and clarity.

What a freedom wall this is, Salam thought to himself, completely oblivious that just outside that door his future was being not-so-gently directed.

Julia continued her announcement, even with Emily's signals and pleading to stop embarrassing her...

"Here he is, ladies and gentlemen. Here is the man of the hour," Julia's voice echoed as Salam walked out of the men's room having given up on David following him.

He looked around and realized that everyone in the bar was looking at him.

"Can you come up here, please?" Julia asked him.

He looked at Emily as he walked toward her, looking for salvation from Julia's wrath. She smiled at him and joined the crowd in cheering, letting him fall in the trap of innovative drunkenness and the joyful gathering of strangers.

He walked toward the small stage. He pushed the long curl on his forehead backward and stood closer to Julia as the cheering of the crowd grew louder.

"You are cute. You want to marry me?" one woman shouted from the dark end of the bar. Laughs and cheers covered the comments Julia was trying to make.

The earth felt like it was turning underneath him. He was never as embarrassed as he was at that moment, but he completely surrendered himself and his destiny to Julia in hopes that she would have an iota of mercy in her Irish heart. She did not. Julia grabbed his hand and said, "Come closer, you big dork...and testify!" He smiled nervously, not knowing what to say.

"Come on you...dark-haired...wherever you are from, just say it...say it like you mean it...tell that woman over there that you love her." He looked at Emily, wondering if she planned this...with the help of David, he suspected...but what the hell, he thought, it's either submit or prepare for more creative comments from Julia. He leaned toward the microphone, looking to Emily for support as he bared his soul publicly.

Emily looked at him with anticipation and acceptance that allowed him to calmly and clearly say, "I love you, Emily. I love you very much," he assured her, hoping that was the end of that show, as the crowd cheered and whistled, with shouts of "yeah" coming from invisible strangers hidden by the haloed colorful lights and smoke.

Julia, feeling the rush of impending victory, pressed forward on her campaign. "And you will tell her that you want to marry her...plain and simple...just because you are a man...or a chicken that is afraid of commitment...Like all men, so it's your choice. Honey, are you a man or a chicken?" Julia asked as she drained the last drop of Middle Eastern dignity out of Salam.

"Be a man, and say no!" One man shouted...cheers from the men rose from across the bar.

"Say it... says it!" chanted a group of middle-aged women, soccer moms.

He had hoped for a more civilized and merciful setting, not this Viking-like melee. At this point, David's skydiving idea was beginning to sound almost rational, but it was too late now, not because of Julia, but because of Emily. He looked at Emily and realized that his fear of commitment was neither her fault nor her reward at this devilish setting that Julia's brain had created. Nevertheless, it was Emily who would suffer from whatever his next action or words would be, and it was time for him to stand by her as she had relentlessly stood by him for the last five years. For better or worse, come rain or shine..."OK...OK," he told himself.

"Emily, I love you. Can you marry me?" he proposed with a firm quiet voice.

"It is WILL you marry me, you idiot!" Julia screamed with laughter.

"Say it right...hahaha," Julia added.

"OK...Will you marry me?" Salam said with the same tone.

Julia then unceremoniously snatched the microphone from him and ran toward where Emily was standing next to David, Amy, and Russell, by the bar corner close to the door.

"What is your answer, young lady...?"

Julia asked Emily as many women and men were shouting, "Yes! Yes! Yes! Yes!"

Emily gently took the microphone from her over energized friend. The crowd slowly grew silent in anticipation of her answer and she said..."I love you, and yes, I will marry you." She spoke with a sincere conviction and arrested voice, as if she just had a stone removed from her chest. She then walked like a trained actress with a simple and well-rehearsed role, toward the stage...waltzing to the synchronized shouts of the crowd...

"Kiss! Kiss! Kiss! Kiss!"

She climbed the stage, looked lovingly at Salam, and they kissed... a long and true kiss.

The crowd cheered as the two exited the stage hand in hand, and the manger announced that drinks were on the house for the group of friends. The rest of the patrons went back to their private parties, except for the group of middle-aged women who came to where the group was standing. They hugged Emily and Salam and wished them happiness.

"That was so cool," one woman said.

"That was so romantic... you guys are so cute... you will make a great couple," another woman commented.

He noticed that Emily was looking at him, trying to make sure he meant what he said instead of simply bowing to Julia's unstoppable power of making people do strange things by the force of public humiliation and her self-given right of manipulative exposure and invasion of private lives and secrets. She was looking for the right proposal from him...quietly... and he was not slow to assure her as he read the wondering in her eyes. He leaned and whispered in her ear, "Emily, you are beautiful. I truly love you, and I want to marry you."

She smiled and kissed him and whispered in his ear, "I've always loved you and always will. Yes, I will marry you."

To him and to her, this whispered admonition was more exciting and honest than Julia's drunken carnival. But the two events linked them, and the rest of the patrons, to an unforgettable night with unbreakable vows of partnership that withstood differences they never seemed to understand or care about as they had never felt the need to ever address them. They always had an unspoken agreement to talk about finer things in life like art, movies, places, or books instead of having to waste a single moment of their lives discussing the differences between East and West; black and white; Islam, Christianity, and Judaism; soccer and football; man and woman; or right and wrong. They just thought or believed that in many ways it was a match made in heaven or at least on the way there.

"The only difference between us is that you are from the Midwest and I am from the Mideast," Salam had often said to Emily.

The two set the wedding date after he managed to give her the engagement ring that wiped out half of his savings account. They set the date of the wedding on the ninth of April, 2001.

"I hope it will not rain," Emily commented.

"April is my favorite month, and the ninth is my favorite day," Salam said, and Emily agreed because she had no significant day in mind.

Julia appointed herself as the wedding planner and the bride's maid of honor because Emily's only sister, Stephanie, did not make a clear commitment to attend the wedding. Reluctantly Emily accepted that Julia would be the maid of honor, hoping she would not do anything too outrageous. To her relief, Julia proclaimed that the wedding should be simple. In spite of this declaration by Julia, she was loaded with alcohol two hours before the wedding. She also insisted the night before the wedding to have the bachelorette party at Barleycorn. Both Salam and Emily agreed, remembering Julia's unforgettable part in their marriage proposal at Barleycorn. The wedding was simple. They had the reception at the Botanic Garden, as she wanted, and they had a church wedding, as her family desired, and he kneeled and accepted the Catholic ceremony to make her happy. Unknown to their friends and family, they also met secretly three days before with a very thin sheikh who married them in an Islamic ceremony. Emily did not mind wearing the scarf and saying the ritual in Arabic, especially the part where she said, "I accept."

Salam looked at her with eyes full of love and admiration as she sang it in Arabic with her sweet American voice.

"Na'am."

He felt obligated to be a real husband, an Arab-Iraqi husband who would defend his wife's honor until death and all of the other responsibilities of providing and taking care of a household, which, in a way, filled him with strange joy, fake courage, and inescapable anxiety. Her parents, who helped greatly with the wedding expenses, had flown in from Youngstown, Ohio, and were extremely gracious. Her father, who was warm and genuine, joked with his new son-in-law about what number in his harem his daughter would be, ending his joke with, "As long as she is number one and only in your harem, or I will kick your ass...hahaha."

Many other family members he met for the first time at the wedding were filed under the first-timer and one-timer categories in the book of their lives. Most of them would always remain as one-timers, Salam thought to himself. Surprisingly, Stephanie called one day before the wedding and said that she would attend the wedding. On the wedding day, Stephanie, who had never kept a commitment in her life, flew from New York. She was on her seventh boyfriend after breaking up with Dutch Karl a couple years earlier. Now she was into Buddhism, and her new faith had overshadowed her behavior more than her involvement with politics and feminism. She also had gained a little weight, and she was thinking seriously of leaving New York and going to live in India or Morocco or...

"Wherever, as long as I don't have to ride the trains every day in order to breathe freely," Stephanie said without offering any explanation of her decision.

Over all, everything went as planned with the help of David, Amy, Julia, and Russell who was forced into the lineup of the groomsmen with a decree from Julia. At the end of the night, Amy and David, who were too drunk to drive, drove the newlyweds to O'Hare, to catch a flight to Acapulco for their honeymoon. Salam wanted to go to Morocco and Emily wanted to go to Hawaii, but they were going to Acapulco since they had received the Acapulco vacation package as a wedding gift from Emily's grandmother. Because he was practically broke, their vacation decisions remained open ended. The community college he was teaching at had reduced his hours by almost half due to class reductions and budgeting. This reduction in income was explained to him with the usual reasons that he never understood.

"Republicans in the White House," was how the long-haired, bearded, communist-wannabe dean put it. The minimal sales, and sometimes no sales, of his paintings for months did not help his financial situation.

The first year of their marriage was uneventful, except for the time when he received an invitation from the famous art dealer, Roger Goldstein, who later became a very close friend of the couple and a vital supporter of Salam and an enthusiast of his art. Later Salam found a very good real estate deal, both price and location wise. Emily was so excited because it was her way of showing her family that they were on their way to a serious and secure future. She was in her last year of residency at Evanston Hospital. Compared to her fellow students, she was going to be an older doctor. She was thirty-three, having spent her later twenties searching for a career path. Emily had given up on the corporate world when she broke up with her last boyfriend, Josh, who was also her boss. For a complete change of pace she took and passed the MCAT and attended Loyola medical school. At the age of thirty-one, she graduated.

Five years before that, she and Salam met at a small party gathering at her friend, Kimberly's house. He talked to her briefly that night, and later that week Kimberly called her to ask if she was interested in going to the movies with her and Salam. The three went to Piper's Alley Theatre and watched a Turkish movie called *Hammam*, which means Turkish Bath. Emily liked the movie, which had been his choice, and they started dating after that. She never looked back, and to her that was a sign of real love and a true match. She liked his directness and genuine sense of humor, his long hair, and scruffy looks. Most of all, she liked knowing that he had been alone for a long time, misunderstood most of the time, yet secure in his own existence and in his relationship with the world and with others.

One month into their relationship he asked her if he could paint her in the nude and she agreed. Later, he confessed to her that he had two reasons in mind to paint her in the nude; first, he wanted to see her naked, and second, he was wishing that she would sleep with him. She confessed to him that she would have slept with him, if he had asked her that night, but of course he did not, fearing she would be offended and stop seeing him, and they laughed about it.

After two months of convincing and a solid commitment to repay the loan that Emily's father had given them for the down payment for the house, they bought a two-story building on Grand Avenue. The couple converted the first floor into a magnificent setting of art and music: a hangout place using his design, David and Julia's free labor, and Emily's impeccable attention to detail and money management. David and Julia helped graciously, and Emily kept a nonstop supply of food and drinks coming. Even with the stream of gifts and advice coming in from Emily's family, nothing meant more to her than knowing that Salam drew the entire structure on a piece of paper and told his wife, "This is our home, for the next ten years at least. Let me know what you want to change or what you want to add."

She did not change or add anything...because she very much liked what he drew and was looking forward to the final product. Within two months, they managed to rehabilitate the two-story building into a beautiful art studio and a living loft. Their best friends became like furniture. David routinely showed up for one reason or another, and Julia decided the layout made a perfect party location and managed to host many of her nonstop parties at their place. Sometimes they had to say no and draw the line, because having two or three parties a week was a little bit too much.

2

It was shortly after nine o'clock in the morning as he and Emily drove to Evanston Hospital. Salam had begun to drive her to work every day since they started living together, long before they got married. This drive was a duty that he never complained about no matter the weather, traffic, or earliness of the hour. He never wanted to stop driving her to work. It was their time that no one could intrude upon.

"Mornings are too important in a human's life and too beautiful to waste in sleep. They need not be wasted on the most disturbing part of making a living, which includes running after trains and walking like zombies to work with coffee in one hand and a handbag in the other," he told his wife. "We can have a good cup of coffee and listen to music or the world news, and at the same time, we can observe our surroundings and the people from a very warm place in the winter and air-conditioning in the summer."

She did not mind at all, as he sat in the passenger seat while she drove. That was the arrangement going to work, and he would drive back. He turned on the radio; there was something wrong about that particular morning. The couple noticed that more than one police car was speeding eastward on Grand Avenue, toward the downtown area. Something was not right, or at least not normal...

"Is it a fire?" Salam asked.

"I don't know," Emily said.

They noticed that all of the pedestrians were talking on the phone...All of them. He turned the radio to their favorite station, Chicago Public Radio, WBEZ. They heard a familiar voice talking about a tower falling down and the other burning. They did not understand what he was talking about, and then Emily's phone rang. Emily answered it while driving. It was Julia screaming on the other end.

"Hey, Julia," Emily said with a calming voice that had no effect on the overanxious Julia.

Julia's voice came from another world; she was more frantic than usual.

"You're kidding me," said Emily. "Oh, my God...you're kidding me...no way...oh, my God!"

Salam waited patiently for her to tell him what that was all about. She kept saying, "Oh, my God...Are you OK...Julia, did you call your parents? Oh, my God!"

He looked at her. She looked at him with a weary gaze as she tried to finish her call with Julia and safely maneuver in traffic.

"OK, sweetie, please do...and tell them I said hi...I will...OK...bye."

She hung up her phone and looked at him with accusing eyes, "They attacked the World Trade Center in New York."

Without asking who attacked the World Trade Center, he looked at her, questioning the accusing look in her eyes that demanded an explanation. Deep in his heart, he knew who attacked the World Trade Center. Who else would attack the World Trade Center, other than his people, the Arabs or the Muslims?

"The terrorists hijacked planes and flew them into the World Trade Center. Almost ten thousand people are dead," Emily said as she tried to appear calm and neutral.

Who else would hijack planes full of people and fly them into buildings full of people to prove a point, whatever that point might be? He took the phone from her hand and turned the radio volume louder, as they were passing under Michigan Avenue, making their way to Lake Shore Drive. The public radio announcer was the calmest among those on all the radio stations that day.

The ride to Evanston Hospital was longer this time. For some reason, he felt that she had suddenly become distant and untrusting. He felt that she wanted to say something or many things, and wanted to ask many questions and demand many answers. She wanted explanations for herself. She wanted to use this as a defense mechanism to the chain of effects that she could see, coming their way, of the many accusing and unforgiving eyes and words of her friends, family, and colleagues at her job who knew that she was married to a Middle Easterner or a Muslim or an Arab, let alone an Iraqi. Salam kept silent. During his silence, Emily realized that she had overreacted and had wordlessly connected the Salam she loved to something truly heinous. Throughout the ride, she knew he was worried. When they arrived at the hospital, he jumped out of the car to take her place in the driver's seat. She grabbed her bag and opened the door. They met as she exited the car; they met with their hearts in their eyes and the uncertain feelings of that moment. This was that key moment where the right words could salvage their world, and the wrong ones could tear it apart. She was the first to speak.

"Are you OK, babe?"

"No," he answered. "I am worried."

"About what?" she asked.

He did not want to go back to the accusing looks he felt back in the car. He wanted to hang on to the threads of truth he had known for the past five years with her.

"About what this thing will do to the world... and to us."

She wanted to assure him and herself that the world was the world's own thing and their world was theirs alone, and that the two did not tango.

"We will be just fine... I love you."

She wrapped her arms around him and kissed him. He kissed her back with a strange force. He needed that warmth... to ease his fear or fears. He kissed her and did not want to let go... then he did.

"You know..." he called as she was walking away.

She looked back.

"What, honey?"

"This morning when you told me about what happened, it was the first time in years... that I felt... that I was an Arab all over again."

She did not understand the reference, or maybe she did. Her smile was strained as she made her way into the hospital. He got into the dark green Land Rover and tried to avoid looking at the people in the other cars. He was hurrying back to the studio. Although he had nothing to do, he just wanted to close the doors and stay inside, light the fireplace, and not leave all day, maybe all week, or maybe forever. All he needed was some alcohol for company, and he would be just fine. He called David, who was watching the only subject covered on television that day, and asked him if he could pick up some beer and whisky and come to the studio.

David, with his untimely yet daring humor, said, "I don't know, dude, if hanging out with you today is a good thing. Man, you know what I mean?"

"David, don't be an ass."

Salam's tension must have seeped into his voice, making David realize that his usual smart-ass approach was not appropriate. "Yeah, sure, man. I will be there... Heinekens ha... OK. Will be there within an hour or so," David said.

They spent the day inside watching television and eating leftovers from Julia's last theme party, the Irish Nirvana, which was basically a cuisine made of spiced Irish food, if there is such a thing. It was, at least, tolerable and edible. The two men munched as they sat and watched television and talked about possibilities, theories, and conspiracies. They talked about Osama bin Laden and al-Qaeda. They talked about Saddam Hussein and Iraq. They talked about history and the link between oil cartels and royal families and all the secret and weird relationships and connections of all the secret organizations that may exist, but no one really knew.

David liked five things in life: living in a capitalist society without actually working, food that he did not have to pay for or prepare, women, politics, and imbibing in alcohol and marijuana. Even after these recent worldwide traumatic events, he stated that he would not change his way of living or his way of thinking until his glorious death. Others were rushing to join the armed service or donate blood because they felt helpless to change the situation, so they gave the only thing they knew to give. David felt no such compulsion to improve himself or the world around him. He loved not working long hours; he loved existing without much effort to exist. He loved it because he wanted to prove his revolutionary theory of surviving in a capitalist system without working. There was never an event before the attacks of September eleventh that gave him the intense magnitude of material to discuss and to sound smart and intellectual about. He always reminded people that even the numbers sounded like a movie title.

He would say, "It's 9/11, like nine one one, the numbers people dial when they have an emergency."

Or he would ask, "Did you know that there were no windows on the planes that hit the towers?"

"If you look closely, did you know that if you fold a dollar bill in a certain way, you will see the two towers and the pentagon burning?" he would say while pulling a twenty-dollar bill out of his pocket and folding it in a certain way.

"It's all in the prophecies of Nostradamus," David would say, and he would go on and on whenever and with whomever.

A short while later, Emily decided to host a party to test the waters to see who their friends were. She never stated that her real reason for the party was to see how their friends were feeling about her husband. She wanted to know what they had to say and how they would react to the invitation. The idea for a party came to her when her mother called two days earlier asking how she was doing.

"I am fine, Mom."

Her mother asked about her husband. "Is he...?"

Emily said that they were both well and that nothing and no one was bothering them. However, her mother kept pressuring her about her husband. "Is he OK? Is he worried? Is he acting in a strange way?"

She did not drop the subject until Emily stopped her with a curt and determined voice.

"Mom, what is the problem? Is there something you want to say?"

Her mom did not want to take all the blame herself, so she ratted on everyone who put her up to the questioning.

"See, honey, you know your father's friend, Richard Zlotcik. He called your father and told him that we better make sure that our son in-law, your husband, is not a sleeping cell, or a member of some group... you..."

"A sleeping what?" Emily asked with barely repressed anger.

"A sleeping cell, like the one they talked about on television... you know..." Her mother's voice trailed off as she realized she might have pushed too far.

Emily had repressed a lot of anger in the last week or so. She had listened to colleagues, friends, and strangers talking about the events, and she did not associate herself with any of them because she knew that she was shielded with her own beliefs and her own way of explaining the unexplainable. She did that for a long time, and she was not about to go down in shame, so she let her mother have it.

"Mom! First of all, it's a sleeper cell, not a sleeping cell. Second of all, this is the last time you call me asking me these stupid questions about me and my husband. You know, I thought you were calling because you were worried about us. Then you tell me that Richard Zlotcik, that ignorant moron, had called you and Dad and convinced you guys to investigate us. What is your problem? You know... don't call here anymore unless... just don't call here."

The usually calm Emily was furious, but she never told Salam about her mother's phone call. She decided to throw a party instead, "to have some fun," as she said, and to ease the tension, as she did not say. Julia was the first to announce that she would come up with a theme for the party, and David was excited just because Kelly would be there. Kelly had just started working in the gallery as a part-time framer and assistant manager, a grocery getter, janitor, and coffee maker. She did things at her own pace, but she was helpful when she was needed, and that's what mattered most. The party was set for the twenty-fourth of September and went very well. It seemed like everyone had already forgotten about the events of the eleventh and looked toward the future, which seemed to promise an imminent war. Only David kept repeating like a crazy prophet...

"It's the ultimate bridge between the East and the West; it's the ultimate bridge."

No one really knew or cared about what he was saying. David himself did not care that night about his own words because he was trying to impress the not-so-focused Kelly and no one else. The party was Emily's way of saying to her friends, "If you have anything to say or if you want to say anything, say it now, and say it to our faces, not behind our backs." Luckily, none of their friends really had anything to say, nor were they thinking of anything to say, except for words of support to Salam. Even with the supportive environment, he felt cornered in his own home, because he was the only Arab among Americans, and the only Muslim among Christians and Jews. Little did he know that all of his insecurities were only the work of his worried mind. The party was a test, a test of true virtues, actions, and attitudes, and they all passed. Emily was relieved, and Julia's effort to find a theme for the party dwindled, as she found it difficult to find a suitable one. She just called it "The Party Where She Did Not Find Anyone to Take Home Because Everyone Was a Bore."

The party was an event to heal wounds... wounds that were real or imagined. No one at the party looked at him as though he knew something or knew someone who knew something. He concentrated on helping his wife and chatting with David. After that party, neither the couple nor their friends threw another party other than to occasionally hang out at a bar or at the gallery for some time. Large crowd gatherings had almost become a thing of the past as the country and the people around the world were waiting for the inevitable war. The news from the East and the many theories, conclusions, plans, and expectations presented an environment of an unstable march toward self-examination of values and standards that set the stage for many uncorrectable mishaps and many lasting atrocities.

Salam and Emily became like two estranged birds trying to sustain the most precious nest. They were protecting their souls, their home, and their marriage, their unity and their partnership, as they saw fit. It was during that time that she suggested they have a baby, a son or a daughter, that would strengthen their bond and unify them forever with blood, to share something ultra-earthly between them. He suggested waiting for better times... and more comfortable finances, or as he wanted to say, until he started making more money so she could stay home with the baby. As he thought that all women must do when they have children at least for the breast-feeding and early nursing period, even though he was not sure of his logic. He based his logic on a story he heard in his home country when he was young, a story of a child of a poor peasant who could not drink his mother's milk; that boy grew up to be estranged and prevented from love.

3

The first air strikes had begun, and the world would never be the same. The coalition forces had entered the Afghan war and pictures of long-haired, long-bearded Muslim men became the favorite theme of all magazine covers as the face of the enemy, and new names and realities were the daily bread for the world. This turn of events prompted Salam to shave his short goatee, but he left his long wavy hair alone. David spent much of his time at the recording studio, where he worked part time and sometimes slept. Then he showed up in the afternoons at the gallery with news and new conspiracy theories.

The two men went to a rally against the war in downtown Chicago. Salam was neither against nor for the war. He just went there to get out of the art studio and to meet people. Maybe he would meet an art dealer who could help him with the pile of paintings that had not moved in the last two months. He needed the money to give to Emily, who was struggling with student loans and everyday living expenses. He managed to pay almost half of their expenses, but he needed to pay more as the unwritten Middle Eastern husband doctrine dictates. At the rally, he was surprised when he saw that there was a large mix of people with diverse ethnicities, faiths, and backgrounds. They brought with them a message of unity and forgiveness. Every one of them hated President George W. Bush for one reason or another. It was a preemptive hate that he never understood. Suddenly, the crowd became larger and larger as almost two hundred people joined: whites, blacks, Hispanics, Asians, Christians, Jews, Muslims, and Arabs. All were "Americans" in his mind.

Many were wearing the Palestinian scarf or the PLO scarf in reference to the Palestine Liberation Organization, but one person was distinctively louder than the others and taller than most of her peers. She looked familiar. After a careful examination to be sure who she was, he shouted, "Stephanie...Stephanie."

Stephanie looked at him and waved as she kept screaming into her bullhorn, "And when do we want it? Now...now."

She handed the bullhorn to the person next to her and made her way toward where Salam and David stood. She looked thinner and pinker because of the cold. She wore a green jacket with jeans that had a multitude of colorful designs on them and a sweater with the scarf. She asked for a cigarette, which David was quick to offer.

"So this is the famous Stephanie," David said.

"How are you?" She hugged Salam and only looked at David. Salam kissed her on her cheek and said, "You remember David from the wedding; he is a friend of Emily's and mine. What are you doing here?"

"I don't know," Stephanie said with a wide and sincere smile. "I was in New York last night, and Jodi suggested we join a group of activists coming here for the march." She pushed a large cloud of smoke mixed with steam from the side of her mouth.

"Where is Jodi?" David asked.

Stephanie ignored David's question entirely and continued her conversation with Salam. "So how is my older sister? You guys still married, huh?"

"Yes... we are... it's only been seven months. Why don't you come to visit today?"

"I can't, babe. I am on caffeine, Red Bull, and weed. We are going back this afternoon, and there is another rally in Philly tomorrow, but listen, you tell her that I said hi and will call her. OK, can you give me one more cigarette... Danny?"

"It's David." David was not used to being so callously overlooked and the experience was making him angry.

"Here, you can have my pack," Salam said. "Do you need money?"

"No, I am OK. I mean I will be OK... thanks. Tell Emily I said hi and I will call her," she said as she disappeared in the crowd. She never called that day; it was almost a year later before she called.

He and David left the rally and headed back toward Emmitt's for a drink. David, who was still peeved at having been blown off so completely, commented, "With all due respect, your sister-in-law is some kind of a freaky bitch."

Salam's only response to David's comment was to laugh. They spent the afternoon at Emmitt's.

Over the next year, Emily was able to secure a permanent position with the hospital. Things were getting better within the inner circles of friends and family; even Emily's parents decided that maintaining their relationship with their daughter was more important than the views of some anarchistic friend, so they stopped talking to the person. David started dating an Arab girl from Morocco that he met in a small Middle Eastern gathering at the University of Illinois. He was working part time in a coffee shop and spending his afternoons at the art studio. Kelly was going to school to be a masseuse while maintaining her unscheduled schedule at the studio. Emily was settling into her career, and Salam's work was picking up for the first time. It seemed to be by chance that he received a call from Rob Gibson.

Rob Gibson was the unofficial link between Chicago artists and the rest of the world. He knew the who, what, where, and when of the art world; he could create the conduit for success for a starving visual artist. In addition to being the known link, Rob himself was an artist turned businessman; he was an art dealer with a heart. The phone conversation was brief, and they would meet for only five minutes.

"If you have the time," Rob had finished the conversation with Salam. Knowing Rob's reputation, Salam would have forgone lifesaving medical treatment to make time.

The two agreed to meet in the bar of the Sheraton in downtown Chicago. Salam took a taxi, and when he arrived, he recognized Rob sitting at the bar wearing the ponytail that had long been his trademark. He greeted Rob with a wave and sat next to him, listening to Rob talking on his cell to his mother.

"Yes, yes, Mom, and tell Dad to make sure to take his pills. I love ya." Rob concluded his phone call and turned to Salam with a sincere smile.

"OK, here is what you want to hear. We are putting together a huge collection of artwork that we will showcase around the United States and the world, and you have been selected to be one of the artists," Rob said with a calm and firm voice...

"Why me? I mean, who nominated me?" Salam asked.

"I did," Rob said. "I got your information from Stephanie. She said you are her brother-in-law, and she showed me some of your paintings on the Internet. You are good. Here is my card. I am sorry. I don't have lots of time. I have other appointments. Call me within twenty-four hours to let me know if you are interested. Ciao," Rob said as he shook Salam's hand and walked away.

"Ciao," Salam said to empty space. He numbly held the coveted business card. Salam left the bar and walked back to his studio on Grand Avenue with newfound respect for his bratty sister-in-law. After some of the shock wore off, he tried to call her, but her phone was disconnected. He told Emily about it, and she told him she was very happy for him, but he had the sensation that Emily was not entirely behind the idea.

"How did Stephanie meet Rob Gibson?" Emily asked twice.

"I don't know, but it does not matter," he replied, trying to avoid getting into the sibling rivalry thing. He knew the history of resentment, jealousy, and competition between the two ever since high school, and he was not interested in wasting precious energy on that.

"I can take some time off and go with you," Emily said.

He smiled and kissed her, realizing that his wife always said the right thing at the right time. Even with her insecurities, she always had the upper hand on things. She had the world within the warm, soft swing of her palm.

The next afternoon, he went out on his weekly run around the industrial district nearby when David called him on his cell and told him to turn on the television to see something extremely important. David refused to give any clue as to what this all-important subject matter might be. He insisted that it was something he had to see for himself.

Salam thought the urgency in David's voice was his usual intensity over trivial matters and finished his workout. When he went back to the art studio, he found Emily downstairs with Kelly framing one of the paintings and talking about what sounded like clothes, Kelly's favorite subject. He greeted them and went to where the television set was, pushed the button on the remote, and flipped through the channels, deciding that he might as well check up on what had David so excited.

"Babe, what channel is Fox news?"

"It's twelve," Emily answered.

The news anchor sounded like he was talking about a very important issue, and the commentators acted like they really knew what they were talking about.

After a couple of minutes, he realized that for once David was not simply trying to get a reaction for his own amusement. The newscasters were talking about Iraq. Correspondents and the analysts seemed to have little or no real knowledge about what they were discussing. They were educating the American public about the upcoming military involvement in Iraq. They were talking about an invasion, another war. The wounds of the first Gulf War had not healed yet, at least not for the Iraqis. It was only ten years later, and the Americans were about to go back to Iraq.

"I guess the old theory was right," he thought aloud. "If you enter Iraq, it will stay with you forever."

He sat and listened. Then his mind wandered back to distant memories he had hoped to keep in the past. He realized that if the Americans went to Iraq it might open a way for him to go back. These past ten years, he had protected himself from the slightest chance that this kind of challenge might present itself. He had avoided telephone calls, letters, or news on the radio or television that might remind him of the home he had left and the people he thought were cut off from him for eternity. This had been a one-way road that he traveled down, and he wanted it to stay that way. He did not want to travel the other way.

He had severed ties to the land that he had once called home. The letters from his father were left unopened after he received a letter telling him that he was no longer worthy to be a son, because he chose to study art over medicine, and that he no longer would receive any funds that would help to sustain him. He had replied like an idealistic, arrogant young man who could not yet see the future effects of his current reactions. He had sent a reply with only four lines:

Dear Father:

I fail to see where your anger is coming from. Is it because I chose what will make me happy or because I chose what would not make you happy? I don't need the money. If you say that I am not your son, then I am not your son... don't send anything, not even letters.
Salam

After that letter to his father, he received many letters from his family and from people he had long forgotten about. He had opened only two: one from his sister telling him that she was getting married to her classmate and they were leaving Iraq to find another place to live, and one from his brother telling him that his father had passed away. He stopped opening any letters or reading postcards that came from Iraq. He kept everything, including other letters from people he knew and people whose names he did not recognize, in a shoebox labeled "Payless," and called it the "Payless attention to emotions box." He never knew how many letters he received because all of the letters made it to the Payless box directly from the mailbox, and there they stayed. When the letters stopped arriving, he wrapped the box securely in several rolls of clear tape.

He shook himself out of his reverie and reminded himself that he had no time for politics or military invasions and definitely no time for emotions and shadows that he had long forgotten about. He had Emily. He had his art and his work, and he had Rob Gibson to answer to in twenty-four hours. "Why wait twenty-fours?" he asked himself. He looked for the phone and dialed.

"Hello, you've reached Rob Gibson, leave a message after the beep." So he started to leave a message.

"Hello, Rob, it's Salam. Yes I will do it... you let me know what the next step is, and I will do it."

When he finished the phone call, he redirected his attention completely from the nonsense that was on the television that day.

The next day he received a call from Rob's secretary, telling him to come to the gallery on Grand and LaSalle streets. There he met with Rob and one other person. The other person turned out to be Roger Goldstein, the emperor of the world of art, the one who could make or break an artist with one comment or review: the gold if he liked you and the stain that could not be removed if he disliked you. The tour was to start in two weeks, and New York was to be the first stop. Salam would have to have at least thirty paintings ready for display. He went home and waited for Emily to tell her about the meeting. He called David, Kelly, and Julia, and he asked Julia to search for a theme for a small party. When Julia asked what the party was about, he told her it would be about making it.

Julia never found a theme for the party, but she did find various types of liquor that were sure to make everyone at the party feel like they had made it, or at least died trying.

David likened Roger Goldstein as being to painters what Steven Spielberg is to actors.

"New York, I hate New York," Emily commented.

"I hate it too. But it's only a week. After that, it's Montréal and maybe even Paris... you like Paris?" Salam asked.

"I've never been there. It will be great, but I can't take more than ten days off, you know," she said.

Within a week, an entire team of artists had assembled from all over the world. There were some heavy names like Elijah Anderson, Emil Procheier, Gennady Tarrssof, Gilda Huffman, Henrico Menendez, Gerald Abbatcho, and others that he had heard of and watched with envy. He still could not believe that his name was now with theirs. The artists met at the Hyatt Hotel in Chicago, and they took off on the tour from there. Emily was with him the entire time, and he even managed to get David a part-time assignment as a crewman. It was the best time of his life, the achievement of his lifetime that he had been waiting for. Newspapers, magazines, and radio stations interviewed him. His paintings were mentioned in many artists' review magazines.

In Montréal, one Lebanese millionaire paid sixty thousand dollars for two of his paintings, and in California a well-known film producer paid eighty thousand dollars for another two. It was like a dream. He was now an artist through the recognition of the forbidden kingdom of the elite that he always claimed he despised. It upset him to learn that he had always actually been after the money, although he stated many times that he lived for art. He realized that without money, art was like... like... well, it was like art without money. It was the same thing as having senses without being able to see, taste, hear, or touch. Without money, you are an anarchist. With money, you are an artist. He tried to control the annoying intellectual pride of the self-righteous artist and gather what was left of the staunched castle of self-made artistic defeat.

He wanted to be a better artist, a happy artist, and an artist who could afford to buy his wife something that she wanted instead of giving her paintings as the standard gift for every occasion. He wanted to buy her a gift that she could go back to Youngstown, Ohio, with and tell her parents about, especially her mother. She could say, "Look, Mom, my husband bought me this for my birthday!" as she showed off some expensive bauble.

Taking care of Emily was all he had wanted to do since the day she said yes in Arabic in front of the Muslim sheikh who performed the Islamic marriage ritual on the South Side of Chicago. He wanted to quit the job that he was laid off from more often than he labored at. He would be able to quit teaching young "artists" who had more of an interest in looking like artists than having any real talent. With money behind him, he would be able to concentrate on his own art and paint pieces that would last, and maybe one day his name would be recognized as the artist who left Iraq and became one of the most famous and respected artists that Iraq and the Arab world had ever birthed.

Oh, what a joy it would be: the joy of making it, the joy of success, and the joy of not needing to work anymore. Before the tour was over, he had a brief meeting with Roger Goldstein, who told him that they would do this more often, at least once a year, and that he, Roger, wanted to take him under his wing. Roger's wing was the safest place for a new bird in a sky full of ruthless hungry hawks and carrion-eating buzzards. Before the end of the tour, which included London and Paris, Emily had to leave. The ten days Emily had to spare were at an end, and she declared that Paris was completely overrated anyway and that she would wait for him to return home. He kissed her in the Charles de Gaulle Airport and told her that he would be home soon and that the best was yet to come. When the tour was over, he had sold half of the paintings he started with in Chicago. He could not wrap his mind around the sum of money that he would get from the tour. He was more than happy with Roger's commitment to him. The one thing that upset him was that in New

York he and Emily did not have the chance to see Stephanie. She did not even answer their phone calls.

"She must be somewhere saving a whale," Emily said, with a sarcastic, insincere half smile.

4

After the art tour was over Salam arrived at O'Hare with Rob Gibson on the ninth of November, 2002. The two shared a limousine that Rob Gibson had chartered for the night. As the limousine drove them toward the magnificent Chicago skyline, down on I-90, Rob planned to have a night out with some friends. He tried to convince Salam to come with him, but Salam was anxious to get back to his home and to Emily. Then Rob commented that from now on they would hang out more often, which was more promising and assuring than the tour itself and any publicity campaign. An artist like Salam could only dream of someone like Rob Gibson wanting to hang out; that meant it was a smooth ride from now on. He arrived at the studio to find Emily asleep. He let her sleep, gently kissing her on her forehead, then sat downstairs for two hours drinking whisky, contentedly thinking to himself, *So this is how it feels to be somebody.*

Whoever that somebody was, it felt good, he thought. It made him feel comfortable and at ease, something that he'd yearned for many years ago. It was funny that Rob Gibson said they would hang out. It meant that he would now hang out with people who knew people, who knew other people who had influence and the money to spend on art. That was the missing link in all artists' lives. And it was all made possible by Roger Goldstein, a man who was able to look beyond things that others could not look past. He smiled and went to lie down next to Emily in the heavenly, warm bed.

The next day he was up early and took a shower while singing "Proud Mary," by Credence Clearwater Revival, his favorite song of all time, as Emily waited at the breakfast table. On the drive to the hospital, he told her about the amount of money he made from his tour and the amount of money he could possibly make once his gallery was all set and ready for business. He also told her something else that took her by surprise. He told her that he would invest the money he made by turning the studio into the gallery he always wanted. He would turn the studio into a full-fledged gallery with the help of David and Kelly.

"And you, of course, can manage me and the gallery," he concluded.

"That will be great, babe," she said with less joy and even less approval in her voice than he was expecting. Salam did not know why Emily sounded a little upset, so he waited for her to say something further.

"Well?" he said.

"Well what?" she answered.

"Well, you know what, Emily... you are not... you are not totally approving of the idea," said Salam.

"No... but, you know... it's OK," she answered unenthusiastically, confirming his belief that she did not fully approve of his idea.

Her answer did not sit well with him... not in the least. And he knew that when she OK'd things with this tone things were not OK, so he wanted to scratch below the surface. "OK, Emily, what do you want? Do you want us to buy a new car? Do you want jewelry? Do you want a house in the suburbs, so I can mow the lawn and have barbecues wearing khaki shorts and a stupid polo shirt that says 'greatest husband in the world,' or do you want us to move to Youngstown, Ohio, and buy a bigger house than your parents'... do you want"

She did not let him finish. She looked at him and said, "A baby!"

He had not expected that answer at all, and he had no clear response to it. He searched for a dignified reply, but he was only able to croak out a faint "What?"

He cleared his throat. "A baby?" he further questioned, hoping he had misheard her.

"Yes... a baby. I want to be a mother. I want to have your child," she said with the unquestionable certainty of a woman with a massive clock ticking in the center of her being.

Salam was desperately looking for the appropriate words to this unexpected wrench and, quite frankly, could not find any. They reached the hospital and he did his customary exit from the passenger seat and went to her side. She exited the driver's seat and he kissed her lips. They were cold and unresponsive. He looked into her eyes and said, "Promise me that you will give us the chance to talk about this before you start thinking more about it, because the only thing in the world I cannot handle is that you spend one minute of your life upset because of something I said or did."

"I promise," Emily said. She hugged him and went into the hospital, leaving him in the middle of the cold breezy morning in the lonely streets of Evanston.

On the way back he started thinking of a way to manipulate the situation to his advantage, in direct contradiction to his recent comments to Emily. Salam had always used a method of organizing the important things in his life that he referred to as "Hierarchy of Things in My Life." This was a self-centered way of organizing what was most important to him so he knew what to focus on. After a few moments of organizing his list, he concluded that there were only two things to consider: the gallery that he always wanted to have was first on his list and his wife's love came in second.

"It will hurt no one," he reasoned, "if I open my gallery, and then maybe in a year or two Emily and I will have one or two children. I mean, by the time we pay off our debt and renovate the studio, make it larger, decorate it, buy the necessary equipment like lighting, and pay for advertising, all the fees, memberships, permits, the grand opening expenses, the salaries of two part-timers, David and Kelly, and all necessary things to start the gallery, we would have little or no money left for whatever a baby needs, and what about the time?" Salam assured himself, as he smoked for the first time in the car while he was driving, and tried to let the smoke escape from the window so Emily would not notice the smell. Then he said to himself, "What about the time, the dedication, and the responsibility? What if the baby is born deformed or what if he or she requires special help? What if something happens to Emily during the pregnancy or delivery, and what if... can I handle all of that?" Even to himself he was beginning to sound like a man talking in circles, avoiding the prickly center. Then he realized an unpleasant, but very possible outcome of focusing on just his own wants. What if Emily left him? Could he live without Emily?

"OK, that's not the plan," he said to himself. The new plan would be that he would talk to her, and they would agree on something. They had always agreed on things. They would agree, and she would stay with him. She would support and love him forever, and they would have children, and that's the way it would be. Salam told himself this to assure his shaken confidence as he drove. He called a heavily sleeping David near home and asked him to come meet him at the coffee shop. When he arrived, David was sitting on the steps of the coffee shop with a large cup of black coffee in one hand and a cigarette in the other in his usual effort to nurture a perpetual hangover. He looked and smelled like he hadn't showered for a month.

"So, what is so important that you needed me to meet you at such an ungodly hour?" David asked through a swirl of smoke.

"Let's go inside. It's cold out here. You look like shit," Salam said.

"I feel like it too. It was a surreal night last night. I don't remember a thing."

The two men entered the coffee shop. Inside they sat and talked about Salam's plan to turn the first story of the building into a gallery with a studio in the back with a small cafe in the corner, a fireplace, a bathroom, and a sitting area with Internet—the whole nine yards. David would be the assistant manager. "You and Kelly will have permanent part-time jobs. Only because I cannot afford to pay you full time," Salam justified the offer.

David perked up, agreed, and immediately said, "Let's go look at the old dump."

The two friends looked around the art studio for possible expansions, grabbed a paper and a pen, and wrote things down. Then David asked what Emily thought about Salam's newest project.

"She is OK. She will be OK," Salam said, studiously avoiding David's eyes.

"Uh oh," David said. "Dude, I will not lift a finger unless I know that Emily is OK with it. You know me. I don't want to be part of any marital mess."

It took Salam almost two weeks to make sure that Emily was OK or would be OK. He bought her a peace-offering ring that she put aside in a jar by the bed and did not wear for three days. He took her out to several expensive restaurants and a car dealership to trade in the old Land Rover for a newer one, and he agreed to join her in doing the thing that he hated the most, Christmas shopping, or just shopping in general, especially when it involved buying for someone other than himself. He talked about how much he loved her, how much she meant to him, how she was more important than the gallery or anything else in his life. He wanted a baby even more than she did, but, "The timing is not right, babe." Salam used this phrase as he smoked his Marlboro. He tried to reason that they were just starting their careers and their lives together and that they should be a little more settled; he asked her to wait just a year or two.

"I am thirty-five, you know," Emily reminded him.

"So what? With medicine today, women can have babies at the age of fifty," Salam said, not sure of the facts of his medical statement.

"I don't want to have a baby when I am fifty," she said.

"Neither do I. It's only a year or two. Not even. A year or a year and half max, and we will have a baby and the gallery. Everything will be just fine," Salam said and waited for a positive reply. But before he gave Emily a chance to reply, he did what he always did. He made a commitment to a promise that he knew he might not be able to keep.

Finally, he said, "OK, from this day, December fifteenth, you count a year and half. If you are not pregnant, then you will decide what we will do, where we are going to live and everything else. I will put that in writing, if you want... and if I do not meet the agreement..." he paused. "If I do not honor the agreement," he stopped, looking for an appropriate ending to his pitch.

"I will leave you," Emily said with a quiet voice.

"What?" he asked with real shock.

"If you do not honor the agreement, I will leave you. You will have the gallery and I will give you a year and a half. If I am not pregnant by that time, I will leave you," Emily assured him.

He knew his wife very well and knew that she was as serious as the threat she had just made. So without stooping to any conniving skills of schmoozing and deal making, he looked at her and said with what he believed to epitomize the total American attitude in agreements, "Deal!"

He looked at her moments later as she gazed at the waves of the freezing water of Lake Michigan. He calmly said, "You know I will die if you leave me," as they turned westward onto Oak Avenue.

Without moving or turning her eyes or her face toward him, she replied quietly, "I know."

5

Renovation and new additions to the gallery and studio were more expensive and time consuming than Salam and David had anticipated or prepared for. Even with the hiring of nonunion construction workers, which were owned by a skilled and extremely hardworking Polish contractor that David knew, they were over budget by the first week. Nevertheless, Salam watched the entire process with great pleasure; finally, his own space, his own sanctuary, his own podium, where he could address the world with a brush, oil paint, and canvas. Surprisingly, the normally unfocused David was an experienced businessman and a decisive director with the construction workers. He followed up on the floor plans and other details that Salam did not have any clue about. David even made several trips to the lumberyard to save money instead of having the contractor buy the materials. Emily tried to stay away from getting involved. She spent her free time moving boxes and covering furniture with plastic sheets with Kelly's help. They stashed all of the boxes in the back room where they kept all the stuff they thought they would need one day but still had not touched since the day they moved into the place.

One day, just before the construction workers were about to leave, the foreman asked if Salam could move all of the boxes from the storage room. The room was to be turned into a glorious bathroom with murals of an ocean on the horizon and with dolphins, small fountains, stones, and some real sand, where "a person could have an out-of-the-world experience as he releases something out of him or her." So he and David, with help from Emily and Kelly, started moving box after box to the middle of the main room. They sorted the boxes into three piles. The first was for what they would keep. The second was for what they would give away. David quickly claimed that as his pile, and the third would be what they would throw away. Emily handed a small box to Kelly. Not a very big or ornate box, it was nothing more than a small red shoebox with black and white stripes and the word "Payless" on the side and top of the box. It was wrapped in yards of clear tape to keep its contents intact. As Kelly placed it on the top of another box that she was ready to move, Salam's breath caught, and his mouth went dry.

"Wait, can I have that box...please?" he asked Kelly who was already on her way up the stairs. Kelly handed him the box and continued up the stairs.

"Is that your secret stash, dude?" David asked seriously without getting an answer from Salam, whose face turned grim and sad all of a sudden as he sat on the tan leather chair looking at the box and wondering if it was the same box that he thought it was: the box that he kept all of his father's letters in and all of the letters that people had sent him throughout the years, letters that he never opened; all the links of a past he had avoided and wanted to avoid for the rest of his life. He sat there, wondering if he should open the box. He was sure that no matter what was in the box, it would have the effect of a golden necklace on a monkey's senses. He wanted to make sure that he put this box in the correct pile; the giveaway pile or the throwaway pile, but before he did he wanted to do one last inspection of its contents.

With worried fingers, he untaped the box, and his doubt about opening the box started to grow more and more unsettling as each section of tape was pulled from the once shiny box. He opened the box and looked inside. There was indeed a stack of letters that looked very old and dusty. They were thrown over one another in no particular order. The envelopes looked foreign with light blue and red stripes and covered with stamps that looked cheap and fake. All of the stamps were pictures of the dictator that he had known as the president of his birth country for so long. The faded egg-shaped seals on the envelopes appeared to have been opened and resealed many times. He carefully touched the stack of envelopes and imagined the dust from the envelopes entering his pores.

He began looking at the names of the senders. The first was from his brother; the stamp on it showed the date the letter was sent, January 18, 1989. The second letter was from his father, dated July 5, 1987. One letter had no stamp on it. The name of the sender was not familiar at all, and the sender's address was almost completely faded. The next envelope looked flimsy and old, with blue and red lacings and the French words "PAR AVION," with two stamps of a man in a military suit. Calmly he tore the envelope open and took out the piece of paper that looked like it was ripped from a cheaply made school notebook. It had a distinctive scent, a scent that he had long forgotten. He looked at the writing, which was in Arabic, in a blue ink pen that skipped many letters in between words. He began reading the letter as David commented that he needed help with some of the larger boxes. Salam barely heard his request as he sank into the world hidden in that flimsy shoebox, not certain what he was getting himself into or what monsters the locked doors he was now opening were hiding. It read:

In the name of God the merciful and the most compassionate.
In the name of everything that is true and sincere.

Dear Salam:

It has been awhile since we have heard any news about you. I asked my brother Hamid if he had any news from you, and he told me that he had not heard anything from you. By some miracle I was able to get your address from your sister, who I called from the police station, where they have the only working phone. She gave me your address and told me that you have been in America. How is it there? Did you fall in love with your dream woman with blue eyes and blond hair? I am sending you this letter to inform you that we are all right, and all thanks to Allah. I have passed the fifth grade secondary and next year, I will be in the sixth grade

secondary. So pretty soon, I will be attending college in Baghdad; at least this is what I am planning. I don't think my brother Hamid will allow me to go. Plus, we don't have the money. My mother and I still sell candy in the small shop in our home. Hanan and Kamal have gotten engaged, and Abdullah and Basima married five months ago. I read the entire book of Bader Shaker Al-Sayyab poetry and read Muhammad Al-Maghoott's entire work of poetry. I like the poetry of Al-Sayyab better, because it reminds me of you, and because he is from Iraq. When I read it, I feel like he is telling my story, our story, and the stories of all the people I know. If you are able to send a letter and maybe a picture of you, this will bring much happiness to many people here; so many people here miss you greatly. May Allah protect you, and I will be waiting for your response.
The ever devoted Amel.

P.S. Here is something to read on a cold night. We used to read this together.

Sparrows or playful children
Or is it water oozing from a rock
Wets the grass, splashes the flowers
A singing raven
Dances in between the hills
Swinging in an imaginary swing... to dream.

"Who in the hell is Amel?" Salam said to himself.

He shook himself off mentally, put the letter aside and got up to help David with a large box. That night he did not sleep well. In the forgotten corners of his memory, he knew the name Amel. It sounded like his wife's name, Amel. He was sure that he knew her from his home country; however, he could not associate the name with a face or a memory. "It has been a long time," he said to himself, and that letter meant nothing. He wanted to drink whisky and go to sleep. He swallowed two sleeping pills with his drink and waited for sleep to find him.

As he started to slip into his dreams, he felt that he was awake while swinging within the pages of the dream book. He felt something caressing his skin, starting at his heart and then up his neck, face, and hair. He thought it was Emily, but the touch was different, unfamiliar, smooth, and silky like the touch of a gossamer wing. He could not wake up; he tried but couldn't. He felt the touch penetrate deeper than the skin; it was inside his flesh and in his blood. He felt two hands caressing his soul, two needy hands, two forceful and relentless hands touching him and holding him hostage to the dream. He wanted to scream because the hand started to press on his neck none too gently. He knew it was a dream. It was a nightmare that was relentlessly holding him, and he wasn't sure he wanted to leave it even though it terrified him.

Suddenly, he woke up to find his wife, Emily, shaking him and saying, "Honey, are you OK? Honey, what's wrong?"

"What...?"

"I don't know," Emily said. "You were...making noises like you were crying... in your dream. Are you OK?"

"Yes, I am OK. It was a nightmare," he answered, still mentally shaking the oppressive hands from his neck. "Babe, did you touch me on my neck while I was sleeping? I mean, did you caress my neck and face?"

"No. Maybe it was your dream girlfriend," she said with a smile. "Why are you asking me that?" she wondered with a suspicious look in her sleepy eyes.

"Oh, nothing. Go back to sleep... I love you," he said as he jumped out of the bed looking to calm his fears with another drink.

"I love you too. You should get some sleep. We have a lot to do tomorrow."

"I will," he said as he ran down the stairs to where he left the box of letters. He stared at the box, not knowing what to do. He knew that the box contained his past, a past that he did not want to get back to, a past that he had disengaged from a lifetime ago, a past that was calling him back, urging him to read more letters, taunting him with the mystery of their contents. He needed to read the words that had been sealed in that box with the voices on the pages muffled by cardboard and many feet of clear tape. It was becoming a thirst that he started to feel in a vivid, physical sense. A desire that opened his pores and needed to be filled with that dust of a distant land in the past mixed with the dust of the present and every land between. He was afraid. He felt much weaker than he had a few hours ago, before he read the meaningless letter with that strange poem. He had no clue of what to expect next. He only knew that he needed to read more letters. No amount of tape could silence the voices any longer as they all clamored at once to be heard. He placed his whisky and lime on the table, lit his cigarette, and pulled out another letter.

In the name of God the merciful and the most compassionate.
In the name of everything that is true and sincere.

Dearest Salam:

You are truly missed by me and the others who remember you. How are you and how is America? Life here became unbearable due to the embargo. Many people have suffered beyond acceptable human standards, but it seems like no one cares about Iraq or Iraqis, and everyone wants to put this thing called "the Iraq issue" behind them and move on. The world has forgotten that we are suffering. Some families had to sell their homes and their belongings. Some women have had to sell their underclothes just to survive one more day. The other day I saw Bushra and Adawya, the Hillaly girls, selling their undergarments in the street and could not keep myself from crying. One man in the big city killed his entire family, his four kids and his elderly mother, and then shot himself because he was unable to feed them. I don't know what you can do to help, but if you can send letters to the American president, telling him about these stories, please do so. I don't know if you remember many of our friends, but bad things have happened to them and their families. We have not heard from Basima and Abdullah for almost a year now. One story is that Abdullah had died and Basima was still in Jordan. I don't know if you heard about what happened to Hanan and my brother Hamid, but it was tragic, and poor Ahmed. Sometimes I feel like everyone is leaving Balluria for one reason or another, but no one wants to take me with them. For me, I am still helping my mother in the candy shop. We are barely alive, but poetry and Fairuz's songs keep me going. I wish I could fly the oceans and be next to you so that I would not have to live this life here. Please remember me in your prayers, and whenever you hear Fairuz's song:

> *Tomorrow when the riders return*
> *You will return, my love*
> *Tomorrow as I wait for you*
> *Looking at the stars*
> *Don't leave me waiting*
> *Alone with the stars*

So as you can see, Salam, I guess I can live on poetry and love songs forever.
The ever devoted, Amel

It was her again. That name sounded more familiar now. She must be someone he knew, a girl from his homeland. It was someone he had must have shared moments with that were not of this world, his world. Yes, it was her. It was that girl who used to read poetry with him in the hot, sweaty afternoons in the shade of the mud hut.
"Oh, my God."
"It has been a long time."
He was not able to sleep at all after that.

6

David and Salam moved almost thirty boxes filled with stuff he and Emily never used. Emily was surprised at how much junk they had. She was not aware that they had that much.

"I thought my parents had a lot of junk... look at us!" she said. "We are so spoiled."

He was numb to her comments, David's sarcasm, and Kelly's airheaded remarks. He wanted to go back to his box and read more letters. The box had become an addictive drug. He was hooked. It was as if the dust from that box had entered his senses like the first hit of a line of the most pure and expensive cocaine. They finished moving all of the boxes. Then Emily announced that she wanted to take a shower. Kelly left and David sat on the floor drinking a beer and watching television. Salam went back to the box. He touched the letters and felt the spirits entering his fingertips, his veins, and his heart. He was entering this trap of his own will, letting the long shreds of thread from the witch's dress tie ropes around his hands. The shreds were pulling him further into the abyss of the unknown spirits he was yet to encounter. He grabbed a letter that clearly was from his father.

Allah's peace, blessings and mercy be upon you.

Dearest Salam:

Dear son, may Allah protect you, save you, and guide you to the path of the righteous and the good. All prayers will be for the prophet Muhammad, his family, and his companions.

I have retired from my job because the salary was not enough to feed us. Imagine that they are paying me three thousand dinars a month and the transportation costs three thousand dinars a week. So, I opened a small shop with Abu Khaldoun. He is a good man, and he and I are working very hard to secure a dignified living for your mother, sister, and brother, but nevertheless, we still need assistance just to keep up with the hardships of our lives. The embargo has inflicted extreme harshness on all of the Iraqi people. I know that you are depending on yourself for support, and I know that I am asking a lot of you, but if you could send us two to three hundred dollars a month, it would be very helpful. May the lord almighty bring you dignified riches and wealth, and grant you health and wisdom. May peace be with you and Allah's mercy and blessing be upon you.

Your father
Abdul-Kareem Sultan
August 19, 1993

A lump choked his breath as he tried not to cry. He had never opened that letter. He stashed it without knowing what was in it. He had automatically assumed the contents would be like the earlier letter that belittled his life choices. If only he had known, if he had just opened the letters. He was spending two hundred dollars on cigarettes alone, another two hundred dollars on other things that he did not need. But it is too late now, he thought. He grabbed another letter, opened the envelope, and read.

Allah's peace and blessing be upon you.

Dear Brother:

It has been almost three years since we've received any letters or phone calls from you. Are you that busy? I hope what is preventing you is a good thing, and we hope that you get and achieve all that you have ever wished for. I am sorry to inform you that our father is ill and that he needs surgery. The public hospitals here have no medications, and conditions here are dire. If we take him to the public hospital, I cannot speak of what the results and complications may be. So, I suggest that we take him to Jordan. I can get the required approval from my professors in the medical school. I am now in my third year of medical school and I am doing well, but the problem is that I have no money, and I only have one set of trousers and one shirt that I wash and dry every day. Our father's health is deteriorating, and he needs surgery, so if you can help us with some money, please do, and I promise you that I will pay it back. The traveling expenses will cost about a thousand dollars and the surgery will cost about three thousand dollars. Mother had to sell the jewelry she received from our father on her wedding day; she received two thousand dollars, so we need three thousand more. I know that you need that money as well for your living expenses in America, but we need it to save our father's life. I do not mean to bring sadness to your heart, but I need to say this, because I have no other choice. By the way, our sister is engaged now to Ali. You know our neighbor from Baghdad in the old neighborhood. He asked for her hand, and the two seem to like each other a lot. Ali told me that he will leave Iraq after their wedding and will take her with him. He is planning to go to Malaysia and then to Australia. I wish I could go with them, because life here is becoming unbearable. Accept my love and my respect. I will be waiting to hear from you.

Your brother,
Wisam
March 12, 1996

That night he was sickened by his selfishness and his self-absorption. He wanted to stop reading because he knew he was sliding into an emotional and physical abyss that would change him forever, but he had no choice. Even when he tried to take a nap in the afternoon, the two hands from his dream were there caressing him, and songs in a strange language started to play in his ears, songs that called the names of people whom he never knew. He tried to stay awake for as long as he could to avoid the nightmares and he woke up always drawn to the box. Emily started to notice his facial expressions and his new habits. She was first worried that David might have introduced him to drugs, but she knew her husband well, and she knew it was not what she was thinking. Also she noticed how protective and obsessed he was with the old shoebox. She did not want to initiate any arguments so she waited for him to tell her about what was in it, but he never did. Finally, she suggested he see a doctor when he walked through each day unfocused, speaking less and less.

To this he replied, "No, I am OK. I am just tired of all the construction and work," he lied.

For him it had become an addiction. He wanted to quit everything he was doing to read the letters. What he felt as he read them was a strange sensation that he had never experienced before. He felt like he was moving from a cold shade into the toasty, warm rays of the morning sun that he always longed for. He wanted to keep that warmth; letter by letter, word by word, he was parting ways with his familiar surroundings and letting himself slip into the unknown, the unknown that he somehow knew.

The next day David announced that they were almost finished with the renovations and they needed to start planning for the grand opening. He said that he had already started contacting some friends about the party, and he said that he called Julia to come up with a theme for the party.

"I think the theme should be success," Kelly said. The three looked at her, as if she were talking a different language; for the first time since they had met her she sounded intelligent.

"We need to start putting together the invitation list and the menu," Emily said. Everyone was waiting for Salam to say something. He said nothing.

The night before, he had been in the glorious new bathroom alone choking back tears, reading the letter from his brother, the brother that he had not seen for almost twenty-five years. That night he was finishing up with David, going over receipts of the month's work, when he suddenly said, "David, you go ahead and finish the bills. I have something to do." He sat on the couch by the television and read the letters, drinking whisky and lime juice.

May Allah's peace, mercy and blessings be with you.

Dear Brother:

I really did not want to send you this news in a letter; I wish that you could be here, because I could not bear to bury our father alone. But it seems like you have gone to a place where the letters do not reach you. Our father died three days ago; he suffered a lot. He wanted to see you very much. He was talking about you in his last days and on his deathbed. I had no choice but to bring him home from the hospital because the doctor told me that

there was nothing they could do. His kidneys had failed, and he was in a lot of pain. The hospital had no medications that could ease his pain. The most painful thing to see him through was his sadness, because you were not there. He kept asking me if I had sent you letters telling you that he needed to see you for one last time. Our mother is devastated, and our sister and her fiancé, Ali, stayed here and postponed their trip to Jordan to attend the funeral. I don't know how to tell you, but I managed to sell our mother's last stash of jewelry and china to cover the expense of the funeral. It was very hard on me to bury him alone. Although our mother and sister and her fiancé were there, I wanted you to be there. I miss you so much, brother. I feel all alone now and responsible for many things that I cannot handle. The country is bleeding with tragedy, and my studies have become demanding. I can barely finish my day and crash in my bed, but I have to support my mother and console her. Our sister and her fiancé still need help. Why are you not responding to our letters? Is it the life in America? My condolences to you and to myself; I know you will cry. I did. In our tradition, men do not cry, but sometimes I wonder if that is why we are so unfortunate in not having a peaceful life. Please try to call or send a letter to our mother. She needs to know if you are still alive.
Peace be with you,

Your brother
Wisam
June 5, 1996

"Oh, may Allah have mercy!" he cried.

He had learned of his father's death, but not from this letter. He learned of his father's death from a phone call from a stranger in Jordan. The stranger told him that his family wanted him to know. At that time, he was finishing his master's degree and wanted no interruptions. He cried alone for two hours, and then he stopped and continued his life uninterrupted. Oh, my Allah, oh, my God, oh, my Jehovah. *What's wrong with me. Am I that cold?* He asked himself. Does the life in the West make people like this? Was it his love and devotion to Emily and her world, or was it the talent of painting that absorbed him and left him senseless? He started to question his staunchest beliefs. But before searching for the answers, he continued reading the letters.

Dearest Salam:

It was by coincidence that I got hold of your address. I did not know that you were in the United States. One of my tent mates was talking about you and said that he knew your brother, the one who is studying in medical school. He told me he had your address in the States for many reasons I don't want to mention, because they are not of my concern. As for me, I

have been in the Rafha refugee camp for the past two years. It has been long, and the years have been hard. We have been here in the middle of the desert with no hope of leaving this place. The Saudis are treating us worse than they treat the other nationalities. I am afraid to say anything more because the Saudis open our letters before sending them to the outside world. After an incident where some refugees attacked the aid station because there was no water for three days, the Saudis attacked and killed almost fourteen of the refugees. It was very tragic. The Saudis beat them to death with sticks and rubber hoses, strangled them, and left their bodies in the street. I hope that you can reach out to the media or the international authorities in the United States or the United Nations to let them know of what happens here. We are waiting for the outside world to hear about us. Either that or one day some anthropology students will find the remains of the one hundred thousand Iraqis who have disappeared in the desert. I have to tell you that what is happening here is unbelievable. Why has the world had forgotten about us? It's been two years already, and everyone has had their celebrations. The Kuwaitis are back in their country. The Americans had their victory. The Saudis are safe now, and the tyrant is still in power. So how come the only people who are still suffering are the same people who suffered all along, us. Dear friend, if you can help me to find a way out of this death camp, I will be in your debt forever. The Saudis are treating us like nonhumans. The other day, they tortured and killed six people, because they asked for water. After they boycotted the camp for three days and did not provide water, we staged a protest, but the Saudi guards opened fire on us, and they killed six people. One of them was a woman. The Saudi soldiers just opened fire on a crowed of unarmed Iraqi civilians just for protesting because for days we had no drinking water in the camp. The bodies stayed in the sun for two days, and a curfew was imposed. The Saudi soldiers roamed the narrow streets of the camp, and they beat anyone who was outside his tent. How come no one knew about this? I don't know if this letter will ever reach you, because I have given it to the United Nations representative who is basically a servant for the Saudis and never helps us. Why has the Iraqi blood and soul become so cheap like this. So many people have died, and until now none of the world's governments or media have said or done anything. I am hoping that you will do something about it, and if you need more letters or photos, I will be glad to send them to you.
Peace be with you.

Sincerely,
Murtada
Saudi Arabia–Rafha refugee camp
October 11, 1996

He had no clue about who Murtada was; he must have known him long ago, but he did not spend too much time trying to remember. There would be time later to remember. The next two letters looked the same, and they had the Red Cross emblem stamped on them. He opened the second letter.

Dearest Salam:

I have written you almost twenty letters, but with no answer from you. My guess is that the Saudi authorities in charge of the camp have confiscated them, just like the old days of the tyrant in Iraq. It has been very scary and hard here. The Saudis started to pick people out at random and throw them back on the Iraqi border to face the death squads waiting for them on the other side. Everyone is talking about an agreement between the Saudis and the dictator to apprehend all of the resistance figures and activists of the uprising. In the camp, last month we found bodies of sixteen refugees shot in the head and buried right outside the camp. It's puzzling how the outside world does not hear of these tragedies. Aren't we humans? Aren't we under the United Nations' supervision and protection? Didn't we do what the American president had asked us to do? Then why is it that no one cares about us anymore? Many people have committed suicide here. Others have wandered into the desert looking for faraway cities and harbors, so they can get on a ship to somewhere else in the world. But I am still here because I cannot leave the others that are still here. I don't know, friend, but to me I feel like we were part of a big game. They called it the Gulf War. Was it so they could get more money? Maybe it was just for the joy of killing others. We people at the bottom, we are just pieces in this game. I feel that my heart is enraged with hatred toward everyone. My family back in Balluria has no way of living. No medicine, no hope, and I am here chewing my youth away, while the rest of the world is having a party. I try not to hate, but it is so hard to accept this reality. Once again, if you have any way to help me out, please do so, because if you live one day in this camp, you will understand why I am asking you to do this for me. I will wait for your reply.

Yours truly;
Murtada
Saudi Arabia–Rafha refugee camp
February 4, 1998

Balluria, oh, that was the place. That was where he sat listening to poetry and songs in the sweltering shade, but he still did not remember who Murtada was.

Every night for the entire month of the renovation of his dream, he was distracted and absentminded as he read the letters, one by one. There were letters from people that he never heard of and others from people that he barely knew or remembered. He read letters from a man named Abdullah, telling him of his true need for money so he could travel to Turkey, Denmark, and other European countries, and another from Basima, Abdullah's wife, asking him to help her while she was waiting for the return of her husband, who had traveled and never returned. He read many letters from Amel filled with poetry and love, and many letters from his brother telling him about the family. He learned that his sister had gotten married to a man named Ali, a man whose face he could barely put a name to. His mother had moved to Jordan to stay with her daughter. The family had lost their house because his father did not have the money to pay back the loan he took out against the house many years before to pay for Salam's travel and education in America. Many letters were from the refugee camp in Saudi Arabia from this Murtada, whom he tried hard to remember or put a face to, but he could not. The letters told the tales of despair, torture, and tragedies with strange persistent cries for help, asking if he could contact the United Nations or the American president. The real pain that he felt came from the letters from Amel, the girl who sent pieces of poetry and songs that he had long forgotten.

Amel, he remembered her. She was the girl with sad and accusing big black eyes, the younger sister of his boyhood best friend, Hamid. Salam remembered her and the poetry also. The words of the short poems she had sent started to come alive with meaning and feelings that scared him. He tried not to let the past sneak back into his heart, but it was too late. The mysterious hands of the Gypsy witches who waited for him whenever he closed his eyes to sleep touched his heart, and her scent had filled his lungs with the dust particles from the past that he always tried to escape. It was like a divine revelation to a lazy prophet who did not want to carry the message to anyone, and he was that lazy prophet. He started looking for anything that would link him to his home country. He was looking for temporary remedies and quick fixes that could save him from slipping back into the heavy past and the unavoidable trap of yearning. He followed the news and read the newspapers to learn more about the unavoidable future that was near. He paid attention to the upcoming events that the entire world, except for him, was talking about. He knew that for the past six months the president of the United States had made it clear that he would go to war with Iraq. Another campaign of pain, another ten years of uncertainty, was about to include Balluria in the whirly will of the outsiders.

David tried hard to keep him notified about every little detail and expense from the renovation of the studio and the building of the new gallery in order to keep him involved. He tried to make it sound like the grand opening was the talk of the town. David laid out the plan of the grand opening with the help of Emily and Julia. They had put together a long list of invitees without his input. She even claimed to have sent an invitation to Mr. Zlotcik in an effort to get a reaction from him, without any success. He was drowning in the abyss of images and voices that kept luring him and showing him the realities of the past that he tried to ignore. He did not recognize for the longest time that he had started drinking heavily every day after work. Emily started to worry more and more about him, so again she broached that prickly subject.

"Babe, I think you need to see a doctor. Or I can check you to see..."

"No, I am OK."

She did not reply, but she told Julia that she was afraid that he was slipping into depression, an artist's depression. Emily started thinking that it was not his fault that he was feeling this way. She blamed herself for not being more supportive, and she blamed David because she felt he was a bad influence on her husband. She blamed the world, the president, and the Middle East. She blamed everyone and everything that she could think of, but she never suspected that the cause could be a stack of letters that he read so often in solitude.

7

As the day of the grand opening slipped closer and closer, so did the day of the invasion. It was virtually impossible not to follow the president's threat of the invasion of the Persian Gulf on the news since every television network and every radio station broadcast an unending supply of "can't-miss" information on the upcoming military campaign. It was in early March when David called and said, "Dude, aren't you from that country, man? I think they are invading your country."

"Yes, I saw the news. My gallery is my country, David, and you are welcome to invade it anytime."

"Dude... that sounded so gay. I know that, but this is some serious shit... do you want to go somewhere for a drink and watch this?" David asked with keen interest in the live drama.

"Man, no, but you can come here if you want." David was at the gallery twenty minutes after the telephone conversation. The two men spent the day drinking beer and watching television. David did not stop his stream of commentary.

"Man, this is unbelievable. I mean, in this day and age, an invasion of a country! Are we living in medieval times?"

Together they watched the unfolding events. They watched the coalition forces enter the country from the south, making their way to the capital. David's comments turned sarcastically to comparing this invasion to the empire and the rise of the new Rome, all of the other historical similarities and the possible scenarios and ultimate conspiracies that could be. Salam did not reply to any of David's theories. He was asking himself quietly about the timing, the irony of finding the red shoebox of letters, and what was happening in his homeland. Was it a coincidence that he found the letters after years of travel restrictions to his homeland? Those restrictions had made it so convenient for him to not think of going back to his home country. After all of these years of feeling safe being away from the past, he was now able to travel back to his homeland. Also he started questioning the nightmares he was having every night. Was everything somehow connected? Why the shoebox? Why the war now? Why was the poetry that he had long forgotten starting to make sense? And what about the two silky hands in his nightmares?

"Was this all a silly conspiracy?" he asked himself, avoiding saying anything to David, who could easily make things more complicated, more frightening, and more confusing. He kept reading and rereading the letters and numbly watching the events on the television. He allowed himself and his senses to slip into the trap of yearning, yearning for a life he left, yearning for the people that he once thought he could live without, yearning for what he could not name.

As Salam was sinking into his solitary emotional abyss, Emily watched helplessly. Deep in her heart Emily knew that there was soon to be a real change in her life with her husband, but could not fathom where that change would take them. When she returned from work that day to prepare for the grand opening the next day she looked at Salam, again deep in his secluded world. Something about his posture told her that he had come to some decision and that he would soon ready to share his thoughts. She waited patiently for him to tell her without her asking.

Salam knew that Emily was waiting for him to bare his soul, but he continued to put it off. He wanted to wait for the right moment and his gut feeling told him it was not the time. Salam believed that there was always a perfect time for everything, and this was not the perfect time to walk down that particular path. He also knew that he would never sleep well again until he had reached an unspoken new goal. From the moment he had seen that red shoebox sitting on top of the larger box, he had known it was a trap. He had known that by opening the box and inhaling the dust inside he risked being caught in its web of mysteries and unable to escape. He had known, yet he had opened it.

He was a completely different man just a day before the grand opening of his gallery than he had been just days earlier. It was the day he had waited for his entire life, the day that would alter his life and the lives of many others who loved and cared about him. It was the day that showed the world that he had succeeded, and on that momentous day, his mind was half a world away in the dust of a war-torn land. He did not look like a man who had the world at his feet. He looked like a man with a secret plan, a man with an itch in his heart, a distracted man who did not like, recognize, or have any desire to interact with his surroundings. He wanted to be alone most of the time and had barely even commented on the invitation list that David and Emily had worked on for two days and that Roger Goldstein would be gracing the event with his much-lauded presence.

"OK, so Roger Goldstein and his companion. What's her name?" David asked, switching topics.

"What? I don't know. Just do what you want. I will be upstairs," Salam said and left an actually speechless David sitting on the couch.

8

If it were not for David, Emily, Kelly, and Julia, the grand opening party would have never happened. He was completely disconnected. Emily knew that there was something he was not telling her. He was either sick or hiding something very serious from her. She was certain there were no other women in his life. She knew that he loved her and had never once cheated on her in the five years they had dated. He spent all of his time in the gallery, when he was not teaching. She did not say a word to him; instead, she waited, as she always did, for him to tell her what was going on in his mind and hoped that he had simply slipped into an artist's funk that would clear up once the festivities began. She knew he would tell her in his own time as he always did, but this time she braced herself for the worst, and just twelve hours before the grand opening, she could wait no longer and tried to push him into a response.

"Just tell me that you are not thinking of separating or getting a divorce. Anything else we can work on," she said with a worried smile, temporarily forgetting that she had been the one to threaten to leave him.

"What?" Salam answered with surprised look. "I would never break up with you. I love you, and you always put up with me and my mess," he said with the sad smile of a grown man realizing his shortcomings for the first time in his life. "And because the moment we are not together will be the last moment that I want to live."

Emily tried to accept that answer, but the truth was that she knew there was something more to it, that he was waiting for the right time, and she would just have to be patient. David and she had finalized the invitation list. All of the invitations were sent two weeks prior to the opening date, and many RSVPs had been returned within days of the mailing. The grand opening of the gallery was the talk of the town or at least the artists of the town. Many replied by e-mail, confirming the attendance of over 90 percent of the invitees. Julia had also published an ad in the newspaper and invited all of the journalists she knew from her job at the advertising agency. David and Kelly placed several posters and flyers in the bars they frequented and the anarchist meeting places on Milwaukee Avenue. Emily invited her family and family friends. She even sent an invitation to Mr. Zlotcik, with the wrong address for the gallery. She thought it would be funny for Mr. Zlotcik to travel all the way to Chicago and get lost for hours looking for the gallery. She had told her husband about her devilish plan, hoping to humor him out of his funk. He only looked at her and smiled, but his smile was that of a man who was not really there. The last day of preparations and decorations had passed, and many of the most important people that Salam wanted to ensure would attend had already committed. Roger Goldstein and Rob Gibson both were coming with female companions and bringing with them several journalists from the local newspapers and two magazines. In addition, three independent journalists would attend.

9

The day of the grand opening was a grand day indeed. It was surprisingly warm for the end of March. The exceptional sun, clear skies, and easy wind were all cooperating partners in making this the greatest day of Salam's life. Finally he had his own gallery, his own place in the world where he could teach the world a lesson in art. Emily worked hard to create an aura of excitement. She woke up early and called David to make sure that he was up and asked Kelly and Julia to come over early so they could pick up the many items they ordered from the wine store and the organic food store that had just opened in the neighborhood. She wanted to get started on the food arrangements no later than 10:00 a.m. The plan was that Emily, Kelly, and Julia would be in charge of the food and hospitality. David, Salam, and Russell, who expressed his willingness to help at the last minute, would get the place ready and follow up on the arrival of guests and the music. David declared that he would be the DJ in charge of the music.

The group of people who had supported him through the long and agonizing realization of his dream was working hard on the final details to commemorate the difficult journey to a once seemingly unattainable goal. Salam was the only one who seemed not to be a part of the celebration. He was not in it all; it was though the entire event had lost all meaning to him. Even the usually unobservant Kelly commented to Emily that she had noticed he wasn't his usual self.

"Is he OK? He seems sick or something."

"He is not sick; he's just little tired," Emily replied, wishing that were true.

Emily knew that he was not just tired. She felt like her husband had had a sudden change of mind about everything in his life. She thought he might be going through a midlife crisis and that was the reason for him being secluded, estranged, and shut down from everyone and everything for the past two weeks. She also thought that it could be the artist accomplishment syndrome: when you get excited about an idea, and then lose interest at the end of an extended adrenaline rush at just the moment when the idea is about to become a reality. His excessive drinking had concerned her, but she did not make an issue out of it. She knew for sure that he was not the same man she had known for the past five years. He was not the same man she knew a month ago. He was not the same since he found that shoebox that he carried around their home. The night before the grand opening, he was sitting in the gallery alone reading a letter. She woke up in the middle of the night and found that he was not in bed, so she went downstairs looking for him and saw him crying alone with a letter in his hand. She did not interrupt him. She just watched him cry and then went back to sleep. She did not even tell him later that she had seen him crying. That morning she picked up his clothes from the corner dry cleaner so that he could dress up, and then she busied herself with preparing the food and coordinating things with Julia. She knew that he would tell her something after the party, she just knew, and this time she was right.

With the re-arrival of David, who had mysteriously disappeared for two hours, the party started to come alive. He had switched out of his respectful suit he had been coerced into wearing and was now wearing his famous Jamaican poncho and hat that did not match any of the colors he painted his slim figure with. He referred to his costume as "human display of self-disrespect and unconditional acceptance." He was notorious for making this comment whenever Salam or Emily made remarks about David's often chaotic appearance. These comments tended to intensify when they were meeting with prospective clients who frequented the studio.

The group had put in a great deal of effort to turn the cluttered, paint-covered studio with canvases sitting ten deep on every inch of wall space into an art gallery. They turned it into a space in which men and women in formal evening wear looked natural walking through, sipping champagne. Emily, who always complained about the disorganization of the art studio before the renovation, looked at the new gallery and said, "Now this is what I call a gallery," as she and Julia put the final touches on what looked like a colorful and delicious buffet. Kelly started preparing the bar and organizing the glasses, not paying any attention to David's less-than-subtle attempts to get her attention. As the clock indicated six in the evening, Salam snuck upstairs alone, nursing a glass of whisky with lime juice and all the despair in the world.

Guests started arriving as early as six thirty, and two journalists sat on the wooden bench that Salam designed himself, waiting to interview him. Two hours passed, and he still sat upstairs alone. At that time, Emily's parents showed up more than fashionably late. Stephanie, who had been the catalyst that shot his career in the right direction, was on some kind of self-realization trip to Tibet and unable to attend. The noises from the party got louder and louder, as many guests had arrived and David got carried away with his assignment as the music man. But all Salam could hear was a voice, a distant voice from the past, reading poetry, the voice of a tanned thin young girl with big black wondering eyes reading poetry in a language that no one else in the gallery could understand.

When Roger Goldstein arrived, he was accompanied by a tall blond he introduced as Heather. She spoke very little and drank a considerable amount of wine. Roger Goldstein became the de facto center of attention and was crowded by all of the attendees and journalists and by Rob Gibson and his wife, Jennifer. The party became lively and enjoyable, yet Salam was still not there; he was upstairs watching television and waiting for any news about the homeland, while all of the elite—or, as David called them, the art crickets—had gathered downstairs to celebrate him and his success. His absence from his own party became noticeable and worrying to the point that Emily commented to Julia, "This is embarrassing; he needs to come down now."

Eventually when Roger Goldstein could untangle himself from the crowd he walked to Emily and asked with his pretentious charm that seemed almost genuine, "Emily dear, where is Salam of the hour?"

Emily could not wait any longer so finally she climbed the stairs and saw him sitting in his chair, dressed but without his jacket, drinking alone, and watching television.

"Everyone is waiting for you," she said.

"I know," he answered.

"Roger is here. So are Rob Gibson and his wife and many journalists and media people. I think you've made it, babe. Oh, yeah. My parents are here too," Emily said.

Salam looked at her with a loving yet despairing smile and said, "Did you really send an invitation to Zlotcik with the wrong address?"

"Yes, I did, but this is not the subject," she said with a wary smile.

"What is the subject, Emily?" he asked.

"The subject is that I know there is something you need to tell me about. I know it's a very important thing to you, and I know that you have been waiting for the right time and the right moment to tell me, but at this moment we have a gallery overflowing with people who have come for you. Let's wait till after the party to discuss what has been dragging you down, because right now you owe it to me, David, Julia, and Kelly. Moreover, you owe it to yourself, because we all have worked very hard for this night, especially you. This is your night, so enjoy it, live it, and when you are ready to tell me, I promise, I will listen. So if you love me, then put on your party face and come downstairs with me. Later, when everyone is gone, you can tell me whatever is on your mind," Emily said with undefeatable reasoning.

For a long time, even though he sometimes felt trapped, he always counted on her ability to see through him and to guide him with simplicity toward safe harbors through his troubled emotional oceans. He never doubted the hidden strength of his wife and the persistence of her love. He had always trusted her and believed that everything she said or did was out of love for him.

Although he was emotionally in no state of mind to mingle with the crowd downstairs, he knew that Roger Goldstein and Rob Gibson held his career in their hands. They had been very caring and generous to him, but this night was about him and Emily only, and he felt that he could not let her down. She wanted a baby. He had wanted a gallery, and she had helped him build it. His dream, that was a clear manifestation of her love for him. With the last ounce of faithfulness before he announced his plan that he had been contemplating for the past two weeks, and before he would tell her about the important thing that he felt he had to tell her, he decided to put everything aside and stand by her for once... at least for the three to four hours of the grand opening party. He looked at her and said, "You know, Emily... you know that... I cannot live without you."

"I know, and I love you. Let's go celebrate that fact, and let's go celebrate your dream. It's your dream come true," she said.

"Our dream," he answered.

She kissed him and said, "By the way, I did not send Mr. Zlotcik an invitation with a wrong address."

"I know," he said. "You are too good a human to do such a thing." They held hands as they walked downstairs to the awaiting crowd.

10

The cheering crowd and the flashing lights of the cameras cheered his spirit a little bit, although David's raucous music added to his anxiety. Nevertheless, he appeared to be his usual self while he shook hands with everyone, with his wife beside him. Roger gave him a hug and said, "We need to talk. Many things are developing. This is Heather."

He shook Heather's hand and said some words. Rob Gibson was talking to his wife and eyeballing Kelly. David was engaged in a conversation with a girl who looked Middle Eastern and had a Palestinian scarf, a "Kuffia," wrapped around her neck and was playing music unfamiliar to the assembled crowd. It sounded appropriate for the colorful and diverse crowd in the gallery. Another man was talking to his in-laws, who sat in the middle of the gallery with two other couples, and chatted with him about Stephanie and Emily. He missed his quirky sister-in-law, Stephanie, and wished that she was there, because he believed that she had a lot to do with what had transpired with his career.

He stood talking with Rob Gibson for almost a half hour, talking about the plan for a new international tour. He felt nausea and needed to breathe; he went to the bathroom and washed his face. He wanted to go back to the letters and read more, but he looked at himself in the mirror telling his reflection, "Not now... for Emily... at least, not now."

Before the party was over, Julia had made Russell mad by making several passes at Rob Gibson. David left all of his music equipment and went to continue his night of drinking with the girl wearing the Palestinian scarf. The journalists and general crowd trickled out, and Emily's parents hailed a cab and went back to their hotel room. Roger Goldstein and Heather announced that they were going to a strip joint. Kelly left the party early to hook up with some friends. Five minutes after Rob Gibson and his wife left the party, Salam and

Emily were alone. They were alone and tired. Emily, who had been the first one up energetically directing the masses, could no longer keep her eyes open and decided they could clean up tomorrow. She walked slowly upstairs to take her shower, leaning heavily on the banister.

Salam sat on the couch and spaced out, sipping his drink with the same look he had at the beginning of the party. He began reflecting on the past two months of his life. Although he had waited his entire life for this moment and had worked diligently to achieve this success, he would not be able to enjoy it until he had taken care of long untended business. At the moment that it all came together for him, fate stepped in with that long forgotten past, reminding him that no matter how hard he tried, he could not forget. What he had wrapped securely out of sight would have to be faced head on before he could enjoy life. He knew that he would be letting Emily down for the second time, but he also knew that he had no choice. He was emotionally spent; the letters had opened a hole in his heart that needed to be sealed before the last drop of life was consumed. He smoked his cigarette, not knowing how much time had passed, and then went upstairs, looking for his wife. He saw her curled up in the bed with her eyes closed and a serene look on the face that he loved so much. He stood there looking at her for a while, and then he approached the edge of the bed and sat next to her.

"Emily, are you awake?" he asked.

"Yes, what, hon?" she mumbled.

"Emily, wake up, I have something to tell you," he said with a gentle voice.

"What is it, hon?" Emily replied without opening her eyes.

"Wake up, babe, it's important," he insisted.

She sat up with her eyes half closed and said with her sweet, sleepy voice, "What is it, babe?"

"Open your eyes. Look at me. Listen to me," he said.

Emily opened her eyes and saw him sitting next to her with a deep look of concern and confession in his eyes. He looked at her with all the conviction he had in his entire soul and said, "I know that what I am going to tell you may scare you. You may get angry, and I know for sure that you will try to talk me out of it, but you will just be wasting your time."

He hesitated briefly then continued, "But if I don't do this, I will never be the same man again. I will never be the Salam that you know and love. I have already slipped into a depression that may destroy our lives together, and I may never recover if I do not do this, but I have to tell you," he said, and looked at his wife who was now fully awake sensing the seriousness of this confession.

Salam continued, "Ever since I started reading the letters from that shoebox and with the current state of events, I feel that there is a chance, or a way, for me to return to my home country. I've started feeling like I cannot go on anymore unless I find the answers to the many questions I've had about my family and the people I left behind twenty-five years ago. I think my nightmares are associated with these feelings."

"Babe..." Emily tried to interrupt, knowing that there was nothing she could say that would be an appropriate response to his confession, so she gave him what she knew best: unconditional love and support. "You know I will support you in whatever you want to do, but don't you think it's too dangerous?" she said as she waited for more details of his plans.

"Please, Emily," he begged. "Hear me out and then you can say whatever you want to say."

"OK," she said.

He maintained his demeanor and continued.

"I am going to Balluria," Salam said.

"Where?" Emily asked.

"Balluria, Emily, Balluria. I need to go there," he said.

"Balluria, what is that—is that a real place?" Emily asked with soft voice and half-opened eyes

"Balluria, the small town where I grew up. I am going to see if any of the people I knew there are still alive. I have already done my research and bought the airline tickets. I am going for one reason only, to find answers for myself and for my family. I have been living in America for a long time, and before that in Europe, and never for one moment did I ever think of going back. But now it seems to me like someone or something is calling me back. Every time I fall asleep, I see two hands pulling me and dragging me back to that place. I have no explanation. I don't know if I am hallucinating or losing my mind, but I have these nightmares every night, and I have not slept for two weeks. For the past two weeks I've wanted to leave to go to Balluria, but I waited until we opened the gallery. The day after tomorrow I will be traveling. I know it is dangerous and things are still not clear. I know it is not safe, but I really have no choice. I knew that you would not be happy with this decision, but I have to do this. I leave the day after tomorrow; if I don't go..." he said, pausing, and then he held his wife's hand to feel safe and secure and loved, as he was shaking with fear and emotions while revealing his intentions and trying to choose the right words.

"If I don't go, I will never be the same, and we will never be able to have our family. I have to go to find my own peace," he concluded.

Emily looked at him, and she noticed that he looked like a hundred-ton stone had been lifted off of his chest. He looked deep into her eyes and heart looking for her support, approval, and blessing. She looked in his eyes and saw what looked like more than just determination; she saw a plea for help and a request for understanding. She also saw a tortured soul that longed for redemption. Without searching for words, explanations, or reasons that she knew would be useless at that moment, she smiled and said, "Just don't marry another three women while you are there." Then she hugged him and said, "Try to go to sleep now."

He lay in bed and waited willingly for the two hands to take him to the world of nightmares and a history that would not be forgotten, and he lightly slept for the first time in two weeks.

The Book of Balluria

The Unplanned Birth of Balluria

1

All passersby had the feeling of a strange, devilish energy going through their veins as they passed through these parts and noticed how glorious, splendid, and mysterious the mornings were. The sun rises here before it does in any other place on earth and paints the palm trees with a haze of yellow and gold, adding an extra layer to the mixture of dark green and faded brown and allowing the useless trees that live in the shade of the palm trees to show their celebratory colors. The sun adds gold in the yellow lace of the sharp leaves of the palm trees. The fog that covers the water in the river flies softly and touches the banks, moving to the rises beyond the human-made dirt dams invading the weedy fields and orchards. Mornings here are longer, seeming to last forever.

It was on one of these mornings that the early inhabitants of Balluria noticed something in the river as they tried to earn their daily rations of the khishny and bunnie fish that populated the river. The early inhabitants of Balluria watched with curious, hungry eyes as they saw the strange movement of a creature that looked like a small fish but acted like a snake in the river. There was a new, red and purple fish that kept rising to the water's surface, and then would go back down to the bottom. It had a long and slopped tail, similar to a moustache, long moustaches. They called it the moustache fish, but the news from the big town in the province came with a different name, "the republican fish." It appeared that the fish had invaded the Euphrates. The people in the few automobiles that passed by the gravel road near Balluria told the people in the only open shop in the village, where they stopped for water and tea, strange and sad stories about the fish. They said that the fish was a curse because of what happened to the young gentle king and his family. Allah was angry because they were a holy family, descended from the bloodline of the prophet and their merciless massacre had angered Allah. So the almighty sent the republican fish into the Euphrates and scared the other fish away; for weeks no one in Balluria came home with anything from the river.

A few months before the invasion of the republican fish, a high-ranking general of the royal guards marched his soldiers to the capital and bombarded the sleeping capital city with heavy artillery. His conspirators surrounded the city and closed all the streets. It was a morning of sadness for those who believed in and loved the monarchs. There were only a few people of Balluria who had ever heard of the word "socialism." The word was being used on the radio as the mean general delivered his speeches filled with promises of a new life and plenty of bread for everyone. As the people of Balluria listened to the distant scratchy voice on the radio, ushering in the new era of blood and fear, the voice of the anchorman brought discomfort and mistrust as he announced the end of the monarchy and the beginning of the new republic.

"In the name of the Allah, the most merciful and the most compassionate."

"People of our country, and the great people of this nation, with the help of the almighty Allah and the courage of your sons in the armed forces we had the ability to bring down the rotten and hated monarchy and end the reign of terror that the king, his cronies, and all the spies and agents of the West had inflicted on you. From this day forward, the sun will shine on the republic. Long live the republic and long live the new leader."

With a swift and surprising maneuver that shocked the royal guards, the general controlled the capital city and within two hours had surrounded the palace and demanded that the king and his family surrender with no conditions. To ensure the surrender of the king and his family, the general sent a mean and vicious captain who had no mercy in his heart. Although the general did not order the captain to kill the king and his family, the captain did. The vicious captain entered the courtyard of the royal palace and broke all of the windows with the bullets of his machine guns. He brought the young gentle king to his knees, asking for mercy that the deranged captain had no intention of giving. Many said that the captain ordered his soldiers to fire as soon as the king appeared from the doors of the palace surrounded by scared young princesses and crying royal children. Many knew that the evil captain, Abousy, who was drunk that morning and full of hate to all mankind, was a bastard. The commanders chose him specifically for that part of the coup, to humiliate the young king. His company entered the royal palace on that beautiful fateful morning. They ordered the royal family to line up in the garden. When they saw the beauty and elegance of the royal family, the princesses and the other women, how clean the children were and how proud the young king was, soldiers were filled with rage. The captain in charge ordered his soldiers to fire. The bullets ripped through the soft bodies of the royal family. Soldiers screamed with devilish joy. The streets of the capital swarmed with supporters of the new leader, and they started chanting.

"The leader... the one... the one and only leader."

Most were communists and very young. Many did not believe in Allah.

Travelers who passed through Balluria said one of the stories they heard was that the almighty was angered because they killed the royal family—the grandsons and granddaughters of the prophet—and started praising the new leader who did not believe in Allah.

That is why Allah sent the ugly republican fish, the many travelers told the people in Balluria. For the few households in Balluria that depended on the Euphrates for their daily bread, the hot July of that year was devastating. No one was able to fish, since all of the other fish had disappeared from the water and the fisherman were unsure if the republican fish was edible since no one could catch the ugly, red fish. The highest religious authority of the land had also declared that it was inedible and forbidden to the faithful because it had no scales. This, of course, added to the suffering of the few households of Balluria. At that time, there were only eight households in Balluria, and they were, for no particular reason, all on the west side of the river. No one from the big city of the province had any business in Balluria except to travel through it, as the little town was on the way to the intersection that led to the desert and it was near the road that led to the great city in the south. The eight houses were far from the main, and only, road in Balluria. The main road was full of water puddles from the previous rainy season. The water stayed throughout the entire year until it turned yellow, then green, then purple, then yellow again and then, finally, to gray. When the mosquitoes would nest in the puddles, the water would disappear under the scorching sun over a period of several months. Then with the next rainy season, the puddles came back again with the cycle of colors and the evolution of the mosquitoes' short life-span. The changing colors of the water mesmerized the children who watched them transform daily.

It was during these days that the large household of the Sharify family moved to Balluria, when their father, who was known as Sheikh Ghathban Al-Jassir, was killed in a tribal dispute down south. The story was well known in the marshland that the Sharify family had lost their father and seven of his sons and nephews in a dispute with another tribe led by a famous sheikh known as Nasser the Blond and his tribe. When the dispute developed into several battles in the marshes, it ended with a conflict in which the Sharifys lost almost twenty men because of the famous marksmanship of Nasser the Blond and his devoted slave Achrish, who killed five men: one bullet per body. The members of the Sharify family had no choice but to abandon their homes and move from their beloved stretch of land that divided the marsh. The family was afraid that they would be humiliated into forced marriages and terms of peace that would bring the Sharify name and their tribe to the ground. Most of the tribe members left the marshes and went to the big province in the south where they married into other tribes and then settled in the city of Jubair. Only the Sharify family members who held the title of the paramount sheikh and their closest relatives decided that they would move to Balluria. With them they brought sixteen households. They settled on the east bank of the river and started fishing the river and farming the unfertile land. Their first year in Balluria was harsh and filled with resentment and starvation, but they stayed, as their choices for other places to live were limited.

Sheikh Nasser the Blond had declared that if he saw any Sharifys near the marshes that he would cut their spines and heads off. For almost five years the Sharifys steered clear of the marshes, the small stretch of marsh towns and the fishermen villages all around the marshes. For a change, they enjoyed peace and they prospered in Balluria. Latifah, the oldest daughter of the late Sheikh Ghathban, who was wounded in one of the battles with Nasser the Blond, swore as she was dying from a wound that never seemed to heal that she would burn herself alive if the sixteen families did not build a guesthouse and name it after Sheikh Ghathban. Latifah said that it was her father's dying wish on the battlefield.

"He told me to keep the guesthouse open, so that his name and the name of the Sharify tribe would not be forgotten. Without a guesthouse, there would be no Sharifys," Latifah said.

For a year after her father's death, she insisted that they build the guesthouse and choose a man to head the tribe. So the men of the sixteen households chose a plot of land near the open field that led to the prairie and started putting the foundation down for a large guesthouse. They built it with mud and mudstones and used the branches and the trunks of the palm trees to roof it. Upon its completion, Latifah, who was on her own deathbed, told the tribesmen that the first person to enter the guesthouse must be Badr, the only surviving son of Sheikh Ghathban. On that day, Badr, who was in his early thirties, became known as Sheikh Badr Al-Ghathban in Balluria and in all the surrounding villages. One day before she died, Latifah told her younger brother, "Prepare a big feast, even if you have to burn my clothes to cook the meat and the rice. Invite all of the people of Balluria, Tawsheeha, and the surrounding villages. When they arrive for the feast, you are not to eat. You must stand alone with two of your cousins standing directly behind you with their rifles on their shoulders so that everyone will know that you are the sheikh in these parts. After I die, you are never to fish for your daily food. Instead, do what Nasser the Blond does. You are to raise a herd of livestock, even if you have to steal it. You must have a herd bigger and better than Nasser the Blond's. One day you will have the power to kill Nasser the Blond and avenge your father."

The next day, Badr Al-Ghathban prepared his first feast as sheikh, and that same day he buried his older sister Latifah, who died smiling as she saw the many large pots filled with rice and lamb meat cooking. She told her younger brother, "Now I can die in peace, because I know that my father's name will carry on. Promise me that you will keep this guesthouse open."

"I promise you," said Badr, and Latifah closed her eyes forever.

The men of the Sharify tribe had no money to hire an automobile to bury her near the shrines in the holy city, so they suggested burying her in a place near Balluria. They looked and searched around Balluria and the land beyond the river for a suitable place to bury Latifah, the daughter of Sheikh Ghathban Al-Jassir, but they did not find the proper place. Then one man, a stranger to Balluria whom no one had seen before, appeared from nowhere and suggested to the men, "I know where we can bury her. There is a place where the prairie begins. It has soft sand and there are seven palm trees."

Since they were more interested in burying the dead body as soon as possible so they could return to the feast, they asked him to show them where this place with the seven palm trees was. The men carried the body of Latifah and followed the thin man, who looked like a snake, for miles. When they arrived, they were surprised with how clear the sand was, how glorious the green color of the palm trees was, and how perfect the circle the palm trees made in that spot. One man commented that it looked like a shrine.

The group of men buried the body hastily and left the mysterious sandy spot. They could not help themselves from noticing the strange green glow that shimmered from the tops of the seven palm trees. Each one of the men felt a shiver of cold wind going through their spines, but none of them ever confessed their feelings to the others, and none of them ever returned to that place where the seven palm trees stood.

Sheikh Badr found it difficult and costly to keep his status as a sheikh without a reliable flow of revenue and the only way was to smuggle sheep across the border to the rich country in the south. So he sold some of his father's rifles and with the money he purchased fifty sheep. He then partnered with a young sheep smuggler known as Shershab, who was also a well-known smuggler because he was the son of a notorious sheep smuggler. This was a very opportunistic time as it was when the new general dictator who killed the young gentle king decided to attack the small country in the south. However, Great Britain was there to protect the small country because of its interest in oil. This made the invasion that the general planned a complete failure and forced the closing of the southern borders. The border closing made it very difficult for the nomads to transfer their herds of thousands of sheep to and from the small country. This created a market shortage of sheep for populations that feasted every day on sheep and lamb. Smuggling was the only way for sheep trading and Sheikh Badr Al-Ghathban and his young partner Shershab were dedicated smugglers. Sheikh Badr was greedy and full of courage. In just two months, he bought a hundred sheep, smuggled them himself across the borders and returned to Balluria a wealthy man. He built a new house with many rooms attached to the guesthouse. He then stopped doing the smuggling himself because sheikhs do not smuggle sheep, they sit in the guesthouse and let others smuggle, like Sheikh Nasser the Blond. So instead, Sheikh Badr hired willing and needy men to smuggle his herd, ten or twenty head at a time, dividing the profit fifty-fifty, paying them with money or one or two head of sheep. Each month he would send one or two men at time across the border to risk being eaten by wolves or large snakes that roamed the desert and the bullets of the border patrol. But after years of working for Sheikh Badr, Shershab finally decided that he would not smuggle anymore due to the new restrictions on the borders and news that the general had given an order to shoot any smuggler who crossed the border. Shershab moved to Tawsheeha to raise his herd of lambs and sheep, and he also wanted to find a woman to marry. Although he lost his best and most honest partner, Sheikh Badr was not deterred and continued looking for ways to keep the flow of money coming because it was the only way to maintain his status as a sheikh.

Only money and a guesthouse will make a sheikh, he thought to himself.

Soon enough, Badr Al-Ghathban started paying the border patrol police bribes that made the smuggling business very lucrative and much safer. It was during that time when a man named Irar arrived at Balluria. He was a strange-looking man, thin like a sword but extremely powerful in his ability to undertake tasks. When he first arrived at Balluria, he asked for hospitality customs in the guesthouse of Sheikh Badr Al-Ghathban. Just two days after that, he was herding sheep across the border, and while it took other men almost a month to complete the trip, Irar was back in only seventeen days. He never told anyone his secret. Some said that he was half human and half jinni and that he spoke the language of the wolves, and that was why the wolves never attacked him or his herd, because he was one of them. No one really cared, especially Sheikh Badr, who had found this dedicated smuggler who kept the money coming.

The people of Balluria did not notice any change in their lives since the death of the gentle king. Most stopped listening to the radio because the scratchy voice of the anchorman only told of new conspiracies and new plots to kill the young republic. It seemed like the bloody cycle of military coups did not stop after the killing of the young king and his family. All of the men would gather in the guesthouse of Sheikh Badr Al-Ghathban listening to the radio; the news of the capital told of another conspiracy.

"In the name of God the merciful and the compassionate."

"Oh, our people, the great people of this country and our great nation, by the care of the almighty Allah, your devoted armed forces and its intelligence have discovered a plot of treason. It was planned for by the Western intelligence agencies and the colonial powers of the world. But we were able to stop it and kill it before it started and we were able to capture the conspirators in their rat holes and put them in front of the people to do justice. The people have spoken, and justice was served as the bullets of the righteous and the nationalists ripped through the bodies of the traitors and to hell they will go. God, protect the republic; protect our divine and only leader. Here are the names of the traitors so the people will not forget:

–General Hasan Mashhan
–General Ali Salim Mahmoud
–Colonel Rifaat Hajji Umri
–Colonel Zaid Hayder
–Lieutenant Colonel Ghazi Sayhood
–Major Kareem Shadhan
–Major Jamal Adil Fahad
–Captain Hikmet Abbas Fakar
–Lieutenant Muhsin Humadi

–Sergeant Mustafa Alwan."

To the men in the guesthouse these names were unfamiliar and sounded like they were from another country. To the men mentioned in the death decree, as they faced the firing squad near the great mosque in the capital, Balluria was never significant enough to enter their minds. For some young men who frequented the guesthouse and whispered new terms like "communism" and "socialism," "Israel," "Abdul Nasser," and the name "Fahad," which was apparently the code name of a communist leader, it was a sign of troublesome times ahead and an uncertain future. For Sheikh Badr, it was the closed borders and what the conspiracy ramifications would be to his income. Especially when he heard that the prince of the small country in the south was the one supporting the conspirators to avenge the takeover attempt by the general dictator, who was worshipped as a national hero. The scratchy voice of the anchorman on the radio was the only link between Balluria and the world. It was clear that things would not be as safe or as easy as they had been, and Sheikh Badr was worried.

These people, who called themselves Maoists, believed in and followed a man who lived in China, had moved to the marshes and started an armed rebellion that went nowhere. They stayed in the marshes reading poetry all day while their urban, soft bodies became a feast for the merciless giant mosquitoes. The people would say that the leader had made soldiers of the mosquitoes. At this time, Irar had become the only man Sheikh Badr trusted to run his sheep across the borders. Irar was the only one who would succeed in crossing the borders. Every month he came back with more money, no matter the weather conditions or how many border patrols there were. He was the only one who lived alone in the outskirts of Balluria in a mud hut that consisted of one mud room with a high wall surrounding the hut. When the men joked about him being married to a jinni, he did not answer; he just smiled and mumbled, "No jinni would ever want to live with me."

Although Irar was the only man that Sheikh Badr trusted with his sheep and his money, he never let him be more than his smuggler. He never even raised Irar's share of the smuggling money, even though the price of the sheep had gone up that year. Sheikh Badr bought the orchard of the Merza Khalaf, which was a delight to look at because of its healthy palm trees, and managed to purchase the land near the main road, which later became the market. Sheikh Badr kept Irar on a short leash, knowing that he would not be able to compete with him if he had any amount of money that would allow him to buy his own herd. He paid him small amounts and kept most of the money hidden in a hole in the garden of the guesthouse, fearing that Irar, who looked and acted like a wolf, would attempt to steal it. The first government official had arrived from the big city with an official paper in his hand. He appeared midday and asked where he could find the house of Sheikh Badr Al-Ghathban, who was inside the house eating lunch with his wife and young son Reyhan.

The coffee man Khanger, a black slave that Sheikh Badr inherited from his father who had him since he was a young boy serving the sheikh's family, appeared and said, "May your life be long. There is a man dressed up like city folk waiting for you in the guesthouse."

"Feed him lunch and I will see him when I am done," Sheikh Badr said and kept devouring the leg of lamb. After finishing his lunch, he dressed in his robe and iqal and stashed an old English pistol in his dishdasha (a traditional man's garment), fearing that the man from the city was here to arrest him for smuggling sheep across the borders. He wished that Irar was there with him since he did not have any sons who were old enough to fight. At that moment, Irar was on his way back from the borders being chased by almost half of the entire border patrol force.

When Sheikh Badr saw the man, he had a sudden feeling of comfort because he realized that if the government wanted to arrest him, they would not send a man like this one. He looked like a sixteen-year-old boy who was barely able to stand. He was thin and delicate. Besides that, the guesthouse was filled with men from Balluria. Some were his cousins who were eating lunch, so arresting the sheikh would be close to impossible. All of his fears disappeared when the man, who dressed in city attire, spoke with a voice that sounded like a woman's.

"May your life be long. My name is Abdul Hafith, and I have been appointed as government representative, the mayor, and the magistrate to this town. I need your help; I was told by the mayor of the big city that you are the sheikh in these parts."

"That's correct," Sheikh Badr said, confirming his position and looking at the other men in the guesthouse as he realized the opportunity at hand: a government official asking him for help and protection. It had been declared officially that he was the sheikh and no one else. But even this fear had no basis because no one at the guesthouse thought otherwise. As the sheikh and the men in the guesthouse listened to the clean-cut and well-groomed afendi, as they called the city people, speak with his soft, female voice, he quietly started to explain his new assignment and what was expected of the townspeople.

"As you know, Sheikh, the enemies of the republic are targeting our great country with conspiracies and the great leader has decided that from now on all the people must participate in the honored duty of the protection of the land. Therefore, I will look for a place to establish my office, and I will need you to appoint three of your men to be in my gendarme force. One will be my sergeant, I want him to be one of your most trusted people, and I will need two more men to be policemen. The sergeant must be a tough man. All three will receive a salary of seven dinars a month," he concluded, not knowing what kind of storm he had just created.

The Sheikh welcomed him and assured him that he would do his best to help him and that he would give him the names of the three policemen in a day or two. The tiny afendi thanked him and said that he would return in a week with more official papers, a police car, and a gift from the leader. He left the guesthouse accompanied by two men the Sheikh appointed to the important visitor in order to reach the main road in hopes of encountering a traveling vehicle that would pick him up on its way to the big city.

2

It took the men in Balluria six days, three arranged marriages, and one knife fight to vie for the positions of the policemen. That knife fight almost killed Shaheem, the youngest male of the Saddawys family, who arrogantly said that he was the best man for the job because he knew how to read and write. They spent all six days and nights in the guesthouse debating who should be the chosen three. The sheikh let them think that their arguing would actually get them the coveted positions. As they argued, he decided who the men would be. The sheikh finally tired of their bickering and signaled that he had something to say. The bickerers grew quiet so that he could be heard.

"Jelwi will be sergeant."

No one argued about this selection, because he was the massive structure of a man who had stabbed Shaheem. The fifty or so remaining grown men of Balluria all wanted to be the two policemen. Although the Sheikh had let the men argue, he already had his own plans. He would only choose the two men who would pay him two dinars a month from their salaries without question. So, for one of the two other positions, he chose Qasim Wrewir a man with the body of a bear and the brains of a khishny fish. The other one was Rumthan, the one-eyed cousin, who was a shadow of a man. There was a great deal of loud complaining until they realized it would do them no good, and they just accepted that Sheikh Badr's choices were final. The exhausted and disgruntled men left the four of them alone in the guesthouse so they could take their wounded egos to bed.

The Sheikh gathered the three men and told them he would be expecting six dinars a month from them. The three men slept in the guesthouse awaiting the arrival of the feminine-looking magistrate. The next morning, the sheikh ordered his slave, Khanger, to prepare lunch for the entire town and waited for the magistrate to arrive. About noontime, when the sun was burning the ground underneath the bare feet of the people of Balluria, an English military truck, followed by all the children in the village, blew the dust on the main road driving toward the guesthouse. In it was Salam who dressed like the city folk, the afendi, who spoke with the female voice. He parked the truck in front of the guesthouse and was received like a hero when he stepped down out of the cab. The Sheikh was the first to welcome him; he sat Salam next to him in the middle of the guesthouse and lunch was served immediately. During lunch the afendi whispered in the Sheikh's ear, and the Sheikh turned to Jelwi and ordered him to go to the truck to unload the box. Jelwi jumped and told Qasim to follow him. They returned with a large green box that had English writing on it. They put it next to the coffee corner where Khanger sat on it, as the Sheikh instructed him to do so that no one could steal its contents. After lunch and after they all drank their tea, the Sheikh ordered Khanger to bring the box, but Jelwi jumped and brought the box to the middle of the guesthouse.

The afendi who spoke with a female voice said, "As I have been instructed by our leader... three men will be appointed as the police for the town of Balluria... and with the Sheikh's permission," he looked to the Sheikh for approval, "I will officially open the box and give them their weapons that come with their new positions"

The Sheikh felt as if he were just crowned the king of Balluria and wished that his late sister Latifah and his enemy Nasser the Blond could have been there to see and hear what was being done and said. Then to acknowledge the authority he was just given, he said "My dear afendi, I give you my word of honor that from this day forward, everything that you will need to support our leader, I will do and my men will do the same."

He looked around looking for approval, and Jelwi was the first to say, "We are your eyes, as you wish. May your life be long."

"Then by Allah's blessings, let us open the box," the afendi said.

All eyes were fixed on the lid of the wooden box as Jelwi and Khanger pried it open and pulled out a long-barreled rifle, they all called it the Inglizia, in reference to the rifle's English make and origin. It was known for its accuracy and its loudness. Jelwi pulled out three rifles, and the afendi pulled out three contracts and had the men sign them. None of the three men knew how to write, so he pressed their right thumbs in his ink box and had them stamp the bottom of the paper with their thumb prints.

Then he pulled out a shiny, clean pistol and gave it to the Sheikh and said, "And as for you, Sheikh Badr, here is a gift from His Excellency, the president of the republic, the only leader, as a token of his gratitude for your doing your patriotic duty." The sheikh almost passed out with joy as he took the shiny, clean pistol and looked at it.

At the same time the sheikh was reveling in his legal affirmation, Irar reached the outskirts of Balluria. As the afendi's arrival occurred after his departure, Irar went to his mud hut to rest rather than attend the ceremony. It was also during the initiation that a young boy came running to the guesthouse and told the men that three thieves were being chased by the people of the neighboring village of Tawsheeha and that they were seen walking by the river. The Sheikh was furious with the boy because he did not want anything to disturb his official inauguration as Sheikh of Balluria.

Before the Sheikh could begin dressing down the hapless youth, the magistrate, who was eager to do his job as the new mayor of the town, stood up and with his female voice that shook with barely controlled anticipation, he declared, "We must go and find these thieves. This is why the president of the republic has declared Balluria a town; because he knew we would be able to deal with these villains who would break the laws of the president." The new mayor thought that this was the perfect chance to capitalize on showing the true authority of his presence. He ordered the three men to immediately dress in their police uniforms that he brought with him and to join him on the search for the thieves by the riverbank.

The three men looked ridiculous in their khaki shorts and police shirts and hats; nevertheless, they also looked official. Without any training on how to use their rifles, they grabbed the rifles and stood outside the guesthouse waiting for the afendi, who was talking to the Sheikh about getting some help in rebuilding the only house that was close to the main road, which was deserted, to use as the new government headquarters. The three men stood outside waiting for their marching orders; Jelwi told the other two men who were the acting police officers to put their rifles on their shoulders. Jelwi was the most excited of the three, and although he was known for his previous mischief, years later he became a dedicated guard to the sheikh and a respected and feared lawman in these parts. He performed his pilgrimage to the Mecca that year and every one called him Hajji Jelwi. He was in his mid-forties, when he became the gendarme sergeant. Years later, when he was well known as a ruthless police sergeant, most people who saw him in the street or in the guesthouse of Sheikh Badr greeted him with fear, as stories of his courageous chases of thieves, smugglers, and wild animals were told around all the coffee and tea fires and in all the guesthouses in Balluria and all the villages near the marshland. All of those who greeted him made sure to use all of the titles he was known by. His eldest son's name was Hatem, so everyone got used to calling him by all of the occupational, traditional and religious achievements as well, just to be on his good side. They would greet him as "Sergeant, Hajji Jelwi, Abu Hatem, Salam Alykum."

When the new mayor walked out of the guesthouse, he saw his new police force waiting for him, and he climbed into the truck and sat in the passenger seat assuming that one of them knew how to drive. The three men stumbled into the back seat, and they all sat there waiting for the man with female voice to move the vehicle. He was stunned, but finally realized that none of them, and possibly that no one in the village, knew how to drive so he moved slowly to the driver's seat and asked Jelwi to move to the front passenger seat. He started the truck and the men of the guesthouse began chanting, "Praise the prophet and his family!" Their jubilation was evident with their rising cheers.

The tiny new mayor waved his hand and drove off to go search for the three thieves. Jelwi shouted to the sheikh, who stood in front of his guesthouse.

"May your life be long; I will bring the thieves with their hands tied to your guesthouse."

The truck took off toward the river; the direction the boy had told them that he'd last seen the thieves. The three men and the mayor drove back and forth along the river for almost half an hour. They reached the beginning of the neighboring village of Tawsheeha, but found no trace of the thieves. They stopped in Tawsheeha and the villagers were surprised when they saw for the first time the well-dressed man in civilian clothes and the three strange-looking policemen. They knew who Jelwi was, and they were willing to give any information they had about the thieves. The four men drove back to the river as the sun was setting. The darkness made it impossible for them to track the thieves, but in his mind the mayor felt he had achieved more than what he was aiming for in one day. The villagers in Balluria and Tawsheeha had seen him and had taken notice of his new authority. He went back to the guesthouse and ate dinner with the sheikh and they discussed the repair project of the new government house. The next morning the mayor accompanied six of the sheikh's men and cleaned out the old Ottoman Empire gendarme house. He went to the roof, made a pole out of a long eucalyptus tree branch, unfolded the red, white, and black republican flag, and flew it high. With a rope and three nails, he mounted a wooden board on the entrance of the building. On the door in a distinctive red color, like fate itself, there were three words that meant nothing to him, but would have great meaning to many people in later years. The three words on that wooden board were "Town of Balluria."

The Book of the Man

The Black Hole of Scum

1

It was a lazy and sleepy Monday when my father came to the house with the news. My younger brother, Wisam, and I were playing with soccer trading cards after we finished watching *The Big Valley*. The episode was disappointing because it was not about any one of the three boys, Jarrod, Nick, or Heath. The youngest was my favorite character in the show and was played by Lee Majors. Rather, it was about the mother, Barbara Stanwick, which meant that there were no shootings and no fistfights. So my brother and I tried to bury our disappointment with our soccer playing cards, trading cards that carried the photos of the most popular soccer players.

I had collected almost two hundred cards by playing with other kids in the neighborhood. I had this secret my whole life that I kept from all the kids in the neighborhood and from my brother. They never knew that the reason I was winning all the time was because I had marked my cards with very tiny and almost invisible signs on the backs. These signs let me know what player was on the other side of the card and what number the card was. One point made with a blue ink pen. "OK, it's Ali Kathum, number ninety-six." Three points made with a pencil. "OK, it's Falah Hassan, number ninety-eight." This way, when I threw my card, I would know exactly when to call it, and I was able to win almost the entire collection of the neighborhood kids' playing cards without anyone noticing the little ink dots. My brother, the poor kid, had only twenty-five cards, and he was losing them to me one by one with almost teary eyes. My mother was in the kitchen preparing lunch, and my sister was sweeping the staircase when we heard the roaring engine of my father's Fiat GL, one of the few cars on our block.

We knew that my father was home, and we knew that we would be in trouble if he learned that we were playing cards instead of studying for next year's school curriculum, something he always made us do during the summer holiday. We did not understand his insistence that we go about as if school were in session since we were in the middle of the summer holiday and all the other kids of the neighborhood were allowed to do what they liked. My father shouted from the driveway for us to come assist him with the groceries. We hid the cards hastily under the couch and went to carry in bags of vegetables and a big watermelon. There was one item that my father insisted on carrying himself. It was a case of twenty-four eggs, something so precious those days that my father himself took the time to place them one by one in the fridge. He even went so far as to give my mother strict instructions about the consumption of the eggs.

"There are twenty-four eggs here. That's four eggs each day, and Inshalla (God willing), next week we will be able to get another stack of eggs. I had to pay the shop keeper a quarter of a dinar extra for this one."

During those days, every household was looking for two precious rarities: eggs and matchboxes. My parents always talked about how items disappeared from the market and then suddenly everyone in the country would be looking for them. One year it was the sugar, and another year it was the cooking oil, but at that time it was eggs. I never understood this, so I asked my mother.

"Did the chickens stop laying eggs or what?"

My mother looked at me and did not reply, which made me spend many hours thinking of reason the chickens decided to stop laying eggs.

My father was a good man, well dressed, and he had the respect of all the people in the neighborhood. Compared to other fathers in the neighborhood, my father was a good one. Other kids talked about their fathers and told many stories of beatings for such minor infractions as sneezing without covering their mouths or playing cards or dominos. My father, on the other hand, beat us only when we deserved it, like the time when I stole a duckling and kept it in a bucket in the bathroom, hoping to raise a family of ducks that I could sell to buy a soccer ball or lots of soccer player trading cards. Or the time when my younger brother and I broke into my father's secret cabinet and drank some of the strange yellow liquid that made us talk and walk funny. Later, my younger brother vomited just in time for my father's arrival. Or the time I failed my math midterm exams and tried to erase the red circle around the number, so I could change the four into a six. I tried to do this with my thumb; the dirt on my thumb made a huge dirty black stain on the report card. When I tried to remove it with a razor blade, I poked a hole in the report card. After all that, there was no way it could be corrected. When my father asked me for my report card, I told him that they did not give me one. So he asked my sister, who told him the truth. I was so mad at my sister. Nevertheless, I got the beating of a lifetime. He never let me forget that it was worse that I lied. And he never stopped reminding me of the ramifications of lying, especially to my parents, and how Allah would punish me forever, because lying to your parents is like lying to Allah.

The only other family in our neighborhood that had a car was the Abu Hazim family. They had a Volkswagen Beetle, which everyone called the turtle.

It was broken all the time, and my father and Abu Hazim had spent many afternoons sitting in the middle of the street trying to fix it.

My father worked in the ministry of municipalities. He held a degree in political science and management. By current living standards, we were considered a little above middle class. We were a lighter-skinned family because my mother's side of the family was part Turkish and part Lebanese. They were the descendants of Joan Pasha, who was a Turkish military commander four hundred years ago, something I could not have cared less about, but that everyone else seemed impressed by.

We knew other fathers in the neighborhood. Some of them were mean like Abu Jaleel, the father of my friend and schoolmate Ali, who always wanted to hang out in our house and give my sister strange looks. Abu Jaleel was a man who beat his wife, sons, and daughter every time he drank, and he drank every day. Sometimes it required the intervention of the people in the neighborhood to save his wife or his daughter from his wrath. There was Abu Mizied. People talked about how his wife cheated on him with many other men. Although he knew about it, he kept quiet because she was the breadwinner.

Summertime in Baghdad was a beautiful time of the year. The ambience was filled with Qiddah, the aroma of the orange trees and the natural scent of the Joori flowers, which were in every house; the grass was green and wet all the time. The scent of the earth filled the senses with an overwhelming feeling of content and security.

We were the first family in the neighborhood to get a color television. My father, through his job and his many contacts in the ministry, was able to get one. It took the other families at least two months to get one, and for almost the entire two months, all the kids in the neighborhood camped out at our house from eight o'clock in the morning until my father arrived home from work. My younger brother would announce his arrival. "My father is here!" Then the neighborhood kids would jump frantically and start a nervous search for the nearest exit to leave the house. When my father would leave for the teahouse in the evenings, teenage girls and some of the younger and older women of the neighborhood would come to our house to watch a movie. The movie was usually Egyptian, and almost always old with Faten Hamama and Omar Sharif but sometimes a new one with Adil Imam and his group of funny castmates. My favorite television days were Sundays and Wednesdays because they played American movies. On one Sunday night they played a movie that I liked so much, called *The Alamo* with John Wayne and Richard Widmark, and on Wednesday, they played the *Butterfly* with Steve McQueen and Dustin Hoffman. Many other days, they played cowboy movies with Gregory Peck, Gary Cooper, Kirk Douglas, Lee Van Cleef, and the ultimate, Clint Eastwood. Sometimes they played French movies with Yves Montand, Alain Delon, Jean-Paul Belmondo, Simone Signoret, and Anouk Aimee. Oh, Anouk Aimee, I fell in love with Anouk Aimee the first time I saw her eyes. I decided that no matter what, I would go to the outside world and marry her, and we would go on many adventures just like the one she went on with her husband in the movie.

By the time summer was over, almost every family on our block had a color television set, and the neighborhood kids had deserted our house. Everything was back to normal as the other kids either stayed home or went to other houses. It was during that time that I heard my father telling my mother that it would be better if she did not go to Abu Hazim's house anymore, or at least for a while. I was upset with my father, not really knowing why he asked my mother not to let me go to Abu Hazim's house. I really did not want to know, but to me it was a sad thing because Khawla, their middle daughter, was extremely beautiful and witty. She was fourteen years old, with big black eyes and long wavy hair, and she always wore a tight dishdasha (traditional dress) that revealed the exotic terrain of her body. She would tuck her dress in the sides of her underpants as she swept the door front, and I would watch her from the rooftop, peeking through the holes of the stone decorations of the fence walls. One day she noticed me, and she smiled and kept sweeping. Not only that, she kept sweeping for a longer time than usual, and later she changed her dress and pretended that she was studying. She leaned forward many times and would glance out of the side of her eyes to where I was.

One day my mother said she wanted to go to visit the Abu Hazim family. I said, "I will go with you to see their son Imad," whom I barely knew. When we got there, Khawla walked into the garden while my mother was talking to her mother and older sister. I went after Khawla. She was standing under the orange tree. She looked at me, standing there with no plans to talk or to move. I was just looking at her, waiting for a sign of mercy, a clemency, or anything. I believe at that moment that if she would have asked me to lie on the grass and roll over, I would have done so. Instead, she extended her hand to the orange tree branch, picked an orange, and said, "Do you want it?"

"Yes," I answered, trying not to appear like a lovelorn oaf.

"Then come and get it," she dared me.

I walked toward her. She put the orange behind her back. I put my arms around her, faking trying to get the orange. She pushed her chest toward me and pushed her hands farther behind her back. Our bodies had touched in every possible spot. I smelled her hair and her skin. The scent filled my senses with the smell of women full of desire and heat. For almost fifteen seconds, which felt like an eternity, I was not able to breathe. I almost died. I wanted to die. Then she dropped the orange behind her and kissed me on the lips. My knees were shaking to the point that I almost fell to the ground. I was about to grab her waist and move my hands to where she always stuck her dress in her underpants, the spot that haunted my dreams and tortured my nights, but then her mother's voice came crushing through my adolescent fantasy turned reality.

"Khawla! Where are you? Come here."

She ran, leaving me numb and unable to recognize my surroundings. I almost passed out on the grass when my mother's voice shocked me back to coherence. That was the last time I saw Khawla, but she was always in my memory, along with her scent and the smell of the orange tree. As I grew through the remainder of my childhood, whenever I asked myself what would be the best time for me to die, without a doubt in my mind, that hot early evening with Khawla was the time I would have chosen. That kiss, which lasted only a few seconds, in reality lasted a lifetime in my memory; I wanted time to stop right then and there. I wanted everyone to disappear, and she and I would die and go to the other world. I felt that that unplanned moment of love that Khawla and I shared was the only moment of true love that I really ever had. Khawla stayed with me forever.

2

In the world of a twelve-year-old boy, it was hard for me to let things that I did not understand interfere with the thirst that I had for the world. It was hard for me to deal with other issues that were beyond the rosy picture that I had painted in my mind about the next possible visit to Abu Hazim's home. The chance to be alone with Khawla was again in my mind, and I had decided that I wanted to marry her, but I kept hearing my father telling my mother to stop visiting the Abu Hazim family. I was sure he was trying to keep me from my true love. It did not make sense that was he trying to prevent me from drinking from the fountain of love that Khawla had in her body and her lips. Why was he doing this to me? I hated him for this, and I decided that nothing in this world would prevent me from being with my love, not even the most painful beating a father would give to his son.

One night, I remembered seeing my father peeking from the window with the lights turned off. My mother was standing next to him, as they whispered in the dark. Quietly, I went to the kitchen and looked from the window. The kitchen lights were turned off. I saw what my parents were looking at. They were looking at the four vehicles parked in front of Abu Hazim's house. So infatuated was I that my first thought was of Khawla and the hope that she was not being married off to another man that night.

I soon learned that twenty or so secret service police agents raided the Abu Hazim house quietly and arrested their older son Hazim, who was an officer in the Air Force and a very well-liked young man in the neighborhood. This news saddened me because since that night my mother and I were strictly forbidden by my father from ever visiting the Abu Hazim family. My only concern was that I might never get to kiss Khawla under the orange tree again. The next day my father looked worried; he was visibly afraid, and I did not really understand why he was so worried. When he sat in the main room of our home waiting for lunch to be served, he looked like he was just about to say something terrible.

My mother was setting down the rice, okra stew, salad, and fresh bread on the table, and my sister was stirring a pitcher of fresh yogurt when my father looked at my mother and said, "They have transferred me to another province to the south. We will need to move soon."

My mother, who never usually showed much emotion when dealing with serious issues, nervously put the food on the table, looked at him, and said, "Oh, Allah. Where to?"

"A small township... Balluria. I've never heard of it before. We will be moving there in two weeks," he said. My father gave my mother a pleading look and continued, "I cannot do anything about it. We are moving, and don't make this harder on me than it already is."

So she kept setting the table and called my brother to come to eat.

That was the first time that I had heard the name Balluria. "What a name," I remember saying to myself, and then I asked my father, "Is it a real town?"

I thought my father was making the name up. I tried to convince myself that it was a trick. He wanted to see if we knew the place. Maybe he was quizzing me, trying to see how well I knew my geography. Maybe it was a conspiracy against me and my newfound love of my life.

"We are not moving," I said to myself. "It is just my father trying to scare me from going to Abu Hazim's house after what happened to their son. That was it, but soon things would be back to normal, and I would have many love encounters with Khawla under the orange tree. She would not be sad because soon her brother Hazim would be released from wherever he was, and things would be just be fine. It was only a fatherly conspiracy, so I smiled within.

My theory of a fatherly conspiracy was shattered the next day when I saw my mother packing the first set of boxes, stacking mattress on top of mattress, and getting the china wrapped in newspapers, making sure not to use the front page that had the picture of the president on it. To me these two weeks went by very quickly and were much too short for a twelve-year-old kid to wrap up his love life and move to the unknown. The pillars that support the existence of a twelve-year-old boy are his knowing the world around him, knowing his surroundings and companions, and most important, knowing himself and seeing his own way on his dangerous and eventful trip to manhood. For me, I almost had a beautiful fourteen-year-old full of life and full of desire, with the will and ability and attentiveness of a mischievous guardian angel. She would have guided me through that trip to manhood. She was living just four houses down the street from me and now all of that would be shattered. I could not move anywhere, not at that moment in time. I would stay here in the capital. Maybe I could live with the Abu Hazim family to stay near Khawla. Day by day, the unavoidable reality edged closer and closer. Each day, I heard my father tell my mother something that was related to moving.

"Make sure that all the china is stored in boxes and wrapped with a blanket so it does not break."

Or

"I have already transferred the children to the school in Balluria."

Or

"We will need to buy all the eggs that we can because I don't know if they will be available in Balluria."

My mind shut down and I was not able to hear any more bad news because I was enraged with the sadness of my lost love that was never given the chance to blossom. For me, knowing that I would never see Khawla again was more devastating than my family's ordeal, even after I found out that the reason for my father's transfer was that the Ba'athists regime decided he was to be punished for not informing on Hazim. My poor father was facing the lie that he lived as a Ba'athist because of his job in the ministry and that he paid no attention to his party duties. While the party superiors instructed lower-ranking members to watch their neighborhoods and their city blocks, my father instead enjoyed his evening drinking with his friends in the cafes by the famous river. At the same time, one of the most wanted men was living just four houses down the street from our house. That man was the young Air Force captain Hazim, who was the pride of his family and the neighborhood. He was the oldest brother of my beloved Khawla. Hazim was wanted because apparently he was a member of a cell of officers who were secretly organizing to overthrow the "divine leader" and who called themselves the "Warithon" (the inheritors), as I later found out.

It turned out that my father really had no idea of this conspiracy and even if he had known, he would not have told anyone about Hazim. But, someone had told the secret police that my father was a close friend of Abu Hazim (Hazim's father) and that my mother visited the Abu Hazim home on many occasions. Since my father was a government employee who failed to detect the political affiliation of Hazim, my father was dismissed from his ministry job and further punished by being sent on a faraway assignment for four years. I hated the government for doing what they did to us. And I hated my father, which was not fair of me, for not informing on Hazim, who had joined the forbidden political party. For these reasons, I would never see, touch, smell, or kiss my beloved Khawla again.

Throughout the week, we had many visitors who came to wish us luck and help with the packing. Khawla, her mother, and her sister came too, but it was my luck that I was out with my father buying sacks to put the clothes, shoes, and other stuff in for moving. I had lost my last chance to have a moment of love and to say good-bye to Khawla. Many people had come by because my mother was selling a few things. I hoped that Khawla and her mother would arrive to buy a thing or two, but they never did.

Two days before our journey, I found out that the reason the Abu Hazim family was unwilling to accept visitors or to visit others. They had received two visitors in the early morning hours who accompanied Abu Hazim to the fearsome Secret Police Headquarters, where they handed him the body of his executed eldest son, Hazim. He was ordered to do two things. First, he was not to have a funeral for his son and was told not to let anyone in the neighborhood know about the execution. Second, he was ordered to pay for the twenty bullets that shattered the head and shredded the body and the beautiful face of his son.

Abu Hazim did what they ordered him to do and never told anyone. He took the dead body of his beloved son, by himself, and buried him in the great cemetery in the holy city near the shrines. The family had a very private funeral that was only for them; they shut their doors for three days and cried alone. None of the people in our neighborhood dared to give their condolences in fear of what the divine leader might do if he found out. I certainly did not try to convince my mother to go to visit for the last time. I never gave much thought to the devastating impact of the event on the Abu Hazim family and on all of the families of our neighborhood. The only thing I could think of was the image of Khawla weeping over her brother's body. I imagined the thick black eyeliner coming down her cheeks mixed with tears and how beautiful she looked in her black dress of mourning.

3

The day of the move was chaotic. My father was up very early; he watched the movers load everything onto the large truck. He tried to look as dignified as he could, and so did my mother. I was late to rise, because I had spent almost the entire night waiting to see if Khawla would leave her house. To my extreme disappointment, she did not, so I went to sleep late, brokenhearted and as lonely as a loveless twelve-year-old could be. I woke up when the sun started to pinch my cheeks through the window of the bedroom that I shared with my younger brother. He was already awake and helping the movers load our belongings onto the truck.

While I wandered through my morning routine, my father was shouting, "Bring that box... take this bag... empty that one into this... make sure we left nothing in the bathroom."

My feet took me to the kitchen, just as they did every other day of my life, so I could look for breakfast. There was none. All that was left was a piece of bread and cooling dregs left in the teapot; that was all I had to eat the day I left the love of my life, Khawla, and set out to travel to Balluria. Balluria, whatever that name meant and wherever the place may be.

I remember the day we moved to Balluria like it was yesterday. It was an extremely hot day. My father was angry from the moment he woke up. He was angry with the laborers he hired to help us load the large truck. He got mad at the truck driver because it took him a long time to back up the truck into the spot that my father had designated as the loading point. I guess he was angry with us too just for being a part of that day. He was angry because he liked his job and the neighborhood we lived in, and he would no longer be able to join the pack of government workers every Thursday on Abu-Nowas Street to drink the Iraqi moonshine we call areq. Although his origins were from the south, he had not been there since he was a child, and he always considered himself a Baghdadi. When the workers finished loading the truck, he angrily handed them their money and said, "Mashallah...May you will always load trucks for a living."

They did not pick up on his sarcasm. They thought it was a compliment, and they answered, "Inshalla...God willing." Then they left us alone with the truck driver who had a strange habit of spitting on the ground every two minutes. The plan was for me to ride with the copiously salivating truck driver. My father, mother, brother, and sister would ride in the Fiat GL and drive in front of the truck all the way to the south. This was my father's way of ensuring that the driver did not steal our belongings.

"You can never trust these truck drivers," my father said as he instructed me to make sure the driver followed the Fiat GL. I sat in the passenger seat of the truck and as my father, my mother, and my two siblings kissed and said good-bye to the many well-wishers that gathered next to the Fiat, I desperately searched the small crowd to see if Khawla was there, knowing in my heart that she would somehow manage to look for me one last time. She never joined the crowd. My disappointment was interrupted by the weirdly loud and extremely annoying high-pitched grating-shriek-rattle of the truck's engine starting. The noise all but covered the voices of the people who waved their hands and shouted good wishes to us.

"Go with the safety and the keeping of the almighty Allah and with peace."

The truck started moving slowly and my eyes were still fixed on the light blue door that held behind it Khawla, the love of my life. As the truck passed by the door, I looked and saw that the light blue door was slightly open. From the slight opening of the door, there were two incredibly beautiful eyes looking out. She was there, Khawla, my love, my only love. She was there looking at me. I looked at her for a brief second and saw the lines of tears mixed with thick black eyeliner rolling down her face. The truck driver sped up, covering my life and my only love with the ugly black smoke that coughed out of the truck's exhaust.

On the way out of Baghdad, the driver lost track of the Fiat. He and I waited alongside the road for my father to drive back to us, yelling. The driver was intimidated by my father, but not enough to keep from losing contact with the Fiat two more times on the highway. It didn't help that my father's way of driving was to speed and zigzag through traffic and get ahead of everybody, causing my father to return again, and he would curse the driver each time. The poor driver wisely did not point out that the rickety old truck had no chance of keeping up with the sporty little car; it was obvious that my father was not in the frame of mind to listen. I realized that my father was extremely angry that day, and I knew that my poor mother and siblings were uncharacteristically quiet in the Fiat the entire time, so I said nothing either.

During the six-hour truck ride, the driver kept spitting out of the window. He must have spit a thousand times. Between the continuous streams of saliva, the merciless heat, and the noisy folkloric songs the driver liked listening to, I felt as if I was on the verge of having an ulcer; it was pure torture. By the time we reached Balluria, the sun had painted it with a bright color of severe nothingness. There was nothing on the horizon: no orange trees and no big buildings like in Baghdad. The one and only paved street was the road that connected the big city in the north with other big city in the south. The rest were meandering dirt roads; solid dirt that turned into a rocky yellow and white mud in the rain. All the houses were built with no plans whatsoever. There were only six houses on the main street. The rest of the town's houses were scattered here and there, making it look as though a mysterious hand had thrown all of the houses in the dice game of sagla, where kids in these parts throw stones and the ground and start picking them randomly.

From the passenger seat I looked to the left and felt a wave of fresh promise. I saw the river, the Euphrates. There was no one in the streets, which was normal since it was three o'clock in the afternoon. The only people who were out were those who did not mind the risk of heat stroke. Everyone usually stayed inside until the late hours of the afternoon when it was tolerable to go outside. When we reached the government house designated as the living quarters for the new mayor, the house that we would be living in for the next four years, I realized the reasons my father was getting angrier with each passing second. The house was close to the main road and facing the police station, where my father's office would be. The other five houses the government built for its officials were similar to our house, but smaller, and there were only twenty meters between each of the homes. Our house was painted yellow and gray like the other five, which looked out of place and secluded from all the other houses in town. I jumped out of my seat as my father was opening the gate to the house. The garden was an empty piece of salty dirt that I knew would cause my mother a lot of grief since she had been the caretaker of our beautiful garden back in Baghdad. Only one palm tree and one bushy weed grew in the shade of the kitchen's awning outside the door. My father, who thought he could find some daily laborer to help us unload the truck, was extremely upset when he looked around for someone, but found no one that could help. He put both of his hands on his waist as he usually did when his anger had reached the point at which the slightest action or word would set him off. My mother quietly carried the bag that had all the important papers and jewelry with her, and my sister and brother carried their schoolbooks. The three looked exhausted and extremely dehydrated. The driver, apparently oblivious to the mounting tension, again missed the spot where my father wanted him to back the rear of the truck into, and he slightly scraped the open gate.

Thankfully, by now my father was too tired and too angry to shout, so he just shook his hand and his head and said with a quiet voice, "What a donkey."

My mother came out of the house with a gray, metal jar of water and told me to give it to the driver and to my father, who at that moment started walking toward the only open store in town across the street near the police station. I looked in the direction he was going. There were only two people at the shop: an old man, who kept looking at us, and next to him was a skinny kid, who appeared to be my age or a little older. The driver drank the entire jar of water, no doubt so he would have the ability to continue spitting on the return trip. I went to the house looking for more water and found a metal bowl on the sink. I filled it with water from the cooler, which my mother insisted on filling with ice before we left Baghdad, and went outside fearing my father's wrath if I acted with my usual laziness that day. On my way out, I noticed that the bathroom and the toilet were in the same spot, and they looked dirty and neglected. It was obvious that hard labor and cleaning days were ahead. I went outside to where the driver was smoking his cigarettes, waiting for my father to return. When my father walked back, I noticed that the skinny boy followed him. As they got closer to the rear end of the truck my father said with disgust, "There is no one to help us in this black hole of scum. Only this boy, he will help us."

That was the first time I saw Hamid. He was thin and naturally muscular. He had no meat on his bones, only dark skin with many wounds on his hands and arms and scratches that made faded white lines on his dark hands. His hair was dark with yellowish blond ends. His eyes were more hazel than black, and they flickered with a wild energy. He looked at me with the look of a beggar and greeted me with, "Shloneck (How are you)?"

"Zein (I am OK)..." I replied.

"I have ten pigeons. Do you want to see them?" he said it as if he'd known me for years.

My father was against having pigeons in the house, so I never had any. All the other kids that I knew had pigeons, but my father made it clear that he would kill any pigeon if I ever thought of getting one, because they brought bad luck and hate among families as the legend suggested. Before I could get a fully formed idea in my head that my mother would help me in my quest for a feathered pet, my mother added to my father's comments by saying, "They shit all over the house."

Unloading a truck full of furniture and kitchen stuff during a midsummer day in the south was the hardest and most physically demanding job I had ever done in my life. I had smashed my fingers many times between pieces of furniture and wanted to shout from the pain. A heavy wooden bedpost fell on my foot and pushed me to the edge of screaming, but I did not because the little boy, Hamid, was doing more than I was, and I did not want to look weak. He was jumping in the truck, picking up pieces that I thought he would never be able to lift, putting them on his back or his shoulders, and slowly carrying them into the house. I thought he was trying to impress my father to convince him to pay him more than what they already agreed on. I hated him, and then I later learned that he had been doing this kind of backbreaking labor daily since he was nine. That was one of the ways he earned his living and supported his mother and his younger sister. That was the day I decided that I would never help anybody move nor would I move any house furniture by myself anywhere. After that, I always hired laborers, which I nicknamed "the Hamids" of the world, to move my stuff. Even when my wife insisted on packing and wrapping everything herself, I sat watching television and let her deal with the moving company when we moved to where we live now.

"That kid is strong," my father said, looking at Hamid as he moved a stack of boxes into the house. I was upset because the day was not going well at all for me. First, it was leaving Khawla and now here was this filthy kid who was getting my father's admiration. I was angry and jealous.

When we were done unloading the truck, we were closer to death from pure exhaustion than we were to life. Even the poor driver helped unload the truck. I decided it was because he just wanted that day to be over with so that he could leave to escape my father's wrath. The entire time we moved the physical pieces of our lives from the dilapidated truck into our new home, Hamid talked endlessly about his pigeons and was smiling at me. He performed twice the labor that I did. "I have two Zajil pigeons, a male and female Zajil," he said as he carried a stack of blankets wrapped together.

"Be careful with that bookshelf; it's mine," I said, trying to make sure my father heard so he didn't get too carried away with his admiration for Hamid, as he slightly touched the only bookshelf we had.

"I also have two Aalljie pigeons," Hamid said. I kept quiet and looked at the thin kid with a superior look, but he just kept smiling.

My mother came out of the house with two pitchers of water. They were the last two pitchers left in the ice cooler. We were tired, hot, and covered with layers of dust that seemed to coat every inch of our bodies inside and out. The water tasted like it was poured from heaven. My father was talking to the driver and handed him the money, and to my surprise, they shook hands. I figured that my father was grateful for the help he got from the driver since no one else was there to help except for the sweaty kid, Hamid, who was standing next to the door, waiting for his money and for me to give him some water. For a few moments, I intentionally ignored his silent plea for water and kept standing there waiting for my father. Hamid was out of breath and sweaty. His shirt was very dirty, and so were his feet and the mismatched pair of sandals that covered them. My father and the truck driver drank the entire first pitcher of water. I drank half of the other pitcher and held it in my hand.

Hamid looked at me and asked politely, "Can you give me some water, please?" he said as he breathed heavily with his shoulders beginning to droop from exhaustion.

At that moment, I felt extremely guilty, so I forgot about how I believed he tried to impress my father and how he tried to show that he was stronger than I was. Here was a kid who was desperately trying to be my friend in this godforsaken place, who just helped me unload the heaviest furniture, a refrigerator and a stove, and was still able to keep a smile on his face even though he had done twice the labor I had. Also, if there was anything that I needed in this black hole of scum, as my father called Balluria, it was a new friend, a friend that I could talk to about Khawla and the capital city. I looked at him and saw the sincerity of his plea when he was asking me for a drink of water.

"Sure," I said. "Do you want to sit?" He squatted next to me waiting for my father, who was directing the driver to the highway back to the capital city. My father then walked by us and said to Hamid, who stood up in respect, "You are a good boy. What is your name?" my father asked.

"Hamid," he answered with this strange energy that he seemed to have regained after drinking the cold water. My father gave him five dinars, and I guess that was more than he had expected. Hamid was so happy and started thanking my father with a stream of. "Shukran ammy, shukran jazeelan ammy, thank you" (thank you sir, thank you very much sir, thank you).

"Afwan" (you are welcome), my father said and added, "You deserve it. Your father should be proud."

It wasn't until some time later that I understood the strange look on Hamid's face. He just looked at my father, then at me, and smiled slightly. He held the pink reddish five-dinar bill and looked at the drawing on it as if he'd never seen one before. The sound of the truck leaving ushered the end of my life in the capital. It drove off, taking the last hope for me to leave this trap called Balluria. As I saw the truck mount the paved road that would take the eternally spitting driver to the big city then to the capital city, I felt the desire to run all the way to my old neighborhood and back to Khawla and her magical kiss that I would now be eternally deprived of. I felt like I could run and hang onto the back of the truck for the six hours it would take to return home. I just wanted to leave to go back to Khwala, the orange tree, and the things I knew and loved. The truck quickly disappeared in the haze of the merciless waves of heat rising from the black paved road that led to nowhere. I looked around. My father had entered the house, and Hamid was still standing there. He smiled again and started to walk away. I looked for someone to talk to console myself. He was the only one there, so I called him back.

"How many pigeons did you say you have?"

He turned toward me with a large smile on his face, happy to receive my attention. "Ten...two of them are Zajil," he answered with undeniable pride.

"I would love to see them sometime," I said.

Hamid's eyes brightened with a wild glow, and he quickly disappeared through the palm orchard behind our new home.

71

ARMAND NASSERY

The Book of the Gypsy Witches

The Road to Balluria

1

The trip to Amman, Jordan was long and tiring. The flight was completely filled with Arabs who were going to the Middle East to visit family or go on vacations and Americans who were going on vacation or in some cases to work. "The man" sat next to an Arab woman with traditional dress, and other than a courteous smile, he did not exchange a single word with her. She made several trips to the bathroom, so he offered her his seat in the aisle to avoid waking him up every time her bladder answered the call of nature. He did not want to talk to anyone. This was the first time he had returned to the Middle East since he left twenty-four years earlier. The overwhelming feeling of being a stranger and the fear of things that he did not understand prevented him from starting the process of ice melting with his people, the Arabs. On the contrary, he felt a closeness and comfort whenever he turned and saw the old American couple sitting two seats to the left or the young man who looked like a soldier. He thought to himself that the strikingly beautiful flight attendants of the Royal Jordanian Airlines looked so paintable; they made the trip tolerable and to a certain extent easy.

He wanted a drink of any alcoholic beverage they offered, but realized the insensitivity of the situation being next to an Arab woman with traditional dress. So he asked for his drink to be poured into a can of Diet Coke, and with his drink he swallowed four sleeping pills. He did not wake up until the flight arrived in Amman. He felt an overwhelming sense of being lost and scared; it was inked into his heart in a gloomy fog of uneasiness and made him lose his composure. He suddenly wanted to turn around and board the next returning plane to Chicago; he missed his wife very much and wanted to call her. Instead of bolting for the undeniable security of an immediate return flight, he made his way to the café, where there were many pay phones, and started dialing using his credit card; after three tries, he gave up. He understood what the operator was saying and knew it would be easier just not to try. He wished he'd brought his cellular telephone with him, so he did not need to follow the extremely long and complicated instructions of the billing cycle. He sat in the café and asked for a beer. The cold sensation of alcohol calmed him down, and he started planning his trip.

OK, he said to himself. *Do I want to continue?* he asked, as he watched the many departing passengers with envy.

Yes, he answered himself.

OK, what is the most harm that could happen? he asked.

I could be killed by a group of thugs, he said to himself wryly as he started walking through the long corridor to the arrival terminals.

He thought that since he could speak the language, and after all he was going to his home country, that he could impose tribal or traditional customs. He had heard stories of lawlessness and looting and watched the chaos that was ravaging his home country on television, but he realized that he would be able to handle anything—any situation and any ordeal. *After all, I am going to my homeland,* he said again, trying to reassure himself with the dwindling light of safety. He exited the terminal after getting his only bag, cleared customs, and was in the streets among the noise of the taxi drivers, who tried to welcome him to their vehicles, and the other people, all conversing in Arabic.

He looked around and noticed that he was being enriched with the life and warmed up with the vibration of closeness and to the smells and texture of these humans who led a much simpler life than he did. The faces of the people at Queen Alia's Airport were different than the faces in Chicago and New York. He felt closer to the "colors," as he always put it. Then he thought that he might be inspired in the most exotic and creative way if he would continue on. He gathered his shattered courage and went back to the counter where he exchanged dollars for local money, telling himself again, *What is the worst that could happen?*

"Jordanian dinars?" the thick-moustached clerk asked.

"Yes, please," he answered.

"How long will this visa allow me to stay? I am an American citizen," he asked the man in the tiny booth, realizing that he should have asked that question at the visa counter.

"Forever," said the Jordanian clerk, revealing yellowish smoky teeth when he flashed a very sincere and comforting smile underneath a grayish, bushy moustache that needed trimming.

The jolly Jordanian man counted the money loudly and quickly, gave him the exchange of money, and said, "Welcome to Jordan."

Jordan, the country that seemed to be a link between what is familiar now and what was familiar then: a link between the past and the present. It was a link between the East, all of its troubles, spontaneous impulses, and mysteriousness, and the West, with its settled arrangements, guarantees, and boredom. He wished to stay in Jordan because it was the last piece of safe ground before the unknown. For some reason he felt at ease in Jordan; the mixture of yellow and white stones and the dark green color of the trees over the hard rocked land felt like a familiar setting from other times and other dimensions of existence that he had long since forgotten. The sun was shedding its rays on his cold soul as he looked through the terminal window and saw the life outside. Here in Jordan, where he'd never been before, he could stay and maybe go see Petra or the Dead Sea, anywhere but the homeland. That homeland filled him with a very distinctive fear; he thought to himself as he looked at the faces of the people waiting for their loved ones to exit the arrival gates; old and young, men, women, and children, and they all smoked and talked loudly. He felt dizzy and hung over; he looked for a familiar face, just to avoid this overwhelming feeling of being a stranger among the people, his people, his native people, the people that he always felt obligated to defend and advocate for back in the United States, the same people he felt obligated to show solidarity with and to politely escape his wife's flavorless Midwestern cooking by going to their restaurants. These were the people he always bragged about whenever he found himself willingly or accidentally involved in a conversation about Arabic culture with an American who considered himself educated about the Middle East.

He preferred to call them the "fortunate luxurious elite by a stroke of luck and mind-boggling selection of time and topic." The elite liked to start the conversations with the phrase, "in my opinion," regardless of the accuracy or the validity of their opinions, and regardless of the level of care or carelessness they showed to the matter itself. They liked to talk about the Middle East just as they liked Middle Eastern food as an occasional cuisine. The conversation always steered toward using terms that meant nothing, as he always realized a certain disrespect that arose just minutes into the conversations toward many of the elites as they all suddenly became experts in religion and culture with the help of two or three glasses of wine. He learned early on to exit those conversations as quickly as possible. It was during his first year with Emily, when she invited him to a Thanksgiving dinner and to meet her parents in Youngstown, Ohio.

They arrived there the day before Thanksgiving, and he stayed in a hotel and insisted that she spend the night with her family. When she asked why, he told her, "You can't stay with me tonight. Knowing your father is in the same town—it's just weird."

She never understood that, so she went home and told her parents that he would be staying in a hotel.

"What, is he—Catholic—haha?" her mother said and laughed, because she was from a strict practicing Catholic family.

"Even though he is Middle Eastern, I like this guy," her father roared. "At least he understands that I do not appreciate that a jerk like him is touching my daughter, and I hope he knows that I will kick his ass anyway when I see him for keeping you away from me," her father added with his notorious body-shaking laugh.

The next day they went shopping for a gift for her parents. They finally agreed on a painting after arguing about it for two hours. It was by a Latin American artist, Pedro Alfaro, he was not famous at all, it was just a coincidence that he and Pedro met in New York three years ago at a gallery opening. He tried to convince Emily that their meeting in New York was true, and it was, but she just could not figure out how the painting made it to Youngstown, Ohio, plus she was just tired of arguing. By dinnertime her father had forgotten about the ass-kicking promise; he and her father were engaged in a very interesting conversation about the Middle East.

Her sister Stephanie was there as well, wearing her Palestinian scarf. He liked Stephanie for reasons that he could not explain. To him Stephanie was a female version of himself. He liked her as a friend, because she was not ordinary. She lacked the depth and perspective of an intellect, but she seemed to be what most people would call "cool." At that time he learned that Stephanie lived in New York and politically she opposed everything; the man, the machine, the government, and simply the way things were. When her boyfriend, Dutch Karl, tried to voice his opinion with his heavy accent, Stephanie rejected everything he had to say.

Emily's brother, Steven, from Vermont, and their cousin Blake, who lived in Youngstown and managed a drug store, were there. Also there were the Zlotciks, local longtime friends and neighbors of Emily's family. The mother, Terry, was a delight. She was making sure everything was just a joy with her jokes and talking about the food she prepared. Their oldest son Chris was there so was their youngest, Jonathan Zlotcik, was there from college, but it seemed that he did not want to be there. Their daughter, Melissa, who was infatuated with Stephanie and her rebelliousness, was also present. Everyone seemed to have a very keen sense to make the evening go by with as little damage possible to their emotions and their future relationship with their own families. He liked these "public conventions," as he called them.

Then there was Richard Zlotcik, the father. He had been a law enforcement officer for twenty-three years before he became a public prosecutor. When Mr. Zlotcik and Emily's father finished their conversation, Emily was worried about her two men. She knew her father, and she knew her boyfriend. She knew that both were kind and understanding, but she also knew that her father was hardheaded and opinionated about many things. He had prejudices, maybe a just few, but enough to scare the outsiders. And she knew her boyfriend with his shielded feelings and how he was extremely defensive about his thoughts and beliefs.

"They may not look good to you or sound logical, but they are the things we grew up with and believed in, so unless you go back in time and rebirth me, then let's not waste our time." That was always the closing line he used to finish an argument with her father.

At dinner Mr. Zlotcik dove into his choice of topics with all the grace and dignity of a charging rhinoceros. "So, you are from Arabia?"

"Originally, yes," he answered, already looking for his escape route from this doomed conversation.

"That is one strange place."

"As strange as Youngstown."

"You got that right!" Emily's father said, trying to cool down the little fiery conversation starting to heat up at the huge dinner table. "With the way things are in Youngstown, with all the gangs and shootings, I feel I am in Arabia," Emily's father added, as he laughed his usual roaring laugh.

Emily looked at him with a smile, acknowledging his attempt to neutralize the atmosphere by adding. "To me, every place on earth is strange to some and familiar to others. It's like your house is familiar to you, but the neighbors' house is not."

"But not like the Middle East and especially Iraq. That place is a hellhole," Mr. Zlotcik said.

"Unless you have been to Hell, you cannot describe any place as a hellhole," he answered with a familiar feeling of battle ahead. For Emily's sake and because he was enjoying the food, he felt the need to raise his white flag and surrender to solitude as he had learned to do his entire life, but he felt like he could not let Mr. Zlotcik win. He figured he would defeat Mr. Zlotcik intellectually and eat the food that Mrs. Zlotcik and Emily's mother spent an entire day preparing, and that combination would construct a Napoleonic victory.

"I have one thing to say. The people from the Middle East can learn a lot from us," Mr. Zlotcik said as he shoved a piece of turkey covered with gravy into his mouth.

Salam looked at him calmly, and although he agreed with what Mr. Zlotcik said, he did not like the way Mr. Zlotcik said it, so he replied, "People everywhere have a lot to learn. Some need to learn democracy, some need to learn hospitality, and some just need learn how to talk to others."

"You have to try the pie," Mrs. Zlotcik said, as she was cutting and placing the pumpkin pie slices onto the paper dishes.

"I definitely will, ma'am," he said, smiling at her and hoping that was the end of that conversation with her husband.

To his credit, Emily's father was trying to steer the conversation into another direction when he suggested that the election of 2000 would have the Republicans back in the White House. Mr. Zlotcik tenaciously refused to drop his chosen subject. "It has been proven that people from that region have their minds twisted somehow. I mean, like they just don't want to get along with anyone. They are less intelligent than anyone else in the world. They are... they are."

"Dad, you are a jerk," Jonathan said as he stood and went out for a smoke.

"Why? We are just having a conversation," Mr. Zlotcik said and added, "All I am saying is that they are... they are."

"Is inferior the right word?" Salam asked.

"Yes, inferior in some way," Mr. Zlotcik said.

"Oh, Richard, I told you to take it easy on the scotch," Emily's father said.

"No, Don... it's OK, we are just having a conversation... Aren't we?... What was your name... was it Salami?" Mr. Zlotcik asked.

"Mr. Zlotcik, I think it's time to stop this nonsense," Emily said with a distinctive anger in her tone.

"Why?" asked Mr. Zlotcik and concluded, "We are just having an intellectual conversation."

"Too intellectual for my taste, frankly," Salam said, "and the word inferior is not accurate, but let me ask you this, Mr. Zlotnick, or whatever you name is."

"Babe, please," begged Emily.

"Wait, Emily," he said, confirming his desire to fight back with a deep look in his eyes. "His argument is partially true... being inferior is a standard set by societies that have achieved great advancements in many fields. However, it is different in this case, especially since the standards are not proven to be accurate in their results as to the achievement of happiness and self-satisfaction as humans. For example, many Western philosophers have wasted their entire lives searching for the road to total satisfaction of earthly happiness, while many Eastern and Middle Eastern thinkers just drown themselves in earthly pleasures instead of asking the same questions. And to set the stage for a debate, to ask this question and have answers between these two groups, it will require a lifetime not a cold night in Youngstown, Ohio, over a very delicious and pricey meal that could feed an entire family in Asia or Africa for ten days or fifty homeless people in Chicago. It's just not intelligent enough for me.

"Also, why ask questions? To me it's an equation of time and events. It's how long you live and how you live your life, regardless of color, ethnicity, or religion. I choose neither to participate nor to justify it with an answer at the risk of losing some precious time enjoying myself as a guest, especially with this delicious-looking pie that your wife has baked, but I must say one thing. It has been suggested that some Eastern philosophers have recommended that we eat the monkey's brain, because it's a recipe for happiness since monkeys don't seem to be sad at any given time. So, until and unless you prove to me that this theory is wrong and convince me that a life wasted working a job and mowing a perfect lawn is happier than the life of a monkey on a tree, then I think our conversation will have neither fruitful results nor satisfying answers."

Salam was not sure of the validity of his comments, nor was he sure of the scientific reasoning and the historical references of his speech, yet he felt relieved to see its effects on Mr. Zlotcik's face. He did not want to stay for dinner anymore; a massive feeling of being a stranger and not welcome reigned over his heart

He stood up, smiling as he looked at Mr. Zlotcik who looked at him and said, "Whatever...Can I have some pie?"

"Whatever, f***ing whatever," Emily mumbled and stood up.

Stephanie, who was impatiently eavesdropping on the conversation in the dining room and had just come back into the house from the porch with Karl and smelled of reefer yelled, "So now you will say blacks and Hispanics are inferior and Latinos and others too."

"Hispanics are Latinos, babe," said Karl.

"Shut up, babe..." said Stephanie with an assuring voice and looked at Karl and added, "I love you."

The meal was over by normal dining standards, Salam looked at Emily, then said, "It was a wonderful evening." He looked at Emily's mother then at Mrs. Zlotcik." That was a very delicious meal. How come Emily is not as good a cook as you are?" He walked to the door with the false smile plastered uncomfortably on his face.

"Whoa, that was something," Chris said. "I am gonna watch the game." He stood up and escaped to the basement.

Salam wordlessly jerked his coat on he passed tightlipped through the entryway lighting up a cigarette, without waiting for Emily's father, who tried to shake his hand and offer a word of peace. Emily's father looked at Mr. Zlotcik with disapproval for what he did, and tried to catch up, but Emily was too fast, and she put her hand on her dad's shoulder and said,: "It's OK, Dad. He will be OK. I will go with him."

Outside he started thinking that he would need a ride to the hotel, so he looked for his cell phone and dialed information. Just then, Emily's voice warmed his cold loneliness on the freezing front porch.

"Listen... babe... don't pay attention to that asshole. He is always like this. Please don't let it upset you. He is just a grumpy and angry old man."

He looked at her, letting the smoke from his cigarette curl around his fingers. "Your father's name is Don?"

"What? Yes... Donny... Donald... Listen... Please don't go. Can you just calm down and come inside? It's too cold out here."

He looked at her with firm eyes and a wondering look, trying to guess what her reaction would be. He didn't search for the right words. As he always did, he spoke from his heart: "Emily, there is no force on this earth that will make me go inside that house again. Not because I don't want to, but because I can't. This party is over, but I have to ask you something."

"What is it?"

"Do you think I am inferior? I mean to you."

Emily was incredulous. "Are you kidding? Are you really asking me that question?"

"No, I am not kidding and, yes, I am asking you that question. See, I don't really care what people like Richard Zlotcik think of me, but I care deeply about what you think of me," he said.

"Babe, you can't ask me this. You know me, and you know how I feel about you," Emily said.

"That's why I need to know, Emily," he said. "Let me tell you something, Emily. I left Iraq when I was seventeen. My father had to sell our house to pay the bribes to the many government officials and to pay for the traveling expenses for me to go through Europe and then to America. He was hoping that I would become a doctor. He sent me so many letters encouraging me to do so, and he was very disappointed when I told him that I would be studying art and oil painting. He begged me not to do so and tried to change my mind. Then he threatened to stop supporting me by discontinuing the monthly allowance he was sending. However, I did not change my mind. I thought it was up to me to choose what I wanted to do, because it is the civilized way of living and thinking. I knew that my father had lost hope and faith in me, and I cut off my ties with my father and my family, but I knew that they had sacrificed a lot for me. It was their choice to send me here to America to become someone and to do something that would impact this world in some way.

"My father passed away, and he was still mad at me, but I believe that my quest in the West is simple, because it has a significance of its own. Whether I became a doctor or an artist, it was all for one noble goal: to achieve the status of becoming a total human and I wanted to do that through art. That was the only ambition I ever had in life, and at events like these and when meeting people like Richard Zlotcik, I feel like I have failed in doing so. Moreover, I feel like I have failed my father and my family for the second time over. So it makes me look for assurances for my steps and my beliefs and assurance that I am on the right track. That's why I am looking for reassurance from you, in myself and my goals, my surroundings and my companions. Maybe it's just to reject or at least escape the feeling of massive guilt and disappointment in myself and in life, but it will help me to know the true feelings of others toward me."

Emily watched him in the dim porch light. His body was tense with hope and uncertainty. His eyes glittered with emotion and because of the cold breeze of the Ohio autumn.

"Salam, I will answer your question if you answer mine."

"What is your question?"

"Am I just a companion to you?" she asked with just as much uncertainty as he showed.

He looked at her, searching for the right answer and the right words. He did not trust his English, because he really did not have it. He saw in her piercing blue eyes a flare of wondering in the midst of collapsing waves of emotions through the dimly yellow lights of the front porch. "You are not only my companion," he said with the voice of a young foreign student who was learning his first words in English class. "You are my lover, my best friend. You are my only friend in this world, my girlfriend, my partner, and you are the only human being that I trust with my life." As he said the words, he looked in her eyes to see the effect of his reply, knowing for a fact that he was telling the truth, and then added with a serene voice. "You are my one and only inspiration." He said that, wondering if he said the right thing, if he said enough, or if he needed to say more or use different words. Her warm smile and unexpected lingering hug brought all the warmth and assurance he needed.

Jonathan, who exited the house, interrupted and said, "Sorry, ohh, isn't that sweet. What's up, crazy lovers? I am going to get some beer. You better get inside before you freeze your butts off." Then looked at Salam and said, "Hey, dude, don't mind my dad; he is really a nice guy, but sometimes he acts like a jerk." He got into his Jeep Cherokee and drove off.

At that moment, Emily let go of him and stood there; she looked at him and said, "I will give you my answer tonight. Let me just get my dad's car, and I will go with you to the hotel... and I don't care what or whose ass my dad will kick tonight." They drove to the hotel, and she spent the night with him. That night he realized how much he really loved her. From then on, she was his partner in everything. She was his partner in his thoughts and his goals and in his despair and overwhelming loneliness. But that sense of failing his father and the massive guilt never left him.

2

While he sat in the coffee shop in Queen Alia's Airport in Amman, Jordan, thinking of his purpose when he set his plans to come to his homeland, he thought of his father and thought of Emily and who would be more forgiving and more accepting. He thought about his trip and what might come of it, as he knew that his father had waited for him to return for many years, Emily was waiting for him to return now. Was the trip just another mistake that he would make or another self-searching journey that could be his last? Emily was there for him twenty-four hours ago, and his father was there twenty-four years ago, yet the wait felt the same; on one end, there were Emily's hopes and dreams that longed to become true and on the other end were his father's dreams and his mother's hopes that never came true and never would. Also there was his home country that he never missed and never thought of going back to. Or was the trip the closure that he needed, since he left Balluria and the end to a journey that he started nearly twenty-five years ago? He finished his tenth cigarette and put it out in the overflowing ashtray. He picked up his bag and made his way outside to find the sun shining on the glorious Jordanian morning.

"There are two ways to go to Baghdad," said the taxi driver, who was stunned by the question and by the opportunity of a lucrative fair. "I can take you there... I mean to the border, and then you can take any taxi or bus to Baghdad, or you can go to the traveling company that goes there, to Baghdad, by bus."

"Will I need to go to a hotel to find a traveling company?" The driver did not answer. However, the trip to the border sounded less troublesome and in a sense closer to his salvation, at least this way he would see the border and could make up his mind there. So, with his mind made up, at least on this leg of the journey he asked, "How much? If you take me to the border, how much it will be?"

"Whatever you want to pay me is fine, but no less than two hundred and fifty Jordanian dinars, sir," the driver said, preparing for some haggling.

"That's fine... let's go," he agreed with the stunned driver's demands.

The driver was quick to stash the bags in the trunk to ensure no changing in the deal and opened the door. He got inside the car and realized that it was a smoking car. Smoke and cigarette butts were all over. He sat in the backseat and waited for the driver, who was talking to a policeman, slipping him some currency. Then he got into the driver's seat and said, "Bism Allah Alrahman Alraheem (In the name of God the Merciful)...you have honored us, sir...we will be there in three hours, Inshalla (God willing). You just make yourself comfortable."

"Do you mind if I smoke?" he asked.

"Not at all, sir. Do you need cigarettes or a lighter?" the driver asked.

"I am OK. Thank you."

He smoked his cigarette quietly, looking at the street signs and billboards, searching for familiar billboards, and it was comforting to see a McDonald's sign. He smiled as he realized just how long it had been since he had been away from the Arab land, or Arabia, as his father-in-law called it. He was upset because he really wanted to call Emily and tell her that he was OK. She must be very worried about him, he thought. Jordan was warm and the people seemed less tense. He could stay here for a day or two, maybe call Emily and she could fly here to join him and be closer to him when he needed her. They could go to the Dead Sea. He saw a brochure once, and his in-laws had told him a lot about it when they took their trip to Israel to visit the site of John the Baptist two years ago; or they could go to see Petra. "Yes," he said, as he thought to tell the driver to go to the nearest hotel, counting on the disappointment of the enthusiastic driver, who never stopped talking. Then the old voice and the mysterious feeling that he would get when he saw the old photos came storming into his senses; the scent of the dust of the letters filled his soul again, and he started to feel the spider web of longing and a strange thirst that he tried to resist by repeating the unknown and unsuccessful suggestion of peaceful defeats of this calming artificial retreat.

I could go see Petra. Petra...? he asked himself.

What's Petra got to do with my soul? he wondered. *I need to see Balluria...* The mysterious voice and the amazing scent overwhelmed him and calmed his soul and finalized his decision.

"You don't mind if I sleep until we reach the border?" he asked the talkative driver.

"Not at all, sir. You just make yourself comfortable, and I will wake you up when we get there," the driver said.

He woke up when the driver was shouting. "Mister...Ya...sai'yed (mister)...ya... sai'yed...we are here." He opened his eyes to the unrelenting noon sun. The border checkpoint looked busy. Many taxies and many old and new GMC Suburbans that were painted with black and white, or orange and white, with the taxi insignia and colors lined up waiting for clearance to get into the country. Buses full of mostly women and luggage piled so high on top of them made him think that any policeman in America would have a field day issuing safety tickets and citations. To him, this was not only the border to another country or the border to his home country; it was the beginning of a journey a person only took once in a lifetime... After this journey he would never be the same and that would stay in his mind forever, if he made it back alive. Just as he was never the same and did not forget about the time when he was twelve and his family moved to Balluria... or the time when he was sixteen and his family moved out of Balluria, and just like the time when he was seventeen and set sail alone to America. For some reason, he knew that this trip would be the last trip for him, and then he would have inner peace and would never embark on another trip, not anymore. After this trip he would go back to Emily.

3

The borders were not only invisible lines that separated people, customs, behaviors, and loyalties; they were meaningless proximities of fake self-ratifications. To him, however, they were the gates to another dimension. From this point on people would look differently, talk differently, and look at him differently. It was almost two o'clock in the afternoon when he paid the driver the taxi fare and walked toward the checkpoint just as many others went to the checkpoint to enter the borders with their vehicles. He was directed by a soldier who looked very familiar and reassuring. He was an American soldier, a man who could help him bypass all of the third world procedures and humiliating treatment if he showed him his dark blue American passport. He flashed his passport, and it actually worked; the soldier waved for him to get closer and greeted him.

"How can I help you, sir?" He heard the familiar language spoken with a distinctly American accent. He smiled and for the first time, he felt safe and comfortable.

"I am here on a short visit... I am from Chicago," He said to the soldier.

"Where are you going, sir?" the soldier asked politely.

"My hometown a small town, Balluria, maybe you've heard of it," He replied.

"No, not really... is it a real town? The name sounds strange," the soldier said. The man looked at his name tag. It read Zeller.

"Yes, it is a real town, Mr. Zeller," He replied.

"My advice, sir, is that you spend the night here and in the morning we can direct you to one of our local bus or taxi drivers that we can trust," the soldier said.

"What do you mean, that you can trust, Sergeant Zeller?" he asked after taking several seconds to see the three stripes denoting his rank and to read the tag on the soldier's uniform one more time.

"Well, sir. There have been some incidents on the highways, and it's better to travel during the day," Sergeant Zeller explained.

"Where can I sleep or take a shower, then?"

"There is a tent right there, sir. I don't know about a shower, though, but let me see what I can do later."

"Thank you, Sergeant Zeller. Thank you so much," he said with sincerity.

"Oh, no problem, sir My pleasure. And if you need anything, let me know," Sergeant Zeller replied with his noticeable Texan accent that sounded so assuring.

The courteous sergeant directed him to another soldier of lesser rank, who walked him toward the tent. He noticed that there were many locals and other Middle Eastern people sitting in an area where there was no tent. They sat there waiting for their paperwork. They had spread colorful blankets on the ground and put their luggage and other belongings on them and waited. It was getting closer to darkness when he asked the soldier who was guarding them, "Are they staying in the tent?"

"No, sir," the private answered.

"Why not?"

"They are local nationals, sir," the soldier said.

"But, I am too," he said not thinking of the privileges that he could lose.

"Well, I was told that you are an American, sir... and Americans and some other nationalities stay in the tent. The rest stay out here because they can leave whenever they want to," he explained.

"But it's really cold out there," Salam said.

"I know, sir, but this is the way it is."

"I am an American," he said.

"Roger that, sir," the young soldier replied.

The way it is, he thought. He went to use the latrine outside the tent and looked at the large number of people gathered around what looked like a small brown hill of plastic bags. They were the MREs provided by the soldiers to the local nationals and those of third world nationality at the border entry point, and it was dinner time. He stayed outside looking at men, women, and children storming the pile and taking as many meals as they could.

The wind started to sing its songs. It was late April, the season when the orange trees blossomed in the capital city and the palm trees started to let out the aroma of growing dates. Birds started to leave their nests. *Balluria...* he thought. He learned this long ago, but it did not feel that way in this spot. Something was not right. Something had changed. Is it because American soldiers are here? Did that take away from the romantic sense of the moment or the place? Did the uniforms and the many armored vehicles prevent the romantic senses of his memories from peaking and reaching out to his long-awaiting heart, or was it that it had been so long since he felt innocence or normality? He did not know, but he needed to smoke; he stayed outside the tent to smoke and did not want to go inside, which was starting to fill up with civilians. Most of them were Americans and some Europeans, British, and Australians. Some of them hung outside the tent smoking and talking about the new reality in his homeland. They all looked at the mass of people eating the packaged food. He felt a sting of shame inside and treason as he realized what he really shared with the others who stood there watching the locals eating MREs. What really shamed him was the feeling that he was safe while he was with the Americans, although he wanted to touch the locals and ask them about Balluria and maybe about Amel and all his friends from the photo of the soccer team. He might be lucky and meet someone who knew where to direct him, but he did not really need any direction. He would get there somehow. For now he was more comfortable standing with a group of Western strangers, smoking cigarettes, and watching the locals eating the MREs.

4

It was a very noisy morning when he woke up. All the civilians in the tent were getting ready to depart. They rearranged their backpacks and bags, and some started to move outside the tent looking for a cup of coffee and transportation eastward. He was slowly rising, and before he did anything, he went outside to see if the locals were still there. They were all gone; he was disappointed. The soldiers had a portable kitchen, and they served coffee and some kind of biscuit. He grabbed his bag, which he had used as a pillow the night before, and went to where some civilians were standing with their Styrofoam cups and cigarettes talking about the road ahead. He heard a big-bellied American, who had a long moustache and a tattoo of a very well-drawn naked mermaid peeking from the blue T-shirt he was wearing, say, "The safest way is to wait for one of the convoys and ride with them if you have no one coming to pick you up." That was the answer he was waiting for without asking.

"Do you have someone picking you up?" he asked the big-bellied man.

"Yes, sir. It's my company. Their convoy will be here at 0800 hours," the big man answered.

"At 0800 hours. Does that mean eight in the morning?" he asked.

"Yes, sir," the fat man answered, taking a deep inhale from his cigarette.

"If I get a taxi, can I follow the convoy?" he asked again.

"Where are you going? Are you an American?" the fat man asked as his voice changed.

"Yes, I am. I am an American, and I am going to Balluria. It's a small town," he replied.

"Never heard of it," the fat man said, adding "Ah, hold on. Let me make a call. Maybe we can get you a ride on our convoy," the jolly American fellow said as he grabbed his phone and took a few steps away.

"That will be great and I really appreciate it," he to the fat American and waited. He tried to remember the dream he'd had the night before and wondered why an old woman he did not recall ever meeting would appear in his dream, calling him to enter her house and when he did, she locked the door. He wandered in thought until he was shaken back by the voice of the fat American man.

"Good news, buddy," he said. "You are in. We will take you with us to Baghdad. Then you are on your own to that town you are going to. What was its name again?"

"Balluria."

"Yes, is it a real town? It sounds very strange."

"Yes, it is, sir," he replied. "But that's wonderful that you are offering me the ride," he added and waited for the man to say something. The fat man said nothing in reply and went back to talking on his cell phone.

At eight o'clock, the convoy arrived, and extremely tough-looking and fully armored men exited their trucks and went straight to the latrines. A young man, who looked and acted like he was in action or in a war movie, shouted to the fat man, "Come on, Bill, we don't have a lot of time."

"I'm coming. Hey, Shawn, this is the man I told you about."

Shawn, the young man, greeted him and grabbed his bag and said, "You can ride with Diablo, third truck. Let's go."

Bill, the fat man, instructed him to go to the third truck and said, "There is Diablo. Well, I guess I'll see you in Baghdad."

"Yes, I will see you there," he replied and went looking for Diablo.

The highway between the western border and Baghdad looked busy with trucks loaded with goods and buses filled with people and material as well as endless military convoys. He did not pay attention to all of that; he was waiting for the right feelings, the feelings he had in his nightmares, that silky feeling of being at home to sneak back into his heart. He knew that it would be in Baghdad only or in Balluria, but not in these parts or this western desert. That desert was the opposite of his two worlds, and it held no emotional connection to either of them. Looking from the window to the desert and the people, he thought that he might have been able to paint it with the craft of a nomadic wonderer, but his heart was not touched. He was safe in the shell that he created for himself and was just looking outside at his homeland, but with no feelings whatsoever, until the convoy passed by three women carrying firewood. He looked at one young woman, who looked tortured, and when his eyes met with hers, he saw how deep her eyes were and how black they were. At that moment, he felt the thrust of the color of her eyes as they started to come alive. Even the sand started moving. He felt the hands of the old woman from his dream again pulling him and directing him. His search for the right and the true feeling ended as he felt his heart weaken with the blackness of the nomadic woman's eyes. It stayed with him long after the convoy passed by the three women. "So it is here, the magical feeling of being home," he said to himself as he buried himself in the seat and braced himself for whatever might come. He leaned on the window and fell asleep, hoping to see the old woman again in his dream.

He woke up when the convoy stopped at a checkpoint. American soldiers were in the streets walking around, and everything seemed just normal. He looked at the horizon and saw the minarets. "Oh, my God, it is Baghdad... Baghdad, the ultimate city of love and betrayal." He started to sing the old song of Fairuz, a song he had heard a long time ago, a song from the Lebanese songstress of love who sang for Baghdad:

Baghdad, the poets and the paintings,
The gold of the ever-lasting glory,
And
Its Aromatic fragrance,
Oh, your thousand nights,
Oh, your ultimate celebrations,
The moon washes your face,
Oh, Baghdad.

Baghdad looked dusty. It seemed like an invisible wizard had waved his wand and painted the city with a coat of dust and mud. He yawned and looked at Diablo, who was talking on his radio. He looked out of the window and there were people, Iraqis, his people. He searched for the right words to describe what he saw in the people's faces, as they looked at the convoy, and two words came to his mind. Tired and careless... and one more word... naturally, sad... as sad as sadness itself. They just knew how to hide it behind the colors of their eyes. That realization scared him because he never noticed that before, when he was one of them, when he was an Iraqi. He heard Diablo screaming.

"Sir, where do you want to go? We are close to the palace, the republican palace."

"Is that close to the main bus station?" He asked.

"I don't know, but I think it is. Is it in the Allaawy garage?" Diablo asked.

"Yes, exactly, the Allaawy garage. The bus station," He confirmed.

"Yes, sir, it's just one hundred feet from here. We will drop you off; we will get there soon."

"Thanks, I really appreciate it," he replied. He looked for his bag and started telling himself that it would be all right. He felt the hands of the old women wrapping firmly around his heart.

"Here we are," Diablo said and smiled.

"Thank you, I really appreciate it. Say thank you to Bill and be safe," he said to Diablo.

"No worries. Good luck," Diablo replied.

When the convoy left, he felt extremely lonely and vulnerable. Although he was not as afraid as he thought he would be, he was lonely. He wanted to say something to the people who looked at him, but did not know what to say. He thought he could say, "I am an Iraqi. I am one of you. I need to go home... I miss home," but he realized how stupid he would look if he said that, so he pulled out a cigarette, lit it up, and waited. He saw the taxis lined up in more than six lines. He walked toward where the taxis were and looked for any familiar faces among the taxi drivers. There were none, so he looked for the one with the most civilized appearance among them and found one who looked weak and poor. At that moment that taxi driver was looking at Salam too. Their eyes met. The taxi driver smiled, and that was enough for Salam. He walked toward him and said, "I need to go to Balluria."

"Balluria? I have never heard of it. Where is it?" the taxi driver asked.

"It's a small town in the south on the bank of the Euphrates. I need to go now," he said, realizing that he was losing the initiative in the conversation and the chance to price bargain.

"Well, if you know where it is, I will take you there. How much will you pay?" the driver asked.

"No. No. You will stay with me because I need to come back to Baghdad. I am only here for... I mean I need to go there and come back the same day."

The skinny driver looked at him and assessed that he must be from "The Outside" (a name Iraqis used to describe the world outside Iraq), and immediately realized that the fare would not be karwa taabana (a cheap fare). He realized that this fare might be equal to what he would make in an entire week of work. Therefore, he moved right away to negotiate. "How much will you pay me?" the driver bluntly asked him about the fare and waited for an answer.

"I don't know, but you will be satisfied with what I will pay you. It's a family affair, and I need to go immediately," he said trying to convince the driver of a deal when he had no idea about its details.

The driver looked at him and asked, "You look like the son of good people. I will take you there."

"That's good. What is your name?" he asked.

"Alwan... Abu Hassan," the driver answered... and continued, "Let us drink some chai, and then we will depend on Allah and will travel to... to, what is the name of the town you are going to?"

"Yes, let us do that. The town's name is Balluria," Salam said.

"Balluria?" Alwan, the driver, asked, and continued, "What a name. Is it a real town? It sounds like a mirage to me."

He looked at the driver and replied, "It sounds like a mirage to me too... but it's real." He followed Alwan to the tea stand to drink some chai.

The Book of Balluria

The Eagle and Balluria

1

The gendarme patrol gave up after they waited for an hour by the other side of the river. It was getting darker, and it seemed that all three thieves had vanished. Sergeant Jelwi, who was known as the best tracker in these parts, walked out of the old English truck and looked around. He glared at the river with his hawkish eyes, searched the thick bushes of reeds, but he saw nobody. There was no sign of the three thieves. He went back to his squad of two men, and the slim afendi who spoke with a feminine voice and told him that he did not see anything or anyone.

"Maku, there is nothing here."

The civilian man looked around and ordered with his woman-like voice, "Yalla imshoo (come on...let's go), let's go back to the town."

"What a first day for me," he concluded.

Several hours before, when dawn broke the serene darkness of the orchards and removed the only cover the three thieves had, the oldest of the three-thief posse had parted ways from the other two when they were near the outskirts of Tawsheeha, the a small village south of Balluria. The oldest of the thieves walked parallel the train tracks that led to the south. The second man, who was wounded by a bullet fired by a shadow of a woman in the darkness of the night before, could hardly run or walk fast enough to keep up with the other two. He was bleeding ferociously from his wound, so his two cohorts left him in a dried-up creek, covered him with fallen palm leaves and grass, and left him bleeding to his death in the orchards of Sheikh Waitan. The youngest of the three thieves decided to hide near the town of Balluria and stay close to the banks of the river because he knew that this was his only way back to the outskirts of the big city in the province. He never made it there. None of the three thieves, and for that matter, none of the people in Tawsheeha realized that the government had dispatched gendarmes, or provincial police, to these parts and none of the thieves expected there were that many rifles in the hands of the peasants.

Jawad, the youngest of the three thieves, walked by the river's bank on his way back to the outskirts of the big city in the province where he lived near the ruins of Ur. He was thinking of how he must walk for almost a day to reach the big city when heard the distant roaring engine of the gendarmes' English truck behind him. He started to run, wanting to reach the wooden bridge near Balluria, the only bridge that could lead him to the dirt road where he could walk to the big city. The gendarme patrol was faster than he was; they drove to other end of the bridge on the river and waited there, blocking his only possible passage to the big city. When he saw the gendarme patrol was closing in on him, Jawad dove into the river and hid in the snake-infested reed bushes on the other bank, watching what looked like a four-man gendarme patrol. An unusually large man walked slowly by the bank looking for him. The man's rifle looked like it could end a man's life with a single shot. From where he hid across the river, Jawad could see the features of the large man; he looked hardened and angry. Two nights later, he learned the man's name was Jelwi and he was the newly appointed sergeant of the gendarmes in Balluria. Jawad hid in the reeds for almost an hour. The dark and chilly water of the southern winter made him shiver, but he stayed until all was quiet. He was first to notice the red and dark purple fish that kept stinging him. He had never seen that fish before. Later he learned that people in these parts called it the republican fish. He crawled out of the water trying to keep from screaming from all the pain of the tiny stings of the republican fish.

Jawad, the young thief, waited for the first call to the evening prayer to end before he started walking toward the small town, not knowing where to go, not knowing what the real name of the small town, and not knowing who the sheikh of the town was. He had heard before that the town's name was Balluria, but he was not sure if he had reached it. He always wondered if the name was real. He knew that whatever the town's name was or whatever might be, eventually he would look for a big guesthouse of the sheikh and ask for hospitality rights for the night. In the morning he would know what to do. As he walked the tiny dirt path that split the orchard, vigilant as a wounded wolf, he heard a movement behind him. He stopped and looked back, thinking the gendarme patrol was following him, but he saw no one behind him.

Although he knew there was no chance for the gendarme patrol to catch him, his gut feeling told him he was not safe. He was right; it was the beast that everyone in these parts feared, the vicious black wild boar that could rip a man's belly with its sharp and curvy fangs. Without hesitation and with one leap Jawad jumped to the first palm tree and within seconds he climbed the tree. "That was a good luck sign," he said to himself. He had survived death twice that day, and the night was not over yet. While he was on the tree waiting to make sure that the ugly, wild, black beast was no longer waiting for him at the bottom of the tree, he looked over toward the small town, which was slipping into the new darkness of another forgotten night. The lights from the mud huts were dim yet inviting and welcoming; he had a strange feeling of fresh energy and a feeling he had not had since he left his mother's house after stabbing his stepfather three times with a rusty knife.

As he sat on top of the palm tree looking at the few dim lights Balluria, Jawad felt that he was at home. It had been a long time since he felt that way. He looked at the houses and realized that he might never leave this town; after long years of being homeless thief, he had the feeling of being home at last

He had been in constant fear, always on the run, in the cold, in the rain, in the dust storms that seemed endless, in the merciless sun of the utterly exposed ruins of Ur, he lived with constant hunger and constant yearning for a place he could call home. Jawad never was at home until he looked at Balluria, not knowing that just a short distance away there was the spot where his father was killed, his father who was also a thief, and who also tried to steal sheep from Abdulwahed the Brave. Jawad knew that his father was killed by another thief in a place near the marshes. He also knew that it was near a place that made evil men feel safe. He thought it was somewhere near Balluria. He did not give much thought to his father as he looked at the town from the top of palm tree. Later that evening, when the call to the evening prayers ended, he walked toward the dim lights of Balluria and looked around for the largest guesthouse and asked for hospitality customs. When he sat down in the guesthouse, looking at the delicious fire in the coffee pit, he felt at home and, for the first time in his life, he felt that he never wanted to leave.

"Balluria, what a name for a hometown," he mumbled to himself.

2

Long before that night when he walked out of the river and saw Balluria for the first time, Jawad learned to hate, he learned how to hate fast and steady, and never let go of his hate to others. Since he stabbed his stepfather and ran away from home, he had lived on hate. For four years, Jawad roamed the outskirts of the big city in the province fearing that if he returned home and found that his stepfather had survived the wounds he had inflicted on him that his stepfather would kill him. If he had died from the wounds then there was the very real fear that his stepfather's brothers, cousins, and tribesmen would seek Jawad's blood for revenge even at his young age.

Jawad could not risk returning home even to learn the fate of his mother. He hid for days in the ruins of Ur living in an archeology hole, dug long ago by the British, and survived on a nearby garbage site where local butchers would throw out the inedible remains of slaughtered sheep and cattle. Jawad and other homeless thugs picked the guts, skins, and bones, and then cooked it with only water and salt. He supplemented his diet with what the mosque of the big city offered needy people, primarily at religious holidays when the wealthy people cooked the traditional meal called qima, a thick red stew filled with lamb and chickpeas. When this was not enough to fill his growing body he stole food to fill the void that never seemed to go away.

For brief period, Jawad worked in the seasonal mud brick factories near the ruins of Ur and stayed near the factories under the shelter of fallen buildings with several other homeless boys. In the mornings he and the boys would chase wooden carts pulled by donkeys. They would then unload the freshly baked bricks from the carts burning their hands as they piled endless stacks of hot bricks for the buyers who came from the big city.

By the time he was sixteen, new brick buildings were being constructed next to the old mud and reed homes on the outskirts of the big city.

One day while he wandered through the partially built structures he met with two men who looked older than he and who changed the course of his life yet again. Without proper introduction, they approached Jawad and asked him to join them in their occupation. Jawad didn't ask what the occupation was; he was certain that they were thieves. Young Jawad did not ask much. Rather than spending the rest of his time burning the skin from his hands on hot bricks and eating other people's garbage, he agreed to join the two thieves and they became a three-man posse. Young Jawad spent the next years of his youth with his new companions stealing anything they could steal. They stole food, weapons, sheep, jewelry, clothing, and whatever else they could from the unfortunate peasants on the outskirts of the big city in the province.

On a clear day, as they sat on the magnificent steps of the ruins of Ur looking at the desert, the oldest of the three men claimed that he knew of a secluded mud hut with four sheep in it. It belonged to a man named Abdulwahed the Brave who lived there with his family west of the village of Tawsheeha near a small town called Balluria.

"It is a small grouping of buildings that had just recently been declared a town," the oldest of the three thieves said. "If we can steal the four sheep we will each earn ten dinars, enough to live on for months."

The thieves knew nothing of the fierce reputation of Abdulwahed the Brave, nor did they know about the many failed attempts of other thieves who tried to steal the sheep of Abdulwahed the Brave. Moreover, the three young thieves, as they walked toward the outskirts of Tawsheeha that night, had never heard of the story about a curse that follows whoever tries to steal from the poor and honest peasant who was known for three things in these parts. First was his exceptionally strong faith in Allah, second was his fearsome thick eucalyptus stick which was his only weapon to defend his small herd of sheep, and third was his older daughter Nahda who was known to be beautiful and as brave and fearless as her father. They were unaware of his famous stick and how he had bashed many bones of many thieves through the years, thieves who thought it would be no difficult task to run off with his small fortune of sheep. Though he knew nothing of the violent reaction waiting for him and his two companions, Jawad had a premonition that he was walking to his fate, a fate that would take him to a greater destiny. He had no fear in his heart, only anticipation.

The three thieves walked half a day and reached the village of Tawsheeha by nightfall; they cautiously approached the secluded, mud hut. Jawad and his two companions could see that the dimmed ceresin lamp lights of the mud hut were still lit so they waited to see the opportune time. They waited, hidden in the orchards of Sheikh Waitan, before deciding that it was time to make their move. Without knowing what they are about to encounter, the three dark-hearted thieves, who were armed only with small daggers, took the first step onto the path that brought a curse upon them and upon many people in these parts.

They slowly crept to the mud dwelling and attempted to enter the corral where the four sheep were being kept. They entered the corral that was made from palm tree trunks only to have their ears and nerves assaulted by the loud blast from a new rifle that was called Ingilizia, an English rifle, a new weapon that was admired by the locals. A rifle was a precious commodity in these parts and only sheikhs and gendarmes possessed them. This rifle made a very loud and distinctive noise when it fired, and it had become the favorite of all aspiring sharpshooters in these parts because of its accuracy. When the rattling sounds of the round pierced the silence of the night, the three thieves dove to the ground and looked around for the source of the assault.

They did not believe that Abdulwahed the Brave had such a weapon. They had heard that he lived alone with his family and he had only an older daughter and a sick son who was unable to nurse. As they retreated back to the spot where they were hiding, the three they saw the shadow of a woman with crazy hair in the steps of the doorway of the mud hut aiming her rifle at them. It was Nahda, the older daughter of the brave peasant.

She held the rifle to her shoulder looking to see any movement or a sign of the thieves. The three thieves waited for a while before trying to move. When they made the slightest move to change their position, another shot was fired. The round pierced the air near Jawad and landed in the exposed chest of his hapless cohort as he stood trying to flee.

It seemed that all of the local peasants had been alerted of the thieves' presence and were coming after them. Unbeknownst to them, a few weeks ago the new magistrate of Balluria had declared the village of Tawsheeha as part of the administrative vicinity of Balluria. The new town had armed the peasants as the People's Resistance Army. It was the government plan to fight conspiracies against the leader of the new republic and ultimately to be ready for the war with Israel to liberate Palestine from the Jews.

That night Jawad came close to death for the first time in his life and he was not afraid of it. It was the same feeling his father felt years ago, when a skilled and notorious thief named Shiaa learned of a small fortune of four sheep, when he saw a young, beautiful girl herding the sheep at dusk, returning back to her father's mud hut by the outskirts of Tawsheeha.

3

Long ago, many years before Jawad walked out of the Euphrates and saw Balluria for the first time, another three thieves had succeeded in stealing the four sheep from Abdulwahed the Brave, a man who lived alone with his family on the outskirts of Tawsheeha, five miles south of Balluria in a secluded house in the middle of nowhere. The three thieves managed to steal the small herd of sheep while Abdulwahed the Brave, who never slept through the night, had gone to sleep for a few minutes because he could not resist the numbing sounds of the southern rain. He had tried to stay awake, but rain poured slowly and softly, and the sound of raindrops on the rusted tin roof of his secluded mud hut made him fall asleep briefly. He awoke and realized that he had been robbed of his livelihood, and with a heart of a fearless southern peasant he grabbed the only weapon he had, a fearsome long thick eucalyptus stick. In the middle of the night, he screamed, "I am the son of my father."

He chased them in the middle of the dark night. The three thieves tried to keep the sheep silent by tying their mouths and they hid in a dry ravine as Abdulwahed the Brave passed by them looking for the four sheep, which were his only fortune. Losing them meant certain starvation for his family in the hunger days in the south when the gentle young king was only sixteen and was officially placed under the care of his uncle prince.

Days before that night, Shiaa asked his partner Sakran, a loner of man and a hardened thief who lived in reed hut near the marshes, if he would join him in the theft, and Sakran agreed, but he did not agree when Shiaa suggested that they bring another man with them.

"Who is he?" asked Sakran.

"He is a distant cousin of mine, a young brave man. He has a wife and young son, so he will not escape with the loot," said Shiaa.

"What is his name?" asked Sakran.

"His name is Abu Jawad," said Shiaa. "I will sponsor him. He is on my guarantee."

When Sakran met Abu Jawad he had the feeling that something in the fate of the two men had been written a long time ago and he did not like that feeling, but he could not be cowardly. He had the feeling that blood was to be shed, as he always knew when blood was to be shed, since the day he first killed a man.

For two nights the three thieves had stalked the isolated house to steal the four sheep. They waited and waited for Abdulwahed the Brave to sleep. He had been awake for three days and nights caring for his ill son, Rahman, who for no obvious reason could not drink the milk of his mother. He later became the only young man who could speak fluent English in these parts. The three thieves quietly managed to sneak in and took the four sheep away from the tiny corral at the mud hut when Abdulwahed the Brave slept for a few minutes. He was dreaming he saw a young Gypsy woman singing a strange song telling of the fate of a young man who one day would be the ruthless sheikh in these parts. As he slept, the three thieves hurried away from the mud hut and toward the abandoned train station that had been abandoned since the defeated soldiers of the Turkish army boarded the last train fleeing from the British troops advancing to the north after the battle of Shuaiba.

Breathless they were, when the three thieves with their loot of four healthy sheep, ran through the darkness and the many muddy puddles of rain. When they neared the abandoned train station, they saw a magnificent place. It was a perfect spot of sandy hills surrounded by seven palm trees, beautiful and glorious palm trees. The glowing green light from the tops of the trees distracted the three thieves and left them infatuated by the scene for hours. They stayed there looking at the trees they had never seen before and, rather than escaping the wrath of Abdulwahed the Brave, they decided to divide the loot in that spot, not knowing that stealing from Abdulwahed the Brave was the worst thing they could have done to themselves. It was like a curse that followed the three thieves from the beginning.

When they entered the mud hut of Abdulwahed the Brave, Shiaa, the oldest of the three stepped on a spike that went all the way to the bone of his foot; he managed to swallow the pain, wrench the spike free from his foot, and steal the sheep with the others without telling them about his injury. He was bleeding profusely and could feel his body drain of blood. When they reached the train station and the seven palm trees, he told the others that he could not walk anymore. They knew that Abdulwahed the Brave would soon find them; even if they went to Hell, he would follow them. Nevertheless, Shiaa realized that he was dead anyway, and he had a better chance to ask clemency from Abdulwahed the Brave. Shiaa was too weak to walk. He felt like he was drained of his own blood, so he sat leaning his back on the soft cold sand of the tiny hills by the heavenly looking palm trees. He stared at the tops of the palm trees and he thought he saw two men with wings, wearing green shrouds, two magnificent-looking men with long hair and groomed beards. He thought he was dying and seeing angels, so he accepted his fate and stayed there waiting for Abdulwahed the Brave to find him and finish him with one blow of his stick.

The other two continued without him, leaving him to an uncertain fate if Abdulwahed the Brave found him. The two tried to alter their getaway route by taking the road that led to the village of Midan, the water buffalo herders' village closer to the river and to the marshes, On the way there, Sakran started to experience the same feeling he had when he first saw Abu Jawad, and for some reason, Sakran had an attack of greed after he realized that this young associate of his, whom he had met only a few days ago, had no one but a young son to avenge him, so he bluntly said, "Shiaa's share would be mine."

Jawad's father looked at him and realized that what Sakran said was not a statement; rather, it was a threat and a deadly challenge. He did not say a word until he made sure that his tiny dagger was in his hand and out of his belt and then responded with, "That's not acceptable. We will divide Shiaa's share."

Although he had prepared himself for a fight, he was not able to react quickly enough to Sakran's lightning-fast hand as it landed a deadly stab to his neck. Sakran was known among thieves and thugs in these parts for the deadly speed of his hand to the point that it was a common phrase to say, "Faster than the stab of Sakran." Before he was killed, Jawad's father did manage to slash Sakran's right cheek deeply, so deeply that it left a scar on Skaran's face for the rest of his years. It looked like a deep brownish gorge, and that was the sign that Jawad looked for in later years to find his father's killer.

Jawad's father fell to the ground kicking and violently screaming from pain before the calmness of death quieted him as the blood oozed from his neck. He tried to stop the bleeding with his hands and by pouring sand and dirt into his deep wound but he was dead within minutes. Sakran stood there watching him and waiting for him to die. Sakran then went to the four sheep they stole and used his dagger to cut a roll of wool from the brown-headed male sheep and burned it quickly. He smashed the ashes and filled the wound in his face with it; the bleeding stopped. He rounded up the sheep and pushed the body of Jawad's father into a shallow puddle of water and pushed it, hoping that the body would float to the marshes.

Before the night was over, and for a reason that no one in these parts could ever understand when they told the story of the three thieves, and although Sakran claimed that he went back to make certain that Shiaa was dead, people in these parts believed that Sakran went back to Shiaa's body because he wanted to loot his dagger and his money, if he had any. But when he reached the magnificent spot where the glamorous green light of another world had filled that bloody night with strange warmth and human calmness, he not only found the dead body of Shiaa, he found Abdulwahed the Brave waiting near the dead body of Shiaa. Abdulwahed did not hesitate when he saw him with four familiar sheep. He struck Sakran with his fearsome thick stick.

Before bleeding to death, and as he kept staring at the top of the seven palm trees where he thought he saw the angels, Shiaa decided to cleanse his soul by confessing the names of his partners to Abdulwahed the Brave, who stood up next to the dying thief with his fearsome stick After he heard the confession, Abdulwahed the Brave waited and watched as Shiaa appeared to die peacefully looking at the top of the seven palm trees and smiling. He waited by his body for the two other thieves to return. For some reason, he knew that they might return; *this is what thieves do*, he told himself.

When Sakran showed up to loot Shiaa's dead body of its possessions he did not have the time to explain or to apologize or to save himself from the wrath of Abdulwahed the Brave who sent Sakran to a near-death coma with one blow to his head. He was certain that Sakran was dead also but when the local gendarme patrol searched the area they stumbled upon Abu Jawad's corpse with a knife wound that was fresh enough to be made by the still-bloody dagger on Sakran's belt when the gendarme patrol later found him nearly dead by the seven palm trees. Sakran woke up a day later. He woke up with dried blood covering his face in the provincial gendarme prison, where he was charged with the murder of Jawad's father but he was not charged with the theft of the sheep.

He was sentenced to twenty years in prison for his crime. He was sent to serve his sentence in a dark cell of the Salman Hole in the desert prison for many years. When he told his story to his prison mates who were mostly thieves like him, one of them always asked him, "Why did you go back to where you left your dead partner by the seven palm trees? Did you want to loot his dead body?"

Sakran always said no, and then his expression turned softer and his eyes glowed with a human glare and he mumbled, "I don't know. For some reason I felt safe at that spot."

He was released when he was almost sixty-five years old, broke, with no home to go to. He went back to Tawsheeha, found an abandoned mud hut, and lived off the fish and food that he hunted. He wished every day for death to visit; he did not have to wait long.

4

While Sakran was barely surviving his sentence in the desert prison, that everyone called the Salman Hole, from which only few men left alive, the young Jawad was surviving the sentence that Sakran had imposed on him by killing his father. A sentence of a long and agonizing waiting for revenge that was sustained only by nurtured hatred. Young Jawad survived it listening to his mother telling him every day about his father, how he must avenge him, and how he must search the Earth to find the man with a red scar on his face. Jawad was two years old when, after searching the dirt road by between the train station and the marshes, the gendarme patrol found two bodies and a nearly dead man. The gendarmes found the body of Abu Jawad and brought news of his death and the name and description of his killer to his widow. Upon learning about the death of her husband, she cried bitter tears for one day. She then wiped the tears from her eyes and sat her two-year-old son, Jawad, down. She held his tiny hand, placed the blade of a small sharp knife against the soft skin of his palm, and with a swift slash she sliced his hand. When his cries of pain subsided, she again grabbed his hand and poured salt into the open wound. The sting of the salt entered the little boy's heart and burned his innocence. As he screamed in pain, the widow cried with him as she chanted with sadness and sorrow.

Hours later, when the tears were drying on their cheeks, the widow looked in her young son's eyes and said, "Here, my little boy, my little man. Don't cry. Only women cry, but from this day on, you will feel this pain in your hand as I feel it in my heart. It's the pain of losing my husband and your father. People tell me that another man killed him, a man who has a deep brown scar on his cheek. Remember that, my son, a brown scar on his cheek. I want you to carve another scar in his heart when you meet him. Remember that, my son, my only man."

The widow repeated those words daily to her son for the next eight years. The words were his lullaby as she put him to sleep every night, they were his only memory and the one connection to his father and gave him a purpose to live for since he started to understand and realize what they meant. After eight years, the widow remarried. Her new husband moved in with them and assumed control of their world, a situation that Jawad visibly resented. Jawad was no longer the center of her world, and she no longer recited the story about his father. When young Jawad questioned his mother about this man and his father she replied, "He is like your uncle, he is my husband, he is like your father, so you must obey him."

For six years, her new husband, who had tiny and fleshy body, saw Jawad as little more than a disobedient beast to be beaten when he did not move fast enough or well enough, or just when the mood to be violent amused him. Jawad suffered six years of welts, bruises, broken fingers, and black eyes. When he came home one day and saw that his stepfather had beaten his mother nearly to death, he grabbed a rusty knife at the beginning of one of his stepfather's rages against him. He complained that Jawad was not bringing home any money that he could earn by working as day laborer near the site of the company that was building the new long, iron bridge in the big city. Jawad garbed the rusty knife his mother used to clean the fish and stabbed his stepfather's fleshy tanned body three times. Jawad did not wait to see where he landed his stabs, nor did he wait to see if his stepfather would live. He ran as far as his feet would carry him. Whenever he needed a purpose to go on, all he had to do was look at the fading scar on the palm of his hand and remember his mother's words and all of the pain he had suffered from his replacement father, and he again had the energy, anger, and hate to continue.

As he hid in the water of the Euphrates waiting for the gendarme patrol to leave, Jawad was unaware that he had been only several hundred meters from where his father was killed. All he knew of his father's death was that his father's killer was still alive and had a brownish-red scar on his face. Jawad had lived his young years thinking of what he would do when he met his father's killer and that thought had mustered the hate that eventually engulfed his heart and prevented him from loving.

For almost three years after first arriving in Balluria, seventeen years from the day when his father was killed, three years after he killed his stepfather, and only a year after he kidnapped the most beautiful young Gypsy dancer, Jawad saw his father's killer for the first time he stood there looking at Sakran and stared at the brownish scar his father's dagger left on Sakran's face.

For a year before Jawad met his father's killer, he and his partner Irar, who he met at the guesthouse of Sheikh Badr Al-Ghathban, had tracked and searched for Sakran. They found him nearby. They found him waiting. Sakran was waiting for that moment since he learned that the man he killed had a young boy named Jawad. Sakran was hoping that death would visit the young boy before him, or before he was released from his prison sentence.

It was two years before Irar noticed that his partner and protégé, the young Jawad, started to lose sleep, and he watched him stay awake for nights. He had asked him if he was in love.

"No, I had a dream some nights ago, and I cannot sleep," Jawad answered.

"What was it about?" Irar asked.

"It was about my father," Jawad said.

"Men like us, if we do not sleep, it is due to one of two reasons. Either we are in love with a beautiful woman or we seek revenge... so let's talk about the revenge," Irar said with a voice that sounded like fate. Jawad told Irar about what his mother said to him about his father's death. Irar kept making the same sound.

"Mmm, mmm, mmm," as he listened to Jawad's story.

"The only way you can sleep again is if you kill your father's murderer and watch him die. So, are you ready to kill?" Irar asked as his eyes pierced Jawad's soul searching for the animal inside.

"Yes, I am."

"If you are ready, then finding him is the easy part," Irar said.

That evening, when Irar and Jawad knew the whereabouts of Sakran, they chose two weapons to kill him. They packed an old pistol that Irar stole from an English army barracks weapons depot in the southern province and a black dagger that looked like it was made of death and designed by a hellish demon from centuries ago. When Jawad saw the dagger, he had a massive feeling of connection to the dagger. He felt that it belonged to him, he felt that it was his to own, to have, and to kill with. Jawad looked at the dagger and did not ask his older partner about it. The blade looked fearsome with its dark silver color that revealed many chips, the grip was dark and wrapped with black leather, which was faded from the effects of friction of the many hands that may have once held it, as they delivered their death blows to many men who faced their final moments as they received its cold metal taste into their bodies. On the grip there was a writing that was neither Arabic nor Persian. Many owners of the black dagger tried to read the writing, but none of them could ever do so.

Irar never told the story of the black dagger to anyone in his life. And since they met, and as much as he liked and trusted Jawad like his own son, Irar never told Jawad the story of the black dagger and how he came to possess it. Irar never told his young partner and protégé that when he was twelve years old, he left the home of the family that cared for him and fed him for three years, after they found him sleeping next to his father's dead body in the battlefield of

Shuaiba three days after the British swept through these parts. The family of nomads kept young Irar and adopted him in exchange for him being a servant and a shepherd. Many nights they forgot to feed him; he slept with the herd and ate what they fed the sheep. Once, Irar did not eat for seven nights, so one night he slipped into the tent and stole seven Indian rupees, which was the currency at that time and was the only fortune the nomadic family had, and he ran away through the desert. Irar jutted left and walked through the prairie for several nights and days until he reached the outskirts of the big city. He stayed hiding in the ancient ruins of Ur for two years. He stole whatever he could to eat, and if there was nothing to steal, he ate grass and drank the water of the Euphrates, but he never spent the seven Indian rupees.

One night he saw a strange-looking man standing near the ruins of Ur. The man looked as if he was waiting for Irar. Irar, who had no fear in his heart, approached the man whose head was covered with a black shroud. The man turned his head to Irar, who noticed that the man's eyes were not like other people's eyes; they were upside down and looked like cats' eyes.

The man looked at Irar and asked, "Where are you from, kid?"

"From the desert and the strong back of my father," Irar replied.

"I was waiting for you. I have this dagger for you if you want to buy it for the seven rupees that you have," the man with the long and turned eyes said.

"Who told you that I have seven rupees?" Irar asked.

"No one... Look at this dagger." The man pulled out the fearsome dagger and showed it to Irar.

"Do you see the writing on the grip? Can you read it?"

"I can't read," said Irar.

"Doesn't matter," he said. Then, without being asked, the mysterious man said to Irar, "The codes on the dagger grip were those of an ancient language long before the Arabic language; it was what the people of the ruins of Ur spoke. The dagger itself was made a long time ago, and it has ended the lives of many people in these parts since the beginning of time. The dagger has the blood of many brave knights who faced their final fate as they felt its sting; and many princes and brave Arabian knights tasted its cold blade piercing through their hearts and necks." The mysterious man told Irar that he had been waiting for the right man to sell the dagger to; he said that only a man with a heart of stone was worthy of owning the dagger because it would lead to blood.

"Do you fear blood?" the mysterious man asked.

"No," young Irar answered.

"Then, the dagger is yours," the mysterious man said and took the seven rupees and disappeared in the darkness of the ruins of Ur. From that night the dagger never left Irar's side; it was on his waist when Jawad and he packed their weapons and mounted two horses and went to kill Sakran.

"We can kill him with the dagger," Jawad said.

"The dagger is to feel the death of the person you kill, the dagger is to kill enemies that you truly hate, the dagger is to kill sheikhs and knights and wolves. But this bastard, the man who killed your father, he is thief and he may be good with a dagger," Irar said.

"Use a pistol to kill him and watch him die," Irar continued, "because he may be faster with his dagger than you with yours but when you shoot him with your pistol, wait until you see the light of life still gleaming from his eyes, and then drive the dagger into his heart."

Irar and Jawad rode their horses and searched for Sakran. They asked about him near villages by the marshes, and they searched near the train station where a group of nomads had set up camp for the season. They were almost ready to head back to their mud hut when a peasant who was walking his donkey from the village of Tawsheeha told them about the strange man who lived alone on the outskirts of the village, a man with a reddish-brown scar on his face who lived off fishing and barely met with anyone. They knew it was he. They knew it was Sakran, the killer of Jawad's father, the man they had been looking for.

5

After spending fifteen years of his sentence, Sakran was released by a presidential pardon on the first day of the Big Eid, the holiday that comes after the fasting month of Ramadan, a tradition that many presidents and kings practiced in the Arab world. He left the prison a broken, weak, and scared man. After spending two nights in the streets, he traveled to the only place he still knew, the outskirts of Tawsheeha, near the Euphrates, where he could see the seven palm trees from a distance. Not able to go there yet, he could still feel safe when he looked at the spot where the seven magnificent palm trees stood. Hiding from people, he lived on the fish the Euphrates offered and what the marshes gave away from its black birds that they called water chickens. There he lived in a tiny secluded mud hut and waited, waited for the fate he knew he would face no matter how long it took for a certain young man to find him.

One day Sakran saw a steely thin, dark-skinned old man and a similar-looking, younger man waiting for him with their horses by his mud hut as he returned with three water birds hanging from his belt. He did not know the men. He took them to be strangers from another town and welcomed them with the usual greeting.

"Welcome to the guests."

"Peace be with you," they replied.

There was no peace in their eyes.

Initially Sakran thought that they were lost smugglers who needed to stay in the shade until nightfall, and then they would make their way to the endless desert, but something in the eyes of the younger one suggested otherwise. He then thought they might be a couple of thieves staging themselves closer to Balluria, but he was wrong. The two men looked at him silently, and they looked at his scar more than they looked at him; they examined it. Sakran touched his dagger, making sure that it was there, and just when he was about to pull his dagger out of its sheath, Jawad pulled his pistol and aimed. Sakran's dagger was no match to the pistol the young man drew fast and with firm grip. Jawad shot Sakran six times in the face and chest, as Irar stood and watched. Sakran fell to the ground motionless, and blood poured from the carnage that was once his head and face. Jawad sat there next to the body and looked at Irar, who insisted that Jawad must keep looking at the dying man.

"Keep looking at him dying. Now use the dagger and drive it into his heart, so you feel his soul departing his body, and when you know he is dead and you can sleep at night," Irar calmly explained.

Sakran died fast. Jawad's bullets shredded his face and tore his head apart; Irar kicked him to make sure that he was dead, and then they wrapped the body with the only dirty carpet that covered the dirt floor in the secluded, mud hut. The two men put the body on Jawad's horse and walked for miles, looking for a place to bury the corpse of Sakran. They went to the river, but Irar did not want the body to be found, so later that night they searched for a spot where no one would look for it. They carried the body toward the train station that saw traffic only once every two weeks. Miles after they passed the train station, they found a flat, sandy spot surrounded by tiny hills that hid a perfect piece of land that was circled by seven palm trees. The seven palm trees looked like they were planted by a meticulous farmer. The colors of the palm trees were exceptionally bright and glowed in the darkness of the night. They were within equal distance from each other, forming the shape of a big heart. They were all about the same height and had almost the exact same number of leaves. The trunk of each palm tree was clean and shaped the same. They had no bushes around them, nor any dates hanging from their fronds. Between the palm trees the sand smelled differently; it was the smell of earth and soil after it rained, even though it had not rained. The two men were mesmerized by the color of the palm trees and momentarily forgot about their evil deed. The body of the dead old man was heavy; the two men took it down from the horse's back. They dug a shallow grave and buried Sakran's body in it; that spot seemed to be the perfect place to bury it.

Jawad broke the silence that had hovered over them until now. "Should we read the Fatiha (prayer) on his soul?"

"I don't think that will do any good for his soul, nor will it do any good on our souls." They sat there and smoked cigarettes and could not help but notice how serene and peaceful the surroundings of the seven palm trees were and how soft the sand on the small hill was.

"There is something about this place," Irar proclaimed. "It's either blessed or cursed or both."

Jawad listened to him intently like a good son listening to his father. Then he asked, "What do you mean?"

"There is something about this place; it makes me feel like I only belong here," Irar said.

Jawad looked at his old friend and mentor, trying to comprehend his meaning. "Irar, this is the first time I've heard you talk like this, and if I were asked who is the bravest man in these parts, my answer would always be you, but you are talking like a child now."

Irar looked at him, moved his eyes toward the palm trees and listened to the sound of the soft wind as it touched the palm trees' leaves, synchronizing the movements of all the leaves in one directed dance. He tried to comprehend why this place felt so familiar. Perhaps he had been here before, maybe when he was a child or maybe even before he was born. For some reason he knew that he would be coming back here again; he knew that for sure. Again taking the risk of sounding soft he said, "Don't mind me, Jawad... but this place... these seven palm trees... this sand... they are strange. It seems to me like they have existed for a long time, a very long time... since the time before Balluria. I feel like the palm trees are looking at us and hearing what we say... I feel like they know us."

"Maybe it's inhabited by jinnies or demons," Jawad said.

"No, if it is inhabited by jinnies that would be a simple thing... I can deal with jinnies and demons... but it's not a bad thing. Souls... that's what I feel... there are many souls around us. They are looking at us and listening to us," Irar said with the deep voice of a faithful person who vividly saw what he believed in.

"Souls or no souls... we need to head back to Balluria," Jawad said as he stood up shaking his robe and dusting it off from the sticky particles of sand and small pieces of rocks.

From that night, Irar on their many trips to the borders, never talked to Jawad about the seven palm trees again. He avoided the subject because he felt that he looked and sounded weak in front of his young friend and protégé. Also, he always avoided passing the seven palm trees; even in daylight, he tried to steer away from them as far as he could, something that Jawad never understood.

Coming back from the seven palm trees, Irar changed the topic far from its original course and asked Jawad, "When are you getting married?"

"To whom?" Jawad answered.

"Do you want to choose or should I choose for you?" Irar asked like a father keen on marrying his son.

"You choose for me. You are like my father," Jawad said courteously.

"You will marry Sabrya, the daughter of Sheikh Badr Al-Ghathban."

"Who? How? I have no money, and no one even knows who my father is. I have no family," Jawad argued.

"Money will come, and you will marry her... Sheikh Badr Al-Ghathban has one son, Reyhan, and he is weak. So if the sheikh dies, you will be the sheikh in his place, and you will inherit all of his fortune," Irar said. "You just need to harden your heart and not look for love or beauty. Later you can find love and beauty with another woman or you can be satisfied with the Gypsy woman," Irar said as he looked for an answer from his young partner, who was deep in his thoughts. "This is how all the brave Arab men have done it. A man without a fortune and status is nothing but a thief," Irar explained, and then added, "just like the bastard we just buried. Jawad, I don't want you to be like him... or like me. You need to start thinking of these two things. Fortune and becoming a sheikh with a name that makes men shake in their sandals when they hear it. I will help you. I am getting old, but I can help you," Irar said as he coughed.

"I am from your right hand to your left hand; I will do what you say," Jawad said.

"Keep your secrets from the Gypsy woman; never trust a woman, and let me worry about the money and where I will get it from," Irar said. "Let's go tomorrow for coffee at Sheikh Badr Al-Ghathban's guesthouse. And one day, when the time is right, that guesthouse will be yours," Irar concluded with a firm and confident voice like a father showing his son the righteous way in life. The two men walked toward the end of the town to where they lived with a young Gypsy woman named Barrya in a deserted mud hut near the empty field. That was the only empty field near the town with no weeds, bushes, or palm trees, where they had seen some boys the other day running after a well-worn soccer ball.

The Book of the Man

Snakes and Pigeons

1

Hamid's house had only two rooms. One of the rooms was built with mud bricks and roofed with the trunks of eucalyptus and palm tree branches. For some reason, warmth and the smell of food filled the room all the time; it was the main living, sleeping, and dining room. The other room was built with mud and strongly shaped cement bricks and it was roofed with palm tree trunks; this was Hamid's room. It was empty of any furniture; there was only one old and dirty carpet on the floor, but the room was filled with a strange collection of many things, such as nets, birdcages, empty drums and boxes, and a large collection of fishhooks. The room always reminded me of my vision of Robinson Crusoe's home or the room of a pirate who was marooned on an island by himself.

"I found all of these things floating in the river," Hamid explained.

Hamid's house was basically an open space surrounded by a failing fence made with palm branches and supported by short palm tree trunks. The house's open space was a joyful field of natural coexistence. It was filled with many cages of birds, chickens, and ducks that were allowed to run wild making all their natural noises. All of the animals lived on one side of the open space gated with a small tree branch that looked like it was from a children's book. It was like small bird garden with sparrows, ravens, pigeons, and crows, and it even had one white and blue cockatoo; it was a mystery as to where he possibly could have found that exotic part of his menagerie. The house's gate was filled with more baskets and fishing equipment than I had ever seen in my life. Compared to our very clean and well-kept house that was too organized to allow an imaginative thought, Hamid's house was the perfect setting for my natural daydream adventures. When I told him that I would love to see the pigeons, I did not plan to go see them next day, but Hamid was at our house before I awoke. He knocked at the door, and when my mother answered the door, he told her with his wild innocence, "I am here to take your son to see my pigeons."

My mother let him in and offered him breakfast. My father had already left home for his first day at work, and my brother and I were sleeping in the bedroom under the ceiling fan that did little to dispel the growing heat. Mother came and woke me up, telling me that the kid who helped unload the moving van was here talking about some pigeons. I rubbed my eyes and went to the kitchen, where I saw him wearing the same clothes that he'd had on the day before and was drinking the chai that my mother gave him.

"Do you want to see my pigeons?" Hamid asked me with a strange energy that I soon realized was characteristic of him.

"Now?" I asked, wanting nothing more than to drink cool water under the worthless fan.

"Yes, I will show you all the birds, and maybe we will see a wild boar."

"What is a boar?" I asked, trying to keep my eyes open. I grabbed a glass of tea and listened to my new friend tell me all about boars.

"A boar is a black male pig and it can rip you apart with its teeth. I have killed two of them." I decided that my new friend had a talent for making things up, so I waited for him to show me the evidence before saying anything. When we finished our tea, I put my blue shoes on and followed my new friend. He walked in front of me with confident steps, and I walked like a delicate city boy trying to avoid the thorns and branches that paved the way as we walked between the trees in the orchard behind our house and halfway to his house. It was the first time I had walked through an area that looked like the scene from *Big Valley*...or *The Little House on the Prairie*. Balluria was a black hole of scum to my father, but it was starting to look very promising to me. I saw a glimpse of the river that was close to Hamid's house. Just before the dirt walkway that protects the town from flooding sat Hamid's house.

The river looked so majestic; it left me speechless. I stood there looking at it. Its water was closer to green than blue, perhaps even closer to white than green, and its waves looked like the shiny skin of millions of snakes. It looked so mysterious and inviting.

"What river is this?"

"This is the Euphrates," Hamid said. "The Euphrates is my friend. I found my things floating in it. Once I found a dead woman's body floating. I think she was killed because she slept with someone."

Oh, the Euphrates? I thought. For some reason I felt the river was different than when I saw it in Baghdad. It was wider and clearer, and I felt a strange connection to it. I felt the urge to dive in it and hug the water as though there was a relationship between the people and the river. I was not sure of its merit, but it felt real and unbreakable. "Do you swim in it?" I asked as the two of us walked toward Hamid's house.

"Yes, I swim, fish, and spend my whole day by the river," Hamid said as he opened the half-wood and half-tin door of his house.

"I hope your father is not home, I mean, so we don't bother him," I said trying to be polite.

He did not answer me at first, but then he stopped and turned to me and said calmly, "My father died a long time ago... When I was really young... I don't even remember him." I sensed sadness mixed with carelessness. At the door Hamid yelled, "Mother, I have someone with me," and he pushed the door open. I waited outside and listened as he spoke to a woman. Then he invited me in. "Tafathall (come in)." I entered and looked around, feeling shy and embarrassed. I saw his mother and what looked like a younger sister of his; she was dark skinned with exceptionally big beautiful eyes. They were sitting against the wall of the main room eating their breakfast of warm bread, white cheese, and tea that smelled delicious. The food was on the plastic sheet that was spread on the floor. They also had fried tomatoes and fried dough. In the corner there was a grayish-green hibb (a clay water jar) sitting on a stand and a little dog sleeping underneath it. Outside there was a garden that had vegetables growing in a disorganized and wild way, but the vegetables looked so fresh and colorful.

Then I saw ten of the most beautiful pigeons I'd ever seen in my entire life; they made my head spin. Hamid pointed to the corner and said, "There are my pigeons." I looked at the pigeons; they looked so mythical to me, especially the white ones with the fluffy feathers on their feet. They were so close to me; to the point that I could just reach out and touch them. I walked two steps toward them, but Hamid stopped me and said, "Not now. We will feed them after breakfast."

I realized then that he came to my house before eating breakfast, and his mother, who looked like the most innocent, poor, and defenseless person on earth, said to me, "You can sit here, son."

With my city boy manners, I kept my shoes on and sat on the edge of the dirty stained carpet. In their house, there was complete harmony between the humans and the animals; I saw Hamid's sister throw some food to the animals, and they all ate together. At that moment, I felt like I belonged to Hamid's family. His mother handed me a piece of bread that was fresh out of the clay wok. It tasted sumtuous and, along with the fried tomato, fried dough, and dark sweetened tea, it was the tastiest breakfast I had ever eaten. She also had yogurt that was cold and delicious. I could not help but notice the young girl, who I suspected to be Hamid's sister, looking at me from inside the room. I knew it was impolite to look back at her. She entered the room when I started eating my breakfast, and she just kept looking at me. I looked at her big black eyes and saw how sad they were. That was the first time I really saw Amel, Hamid's younger sister. Although she appeared to be shy, she kept staring at me. Judging from her height and the way she acted, I guessed she was maybe eleven years old or a few months younger than I was.

Hamid finished his breakfast fast and went back to the pigeon house, so I followed him. He squatted in front of the pigeon cage and started explaining to me like a pigeon expert, "Look at these two right here; one is a male and the other a female. They are the Allajie kind. I love these two birds," he said. I looked carefully at the birds; they looked clean, royal, and fluffy. They had long white fathers over their feet and spots of silver and black on their wings. "I love these two birds. They are expensive and very rare. They used to be the favorite of all the Arabian kings. Although they cost a lot to buy, I got these two for free; one day I woke up, and the two birds were here. The other two are the Zajel kind. They are the smartest. They can take messages and deliver them to other people. Arabian knights used them to send messages to their beloved princesses."

"Have you ever sent them with a message to anyone?" I asked.

"I could, but I have no one to send a message to, and right now they are nesting to lay eggs. As for the other two, they are the Hamrawis kind. You can tell by their red color," said Hamid.

"I hate these two birds," Hamid said. "They are lazy and don't fly very high. Look, look. Do you see the Allajie gathering hay for its nest? Did you know that the Allajie birds would abandon their nests if a human touched them, and they would start a new nest all over again? They are very clean. I think they are the kings of pigeons. And do not touch their eggs, because they will peck them with their beaks and kill the baby pigeon before it is born. So never touch them," Hamid explained.

"I will not touch it," I replied.

"When it hatches, I will give you a pigeon," Hamid said.

"Are you serious?" I asked, unsuccessfully trying to hide my joy.

"Yes, I will, I promise," he answered.

From that day Hamid and I became friends. We were more than friends. He was my partner in everything. I started to like him more and more, and each morning I woke and dressed faster than anyone in my family had ever seen me move, so I wouldn't miss a waking moment of adventure with Hamid. I had even stopped showering, just like him, and wore my clothes for days a time, which made my mother furious. She said many times, "Look at you, looking like a shroogy boy." That is what city people called the southern folks. I did not pay any attention to her because Hamid was filling me with stories and adventures that made me hope and pray that school would never start. Pigeons were not the only animals in the house; they also had the lazy dog that was asleep under the hibb during my first visit. The puppy didn't do much more than sleep. Hamid said that the dog was his sister's and said that she called the dog by a foreign name.

"What is the dog's name?" I asked.

"Lassie," Hamid answered. Lassie was a familiar name to me.

"Where did he get the name from?"

He said that he did not name the dog, that his sister Amel named it when she saw another dog on television. "She saw the dog on the television at the Hillaly's house; they were the only family in town that had a color television. The brave dog could save people's lives," Hamid further explained. I knew exactly what he was talking about, because *Lassie* was on Tuesday evenings at eight the previous summer. His sister's dog was dirty, gray, and lazy and didn't have the inclination to protect himself from his own fleas, let alone rescue anyone from a burning house. It did nothing all day except move from one sleeping place to another cooler sleeping place as the sun's rays moved throughout the open space of the house. Amel also had a cat and three kittens.

"You know I saved the mother cat from drowning in the Euphrates," Hamid said, pointing to the yellow and white cat.

He had two lovebirds and a colorful majestic looking bird that was quiet. I had never seen a bird like this before in my life and asked Hamid where he found it.

"I hunted it. I trapped it," he said with confidence.

"Where?" I asked, completely in awe of my friend's skills.

"In the orchard near the river. I will take you there to hunt for birds." That was the statement that ushered the start of the most exciting and extremely joyful three weeks in my life. In a way it was the only adventure that rose to the status of a book worthy of reading by all the boys in those parts. Not only did he offer to take me hunting for birds and animals, he also offered to teach me how to swim and give me my first pigeon. My father was busy with his new post as the mayor of the town. My mother was busy making our new home as livable as possible, and my brother and sister had the duty of helping her and preparing for the new school year. I was left out from the duties of the house because my father had mentioned many times that he wanted me to come with him to work to be his unofficial assistant, but he never really acted on this request since he had several policemen and three male secretaries. I would pretend that I was sleeping until he left the house, and then I would eat the leftovers from breakfast, hastily put on my track suit, and go directly to Hamid's house, have another breakfast, and then look forward to my friend's surprises.

One day, my father waited for me to wake up. He instructed me to dress to go with him to his work. We walked into the building that contained his office, the post office, the municipality's manager, and the only working public telephone in town. I walked behind him, carrying his briefcase. As he approached the main entrance to his office, the four policemen who stood in a line on one side of the walkway saluted him. They used a military salute, which gave me the impression that my father was an important man; he looked and acted as if he was the boss of the town. I later learned that my father was just a figurehead; the real powers were in the hands of a man called Comrade Uraiby, who was the head of the governing political party division in Balluria. His office was in another yellow and gray building that housed the offices of the political party and a small jailhouse. Comrade Uraiby's office was about a kilometer from my father's office. Years later, I learned that my childhood friend Haleem stormed that building alone with his Kalashnikov and burned it to the ground. I also learned that four of my childhood friends were housed in the small jailhouse for one night before they faced the firing squad.

That day at my father's office, however, was the most boring day in my life, and I hoped that it would end quickly. I sat outside on the bench, and one of the policemen brought me tea and asked me about the capital city. He looked very old and close to death. As I sat with him telling him about the capital city, he smoked cigarette after cigarette and coughed like a dying man. He looked older than my grandfather when we saw him on his deathbed.

The old police sergeant man asked me, "What grade are you in?" He spoke with the concern of a loving grandfather who reeked of the smoke of thousands of cigarettes smoked one after another.

"I passed the sixth grade in the capital city this year and I will be in the first grade of middle school," I said.

"So you passed the sixth grade of elementary. Is that right?" the old policeman asked.

"Yes." Then another policeman called him.

"Sergeant Jelwi, do you want chai?"

"Yes, I am coming," the old relic said to the calling voice, and then he looked at me.

"I am Abu Hatem Hajji Sergeant Jelwi," he said and left me wondering about how old he was and how long the day would be.

My father walked out and said, "Let's go have lunch." I was not planning to come back to his office after lunch and as soon as we reached the house, I changed into my raggedy clothes and went straight to Hamid's house. It was lunchtime, and the streets of the town were deserted, as everyone sought shelter from the August sun. I reached Hamid's house breathless and knocked on the door. There was no answer. I was beginning to get frustrated when his sister, Amel, opened the door.

"Is Hamid home?"

"No, he is not. He went to the Hillaly house to get something for my mother. He will be back soon," she said and looked at me. "Do you want to come in?"

I did not know how Hamid would feel or what he would think of me entering his house without his permission and without him being there. I mean, after all, we all know the limits and boundaries of the Arabic traditions, and we were not in Baghdad, where people could enter their neighbors' houses unannounced. Some people killed for things like looking at their sisters or mothers in a disrespectful way. The heat of the sun and my not wanting to return to my house, because I knew my father would take me back to his office, were my only justifications to cross over that line. So I entered Hamid's house, but I decided to stay in the courtyard. I did not go into the room where his mother and his sister were. Instead, I went over to the pigeons' cage and watched them sleep. They looked at me like I was a mite that jumped up into their feathers just after a cleansing dust bath. I felt someone behind me. It was Amel, Hamid's sister, with a metal cup full of fresh cold yogurt. She stood there, looking at me with her big, black, sad eyes that seemed to hold many meanings that I did not understand, and she asked me if I was hungry.

"No," I replied, trying to avoid looking at her eyes.

111

She handed me the cup and said, "You must be thirsty."

I took the cup from her and prayed that Hamid would arrive soon because for some reason I felt that Amel knew everything I was thinking. It was as though she could see through me with her deep black eyes, straight inside me. At that time, I did not know what to call that feeling or how to react to it; to me she was just the younger sister of my friend annoying me with her constant stare. I drank the yogurt and gave her the cup, wishing that she would leave me alone with the pigeons, but she stood there staring at me.

When I was ten years old, I read a story by an American author. His name was Mark Twain, and he told the story of a kid named Tom Sawyer with his friend Huckleberry Finn and their adventures on the Mississippi River. I had long wished that I would get a chance to live the same adventures the two American boys lived, but there was no chance of that in Baghdad, because the river was too far from the upscale neighborhood where we lived and because I did not have a best friend there. Now after only one week in Balluria I knew that I was given that chance with Hamid, the chance to live like Tom Sawyer and Huckleberry Finn. But there was no annoying eleven-year-old sister in that story. She stood there waiting for me to say something but I did not say anything, trying to block out her silent staring by thinking of what Hamid and I would do that day. Would we go hunt for birds? Or would we go to the river, so he could teach me how to swim? I knew that if my father found out that I was swimming in the Euphrates, he would beat me and possibly forbid me from ever spending time with Hamid again, but I was willing to take that chance. Maybe Hamid and I would go fishing, or was he going to show me the snake he told me he made friends with? He told me many times that snakes are good friends because they understood people. Amel was still standing there looking at me, waiting for me to say something. I was going to say something when she surprised me with a question.

"Are you from Baghdad?"

"Yes."

"What is your name?" she asked.

Just then, Hamid entered the house with a bag of rice in one hand and lentils and peas in the other. He looked at me sitting near the pigeons' cage and his sister standing there with the empty metal cup. He did not get angry or upset about his sister standing next to me; rather, he asked right away, "Did you touch the pigeons' eggs?"

"No, I did not," I answered.

"Where have you been? I waited for you all morning," Hamid said to me.

"I was with my father at his office, and I was talking to an old police sergeant; his name was Jelwi," I replied, trying to explain my tardiness.

"Oh, Jelwi, he has been a police sergeant for many years; he is older than the town."

Amel took the bags of food from her brother and went inside. Although I was relieved that Hamid was there, I felt an unexplainable disappointment because Amel was no longer standing there staring at me.

"What are we going to do today?" I asked.

"We will go swim and fish," Hamid answered.

That was the perfect answer. It was almost two o'clock in the afternoon, and it was a mercilessly hot August day. We still had almost three weeks until school started, so I had plenty of time to learn how to swim.

"Let's eat lunch first," Hamid said.

"No, let's go now," I suggested, unaware that Hamid and his sister and mother had had nothing to eat that day. I also did not know that the food they got from the Hillaly family was a charity that Haji Hasan Al-Hillaly would give them whenever he felt like giving. But Hamid was not about to disappoint me, so he grabbed a fishing rod for himself and gave me one that he made for me and said, "Let's go. I will eat later. Are you wearing shorts to swim in?"

"Yes," I replied. I was so anxious to get to the river and try to swim for the first in my life that I was not afraid of drowning after listening to Hamid's expert instructions; he made it seem so natural.

"We are not going to swim in the deep parts. We will start in the shallow banks and if you start to drown, don't do anything. Don't even move, because I will save you. Just let me pull you out, and don't take me down with you," Hamid said.

My first time in the river was a delivering experience. Hamid held me by my waist with his two hands and explained to me how to stroke the water with my hands and my feet to stay afloat. I was like a heavy sloth and a slow learner. Compared to the amazing swimming speed that Hamid had, I was an embarrassment. If my father had seen me, he would have been ashamed, and he would have beaten me for being so slow. Hamid was very patient, and he did not give up on me. After three and half hours of coaching me, he proved to be a skilled and dedicated teacher and lifeguard.

"Don't put your face in the water; you need to breathe. Kick with your feet and look every other stroke," Hamid would say, and when I first floated in the water and swam for two meters, it felt like I had just crossed the Atlantic Ocean.

Hamid exclaimed like a proud parent, "There you are. I knew you could do it. Just don't stop breathing. You need to breathe."

I was so proud of myself that I thought about telling my father that I learned how to swim on my own, but I was afraid he would beat me for swimming in the dirty water of the river and risking the possibility of drowning. When we were done swimming, Hamid and I sat in the shade of the palm trees, and he taught me how to fish.

"You place the dough on the hook like this, because if you place it like that, the fish will know what you are doing, and it will eat the bread and will get

113

away. To this day, I think Hamid was the luckiest fisherman in the world. He knew exactly where to throw his hook and within seconds he would catch a lively fish that looked so fresh and tasty. I was just mesmerized by the way the fish started jumping around and how right away Hamid would grab a palm tree leaf, twist it many times in a way that I could not follow, making it into a knot and hung the fish from its gills. My luck in fishing was similar to my slowness in swimming. Hamid tried to help me place the bait on my hook the right way, but I had no luck. I did not catch any fish. Hamid caught his sixth fish within half an hour. I was jealous and a bit embarrassed, but he did not let me feel it. He traded his rod with me and said, "Maybe it's the rod that is unlucky." He gave me his favorite fishing rod, and he skillfully placed the bait on the hook.

"Now throw it like this, to that spot," Hamid said. I did just as he told me and seconds after I threw the hook into the Euphrates I saw the cork floater bobbing. Amazingly, I felt the first fish nipping on my bait, and my friend and fishing mentor was watching and said, "Not now. Don't pull yet. Let the fish eat the bait." When I saw the piece of cork floater sinking, he shouted, "Now!" So I pulled with all of my strength, and for the first time I saw a nice-sized fish jump out of water and go right back into the water as it freed itself from my hook. The feeling of the fish's weight at the end of the fishing rod was so uplifting.

"I think you ripped the fish's mouth with your strong pull. You need to be a little gentler," Hamid said.

Hamid and I returned to his house with his six fish and my overwhelming disappointment. While we were walking, he stopped and pulled off a palm tree leaf, and with his amazingly quick twisting, he made a perfect knot and took three of his fish and hung them from their gills and gave them to me, saying, "Carry these three so my mother and Amel will think that you caught them."

Although I wanted to do that so badly, I objected so I would not lose my new friend's respect completely. "But I did not catch them. They are yours," I replied, hoping that he would not take me too seriously.

"It does not matter to me. I catch fish every day, but it's better for you to walk into the house with something in your hands," Hamid said. So, I gladly agreed, and I did not argue anymore. I wanted to look like I was as good as he was, at least in front of his mother. I absolutely did not care about what his little annoying sister would think of me. I just wanted his mother to respect me. However, when we got to his house, I was smiling with a pride that felt a little fake. Hamid's mother did not even notice what I had in my hand and that I had participated in the bread-earning process for that day. She did not even look at us since she was busy trying to keep from burning her hands while she baked the most amazing fresh bread in the world. On the other hand, Hamid's annoying younger sister was so excited and happy. She walked toward me like a loving wife welcoming her victorious husband, who brought the riches of the world back to her after a long journey at sea.

"Mashalla (God bless)!" Amel said. "How did you catch all these fish?"

"With a hook," I said, hoping that she would stop asking me questions, because I did not know how to keep the lie going. His mother finished preparing lunch, and she brought the freshly baked bread to the room and started setting sufra (placemats) on the floor, with rice, pea soup and vegetables. We all sat there eating lunch, and for the first time, I did not feel shy or like a stranger. In fact, I felt like I did not want to go home. I wanted to stay with Hamid and his family all the time, except for his sister, who kept looking at me with her deep, black, wondering eyes as if she were looking at an animal from a mythological tale. At that moment, I remember wishing that I were Hamid's brother. I wanted to stay in his house and be adopted by his family. Later, when we were done with the lunch, Hamid asked me if I played soccer.

Do I? I said to myself. Next to the television and American cowboy movies, I had only one other love in my life, and that was soccer. My dream was really to play on the national team or even make it to the world cup and to win the cup for Italy, because they were my favorite team. "Yes, I love to play soccer. Matter of fact, I am a very good player," I replied, waiting to see if this would be the most perfect day in my life: swimming, fishing, and now soccer.

"I will take you to meet with my team. We have a game against the Wild Lions. Do you know the Wild Lions?" he asked.

"No."

"They are from the next town over, and their captain is Mazen Uraiby. He is the son of Comrade Uraiby, the party boss. They've won every game we've played against them. They are good. We will play today," Hamid said. "We need good players. Our team captain is about to lose his mind because we have lost almost fifty games against the Wild Lions."

I was listening to Hamid telling me about their team's foe when someone knocked on the door. My heart jumped from fear, because I thought my father might be looking for me. Hamid stood up and shouted, "Mino (who is it)?"

"It's me, Hisham," I heard a voice similar to Hamid's.

"It's Hisham. He is our team captain, and he usually goes to all the team members' houses to make sure we all show up to the soccer match." Hamid and I walked to the door, and he opened it.

"Al Salamu Alykum," said Hisham.

"Alaykum Al-Salam," replied Hamid, and right away he introduced me to Hisham and said, "He is new here in town. He is the son of the new mayor. He will play with us."

"Salamu Alykum... shloneck (how are you)?" Hisham said to me and extended his hand to shake mine.

"Zain (I am fine)," I said as I shook Hisham's outstretched hand.

Hisham looked like he was just about to burst into tears from the heat, but he was firm in telling Hamid, "Four o'clock. Swear to me on the Qur'an that you will be there."

"I swear to you, Hisham. Did you tell Kamal, Ahmed, and Adnan?" Hamid asked.

"Yes, even Salah, Ashraf, and Haleem, and I hope that Abdullah will show up as well. I know that his uncle passed away yesterday, but we need him. He is a good defender. I will go to the funeral and ask him if he can make it to the game. So your friend here will be there, too? What position do you play?" Hisham asked me.

"Striker," I answered.

"OK. Can you give me some yogurt? I am really thirsty," Hisham told Hamid without commenting on my answer.

"Yes," Hamid answered and went inside to get him some yogurt.

2

When I first started playing soccer with my new team, I had no idea about their ordeal with the Wild Lions. It appeared that my new team, that had no name, had lost every game they played since they had started playing. Hamid told me about my teammates.

"Kamal, he is a bad kid. I hate him. He once threw a sack full of kittens in the Euphrates, and I had to save them, but he is a good player. He is related to Sheikh Jawad. Ahmed is Sheikh Jawad's son. He is a bad player, but we keep him on the team, because we don't have enough players. Adnan is our goalie. He is my friend, and Haleem is the best player on the team, but his big toe is always injured, because he never wears shoes. That is Hisham. He is our captain. He is not really a good player, but he keeps the team together."

Then he started telling me about the other team. "The Wild Lions, they are the best team in this area. Mazen is the son of Comrade Uraiby. His father got all the kids on the team their red jerseys and many soccer balls. Mazen likes to act like he is the best player in these parts, but in my opinion, Hisham and Haleem are the best players. The Wild Lions have shoes called Pumas that were imported from Germany. Mazen always brags that his shoes were made in Germany by the same company that made Franz Beckenbauer's shoes," Hamid said, looking down at his feet that had so many cuts and darkened scratches, and he added, "I don't have shoes, so I play barefoot. I wouldn't know how to play with soccer shoes."

Hours before that and then again when it was almost time to get ready to go play soccer, Hamid asked, "Do you want to go hunt for birds? And maybe I will show you where my snake lives." There was nothing in the world that would have prevented me from going with him, even though I knew that I would get a beating or, at the very least, a lecture from my father when I returned home. Since I would probably get a beating no matter what my decision, I decided to do all the things that I would be punished for.

"Yes," I said. "Let's go hunting." Hamid grabbed his slingshot and a bag filled with ropes. I was curious about what the ropes were for, but when we reached the middle of the orchard, Hamid took out of the bag a web of threads that he designed. He laid the web on the ground and tied the ends of the ropes to a tree. I had no idea what he was doing, but he was quick to explain, "I don't like to kill the birds. I like to catch them alive, and this net will do that." He then took out of the bag a small thing that looked like a bird, placed it in the middle of the net, and told me, "OK, we will hide here. As soon as we see the birds gathering inside the net, we will pull this rope." My heart was filled with a joyful thrill, as I was hiding in the dry creek that was filled with small plants and ants. I felt just like Robinson Crusoe hunting for his supper. I watched the birds descend from the treetops and check the decoy that Hamid made with clay and feathers. The fake bird was moving like a real bird, because Hamid was pulling strings that he attached to its wings. I saw doves and ravens come close to the bird and disappear. Also there was one crow. I tried to convince Hamid to pull the rope so we could catch it, but he whispered, "Crows are bad luck; let's wait for a fukhtaia (dove)." He was watching them with the look of a kid who knew what he wanted and how to get it. Suddenly, we saw a movement by the decoy. It was not the movement of another bird, because all the birds on the net flew away. The net was moving on the grassy ground, but we could not see what was causing the movement. We rose up to see what was making all the movement, and my heart stopped when Hamid pointed to the net.

"Look, it's my snake," Hamid said with a disturbingly calm voice.

"Oh, my God!" I shouted, then froze in my place and reached for Hamid's hand, looking for safety. I was scared beyond redemption. I thought that if I were to make any sudden movement or produce the tiniest of sounds, I would be eaten by the magnificent snake or that it would simply kill me by spitting venom from its mouth.

"Hamid, let's leave," I begged.

He smiled at me and said, "What's wrong with you? She will not harm you. It's my snake, and she knows me." He rose up higher, and his eyes widened. I thought that he was going to reach out and catch the snake. We were only ten meters from the deadly slithering giant. A magnificent beast, it had brown and black spots and looked like it could kill both of us with its unblinking stare. The snake did not eat the fake bird; instead, it lifted its head and looked around. I was sure that the snake had seen us or at least saw Hamid, who looked at it as if it were a cuddly little puppy and not at a giant deadly anaconda; at least that is what I had decided it was. Shaking and close to tears, I begged Hamid to get me away from the slithering terror.

"Please, let's go." He must have felt my fear and agreed to move on.

"OK, let's go." By the time we reached the end of the orchard, I must have looked behind me a thousand times to make sure that the snake was not following us. It was the most fearsome thing I had ever seen in my life.

"Did you see the size of that snake? It was huge," I said, trying to justify my embarrassingly cowardly behavior. Thankfully, Hamid did not comment.

"No, she is not huge. She is about a meter long... and I told you she is not harmful. She is my snake and she knows me. I feed her palm tree rats," Hamid said with strange adoration and confidence. I did not know why he was referring to the scary monster as "she" and how he knew that it was a female, but I figured that I would drop the subject because we were almost back to his house. Hamid opened the door, went directly inside the room, grabbed a jar full of yogurt, and handed it to me. Then he called out to his mother, "Yom'ma (mother), I am going to play soccer." We left the house and I saw Amel walking outside the room and following us with her sad eyes. I tried to avoid them, but she looked at me as if I was leaving forever and she did not want me to.

What an annoying, strange girl, I thought to myself and hoped that Hamid did not notice her look.

On the way to the soccer field, I asked Hamid what grade he was in; school was starting in twenty days, and I wanted to know if he would be in my class.

"I don't know. I may not go to school this year," Hamid said with a sad voice.

"Why is that? And how could you not go to school?" I asked.

"I need to work," he answered.

"Why doesn't your father work?" I asked. Before he answered, I remembered that he had told me before that his father died. I tried to retract my comment, but he surprised me with a new story and said, "I don't know where my father is. He is gone. My mother said that he is in Kuwait, but I know that he is dead. However, I don't care. I can work. Who needs him anyway?" Hamid said and shook his shoulders. He was right. Who needs a father anyway? I wished I could work and never go to school again. I wished that I could fish, swim, and hunt birds for a living with Hamid, who then explained the reason that he might not be with me in class.

"I don't know. My mother tells me that I cannot go to school. I need to work, and I don't like school much anyway. My sister, Amel, likes school a lot, and she says that one day she will go to college to be a doctor or a poet. You know, you should take one of the pigeons to your house and tell your father that you caught it and then maybe he will forgive you for being outside the house all day," he concluded.

"If my father knew I was hunting birds, he would beat me and kill the pigeon," I said as I braced myself for the inevitable punishment coming this evening.

It was not long after this that I learned from Adnan that Hamid's father had been the best horse trainer and rider in these parts. "He is a legend," Adnan told me. He also told me that Hamid's father made a living by going deep into the desert where no other man had gone before, and he would come back with one or two purebred Arabian horses that no one had ridden or seen before. No one really knew where to go to get them. Many said that there was a secret cave in the deep heart of the Arabian Sahara that could be opened with a secret phrase that only Hamid's father knew. It was also said that in the cave there were thousands of Arabian horses that lived free and wild and drank from a secret river that ran under the ground and flowed with the water of life. One time the two most powerful sheikhs on the prairie had disputed whose horse was faster; they both bought their horses from Hamid's father. So when Sheikh Miteb Al-Thary challenged Sheikh Muhsin Al-Harchan to race their horses, the prize was that Farhan, Hamid's father, would commit to serve as a horse trainer for the winner for the rest of his life. Not only that, but Farhan must tell the winner the secret words that would open the gate of the hidden cave and that if he did not, then the sheikh who lost would kill him. Hamid's father was not pleased with this deal. So, one night before the race, Hamid's father stole the two horses and disappeared into the desert. Some suggested that he sold the horses to the prince of one of the wealthy small countries in the Gulf and that he was living like a king in one of them.

"That was one month before Amel, Hamid's sister, was born," Adnan told me. I also learned that Hamid's mother was not from any of the nearby villages. She was a nomadic woman, and Hamid's father had met her and her family as they were crossing the southern desert. She was sixteen years old, and Hamid's father was forty years old when they got married.

Later and throughout our four years of friendship, I wanted to ask Hamid many times about his father and the secret cave full of Arabian horses. I thought that he and I might be able to go there, open the cave, and free all the horses. But from the look in his eyes, I knew that Hamid was not willing to talk about his father. Moreover, whenever the other boys and I talked about our fathers I saw a burning cry in his eyes, but he always managed to keep it covered with this enormous energy that he seemed to have gained from the secret water of life that his father found in the secret cave.

3

The soccer field was a very hard and stony ground with ankle-twisting potholes filled with a thick, fine dust. My feet began to unintentionally curl into my shoes away from the harsh playing surface. The two goals were made of twisted eucalyptus tree trunks tied at the tops with rope. I was surprised to see so many boys at the gathering. I thought that Hamid and I were the only twelve- or thirteen-year-old boys in the town. There were seven boys, and they were all by one goal. One of them was practicing his corner kicks, and the others practiced scoring with their heads. I followed Hamid to where they were.

The soccer field was an unattended piece of land full of weeds, roots, and small stones. Luckily, I was wearing my training shoes. No one else had shoes, not Hamid, not Ashraf, and not even the captain, Hisham. None of the boys on my new team wore anything that looked like or even came close to a soccer uniform except for Hisham, who had a faded red jersey with Manchester United misspelled and written in pastel colors with the number 10 on the back. Kamal wore a track suit top with shorts that were ripped from behind, and I wore my blue training shoes. The others wore their normal daily clothes. Hamid started to roll up his pajamas, nodded his head once in the direction of the far end of the field, and said, "There, they are coming."

We looked to the end of the houses, and we saw them, the Wild Lions. They were all wearing yellow jerseys and black shorts. They were the closest to a world-class soccer team I had ever seen. I was from the capital and attended many soccer games at the main high school. And I had seen some great playing teams, teams that were the talk of all the neighborhood kids, teams like the Storm, the Cubs of Baghdad, and, the ultimate team, the Seventeenth of July. This team had the legendary goal keeper, Kadhum Wadda, who was impassable. They all were good teams, but they were all disorganized, and sometimes several teams would play on the same field. One time I had counted ten soccer teams, and they were all playing against each other on one soccer field. Many times, players from one game ended up chasing the wrong ball, because the teams played so close to each other, and they would cross the other team's lines. I also remember that one player scored a goal for a team that he was not playing against. However, none of the teams I saw play in Baghdad compared to the sight I saw as I looked at the Wild Lions; just then, I realized what Hamid was talking about. The captain of the Wild Lions, Mazen Uraiby, the son of Comrade Uraiby, carried a net with a soccer ball inside it, and he kept kicking it over and over.

I looked at my new teammates and could see the look of fear in their eyes. My worry of being new disappeared when I realized that I was not the only who was scared. My entire new team looked like a group of pirates who had just lost their ship to the other team, along with their raggedy clothes and bare feet. We were all scared, but I knew how good I was and was confident that I could help. But I still needed an invitation to play and waited for Hisham to ask me to join them. Hisham was worried because half of our team was not there yet, and not only would he be short of players, but he would have to allow anyone who offered to play, even bystanders who came to watch the game. He was very annoyed because he had gone from door to door to all the team members' houses and made them swear on the Qur'an that they would show up to the game. He continued this practice of going to each member's home for four years. Hisham asked everyone, "Where is Adnan? We cannot play without a goalie, and where is Abdullah? Where are Kamal and Ahmed? They are always late." I think it was Haleem who said, "I think they are coming."

"Where?" Hisham asked.

"Over there, next to the pile of gravel," Haleem replied. Soon enough, three more players showed up, and that completed the nine players on our team.

Still, we were one player short, but Hisham said, "We will play one player short; I don't know how anyone can swear on the Qur'an and then not show up." He said this with great disappointment. They all got ready, but I was still waiting for Hisham to invite me in. I learned that Hisham was a great kicker, probably the best kicker in these parts. Most positively he lacked any other skills. He had great speed and a strong kick that would make the ball cross from one goal to the other. Although Hisham and the other boys never really picked a name for the team, I was surprised to know that each one of the kids had chosen a name for themselves. They had each chosen the name of a famous soccer player. I was waiting for Hamid to introduce me, but he kept running to the corner to warm up, as if he really needed to warm up after the eventful day of swimming, fishing, and hunting for snakes and pigeons. Finally, Hisham turned and acknowledged me. "You. What's your name? You will play defense," Hisham said to me.

"I cannot play defense. I am a striker," I answered, hoping that he would remember our conversation from earlier that day.

"You will play defense first, and then I will push you to the offense line," Hisham said.

I did not like the defense line, and I knew from experience that once a person plays a position, it would be very hard to change, because everyone would try to keep the position he is in and likes, but being the new kid and losing the chance to be in the game made me grateful for the invitation. When the other three players reached the field, we had our team of ten players. Now I was part of the team. Kamal, whom Hamid had told me he hated and that he was a bad kid, was acting like he was the only player on the field. He started warming up, and Hamid, who looked like he was playing against his will, just stood there waiting for the game to start. Adnan, who looked like he had a bad case of anemia and wore thick glasses, started measuring the distance to the goal with equal steps of his feet. I was sure that he measured the goals in every game they played; it seemed to be a ritual. For some reason, all the kids either respected Hisham, or they were afraid of him, even though later I learned that Hisham was not the best or the strongest player on the team. The other team was also warming up and getting ready.

Hisham, for his part, went running to where Mazen, the captain of the other team, was and shook hands with him. They tossed a ten-fils (cent) coin in the air. I guess they were deciding which goal each team would get and who would start the game. We kept the same goal we were playing on, and we got to start the game. Before the game had even progressed, I knew why they needed me. My new team was very weak and disorganized. Hisham started screaming from the get-go. He screamed at everyone, shouting curses and bad names.

"You idiot! What a donkey. Kick the shitty ball. Run faster, you slow donkey. What a dog. What an idiot," Hisham started screaming at us from the moment the game started, and they all accepted it, so I did too. Although he was the captain of the team, I realized that he was the main reason we lost the game. Rather than call them by the names of the famous players they all chose for themselves and loved, Hisham instead used the demeaning names. The names the players chose were inspiring; Hisham was Revelino, after the Brazilian midfielder who shot the soccer ball like a canon. Kamal was Beckenbauer, the German player who was known as the Kaiser (the emperor), and Ashraf was Kevin Keegan, the English player who no one could stop. Haleem picked the name Michel Platini, the French magic maker, who could pass three players at the same time. After the first game, I chose a name that no one really knew about, including me. I was the devoted fan of an Italian team, and the name I chose was Vakity because the name sounded musical and very Italian. Neither my teammates nor I had ever seen Vakity play, but I knew that he was a famous Italian player. I did not even know what he looked like. The only photo I had ever seen of him was a black and white faded shot of him running after a Spanish player. Underneath the picture was the caption, "Carlo Vakity, the captain of the Italian team, chasing a Spanish player after Italy lost 2 to 1 in the match."

So, I named myself Vakity. The others had chosen names that were more current. We had chosen those names to inspire us to greatness. That day the famous names that we had chosen for ourselves, that Hisham seemed to have forgotten, did not save us from the claws of the Wild Lions. It was a miserable defeat, which started with back-to-back goals scored by none other than Mazen, the captain of the Wild Lions. I thought that Hisham would go to the insane asylum after all the yelling and shouting he did, and when the Wild Lions were about to score their third goal, Hisham jumped and fell to the ground, and he shouted. "After him! Stop him. Don't let him score." But when the skinny boy from the Wild Lions shot the ball into the goal, and I saw our goalie, Adnan, covering his thick glasses with his hands, Hisham sounded like he was crying when he screamed.

"Waaaaaaaaaaaaaaa!" Then he called Adnan by a name that I heard for the first time. "You moron! You donkey with glasses. What's wrong with you? Are you scared of the ball?"

The day was almost done, and the game was almost over when another boy from the Wild Lions sent a shot that zoomed over our heads and landed in the left top corner of our goal, as our goalie Adnan pretended that he jumped trying to save it. Hisham fell to the ground again. "I can't believe it. How could you let that ball pass you?" he said to Kamal, who, to his credit, tried to stop the ball from entering our goal with an unsuccessful head kick.

When the game ended, the Wild Lions bounded away, slapping each other's backs and joyously recapping the high points of the game while we were left licking our wounds. The score was 4 for the Wild Lions and 0 for us. I was extremely tired and sat next to our goal trying to catch my breath. Hisham was still blaming everyone on the team for the loss, and beside him stood a thin, dark-skinned man who looked ten years older than us. He had been watching the game, but instead of cheering for us, he was calling us all kinds of names that rivaled Hisham's choices of insults. I learned later that he was from Balluria and everyone called him Fathil the Liar. When the game was over, Hisham stopped shouting and laid down near our goal to rest, and the thin, dark-skinned man walked away toward the homes.

Even though we lost 4 - 0, my day was a complete joy. I was sure that I would get punished by my father and that my mother would call me a shroogy when she saw the amount of dust and dirt I had collected on my clothes. But I will never forget that day in Balluria, where I saw a snake for the first time in my life, the pigeons, Amel's big, black eyes, and Hisham screaming at the team and calling us all donkeys. It was the closest I had ever come to being like Tom Sawyer and Huckleberry Finn. I still remember Hamid, my friend, who within twelve hours, showed me what it was like to have a true best friend. In my heart he was the only true friend I ever had.

The Book of the Gypsy Witches

House on a Chicken Leg

1

Salam did not know what to call the feelings that claimed his soul after reading the letters, but he was sure it was not remorse. He was incapable of remorse without logical reasoning, or so he thought. It was not yearning or longing for a human connection that would last, because he already had that with his wife; he thought and hoped. It was not the need for redemption and repenting, as he never felt the need for them, so certain was he that he never wronged anyone, at least not intentionally, in his entire forty three years on this earth. It was a feeling of true need that was deeply rooted in the empty corners of his soul that needed to be filled. Without it he could not go any further. He had many questions that needed answers. He felt the unchained stream of emotions run through him like a crippling emotional sickness that took away his ability to sleep, think, and live normally. He wanted to satisfy the thirst, to fulfill the unfulfilled emotional leftovers and psychological discrepancies that he had long ago shoved aside. He needed to hear answers from the source of the questions; it was an end that he must reach from where it all started. He knew that if he did not confront his fears, then the things he had sensed, lived, and experienced for the past twenty five years of his life would suddenly lose their relevance and validity. He felt that in order to salvage his sanity and his inner peace, for his remaining years, he had to come to his homeland.

Since he began reading the letters, he had felt as if someone were watching him. A pair of unseen eyes constantly looked at him and watched his every move. Even as he sat in his empty home during the day, he could not stop looking over his shoulder, expecting to see a pair of disembodied eyes hovering behind him; the relief from not seeing them was short-lived as the sensation returned as soon as it had left. He never told his wife or his close friends about the eyes, as he thought they might think he was hallucinating, schizophrenic, or even mad. They might have him committed. He had no doubt that someone waited for him; someone had been leading him ever since he felt the soft touch of the two hands. The hands were not human; their softness was that of a dream fairy or a nightmare demon; their touch was not of this world. Nightly the two, silky hands dragged him back into the abysmal past; they appeared in his dreams as soon as he closed his eyes. Whenever he fell asleep, they were there, waiting to take him back into another dimension, a dimension in which none of the realities that he trusted were viable or even remotely conceivable. He was being pulled into the past, not of his own will, and he did not like it. He wanted to control things; he wanted to choose his own destiny and actions. He wanted to know what was happening to him, so he tried to impose his Western education and his American experiences on a world with no connection to logic. He wanted to find a link between his current realities and those of the past, a mutual understanding of things.

He had intentionally escaped many of the realities from the past. He even changed his last name when he obtained his American citizenship, so he could escape further from a land and a time he wished to forget. In public he always insisted on speaking in English instead of Arabic, even when he and his wife ate a meal at a Middle Eastern restaurant. He even spoke English when he arrived at the airport in Amman. Many times he avoided talking about the earlier part of his life, even when his wife would ask him a direct question about it. For the longest time he was afraid that the past would reappear in the form of a person or an event and that somehow he would be pulled back into it. The past would become the present and the unavoidable future, in disguise, and nothing could change it. The past, present, and future would all meet at the same time in a mixture of chaotic emotions, self-rediscovery, and rationalizations. He was afraid of reaching a state of mind where he was a fake, or a fraud, or at least not genuine. Too many, maybe even his wife, it did not matter, but it mattered a lot to him.

Aside from his sensitive and paranoid nature about his right to exist and the two silky hands that tormented him in his nightmare, he thought that the trip would deliver him to a new stage of his life, in which he could be normal and at peace. He thought the trip to his homeland would be an evolution of his soul and a chance to extinguish forever the light that flickered in its forgotten corners. The corners that represented his barely admitted guilt for abandoning his family, his friends, and his homeland. In the beginning, when he first thought of making the trip, he was afraid that his ultra-kind nature and his self-imposed isolation would affect his ability to achieve total redemption, but he thought he could control his final destiny by applying his mind and his senses whenever he felt the absence of logical reasoning. He cherished knowing that he was protected with his own beliefs and actions in a way that made him immune to any acts that could, or might, bring the past to interfere with his present or his future. He felt that he had to walk a thin line to live up to what a person was expected to do to escape the reactions the world would bring on that person. A person must understand that life was a number of tasks and actions that would bring about various reactions by other people.

His entire life he had found comfort by closing the door to the reactions of others and opening the door to his creativity and art, instead of wasting precious moments of his life on issues like Islam, terrorism, the Arab-Israeli conflict, the hidden prejudices of people like his own in-laws, or the more obvious ones like those he encountered with Richard Zlotcik at the Thanksgiving dinner in Youngstown, Ohio; he was more keen on living his life away from current events and ignoring the reactions of other people. He always told himself it was not his fault that angry Muslims attacked the World Trade

Center and that it was not his fault that the Arabs and Israelis could not figure ways to get along and live in peace. Not only was it not his fault, but he also felt that it was not his business; he had no time for that. He kept telling himself these were parallel lines of events, time, and people and the best way for him to deal with this was by applying his own rules with his own timeline and responses. Then, and no matter what, time would pass, and life would go along with absolutely no need for him to explain things to anyone, and in the end, death would be the final result.

Before he had opened the red shoebox containing the letters, the parallel lines of his life were very simple and understandable. Emily was his base line; his love for art and his career as an artist and teacher were his world away from this world. This was his comfort zone; he liked things the way they were, and he was able to find the balance he needed with that mix. Before he inhaled the dust from the old letters in the shoebox, he exerted control over his life. He truly felt that he was being led by a mysterious rope, forced to face the past, and he did not like it at all. But if the trip would result in him being better equipped to maintain the world that he created for himself, then so be it. He would face the past. He would go back looking for his friends to see if they remembered him, and if they did not, then everything would solve itself. Then he would go back to Emily's arms, and this time he would never leave again. Instead of trying to understand these things, he would wait for them to explain themselves. This would be his only trip to the past and he would be a better human being after it.

Although he never understood the two hands, he was sure he had felt their touch once before when he was young. It was the touch of an old Gypsy woman who lived in Balluria, a woman whom the people of Balluria used to call "Mother Barrya." He knew that she was a Gypsy dancer and the mistress of a powerful sheikh who ruled Balluria with an iron fist. She lived alone and told many stories about lovers and Arabian knights who traveled the Sahara looking for love and fortune. She had touched his face once when he was injured in a soccer game. He had never forgotten that touch; her hands were softer than silk and warmer than blood. He felt a strange desire to sleep and never wake up when she touched his face. "But it had been so long ago in the past; it could not be the same woman," he said to himself. "She could not still be alive, and even if she were, how could she have found her way into his dreams? How could she have put a curse over the letters that were sent to him, and what kind of a curse was it?" He once heard the Gypsy woman say to a wide-eyed group of his boyhood friends, "In the Gypsy world black magic is used only for love and loving purposes. We live only for pleasure. Gypsy Arabs live for lust, dancing, and at the same time, we have poisoned the society that has rejected and loved us simultaneously."

He did not understand how love might fit within the context of his nightmares. If the two hands were those of the Gypsy woman, why was she using her magic to bring him back to that past? Was love the reason behind it?

He knew that the depth of history in his roots, as human being, was strangely the opposite of his beliefs, and the inheritance of his culture was somewhat a mixture between the words of the Gypsy woman and his beliefs.

"Tyrants, kings, and brave Arabian knights had licked the thighs of the Gypsy women, right after executing the divine clergymen, who showed the faithful the way to heaven. They danced until the early hours of the mornings in their quest for satisfaction," the Gypsy woman once said to the group of teenage boys, whose imaginations were fixated on the word "thighs." But he knew for sure that the desire to strive for heavenly rewards after such physical satisfaction was very devious in its presence and like a mirage in its appeal. It might be what he felt at that moment, when he looked out of the car window and saw the lines of dust shaping themselves, blowing on the side of the highway, in the direction in which Balluria waited for him. There was something in the way the dust moved here in the corners of the forgotten walls of mud houses. Magic hid its shyness because of its Gypsy origins. The mythical call to summon all the jinni fairies, who wanted to marry men of the living world, only lived in the hearts and minds of the lusty teenagers in the mud huts: tanned young teenagers, who somehow would always be misunderstood and oppressed and would always live their entire lives looking for that window, which they call life, so they could escape through it. He knew that the big, black eyes were imprisoned within the mud walls, and the long, black hair with ends that reached out to the end of the world were also imprisoned within the boundaries of the mud walls. Love and lust were imprisoned together and always would be, because they could never break free from that ethereal prison made of mud walls.

He felt sadness and wanted to scream; he started to feel that for some reason he loved the mud walls for what they hid within them. He was sure that this feeling was an illusion and that it would change and maybe even disappear forever. He knew that many things would change once he arrived to Balluria. He knew that all of this nonsense would be over soon and that he would be on the plane back to Emily; then he could leave all of this past behind him once and for all. But for now, he wanted to sleep in order to feel the touch of the two silky hands; he did not care anymore if they were the curse of the Gypsy woman. He wanted to feel them on his face and on his neck. The hands would prevent him from breathing the familiar air. They would give him an air of a different kind; he wanted to inhale that air full of dust from the past.

He was not sure of the destination, but for some reason, he was afraid of his destiny. He was scared of his driver and the way he drove, but he was surprised when the driver asked him," Are you from America, sir?"

"Yes," he answered.

"Can I ask you something, sir, if you don't mind?" the driver politely asked.

"Yes, as you wish," he answered.

"Is it true that in America a man can walk to a bar and take any woman he wants and have sex with her?"

"No, that's not true," he answered as he tried to remember where he heard this talk before.

Then the driver asked, "Is it true that American blond women like Arab men, because they have tanned skin and they can have sex many times in the same evening?"

"No, that's not true either."

"OK," the driver answered, unable to hide his disappointment at the answers he received. "You can sleep, if you want. We still have a long way to go. I will wake you up when we get there."

"What is your name again ?" he asked the driver.

"It's Alwan, Abu Hussain," the driver answered.

"Alwan, if you don't mind, I need to sleep for an hour. Can you please wake me up an hour from now?" he asked politely.

"Yes, Ustath to'morny, your wish is my order, just relax and go to sleep, and I will wake you up, sir," Alwan said.

"Shukran, thank you," he said and tried to close his eyes to escape any other attempt by Alwan to restart the conversation. He looked to the side of the car door, searching for a comfortable cushion to rest his head on. He put his head on his hand, and he leaned sideways on the door's leather covering. Then he closed his eyes and vigilantly waited for the hands, the soft hands, to take him into the magic swing, the soft hands that would caress him into a flimsy cradle of dreams.

The first thing he felt was the scent of heavy smoke that filled his lungs with the burnt, dried aromas of the southern evenings as every household tried to rid their homes of the evil spirits and let in the good ones. The smoky scent always reminded him of the sexual desires that invaded him every time he smelled that scent at the Gypsy woman's mud hut and in all the houses that he went to when he was young, yet he never understood why. He saw the hands waiting there for him, to guide him again to the past, the past that never was his nor was he willing to claim it as his. For the first time since the hands reached for him, he let his guard down without any attempt at resistance. This time he let the soft hands of the Gypsy witch guide him back to the past. In a way he was ready for the consequences. This time he saw her face in his dreams. Before he only saw the soft hands of desire and lust, but this time he saw her face, her hair, her eyes with the thick black eyeliner, the dark full lips, and the mole on her cheek. It was she, the Gypsy witch. She was inviting him to sit and listen to her stories, the same stories that he listened to when he was a teenager in Balluria, with a group of human beings that shared the fate of living and being born in the same place as he. In the dream he was a baby, who understood words and the meanings behind a look in the eyes.

He could smell hair, the hair of a woman, and he could also vividly feel the impulse of a woman's nerves, when she is touched, in the bottom of his feet. He looked at her; she smiled at him, and then he realized he was sitting in her lap; she caressed his hair and said, "Kan yama kan, once upon a time, in the deep desert of the Arabian Sahara, there was a brave, young prince who was looking for love and fortune. The young prince searched every place that he could for the love of his life. He looked for a woman who could offer him happiness and satisfaction of all of his desires, but he could not find her. One day he learned that there was the most beautiful woman that had all he was looking for, and she was living in the great city by the two rivers. The brave prince decided to go on a journey to find the beautiful woman and marry her. Many of his friends and family did not want him to go and asked him to stay, because they needed him, but he ignored all of the feelings, emotions, and unconditional love they had for him and decided to go on the journey in search of her anyway. He was told that, in his way, there would be one obstacle that would test his true love and that he must face it in order to test his manhood, his courage, and his abilities as a man. So he set out on his journey to the city by the two rivers. He walked for months in the desert until he arrived at the intersection of two roads; they were both dusty, and the wind blew forever.

"He saw a house, which was standing on a chicken leg, and in the house, there were three Gypsy witches who sang the songs of the desert. Many men were mesmerized by the sounds that came from the house on the chicken leg, and they decided to stop and see what was in the house, but when they entered the house, they never returned; they were cheated out of their fates and their destinies, and that is what happened to the prince too. Son, a man should know how to love first, and if he does, then nothing can stop him from pursuing his true love. That was the obstacle the prince could not pass, and that's why the prince never found his true love and why he forever roamed the desert looking for the satisfaction of happiness and love."

Then the Gypsy woman stopped, as her demeanor changed and she started staring ahead, not paying attention to him.

He waited for her to finish her story, but she simply stared. He wanted to beg her, but he realized that he was dreaming and could not talk. He wondered what his voice would sound like if he were able to speak in his dream; would it sound like Salam he was now or like the baby he was in the dream? So he started to cry like the baby in the dream, and maybe she would finish the story of the house on a chicken leg. He wanted to know if the prince would be able to redeem himself and find true love. He wanted to know if the prince could explain himself before he was doomed to a life of loneliness and misery. He wanted to know if he was that prince, but she kept silent.

He looked at her and saw that she was crying too, and her tears dragged the thick black eyeliner down her cheek to her neck and then to her breasts. It was then that he realized that he was nursing from her all that time.in this dream he was her child.

Her tears and her black, thick, sinful eyeliner were mixed with milk. The feeding calmed him down, and he stopped crying as he looked at her. She was sad, but calm and because she was breastfeeding him the mythical mixture, he was able to hear her thoughts; she was thinking of her loved ones that had departed on a journey similar to the journey of the prince in her story. She was crying because she missed them and wanted to find her true love too, but she knew that they would always end up being cheated of their destinies. That made her sad, and that was why she was crying; the tears poured from her eyes even harder. She wanted to tell her loved ones that it was not her fault, and although many of her stories had happy endings, none of the real-life stories of her loved ones had a single pleasant ending. They always had open endings of suffering and grief. She wanted to say to them that she was a weak Gypsy woman full of two things, love and lust. She wanted to say she was a weak woman who was unable to protect herself from the cruelty of the world and the viciousness of others, because the only things that she could do and wanted to do were to dance and teach others how to read their fortunes in the bottom of a coffee cup. She wanted to teach the young Arab women the most devilish techniques of making love to the many young princes who would cross the desert looking for true love. She only knew how to teach women how to give their princes satisfaction and happiness, so they would never look at another woman in the world.

"That was the Gypsies' magic, my son," the Gypsy woman said to him as he was falling asleep in her lap. That was the only thing that she could do well. Yet she was still caring for the eternal children who never wanted to grow up and never wanted to leave the security of her lap because they were afraid of the outside world, a world that never forgave them for being tan skinned and full of love and lust. He was the only one who made it.

He went to the outside world. He did not need magic or prayers. He did need not family or friends. Then he stopped nursing, because he felt that he no longer needed the tears mixed with thick, black eyeliner. Although he could offer his heart as redemption for the look in her eyes, it was time to wake up from the dream. He no longer cared if the brave prince would always be stuck in the house on the chicken leg, tormented by three lustful, mischievous Gypsy witches, who never wanted him to leave because they had spent all their lives in solitude waiting for love . It was just like the people in these parts who mistakenly thought that the world knew about their existence and the validity of their lives and dreams. They thought that the world cared about the dusty corners of the forgotten streets and sunny mornings of the riverbanks, where birds and fish talked about the muddy currents and complained of waiting. It was here that he realized his fears, as they were clear to him, and maybe they were just a very clear and authentic reason for him to come back to assess the logic of the feeling of being secure and to see if it brought peace to his troubled heart and mind.

Between what Emily, his friends, his gallery, and his art had offered him, within the cold pages of the Western civilization, and what these parts could offer him, these parts that never left him alone, he was to find his happiness in between the two worlds. He was ready to live again as an adult, as a man in his early forties, not as a young boy who chased pigeons and listened to poetry. He had no way to tell in which land or which setting and among who he would feel that he was home. At last, he tried to convince himself that Emily and her settled ways were the ultimate secure nest, but deep within him he always knew that the smell of the skin of the women with dark lips and long black hair offered a more exciting and lively sense of security. That was a sense of life and security a man could never ask or look for in his entire life, even with the very possible risk of following the footsteps of all the lost ancient passersby who once passed near the house on the chicken leg.

2

"Ustath, sir. Wake up. I think we are there," Alwan shouted. Salam opened his eyes to the slap of the rays of the eternal sun. He was alive; that was the first thing that entered his consciousness as the two hands faded away.

"I think there is no place to go after this. I guess this is the place," Alwan said. "Is this the place, sir?"

The man looked for familiar sights. He looked for a school where he and his childhood friends discovered the smell of the gardenia flowers on the girls' left ears. He looked for the police station, where he had sat listening to the most ancient police sergeant who ever lived in these parts tell tales of bravery with his smoky breath and scratchy voice. He looked for the sleepy house where he listened to poetry and the pothole-ridden soccer field where so many games had been played and lost. None of the buildings he saw looked familiar at first. All he saw were pockmarked houses covered with dust which was quickly turning to mud in the light rain that had begun to fall. The houses looked as if they had been deserted by life and people for quite some time. It had all changed. The entire town was covered with a haze of muddy dust that had settled on every surface, making it look like a field of cubic lumps that jutted from the mis-shappened earth. The tasteless painting habits of the unskilled construction workers made the place look like an oil painting, painted by an amateur artist using only one color: the color of despair. Everything was still in its place, but only because of the mere carelessness of existence. He finally saw the school with its faded light blue color, and he saw the police station with its dirt-like beige color. He looked to the furthest corner of his memory, searching for a landmark that would never fade away. He looked to the end of the town, and there he could see the seven palm trees on the horizon, in the wavy heat released from the packed ground by the faint rain, on the line of existence between reality and imagination, just between the end of the town where the mud houses ended and the wide open Sahara began. There stood the seven palm trees between the harsh earthly reality and the divine unexplainable mystery.

"Yes... this is the place. This is Balluria," he mumbled.

As Alwan drove slowly through the streets of the dusty town, Salam tried to see more of what he thought he could remember from his boyhood days. He looked at the houses and the buildings that he once knew. They had all changed to an unrecognizable state. At the same time, he looked within himself for a feeling, the feeling that he had been searching for a long time, but it was not there. He was afraid that he had wasted his time chasing a yearning trap, but he wanted to make sure. It comforted him to know that he still had the alternative choice of turning around and leaving at any time he wanted, even if the two mysterious hands tried to keep him there. So, he wanted to do it fast; he wanted to prove to himself that it was just an illusion and he could just turn around and leave this place; defeat was not a bad thing, as long as he no longer had to fear.

He begged the driver, "Alwan, please drive me to the end of town. There is a soccer field."

The car drove through the ever-dusty streets of the town. He was awakened by the scent as he breathed the dust of the eternal wasteland of life and time. It was the same. The corners had not changed, and they still held the souls of the people lurking and looking at passersby. He passed the corner where Adnan's house used to be, with the colorful water puddles filled with all the germs and mosquitoes of the world. The house was still there. He wondered if Adnan was there too, reading his books. He passed the street where he and his friend Haleem walked back and forth for hours, pretending they were studying and doing their homework, while in reality they were waiting for a signal from the windows where two beautiful sisters had lived. *What were their names?* He could not remember. Was it possible that people would have stayed in this place all this time and waited for his return?

Alwan stopped the car almost half a mile from where the soccer field used to be. "Ustath, this is the farthest I can go because of the rain. You see, my tires will sink in this mud."

Salam looked in the direction of the field and thought to himself, *Oh, my God, it's still there.* The field was covered with a shallow puddle, and many small canals had been dug to empty the many holes of their muddy waters. The goals had been replaced by 2 x 4 wooden goals that were broken, twisted, and abandoned. The nets were gone, and only little threads that danced with the easy wind still hung from the edge of the twisted frames. But it was still there.

He could still hear the echo of Hisham screaming. It seemed like no one had played soccer there for a while.

"All right, I will walk from here. I want you to wait for me and don't leave me here," he said to the driver.

"But how long you will be gone?" the driver asked and added, "I have to go back to Baghdad."

"Just wait for me, and don't leave town without me; I will pay you what you make in a day," he said.

"Well, that's not what I meant. I mean it will be like three notes, I mean three hundred dollars for the day," Alwan said as he readied himself for a good session of haggling.

"That's all right. Here is one hundred, and I will give you two more if you stay and wait for me to return."

"But where are you going in the rain, Ustath?" Alwan asked, blinking at the so easily procured fare in his hand.

"To look for people," he said as he exited the car and looked toward the end of the town, where an open field stretched all the way to prairie and the old train station that seemed deserted. The tiny droplets of rain began to cover his exposed skin. He did not mind it at all, as he felt that the soft and refreshing southern drizzle washed his face and his soul from the tremors of despair and boredom, as he started to walk toward the end of the town where a single, secluded mud hut stood alone. The mud hut appeared as if it were standing on a chicken leg just like in her stories about the three witches in the desert where many brave young Arab men disappeared when they searched for fortune and love in the Arabian Sahara. The mud hut was where he and his friends had drunk fresh yogurt, and he wondered where the Gypsy woman had gotten it from since she never owned a cow; the place where he and Adawya kissed for the first time. "Oh, that was her name," he said to himself as the memories of things, names, and events drifted into his mind. He looked at the soccer field; it was there, almost disappearing in the fog that started to rise from the raindrops of the early autumn of the south. He took off his jacket and walked through the dirt that was starting to turn to a slushy mud. He felt the silky hands starting to let go slowly and gently as he walked toward the mud hut. Then a strange freedom began to overwhelm his entire being.

"She must be here, I must be getting closer," he said to himself as he walked through the soft mud, guided by the Arabian Gypsy sirens with their tones of bloody weddings and tales of virgins with broken hearts and of the insecure rugged men who never knew how to love. He approached the door that looked as though it was not completely closed, just as it had always appeared before, forever slightly open. He walked that path so many times before with his friends when they were dying of thirst and fatigue after a humiliating soccer game against the rival team from the other village. He touched the door; the rain added a pleasant coldness to the faded blue colored tin door. Suddenly he froze. She called him. She welcomed him with her devious, yet motherly, voice.

"Come in," she said.

He cautiously entered and looked around to make sure he was still in the world of the living. His instincts told him to turn around and leave, but instead he entered the house. Many tiny rivers started to stream into the empty spaces of the walls of the mud room, where the scratchy voice came from behind the door. There was nothing in the house except for the wild weeds that seemed to have once grown with abandon, but were now dry crumbling remnants of life. He looked inside the mud hut and saw her. *Oh, my God, she is still here with her dark wild hair, shiny eyes, and the voice that scared the shadows off the walls.* She was sitting directly facing the door, as if she was waiting for him. He gathered his scattered thoughts and said, "Al-salamu Alaykum, I am looking for..." and before he finished what he was saying she finished his thought for him.

"Come in. You are looking for me. I know. I had a dream about you two nights ago, and I have been waiting for you since then," the Gypsy woman explained.

He was shocked, but he did not respond. He walked toward the silhouette of the woman. The smoke from the little fire she had in front of her filled the room with the aroma of a heavy past, a troubled present, and an uncertain future, and it added to his standoffishness. He sat silently and waited, because he believed after what she said about waiting for him that she was somehow a devilish divine.

"Come closer," she said to him. He moved slowly, and she persisted. "Closer, I want to touch your face." Her request rattled his body with fear of everything around him. He wanted to know the reason for her request and before he spoke the question, she said, "I am blind. I need to see who I am talking to, with my hands. No one has visited me for a long time. I can smell your skin. I like the smell," she added with her scratchy confident voice.

He started to feel the heaviness of the past in her breath and saw the memories lurking in every corner of that mud hut, small memories that he wanted to shelve in a forgotten corner of his entire being.

"I am not a stranger," he assured her, and tried to open the door to the dialogue that scared him to the point that he started contemplating his escape as he felt the heavy weight of the past starting to crush him with its gentle enormity. She lifted her hand, reaching to touch him, as she sat by the fire. He extended his hand and held hers to greet her. She protested.

"Not your hand. I want to touch your face."

"I am not a stranger," he said again, bracing himself and swallowing hard.

"Don't talk and let me know you first." She stood up like a gracious host and walked toward where he was standing, blocking the door to the empty space in front of the mud hut and, at same time, blocking his exit path. She walked in a circle around the fire and the tea set and closed in on him. He wanted to flee, but the trap was set, and he was in it. She lifted her hand; he could feel her breath, and the smell of her skin penetrated his senses, causing his blood to race, filling his empty heart. Her hands wiped his cheeks and hair with blessings of witchy prophecy. The rain started falling in the house and on the roof, producing music from another world. He felt relaxed and comforted by her touch as she kept stroking his face and hair. He remembered that touch. It was familiar. It felt the same as the touch from his nightmares. She put her hands down and stood there, leaving him in a state of unconsciousness. He wanted to say something that would save him from the numbness that overwhelmed him. But he did not want to lose that feeling, the feeling that he had been searching for the past twenty-five years of his life, the feeling of being at peace. The feeling started to enter his veins slowly. He never wanted it to leave his heart again. It was as if she scratched with the tips of her fingers all the shells covering his ability to sense things and his ability to feel the true touch of belonging. He felt that he belonged in that mud hut with the smell of smoke rising from the little fire that she started a long time ago that kept burning.

He asked with sincere and innocent stupidity, "Do you really remember me?"

"You are Salam, the son of the family that came from Baghdad. You are the clean-clothed boy. You are the handsome, groomed boy. You are the son of the mayor who never liked us or liked the town. Your father. Is he still alive?"

"No, he died many years ago," he answered with a strange submission.

"I have nothing to offer you except tea," she said. She offered her genuine hospitality and continued, "I have no areq left, so don't ask. And I have had no fresh yogurt since all the boys have grown and left town. Here we drink tea; people in these parts drink tea so they can forget."

"Forget what?" he asked.

"Their lives," she answered.

The rain poured harder, orchestrating a siren and sad noise like millions of tears hitting the tin and palm tree leaf roof. He chose to sit next to the door so he would have the chance to escape and to breathe fresh air. The space between the mud hut and the faded blue door started to fill with bubbles swimming on the muddy surface of the many tiny lakes and rivers that flowed within the prehistoric setting of plants in the shadows, giving the mud walls a teary look. He did not want to go inside the mud hut, as he feared mysterious gates might open. Then out of nowhere, small peaks of memories started to scratch his conscience as he inhaled her heavy presence. She walked back and sat across the fire facing the door, looking into the space where he sat, closing it halfway, looking at her and then looking at the rain outside. Nevertheless, he felt the feeling, that strange comforting feeling of the absence of plans, no plans for the evening, no plans for tomorrow, any plans for the future, and no plans for life at all. His weight was his compass. He felt heavy and comfortable. The sensation of yearning had ended. He felt that she had the time of existence to spend, so he did not argue. She smoked her cigarettes and offered him one.

"I have my cigarettes, thank you," he said and kept looking at her. It was Barrya, Mother Barrya, as many of his boyhood friends called her, but he never called her by that name. Barrya, the Gypsy, he and everyone once knew and talked about, the Gypsy witch who made everyone drink the mysterious yogurt. He remembered that he and his boyhood friends whispered that she got it from her jinni friends, her ghost friends. It was her, the same woman who awakened the buds of his manhood when he saw her dark breasts streaming from the dress she wore. It was her. She knew all the secrets of the town and kept them so she could laugh at them and be sarcastic, as she tried to teach the secret lovers how to love, offering her mud hut and her bed to all of them. She was the mother of all of them. It was her, Barrya, the mother of all the wolves.

He watched, as she slowly poured the tea into the small cups. She did not look the same; she looked old and weak and drained from the wild energy of life she once possessed. She did not look like the image that he had of her when he thought of all the stories he heard about her when he was young, stories about the men who slept in her bed and the ones who drank her areq and the ghost friends from the afterlife and all the jinni fairies that frequented her mud hut and the many sheikhs and sheep smugglers who fell in love with her. He started to feel the presence of historical souls that had passed through the doorway where he sat.

He smoked his cigarette and said, "I am here to ask you about some people I knew. I am here to find them. They were my friends, and we used to come here to your house." He was not sure if he had said the right things.

"After school when you finished playing soccer, I remember... when you were all thirsty and wanted fresh yogurt. I always wanted to keep you boys here for the longest time. I did not want you to leave. I wanted you to stay here," she said with the familiar voice.

He was amazed with what she was saying to him. She was right. When they finished playing soccer and they were licking their wounds after one of the many humiliating defeats with the Wild Lions, their only consolation was the fresh yogurt and Barrya's mud hut. Even before washing the dust off of their feet and the sweat from their foreheads, they went to Barrya's hut to wash from their souls the massive feeling of defeat and nothingness and to prepare for another day in these parts, where humans needed a spiritual cleansing every day just to go on in life. He started to feel the ropes around his neck again. He wanted to escape, because he knew that it was his last chance to do so. He vividly felt the words, the touch of the hands, the smell of the smoke, the little fire penetrating his ears into his brain, and it was becoming unbearable. He knew that if he sat and listened he would never be the same again. He was afraid of the past and knew that the current setting was perfect for him to get lost in.

The rain made the mud hut and the courtyard look like a confusing canvas. The town was in his sight in its entirety; he could see it from the door, like the doors of the house on the chicken leg with the three Gypsy witches waiting for their young prey. Was he that prey? Was she one of the three witches? Was she the last surviving witch of the three that longed for a young man's love? She certainly had the laugh and all the abilities of a Gypsy witch. This is what everyone said about her when he would listen to his childhood friends talking about how she had the lust and the imagination of a thousand women and had the mystic and irresistible power to lure men into her bed. Moreover, so many people confessed to her about things they would never tell the clergy who prepare them to meet Allah. They told her everything. Some men never returned to their normal lives after that. Instead they chose to disappear in the Arabian Desert, wandering aimlessly. Or so the legend says.

He once heard a man everyone called Fathil the Liar say, "Barrya, the Gypsy woman, she slept with the president himself, and she has sisters from the jinnies and ghost brothers. I know that she is not a woman." Fathil the Liar then concluded by saying, "I know that because the president himself told me."

With all of his fears of falling into the abyss of memories and stories of people who were long gone, that would never return, he realized his strength as a logical processor of things, and this sleepy part of the world would never captivate him, but for some reason he thought that the distance between her mud hut and the threats of the house that looked faded in the rain and smoke was the distance between reality and imagination, and between life and dream. He felt that the struggle between him and her would be decided in hours. He would spend some time at the mud hut, and it would be between what he had built his life around, solid logic, and her world of myths of the ancient past or the mesmerizing world of lies that she was trying to pull him back into. He had prepared his arsenal of Western tools to deal with such things, and he was skilled in using them to maintain the shell of not belonging: fake smiles, carelessness, silence, and the certain and undeniable faith of not paying attention to anyone he did not want to be a part of his life. He had Emily. He had David and his art, and that was enough to last him a lifetime. All the other historical mistakes that the world had thrown at him did not matter. Realizing that, he asked himself, *What the hell I am doing here, then?* And before he looked for the answer or walked out into the rain and the safety of the waiting taxi, she provided her silky rope to him to tie him down.

"Do you remember Amel?"

What...What...Amel? The one from the letters... The one from the poetry letters? He asked himself. "Yes... I remember her." *Vaguely*, he thought.

"How is she doing? Is she still alive?" he asked.

"Allah forgives you... you broke her heart to pieces. She never healed from your love. She is alive, and she is still here. She is the only one who stayed here. Everyone else has left, except for her."

What love? I broke whose heart? What was this Gypsy woman talking about?

"Do you remember her?" she asked again.

"Yes, I do," he answered with less protesting in his voice. "Her brother, Hamid, was my best friend." He tried to remove the guilt that had suddenly immersed him.

"She used to read you poetry and made you listen to songs by Fairuz," the Gypsy woman said. "She cried for you for ten years after you left. She did not know that you would not return," the woman said.

"Listen, ma'am. The people you are telling me about were my friends, but that was a long time ago. I mean, many things have changed, but I do remember them. Amel used to read me poetry in her house," he said, and then she interrupted him.

"You never cared," the old woman said. "You never cared about many things. You were always like a stranger. You had your nose in the sky. You looked down on us. You resented our poverty and our level. I did not love you as much as I wanted to or as much as I loved the other boys and girls; you were just a guest in our lives," the Gypsy woman said.

He did not want to comment on what she said and realized that she would say what she wanted anyway, so he used his adopted Western manners and simply said, "Amel, that was her name, yes. I went to their house many times when I was a young boy. What happened to her?"

"She is still in town... waiting," the old woman said. He did not know what to say after that, but she would not let him escape. She knew that he wanted to escape. He was one of many men who came to her mud hut and wanted answers to their lives, but did not necessarily want to hear the harsh truths that made them less than perfect. "You have grown. When I touched your face, I wanted to know if you were Salam from my dreams. I had dreamt that you were coming here. You have gotten older, but you are still handsome, as you always were," the Gypsy woman said.

She had him right where she wanted him to be, or maybe it was where he wanted to be. He knew that he needed guidance like a baby on her lap.

"Well, you know, ma'am. That's life. People get older," he answered, still halfheartedly trying to deny his need to be in this rough-hewn mud room.

"But the hearts stay the same if they are true," she said. "In all of my dreams about you, you wanted to talk to me. You wanted to talk to me, but you couldn't because you think that I am a witch." The Gypsy woman let out a laugh, the same old laugh that chased the shadows on the mud walls. "Yes, I am a witch, a witch of love and broken hearts, a witch that can drink your sorrow together with your tears. After I do that you will leave me brokenhearted forever," she said with a smile that revealed a perfectly white set of teeth.

He looked at her and started to discover the infinity of her beauty, a beauty that faced the mortal enemies of time and life, in these parts, yet it continued to shine like a perfect stone in the desert.

3

The rain stopped and the sun shyly poked out from behind the clouds, sending its warm rays through the window and the small holes in the walls. Millions of dust particles started dancing in the spectrum of the light coming from the holes in the walls and the open door toward the empty ground of the mud hut. Salam buried his head in his hands and leaned toward his knees, realizing that even if he tried to stand up to leave he would not be able to.

The old woman said, "Ask me about them. I know you want to ask me about them. You have traveled all this distance after all of this time, because you want to know."

"Yes," he said. "I want to know what happened to my friends. I have a photo."

"I'm blind," she said. "I can barely see. I only see shadows of colors."

"Oh, I'm sorry. Forgive me. But, I don't remember all of their names," he said.

"I do," she answered. "I remember all of their names, their faces, and their smells. They are my children."

"Your children?"

"Yes, just like you were one of them," she said.

He smiled at that refreshing gesture of love. "I am honored," he said.

"No, you're not. Your father never was pleased with having me in town. He wanted me out, but when Sheikh Jawad heard he sent your father a message saying if I left town that your father must leave town the same day. After that your father stopped harassing me, but he never liked me, which made me sad, because I liked your mother, your sister, and you," the Gypsy woman said.

"My father is dead now."

"Yes, you've told me. Your mother was a good woman. She asked me once to read her future, and she did not like what I told her, so she never welcomed me back into your home again. How are your sister and younger brother?" the Gypsy woman asked.

"They are OK. They are grown and married."

"What do you want to know?"

"I want to know what happened to my friends. I found this photo and want to know if they are still alive, especially my best friend, Hamid."

"So, you remember his name. He is still alive, yet dead. He went to the desert."

"To do what?" he asked ignorantly.

"To live and die. He is in the desert. Sometimes we see him on his horse. Some say he turned into a jinni or a wolf, but I know that he just went to the desert so he can always be free."

Salam did not understand what she was saying. He sat there waiting for her to explain, but she did not. She wanted him to understand that he must be willing to accept her ability to tell mythological lies tied in with truth and to accept her explanation of things because that was the only way she would be able to heal him. She repeated what she had said earlier. "In these parts, people go back to the desert, where they came from, to live and to die. There is no reason for that. They just do it when they realize the real purpose behind the agonizing, endless waiting of their lives."

"So he lives in the desert like a nomad?" he asked foolishly.

"No, my son, he lives in the desert like a wolf."

He sensed truthful sarcasm in her voice when she mentioned the wolves. She was the mother wolf, but without asking another question about the reference, he quickly anchored his lost ship of memories. "Yes, the Wolves. That was the name of our soccer team and the photo I brought with me is that of the soccer team. I was on that team, and so was Hamid," he said triumphantly.

"So were Hisham, Kamal, Haleem, Ashraf, Salah, Adnan, Ahmed, and Abdullah. You were all the Wolves,"

"Yes, ma'am. You are right. How do you remember all of them?" he asked foolishly again.

"How could a mother forget her sons?" she replied. He looked at her and realized how naive his question was.

"Do you remember the girls?"

"Some of them."

"Do you remember Amel, Hanan, Basima, Suaad, and Bushra and Adawya, the two Hillaly girls?"

"Yes."

"You kissed Adawya, the Hillaly girl, right here in this room." She pointed to a spot on the floor. He remembered his first kiss in the mud hut, and he remembered that the Gypsy woman Barrya arranged it. It was one afternoon, when the Gypsy woman asked Adawya, the younger of the Hilally girls, to come to the mud hut so she could dye her hair with henna. At the same time, she asked him to come to the mud hut, because, as she claimed at that time, she had something that she wanted to give him to take to his mother. When he and Adawya were in the mud hut alone, the Gypsy woman closed the door of the room that many men and women had their first kiss in, so they could talk and kiss. He still remembered her words as she closed the door on them. "You are now free to love and no one in this world will ever know." He remembered that he was shy, scared, and more nervous than Adawya, who was at that time his sister's classmate, and he and she were exchanging love letters, and she was more eager than he was to learn how to kiss.

That was a long time ago. Salam looked at the Gypsy woman and realized that she knew more about him than he knew about himself. He also realized that no matter how high his guarding gates might be, he knew that the blind Gypsy woman would be able to climb inside him and find her way into his soul. He knew that in a way she had been inside him for a long time, just as she was inside him at that moment. So, he thought that maybe it was time he let down of all of his guarded perimeters and let in this old blind Gypsy woman, who possessed the secret key to his heart and his past, the past that he was running away from and not wanting to go back to. Even with all of his fears, standoffishness, internal disapproval, and rejection of her and whatever Gypsy witchcraft she might have used to bring him to this mud hut from across the Atlantic, and whatever curse he might leave the mud hut with, he felt that he must let her in; he must trust her. He traveled all this way from his secure world of logic, where things were clear and recognizable, that secure world where many people who loved him and cared about him had asked him not to go on this trip in search of answers, just like the young Arabian prince who roamed the desert looking for true love.

In many ways he was that young Arabian prince. She was the Gypsy witch who had imprisoned him, and the mud hut was the house on a chicken leg. Unlike the prince in the story, he would leave the mud hut and he would find a way back to Emily; he would find his way back to his world. For now he must listen to the blind, old Gypsy woman, because she was the key to the redemption that he needed in order for him to go back to America with self-satisfaction and complete peace, so he could live without the nightmares of the silky hands and the strange woman who reads poetry in Arabic. He wanted to face his ultimate fears and his guilt-stricken conscience, even though he knew that it was not his fault, it was not his doing, and, certainly, it was not his obligation to search for answers, but he wanted to so he could continue to have peace of mind. He was sure that none of his friends would waste even a moment listening to his stories when he returned to Chicago.

David would laugh and would say something like, "Dude, that is messed up!"

His wife, Emily, would listen for a while then she would change the subject to talk about the house or the baby. Even Roger Goldstein and Rob Gibson might listen for a few minutes and then they might ask him if this is the theme he's planning for his next show.

It did not matter what they thought; he was the one who needed answers, he was the one looking for redemption, he was looking for legitimacy for his purpose in life and that was enough for him. It was true that in many ways he was the young Arabian prince roaming the desert for years, looking for true love, and ending up as the love hostage of the three Gypsy witches living in the house standing on a chicken leg. But he was not young anymore. The gray hairs in his long curly mane overcame the myth of love, and only one Gypsy witch lived in the mud hut. He must pass this obstacle to get to his true love, so he could once and for all get rid of that feeling, the feeling that poked him in the heart like sharp little stones in his shoes penetrating his skin with each step. It was because of this that he remained seated to hear the Gypsy woman's stories. He was ready to listen to this old lady speak her piece, with all the sarcasm in the world, just like he remembered her, and he was sure she would laugh, many times over, the same laugh that chased the shadows off the mud walls.

"So," she said, "are you ready to listen?"

With that simple statement, she released his heart and his mind and untied the ropes that bound him. He felt a sense of familiarity, belonging, and a comfort in the smoky mud hut. The rain started to play its tragic symphony again, over the tin roof, and millions of bubbles started to dance on the surface of the muddy walls like tiny lakes and rivers in the space between the mud bricks.

"Yes, ma'am. I am Salam, the son of the mayor who never liked you, because he thought that you were sin itself, and we were the family that came from Baghdad. I had been to your house many times before, when I was a kid, and I drank the yogurt after my soccer games, and for many years I have been living faraway in a country that you may never see and you may have never heard of. I was living in peace with my wife, and one night I opened a letter that I received from a girl. Her name was Amel, and I found a photo of my friends and me on the soccer team. Ever since that night, I've had dreams about two hands choking me, preventing me from sleeping. Every time I close my eyes: the two hands appear in my dreams and keep me from breathing. Sometimes they caress me. Sometimes they guide me toward a house in the desert, and other times they wrap a rope around my neck and drag me. I was not able to sleep until I decided to come here; that was when the hands started to leave me alone, and then I was able to sleep again. I am not a stranger, although I am acting like one. I need answers, and I've come here to see what has happened to my friends in the photograph. Who is still alive, and who is still living here in this town? I want to know about all of them. What has happened to all of them?" He paused. Neither of them spoke or moved as the sound of his voice faded, "Yes, ma'am. I am ready to listen."

"Well then, let me pour you some tea," the Gypsy woman said as she smiled.

The Book of Balluria

Dusty Feet of Fate and Fortune

1

During the time when the general massacred the royal family and the young gentle king, it was known in these parts that to be a smuggler was to play with death. But smuggling seemed to be the only way for those who had very little to nothing to survive, and there were many folks in this position. A real man did not allow himself or his family to die from starvation. The smuggling business was the only way for any man who had an ounce of courage not to starve and to keep his family from starving in these parts. The ounce of courage meant to be as close to death as any other human had ever been or ever would be. A man would walk the distance of three hundred miles through the predator-infested wilderness using the stars at night for direction and guidance. He would risk the possibility of being devoured by the desert wolves, wild dogs, and other smugglers, who would kill for a herd of ten sheep or those who would kill for even one sheep. Also it meant risking the chance of being chased by border patrolmen who pursued the unfortunate smugglers into the deep deserts and left them to die of thirst after roaming the merciless wilderness.

Any man who would travel that road usually went in one of two ways. One way was herding ten to twenty sheep, avoiding border patrols, which had orders to shoot on sight, and entering the neighboring oil-rich country and staying there for a day or two to sell the sheep in the livestock market, avoiding the interior ministry agents who vigilantly looked for smugglers. Then they spent the second day buying goods needed in the homeland and prepared for the return trip with a pocket full of money and a bag full of goods: all within a one-month period. Then they would pay the sheep owner his portion, and they would keep the rest. It was not only an admirable profession, but also the solution to any young man's dilemma for getting funds needed for marriage and the possibility of settling down to start a family, build a mud hut, and have children. Many men in Balluria, Tawsheeha, and throughout the marshland had worked for the sheikhs, in these parts, who lent their sheep to the desperate men for half of the profit.

A few months after the massacre of the young king and his family, a young man showed up out of nowhere and asked for hospitality at the guesthouse of Sheikh Badr Al-Ghathban. That young man was Jawad himself. Khanger, the coffee man, was surprised to see this young, tough-looking man asking for hospitality, because he looked like a thief, a suspicion that was not far from the truth. What Khanger did not know was that Jawad had been hiding in the riverbank all day while the new government official and his new police patrol spent hours looking for him and two other men. When he walked to the guesthouse, Jawad knew that he would be under the protection of the town's sheikh and that the police patrol would not seize him. He walked to the guesthouse after he learned from an old man near the river who the sheikh of this town was and where his guesthouse was.

It was the only guesthouse in the town. After that night and for many years, the townspeople speculated where he came from. Some said that he was a royal family guard who escaped the firing squad. Some said that he was not even human and that he was a jinni, who walked out from the river and came to the village to torment its people. Some said he was a thief who killed all of his gang and made away with the riches they looted from the prince of the oil-rich southern country. That evening when he sat in the guesthouse, Jawad looked at the town sleeping in its dimming lights and said to himself, "Balluria... what a name. But you look like home and you feel like home."

It was while Jawad had decided that he was finally home that Sheikh Badr Al-Ghathban walked to his guesthouse and saw the young man. The sheikh signaled to his slave and coffee maker, Khanger, to come close, and when he did he asked him, "Who is this man, and what does he want?"

"May your life be long. I don't know. He just appeared and asked for hospitality," Khanger replied.

"Wallah, by God. I can't trust the look in his eyes. They look like the same eyes Irar had. I think he is a thief," the sheikh said.

"Long life to you. We can't ask him to leave. It's not our custom," Khanger said.

"It's also not our custom to let a wolf into our family's home. Let him stay three days, and then he must leave." Sheikh Badr had the same feeling about Jawad that he had had when another man showed up a long time ago. That man's name was Irar, who at that time was on his way back to Balluria after a sheep smuggling journey.

There were three nights of heavy rain in Balluria, and most of the townsmen stayed home and were not able to go to the guesthouse. Only a few of them showed up to sit around the fireplace, drink coffee, and talk about how a colonel in the north tried to overthrow the mean general, but was killed and his body was dragged through the streets of the great northern city. That night was the third night of the three days of hospitality for Jawad, who was not ready to leave. Hours before, at sunset, Sheikh Badr had tried to hint to the stranger that he had overstayed his welcome by saying, "Al Khala Makhly (the prairie is wide and welcoming for some)." But Jawad did not answer; he was keen on staying, so he kept quiet and waited. Sheikh Badr was engaged in talks with the new magistrate about how the Israelis were killing Arabs and how the new government was planning to draft more soldiers to go fight against Israel. Sheikh Badr hoped that that the young stranger would leave soon, and he hoped that somehow the young stranger would be captured and drafted by the patrol of gendarmes and the new magistrate, who were already looking for people on the draft list. For some reason Sheikh Badr did not trust the look in the young man's eyes; it was that of a hungry wolf. Jawad did not pay any attention to the political conversations; he paid attention only whenever they mentioned the patrol of gendarmes. His fears vanished that night when he sat next to the big Sergeant Jelwi, who looked at Jawad briefly, but did not recognize that he, Jawad, was the thief they were chasing.

The men spent the evening talking about the military coup in the north and how a colonel, who hated the new general whom every one called, "the only leader," tried to take over the great city in the north. The colonel's coup was not successful and he was killed along with many of his coconspirators when two fighter planes bombed the air base where the colonel and his supporters were.

That night, just about the time everyone wanted to leave the guesthouse and go home, a bald tough-looking, thin man, who appeared as though he just walked out of a grave, walked in from the darkness outside. Everyone welcomed him and the man walked directly to where Sheikh Badr sat, leaned down, kissed the sheikh's hand, and whispered something in the sheikh's ear. Then the sheikh ordered his servant, "Prepare dinner for Irar."

When Jawad saw how the men in the guesthouse greeted Irar and how the sheikh welcomed him, he asked the man who sat next to him, "Who is the man?"

"That's Irar. He just came from the desert," the man replied.

Jawad was more interested in the way the thin, steely man looked. He looked like he was the offspring of a snake and a wolf mated in a hellish desert. He learned that the man was the main smuggler and sheepherder for Sheikh Badr, across the borders to the rich country in the south. In addition, he learned that Irar was a loner, but he did not speak to him that evening. That night, he sat and listened as Irar told of the chase he encountered with border patrol. Jawad was mesmerized by the story, even though his own life was a streak of daring chases and many encounters with the law and the rugged border patrolmen. Irar's adventures were different, and they were braver than his were. He learned that Irar crossed the desert once every month and he did that alone, and when Irar said, "Men, I tell you the truth. After two nights, the border patrol gave up chasing me and it was me, my ten sheep, the desert, and its wolves."

Jawad thought about what Irar said and thought to himself that he could do that; he could smuggle sheep across the border. He listened to Irar, but he did not talk to him, nor did he try to initiate an interaction; rather he waited for Irar to take the initiative. Jawad could not wait long though, because that night was the last that he had hospitality, and he did not know if Sheikh Badr Al-Ghathban would let him stay in the guesthouse any longer. Jawad spent his nights in the guesthouse, but during the day he walked around the town, exploring it and looking for an opportunity to make a living, so he could stay.

145

He knew that he could never go back to the big city, because he was wanted there for many thefts, and he knew he could not stay at the sheikh's guesthouse. He resented that the sheikh allowed him only the three days, and he thought to himself: *If I were the sheikh, I would not ask the strangers to leave my guesthouse.* But it was impossible for him to be a sheikh; he was young, penniless, and without family roots. Besides that, he had to find a place to live; he had to find it soon, and it had to be here, in this town.

Balluria... what a name for a hometown, Jawad said to himself, as he stood outside the guesthouse looking at the desert and at the end of the town, where he saw an abandoned mud hut. The prairie began there, and after it was the desert. Jawad looked at Sheikh Badr's house and wished that he had one like it. How would it feel to have a house, to feel safe, and to be rich? He would never again need to ask anyone for hospitality and would never again be a Leffu from any sheikh. For a strong and tough, young man like Jawad, these soft feelings and self-pity were unknown, but at that moment, he felt alone, and he recited an old poem by a poet who spent his entire life searching for a home.

When will a tired stranger rest in his home
And when is it that he never has to leave his home again?

He wondered how it would feel to have a house, a place where he felt at home; he wondered when he would have a wife, or many wives, and a slave to make the fresh, dark, thick coffee in the morning, and a guesthouse that others could stay in. He wondered how it would feel to be addressed by other men as "long living" or "may your life be long" or "Ammy Al-Sheikh." How would it feel to be a true man with respect and status? *Oh, what would it take?* He did not want to be like his father, who had been weak and penniless his whole life, and he did not want to be like his stepfather, who was penniless and angry all of the time.

Jawad took a very deep breath, as he looked at the house of Sheikh Badr and looked at Balluria, and wondered if he could ever have it, the house and the town, for himself. Jawad dreamed the impossible, of being the sheikh of Balluria.

2

It was during that time that a group of Gypsy women dancers and musical players who were chased away from the outskirts of the capital, appeared in the villages near the marshes and started going from one village to another, begging for food, goods, and any money they could get by showing their talents in dancing and mischievous behavior that left many children infatuated. While those shows made young men in those parts dream of the Gypsy dancers who moved their hips and their shoulders in very suggestive ways, they left many peasant wives and women angry and jealous when they heard their men telling of the beauty of one of the Gypsies. The large Gypsy family came to Tawsheeha and camped in a deserted orchard with many dead palm trees, on the road to Balluria. Many young adult men spent several nights in the small camp of the Gypsies, listening to the men as they played instruments and watched as three women danced—two were older, and one was beautiful and young.

One man who was from Tawsheeha told the villagers about the young Gypsy dancer and how beautiful she was. "She moves the ground underneath her feet when she dances," he said, and added, "I must bring the Gypsy dancers so they will dance in the wedding of Sheikh Waitan's son, Ra'ad."

The large Gypsy family consisted of six men, four women, and many children. The children were so varied in appearance that it was impossible to believe that they shared the same parents. For days the Gypsy family made the crowd of villagers, who followed them around, dizzy with their floats, drums, and three of the women, who danced like three snakes moving harmoniously to the sound of the mutbaq. The three women wore flimsy black dresses and lined their big, beautiful eyes with thick, black eyeliner that made their eyes look like those of the desert deer. Although all of them moved with sensual ease, it was clear that the youngest woman was the center of attention of all men who followed the group of the Gypsies, cheering and whistling. The large Gypsy family had traveled to these parts in a caravan of three donkeys pulling three carts filled with junk and colorful goods that looked as if they were stolen from all the imaginary places that the Gypsy men told their stories about. In reality, the goods were stolen from the many houses they frequented in their travels. The elder Gypsy woman, with her second sight, read fortunes and dropped the future-telling Gypsy stones for many of the women in Tawsheeha and Balluria. In the daytime, while the young, beautiful woman stayed in the camp and received her secret visitors, the elder woman never left the camp in order to ensure that the young, beautiful woman only lay with men who would pay a high price. Many people said that they saw with their own eyes Sheikh Badr Al-Ghathban visiting the secluded camp one afternoon and entering the young woman's tent as the elder woman sat in front. The other two older dancers spent the day going from one house to another, begging for anything. The villagers harshly chased them out of their doors and called them sinners and dishonorable. That harsh treatment seemed not to deter the two women and the four Gypsy children who followed them, holding their black robes and determined to collect anything that made itself available.

After a long day of constant begging, the Gypsies retired to their two tents between Balluria and Tawsheeha, where they prepared themselves to entertain the young men who had frequented the camp for days. One day, two men with rifles on their shoulders showed up in the camp and announced that the Gypsies belonged to Sheikh Waitan, because he wanted them to dance in the wedding of his older son, Ra'ad. He was marrying a girl from the Sharify family, but she was not from Balluria. After that announcement, no man showed up at the camp for quick entertainment, and the Gypsies were left alone for two days to prepare for the wedding. Many women had said that the bride-to-be was not beautiful at all, and rumor had it that she was crazy, but she had inherited almost all the land by the southern, narrow banks of the river after her father died. All the people in Tawsheeha and Balluria were stunned when they knew that Sheikh Waitan had invited the Gypsies to dance in the wedding. That was not an honorable thing to do; at least that's what Badr Al-Ghathban had said in front of the Sharify men in his guesthouse that afternoon.

"Gypsies sitting with sheikhs? What will we see next?"

Nevertheless, Sheikh Badr Al-Ghathban planned to appear at the wedding, and he made sure to have at least twenty men with him, all armed because the old feud with Sheikh Nasser the Blond and his tribe had not ended yet. He made sure to invite the new magistrate with him as a show of his new status as the government favorite and because he was the sheikh of Balluria, which was an official town, whereas Sheikh Waitan was the sheikh of Tawsheeha, which was still a village that administratively belonged to Balluria. Moreover, Sheikh Badr wanted to show Sheikh Waitan that he was the official sheikh of these parts and wanted to make sure that Sheikh Waitan would see that with his own eyes and would have no doubt about it.

On the wedding night, at least forty men from the village of Balluria had accompanied Sheikh Badr Al-Ghathban to the ceremony. Jelwi, the sergeant of the gendarme patrol, was, with his fearsome rifle, standing behind the magistrate, who sat next to Sheikh Badr Al-Ghathban. The magistrate had ordered Jelwi to dress up in his gendarme's uniform and bring the other two gendarmes with him as well. Sheikh Badr Al-Ghathban did not like Irar and did not like Irar's new friend, Jawad. However, he knew that Irar knew everyone and had the beastly ability to read the eyes of humans and know their intentions. Thus, Sheikh Badr asked Irar to come with him for one reason: to see if there were any of Sheikh Nasser the Blond's men in the wedding. Sheikh Badr knew that if Irar saw any of Nasser the Blond's men, he would be able to identify them, so reluctantly he asked Nasser to come with him and bring his new companion, the young, strong man, Jawad.

Two months before the wedding, Jawad had moved from the sheikh's guesthouse and lived with Irar in his mud hut outside the town. Two months had elapsed since the day when the gendarme patrol failed to capture the three thieves by the riverbank. Since that night, when Jawad saw Irar for the first time in the guesthouse of Sheikh Badr Al-Gathban, the two men, Irar and his companion, Jawad, became inseparable. During the last two months, the two men had traveled twice with Sheikh Badr's sheep to the neighboring country and brought back a better profit than that of all the other smugglers who worked for the sheikh. At the very beginning of this companionship, when Irar paid attention for the first time to Jawad, a stranger who was sitting in the corner of Sheikh Badr's guesthouse listened to the men talking about the borders without opening his mouth. He looked at Jawad's face wounds, and he saw many small ones. Irar also saw that the young man's eyes were those of a wolf; he knew this from only one look at the young stranger. At the time, Jawad had run out of his three days of welcome, and he had nowhere to go.

That night, when Irar finished telling his story, he asked Khanger, "Who is that young stranger sitting at the end of the guesthouse?"

"He is a leffu," said Khanger.

Irar knew how to tell what men were made of from their appearances and wanted to examine the young man to confirm his initial perception of him, so he excused himself from the sheikh, stood, and walked all the way to the end of the guesthouse, where Jawad was sitting, and he sat next to him and asked with diligent curiosity, "Where is the man from?"

"From the strong back of my father," Jawad answered with the look of an angry eagle in his eyes. From that moment on, Irar never spoke to him with the same tone. Rather, he wanted to offer his willingness. He realized that Jawad was like him, a loner with a past that would never be revealed to any other human, a sad soul who would kill because its fate is to be lonely, and it has to survive with its bare minimal tools.

He waited for a moment and then said to Jawad, "A real man does not sleep in another man's guesthouse." He was trying to get Jawad to reply with the answer that he was looking for.

"A man like you will not say such insults without preparing a house for a man like me," Jawad said with his hand on his dagger.

"I figured that much," said Irar. "My house is the mud hut outside the town near the prairie. You need to ask the sheikh's permission to leave his guesthouse and come with me."

"I ask permission from no man, but I will tell him that I am leaving after dinner tonight."

Later that evening, the two men walked from the guesthouse to the secluded mud hut near the prairie and stayed up all night talking about the town, the borders, the sheep, and about women, but it seemed as if they both had not much interest in women. Rather, they both wanted to talk about Sheikh Badr Al-Ghathban and his fortune and the fortunes of Sheikh Waitan and all the other sheikhs. For them, those sheikhs were sending men to their deaths in the merciless desert while getting rich and having large houses with many women, guesthouses that served three meals a day, and the respect that the sheikhs get for being greedy and merciless. Many complained, but no one dared to challenge the sheikhs. That night the two men had unwittingly opened their hearts to each other, and they discovered that they had the same abstract of darkness. Jawad, who listened most of the time, found in Irar the older version of himself, formed from unfortunate events and a misguided future. Irar found in Jawad the young man he had been twenty years before. Irar did not want to sit at the end of the guesthouse all the time.

"By the sandals, always by the sandals," Irar said with anger.

He had always resented sitting at the end of the guesthouse and having to stand whenever other men entered. He did not want to kiss the sheikh's hand. He did not want to be served the food after the sheikh and other men had eaten the best meat. But he also felt that he was just not as strong as he had once been, when he used to cross the desert once or twice a month. He said that he was getting tired, old, and extremely lonely. Irar told Jawad that he had never married because "no woman will accept a man like me, walking the desert all of his life." He said, "So don't be like me, Jawad."

Many people said that the reason he did not get married was that he was not human at all. The children in the town said that he was a jinni or a wolf that became a man so he could take sheep to smuggle and eat some of them. No one knew that Irar's father and his mother had walked for miles with the grand ayatollah's clergy and had joined the tribes that charged the salty fields to the north of the southern great city with old rusty rifles and pitchforks. It was in that battle that Irar's father was shot and killed by the Gurkha, as they ransacked the entire stretch of villages and massacred the poorly equipped army of the grand clergy. Thousands of poorly armed but faithful tribesmen were killed and many women were raped and then killed by the Gurkha, who then burned the mud huts of the peasants. No one in Balluria knew that during the tribal rebellion against the British, Irar was the only child of his poor parents, who lived in a one-room mud hut near the marshes and lived on what the father caught fishing and hunting during the day. No one in Balluria knew that when Irar saw his father's face shattered with bullets of the Gurkha's modern rifles, he lay on the ground next to his father's body until the battlefield quieted down. He cried and stayed with his father's corpse for four days with no food, and he drank water from the nearby marsh and slept by the body, feeding only on what he found near the many dead men's corpses. He tried to feed his father, whom he believed was sleeping. No one in Balluria knew that Irar stayed with his father's dead body, waiting for his mother to come and find him, not knowing that his mother had been ravaged and raped and killed by a group of hysterical Gurkhas, led by a young British lieutenant, and that her body had been thrown into the marshes. No one in Balluria knew that on the fourth night after the massacre, the wolves started to show up to eat the dead bodies in the battlefield of Shuaiba. Irar was not afraid of the wolves, and he was not afraid of death. He tried to chase the wolves away with a stick but after two tries, many wolves showed up, trying to devour him alive, and he was barely able to jump into the marsh and into an abandoned small boat that held the body of a dead woman, and in that small boat, he pushed his way to the marshes. He slept in the boat after he pushed the dead woman's body into the water. He survived by eating whatever he caught in the marshes. He dove after fish and learned to fish and hunt birds. He stayed in the boat for almost a month. One day he encountered three men who were looking for the biggest snake that mankind has ever seen in this world.

"The gates of heaven are here and the snake is preventing the dead from entering heaven," one of the three men later explained to young Irar.

"They say that it was a black snake that had eaten a buffalo and an unfortunate boy who was swimming in the marshes. It could eat ten men at the same time, and it could spit fire from its mouth; it had horns like the devil, and it had hair around its mouth. They had made a challenge with other men to find it and kill it. When the three men found the young Irar, they saw a boy who looked more like a snake than a human. He was thin, nervous, and extremely vigilant. They did not know what to do with the boy, who looked hungry and dirty and about to die, so they took him with them. After a week of looking for the snake, they headed back to their village disappointed and ashamed and were not ready to face the questions and sarcasm of the village and accusations of cowardness. The boy, Irar, stayed in the house of one of the men until the man's wife kicked him out for no reason other than she was afraid of this wolfy-looking kid who refused to talk. She told her husband that she was afraid that he was a jinni and not human and would bring bad luck and curses. She also told him that she saw young Irar eating a dead animal. When he left the man's house, Irar walked almost fifty kilometers to reach the small city, where he slept in the streets as he watched the same British soldiers and their Gurkhas entering the town again. He hid in a small barrel outside the fish market and watched the Gurkhas marching in the streets of the small city to the south, looking for the clergy who declared Jihad against the British. And for the next three years he lived in a small shack in the fish market, working for his food, doing whatever job he could do for some Indian rupees.

It was during that time that he heard of how men started to bring riches by crossing the borders with some sheep. He asked how to go about making such a living, but he never got the answer that he wanted so he left the fish market with his belongings—a dirty blanket and small dagger that he had bought from a mysterious man—and went looking for the sheep market. Only there was he able to find one person, who told him that if he really wanted to smuggle sheep, he needed to talk to Hayyan, a smuggler who did not approve of this young kid asking to smuggle. He thought that Irar was either crazy or an informant of the British. Hayyan looked at him and asked, "What are you? A jinni? How come your eyes shine like a wolf's?"

Not deterred by that treatment, Irar begged Hayyan to show him how to smuggle sheep. After days of constant pestering and persistence, Hayyan agreed to take him on a trip to the southern country, with one condition: when Irar learned the trade, he would start smuggling sheep for Hayyan. At the age of fourteen, Irar crossed the borders for the first time and became one of the best known and most respected sheep smugglers in these parts. Never striking a lucky deal in his life, he always worked for others, from the days of Sheikh Miteb Al-Harchan , the estranged father of Sheikh Muhsin Al-Harchan to the days of Sheikh Badr Al-Gathban. He was just a sheep smuggler with no sheep of his own. He never married because he knew that no woman would be faithful to a wolf-like man with jinni eyes who was absent from the house for months at a time. He never bothered looking for family members, nor did he claim to be of any tribe. He built the mud hut away from the village and lived there alone until he stumbled upon his new friend, Jawad.

For Jawad, who knew nothing about Irar and did not want to know anything, it was enough that he had a place to stay instead of staying in the prairie indefinitely or the unwelcoming guesthouse of Sheikh Badr. Since that night, he had wanted to be with Irar all the time; the two walked together everywhere. They ate together, and for once, they shared a laugh. But for both lonely men, it was a partnership that waited for so long to happen since it was written in the twisted lines of henna on the hands of Gypsy witches. When Sheikh Badr agreed to let Jawad to accompany Irar in his smuggling trips to the desert, he also agreed to let him stay in Balluria and granted him the statues of a leffu, which meant that Jawad would be under the protection of Sheikh Badr. But it also meant that Jawad would come to the aid of Sheikh Badr if the sheikh decided to feud with other sheikhs, and it really meant that Jawad was at the mercy of Sheikh Badr, who could tell Jawad to leave Balluria whenever he wanted to.

"I have been a Leffu for more than twenty years," Irar said. "But Sheikh Badr never asked me to leave because I have never disrespected him and have always worked for him."

"No man will make me leave Balluria," Jawad said to Irar, who looked at him with wide-open eyes and felt the willingness of the young man to do whatever his stone heart would tell him to do.

"Let us hope that day will never come."

3

For Jawad. The wedding of Ra'ad, the son of Sheikh Waitan, was his first recreational event. He had never gone to a wedding or any other celebratory event, not even funerals. Moreover, other than his gray robe and kuffia and iqal, he never really had any new clothes to wear for a wedding. The only new thing he had was a kuffia that he acquired on his last trip to the southern oil-rich country with Irar. The only things that Irar and he had bought with the little money they received from smuggling were coffee, cigarettes, and whatever they needed for their smuggling trips. The two men arrived at the wedding as part of the forty-man posse of Sheikh Badr Al-Ghathban and the new magistrate and the four-man gendarme patrol. They found that many sheikhs with their men had shown up early and had sat at the center of the roll of two lined-up carpets facing each other outside Sheikh Waitan's guesthouse. Sheikh Badr Al-Ghathban called Irar to come close to him and whispered in his ear, "Do you see any men in here of that son of whore Nasser the Blond?"

Irar looked carefully at the faces and said, "No, may Allah give you long life. I don't see any of Nasser the Blond's men in here."

"Keep your eyes open, and let me know if you see any strangers not from these parts," said Sheikh Badr as he took his silver-plated pistol from its holster and fired three shots. He spoke in a voice that all could hear. "We came here to congratulate the honorable and the brave, and our rifles are our witness that we did so."

Cheers and bullets shattered the quietness of the evening, and countless trays filled with rice and lamb meat were served. Hungry children waited for the men to finish the meal. Then, like a pack of wolves, they stormed the leftovers as the men stood aside drinking tea and washing their hands. The children rushed toward the carpet and tried to sit near the trays with the most leftovers. They devoured the contents of the large metal plates with their dirty hands, and within minutes, they had emptied the trays. The kids chased the trays as many men carried the food back to Sheikh Waitan's house so that the women could eat. Jawad was sitting next to Irar drinking his tea when he heard the noise of the Gypsy drums and the whistling sound of the mutbag, and out of nowhere, two Gypsy women appeared and started dancing between the two rows of men. When Jawad saw the two women, he felt the thrust of a warm dagger pierce his senses and was numbed by the scene of the women's snaky movements. He had never seen a Gypsy woman dance before. When the young Gypsy appeared with her pink cheeks and her long black dress and started to dance, he was poisoned with the smell of her body as she passed him dancing her way toward where a very clean-looking man, quiet and well dressed, stood.

Later Jawad learned that man was the groom, Ra'ad, the son of Sheikh Waitan. Jawad looked at the young Gypsy woman, with his eyes wide open. He felt that the people and the noise around him had suddenly disappeared and that he and the young Gypsy woman were there alone. Looking like a real jinni, she appeared as if she had mixed in her the bodies of all women. As she mesmerized the men with the bewitching movements of her hips and shoulders, her eyes met his. He felt the Gypsy spirits entering his soul, invading his veins and entering his heart. When the young, beautiful Gypsy woman danced close to him, he smelled the fresh poisoning sweat of a Gypsy mixed with the desires of centuries invading the empty, dry fields of his being. He wanted her. She looked at him, daring him to grab her. As she knew that he wanted her, she danced closer and closer, and finally he could not resist any more, so he reached out to her.

As he did, a deep voice shouted, "Can you prevent your refuge seeker from dishonoring us?"

The voice was from one of Sheikh Waitan's men who had the same infatuation that Jawad had about the young Gypsy woman. The noise of the wedding party was silenced. Men with thick moustaches and eager eyes turned their heads to the source of the voice. The man who provoked the possible feud sat next to one of Sheikh Badr Al-Ghathban's men, and it seemed that the two had talked about the young Jawad, who looked like he was not one of the sheikh's men. Sheikh Badr did not know how to react, and he waited for a few moments to gather his thoughts. The sheikh knew that even though for the past months Irar and Jawad had worked for him and that they were his men, at the same time they were not from his tribe. Rather, they were a leffu. He knew that the man who made the statement knew that about them. In addition Sheikh Badr was not ready for a feud. On the other hand, Sheikh Waitan's man knew that Jawad was a stranger and a refuge seeker and that he was not one of the Sharify tribesmen. For him, Jawad was just a man with no origin, and he would be damned if he would let Jawad, who looked like a thief, touch the young Gypsy woman, whom he had already planned to take for the night because, after all, it was his cousin's wedding.

Jawad looked at the man who made that statement and wished to be alone with him so that he could rip his heart out with his dagger, but Irar, who knew what Jawad was thinking, was quick to say, "With the permission of the sheikhs, my young friend here meant neither insult nor disrespect to the sheikhs, and we all agree to the judgment of Sheikh Badr Al-Ghathban, and whatever he says we'll do."

The entire wedding and the three Gypsy women looked wordlessly to Sheikh Badr and waited for him to speak. He looked at Jawad and looked at the man, and then looked at Sheikh Waitan and said, "My brother, Sheikh Waitan, this is his house, and it is his son's wedding. I will do whatever pleases him."

Sheikh Waitan knew that his son's wedding could turn into a funeral of many men and that a possible feud between him and Sheikh Badr could start and never end for years to come. Although he knew that young Jawad was just a leffu, someone with no family and no roots with the Sharify tribe, and he knew that Sheikh Badr knew that sheikhs do not put their men or their refuge seekers down in front of others. Sheikh Waitan realized that he must do what he needed to do, especially after Sheikh Badr's statement, so he searched for the right words. Then he looked at Sheikh Badr as he smiled and spoke, "The young stranger may leave our wedding, and all will be forgiven. I swear on my honor and the grace of all the dead."

"May your life be long, Sheikh." Shouts rose from the men from both sides of the carpet and Irar looked at Sheikh Badr, waiting for a response.

"I am with Sheikh Waitan," said Sheikh Badr, approving his decree.

4

Jawad and Irar walked by the railroad that connected Tawsheeha and Balluria from the side near the prairie, the side close to the desert. Since leaving the wedding, Jawad was silent with rage. Jawad was the only one who was asked to leave, but Irar insisted on leaving with him after he gained the permission to leave with a wink from Sheikh Badr's eye. For an hour, the two men did not speak of what happened. Then suddenly, Irar broke the silence. "Let us go and sit awhile in a place where only the dead can see and hear us."

Shortly afterward, the two men were sitting in the middle of a sandy hill surrounded by palm trees. Irar, who wrapped a cigarette and gave it to Jawad, was thinking of the possibilities of their tomorrow, whether or not Sheikh Badr would let them stay in Balluria. Irar was more concerned about Jawad, who seemed dangerously angry. He was looking to scratch the iron shell that Jawad had covering his true heart and expose the real wolf in Jawad.

"Tonight you did something that men in these parts get killed for," Irar said. "You have done something that will bring Sheikh Badr's wrath on us, and I need to know what is in your true heart."

"Speak."

"What made you reach to grab that woman?" asked Irar.

"I don't know, but I want her to be mine." Jawad replied.

"She is a Gypsy, and a Gypsy woman would not belong to one man," Irar said.

"She will be mine alone if I find her again," Jawad said, "and I will cut the throat of any man who dares to touch her."

"Are you afraid of what Sheikh Waitan may do?"

"Sheikh Waitan should be worried about what I will do to his cousin who made that statement. I will feed him his own tongue."

Jawad answered with a firm voice that revealed his anger and his willingness to perform anything that Irar might see as the appropriate action, but Irar was patiently discovering the massive ability of his young companion and wanted to learn more about the willingness in the young man's heart, so he asked, "What should we do if Sheikh Badr asks us to leave Balluria?" Irar said, hoping for a specific answer he had waited for since he took this strong, tanned man into his house and into his heart.

"We will say no, we will not leave Balluria," Jawad said.

"What if he tries to force us out of Balluria?" Irar asked, looking for only one answer from his young and ruthlessly brave protégé.

"Then I will kill him," came the eerily even reply.

"That's the right answer I was waiting for," Irar said as he looked around, noticing the glow from the top of the palm trees near the spot where they sat and talked. It was a strange-looking spot. It was a perfect circle of sandy little hills between them. There were seven palm trees forming a perfect circle.

"About that woman, that young Gypsy woman, why do you want her so much?"

"It's the greed of a man who has nothing. She seemed to me to have all the things a man is looking for, just like Balluria," Jawad said.

"I know where the Gypsy women are camping tonight. Would you want to go and lie with her?"

"No, show me where the Gypsies are camping and I will kidnap her tonight and keep her with me and for me only."

That night the two men waited until the night became very quiet except for the howling of the wolves in the desert, and then they walked to where Irar said the Gypsies were camping. The young beautiful Gypsy was sleeping after exhausting herself from all the dancing.

Irar placed his fearsome black dagger on the elder Gypsy woman's throat. "Not a sound, woman," he said.

Jawad woke the young beautiful Gypsy up and signaled to her not to make a sound. The young Gypsy woman looked at him and remembered him from the wedding so she kept silent. Jawad wrapped her in the blanket she was sleeping in, put her on his shoulders and carried her away from the Gypsy camp. The two men with their kidnapped prey walked back toward the secluded mud hut. After walking for almost three kilometers, they were tired, and Irar wanted to rest, so they sat down and looked to see if Sheikh Waitan's men followed them, but no one had.

Irar looked at Jawad and said, "Have we been here before? This place seems familiar."

Jawad dismissed the old man's comment and said, "I don't know. It seems to me like we have, but, just like I said, I am not leaving Balluria, and no one will ever touch this woman again as long as I live."

"You have changed your fortune tonight," said Irar, looking at the blanket where the young and beautiful Gypsy woman lay quietly. "You wanted something that belonged to other men and other sheikhs, and you have it now. I hope this will be your way always. This is how fortunes have been made."

Jawad looked at his partner, then at the Gypsy, who stayed quiet, not knowing what he would do with her now as she was his own.

"She will be mine," Jawad said. "If anyone, whether Sheikh Badr Al-Ghathban or any other, tries to take her from me, or if he tries to force me to leave..."

"Then what will you do?" Irar asked, looking at the palm trees.

Jawad looked around at the silent leaves and murmured, "I will kill him and kill anyone he sends and bury them here. I will never leave Balluria, not for him and not for any other man."

That was the answer Irar had hoped for. He looked at his young friend and said, "You know... if you were called Sheikh Jawad, no one would have dared talk to you like that son of whore in the wedding did."

Jawad looked at Irar with blood-filled eyes. "How would I be a sheikh?"

"Let us take this Gypsy and go to the mud hut. Then I will tell you what it will take to be a sheikh."

They arrived at the mud hut while the exhausted Gypsy woman had returned to sleep in her blanket. The two men spent the rest of the night awake as Irar taught young Jawad how to be a sheikh. "The first thing a sheikh must learn is how to hate, and then he must learn how to kill for any reason, no matter what. A sheikh is like a king, and he must protect his right to his kingdom," Irar advised. "I know that you can kill, but you need to learn how to kill for other reasons. You must learn how kill for greed and maybe for the mere desire to kill."

Jawad listened to his mentor with undivided attention, although the glow from the tops of the palm trees was mesmerizing, numbing, and calling. But the young man ignored the feelings of wanting to go back to the spot of the seven palm trees and sat and listened carefully to the words of his mentor the blade-thin man Irar like a young Greek emperor listening to his wise and devoted teacher.

As Irar spoke, he never stopped thinking of the green glow of the top of the trees in the place where they sat that night and the magnificent seven palm trees that surrounded that place, which looked mysteriously familiar to him like no other place. But for some reason, it seemed like the two evil men decided not to talk about the magnificent glow of the green color of the seven palm trees. Instead, they spent the night looking from time to time at the quiet body of the young Gypsy woman wrapped in a filthy army blanket, sleeping peacefully, as they talked about how Jawad could be the next and the only sheikh of Balluria.

The Book of the Man

Where Wolves Dream

1

No one in Balluria knew what Fathil the Liar's real job was, nor did anyone know if he was a civilian or in the military, or in what branch of service he was if he was in the military as he claimed to be, because he lied about everything, all the time. Not only did he lie about his job, he lied about everything else in his life and what he did when he would leave Balluria and disappeared for months at a time. Fathil the Liar was a slender, dark-skinned man with a thin moustache that appeared to be drawn on his upper lip. He looked like an Egyptian movie star from an old, faded picture I had once seen on a poster from the twenties. The first time I saw Fathil the Liar or heard his voice was when we were playing soccer against the Wild Lions. It was when I was taken by Hamid to play soccer for the first time with the team that later became my team. I learned that my new team had an archenemy from the neighboring town, and I knew that as a new member of the soccer team I must hate our rivals. Before I started to form my own judgment, I understood why my new team hated the Wild Lions, the rival team, and we hated them for everything they had. We hated their captain, Mazin, who was the son of the local party official from the other town. We hated their red uniforms, which we knew Mazin's father gave to them as the official team of the governing party. We hated them because they were good, and to my knowledge, they had won every game had they played against us for two years and with no score less than four goals at any given game. I think it was Hisham's mission in life to win one game against the Wild Lions, just one game in his lifetime.

When I played my first soccer match in Balluria with my new team, it looked like a shameful defeat from the start; we were only half an hour into the game, and we were losing by five goals to nothing. We were tired, and we were beaten to the point that we did not care for the constant shouting and screaming of Hisham, who almost lost his mind when Lateef, who joined our team because we did not have enough players, missed the perfect chance to score a goal by meters. The event happened when he was in the middle of the Wild Lions' goal with no one to protect it. The goalkeeper left it unattended because he was searching for water on the sidelines. The ball passed Hisham and landed by the feet of Lateef, who was too nervous to take the shot, but he did anyway. Not only did Lateef take Hisham's shot, but he also missed the widely open goal by almost ten meters while Hisham was screaming, "Leave it to me... leave it to me!"

Lateef realized that the shot was too good to pass. It was the chance to score. Scoring a goal, one against the Wild Lions, the one that everyone waited for, would be an achievement that would not only gain him fame in Balluria, but also a chance to be permanent member of our team. So Lateef positioned himself facing the Wild Lions' open goal, gave it his best shot, and missed; he missed the perfect shot, the one that Hisham had been waiting dozens of games for, and by missing this shot, he missed not only the goal but the chance to ever again be part of the team. He lost that chance, especially when Hisham struck him on the back of his neck when he missed the only golden opportunity to save face. Our faces were smeared with shame, defeat, sweat, and dust as we saw the ball fly over, outside the field, and enter the thorny field of wild plants stretching all the way to the prairie.

"May Allah give you luck as miserable as your shot, you donkey," Hisham said. "You'd better go get the ball, and I hope every thorn in that field will enter your cracked feet." He said this as he struck Lateef on the back of his neck hard enough to make him cry.

Fathil the Liar had watched the entire game and had screamed more than Hisham.

"You morons are playing wrong. Play four-two-four like the Brazilians," Fathil the Liar would scream. Although he had never played one game of soccer in his life, he screamed as if he were the national coach. He called us losers, donkeys, morons, and stinky when we were only one goal behind. Later, when the Wild Lions scored their streak of goals, Fathil the Liar shouted unacceptable insults. As our only fan on the sideline, he seemed to be turning against us. When Hamid tried to reach the Wild Lions' goal by passing through two of their defenders, Fathil the Liar shouted, "You will never get past them, they will break your leg. Break his leg. Will you?" Fathil the Liar would say that, encouraging the Wild Lions' defenders. Or if the Wild Lions' strikers got closer to our poor goalie, Adnan, Fathil the Liar would say, "Shoot it. He is too weak to catch it. He can't see with his glasses. He is blind. Shoot it like a bomb. Rip that net!"

It was as if he were one of them, coming from their village, not ours. After the game as we were lying down, dying of thirst, fatigue, and sweat, he came near where we made a circle and just stood there as if he were not one of the reasons we lost. He looked down at us and sneered, "What a bunch of weaklings, and you call yourselves a soccer team."

It was after the first soccer game I played in Balluria, that I heard his name. When he left the soccer field and walked toward the town, I asked Hamid, "Who was that man?"

"Fathil. Fathil the Liar is a big donkey," Hamid said.

The name was as strange as the man. Then I started wondering why everyone called him Fathil the Liar. Soon enough, I learned that not only did he deserve the name, there would no other name that could possibly describe him.

Fathil the Liar told many stories about many things: stories about soccer, stories about the countries that he had visited, stories about women he slept with then left brokenhearted. He told stories about the harbors of New York and Marseilles and other cities he knew the names to, or he just made them up, cities that mesmerized our imaginations and occupied our dreams.

Unfortunately for him, Adnan, our tiny goalkeeper who became a close friend of mine, was there to tear apart Fathil's claims, saying such things as, "That city is not a harbor," or "That city is not in that country," or "That person is not from that country," or "That actress is dead already, so how could you sleep with her?" Adnan's comments and his factual statements embarrassed Fathil and resulted in Fathil chasing him away with a stone or telling him to shut up. Fathil told many stories, and we liked them, even though we knew that perhaps all of them were just colorful lies, but they were lies that told of a land that was different from ours, people who were different from us, and faraway countries, towns, cities, and oceans. Fathil's stories opened the doors of a future full of possibilities, and our small group of anxious teenagers liked listening to Fathil's stories. My favorites, my all-time favorites, were stories about America and the Americans actors and movie stars. Fathil the Liar claimed that he had visited the United States of America many times and that he had met almost all the movie stars, all the politicians, and every person who ever appeared on a cover or a page of any magazine that reached these parts. Moreover, he claimed that he had met all the cowboys and Indians, and any actor or actress who had the privilege of being famous or known here.

Fathil the Liar was exceptionally gifted in telling his stories and making them sound believable, but his only problem was Adnan, who was Fathil's only obstacle in delivering stories without interruptions. Adnan, the thin and weak boy who wore thick glasses, was a smart and surprisingly very well-read thirteen-year-old: he was like a dagger in Fathil's side, cutting through the facade and exposing the man's untruths.

The first time I saw Adnan was during my first soccer game with my new team. Later I learned from the stories I heard from Hamid and the other kids that Adnan was the only male child in his family. Adnan's father was crippled with polio, and his mother had not left the house for many years because of what happened to Adnan's older brother, Qahtan, who had been a known communist and atheist. Hamid told me that Qahtan was killed by the national guards, the fearsome party militia, the terrifying groups of masked men who dragged communists and Islamic activists through the streets of Baghdad and other provinces then shot them during the dark years of the late seventies when the bloody rampage of the party militia wrought death and destruction on political dissidents.

During those days, Balluria had one known communist: Adnan's brother, Qahtan. The story told that Qahtan was a handsome young man full of energy and knowledge, and he preached communism just as clergymen preached religion. People said that he talked about places like Moscow, Cuba, and Angola, and he told stories of people no one ever heard of, names like Karl

Marx, Vladimir Lenin, Che Guevara, and Ho Chi Minh. He recited the poetry of Garcia Lorca, Muthaffar Al-Naw'wab, and the communists Aryan AL-Sayed Khalaf. That all ended when in one dark, fearful Balluria night. A group of masked men broke down the door of Adnan's family's house, dragged Qahtan through the street, and emptied the magazines of their Kalashnikovs into his body. Then they dragged him to the main square and on top of his bloody, dead body they left a cardboard sign that read, "This will be the fate of all the communist traitors and foreign agents."

Adnan's family was able to retrieve his body and secretly and quietly buried him in an unknown place. The family had to act as if nothing had happened. They just lived and faced secret looks of apathy in people's eyes for long years, and the family never spoke of their son. Adnan never spoke of his brother, but he inherited two things from him: superb intelligence and a secret library. Qahtan had hidden the books behind the wall separating the outside latrine from the clay oven, where no one would even consider look for them. One day Adnan had noticed that his brother Qahtan was digging behind the clay oven with his bare hands. The young Adnan thought that his older brother was looking for nails in the ashes of the oven like Adnan and almost all the other kids did, running a big magnet through the ashes of burned woods and attracting all the nails. Months after Qahtan's murder, Adnan searched for the spot where he saw his late brother digging with his bare hands, and hoped to find something—nails, hidden money, or anything else of value. Instead, he found almost a hundred books, books wrapped carefully in deteriorating newspapers that had the title *People's Path* written in red. Authors included Karl Marx, Leo Tolstoy, Fyodor Dostoevsky, Maxim Gorky, Kafka, William Faulkner, Charles Dickens, Victor Hugo, Garcia Lorca, Gabriel Garcia Marquez, and Nageeb Mahfouz. The collection also included the poetry of Nizar Qabbani, Pablo Neruda, and Mohamed Al-Maghoott. There were also novels like *Moby-Dick* and *A Tale of Two Cities*. There was also my favorite: *The Adventures of Huckleberry Finn*.

To Adnan the books were a treasure he was emotionally attached to, a mysterious treasure because it preserved the aborted relationship with his beloved older brother, who in many ways, was the only light in the confusing darkness of growing up as a weak and sick young child in a poor family in these parts. After that day, Adnan stayed up late into the night reading the books in the dim light of the fanoos (a kerosene lamp) because his family's house was one that did not have electricity and never would. Nevertheless, he enjoyed very much being the only kid and the most qualified of our group to rebut all that Fathil the Liar had to say.

2

Every evening, after the game and after we ate dinner at our houses, the other kids and I waited for the call, a sign to leave our homes and gather in the public garden next to the main street. For me this meant crossing the street where cars going from one big city to another would travel at top speed. They would cross our small town with crazy speed as if trying to escape a plague. Many people had lost their lives crossing that street. Our call was, "Aria, Aria, Aria," and we could distinguish the voice that was often Hisham's, Hamid's or sometimes Kamal's. It was the start of the second part of our endless summer of days and nights in Balluria. At night we gathered in the public garden, which was surrounded by an iron fence and painted a shiny light green. We chased cats that we found munching in the many garbage piles in town, or we walked to the river and sat watching the water as the moon painted its colors on the many tiny waves.

Other times, we just hung around in the garden, telling stories of the great soccer players of England, France, or Brazil, or we talked about films, movies, and television shows. My favorite subject was the movies. Among the group, I was the only one who had any credible knowledge of movies: American movies, French movies, and some British movies. In addition, other than Adnan, it seems like I was the only person who knew names and could pronounce them properly. That ability earned me some respect from my new friends, who gave me strange looks when I said, "It is pronounced 'Sean Connery', not 'seen canary.'" Nevertheless, all the subjects that we talked about in our endless nights were interesting to the point that we all looked forward to the night and waited for the "Aria, Aria, Aria" call. Although the word meant nothing, to us it meant the call for a gathering of friends and the chance to hear stories about a soccer player or a movie actor, or a completely made-up story from Fathil the Liar.

I had just finished my dinner when the call came. It was Hisham's voice this time. I jumped to the sink to wash my hands and my mouth, and I hastily made my way to the house gate while my mother's worried voice shouted behind me, "Be careful crossing the street!"

When I arrived at the garden, I found almost the entire soccer team there. I was anxious to see my new friends, especially Hamid and Adnan. Hamid stood in the middle of the garden eating cucumber and a piece of bread; I realized that this must be his dinner. He was still in his soccer clothes with dust covering his hands and his hair. Then again, his clothes were the same all the time and for all occasions and activities. I never thought that he had any other clothes. Hisham was lying down on a piece of cardboard to protect his clothes from the wetness of the grass. Kamal stood looking at the millions of mosquitoes hovering around the streets lights and showing Adnan his new watch.

"It's electronic, you see. Look at the numbers. It's very expensive. Don't touch it."

Ahmed was sitting quietly as he rubbed his ankle from the injury he had received in the last soccer game when he tried to stop the seventh goal. I sat next to Hisham trying to catch my breath from running from my house to the public garden when suddenly Fathil the Liar appeared from nowhere, and, without greeting me, he declared, "I swear on my honor that you guys are the worst team in the history of mankind."

That was an insult added to the many injuries that we had since we were still licking our physical and emotional wounds and our overwhelming feeling of shame and defeat. He did not stop there. "Eight goals? Eight goals and not a single one for you; this is so shameful. What do you call your team? The team of donkeys. You should call yourselves the donkeys. That's what you are."

It was at that moment that we realized that we had no name for the team, unlike the other teams who called themselves the Wild Lions, the Fiery Spears, the Knights, or my favorites, the Flaming Bullets. We played with no name, and maybe that was the reason we were losing with all the hardship we suffered and all the little wounds from the tiny sharp stones in the field that pierced our feet and took weeks to heal. We were a team with no name, and that added to our despair. Fathil the Liar was standing like a Greek philosopher talking to his students. Some people said that he was a sergeant in the air force. He started telling us about soccer strategies.

"Your plan is all wrong because you are playing following the English school of soccer. You need to play according to the Brazilian method," Fathil said. "I know that because I studied soccer in Brazil." Then suddenly, when he heard Kamal talking about his electronic watch, he switched the subject to watches and told us about his watch and how sad he was that he had to give it away as a gift. Then he added that it was much better than Kamal's because it not only told the time but also the day, the year, the temperature, and many other things. "It's only issued to fighter pilots. Only the best."

"Why did you give it away?" Adnan asked.

"I had to. It was an order from the president himself. I gave it away to an Egyptian pilot who helped me and the other pilots navigate our way when we got lost over the Sinai desert."

"And how did you give it to him?" Adnan asked again.

"The president sent me to Egypt especially to give him the watch, and in Cairo I went out with Suhair Ramzy the actress and we slept together."

He always claimed that he was a very important person in the government, and he was always sent on official missions and met all the Egyptian and Lebanese actresses and sometimes European and American actresses. He frequently disappeared for two months at a time and appeared with more stories, which kept us dreaming as he told us about different worlds and different people that he claimed either he met or he slept with. I wanted to ask him if he ever saw or met Annok Amie, the French actress, but I waited until the right time, not knowing when that right time will be.

That night Fathil the Liar told us about his latest trip to Europe. He said, "In Poland I saw a tomato that weighs fifty kilograms. It could feed a family for a month." We listened to him, waiting for more details about the giant tomato, but he said that he was late coming on a leave because the government sent him on a special mission to Russia to transfer a heavy black bag that he was not allowed to open.

"Maybe there was a big tomato in it," Adnan interrupted as he always did.

Fathil looked at him calmly and continued, "No, it was either money or a nuclear bomb. I go on missions like these all the time. One day, the president sent me to Cuba to deliver a letter to Fidel Castro and bring back some cigars, and after that I flew to Havana for a party," Fathil said arrogantly.

"But Cuba and Havana are the same place," Adnan said.

"No, you are wrong. Cuba is very far from Havana. I was even afraid that I would run out of fuel between them, so I had to make an emergency landing right next to the party."

Fathil the Liar was creative. He was extremely entertaining, especially to us, and none of us could prove him wrong. If it weren't for Adnan's continuous interruptions, we would have believed him completely.

"Last night I could not go to sleep, so I dialed the number nine, nine times, and guess who was on the other line: King Hussein himself. I talked to him for almost two hours, and he told me to come and visit whenever I come to Jordan," Fathil said.

"What did you talk about, and where did you get the telephone from?" Hisham asked.

"We talked about secret things." Fathil said, ignoring the second part of Hisham's question.

To his credit, Fathil used names we never heard of and referred to them as his friends. I was so anxious to ask him about America.

"Have you ever visited America?"

He looked at me as if he was seeing me for the first time and said with a sarcastic tone, "Hundreds of times. I go to America like I go to the big city in the province."

"Did you see any actors? Have you seen Clint Eastwood, Anthony Quinn, or Charlton Heston?

"Who? No I did not see them, but I saw Trinity."

Oh, my God, Trinity, the coolest of them all, the one who could fire his pistol so quickly that he could basically shoot ten people at a time, I said to myself.

"But his name is not Trinity; it is Terence Hill," Adnan said with clear impatience.

"No, you blind moron," said Fathil. "His name is Trinity and he and I spent some time with him in a bar in America. He even asked me to drink with him, but I told him that I am Muslim and can't drink. I tell you the truth— America is an amazing country. There are many women with blue eyes and blond hair, and they like dark-skinned men like me, especially from the Middle East, and if you enter a bar in America, you can tell any woman to go with you, even if their husbands are there; it's OK with them. Once, I entered a bar and one woman liked me so much that she stayed with me for the entire time I was there. She had a very luxurious car, a Buick, a red one, and she had a lot of money. I think she owned an entire county and she asked me to marry her. She loved me because I was tanned," Fathil the Liar said, with complete faith in his story.

"Why didn't you marry her?" Adnan asked.

"Because I did not think my father would have approved the marriage, plus I was very busy with my job and my mission, and I didn't think the government would approve of the marriage either," Fathil replied with frustration.

"Why wouldn't the government approve the marriage?" Adnan asked with persistent sarcasm as if he were plotting to entrap Fathil in his own lies.

"You are a very annoying kid," Fathil said to Adnan with a firm voice. He continued, "I don't know why the government would not approve my marriage to the American girl. Maybe because she was an Israeli agent. Stop asking me. You and your donkey-like ears."

Besides his manly adventures with virtually all the actresses of the world, Fathil was a self-proclaimed war hero and involved in all of the wars of the nation. He claimed that once the president asked him to scare Israel a little, so he flew his fighter jet very low.

"Right near the house of the Israeli prime minister," Fathil said. "I broke the sound barrier and shattered all the house windows, and the prime minster had to be treated for a heart attack because he was so scared," Fathil said with a strange joy. He also claimed that he had received a medal from the president for his heroism.

"What was the name of the prime minster, and how did you know where his house was?" Adnan would not relent.

Fathil looked at him with warning eyes and said after he thought for seconds, "As for his house... Ha... it was the biggest one in Israel, with a swimming pool and a small airport, and the Star of David was painted on the roof. The prime minister was Moshe Ben-Gurion, and he had one eye covered with a patch."

Adnan jumped with the joy of victory. "There is no such prime minster with that name. It's David Ben-Gurion, and he is dead, and Moshe Dayan is a defense minister."

"Moshe Ben, my sandals. Moshe Ben, my behind. I swear to Allah that if you interrupt me one more time, I will beat you," Fathil screamed and shook his finger in Adnan's face. He looked relentlessly ready for more arguments.

That night, we felt the first breezes of the fall, adding to the magical evening. The moon started to hide behind the small dark cloud playing the hiding game with our sense of peace. As we listened to the tales of Fathil the Liar, we did not pay attention to the conversation between Kamal and Ahmed.

But when Fathil heard Kamal saying, "I swear to Allah. I have gone there, by myself, to the seven palm trees," they all turned to Kamal, as it seemed that they all knew how mysterious the seven palm trees were. That was the first time I had heard of the place. Kamal, in turn, looked at us for approval and some support. "You know the place where the seven palm trees are. I went there by myself."

Suddenly, we heard Fathil's voice as deep as we ever heard it before. "You are a liar," he said to Kamal. "No one had ever gone there at night and come back alive. It's filled with jinnies. They would steal you, and you would never come back. I went there once, but with other friends, and the female jinnies called us to go with them, and they tried to get us to marry them. You know that when you marry a jinni girl, you must die so you will be living in the ghost world like her. Jinnies are just like us, but with their eyes upside down. The jinni girls chased us all the way to the train station, but fortunately we had taken our pistols with us, so we fired and they disappeared."

"I don't think the government would have approved your marriage with a jinni," Adnan said.

Fathil looked at him and grabbed a branch of wood lying next to him. "Are you mocking me, you blind little donkey? Do you know Sabah? You don't know Sabah, do you? You don't know because you and your family were not here in Balluria at that time. Well, Sabah was a brave young man, very handsome. Everyone knew him. Sabah was kidnapped by the jinni girls, and he married one of them. Everyone knew that in Balluria."

"That's rubbish," Adnan said.

"If you don't shut up, I will rip your stinky mouth."

Fathil threatened Adnan with a firm voice, and we felt that he was serious, as we sensed in his voice a longing for a change. He really believed in his own story, and Adnan quieted down. For a moment, we were all ears, and we wanted to hear the story, so we begged Fathil to continue. He looked at Adnan, threatening him with a deep look and warning him not to interrupt. The expression on his face was that of someone about to reveal a holy secret. He even cleared his throat so his voice would be deeper.

"Sabah was at the guesthouse of Sheikh Badr Al-Ghathban," Fathil said. He looked at Ahmed and said, "Sorry, Ahmed, the guesthouse of Sheikh Jawad now. Late that night, Sabah was chatting in the guesthouse with some other young men when he got into an argument with one of the men, who was jealous of Sabah's bravery. The man challenged him by saying, 'They say you are brave and you have a jinni female lover from the ghost world and that you are not scared of the jinnies.'"

A shiver went through my spine as I heard Fathil talk about the ghost world. Hamid was looking at Fathil with extreme attention, squinting his eyes and looking for facts that he could use in real life. Fathil's voice grew deeper, and we all looked at him with unwavering attention. Only Adnan had a smile on his thin face, waiting for the next opportunity to expose the lies of Fathil the Liar.

He looked at us and said, "Just like I said, the man challenged Sabah by saying, 'You are a coward with a shaky heart. You are a liar. You don't have a jinni girl as your lover.' Sabah became very angry, but he was calm, and he answered the man with a firm voice, saying, 'I don't have a jinni. That's true. But you have a tongue that needs to be cut out. You are calling me a coward... You son of a whore. You are calling me a coward.'

"That's what Sabah said," Fathil added and looked at us, making sure that we were ready for the climax of his story. "Both men pulled their knives and almost killed each other, but the others interfered, stopped them, and calmed them down. But the other man challenged Sabah again, shouting, 'I dare you to go to the seven palm trees and spend the night there until the morning. I challenge you. You say that you are brave. Then go to the seven palm trees, and I will give you a spike that you can drive into the ground as a sign that you really went there, and we can all go in the morning and see if the spike is there. But if it is not there, then we will declare you a coward.'

"Sabah accepted the challenge, shouting, 'I am my father's son. I want witnesses to this challenge.'

"The men who were there made the pact and declared themselves witnesses. The pact mandated that Sabah would go to the seven palm trees and drive the spike into the ground. The witnesses with Jabar, the challenger, would go in the morning to see the spike; if it was there, Sabah would be declared the bravest man in these parts, but if the spike was not there, he would be declared as a coward of the town."

As we listened to Fathil the Liar telling the story, we were all stunned and mesmerized to the point that we were willing to beat Adnan if he interrupted. Fathil pulled a cigarette from his black striped, Sumer cigarette box, lit it, and inhaled deeply.

"What happened after?" Kamal asked impatiently.

Fathil looked at him, paused, and then looked at us to see if we were prepared for the chilling end of his story. He continued, "They said that Sabah went to the seven palm trees, alone and with no weapon, not even his knife. When he got there, the jinni people were waiting for him. The jinni princess, the daughter of the jinni sheikh, was in love with him because he was the most handsome man in these parts. She had asked her jinni father to capture Sabah so she could marry him. Thus, they forced him to marry her, but in order for him to be part of the jinnies' world, they had to kill him, so they did. Many people in the town claimed that they heard the jinnies that night as they celebrated the wedding of Sabah and the jinni princess, and many people swore that they could hear the jinni girls as they sang the song of love. But it was sad that they had to kill Sabah, so he could be with them in the ghost world."

"This is the most ridiculous thing I have ever heard," Adnan said.

"Shut up, you blind donkey." Fathil always called Adnan the blind donkey because of the thick glasses Adnan wore. "You are a donkey. Everyone in the town heard that night the voice of the jinnies as they sang in the wedding. They even played their music."

"And who did they hire to sing in the wedding? Umm, Kulthum?"

Fathil lost it when he heard Adnan saying that. It was the last straw; Fathil could not contain his anger and his frustration with Adnan. He got up at the same time as Adnan had already put his own sandals in his hands preparing to flee and jumped over the light green fence. Fathil chased Adnan through the main street that led to the police station shouting, "You stupid blind donkey. You have no manners. You blind four eyes. I swear to Allah if I catch you I will tear your ass apart."

Adnan, who was laughing as he fled, was almost by the police station, almost fifty meters ahead of Fathil, who stopped after throwing a piece of rock that failed to hit Adnan. Fathil came back to where we were, breathing very heavily. He lay down on the grass. I asked with much curiosity, "Tell us what happened after that, Fathil. On your honor, Fathil, tell us what happened to Sabah."

He looked at me again as if seeing me for the first time. He took a minute to catch his breath, tensing to run again as he saw Adnan returning.

"I swear to Allah that I will not interrupt you again," said Adnan.

"You better not," Fathil said then concluded with his short breathless words, "I don't know the complete story, but the witnesses who went to see if Sabah had put the spike where he was supposed to, by the seven palm trees, came back in the morning with Sabah's dead body."

"Does that mean that he drove the spike into the ground?" asked Hisham.

"Yes. He was brave just like I said," Fathil answered as he looked where Adnan was standing, waiting for a sarcastic comment.

Hamid was listening all that time, paying attention to the story. Ahmed and Kamal exchanged looks of disbelief and wonder. Adnan was standing a bit far away so he could have leverage on Fathil if he decided to chase him again. As silence reigned among us, we waited for any comment from any of us. One thing I was sure of: we were all scared.

Adnan said with a sneer, "The real story is that it's true that Sabah accepted the challenge and went to the seven palm trees and took the spike with him. But instead of driving the spike into the ground, he drove it into a part of his dishdasha dress, because he was nervous, and it was dark. Then, when he wanted to stand up, he thought that something was holding him down, so he got so scared and had a heart attack and died. That is the logical story and the only explanation, not mumbo jumbo of jinnies and ghosts."

Fathil looked at him with no patience, but he was too tired to chase him, and he knew how fast Adnan was, so he said with a calm voice, "You are a donkey, a donkey that farts and wears thick glasses that looks like the bottom of the tea cups. Your brain is in your ass."

Then he got up, shaking his dishdasha dress with his hands and cleaned his back from the dried pieces of grass, telling us about how he truly felt about us. "And you... you are not a soccer team... you are a team of donkeys. You need to name your team the Donkeys Who Fart a Lot. You are the worst team in these parts. No... you are the worst team in the world. I don't know why I am wasting my time with stupid kids like you, a group of za'ateet. If you don't believe me, why don't you go to the seven palm trees? Maybe the jinnies will kidnap you. I am sure they can use a group of donkeys to do their chores. They need a glasses-wearing donkey that cannot protect his goal, like this moron." Then he threw a small branch of a tree to where Adnan was and left us among mixed feelings of fear of the story, laughter about what happened between him and Adnan, and anger for what he called us and called our team.

Hisham, who was lying on cardboard all this time, sat up and calmly redirected our wayward thoughts. "Fathil the Liar is the donkey. His father is a donkey too, a big, gray donkey like the donkey the Hillalys had. We will not call our team the donkeys."

Ahmed was lost in a fear that could be seen in his sparkling eyes as he looked at all of us. Kamal was chewing a piece of gum with not the slightest emotion. Salah and Haleem sat next to each other in silence. Adnan stared at the departing figure of Fathil as he disappeared, making sure he would not return to ambush him. I, as the new boy in the group, waited for someone to say something. We did not know why we were quiet. Maybe we did not know what to say. I certainly did not.

I was looking at Hamid, the only one who had not said a word all night. He looked at me and then to the others. With a firm voice and strange determination, he suddenly said what no one expected him to say, "Who wants to go with me tonight to the seven palm trees?"

We stopped talking, thinking, and breathing at the same time. We looked at Hamid, who looked as if he had not suggested anything out of ordinary as we tried to wrap our minds around what Hamid had just said. Go where? To the seven palm trees? Where jinnies kidnap humans and marry them? Where no one ever returned from? Where many mysterious graves are? Graves with unknown occupants, most likely people who were killed by the jinnies. Was Hamid crazy for real, or did he just want to prove that he was the bravest of us? I was new to their group and did not know my place in suggesting, accepting, or refusing to participate in the many adventures the team was about to embark on. Kamal, who appeared to be Hamid's eternal adversary, answered, "I will go. I just need to bring my knife." He stood up and concluded, "I will go to the house, get my knife, and will be back."

He is not coming back, I thought to myself. *He just said that because he wanted to avoid going with us.*

Salah, who was silent and frightened, announced, "I cannot go because my father will be home soon and if I am not there by then he will beat me up really hard."

He is just afraid, I thought, *like all of us*, but that reminded me that my father would be very angry if he knew that I went with the boys to a place where jinnies were.

Like all of us, Ahmed, the gentle son of Sheikh Jawad, looked as if he was facing yet another test of his long struggle to prove that he was tough and brave just like Kamal. Ahmed said, "If Kamal goes, I will go."

In my mind, I thought, *Ahmed is praying that Kamal would not come back.*

We all looked at Ahmed as he explained, "You know that my father will not let me go anywhere without Kamal, plus I don't want Kamal to get in trouble with my father if I went and he did not."

At that point, I did not know what Ahmed's relationship to Kamal was. I thought that Kamal was his older brother. Hisham, our team captain, who looked and acted like the one everyone looked to for leadership and guidance, addressed us as if we were a squad of soldiers and he was the sergeant. "We all will go. No one will turn cowardly on us in this. We will do this together. We will need a flashlight."

"I have one. I bought it for three dinars," Hamid answered. I learned later that Hamid, out of the five dinars that my father paid him to unload the moving truck that brought my family and me to Balluria, had spent three dinars on a flashlight and had given two dinars to his mother.

Hisham continued giving us our marching orders, "We will wait for Kamal and then we will go. We will walk together. I don't think the jinnies would want to kidnap us and marry us. We are still young, but if we go there and come back, we will become heroes and the Wild Lions will fear us forever. You know I don't think their sissy asses would ever be brave enough to do this," Hisham said, revealing his true motive behind his enthusiasm to attempt the impossible.

Besides being their new friend, I wanted to prove that I was not a sissy capital city boy. At the same time I was praying that Kamal would not come back so we did not have to go as I, and maybe the others, would use that as an excuse. But my hopes were shattered when I heard Kamal's voice from a distance.

"Aria, aria, aria." He was running toward us. When he got where we were, he said, "I brought a stick and a knife with me."

"Let me have the knife," Hamid said.

Hisham supported his request, saying, "Yes, Kamal, you carry the stick and let Hamid carry the knife so we will know that we will be protected in the front. Hamid, you will walk in front of us and for the back, Kamal, you will be in the back and I will be the second after Hamid so I will lead if anything happens to Hamid," Hisham decreed

We all got up and started what looked like a new army recruits formation when I heard Abdulla, who was the most religious of us, start to pray. "And say… I will seek refuge in the protection of the mighty lord of the universe from wickedness of what he has created."

We knew that if anything happened, we would all be in great trouble. Knowing we would all be in trouble eased our fears and leveled our anxious hearts as we walked through the street, heading toward the darkness-covered soccer field that led to the prairie. We walked through the soccer field, by the secluded mud hut of Barrya, the Gypsy woman, and crossed the line between the safety of our small town's lights and the houses of our families, and onto the open road to the wilderness, where the seven palm trees stood in the distance, calling us to test our bravery and our blossoming manhood, several kilometers away from Balluria. The seven palm trees looked distant, yet inviting in the moonlight. We walked as our heartbeats increased in volume and the number of shaky and nervous beats. I was the third one in the line, because I wanted to be close to Hamid. Hamid was first. He was walking quickly as if he could not wait to get there. Then after him Hisham, and then me, followed by Abdullah, who never stopped praying, and then Adnan walked next, I think, holding onto Salah's shirt.

Salah kept saying, "Wallah, if my father finds out about this, he will kill me." After Salah came Ahmed; after him walked Haleem; after Haleem, Ashraf walked with complete silence; and in the rear, Kamal walked while hitting the ground with his stick. We were all walking in a group, trying to stay as close to each other as possible.

As we got closer to the seven palm trees, the familiar noises from the town started to disappear and the chill of fear and thrill of courage crept within our veins. We knew that there would be no going back. Hamid led the way with such enthusiasm that made us all follow his lead. The seven palm trees looked deserted, yet so magical. The green halo of light that we all anticipated was barely there. We looked at the seven palm trees, and I had a warm feeling of familiarity. I felt like I had been there before; the strangest thing was that I thought that I had seen the seven palm trees many times in my dreams, or when I was an infant, or in another place or another time. My fear, and I am sure the fear of the others, disappeared suddenly as we got closer. I felt as if the site of the seven palm trees was the safest place on earth and that the trees had a mystic glow that reflected all the lights of all the moons in the world. In my mind, I did not care if we encountered a jinni girl from the world of the dead. In my mind, I felt that the place was perfect for a love story between the dead and the living, and I understood the story that Fathil the Liar told of the jinni princess who fell in love with Sabah the handsome.

Suddenly Hisham said, "That donkey Fathil the Lair will swallow his own words after tonight."

We were about twenty meters from the seven palm trees and we were still walking toward them, but we felt no fear whatsoever. We started to talk to each other when suddenly we heard voices. We all froze. None of us moved and we helplessly waited for the jinnies to appear, to carry us on their wings, and steal us from our bodies. We were all scared. Even Kamal and Hisham, and Hamid, the bravest of us, all stood still and did not move a step forward. We tried to listen to the unrecognizable voices.

Ahmed was the first to say, "Let's go back." He said it as quietly as humanly possible, but before we knew what to do, Hamid was on the ground. He signaled to us to lie down too. We all did like a squad of solders who awaited an ambush. We could not see what was behind the small hills of sand. Hamid crawled toward the seven palm trees. Hisham followed him, and Kamal, who was supposed to protect the rear of the column, was in front trying to catch up with Hamid and Hisham. Soon after we were all on the ground and crawling toward the small, sandy hills between the seven palm trees and us. Meter by meter, we crawled over the soft sand and wild thorny weed. Crawling toward the mysterious voices, Hamid was the first to arrive there, and I saw him as he slowly and cautiously climbed the small sandy hill. He lay there motionless, waiting for us. I realized that he did not move a muscle and did not turn toward us to let us know what he was looking at. I felt the warmth of my blood streaming in my veins as I thought that he was mesmerized by the jinnies that he was looking at, and by the time I reached the sandy hill, I was the sixth person there. Hamid, Hisham, Kamal, Ashraf, and Haleem were already there looking at what appeared to be a fuzzy scene of jinni fairies or ghosts. But it was not what I thought. I looked at what my friends were looking at, and I saw a pack of what looked like small animals; they looked like small dogs, small puppies.

"Are they dogs?" Hisham asked with a quiet voice

"No they are baby wolves," Hamid said with awe. "Wolf cubs, we should be careful because the mother may be near, and mother wolves are very dangerous," Hamid explained, with the firm voice of an expert.

"Where is their mother?" asked Adnan, who had just climbed the sandy hill and laid next to me. He was out of breath.

"I am sure she went hunting to feed her cubs."

That night, the eleven of us had nothing to say and nowhere to go. We did not want to say or do anything, nor did we want to go anywhere else. We just lay on the side of the sandy hill as the moon appeared from behind a cloud, shaped like running horses, and cast a silvery glow on the palm trees and white spots on the bellies of the little wolf cubs. The eleven of us just looked at the scene, mesmerized by amazing, green glow stemming from the tops of the seven palm trees. Our young lungs were rejuvenated and filled with the dry breeze of the Arabian Sahara as it moved the leaves of the palm trees, and carried us to the roots of our being. There, between the seven palm trees and the seven wolf cubs, was the distance between boyhood and manhood.

We watched the young wolves and listened to them. They were making the noises that we thought came from the jinnies. Their voices were those of the true children of unchained nature: a small pack of wolf cubs that lay around and played, unaware of the world around them, unaware of what the future might hold for them, and unaware of our mesmerized eyes, minds, and hearts. The wolf cubs did not notice or sense our presence. For some reason, they all just lay down on the ground looking at the sky or looking at the tops of the palm trees as if they were taking a rest from a long day of playing. They just lay there looking at the same moon and the same sky we were looking at. The only difference was that they were animals and we were humans, and to me—and probably to my friends too—reality at that moment it did not make any difference or hold any validity.

"Are they sleeping?" Hisham asked.

No one answered as the nine other kids and I looked at that majestic setting nature had offered us, away from the realities of our daily strivings, to dream. Clear southern, summer skies, glowing palm trees, moonlight that pierced the scenes of the earth, and seven wolf cubs had presented what came close to being the gate to the other world, the world that all children dreamed of, a world that was not ours forever but was for the moment.

"They are dreaming," said Hamid, "Wolves' dreams."

We all became silent and tried to comprehend what Hamid said and the way the cubs had lain on their backs looking at the silver moon and the deep sky.

Kamal said, "I should grab one of them so I can kill it and take its fangs and make them into a necklace. They say..."

"I know what you will say," Hamid said, interrupting him, "but you will not touch the wolf cubs. I know that if you made a necklace of the wolf fangs, then everyone would know that you are brave, but they must be the fangs of a fully grown wolf, not a baby cub," Hamid said to Kamal, and then he looked at Kamal and said with a warning voice, "The mother wolf will chase you and kill you."

"What should we do?" Hisham asked.

"We need to go back and let them dream. We have fulfilled our challenge, but leave the wolf cubs alone," Hamid said and then decreed, "We will call our soccer team the Wolves."

"Yes, that's good name, "Hisham whispered without thinking long about the name, I guess he just wanted a fast end to our adventures night.

In the moonlight, I thought I saw a tear rolling down Hamid's face as he looked at the cubs like an older brother looking at his younger siblings, and then he said to us. "Yallah, let's go."

One by one, we crawled back to the bottom of the sandy hill. Quietly, we started walking back toward the town, guided by the shimmering lights of the old section where all the mud huts had recently enjoyed the benefit of electricity. Each hut had a light next to its gate. We walked slowly and without line or formation. I was disappointed that we left, as were the others, I am sure. Hamid was the last one to leave the sandy hill, and he walked past me. I held his arm, slowing him down, and said, "Thank God there were no jinnies."

"There was never a jinni, nor there were jinni girls who kidnap young men, but seeing the wolves is the best thing I have ever experienced in my life. I wish I could stay there forever," Hamid said, and his voice turned animalistic and true.

I remember looking at him when we were lying on the hill, and that look in his eyes made me realize then that he was seeing the wolves with different eyes. The sight of the moonlight shining from the fur and the sparkly eyes of the cub wolves had awoken something inside all of us but it had awakened Hamid's entire soul. He was never the same after that night and, although I had always seen the wild glare in his big, black eyes, a glare full of life, after that night, I saw the glare mixed with what looked like a yearning for another life. This yearning lasted all the years of our friendship, and it was a yearning that indicated that he searched for his own wolf, one deep inside him.

That night we came back with more than a story that we were dying to tell everyone in the town; about how we went to the seven palm trees and came back alive and that none of us was kidnapped and forced to marry a jinni. Although all of us feared the punishment of our parents if they knew what we had done, the ultimate feeling of victory was vivid and overwhelming. That night we came back with more than the sense that we reached the enchanted waters of manhood, as we reached the place that was the ultimate challenge of bravery to any boy or man in these parts. We felt that we had passed the challenge that made the difference between a brave person and a coward, which meant the difference between a good man and a bad one, the difference between a man and a boy. We came back with a clear vision of how closely nature touches the hearts and the sense in these rural parts and of how nature offers the riddles that open the window to the unknown worlds of the endless starry nights of the Arabian Sahara, prompting many young men to roam through it searching for answers for many questions to come through a lifetime. That night we came back with even more than that; we came back with a name for our soccer team. That night we came back as the Wolves.

The Book of Balluria

Men and Wolves

1

Irar knew that everyone in Balluria and the surrounding villages thought of him as half man and half wolf. He chose not to reject that image of himself. He thought it was better to be feared as long as fear brought respect. Respect was given to him by no one; even young boys called him names as he walked alone from the guesthouse toward the ends of the town, where he lived alone. For years, Irar lived alone. The first time any human laid eyes on Irar was when he walked out of the desert and asked for hospitality at the guesthouse of Sheikh Badr Al-Ghathban, the only known sheikh in Balluria at that time. After that time, Irar made Balluria his home. First, he stayed for three days in the guesthouse, and when his three days ended, Sheikh Badr Al-Ghathban asked him where he came from.

"From the prairie. May your life be long," Irar said.

"Where will you be going if you leave my guesthouse?"

"Back to the prairie and to the desert. May your life be long," Irar answered as he looked down with complete humility.

Sheikh Badr paused for many long moments as he looked at Irar. "You can shepherd my herd, and I will give you food and shelter," Sheikh Badr reluctantly said to the man, who so vividly reminded him of a slithering, lidless snake.

"I accept, and I am at your service. May your life be long," Irar said. He kissed Sheikh Badr's hands as a gesture of gratitude. After that, Irar shepherded the large herd of Sheikh Badr. He did that for almost a year and did not ask for more than his daily food. He slept and ate at the guesthouse until one day he heard Sheikh Badr saying to a group of men, who sat close to the sheikh, "I need one more man to go with Abed, my trusted shepherd, to take my ten head of sheep cross the border."

At that moment, Irar stood up and said, "Sheikh, no one knows the desert better than I do. May your life be long. Send me with Abed."

Reluctantly Sheikh Badr agreed to send Irar with his trusted man Abed, who smuggled sheep across the border to the country to the south that had more oil fields than people. There the prices of the sheep were four times higher than the price in these parts. Sheikh Badr knew that Irar, with the way he looked, was more than able to undertake the task, but he was reluctant at first for no reason other than he had a bad intuition about the man who lived alone and never spoke.

Sheikh Badr was just recovering from a shameful defeat in a tribal battle with Sheikh Nasser the Blond. This defeat forced Sheikh Badr and almost half of the tribe of the Sharifys to leave the marshland and settle in Balluria. After that, Sheikh Badr did not trust strangers who showed up in his guesthouse, especially those who claimed no discernible roots. He was afraid that one of them was sent by his lifelong enemy, Sheikh Nasser the Blond, to kill him. The feeling he had whenever he looked at Irar, however, was that of pure fear; the same feeling a lamb would feel when seeing a hungry wolf. Nevertheless, he agreed to send Irar with Abed to muscle twenty sheep across the desert, and he wished that Irar would die on the way. However, twenty days later, Irar came back alone, with all the money he gained from selling the sheep, and Abed did not return with him. Irar claimed that Abed was shot by the border patrol as they chased them.

Sheikh Badr could not confirm the story, but he paid half of the money to Abed's widow and told Irar that he would be the only smuggler who would work for him. After that, Irar traveled hundreds of times with ten or twenty head of sheep at a time, bringing all the money that he gained to Sheikh Badr, and not asking for much of it, unlike other smugglers who demanded half of the profit. Sheikh Badr was pleased with that arrangement, but one day he asked Irar, "Why don't you take some of the money you bring me?"

"I don't have anyone to spend it on," Irar replied.

Sheikh Badr was not surprised by the answer he heard since he knew that Irar had eaten and slept in the guesthouse since he came to Balluria and had no other human in the world to give the money to, but he wanted to clear his own conscience when he offered Irar that mud hut that no one lived in. The mud hut was Sheikh Badr's property. It was a secluded mud hut in the middle of open land. It was the last house an eye could see in Balluria. Nothing and no one lived beyond it—no houses and no people—only wolves and desert. Pleased, Irar kissed the sheikh's hand. "May your life be long, Sheikh."

"That's all right," Sheikh Badr said. "Now you have a house of your own. You can leave the guesthouse and move to your house," Sheikh Badr said and ordered his slave Khanger to give Irar one old carpet, some pots, a few jars, and one teakettle - the same smudged teakettle that Barrya had made tea in for the long-haired stranger, who trav`1eled half the globe and showed up at her doorstep looking for answers about his friends. That was years after, during the time when the rain did not stop pouring, the time when the blue-eyed Americans invaded Balluria and these parts. Sheikh Badr was relieved when Irar moved from the guesthouse since the snake-looking man had lived in the guesthouse and the sheikh was weary of him. He confessed to Khanger, "I have never trusted Irar, and I slept every night with my dagger next to me because I was afraid that this snake-looking man would kill me in my sleep."

Irar lived in that house alone for many years, and when he met Jawad, the two men lived in the mud hut. Barrya had lived there ever since Jawad kidnapped her and brought her to the mud hut. When Jawad married Sabrya, the daughter of Sheikh Badr, he moved to live in the large house of Sheikh Badr and left Irar and Barrya alone in the mud hut. Irar lived with Barrya in the hut for one month, and then he asked Jawad, who became Sheikh Jawad after marrying Sabrya, if he could ask the ailing Sheikh Badr to allow him to move back in order to live in the guesthouse. At that time, Jawad became the man who had the final say in many affairs that had formerly been the sole responsibility of Sheikh Badr, including the guesthouse, so Sheikh Jawad allowed Irar to again live in the guesthouse. Sheikh Jawad never asked Irar for the reason he wanted to move away from the mud hut. Irar was the one who said to Sheikh Jawad that it was because he could not stay at one place with the young Gypsy woman that Sheikh Jawad kidnapped in the middle of a night with no moon. He told Sheikh Jawad that it was not appropriate for the latter's reputation. He was starting to become the sheikh of these parts and people would talk. It was during that time that Sheikh Badr died and Jawad became sheikh and took over the guesthouse.

2

"Irar saw the young Jawad sitting in the guesthouse, enjoying the benefit of hospitality in the same fashion that Irar had asked for it years before. Irar looked at the strange, young man who called himself Jawad and he saw himself. He saw himself in the thinly built, yet extremely rugged, dark man who called himself Jawad," the Gypsy woman said. "When Irar saw Jawad the first time at the guesthouse as he returned from one of his many trips across the border, he looked at the young man and realized that he had not seen a man like him before. Jawad looked like a wolf emerging from battle with many wolves after he had left all of them licking their wounds. He saw Jawad at the guesthouse of Sheikh Badr Al-Ghathban and asked Khanger about him.

"Who is the man sitting at the end of the carpet?"

"A guest of the sheikh. It's his third day of hospitality and he has not left yet."

Irar stood up and walked toward the young man, sat next to him, and asked, "From where is the man?"

"From the strong back of my father," Jawad answered.

That was the day when Irar knew that his long wait for the son that he could never have was over, but he needed more answers to learn about the new arrival so he tested him.

"The prairie is wide and welcoming," he said to the young man as a sign that it was his last day of hospitality.

"The prairie is for its inhabitants," Jawad answered with a firm and calm voice, saying, in the nomadic language, that he had no place to go. Irar seized the opportunity.

"The prairie is for wolves and the night walkers."

"I have lived with them all," Jawad said, as he looked straight into Irar's eyes, squaring his jaw and waiting for the provocation. Instead, he received an invitation to a fateful bond and undying friendship baptized with the blood of many men and women in these parts.

Irar was sure of every word as he looked at the young man's face and said, "My house is your house if you wish and you are my guest."

"That night Jawad went with Irar to his secluded mud hut near the ends of all the roads in Balluria, near the beginning of the prairie that led to the endless desert of the Arabian Sahara. That night the two men met as it was planned in the fate of this town and its people," the Gypsy woman said. "It was the fate and destiny of many people in these parts, as it was written in all books of the Arabian monks and in the twisted brown lines of henna on all the hands of the Gypsy dancers. When Irar looked at Jawad's face, he saw that they shared two things, a heart of stone and a humble degrading of peasant roots."

"What's your profession?" Irar asked the young Jawad.

"Any profession suitable for a man," the young rugged man answered, not sure what the thin man wanted to know.

"Even blood?" Irar asked, wanting to know how far the young man, who looked like a wounded wolf, would be willing to go.

"Do I have your word on the grace of all dead?" the young man asked.

"You have my word on the grace of all the dead. Yes, even blood."

"That night, the two men met, as was planned in the fate of this town and its people," the Gypsy woman said, as she wanted the man to believe in her words. Then she continued, "Irar went to sleep that night and closed his eyes for the first time since he was twelve—since the night his father was shot dead in the field and many tribesmen fell to the ground as the British charged the open field of the great southern city."

Irar looked at Jawad. "I have never trusted a living soul before, but something about you is telling me to trust you," said the man who looked like a snake. "I will give you something that a man gave me once, and it kept me alive in these parts." He handed Jawad a long blade wrapped in cloth. "Here, keep this dagger, as it will be the guardian of your life because it will be your last defense, and you will feel the warmth of the flesh and blood when you insert it in the bodies of your enemies, but for tonight you will keep watch the first half of the night, and I will wake up by dawn and you can sleep." He paused and then finished, "This is the first time I can go to sleep without fearing the thrust of a blade or the scratch of bullets ripping through my body."

When Jawad unwrapped the cloth, it revealed a hellish-shaped dagger, with a black grip made of carved woods and stones wrapped in soft black leather. It was shaped with a strange curve and had many little chips in the edges. Jawad realized that the dagger had seen the insides of countless other men and maybe some women too. He held it and felt the rush of the power of being able to kill. After that night, he kept the black dagger next to him until the day he gave it to his son, Ahmed, when he sent him to kill his own daughter, Hanan.

That night Jawad stayed up until the early light of dawn, and when Irar woke up, he asked Jawad if he had gotten any sleep.

"I could not sleep while you sleep, and you said that one of us has to stay awake at night."

"Yes, you have to believe that, from this day on, one of us has to stay awake all the time even if we have to cut our hands and pour salt in them to stay awake."

3

It was a year after the wedding of Ra'ad, the son of Sheikh Waitan, and after Jawad kidnapped Barrya. It was after Barrya realized that she loved Jawad and did not want to leave, even when she was left alone in the mud hut as the two men went on their sheep smuggling trips to rich country in the south. She waited for him to return, and when Jawad returned she laid with him for many nights and she felt safe in his arms. She felt that she had no other men to satisfy, only one man, one man that no other man would dare to challenge him for her. It was then when Irar realized that the time was right to make his protégé a sheikh. Jawad never forgot nor forgave Sheikh Badr for that insult he posed on him in the wedding but he waited. He even confessed to Irar that he wanted to kill Sheikh Badr for the insult, but Irar calmed his anger and told him that it would not be a satisfying revenge. "If you kill him, we will both be killed. Your revenge must last a lifetime, and it must hurt for a lifetime," said Irar who looked like a snake and thought like a fox. "If you want real revenge, you must take his place as the sheikh and strip him of his reputation and his guesthouse."

"And how I will do that?" Jawad asked tensely.

"With the patience of a wolf and the planning of snake," Irar said and told Jawad to wait another week and then ask again for Sabrya's hand in marriage.

"What if he rejects me again?" Jawad said angrily, fingering his knife.

"Then you will wait another two weeks and ask again."

"What if he rejects me then?" asked Jawad.

"Then I will kill him myself," came the cold, quiet response.

Sheikh Badr rejected the second request of Jawad. It disturbed him that no one knew his family or where he came from. As far as they knew, he was a leffu, a man with no history and no family roots. For Sheikh Badr, Jawad was nothing more than a peasant thief who appeared from nowhere one day at the guesthouse, asked for tribal customs and refuge, and never left. Sheikh Badr never trusted the rugged, thin man even though he liked Jawad's personality, apparent decency, and undisputed bravery. He entrusted him to smuggle sheep across the southern borders, but Sheikh Badr always sensed a cruelty about the young man. Jawad had a heart of stone and nerves of steel, and to Sheikh Badr, a man like Jawad could easily kill. Moreover, he did not want his only daughter, Sabrya, who was considered by all women's standards in these parts to be weak, naive, and undependable, to be at the mercy of a man like Jawad. He rejected Jawad, and on the third time he said it bluntly, "What will other sheikhs say about me if I gave you my daughter?"

Jawad's answer was more disturbing than assuring to Sheikh Badr. "If I marry your daughter, I will be your son-in-law. I will be your dagger and your rifle, and if any sheikh says anything about you, I will cut out his tongue and serve him as a lunch in your guesthouse."

Although that answer increased Sheikh Badr's admiration of Jawad's notorious directness and bravery, he did not consider Jawad's request, not until Irar showed up at the guesthouse one windy night and sat where he always sat.

Sheikh Badr waited until most of the men in the guesthouse went home, and then he told Khanger to ask Irar to come closer. When Irar sat closer to the sheikh, he said with a quiet voice, "Night walking has a purpose."

The sheikh looked at him and answered, "A good purpose, God willing."

Irar said as he looked first to the ground and then into the sheikh's face, "It's a good purpose, and I seek your permission to ask for it."

"If I possess it, it's given," Sheikh Badr replied.

"I came here as your servant and on behalf of Jawad. I will not drink your coffee, Sheikh," Irar said as he put the little coffee cup, presented to him by Khanger, near the coffee pit, on the floor.

"Drink your coffee because my answer is still the same," Sheikh Badr said as he looked at Irar with angry eyes.

"Words in private," said Irar, looking to the ever-present Khanger, who was still standing.

"Khanger, go outside," Sheikh Badr ordered. To Irar he said, "State your request."

"He is one of the bravest men I have ever seen in my life. He is braver than me and all the men of Balluria, and our ancestors said, 'The man is not who my father said he was. The man is one who says here I am.'"

"Irar, your friend Jawad is a Leffu who has no roots and no family, and my daughter will not marry a leffu."

"Who will she marry, then? Do you think that Jawad will allow her to marry any other man? I have lived and traveled with Jawad, and I swear to Allah that every time I look at him, I can feel his dagger slicing my throat."

Irar's words reached the heart and mind of Sheikh Badr, not only because Irar was saying the truth about Jawad's intentions, but rather because he had noticed that since Jawad had asked for Sabrya's hand, no other man dared to ask for it. It had been almost three months since Jawad had asked for Sabrya's hand and since then no other man in Balluria had mentioned her name in front of the sheikh, not even her male cousins, who apparently did not want to be Jawad's competitors for the sheikh's daughter. Sheikh Badr, who felt abandoned as he looked for a way out of the spider web that Irar had created around him, resorted to one last defense. "Even if I accepted Jawad's proposal, I don't think her brother Reyhan will accept." Irar was not willing to let Sheikh Badr escape the spider web.

"You are the sheikh, and your word is above all of your men, including your son," Irar said, realizing that the sheikh was about to surrender. "Sheikh, let us start with me bringing Jawad tomorrow to your guesthouse, and he will ask for Sabrya's hand in front of all men. If any of them has a word to say, then we will know how to talk back, and if your son, Reyhan, would have anything to say, then we will know his answer."

"Yes, let us do that, and then we will know. Bring your man, Jawad, for dinner tomorrow."

"Shall we read a verse from the Qur'an for God's blessings?" Irar asked with an ambiguous smile.

"Blessings?" Sarcastically, Sheikh Badr said, "Let us wait until tomorrow, and let us hope that no one will get killed."

"Yes." Irar said with a smile that did not reach his eyes. "Let us hope that no man will get killed."

The next day Irar prepared Jawad for the formal visit, dressing him in a white dishdasha and new keffiyeh and iqal like a proud father dressing his son.

"Tonight, you are not a peasant. You are not a leffu. Tonight, you will sit among men who despise you and me. The men will look at you, wishing they could drive their daggers into your heart. You will look at them, straight in the eyes, and you will see who your enemy is. Tonight, the tongues will speak differently than what the hearts are feeling. You will say what is in your heart, and don't let any man in the guesthouse make you do or say otherwise," Irar said as he looked at Jawad. "You are like my son, and tonight you will be the man that you should be, not a peasant and not a Leffu and not a sheep smuggler. Tonight, you will ask for the hand of the daughter of the sheikh, and soon enough you will be the sheikh. I will make sure of it. We have killed many men for this night, and we will kill more men, so one day men will seek your approval to marry your daughter."

The two men walked toward Sheikh Badr's house in silence. As they approached the guesthouse, Irar asked, "Have you brought your black dagger?"

"It has never left my waist."

"That's what is expected of you. Keep your dagger close to you even when you are seeking to marry a woman because a man can lose a woman, but he must never lose his dagger," Irar said quietly. As they entered the guesthouse, he shouted, "Alsalamu Alaykum, men,"

"Wa-Alaykum Al-Salam." The replies echoed from the two sides of the guesthouse. The two men looked for a place where they could sit, a place not by the entrance of the guesthouse or next to the sandals where peasants sit.

That night, and after the men in the guesthouse ate dinner, Irar looked frequently at Sheikh Badr's face and he saw that sheikh looking worried and very weary as he looked at Jawad dressed in what seemed like a sheikh's attire.

What Irar did not know was that Sheikh Badr was admiring how natural Jawad looked. Sheikh Badr waited until dinner had ended and waited for half of the men of his close cousins to leave. Then he sent his coffee servant Khanger to whisper something in Irar's ear. Later, Irar stood up and said, "I seek the permission of the respected men in the guesthouse, Sheikh, and I seek your permission to speak of a good purpose."

The men looked at him, then expectantly at Sheikh Badr, who replied, "Speak."

"I am here, with young Jawad, asking for the honor of being related to you by marriage."

"Marriage with whom?"

"Jawad and your daughter, Sabrya."

Grunts could be heard from the other end of the guesthouse as the eyes turned to Sheikh Badr, who did not reply. Rather, he waited for his son, Reyhan, to say something. As he expected, Reyhan jumped up and practically snarled in disgust, "What? Have the men lost the ability to talk with sanity? Have they lost their ability to talk properly? Who is asking to marry my sister? Jawad? Our shepherd?"

Sheikh Badr looked at Irar and at Jawad, who stared at him in the eye and touched the vicious dagger at his waist.

"Reyhan, sit down," Sheikh Badr said to his son.

"Sit down?" Reyhan asked his father. "Sit down? You want me to sit down and let these two peasants disgrace our guesthouse with their talk?" Reyhan then stormed out. Silence rang loudly in the guesthouse as everyone waited for Sheikh Badr to say something. Instead, it was the deep fearsome vice of Jawad who broke the silence as he stated what was in his heart.

"I may not be a sheikh or the son of a sheikh, but my roots are honorable, and my heart is the heart of a man. I am worthy of the sheikh's daughter, and any man who thinks otherwise, let him speak now to my face, not behind my back. I am honored to seek the sheikh's daughter for marriage and willing to challenge anyone who thinks of me as a lesser man."

Silence again ruled the guesthouse, and everyone looked at Sheikh Badr, who looked at Jawad and realized that what Irar said about the young Jawad was true; he would not allow any other man to marry her.

Sheikh Badr ordered his coffee servant, "Khanger, go fetch Reyhan and bring him back. Tell him that I need to see him now. And you men, you are all my cousins, I want you to be witness that I have accepted the proposal of this good man, Jawad, and I accepted him as a suitor for my daughter, Sabrya. Keep your tongues in your mouths if you have no good thing to say."

Later that night Irar was so happy, he could not sleep. Even though, when Reyahn came back to the guesthouse he called Irar a worthless peasant and Jawad a rootless, fatherless man. Irar knew that what Sheikh Badr said was the word of a sheikh and that Sheikh Badr could not back down from his commitment, which meant that Jawad would marry Sabrya, just as Irar wanted. As Jawad slept in the space between the mud hut and the door, Irar stayed awake watching the road, fearing that Reyhan could gather some men and come kill Jawad and him, and when Barrya brought him some tea, she asked him why he was so happy.

"You Gypsy woman. Don't you understand what happened tonight? My Jawad had walked the first step to be the lord of Balluria and Tawsheeha and the only sheikh in these parts."

"Why? What did he do?" the Gypsy woman asked anxiously.

"He will marry Sabrya, the daughter of Sheikh Badr, and soon he will be the sheikh. I willed it," Irar said with an intense look of triumph on his snakelike face.

That night Barrya stayed up all night looking at Jawad sleeping alone as she wept.

Many nights later, when the wedding happened, Sheikh Badr did not invite any of the sheikhs in these parts because he was not proud of his new son-in-law and because it was his daughter who was getting married, not his son. Since the night when Jawad asked for Sabrya's hand, Reyhan, spent most of his nights in the big city drinking with his friends and did not return to Balluria until a month after the small, quiet wedding. Only women started playing, with precautions, inside the house and the women insisted on bringing the only Gypsy dancer in these parts to dance for them.

Barrya lived in the mud hut with Jawad, and she wept while she dressed Jawad for his wedding.

Jawad looked at the Gypsy woman and asked, "Why are you crying?"

"No reason," she replied, but he was not fooled.

"You are crying because I am marrying Sabrya?"

"No woman on this earth would be happy as she sees her man going into the arms of another woman. Even a Gypsy woman could not do that."

"You are my woman, Barrya, but I am not your man, I am the man of no woman. You are a Gypsy, Barrya, and you must be a Gypsy tonight, as you will dance and spare me your worthless talk."

"Yes, Jawad," the Gypsy woman said as she continued cleaning his robe and fixing his keffiyeh on his shoulder. She wept silently that night as she lost her only true love.

The Book of the Man

Field of Broken Glass

1

I had never given much thought to the meaning of the term "best friend," nor did I remember that I had a best friend when I lived in Baghdad. All my friends in school were just friends. I liked some more than the others, but I did not consider any of them a best friend. There were Ali, Haytham, and Saady. We were all the same age and attended the same elementary school, but we never did anything exciting or adventurous. Ali was very careful not to get his clothes dirty, because his mother (from the northern city of Mosul) was a clean freak who gave all of her kids baths every day, washed the dishes three times after each meal, and swept the doorway for hours. Haytham was too timid to leave our street in fear of the gangs. Saady was a strange kid who did not want to do anything other than watch television all day. We were not best friends, in spite of what we shared and did together. We played soccer together, traded soccer player cards, and talked about movies and television shows. Occasionally, we stayed after nine o'clock at night in the streets lights, whenever my father allowed me to, playing games and talking about movies and the girls in our neighborhood, yet it wasn't a genuine friendship. When I first met Hamid, I never thought of the term best friend, nor did I know that he was the only best friend I would ever have in my life. When Hamid and I went to the river the first time to swim, I was scared, and I told him that I was afraid of drowning. He replied with confidence, "You are my friend, and I will never let that happen."

I did not give much thought to his words, and at that time they seemed meaningless. Hamid spent two weeks teaching me how to swim, how to bait a fishing rod, which fish are half fish and half water snake, and all the tricks about how to trap a dove or palm tree rats. I felt as if I were in one of my beloved Mark Twain stories and I did not want school to start. Having never enjoyed life so much before, I wanted every day to last forever and I never wanted to leave the water of the Euphrates and its chilly touch. I never wanted to eat any food except the fish that we caught in the river, the little desert sparrows that we trapped, or the gray doves that we hunted with our slingshots. Needless to say, Hamid did all the dove hunting with his merciless slingshot and left me to barely get one dove a day. He packed six or seven of them. Hamid and I crossed the Euphrates when no other kid would. I prayed that school would never come because I knew that as soon as school started it would be the end of my streak of wild living with Hamid. Also, I knew that Hamid might not attend school that year because he said that he needed to work for a living to support his mother and his sister, since their father left a long time ago. My mother commented every day about how the color of my skin was becoming darker and darker and how I had started to look and smell like a shroogy, which was a term the people from the capital used as a degrading description of the southern peasants. She did not, however, notice nor did she comment on my being gone all day. She did not tell my father that I had not eaten lunch at the house since the first day I went to Hamid's to see the pigeons.

To me it was a blessing that because of my parents' distractions, I was able to leave the house in the morning even before breakfast and return after dinner; something I had never done when we lived in the capital. In my first month in Balluria I, with the guidance of Hamid, was introduced to many new things so out of the realm of my previous experience of everyday life in the capital. When Hamid told me that he would show me something the next day that would amaze me, I hardly slept and was so anxious. I thought of the many possible things that he might have meant. Would it be the snake that he said he had befriended? Could it be a mythical bird that he might have caught and hidden away from people? My anxious waiting was over when, the next morning, Hamid and I walked almost three kilometers toward the abandoned train station and toward where the desert started. There was a house, an abandoned mud hut, which stood separate from the rest of the town. It looked lonely, needy, and mysterious. Inside it, from the half-open door, I saw a shadow of a woman. The woman looked so welcoming when she saw Hamid, and she yelled for him, "Welcome, my son!"

Hamid did not go inside. Instead he said, "I will come and see you later." Then he kept walking toward the desert. I was tired and thirsty and asked Hamid who the woman was.

"Barrya."

"Who is Barrya?" I asked.

"She is a Gypsy," Hamid said.

That and left me in the dizziness of his answer. *Oh, my God, a Gypsy woman,* I thought to myself. I had heard many stories about the Gypsies, yet had never actually seen any of them in real life. Then Hamid shocked me with another fact. "She is like a second mother to me. We will go and drink yogurt from her house when we are done." I was barely able to understand the facts of that morning when he stopped me, put his hand on my shoulder, and said, "Swear on the Qur'an that you will never tell anyone about what you will see."

"I swear on the Qur'an."

"OK, look toward the horizon over there," Hamid said as he pointed toward the mirage, and I saw what I thought was just a big black dot.

"What is it?"

"You will see when it gets closer. Just keep looking."

The dot got closer and closer. Then, suddenly, the big black dot became two big black dots, and one of them grew larger. Little by little, I saw the majestic, black hair of an Arabian horse followed by its little baby horse. The rider of the horse was wrapped completely by his robes, and kuffia and I could not see his face. As he got closer, I looked at Hamid and did not say a word, as I saw him mesmerized by the scene, with his mouth half opened and his eyes wide. The horse looked as if it was swimming in the air and its feet were not touching the hot sands. It looked as if it was flying above the prairie and its long, black hair was traveling the distance of dreams. I looked at the horse and saw that the long hair of its tail, stretched further than the imagination.

"That's Kadhum, the horse rider of Sheikh Mutter the son of Sheikh Nasser the Blond. He runs the horse once a month from the big city to the marshes. He is the best horseman these parts have ever known."

I looked at the rider and saw an image that I could never erase from my mind; it was covered with the dust of history and laced by the eternal wind of the Arabian Sahara.

"One day, I will be the best rider these parts will ever know. That little horse will be mine, and I will go into the desert and never come back again," Hamid said as he watched with his almost teary, yet joyful, eyes at the horseman, whose silhouette faded into the mirage. We stood there for a long moment as I waited for Hamid to say or do something. Suddenly he turned to me as he wiped the tears from his eyes and said, "Let us go and drink yogurt from Barrya's house."

We walked back to where the lonely mud hut stood alone. Hamid did not knock on the door when we arrived; instead, he entered the mud hut with a shout, "Barrya!"

From the only room in the mud hut appeared a woman who looked like no other. She was tanned with an amazingly clear texture of dirt-like skin and had a tattoo of many dots on her chin. Her hair appeared from underneath her scarf that was half down her shoulders and barely covered her head. As she looked at me, a piercing chill ran down my spine as if she had entered me with her entire being. I felt that her smell of burnt incense and naturally tanned skin had filled my veins with strange desires and forbidden thoughts.

"Who is your friend?" she asked.

"Oh, this is the boy I told you about. He is from the capital." Hamid came out of the room with a large tin jar filled with fresh, cold yogurt. He handed me the jar, which I lifted to my mouth with my eyes fixated on the Gypsy woman, who kept looking at me and smiling. Her smile revealed a set of amazingly white teeth in between thick, dark lips. I drank the yogurt and looked at her; she was standing at her room's door wearing a long purple dress that mostly covered what she should not reveal to two twelve-year-old boys. For some reason, I dropped my eyes to her chest and saw what I thought was the door to both heaven and hell. She had revealed her breasts and made visible the magically infatuating valley between her breasts that screamed with a strange invitation and remarkable message of forbidden treasures.

I did not realize the time I spent staring unintentionally at her Gypsy body treasure when she let out a laugh. It shook my senses and I saw the shadows on the mud wall escaping as my focus returned to my surroundings. I thought that her pure, wild, and genuine laugh had chased the shadows off the walls of the secluded mud hut. Hamid seemed distant when I wanted him to save me from the deliciousness of her presence, and he did that when he called me, saying, "Hurry up; we must meet the guys for soccer."

Barrya, that was her name I tried to think of the name and then to forget it at the same time so the image of her exposed breasts would stop tormenting me. "Barrya," what a name for a Gypsy, like no other name in the world. *Barrya,* I thought to myself, *Barrya - "wilderness," she could not have had any other name except that name.*

As a part of my new life in Balluria, and as one of the many things that Hamid had introduced me to, the soccer team became an essential element of my daily life. Having a name for our team meant that we needed to prove something to ourselves and to the Wild Lions, who won all the games that we played against them, and they had won all the games since before I had arrived. Because their team captain was the son of Comrade Uraiby, the party's main man in Balluria and Tawsheeha, it was impossible for us to compete with them in many ways. Comrade Uraiby had managed to get the Wild Lions all that they needed: soccer balls, shoes, and jerseys. One thing they did not have was a decent-sized soccer field, because they lived in the small community of houses that the party had built for its high-ranking members. While they did not have a soccer field, they did have a small piece of empty land behind the deserted kindergarten building, which the party used sometimes to train its militiamen. It was not as big and as groomed as our field, which was cleaner and almost close to the official size of a real soccer field, and our team captain, Hisham, spent many hot afternoons cleaning it of pointy and sharp rocks that filled the field and kept appearing time and time again, mostly after minor storms that came from the desert with regularity. We tried to lay official soccer field lines with a bag of plaster that Haleem stole from his father's measly construction storage site guarded by an Egyptian man who lived in Balluria. He was an estranged and lonely Egyptian man who never spoke to anyone. People in Balluria claimed that he was a wanted man back in his country.

Our soccer field was a place where we met every day without appointment and where we played and acted like a pack of wolves on a hunting adventure. It was the place where Hisham cried whenever we lost a game and where Barrya waited for us after each game with a huge, metal jar filled with cold, fresh yogurt. The yogurt's origins were a mystery since she had no cow that she could have milked to make it; yet she seemed to have an endless supply. Our field was perfect, but it needed two things to make it look like an official field, just like the ones we saw on television, a field like the one on which Steve Highway could score a perfect goal for Liverpool against Manchester United, and like the one where Paolo Rossi and Alessandro Alttobelli humiliated Germany with three clean goals. Our field needed two goals made of wood or iron, and it needed nets so we could capture the ultimate feeling of scoring a goal and see the ball as it bounced back. We felt that official-looking goals along with our new name might change our luck in our long struggle against the Wild Lions.

After the last game we had against the Wild Lions, and after we found the name that we had always searched for, Hisham was the most excited member of the team. It was as though his previous all-encompassing negativity had been replaced by an intense optimism. He had even created a trophy to give us a physical artifact to fight for. At this point he went to the house of Comrade Uraiby and challenged his son Mazen, the captain of the Wild Lions, to play one last game against us. He challenged Mazen to a game that would set the record straight, one game that would show which was the better team in these parts, and the winner would take the trophy and the soccer balls from the loser. We did not know that Hisham's plan was to get us a supply of soccer balls that would last us a lifetime, nor did we realize how determined Hisham was to not surrender the trophy that he made, even if we all had to die on the soccer field. We did not know how determined he was to win that game.

While Hisham was busy planning out our fate in soccer, Hamid and I spent two days in constant swimming lessons in the muddy waters of the Euphrates. Able to cross it, I swam like Hamid, who said many times, "Remember to keep your head above water for at least two seconds, then stroke with your hands and feet. You will never drown; I will be right next to you," and for the first time I was swimming like a real southern boy. I was able to swim for hours by myself, to dive for a long time, and to hold my breath underwater for a minute. I was so happy and proud and wanted my father to see me that afternoon. The luckiest kid in the world, I could cross the Euphrates, and I could dive in it. I could do whatever I wanted now. I thought that I would be one of the most famous men in these parts. That afternoon felt as if I had accomplished everything I wanted to accomplish in my life and was ready for another three hours of swimming when Hamid told me we would have to go to Barrya's house.

"Why?" I asked.

"We will make nets for the goals."

Then I remembered how two days before, Hamid's mother complained that two of her yarn balls were missing and that Barrya had shredded an entire pile of old clothes with old rusty scissors and rolled them into balls of threads that she gave to Hisham. We had no time to waste and no energy to spare as we got into the team spirit. We made Barrya's second room into our headquarters. It was not a real room; rather, it was a shade made of two palm tree trunks and covered with palm tree leaves and old deteriorating rugs as a roof. It was the only place big enough and away from the burning sun in her mud house. To make it official, Hisham brought the only soccer ball we had and the team's only trophy, which was not won by our team, nor was it even a trophy made for soccer. In fact, Hisham had found it in the garbage of the big city's Directorate of Education, and on it was written "Champion of the Province's Schools across Country Competitions 1976." Hisham had spent countless hours scrubbing the rust off it. He had then glued a piece of paper right on top of that writing on which he had written, in a messy red and black handwriting, "The Wolves." Other than that, our team's headquarters was empty except for enough balls of yarn to start a small knitting store. Almost twenty balls had been donated or stolen from the team members' mothers, and every color in the world was represented.

When Hamid and I arrived, we found that Adnan, Ashraf, and Salah had already started creating the most colorful soccer goal nets in the world. They had attached the ends of the threads to the palm trees' trunks in the ceilings and started crossing threads from the beginning of the room to the end as Barrya watched with a smile. Later, Ahmed and Kamal came with another pack of stolen yarn balls and other types of threads and started the netting. The threads were twisted in many places and made it difficult for us to get in and out of the room, but we had no time whatsoever; it was only three hours before the Wild Lions would arrive. Hisham and Haleem, who had planned the renovation of the soccer field for weeks, tried to find six pieces of wood or six iron pipes so we could build the soccer goals. They looked for the material in all the garbage sites in Balluria. They even thought of cutting the palm trees, where we saw the young wolves dreaming, and using the tree trunks as goals, but we had no tools, and it would be extremely hard to bring the palm tree trunks all the way to the soccer field. Suddenly Hisham came up with a brilliant idea, an idea he shared with us, but not with Haleem. Hisham's idea was to steal six pieces of wood logs from Haleem's father.

Haleem's father was a construction contractor who was notorious for making bad business deals; deals in which he miscalculated his profit margins and ended up paying from his own pocket to finish his contracts. He was a contractor who built houses and other structures like the concrete wall where the portrait of the president stood in the town's entrance. He had plenty of wood that he used to pour concrete in and build houses for war widows and lucky soldiers who were able to get a grant from the government to build houses just before the war started; thereafter, the government stopped giving the grants, and many houses remained unfinished for the next thirty years.

Our plan was to convince Haleem to let us steal from his father six two-by-fours and enough nails to hold them together. It did not take us much time or effort to convince Haleem to steal the wood from his father's storage lot; on the contrary, he replied right away, joyfully, "Let's go steal them now—today—when my father takes his nap." So we did. Kamal, Haleem, Hamid, Hisham, Adnan, and I went to the gated site where Haleem's father kept his empire of wood, one rusty cement mixer, and an Egyptian guard who slept in a shack made of gray bricks and a flimsy tin-sheet roof. When the guard saw us stealing the wood, he ran toward us with the stick he used as his weapon to guard the storage area but Haleem was quick to assure him, "My father told me to take these pieces of wood to Sheikh Jawad's house."

That was more than what the Egyptian worker needed to hear as he went back to sleep in the small shack where he lived. We later learned that the Egyptian worker informed Haleem's father, and Haleem was beaten up severely. We dragged the long, heavy pieces of wood through the main street to the end of the town and through the empty field as they made an annoying scratching noise. And with many splinters entering our determined hands, we dragged the six pieces of wood all the way to the soccer field. We nailed the top piece, and Hisham and Kamal dug two twenty-inch-deep holes after arguing for an hour about the official width of a goal. We inserted the bottom ends of the goal into the holes and pushed it upward. We did not take any safety measures. The three pieces of the goal fell backward, almost hitting Adnan on his head as the two large nails came undone and twisted from the top piece of wood. Without a hammer, we had to use two bricks to straighten the nails. By the time we stood the two goals up, we saw Salah, Ashraf, Ahmed, and Abdullah coming out of Barrya's house, dragging the two nets on the ground. Barrya followed, carrying a large jar of what we rightly assumed was the much-appreciated, refreshing, ice-cold yogurt. The three of them were about to fly toward us until Hisham furiously shouted, "Pick the net off the ground. It might get caught in the thorns. Pick it up off the dirt... yallaha!"

They did not hear him, I was sure, because they kept dragging the nets on the dusty ground. By the time they reached the other end of the field, it was almost four o'clock in the afternoon. We only had minutes before the Wild Lions would show up and Hisham would lead us in the greatest battle of our young lives. We had all brought our soccer jerseys with us and stashed them in Barrya's second room. Our jerseys were not original. Each one of us had brought whatever jersey we had and dyed it with blue dye that Hisham had bought from a store in the big city. What we all hoped would be bright blue turned a dark bluish color that resembled ink. It left its stains on our necks and backs. Nevertheless it was one unifying color instead of the many colors we wore in our previous matches against the Wild Lions. Only Hisham, Ahmed, Kamal, and I could afford to buy soccer shoes; also, Haleem wore cotton shoes with threads peeling from the sides. The rest of our team members were barefooted.

By the time we managed to tie the loose ends of the nets to the wooden goals, we saw the first three members of the Wild Lions walking toward the field. Hisham, who kept looking toward the end of the town and waiting anxiously for the Wild Lions to show up, smiled and said, "Here they come."

We all looked, and the fear and anticipation for a real battle started filling our stomachs with tingling nausea. Hisham's voice tried to wake the wolves inside us when he shouted, "Everyone get ready with one lap around the field. Let's warm up."

Let's warm up? Is he crazy? We have been working for hours in the merciless sun and he wants us to warm up. Besides, Hamid and I were swimming for three hours, before the mandatory labor of building two goals, making nets and stealing pieces of woods from Haleem's father stock, and now Hisham wants us to warm up, I said to myself and the others probably said to themselves, too. In fact, I saw Ahmed and Kamal lying on the ground as the rest of us took off our pajamas and got into our dark blue jerseys.

We were tired and thirsty, and the only boost of energy we found was in the large jar of yogurt that Barrya held in her hand as she watched us building the goals. The yogurt was fresh and cold, and no one knew how it could stay cold after all this time in the sun, but it gave us a shot of fresh chill before she said, "I will wait for you boys after the game," and she left before the game started.

Hisham was still buzzing with a strange injection of energy when we saw the Wild Lions walking toward us in their matching uniforms with the confidence of a well-equipped army regiment marching toward a guaranteed victory. Hisham reached into a plastic bag and pulled out the trophy. He looked at it, then us, and said to us in the voice of a commander who is preparing his ill-equipped army for a desperate battle, "I wrote the name of our team on this trophy. Don't let them take it from us."

We looked at him with fear and wonder in our eyes. It was Kamal who was able to say something that boosted our morale and forced us into action, "We will wipe the ground with their faces," he said, and then we all stood up and stretched and warmed up, preparing for the game of our lives.

It was amazing to see real goals with nets. Although the nets looked like the raggedy robe of a nomad and the pieces of colorful threads flew as the wind blew, we felt joy as we shot the soccer ball inside the goal, and the ball stayed in the goal as our goalie Adnan dove to save it. To us it all looked as real as what we saw on television. The excitement took us a long way. We felt that we had found the only elements that we needed to win and that we had found the secret elixir that would turn our luck around and beat the Wild Lions once and for all. We had discovered the weapon that would not only defeat our archenemies, but also would make us able to defeat all the other teams that we heard about, the Solidarity, the Arabians, the Brotherhood, and the Knights— all of them. One day they would be here on our field, and we would defeat them all. We were ready.

2

I never saw Hisham cry before or after that day as we sat at Barrya's house trying to lick the wounds from the battle. We looked at each other and tried to make sense of what happened, but no one had an answer. Adnan's face was covered with blood. Barrya and Haleem tried to stop the bleeding from his nose, and she railed at Hamid and Hisham for letting the Wild Lions beat up Adnan.

"It's always my weakest boy because he is so sweet and smart," she said and turned to where Hisham and Hamid stood near the door and concluded, "You should have stopped them."

Hamid stood by the door as he looked to the empty stretch of land between Barrya's house and the rest of the town. He was worried and expecting more trouble. He wanted to chase the Wild Lions and beat them up for what they had done to us, but we all hoped that the day would end and we all could go home. Barrya brought us fresh yogurt and kept a dirty, wet towel on Adnan's forehead. "They will never get away with it," Hamid said as he gritted his teeth, "I swear, I will break their heads."

When the game started, we had very little hope of winning. The most we hoped for was a tie or a defeat with small difference in the number of goals; a two- or three-point difference would be acceptable. That was all we hoped for. In the first ten minutes of the game the back defender of the Wild Lions shot a ball that crossed over our heads all the way to Merheb, the Wild Lions' fastest striker, who stabilized the ball and sprinted toward our goal and our poor goalie Adnan, who was basically defenseless, and with a powerful and accurate shot the Wild Lions scored their first goal. Hisham screamed and shouted with his cracking voice, urging us to act like men and to start playing like real soccer players. His voice and encouragement were different from the shouts he used in previous games. He did not call us losers or weaklings; instead, he used the trophy as the symbol of our resilience and will.

"Do you want them to take away your trophy?" Hisham said, referring to his trophy as ours. It was our trophy now. By the end of the first half, we were so tired. We were dragging our feet and our bodies to defend the relentless attacks and the offensives from the Wild Lions. Almost our entire team was on the defensive, defending the goal, and our poor goalie Adnan jumped from one corner to another just to save as many shots as he possibly could. The left side of his face was covered with dirt, and his clothes had turned into a tanned colored uniform from the many layers of dust that covered them. The field looked as if there was a spread of deadly epidemic on the Wild Lions' half because none of the players were there except for the their goalie, who looked bored because the rest of the Wild Lions were on our half of the field, tormenting us with shot after shot and offense after offense and one, perfect pass after another. Somehow we managed to resist. Hamid dove to the ground so many times that he looked like a dirt monster. The Wild Lions gained almost one hundred corner kicks. Most of these would almost become certain goals if it were not for Kamal, Hamid, and Haleem, who defended the goals with jumps and leaps and double kicks that made them look like warriors defending the most holy of things.

To us, one to nothing for the first half of the game was the best we could hope for, and we were happy with our effort and ready to surrender. The sweat and blood from our feet and our toes had made the rest of the game seem like an eternity of pain and torture, but for Hisham, the trophy and the soccer balls were being protected. Moreover, he wanted a victory, of any kind, to humiliate the Wild Lions. He kept pushing and screaming, "Yallah shabab (let's do it, boys)! Don't give up! We can do it!"

It was the first time ever, and even before my family moved to Balluria, that our team had lost to the Wild Lions with fewer than five goals in the first half of a match. So we felt that we were winning. We would still surrender the trophy and we would not get the three soccer balls, but the game was a victory. Hisham calmed down as he realized that no matter how loud he was and how encouraging he might be, one to nothing was the best score that we could reach, so he stopped talking. We were all tired and wanted to rest, and all the team wanted to go to Barrya's house and drink fresh, cold yogurt. A slight glimmer of hope urged us on.

We started the second half and the agonizing pain of relentless attacks started again by the Wild Lions. Hamid and Kamal, our best defenders, almost put their lives on the line for that half an hour as I saw them sliding on the rough surface of the field to save our weak goalie, Adnan, from the sneaky thrusts of Merheb and Imad, the skilled and fast strikers of the Wild Lions. We were sure that the second and third goals for the Wild Lions were unavoidable. But to our surprise, and definitely to the surprise of the Wild Lions, with only ten minutes left in the game, Hamid, who played rear defender, passed long to Hisham on the left field, who then sent a perfect over pass to Ahmed, a pass too high for the short Wild Lions' defender to reach. By strange luck and ability, Ahmed was alone by the Wild Lions' goal. I saw Ahmed leap to the sky like a bird and hit the ball with his head. I did not know whether to cry or to laugh as I saw their goalie diving to the ball to catch it, but he missed it, and the ball went into the net. We had scored a goal! Ahmed, the worst player in our team, scored the perfect goal, one long awaited. The entire team ran toward Ahmed; Hamid, Abdullah, Haleem, Ashraf, Salah, Kamal, Hisham, and even our goalie Adnan and me. We all ran toward Ahmed, who was not sure of what happened, but he started running away from us, just as Paolo Rossi did when he scored a goal against Germany. That glimmer of hope grew into a blazing fire.

I saw Hisham running like a crazy man chasing Ahmed to kiss him and hug him. We all chased Ahmed, who was a little disoriented; either from the joy of scoring a goal or from the minor concussion that he got from hitting the soccer ball with his head. He did not believe that he had scored a goal against the Wild Lions. The joy was overwhelming, and we wanted to quit the game right then because we knew how angry the Wild Lions would be. We saw that as their captain started to shout at them using all of the demeaning terms he usually saved for us. We knew that he could do that because his father was Comrade Uraiby, and that meant he could get away with calling other kids names like morons, donkeys, and sons of whores. These names showed his real upbringing and the manners he was used to in his house.

We could not play anymore. We were spent by the joy of our goal, and if there had been a fair and just referee, he would have blown his whistle, ending the game at that time because it was the most joyful moment of our lives, the lives of the Wolves. We walked back to our half of the field slowly, and that's when Mazen, the captain of the Wild Lions, declared as he held the ball in the midfield where the kickoff spot was, with a clear authoritative voice, that the game would be extended for half an hour.

"What? No way," Hisham protested.

"It is the wasted time. You took very long celebrating your goal," Mazen said.

"It was only two minutes," Hisham said.

"No, it was longer than that and for all the other time you wasted. So twenty minutes will be added," Mazen said with a wicked gleam in his eyes.

Hisham, who in my mind was ready to quit and keep the score the way it was and keep his trophy, bargained with a plea, "Five minutes maximum time."

"No, twenty minutes," Mazen would not be swayed.

We did not really know what was happening between Hisham and Mazen, not until we saw Hamid running toward the center of the field. It appeared that Samir, one of the Wild Lions who was a known bully, had put his hands on Hisham's chest and pushed him to the ground as they argued about the time extension. We all looked and saw Hamid getting closer to where Hisham had just gotten up and call Mazen a son of donkey, and that was when all hell broke loose. The last thing I clearly heard was Mazen's voice calling Hisham and all of us the sons of whores. That's when I saw Hamid land a powerful punch to Mazen's face, and the rest was a mix of cries, shouts, sweat, tears, blood, and pain. The entire team of the Wild Lions attacked Hamid, like a real pack of wild lions attacking a singled-out wolf, and he barely managed to defend himself until Hisham was by his side aiding him. Kamal and Haleem were the first of us to reach where the fight was, and then I saw two bodies going down to the ground. They were those of Kamal and Merheb, the fast striker of the Wild Lions. They wrestled down to the ground, and I saw Kamal's arm around Merheb's neck, then it was all-out war. For ten minutes, which seemed like an eternity, we used our hands, legs, heads, and some rocks to battle the Wild Lions as they tore our goals and shredded our nets in a clear expression of anger and hate of our team.

In our battle, the Wild Lions lived up to their reputation, and so did we, the Wolves. We managed to exchange punch for punch and kick for kick and thrown rock for thrown rock. Kamal and Hamid were our best fighters. I did not see my attacker's face, but he was a bigger boy who hit my face with his hand, and I kicked him in his abdomen. He fell to the ground as I tried to retreat to where Adnan, the weakest of us, was getting a severe beating from one of the toughest kids, the kid whose nickname was Hanooshy. None of us knew his real name, but we later learned he was Comrade Uraiby's nephew. Hanooshy was not even playing at the time. He had been there standing on the sidelines throughout the game. I thought it was because, as his nickname described his rounded body, he must not be very athletic or prone to anything that involved exerting himself. He got involved, though. During the word exchange and then the first fist exchange when we saw Mazen and Hisham get into a fight, he looked for someone to fight from his place by the goal. He found his prey in our thin, weak goalie, Adnan, who was walking toward the center of the field where the battle was just beginning. Hanooshy pushed poor Adnan to the ground and punched him in his face. I heard Adnan crying for help and felt a fierce adrenalin rush and a boost of courage to save my new friend even though Hanooshy's massive size would normally make any kid think twice before making such a decision. I jumped on Hanooshy to push him away from Adnan, put my arm around his neck, and tried to pull him away. Hanooshy reached out, grabbed my hand, and twisted it. I fell on the ground and looked as Hanooshy went back to prey on Adnan.

That's when I saw Hamid, who had been jumping from one place to another, kicking here and punching there. Hamid was striking Hanooshy in face with his bare foot and saving poor Adnan from what looked like certain permanent body damage. Hamid struck Hanooshy with his foot right on the face, and that's when I saw a streak of darker than normal blood oozing from Hanooshy's nose. Abdullah was chasing one of the Wild Lions with a stone in his hand, and I saw Kamal beating Mazen with both hands. Ahmed was trying to run away from the Wild Lions' short defender, who chased him almost to Barrya's mud hut. Two of the Wild Lions' boys pulled the goal nets along with the pieces of wood all the way to the ground and tore them to pieces. Haleem was kicking his feet karate-style, trying to defend himself from the Wild Lions' fat goalie. Then suddenly it was all over.

We lost our newly built goals with their colorful nets when the Wild Lions' boys pulled them to the ground. For some of us, the victory was complete, as we tied the game fair and square at one to one. And Hisham kept his trophy. As we sat in Barrya's mud, licking our wounds, we braced ourselves for the worst, for punishment from our parents. We braced ourselves for the anger that Comrade Uraiby might have and what he might do, knowing that his son and his nephew were beaten by a bunch of little hoodlums who called themselves the Wolves. It was almost dark when we decided that it was time that we face the unavoidable. Barrya announced that Adnan's bleeding had stopped and that it was time for us to leave. We left Barrya's house and walked silently toward the town, which we thought was waiting for us because we were sure that they must have noticed the blood and tears on the Wild Lions as they walked through the streets and in between the houses crossing our town to their houses with blood, dust, and defeat.

As we were walking, I was sure that I was untouchable to Comrade Uraiby because my father was the mayor. Also untouchable was Ahmed, because his father was Sheikh Jawad and Kamal, who lived as Sheikh Jawad's adopted son. For the rest, and especially for Hamid, things were not looking so bright. Hamid, however, was not afraid at all. In fact, he kept saying that he should have struck Mazen and Hanooshy with a rock and not with his foot. When we reached the town, we saw no sign that anyone had heard of our little battle with the Wild Lions. People who were walking toward the mosque to say their early evening prayers barely noticed our pack of wounded, yet victorious Wolves. We were relieved and felt like they must have been supportive of what we did. Each one of us went to his house and waited for the evening call of gathering that Hisham would sound, "Arya, arya, arya."

That night Hisham was silent as we waited and waited. We could not wait for the morning to come. I woke up and even before I washed my face, I left the house and went directly to Hamid's. I wanted to make sure that my friend was OK. I wanted to make sure that Comrade Uraiby had not paid a visit to my friend's house and arrested him in the middle of the night. Hamid was up when I got there, eating breakfast. The fresh smell of the bread eased my fears as I sat eating the white cheese and drinking the tea. We both wondered about the rest of the Wolves. When we finished breakfast, we left the house and went to the town's square looking for the pack. We met Kamal and Ahmed and were later joined by Abdullah and Adnan. The look in their eyes was that of fear and anxiety because Hisham was not there. We were afraid that something had happened to him, but all our fears disappeared when Haleem and Ashraf joined us.

"Did you hear what happened?" Haleem asked.

"What happened? Did you see Hisham?" Hamid asked again.

"Yes," Haleem said. "We saw him going to the soccer field this morning. We all must go there now."

"Why?" Kamal asked.

"You will see," Haleem said, and we all walked toward the soccer field.

As we got closer to the field, we could see Hisham standing there, looking at what appeared to be a thousand shimmering lights filling our beloved field. Thousands of reflections filled the field in what looked like a large expanse of stunning diamonds, rubies, and sapphires and all the precious stones of the earth. The sight was amazing, and we almost believed it, and as Haleem kept saying, "You will see when you get there." We saw the reality of that morning.

At the field, we noticed that Hisham was looking at the field with the eyes of a farmer who was watching his farm flood with water or harvested by thousands and thousands of locusts. On the soccer field were not small light bulbs, nor were they precious stones, but rather there were millions of tiny pieces of broken glass that came from broken bottles, jars, windows, and almost everything made of glass. Our goals and the nets were broken and shredded to pieces, and there was not an inch that not covered with a sharp piece of glass. We stood there not knowing what to say or what to do. We all knew that it was the doing of Comrade Uraiby, who probably was angry because of what happened to his son and his nephew, so he had undoubtedly dispatched a squad of the party militia to spread our field with an ocean of broken glass. We all knew that there was nothing we could do that would bring us revenge unless my father or Sheikh Jawad were willing to get involved, which was impossible, and it was better for us not even to mention what happened to anyone.

Later we learned the details from Abdullah, who heard the story from a man called Hillaly. Abdullah told us that Hillaly said he was at the party headquarters when he saw Mazen, Hanooshy, and the rest of the team entering the building with blood on their faces and jerseys. He also said that Mazen and Hanooshy went directly to the party headquarters commander's office where Mazen's father, Comrade Uraiby, was holding a meeting. They burst into the meeting crying and with blood on their faces. Comrade Uraiby was furious and wanted to know the names of the kids who did that to his son and nephew, and luckily for us, the first name Mazen mentioned was Ahmed's, the son of Sheikh Jawad, and Comrade Uraiby decided to take another course of action instead of bringing the issue to the fearsome sheikh. Later, and thankfully without asking his son for any other names, he just ordered a group of the party militia to collect bottles and empty jars and broken window glass from all the garbage in Balluria and fill our soccer field with broken glass so no one would ever play there again. Also, he promised his son that he would build him his own soccer field.

As we stood there staring forlornly at our beloved soccer field, we waited for Hisham to say something because, after all, it was his field. It was his game and his challenge that he arranged, and we supported him to the end. It was his battle, and he was the leader who led us to the victory that meant everything to us at that perfect moment. Hisham looked at the field and said with clear and resolute conviction of a true believer, "I will clean it, even if I have to do it with my bare hands, even if they fill the field with nails or bombs, I will clean it and we will play again, but at least the sons of whores did not take our trophy."

As we looked at Hisham, he worked hard to blink back his tears. Yes, at that moment and as we looked that half-rusted, blood-stained trophy in Hisham's clenched hand, we believed in Hisham's words. Every word he said was true. The battle was ours, and the trophy was not his alone. It was our trophy.

The Book of the Gypsy Witches

The Last Dance of the Aging Gypsy

1

"I was in tears as I danced in the wedding of Sheikh Jawad and Sabrya," said the Gypsy woman, "but I had to be happy even if the daggers of pain and sadness ripped through my heart. As I said, we give love but never get it from anyone. I loved Sheikh Jawad and I dreamed many times that he would love me, honor me, protect me, or at least keep me from my degrading life, but to him, he was the sheikh, and I was a Gypsy.

"At his wedding night, I sang and danced until my feet could not carry me anymore. Everyone thought that I was dancing because I was happy or because I was a Gypsy and that's what I do. I was dancing to heal myself from pain, the unbearable pain of lost love, and the eternal wait for true love, love that would never be. When Jawad married Sabrya, I made her up for him; I painted her cheeks with rosy red and painted her lips with dirum, and I put henna on her hands. I made up the woman who would lie with the only man I loved and the only man who loved me." She said this with an emotionless veneer that covered a lingering pain.

"That night I walked alone, rejecting all the men in the wedding who thought they could lie with me because I was a Gypsy who dances in weddings. No one believed a Gypsy could be faithful but I was faithful to Jawad, who was never faithful to me. One night before the wedding, Jawad was here. He lay with me, and he put his head between my breasts and breathed with a fiery breath. I asked him what was wrong with him, and he said that he only felt safe when he was in my arms.

"I never wanted him to leave that night. I wanted to die in his arms," the Gypsy woman said as she blew her gray smoke from the side of her mouth. "Sabrya never loved her husband. She did not like the way he talked. She did not like the way he ate, and she did not like the way he lay with her. Sabrya was a cold woman.

"One night, the moon did not appear, even though it was the fourteenth night of the month. That night Irar and Jawad buried the dead body of Reyhan, the only son of Sheikh Badr, near the seven palm trees."

"The seven palm trees?" Salam jerked to attention as if he were stung by a scorpion. "The seven palm trees?" he repeated.

"Yes," the Gypsy woman said.

"That's where Hamid took us to see the wolves."

"Yes, I know. He told me. He told me everything."

"How did he die? I mean the sheikh's son. How did he die?" the man asked.

"They killed him," the woman said matter-of-factly.

"Who killed him?" the man asked.

"None of the people in Balluria knew who killed him or even that he was dead, but I did. That night, Jawad came to my house and told me to prepare dinner and areq."

"Alcohol?"

"Yes, I thought he wanted to drink areq and lie with me before he went to his house, but he came here with Irar and Reyhan, Sheikh Badr's son. That was one year after the wedding and three years before Hanan was born," the Gypsy woman added. The woman looked at him as if she could see him and said with deep conviction, "If you saw Reyhan, you would think you were looking at the moon itself. Masha'allah, he was handsome and white. His father, Sheikh Badr, loved him so much and wanted to marry him to the daughter of Sheikh Waitan, but Jawad and Irar had other plans."

"But, why did they kill him?" the man asked.

"Oh, my dear son, Jawad was a peasant Leffu with no roots, and Irar was a half-man-half-wolf. These kind of men kill for reasons only they understand."

"Did you see Sheikh Jawad and Irar kill Reyhan?"

"No, son, men in these parts don't kill in front of a woman," she said, "but they made him drink areq. And when he was drunk, Jawad asked him if he remembered what he said when Jawad asked for the hand of his sister Sabrya in marriage.

"'Yes,' Reyhan answered.

"'Do you remember what you said about me?' Jawad asked as his eyes turned blood-red.

"'No, but this is all in the past. You are married to her now, and you are my brother-in-law,' Reyhan said with a tipsy smile.

"'I still remember your words, Reyhan. I still remember them. I have never forgotten what you said,' I heard Jawad say with the stench of death steaming from his mouth," the Gypsy woman said.

"'I think the areq is playing with your head, Jawad,' Reyhan said as he heard the serious tone of Jawad's voice through the haze of the liquor.

"You said, 'I will not let my sister marry this peasant Leffu, who has no roots and has no good family name,'" Jawad said as he fixed his bloody eyes in Reyhan's face. 'I have never forgotten, Reyhan,' Jawad said, and looked at Irar, who fixed his snake eyes on Reyhan as if he was looking at a prey.

"Then they said to me that they would walk toward the prairie and come back later. That night Sheikh Jawad came back, and I saw blood on his dress," the Gypsy woman said, taking yet another drag on her cigarette.

"Why didn't you tell his father, Sheikh Badr?" the man asked.

"Son, Sheikh Badr was ill at the time, and Jawad was his son-in-law. Besides, who would believe a Gypsy woman?" she replied.

"Why would he do that? Why would Jawad kill his brother-in-law?" the man asked with civilized innocence.

"Jawad wanted to be the sheikh. He wanted the lands, the livestock, the status. No one on this earth would have stopped him, and the weak and unfortunate Reyhan was in his way," she said.

Salam looked at her, trying to comprehend how she could calmly sit there, blowing a cloud of gray smoke out the side of her mouth.

"To be a sheikh is to kill a sheikh, and Jawad killed many of them, sheikhs and peasants. He wanted to be like Nasser the Blond. He wanted to be like Salim Al-Thubban. He wanted to be the only sheikh in these parts."

The man ran a shaky hand through his hair. "What happened after that?"

"Jawad and Irar buried the dead body of Reyhan by the seven palm trees. The townspeople looked for Reyhan everywhere. His father even sent men to the marshes looking for his son because he thought he had drowned but he never knew that his son's body lay near him. The poor man died within one year of his son's death. The townspeople thought that Sheikh Badr died of a broken heart, but I know that he died a slow death from poisoning."

"He was poisoned? Poisoned by whom?" the man asked, knowing the answer, but not wanting to believe his uncomfortable feeling of connection to the story he was hearing nor the many dead people in it.

"Who else?" the woman said with a smile reserved for humoring the naive. "Who else would have the poison but the son of a snake?"

"Who?" the man asked, unable to curb the noticeable excitement of his curiosity.

"It was Irar. He could not wait for Sheikh Badr Al-Ghathban to die a slow death while he mourned his only son. Irar wanted Sheikh Badr to die quickly so Jawad would be the sheikh. One night as the ailing Sheikh Badr waited for his coffee after dinner, Irar poured the snake poison he always carried with him in Sheikh Badr's coffee when Khanger was not aware, and the poor sheikh died three days later, vomiting out his organs."

"All of this so Jawad could be the sheikh of Balluria?" the man wondered.

"All of what? All of what?" The Gypsy woman had an angry tone in her scratchy voice.

"Why do you think men in these parts claim to be bravest men on earth? Why do you think men in these parts are incapable of simple love, and if they do love they reach the shores of complete madness and start running with wolves and gazelles in the deserts?" Her anger dripped like acid from her voice. "Sheikh after sheikh and kill after kill, Sheikh Jawad claimed his power in these parts, and for me, I watched him and Irar contemplating killings and watched him and Irar burying bodies by the seven palm trees for thirty years," the Gypsy woman said. "And you are asking, why and for what?"

She paused as she tried to choose the appropriate words to reveal what seemed like a secret that she kept all her life. Then she said with a siren voice and a smile that embraced the absurd, "It's Balluria, my son. It's Balluria, with all of its dust and all of its mystery. Balluria and its secret robes that tie men by their necks and drag them here, and when they arrive, they never depart, and they never get enough, as much as they drink from the water of Euphrates, it never satisfies their thirst," the Gypsy woman said as she poured some tea for herself and her guest.

2

"Do you want more tea?" the Gypsy woman asked.

"Yes, I will prepare it," Salam replied.

"You are my guest."

"No, please let me prepare it," Salam begged, politely. "Please tell me more."

"After the death of Sheikh Badr, the Sharify tribe had no one to claim the sheikh's place because Reyhan, the son of Sheikh Badr, was the only male son of the sheikh, and the sheikh had only one brother who moved to the capital city and became urban. None of the cousins claimed the sheikh's place for fear of Jawad, who made it clear to them that he would slice the foot that stepped on the carpet of the sheikh's place. He killed the sheikh and took his place and with it, he took Balluria and the lives of its people.

"I was there when Sheikh Jawad prepared his first dinner as the sheikh of Balluria. Irar was very happy and jubilant, and I saw him ordering the many guesthouse servants to wear their rifles as they greeted the guests. It was two nights after they buried Sheikh Badr Al-Ghathban," the Gypsy woman said. "Finally, Irar had what he always wanted for himself but could not achieve; he wanted to be a sheikh, but instead, he made Jawad one. That was not enough for Sheikh Jawad, who wanted to be the sheikh of all sheikhs. A dark heart is dark forever. When Hanan was born, I thought that Sheikh Jawad would change. I thought that he would start to learn how to love, but he never did. He waited until his daughter Hanan was two years old and his son Ahmed was born. He waited for few months, and then he killed his wife, Sabrya."

"He killed her?" the man asked, shaking his head.

"Yes, my son. Sheikh Jawad told me that he'd never lain with Sabrya after she was pregnant with his son, Ahmad, because he was afraid that she would kill him because she knew that he killed her brother, Reyhan."

"How did she know?" the man asked.

"I don't know, but she never slept with her husband after her brother's death," the Gypsy woman said as she sneered and said the name Sabrya again.

For the man, it seemed as if she never liked the poor Sabrya, and he thought to himself that it was a jealousy that had lasted forever, but it was apparent that the Gypsy woman resented Sabrya even in death.

"Sabrya had no love for her husband; she told me that and she wished that she could kill him in his sleep, but he never slept," the Gypsy woman said. "She told me that because she thought that I would keep the secret but I told Sheikh Jawad."

"Why did you tell him?"

"Because we Gypsies have no loyalty. I only had loyalty to Sheikh Jawad because I loved him," the Gypsy woman said and let out the same laugh that chased shadows of the palm tree leaves.

"Jawad knew that about his wife, and he wanted her dead. He wanted to drown her in the river after she birthed Ahmad. He wanted her dead because he did not need her anymore after he became the sheikh and after she gave him two children, after she gave him a son."

"He killed his own wife and the mother of his two children?" Salam asked.

"Yes, my son. Sheikhs in these parts had no heart for weak women, especially their wives."

"How did he kill her?" Salam asked, feeling as though simply asking questions about this horrible tale would give him some control over its course.

"It was not he who killed her. It was one of the many women who wore black robes and lived at the sheikh's house. It was Irar who gave that woman the poison to put in Sabrya's yogurt."

"Yogurt?" Salam asked numbly.

"Yes, as she broke her fast after Ramadan, she drank the yogurt, and in the middle of the night she woke up screaming in agony, and by early morning she was dead. I saw her body; it looked as if it were drained of its blood. She looked pale and yellow, the poor woman; she followed her brother, Reyhan, and her father, Sheikh Badr. This fate was better for her, though. To die is better than to be Sheikh Jawad's wife."

3

The rain fell unremittingly outside the mud hut. The drops hitting the roof of the hut made the sound of an aging orchestra, played with invisible instruments as the wind blew gently on the dried palm leaves, dangling from the ends of the crossed branches making the ceiling whistle with voices of the past. Salam sat in the doorway, leaning his back against the mud wall as he wrapped his hands around his knees and tried to create a sense of ease while listening to the blind Gypsy woman telling him the tales of Balluria, the town that he loved as a teenager. He never realized that the tales of blood and pain could be hidden behind the immaculate innocence and the massive currents of love and lust of early adulthood. Salam could not comprehend the evolution of his senses through the spectacular window on a world that looked promising and willing. To his surprise, and to his righteous unwillingness to accept the discovery of an alternative truth to his past, that very truth had clamped on to his heart and squeezed the juices of untarnished memory. Yet, a revelation of truthfulness cleansed his rooted senses and drained his backed-up feelings of nausea, guilt, abandonment, and despair that he had lived with for so long made him willing to listen and learn more. He wanted to hear more tales of people he had seen only once or twice, people who in one strange and unexplainable way were part of his life or his father's life. He had never understood why his father never liked Balluria, not until now as he listened to the stories of the notorious sheikh and his climb to power and dominance of the entire marsh region.

As he inhaled the delicious smoke of his Marlboro, he felt at peace with his familiarity and analogical connectivity to the names and events that came out of a perfect mouth of an aged blind Gypsy woman who once was a goddess of temptation and secrecy. She was the same mysterious young Gypsy woman that made many of his boyhood friends wonder about the secrets she kept under her thin, barely decent garments. He remembered that many times she served yogurt to his entire soccer team after many defeats by the Wild Lions. She was always dressed in a flimsy garment that revealed more than it covered and allowed the treasures of the Gypsy dancer's body to be available for viewing by the many wide-open eyes of the fatigued Wolves as they sat around the mud hut to catch their breaths and talk about why they lost the game. She watched them many times, as they listened to Hisham making another promise that he would defeat the Wild Lions in the next week's game.

He remembered that one time he looked at her breasts as she leaned and bandaged his friend Adnan's wound from a fight with the Wild Lions, and revealed a majestic set of olive tanned breasts that looked like an invitation to a dream. He remembered that it was the memory of the Gypsy woman's breasts that made him start to draw a Gypsy woman's cleavage the next day in lazy fourth-period class when the math teacher, Mr. Mohamed Tabra, was too sick to attend. The man remembered that his memory was vivid and clear as he traced the pencil with dark shades and curvy lines and drew the breasts with unquestionable accuracy and perfect lines. It was then that he realized that he had the gift, the gift of turning paint into live, tempting objects. As he sat in the doorway looking at her, he wondered if she was the reason he had become an artist. The man wondered if the blind Gypsy woman, who never stopped smoking cigarettes and drinking tea, was the reason he chose his path in life and whether she was the reason for his return. She had the soft hands in his nightmares, the same soft hands that wrapped a silky rope on his neck every night, the hands that looked exactly the same as those of the Gypsy woman as she moved the tea kettle on the small fire or when she lit her endless cigarettes.

"Soon enough there was no sheikh in these parts who dared to challenge Sheikh Jawad and no other sheikh made bigger feasts than him," the Gypsy woman said. "People also forgot about his roots and started calling to Sheikh Jawad with 'Sheikh, may your life be long.' Only one man never paid respect to Sheikh Jawad. And that was a mistake that he paid for with his life."

"Who was that man?"

"It was the Sheikh Mutter Al-Nasser, the son of Sheikh Nasser the Blond."

"Who was Nasser the Blond?" Salam asked.

"Nasser the Blond was the sheikh who chased Sheikh Badr Al-Ghathban and the Sharify tribe out of the marshland after the battle of Um Nakhla."

The man realized that if he kept asking more questions he would get answers that sounded as strange as the names he was asking about, so he asked a different question to keep the mind of the Gypsy woman focused on the point of the story that he traveled thousands of miles to hear.

"Why this man, Mutter the son of Nasser, why did he not respect Sheikh Jawad?"

"Son, Sheikh Mutter was a son of a sheikh who was a son of a sheikh, and all of his grandfathers and great grandfathers were sheikhs. It was an ancestry that is as old as the desert itself, and Sheikh Jawad was a peasant who claimed his place as a sheikh with blood and sweat. So there was no way Sheikh Mutter would respect Jawad as his peer. Jawad never instigated the anger of Sheikh Mutter. He waited and waited for an opportunity that would bring the two men into a challenge with him. He waited as Irar continued to remind him, 'Be patient, Jawad. One day we will teach Mutter, who is the real sheikh in these parts. We will show him who really has the heart of a sheikh.' Irar kept saying that to Jawad, and eventually fate brought the two sheikhs to face each other to prove who was the sheikh of all sheikhs in these parts."

"When was that?"

"It was when the party officials needed to name a sheikh to meet the president, and they had to choose between Mutter Al-Nasser, the son of Nasser the Blond, and Sheikh Jawad. Jawad knew that if Sheikh Mutter was to be the chosen sheikh to meet the president, he would be named as the sheikh of all sheikhs in these parts, and that is something neither Jawad nor Irar were willing to let happen." She paused, deep in memory, causing her guest to become impatient.

"So what did they do?"

"They waited for the government to choose."

"Who did the government choose?" he asked, encouraging her to simply tell the story.

"The government chose Sheikh Mutter Al-Nasser," the Gypsy woman said and paused. "That night when Sheikh Jawad knew that the party officials chose Sheikh Mutter, he did not sleep and spent the night at my hut. Irar was with him too. They talked all night."

"What did they talk about?" Salam asked.

"The only thing I remember is Irar saying to Jawad that it was time they take the black dagger out of the cloth that it was wrapped in."

"What did that mean?" Salam asked.

"I didn't know," the Gypsy woman said, "but two nights before, Sheikh Mutter was supposed to go to the capital city to meet with the president. All the people in these parts woke up that morning to the news that Sheikh Mutter was found dead, with his neck cut from ear to ear."

"How did that happen?" Salam asked with apparent curiosity.

"No one knew. Someone had entered Sheikh Mutter's guesthouse as he slept and butchered him in his sleep," she said. "True, no one knew, but I knew. It was Jawad and Irar."

"How did you know?" the man asked

"Because the night before, as the sun was about to dawn, Jawad and Irar came to my hut, and I saw their clothes stained with blood. They had walked all night to Sheikh Mutter's village and killed him with the same black dagger they used to kill all of their enemies and walked back. That's what men in these parts do when it's a matter of honor," the Gypsy woman said.

"The funeral of Sheikh Mutter was the largest ever seen in these parts, and Sheikh Jawad announced at the funeral that he would avenge the death of Sheikh Mutter," she said with a snort of incredulity and a shake of her head. "He kills the man and walks in his funeral. Two days after the funeral, Sheikh Jawad went to the capital city and met with the president, or the divine leader, as they used to call him in those days, and after that day he succeeded in becoming the sheikh of all sheikhs in these parts."

4

"When did Irar die?" Salam asked, uncomfortable with her tears and wanting to direct her to something that would stop them from flowing.

"Who said he died?"

"He's still alive?" he asked with surprised eyes.

"I don't know, my son. No one really knows. He was gone a long time ago."

"Gone where?"

"Back to the desert, back where he came from," the woman answered, content with her belief in such a simple departure.

"I don't understand. Did he die or..."

"No, my son, when Hanan was killed, people said that something had happened to Irar. He started to look for her for many days. He asked about her."

"Why would he ask about Hanan?" The man asked why an evil man like Irar would search for Hanan, the pale classmate he knew long years ago.

"No one knew, but Irar asked about Hanan in the guesthouse of Sheikh Jawad, and when he was told that the sheikh did not allow anyone to mention the name of his slain daughter, who dishonored her father, Irar left the guesthouse and walked the streets, asking if anyone saw Hanan. He asked the children in the streets and asked the women in the vegetable shops if they had seen the most beautiful girl in these parts."

"Was he going mad?" Salam asked again, needing to know why his pale classmate would make an evil man go mad.

"It was the curse of love that Hanan cast over all those who hurt her. She cursed them with love. They all fell in love with her even after she was killed," the Gypsy woman said as her face lit up with the strange glow of the satisfaction of unclaimed revenge.

"I guess Irar was the reason that Hanan was killed, because he was the one who made Jawad a sheikh. If it were not for him, Hanan would have been a Gypsy dancer, and she would have been able to love as she would, and she would have lived the life that was meant for her. If it were not for Irar and Jawad, Hanan would have been the most beautiful Gypsy dancer in these parts, and she would have been loved by all the men. She would have lived a life free of honor, the kind of honor that no one understood. No one understood how to live a life divided between the thrusting desire to love and the heavy inheritance of fake honor," the Gypsy woman said with a siren voice as she looked toward the space in front of the mud hut, seemingly remembering the faces of all of those who had departed.

"Fake honor requires many lives and many, beautiful sacrifices drenched in blood."

"Tell me what happened to Irar," Salam insisted.

"When Irar was visited with the curse of Hanan's love, he roamed the streets of Balluria asking the people about Hanan. Many times people brought him to the guesthouse and told Sheikh Jawad that they found Irar crying and calling for her," the Gypsy woman said.

"What did Sheikh Jawad do?" the man asked.

"Nothing. He told the people to leave the mad old man alone and told Irar to never leave the guesthouse again and never say the name of Hanan again. Then one night, as the men sat in the guesthouse, Irar sat in the place where he had always sat for the past forty years, near the sandals by the entrance of guesthouse," the Gypsy woman said. Then she stopped talking for a moment as she tried to recollect the last night when Irar left Balluria and this Earth forever, never to be seen in these parts again. "That night, Irar looked at Jawad for hours. Then he stood up, looked at Sheikh Jawad, and said, 'You are cursed. I am cursed. All of these men are cursed. We all must seek the forgiveness in Hanan.' The people told me that Sheikh Jawad looked at him with the same bloody eyes that he gazed at all of his victims with but said no words.

"Then Irar said, 'Jawad, it's time for me to leave you. I have made you a sheikh, and we have owned all the possessions a man could ask for in these parts, but one thing we will never have is the love of Hanan, the most beautiful woman here. We will never have it. It's time for me to return to the desert, to my family of wolves and snakes.' Then he looked at all the men in the guesthouse and said, 'Moustaches and daggers, rifles and anger, prayers and chanting, we all howl at the moon like wolves.' Then he started to howl like a wolf, and said, 'Hanan is in the prairie. She is running with the wolves, and I must go with her.' He left the guesthouse running toward the horizon where the prairie began and where the Arabian Sahara is endless. That was when Irar left Balluria and returned to the desert. He left when Sheikh Jawad had no enemies left to fight, no sheep to steal, and no sheikhs to poison. His only enemies were time and the unanticipated deaths of his offspring. That was the last time anyone on this earth saw Irar, the man who everyone thought was half man and half wolf." She stopped talking for long moments, in which only the sound of the rain and wind could be heard.

"So was he really a half-man-half-animal?" Salam asked.

"Does it matter, my son? After forty years of killings, blood, stealing, and destroying the livelihoods and the lives of many people and after inflicting so much pain on the people of Balluria and the people in these parts, the old man realized that what he wanted and what all the men in these parts had wanted for centuries was the love of a beautiful woman." She said this with the comfortable tone of a prophet telling the ultimate truth of a divine revelation. "So does it matter if he was half-man or half-wolf? If he would not be loved by the most beautiful Gypsy dancer in the Arabian Sahara?" the blind old Gypsy woman said, and then asked the man the very same question that he wanted to avoid hearing, "Does anything in this life matter if a man does not have the chance of the love of beautiful woman?"

Salam did not know the answer to that question, nor did he want to know. He forced himself to pretend that he did not understand the question the Gypsy woman was asking, but he could not help himself from thinking about his wife, Emily, who he believed loved him. In his modern way of reasoning, he wanted to seek the truth behind the search for love. He wanted to believe that he was lucky to have the love of his wife, who was a beautiful by all standards American and Arabian. He wanted to understand the necessity of the search for love, the search for the elixir of all elixirs. It was the kind of love that no Gypsy could produce. It was pure love, true and unconditional that makes a half-man-half-wolf, like Irar roam the desert in search of the true love of a young girl. She was the same young girl that once shared meals with his sister, the same girl who looked like a pale princess who was forced out of the royal palace, the same girl who looked lost in thought most of the time and stared at his friend Hamid whenever he was near. She was the same girl that came to their house when his father was the mayor of Balluria, ate meals with his sister and mother, and told stories of Gypsies and the way they danced while he and her brother, Ahmad, clipped soccer players' pictures from the many magazines that Hamid found in the garbage piles of the big city in the scorching heat of the many long and lazy afternoons of Balluria. No one knew that she was also the last Gypsy witch in these parts.

The man stopped asking questions about Irar and Sheikh Jawad and looked at the open space in front of the mud hut. He strained his eyes to see the ruins of the guesthouse of Sheikh Jawad as a convoy of several armored American military vehicles was passing on the main street of the town near the guesthouse of the Sheikh Jawad. The close presence of the American soldiers in what used to be his hometown gave him a strange comfort, a feeling of easiness that his two homelands are not that far from each other, that the world he was familiar with was near and close by. He felt that he missed America, he missed his wife, he missed his home, and he missed his friends and all the people in his life. Although they were thousands of miles away from the mud hut of the Gypsy woman. He wanted to speak to Emily and hear her voice, he wanted to drink from her fountain of reality and assurances she possessed. It was the same feeling he had when he realized that he could not live with Emily, whenever he looked at her eyes and her slender shape. He always felt that she possessed two powers, the power of young and amazingly strong civilization and the inescapable wisdom of an ancient civilization searching for new direction. The tales of the Gypsy woman made him think of the contrast of the two worlds that willingly and unwillingly became the two sources of his life, like water mixed from two rivers, the Mississippi and the Euphrates. He thought how Emily always looked beautiful whenever he looked at her, yet he did not find the scent, the scent that he searched for all of his life; yet at the same time, he could smell it.

He thought of how unfortunate he was for not having both, Emily and the scent. He realized how happy he would be if he could have both, how happy he would be if the Gypsy woman knew about Emily, how beautiful and loving she was. He wanted Emily to hear the tales of the Gypsy woman so she could comprehend his ultimate sadness and his utterly worried mind. He wanted her to hear about all the names and all the people the Gypsy woman told about. He wanted Emily to feel the way he felt as he sat there listening to the tales of blood and revenge and sheiks who killed for mere greed or simple jealousy or even basic lust over woman and power that no one in the world cared about. Who in the hell is Sheikh Jawad in the grand scheme of things? Who the hell is Nasser the Blond or his son Mutter in the grand scheme of things, and who in the hell is Sheikh Badr Al-Ghathban and his son, Reyhan, in the real world, if he can call it the real world. What world is more real to him?

He wanted Emily to be there sitting next to him to understand that he needed solidarity before love. He needed a preemptive promise of understanding and acceptance. He just wanted her there to perhaps catch the scent, and then his two worlds would be one world once and for all.

He never wanted to leave the mud hut like he wanted to that moment but instead he sat and asked for more, more of the tales of blood and revenge and history of his hometown that seemed so alone an abandoned.

He looked at the Gypsy woman as she was struggling to pour tea in the two cups she placed in front of her. He looked at the open space between her mud hut and the guesthouse of Sheikh Jawad in the distance, an Arabian sheikh's guesthouse buzzing with what looked like a frantic movement of soldiers with body armor and a heavy military armored vehicle.

At that moment he realized how different is his two worlds were, which caused him to stop questioning. He leaned back on the door frame of the mud hut, not knowing why he would have a single tear running down his face.

He recalled the many times he was at that guesthouse. Once was with his father when they first arrived in Balluria, when they were invited to eat dinner with Sheikh Jawad as a customary welcome, and other times when Ahmad, the son of Sheikh Jawad, kept inviting him, Hamid, Adnan, and all Wolves of the soccer team to dinner or lunch at his father's guesthouse for various occasions. He neither understood what the Gypsy woman was saying about Irar, nor could he dignify the half-man-half-wolf theory. As a young teenager in Balluria, the first time he saw Irar was on one of the occasions that Ahmad invited the Wolves of the soccer team to his father's, Sheikh Jawad's, guesthouse to eat dinner in the annual forty days' remembrance of the martyrdom of the prophet's grandson. He remembered looking at the man who had a face that seemed carved from the stones of the Arabian Sahara. Salam remembered being mesmerized by the look on the old man's face as he sat in the entrance of the guesthouse like a wax statue with upward little chest and piercing wolf's eyes. The man remembered asking their host, the gentle son of Sheikh Jawad, who the man was.

"That's Uncle Irar. Well, he not really my uncle, but everyone in the house calls him that. He is my father's friend from old times, and he is my father's partner in everything," Ahmad said.

The man also remembered what Kamal said about the stony-looking being of a man: "They say he killed almost thirty men. I wish I could be like him." Kamal said that as he pushed a handful of rice into his mouth. The man remembered that later he asked Hamid about Irar as they lay on the grass in the public garden near the main road of Balluria. "Hamid, who is Irar?"

Hamid looked at him intently and said, "Why are you asking about Irar?"

"No reason, he is just a strange-looking man."

Hamid took a deep breath and said, "He is a thief, an old thief, and the best thief these parts have ever known. He knows the desert routes blindfolded. He can steal anything he wants to, and he is known to be the fastest man with a dagger. Some people say that he killed so many men and others say he killed some desert wolves. He can go to cross the border with ten head of sheep and return to Balluria in ten days. He is the one who taught Sheikh Jawad how to smuggle livestock and weapons, and he taught Sheikh Jawad how to kill."

He saw Irar infrequently, but his name and actions were mentioned periodically. Fathil the Liar said one night, as the group of kids played dominoes in the public garden, "That man was definitely a son of a wolf mother and a human father. I know that for sure. He is too evil to be human." No one disputed his claim this time.

The man remembered that occasionally he saw the bald, thin Irar walking by himself toward the seven palm trees. He saw Sheikh Jawad many times during the celebration of the national days and at his father's office, but he could barely remember the man who looked like a snake and could have been one. He remembered that one night, as he and the boys sat in the guesthouse of Sheikh Jawad listening to Fathil the Liar, who was telling them about how he and Sofia Loren spent the previous week on the beaches of the Mediterranean Sea. In Sheikh Jawad's guesthouse, the dinner was served several times, for whoever showed up at any hour of the night or day. The guesthouse was warm and gave a feeling of strength and security with all the men with faces that looked as if they were carved from the stones of the Arabian Sahara. The man remembered looking at the old man who everyone thought was a son of a snake, or a snake at night and human during the day, the same man that everyone in these parts believed was a son of wolves. The man remembered looking at the old man and seeing something totally human. He remembered seeing Irar as old, tired, and beaten as he sat where he always sat, near the shoes and sandals at the entrance of the guesthouse. He remembered seeing Sheikh Jawad standing up with a plate of food in his hand and taking it to where Irar was sitting oblivious of his surroundings and unaware of his company. Salam remembered that he saw Sheikh Jawad lean and kiss the old man's hand and place the plate in front him. The man remembered that he also saw the old man's snake eyes light with joy as he glimpsed Sheikh Jawad, and when Sheikh Jawad kissed the old man's hand, the old man put his hand on Sheikh Jawad's head, like a good father thanking his good son for respect and help in his old age. As a young teenager in Balluria, he never understood the relationship between Sheikh Jawad and Irar. He always accepted what Ahmed was telling him. "Irar is like my uncle who raised my father. We all call him Uncle Irar in the house."

"He raised Sheikh Jawad. He raised him and protected him like his own son," the Gypsy woman said. She blew the smoke of her cigarette and added, "He raised him to be a man, to be a sheikh, and have a guesthouse. He raised him to be the strongest and the bravest man in these parts, but also the most ruthless and the bloodiest. He raised him to be a sheikh. He taught him how to hate, but he took love and mercy from his heart, and that's why Sheikh Jawad ended the way he did, because he lost the will and the ability to love and to have mercy even with his own flesh and blood."

"Why, and for what?" Salam asked with hidden anger and frustration

"It's the allure of Balluria, and the water of Euphrates; it's the same poison that made twelve thousand men slaughter the grandson of a prophet and his young children, it's the same madness that makes a men in the capital city butcher a young gentle king and riddle his women's bodies with bullets," the Gypsy woman said as she was given a sudden ability to speak mysteriously, wise and articulate. Then she inhaled her cigarette, let out a thick cloud of gray smoke, and spoke calmly as she seemed to reach the conclusion she aimed to reach.

"Irar was the beast who wanted to control other people's lives and fates and to steal away their dreams for reasons that no one could comprehend, and Jawad was his instrument. It did not matter what the people of Balluria wanted for themselves; the two men decided to run the lives of the people in and around Balluria. No human could have stopped them because Irar and his illegitimate son, Jawad, were willing to drink the blood of anyone who dared stop them. It was fate itself. Everything that happened in Balluria was fate, the blood and the pain. It was fate, just like the existence of Balluria itself." She paused. "Look at it now. It's dust, only dust. It numbs the senses and covers the true colors of the faces," she said as she lit her cigarette and stared sightlessly into the space in front of her mud hut.

The man thought that behind the thick black liquid creeping over her sight and preventing her from seeing the world that she loved with her beautiful, Gypsy eyes, she must be seeing all the faces of all the people she had lived with, all the people she once loved, and all those who departed leaving her forever standing in the eternal dusty winds of Balluria.

The Book of Balluria

Birth of the Sinner Princess

When Sheikh Jawad waited for the birth of his first child, he sat in the guesthouse, talking to Irar, his mentor and only friend. The two men sat in the dark corner of the guesthouse as they contemplated the possible ways of poisoning the herd of one of the richest shepherds in the neighboring village of Tawsheeha. The shepherd was a small competitor of the sheikh, but he was selling sheep more cheaply than Jawad and Irar were, and he needed to be eliminated. The two men talked for hours in the dim light of the kerosene lamp and heard the noise of the labor from the dark room filled with women who wore black robes and sat around Sabrya praying and calling the names of the twelve grandsons of the prophet to aid the thin, bleeding woman delivering her first baby.

The noise was not heard loudly in the guesthouse until the women started shouting, "Prayers and praises to the prophet and his holy family! Mashallalah, she is beautiful!"

When he heard the women, Jawad felt a chill in his spine, and moments later, he felt a warm stream of blood running through his veins. He had not had that feeling before. It was a strange feeling of warmth and closeness, the feeling of fatherhood. To him the voice of his firstborn was the first sound of any true human that he had ever heard. He had been alone for such a long time through so many defining events. He was alone when he started realizing the harsh realities of life and when he killed his first victim. He was alone when he watched as his mother lay with a man who was not his father. He was alone when he joined the gang of thieves and when he crossed the Euphrates, running away from the first police force in Balluria. He was alone when he walked into the guesthouse of Sheikh Badr Al-Ghathban. He was alone at that pivotal moment when he met Irar, and he was alone when he saw Barrya and as he carved his name as a sheikh with blood and sweat. He was alone when and killed his father's killer, and he was alone when he killed other men. And he was alone when he smuggled sheep through treacherous terrain filled with wolves, snakes, and border patrolmen who were all eager to kill him.

He had been alone every moment of his life, but when he heard the giggling of his firstborn child, his coldness and loneliness suddenly disappeared as he felt that there was another human being that belonged to him, one that was his and his alone and would love him for himself and not because he was a sheikh or thief or smuggler and would forgive him regardless of all his sins and shortcomings as a human. He wanted to smile, but Irar watched every move, making sure that he would act like a sheikh. Even at the most emotional moment of Jawad's life, Irar sat in the dark corner and contemplated yet another poisoning or another killing, and for the first time Jawad did not want to talk about killing. He was appalled at the idea itself and wanted to say something to Irar, but his sense of reserve got the best of him, and he waited for the right moment, and then he asked Irar to excuse himself so he could see if his wife was all right

"She will be and I hope it's a boy," Irar said as he grabbed his famous stick that had a ball of tar on its end, the same stick that had caved in so many heads. Irar said his words and walked out of the guesthouse after coughing violently.

Sheikh Jawad entered the house and looked for any woman who could tell him the news. He waited for a moment and then shouted, "One of you women, come out!"

His voice spread fear in the many women who wore black robes. They feared his reaction if he were to know that his firstborn was a girl and that none of the many women who wore black robes wanted to be the bearer of such news, but one of them was brave enough to stick her head out from the small opening of the wooden door and spoke in a shaky voice.

"May Allah bless your child."

"Is it a boy?"

"May Allah give you your wish, Sheikh, but it's a girl, a beautiful girl."

Jawad looked at the woman, realizing that he had never seen her before just the same as many other women in the house who wore black robes. Sheikh Jawad was angry enough to kill that woman at that moment, but he felt weak as he heard what sounded like a child's giggles.

"Is Sabrya all right?"

"Yes, Sheikh, she is."

"What are these voices I hear?"

"It's the child. She did not cry. She was born laughing."

"Go inside and send me the Gypsy woman."

Jawad wanted to go back to his guesthouse, but he waited for a moment, hoping that he could hear the voices of his firstborn child again. Jawad could not move, as he felt that he needed to hear the magical giggle of the infant, and when Barrya exited the room she saw him standing in the courtyard as the southern moon filled the it with silver sparkling rays.

"Sheikh, why are you standing here?"

"I was waiting for you. Did you see the child?"

"Yes, Sheikh. She is beautiful."

"Does she looks like me?" he asked with repressed childish joy.

"She is beautiful, Sheikh. She has your eyes," Barrya said trying to cover the sadness in her voice.

"The woman said she was born laughing. Is that true?"

"Yes, and that's a good sign. It means she will bring joy and happiness to you, like I did." Barrya tried to emphasize the validity of her existence.

"Go to your home, and I will follow you."

That night as he laid with the Gypsy woman, Barrya was more sad than happy. She knew that he would love his wife, Sabrya, more than her, and she knew that he would love his daughter more than both of the women, so she tried to claim her place in his heart too; she told Sheikh Jawad that Hanan could be her daughter.

"Because of my water."

"Let us not speak of this matter to anyone. I feel like I have a family for the first time, Barrya."

"Am I part of your family?" the Gypsy woman asked.

The sheikh never answered.

The Book of the Man

Pink Hearts and Flowers

1

What is true love? How does it feel when it enters the heart? Is it the rushing feeling of blood and warm-faced numbness? Is love the feeling of being in the place and time when you want the entire world to stand still? In Baghdad I always attended an all-boys school. The girls' school was next to ours, but there were no mixed classes. My classmates and I looked at the girls' school through the many small holes in the high walls. We made the holes whenever the custodians were not watching. There were other holes that had been made by many students who had walked the halls of our school before us. We gazed at the girls' school from the top of the high walls protecting the forbidden city of golden noise and delicious unknowns, the forbidden world of pink hearts and flowers; girls were in their teen years with ponytails, school skirts, and many chances for love. We could not climb the walls or enter the girls' school because the punishment would have been so severe. The ramification would have been deadly if the parents or the older brothers of the girls knew about any boy who harassed their daughters or sisters. So we resorted to the minimal chance encounters that we could possibly get. We would pretend to be distracted by something on the path home after school in hopes of the girls catching up with us as they were leaving school fifteen minutes after us. I decided that the teachers arranged for such timing so the boys would not mix with girls. This arrangement and that wall only made the girls that much more attractive to our love-starved juvenile selves.

My sister attended the girls' school. She was a year younger than I, and was extremely reticent about all my inquiries about the girls in her school.

"Why are you asking?" she would reply to my questions about the names and my requests to take my love letters to any girl who would accept them. "I will tell Mother that you are asking about the girls." After I begged her for five minutes, she did not tell my mother, so I again tried to get her help in establishing any form of contact with any girl in the forbidden kingdom. Then she gave me a very good reason to never ask her again about the girls in her school. The magic words were, "I will tell Father that you are asking about the girls. This is not appropriate."

When we moved to Balluria, I was in the eighth grade, and as my father explained our new residence and his new job assignment, I learned that our family would spend the next three or four years in Balluria or the "black hole of scum," as my father referred to my new, exciting small hometown. For me, it meant that I would attend the local school for my eighth, ninth, and tenth grades and maybe secondary school in Balluria, and then I would transfer to the big city to attend high school. We moved to Balluria in the late summer that year, and I spent that entire remnant of summer with Hamid, Adnan, the Wolves, my new soccer teammates, and my new friends who did and said more interesting and exciting things than my old friends in the capital. That summer was the most exciting summer I had ever lived. I did not think that the school would compromise my embarking on the many adventures that Hamid and I had planned for, but soon enough it was time to organize the school supplies and leave the freedom of summer for the confines of the classroom.

It was not long after Hamid, Adnan, and I sailed the boat that Hamid found floating in the river. It was a bit strange how Hamid always found such interesting things floating in the river. He found treasures floating on the river every day, but the boat was the grand prize. We spent almost three weeks fixing the boat, and we even painted it with blue and rust-colored red paint. He said that he found the can of paint floating on the river too, which seemed unusual since it was only half full, but he explained, "I found it closed if the can is closed, it will float because of the air inside." Adnan, who had enough scientific knowledge to argue otherwise kept silent, and I did too because we were just excited to put the last touch on our boat. I wanted to write a name on it so we debated on the name for three days. Adnan suggested naming it the *Tetaneek* and I tried to remember the name of the boat of Tom Sawyer and Huckleberry Finn. I looked for the book to find the boat's name but with no luck. Hamid had another suggestion; he wanted to call the boat Hanan. I did not know why Hamid wanted to give our boat a girl's name. Adnan looked very concerned when Hamid mentioned that choice, and he whispered something in Hamid's ear. Suddenly Hamid agreed that *Tetaneek* was a good name; and that was our boat, the *Titanic* or the *Tetaneek*, as Adnan pronounced it. I knew little about the *Titanic*. Adnan, on the other hand, had read about it in a book. Only Hamid had no idea what the name represented.

"What is Tetaneek?"

"It's a ship that crossed the Atlantic Ocean and sank," Adnan answered.

"What is the Atlantic Ocean?" Hamid asked.

"The Atlantic Ocean is the ocean of mystery. It's the ocean between the Arab world and the rest of the world. Beyond it is America. Arabs call it the darkness sea because they did not know what was on the other side of it," Adnan said, and I agreed.

"What is America?" Hamid asked.

"America is where Tom Sawyer and Huckleberry Finn live and where all the people we see on television live," I said and looked at Hamid, who only seemed more confused. I knew he wanted to stop asking because no answer would make sense to him. His world was Balluria, and anything beyond was a chasm.

The three of us planned, at Hamid's suggestion, that when we had a three-day holiday from the school we would go on the adventure of our lives. He had it planned out that we would sail the boat to the marshes, where we would look for the biggest snake in the world. It was called affa, and it was reported to be able to eat three men in one bite.

"Why are we going to look for it?" My private fear of snakes seeped into my voice.

"Because we will prove to the people that we are the bravest," he answered.

I did not want to argue because I knew that I was not going, and that was when Adnan said something that sounded very strange to me. "Do you know that the gates of Heaven are in the marshes?"

"No," Hamid and I answered, a bit confused.

"Yes, they are," Adnan said. "The gates of Heaven, the gates for the seven worlds of Heaven where Allah the almighty created the world, are in the marshes, as believers in religion claim."

Hamid and I just looked at each other, not knowing what to say to our tiny friend who wore thick glasses.

That exciting summer was quick to end, and school was only two days away. Hamid did not seem to prepare for school. He was busy with things that he found floating in the river. I asked if he had bought new clothes for school, and he said with a sad voice, "I have clothes. My mother will wash the smell of fish from these clothes, and I will go to school." I realized that he did not have any other clothes.

"It would be good to have new clothes, especially because of the girls," Hamid said.

"Girls? What girls?" I asked, my curiosity aroused.

"All the girls in town; our school is mixed," Hamid said.

That was the most exciting thing Hamid had ever said to me. It was even better than telling me that we would go on a trip to hunt the biggest snake in the world that could eat three men with one bite. What Hamid said about mixed classes in the new school where boys and girls shared the same desks was the answer to all my boyhood prayers. Finally, there would be no need to climb the walls of the forbidden city. I was trying to wrap my mind around the idea, the mind of an almost-thirteen-year-old boy with overflowing hormones and emotions yearning for the smell of a young girl's ponytail.

"How many girls are there in the school?" I asked, trying to find assuring answers that there would be enough girls for all the boys.

"Many of them; even my sister goes to that school," Hamid replied carelessly.

I did not want Hamid to talk about his strange sister, so I asked bluntly, "Are there pretty girls?"

"No," Hamid said and added, "They are all ugly and smelly. Except for one of them, she is very pretty."

"Who is she?" I asked.

"You will know later, when you see her," he answered, as the look in his eyes changed to a dreamy stare that was the end of our conversation. Adnan said he must go back home, and Hamid tried to get me to go to his house to eat dinner, but realizing that I had not been home since the morning, decided it might be time for me to assure my mother that I was alive, so I walked home thinking of all the girls that I would fall in love with that year.

That night, I spent two hours looking in the mirror and arranging my clothes. The first day of school was only one day away, and I had to be ready for the world of craziness and warmth, the world of pink hearts, rosy cheeks, and lips and beautiful eyes. In the middle of laying out my clothes, I realized I needed more assuring answers from an adult who might know better than Hamid before getting too excited, so I asked my mother about where my sister would attend school. I held my breath, hoping my friends weren't having fun with me. She said, "With you, in the same school." So what Hamid told me the truth; it was a mixed school. Still, I needed to know who would be in my class. I needed answers, not from Hamid, who seemed to be not interested in school at all, so I asked Adnan the next day as we lay near the river after an hour of swimming and waited for Hamid, who disappeared for an unknown reason, "Do you know the girls in our school."

"Yes," he said as he was reading a book that was thicker than his head, barely acknowledging my question.

"Who are they?" I asked Adnan, who just nibbled his cuticle.

"All the girls in town; they all go to the school with us."

"Can you tell me who they are?" I insisted.

"Huh. Oh, the Hillaly girls, Bushra and Adawya, the two sisters, and Hanan, the daughter of Sheikh Jawad, Basima, Zainab, and Amel, Hamid's sister, and many others. Why are you asking?" he asked.

"I don't like to be in the same class with girls and just wanted to know how many we would have to deal with," I lied.

"Me too. I think they are annoying," Adnan said, as he went back to read his thick book that had the title of *War and Peace* written in red on a very old deteriorating cover.

The day had finally arrived after hoping and wishing that school would never come because I wanted to spend more time with Hamid and Adnan by the river. Instead, I was anxious to start school. I barely slept the night before. I knew that the entire town was talking about us, my family and me. They referred to us as "The Baghdadia." I knew that some of the girls must have heard about my family and me. I was the son of the mayor who was the magistrate at the same time, and we were from Baghdad. I was already filled with vanity and a feeling of superiority, and the new clothes that my father had bought for me and my siblings added more glitter to the young peacock that I was.

I woke up early, washed my face several times, and combed my hair. I styled my long hair by splitting it from the middle just like Bobby Ewing from the television show *Dallas*. I wore my blue jeans that people referred to as cowboy, and divided my three shirts into the six-day school week. I was to wear the white shirts on Saturdays and Tuesdays, the blue shirt on Sundays and Wednesdays, and the beige one on Mondays and Thursdays, and since Fridays were weekend holidays, there was no specific shirt for them. Suddenly, I remembered my friend Hamid, who had only one shirt, and I thought about trying to find any of my old shirts to give to him, but I never did.

2

What is love? How does it feel when it hits the heart? I was not able to answer that question and started thinking about Khawla and that afternoon by the orange tree as I walked by the main street of Balluria toward the school with my brother and my sister. The three of us were the center of attention of the entire town, not because we were cleaner and better groomed than the others, but because a policeman, sent by my father, escorted us to school and made sure that we were safe and ensured that all our paperwork was orderly. My heart started to pump faster as I saw the waves of girls. Many were heading in the same direction as we were, to the light blue painted building that was our school. At that time, all thoughts of Khawla left my consciousness. The school looked as if it were an old fortress from another age. Later I learned that it had indeed been a fortress before becoming a prison and then a school. Jelwi, the oldest police sergeant in the world, told me that he had imprisoned many people in that building during the fifties when the general from the great city in the north attempted a coup against his lifelong friend, the general from the south. I did not give much thought to the possibility of finding the spirits of the dead roaming the rooms and the thick walls of my new school as much as I was thrilled to see the many pink cheeks and the lines of undergarments that were visible through the blue and gray skirts of the girls in the classroom. My first day I had to prove myself and set the stage for the entire year. I was so happy to see that Hamid was there, and so was Adnan. The class had not started yet, and suddenly the entire team was there. I saw Kamal and Ahmed entering the class, and I saw Ashraf, Salah, and Hisham, then Haleem and Abdulla. They all were in my class. It put me at ease to see that I was not the new student that no one knew. Even Mrs. Iqbal, the Arabic teacher, recognized me by saying, "Are you the one from Baghdad? Are you the mayor's son?"

"Yes, ma'am," I said, trying to appear calm and worldly instead of excited as I was when I saw the many beautiful eyes of the girls turn toward me.

I sat next to Adnan. Hamid sat at the back of the class. His desk was filled with pencil drawings. Hisham and Ashraf sat at one desk, and Haleem and Salah sat at the desk to the far right. They were lucky because they were closest to the girls.

I don't know what the teacher tried to teach us on that first day. I was too busy trying to learn the names of the girls in the classroom. There was Sa'adya, the beautiful girl from the neighboring village of Tawsheeha. Salma was from Balluria, and she was the younger sister of Salem's, the only car mechanic in Balluria. Nedaa was the daughter of Haji Lafta, who owned a store that sold only sacks of wheat. Zainab was a smart girl who later competed with me for the award of the model student in the class, but she was always sick and limped with polio. Waffa was the youngest daughter of Abdulwahed the Brave, who, legend says, was the bravest man in these parts before he died years earlier; she lived with her family on the outskirts of Balluria and never smiled. No boy in school dared to talk to her because legend said that she had very mean and brave brothers. Maha was a quiet girl who was always by the side of her sister, Balqees, who was tall and witty, and we always saw the lines of her undergarments even when she wore a heavy gray skirt. I was surprised to hear from Hisham, in the first recess, that our class had the ugliest girls in the school, and that classroom B had all the pretty ones. It was then that the students from classroom B came into the school yard.

"There she is, Hanan, the princess of Balluria, the daughter of Sheikh Jawad, the most beautiful girl in the world," Hisham said, his eyes trailing longingly after her.

I looked to where he was staring, expecting to see the most beautiful girl in the world. To my surprise, she was not as he described. She was pretty, but looked pale and distant. She had long, curly black hair and gray eyes, and she walked with a mystical yet apparent elegance.

Abdullah, who was standing with me when Hisham said his words, said, "She is pretty, but she is untouchable."

"Why?" I asked.

"Because she is the sheikh's daughter," Abdullah answered and gave Hisham a look that I did not understand. I thought that it was because I was new and I should not know more than I needed to know, but I did not care, because to me she looked like what everyone said about her. I was more interested in knowing all the other girls in the other classrooms. I saw Amel Hamid's sister, who looked as if she wore the same clothes she'd had since elementary school, walking with two other girls who looked identical, but one of them appeared older than the other. I asked Hisham who were they.

"They are the Hillaly girls. The older one is Bushra, and the younger one is Adawya."

For no particular reason, the sight of the Hillaly girls engraved itself in my mind from that moment. It was not because they were exceptionally pretty or because they wore provocative clothes, which consisted of tighter than usual skirts, but because they had what looked like the longest and the darkest hair I had ever seen in my life.

"You know that they say a jinni woman is grooming the Hillaly girls' hair, and the jinni woman had told them never to cut it," Hisham said.

"That's absurd," Adnan, who just joined the group of lusty thirteen-year-old boys, said as he fixed his glasses. "Under that hair are thick skulls, thick, yet full of nothing, only stupidity."

I did not pay attention to Adnan's comment, because I was taken by the sight of crazy hair traveling beyond my senses. When I found that Haleem was in love with Bushra, the older of the Hillaly girls, I decided that I would be in love with Adawya, the younger one. I do not know how and where or when, but somehow I would figure out how to be in love with her and convince her to be in love with me. I would impress her with my looks and my clothes. I would join the school theater group and become popular, form my own band, or write many love letters to her. That was it. From the first day at my new school, I picked my habeeba (my sweetheart). I had no feelings toward her, nor had I spoken to her or even heard her voice, which I hoped would be soft and feminine. It seemed as if I had to choose a girl then and there before they were all gone. In the second recess, I asked Hamid if he had chosen a girl; he smiled and said, "I chose my girl a long time ago."

"Who is she?" I asked.

He looked at me and said, "You will know when the time is right."

I waited for the right time, so I could learn who Hamid's chosen girl was, but the right time never came. The days of school went by quickly, and just as I had planned, I had joined the theater group in the school. Our activities were to celebrate the many official holidays and the many national holidays the divine president had created for himself. I wrote plays and acted the lead role in all of them. Within two months, my status as a popular student was established, and my love of Adawya, the younger of the Hillaly girls, was on the right path. Although I still did not feel anything toward her, I heard from Basima, who liked Abdullah. Adawya liked me, and that was enough. I could wait for another year or two to tell her that I liked her too, and that was my plan. However, one day, some girl had slipped a pink juri flower in my notebook, and I had no doubt in my mind that it was Adawya; I couldn't imagine anyone but her doing it. I was so excited that she took the initiative, but I did not know how to react so I carried the flower with me all day during all recesses and looked for Adawya, but I did not see her. Instead of seeing Adawya, I saw Amel, Hamid's sister, who seemed happy and kept looking at me as if she were waiting for me to say something when she saw me carrying the flower. Maybe she thought I was giving the flower to her, so I asked Amel, "Where is your friend, Adawya?"

"Why?" she asked.

"Nothing, just wanted to talk to her," I said, trying to avoid any further conversation with Amel.

"Do you like pink juri flowers?" she asked.

"Yes, I do," I answered as I walked back to my classroom when I heard the bell for the second class.

I did not hear Amel clearly as I walked. It looked as if she had a pink juri flower in her hand, and I thought she said, "I have one for you."

The second class was National Patriotic Education. The teacher, Mr. Mehdi, was already waiting for the students in the classroom. He always went to the room one minute before the bell rang, unlike all other teachers, who usually showed up five or ten minutes after the bell. Mr. Mehdi was a boring and extremely slow person. He walked slowly and talked slowly about very boring subjects like "How to be patriotic" or "The enemies of our nation: America and Israel." Sometimes, students joked that he must need to be started with jumper cables in the mornings. That particular morning, Mr. Mehdi had a guest with him, a man who wore the Ba'ath party dark green uniform and carried a notebook with him. After all the students sat at their desks, the only one missing was Hamid. He skipped classes because he had to fix another boat that he found floating in the river. He asked Adnan and me if we wanted to skip school. Adnan, who never skipped, was quick to reject Hamid's mischievous offer, but I considered it for a minute before declining, hoping for my rendezvous with Adawyain the next recess.

Hamid had jumped out of the broken window in the book storage room that no one knew about. By skipping that class, Hamid spared himself from the agonizing half hour the rest of the class endured listening Mr. Uraiby or Comrade Uraiby, as he introduced himself. I thought to myself, *Oh, my God. So this is Comrade Uraiby, the party's strong man in these parts and the father of Mazin, the captain of the Wild Lions soccer team, our archenemy.* All of my teammates and I hoped and prayed that he had forgotten about our little battle with his son, who, luckily, was attending a school in the big city of the province. For our good fortune, Comrade Uraiby did not mention a thing about it, nor did he know who we were. Instead, with his deep voice, thick moustache, and noticeably large belly, which flowed copiously over his belt, he said to the impatient students that the country was at war with a ruthless enemy that aimed to destroy our Arab nation. He also talked about how our country needed us, and duty called on everyone, even the young students of the eighth and ninth grades, to join the party and attend the weekly meetings. He also elaborated on why we must carry the pins with the president's picture on our collars and chests to show the love and support for our beloved leader. He asked if anyone wanted to volunteer for ten days of training on Kalashnikovs so they could fire three rounds each Thursday during the flag raising ceremony. Kamal leaped from his desk and went directly toward Comrade Uraiby, shouting, "Me, me, I will go for not only ten days. I will go for a year to the front if you want me to, Comrade."

I thought Kamal's statement was a mere gesture of bragging since we all knew that shattered young bodies of soldiers were arriving daily in Balluria and the other cities and towns and the marsh villages from the eastern front, but I did not wanted to say anything because I was afraid of the fearsome looks of Comrade Uraiby and I thought it was a waste of time to think about the war or Kamal's statement that he was willing to go to the front. I wanted to focus more on my new love affairs. I wanted to keep my heart occupied with what it seemed were promising love possibilities in my classroom and in the school. I did not want to think of the realities of a war that was so near yet so far away from the beauty of a the world of a thirteen-year-old.

We were embarrassed by what Kamal did, and we thought that was outright brown nosing, but we also knew that the entire class, and perhaps the entire school, must join the party or else suffer unknown and unpleasant consequences. So, one by one, boys and girls, we all walked to the front of the classroom, wrote our names, and signed the form that Comrade Uraiby had in his hand, the form that initiated our status as supporters of the party. The only two who did not sign the form and never attended the weekly meeting were Hamid, who was never there anyway, and Adnan, who said that he could not join. Comrade Uraiby looked critically at Adnan and asked about why he was not joining the party.

Out of the corner of my eye I looked at Adnan, and I could see the fear in his face, but he calmly replied, "I am an independent."

Comrade Uraiby did not like Adnan's answer. "Are you a member of another party?" he asked Adnan with a clearly threatening look from his piercing eyes.

"No, Comrade. I am an independent," Adnan answered with the calm voice again.

"What is your name, your full name?" Comrade Uraiby asked, barely controlling his anger from the civilized challenge he was receiving from a student in front of others.

He gave Comrade Uraiby his full name.

When Comrade Uraiby left, we were actually grateful for the monotone voice of Mr. Mehdi and his dull lectures. Adnan was not paying attention to National Patriotic Education. He never did. Instead, he and I exchanged notes about the girls.

In one of the notes I wrote, "Who does Hamid love?"

"Hanan."

I was surprised with his answer. I thought to myself, *Hamid loves Hanan? How dare he? She is the sheikh's daughter and the princess of the town, and Hamid is a dirty, smelly, poor boy, who spent his time swimming and fishing and does not even have one decent set of clothes.* All that time, I thought Hanan liked Kamal, her cousin. So I wrote on a small piece of paper, "What about her cousin, Kamal?"

"He is not her cousin. He just lives in the sheikh's house."

That answer did not satisfy my curiosity. "Who does Kamal love?"

"Hanan."

Soon I realized that Adnan wasn't going to expound on this, and I would have to ask again, "Who does Hanan love?" I wrote this and passed the note to Adnan, who seemed to get frustrated with my question. He wrote back, "Hanan loves Hamid. She always did." Then he wrote again, "Stop asking me these questions."

I stopped asking the questions and let my mind roam in the mist of perfumes that rose from the necks of the many girls in our classroom. And personally I was happy with the school and the visits of Comrade Uraiby; his threatening presence did not bother me a bit. The Friday weekly meetings of the party were simply extra time for me to be with girls from other classrooms.

My brother, who attended the elementary school, was waiting for me every day so we could walk back together with our sister, who befriended some girls in the seventh grade; one of them was Hamid's sister, Amel, who also waited for me with my sister after school. With them waited another girl. Her name was Naima; she was the daughter of the only nurse in town. The five of us walked together every day after school. I walked alone, followed by my sister and her two girlfriends, who lived near our house, and then my younger brother Wisam, who always slacked behind us as he used his fingers to draw many things in the air and shout, "Salam, wait for me," from time to time.

3

Winter ended very quickly and spring arrived, and with it came the refreshing and promising breezes of the south, and the immaculate morning suns that made the girls' cheeks glow with extra shine, and their eyes flared with wondrous desires. Everyone in the school carried a flower, a pink juri flower, and notes were passed between girls and boys, as through a well-organized postal system. Amel, Hamid's sister, was the messenger of love. She did not mind passing notes from this boy to that girl or from this girl to that boy. She was the love messenger between her brother, Hamid, and Hanan, who seemed to have a holy bond between them as they passed deep looks between them that made us all jealous of the genuinely sparked emotions. Well, at least, I felt jealous of that and hoped to feel the same feeling when Adawya looked at me and winked with her left eye, but unfortunately I did not do the wink back because I was too shy.

Basima and Abdullah did not need Amel's messenger service after they had exchanged their second love letter. They started passing the notes to each other directly and sometimes they just stood and talked as if there were no one else around them and it seemed as everyone had blessed and agreed that these two, Abdullah and Basima, should belong to each other, and they should be together.

Hamid and Hanan went to a great deal of secrecy exchanging their love letters, only because Kamal was watching them like a hawk, even more than Ahmed, Hanan's brother, who never seemed interested in the girls.

Haleem was Amel's most demanding customer and most annoying love-letter sender. He would write three or four letters a day. Sometimes, Haleem wrote love letters between classes or during classes, or he came to school without preparing his homework because he was busy all night writing pages and pages about dying souls and eternal love that would last forever. The first thing in the morning, he would ask Amel to give the letters to Bushra and make her swear that she would deliver all of them to Bushra, the older of the Hillaly girls. Bushra never responded to his letters, but at the same time, she would send him a real message whenever she saw him laughing loudly, acting immaturely, or talking to another girl. She did not send him a note then. Rather, she would send him a verbal message with Amel, to tell him things like, "Bushra said, that's not the way lovers act in front of their loved ones."

Haleem would then stop talking to any other girl or doing whatever annoying act he was engaging in and look at Bushra submissively, asking for forgiveness. She would just ignore him, as if he did not exist. Haleem sent Bushra almost three hundred letters that year. His notebook was as thin as our religion textbooks because of all the ripped papers he used to write the letters. However, he never received one single love letter from her, even when he sent a letter with Amel to Bushra, asking her to answer his question with one word, just one word. Yes or no; did she love him? She did not answer, but that silence did not deter Haleem. He continued writing his ten or twelve pages of messy and misspelled love letters, and Amel never once complained about her duty as the love messenger.

Amel usually seemed happy and content to pass the love letters, but whenever I asked her to give my letters to Adawya, she always appeared reluctant and always looked for excuses not to deliver my letters. I thought that was because she was afraid her brother Hamid might get mad if he knew that she was the love messenger of the entire school and that I would tell him since he and I were friends. I decided it was either that or maybe it was because she never received a love letter from any of the boys. I had always thought that she and Adnan would make a good pair. They both liked books and poetry, and they both seemed lonely. Adnan was more interested in books and talking about people no one ever heard of, people like Karl Marx, Che Guevara, Arian Sayed Khalaf, or the outspoken ayatollah who was executed during those days, and Amel seemed to have no interest in any boy.

Our soccer team stopped playing during school days because every time we planned to play, the rain came and made it impossible for us to play in the soccer field. Hamid always said that the Gypsy woman Barrya was asking about us and told Hamid to tell us that she had prepared yogurt and tea many times and waited for us and she would prepare it again if we would go, play, and visit her in her house. We did not have the time to play soccer all that winter. Hisham instead listed all of our names as the soccer team for the school and worked tirelessly to get us jerseys, but his efforts were fruitless, as the supplies went to the other school, the one that Mazen, Comrade Uraiby's son, attended. Hisham was furious and tried to voice his complaints to the school headmaster, who first ignored Hisham then told him to never step a foot in his office again. We were sympathetic to Hisham and his efforts to revive the glory of the Wolves. However, we, or at least I, was busy with discovering and living the refreshing openings of the ends of long blocked veins of love and desires. I felt the waves of fresh blood invading my senses and bringing with them the warm feeling of innocent adolescence.

Every day in school was better than the one before it because the spirit of young girls and boys filled that old fortress with something other than the building's original, dark purpose. The young girls and boys filled the rooms and thick walls with genuine mischievousness that hid within the lines of the love notes and the immaculate blossoms of physical and emotional buds that manifested between the lines of poetry. They filled the school with laughter of dark cherry lips and promises of the shy, beautiful black and gray eyes. They filled that light blue building, originally built to imprison and torture other humans from another time with the mist of briefly allowed stolen freedom. The spirit of the young boys and girls filled that place with many pink hearts and flowers.

The Book of the Man

Dark Shade of Poetry

1

For the longest time and from the first moment I saw her, with her deep, sad eyes, I tried to avoid being alone with Amel, Hamid's sister. The first reason was out of respect for Hamid, because traditionally I was not supposed to be alone with his sister. Second, she always looked at me as though she had something to say to me and was waiting for me to say something to her, but I did not know what she wanted me to say. Besides, she was always sad and spaced out when she looked at me. I had never seen her laughing, and when she smiled, which was a rare event, her smile was weak, and it made her look more like a tormented female heiress of an Arabian king. I remember she asked me my name, when I visited Hamid's house the first time to see the ten pigeons he had. Then she asked me if I liked Fairuz, the singer from the dreamy mountains of Lebanon. I told her I did, and she said that she loved Fairuz and added, "I have all her songs."

That was the only time Amel and I spoke about something that we had in common. I did not talk to her in school, and I tried to avoid her looks whenever I went to Hamid's house. But I always saw her gazing at me during the recesses between classes with the same sad and unexplainable look.

Amel did not mind delivering love letters and manifestos of undying eternal love from one boy to his one and only true love in the next classroom. And the replies she brought back were always filled with promises of eternal love and happily ever after. Except for my friend, and Wolves mate, Haleem, whose hundreds of letters to Bushra were fruitless, because she never responded with a note or verbal acceptance of his love and devotion. Nevertheless, Amel never stopped delivering his constant love letters in his pursuit of the heart of long-haired Bushra. I, on the other hand, had made the younger of the Hillaly girls, Adawya, my love interest. Only one month into the school year, I asked Amel if she could deliver my love letter to Adawya. After a brief hesitation, she accepted, but she said it would be the last time she would do it. That was enough for me, because the reply from Adawya came without much wait. I got a note from Adawya asking me to tell her whether I was interested in her. Other times, I gave her small notes to give to Adawya, but I did not get any replies. This made me think that Adawya was upset with me; I did not really care, but it was strange that all the notes I had written to Adawya, after the first one, were fruitless. I thought that Adawya and her sister Bushra were two cold-hearted girls. I did not think much about it, because at thirteen I was more consumed with my adventures with Hamid and Adnan, and the renovation and rebuilding of our boat *Teetanek*, than with love. And because I tried, for much of the school year, to avoid Amel and her mysterious stare.

One afternoon during the last period of class, Hamid and I made plans to go fishing, and we told Adnan to come with us. The plan was to meet at Hamid's house around two in the afternoon to go to the river to sail our boat, the *Titanic*, for the first time. We would fish with the net that Hamid found floating in the river.

We ate lunch at Hamid's house. I was very excited. It was the first time in my life that I would fish with a net in the middle of the river. Fishing with a rod and a hook was a plenty of fun, but it was boyish and amateur. To fish with a net was what the real fishermen in Balluria and in the villages in the marshes did. My eyes were wide with excitement when I saw fishermen catch twenty fish in a single throw. I wanted to do it myself, and it was Hamid who said to me, "We will do it, when I find a fishnet somewhere." Only one day had passed when he told me that he found a fishnet floating in the Euphrates, and he asked me if I wanted to fish with it that afternoon.

Many times, I had seen the fishermen in Balluria throw their nets in the river while they were standing in their tiny boats, and seconds later pull out the net, which was filled with silver, shiny fish. Each one of them was ten times the size of the fish we caught with our fishing rods. Hamid was explaining to me how to fish with the net. "You hold the line like this. You spread the net, and then you throw it. You wait thirty seconds, and then you pull the rope, and that's it. Just be careful not to fall into the water, because if you do, you could drown if you get caught in the net. Once I saw a grown man drown, because he got caught in his own fishing net," Hamid said. "When we go to the river, I will show you how to use it, and you can be a real fisherman."

I could hardly wait for school to end that day, and it seemed like time had stretched. By the time school was over, I was so anxious to go to Hamid's house that I did not even wait for Adnan, who was supposed to come to my house, and then we were to go together to Hamid's. My mother was preparing lunch when I got home from school and she said that our father said that "he needs you to clean up the guest room, because he is expecting some guests for lunch." That was not in my plans, and it would dramatically alter my plans for my afternoon adventure.

"But, I am busy... I have to do... I have to go... to school. The teacher said that I had to help." I was looking for any believable lie I could come up with.

"Do what?" my mother asked.

"Help the teacher," I said.

"Help him with what?"

"I don't know. Help the school. Ask the teacher, why are you asking me?" I added, hoping that my mother would stop asking me questions, and I begged silently for her to spare me the expected humiliation.

"You can do that after you clean the guest room. And your father said that you need to stay to serve them tea and coffee. He is excepting some sheikh."

Oh, my God. Why was everyone and everything conspiring against me? I thought and thought of ways to escape the mandatory labor.

"Can Wisam do it? He is not doing anything," I said, trying to implicate my younger brother, who looked at me as if I were sentencing him to death.

"I don't know how to pour coffee," he said.

"Your father said that you need to do this and that's it... and should the teacher say something to you, just let your father know."

My mother sentenced me to an hour of miserable house chores, and I knew that I would be late for my fishing adventure with Hamid and Adnan, the first journey of our tiny boat. I was on the verge of crying. I mean, it was the choice between facing my father's angered disappointment, which he had been showing more often lately, and missing out on the chance to have a Tom Sawyer and Huckleberry Finn-like adventure with my two best friends. But for some reason, I knew that this time my father would not let it go and he would punish me. I weighed my options. I still had almost an hour, and maybe by that time, the guest would leave. Also, I knew that if I did not clean the guest room, my father would be very angry with me and might prohibit me from leaving the house again for a week, or a month, or maybe forever! So I surrendered with a defeated tone.

"OK, I will clean the guest room," I said. "But I still have to go to school to help out," I added, trying to assure my right to leave afterward.

My younger brother and I dusted the guest room rugs and placed the pillows on the couches. We set artificial faded pink and screaming red flowers, which my mother insisted on, in the middle table of the guest room, a habit she brought with her from the capital city. She also wanted us to place a big jug of water and some glasses that were painted with shapes of birds and flowers on the table. I did what she wanted me to do and sat on the couch and waited, looking at the clock on the wall and peeking from the window almost every ten seconds, waiting for my father. Hungry, I started to get very edgy. It was one thirty in the afternoon, and my father did not show up with his guest. I was getting really restless and mad. I thought to myself, *What kind of a father plans things like this? Does he think that a thirteen-year-old has nothing to do with his afternoons? Does he think that sailing the* Titanic *for the first time isn't important? After all the labor hours Hamid, Adnan, and I had put into it, and fishing with a throw net was a waste of time. Why do I need to be involved in this hospitality nonsense? I mean, what kind of a mean, inconsiderate father is he? And then again, my brother, who has nothing to do but study, could do it. He can serve tea and coffee; what am I, a slave?* I was just about to cry when the clock chimed two, and I knew that at that moment Hamid and Adnan probably given up waiting for me and were pushing the *Titanic* into the middle of the Euphrates. I choked as I pictured that image and was about to cry for real when I heard my father's voice and the squeaky sound of the door opening.

"Welcome... you have honored our home, welcome... come in." I looked from the window and I saw my father and a very scary-looking man. Tall, he had a beard and very sharp-looking eyes. His beard was gray and well groomed, and he wore a kafiyah (head covering) and traditional robe. He looked at me with what seemed like a dismissal of my entire being. It was Sheikh Jawad, the most feared man in these parts, the father of my friend Ahmed and his sister, Hanan, and the assumed uncle of Kamal. He owned all the land in Balluria. The many stories I heard about him made me shiver in his presence. My father was extra courteous and nice to Sheikh Jawad and the two men who were with him. They sat in the guest room without speaking, while my father walked to the kitchen and asked my mother nervously, "Is lunch ready?"

"Yes," my mother answered.

"Well, tell the boys to bring water and tea," my father said.

He went to the guest room and continued welcoming the fearsome sheikh and his two scary, armed companions.

My brother and I tried to act as politely as the southern custom mandates. We both walked straight and had a fake frown on our faces to look tough and manly. We did not know the why we did this, but it seemed to be the right thing to do, especially with guests like the ones in our guest room. I carried a pitcher of water and a shiny glass and served water to them, hoping to finish without spilling water on any of them. They looked at me as if I were from another planet.

Sheikh Jawad did not drink the water I gave him, so I passed it to the man next to him, who drank all of it and belched like a buffalo. My brother brought a tray with four cups of tea and placed each in front of the men and my father. By the time the second man drank his water, I was ready to pass out from the heat and the fear consuming me. I noticed that my father was worried too, but I had no time to think about that as I exited the guest room, abandoning my poor brother whose shaky hands were noticeable as he carried the tray of tea.

I looked at the clock in the corridor as it rang at 2:30 p.m. I was ready to escape from the house and run to Hamid's house and suffer the consequences of a severe punishment from my father later, but I wanted to take some food with me, because I did not know if Hamid, Adnan, and I would ever return from our journey. We might get lost in the marshes forever just like Ulysses, and maybe we would end up in the Atlantic Ocean, so I wanted to be prepared. Before I managed to steal a cucumber, a tomato and a piece of a bread to start my journey, my mother said, "Yellah (hurry up), the lunch is ready."

My brother and I carried the china dishes filled with rice, okra stew, bread, and vegetables on two trays to the guest room. If it had been up to me, I would have shoved the food into the scary men's mouths and sent them on their way. Then I would have run to the river, but Sheikh Jawad must have had an important issue to see my father about privately, and not in his office.

Important or not, I had no interest in learning about it at that time, but later I learned that Sheikh Jawad was actually trying to intimidate my father into signing a municipal order that would allow the fearsome sheikh to put his hand on the land beyond the river bend, a piece of land that belonging to a widow and her only son. I also learned later Sheikh Jawad had been trying to buy that land for years, but the widow refused to sell it to him. Barrya had said once that the widow would never sell the land to Sheikh Jawad, because her husband, who disappeared almost fifteen years ago, was Sheikh Jawad's partner in the sheep smuggling business, and something had happened to him, but no one knew exactly what. He just disappeared one night and never returned to his wife and only son; no one dared to ask Sheikh Jawad about the fate of his partner.

The voices in our guest room were getting louder, and I heard one of the men talking about the war and how the last offensive claimed the lives of almost thirty thousand people, from both sides, and how the people in the villages along the marshes had pulled out of the Euphrates corpses of soldiers that had been floating for days. I was disgusted with what I had heard and even more disgusted with the heat of the house and the images of the three fearsome men in our guest room.

I longed for the bright lights of the sun painting the river's surface with tiny shells of silver. I longed for the companionship of Hamid and Adnan, and for the promised adventure of fishing like a real fisherman with a throw net. I thought to myself that if I just left and came back home, victoriously, with a really big fish like a Gattan or Shaboot, maybe my father would forgive me for bailing out on him in the middle of his scariest meeting since we had moved to this town, and he might even be proud of me for a change. So I made up my mind. I looked at my brother, who was trying to watch *Tarzan* on the black-and-white television that we had in the family room and at the same time trying to stay close to the door so he would hear my father if he needed something. Without telling my brother what I was about to do, I put my index finger on my lips, warning him not to make any attempt to tell on me. I snuck out from the kitchen door, to the yard, and with one jump I was on the other side of the brick wall and on my way to Hamid's house. Trying to avoid being seen by my father from the guest room window, I ran on the dirt walkway between the palm trees and the bushes. Feeling the heat of the scorching sun, I realized that I was not that late, but I feared that Hamid and Adnan might have already started the promised adventure without me. I thought to myself that if they had, I would never forgive them. By the time I reached Hamid's house, I was out of breath. I knocked on the door, which was half open, and waited. No one answered the door. I knocked again, and my fear that they left without me overwhelmed me.

"How could they?" I said out loud to myself. Then I heard the sound of two feet approaching the door, and I was starting to cheer up. Two big black eyes peeked out from behind the door, and a lock of black hair crossed the tanned face. Oh, my Allah, it was not Hamid. It was Amel standing in the door, wearing a sky-blue dress. She smelled of fresh soap, as if she had just finished taking a bath. She smiled at me and said, "Hamid is not here."

"Did he go with Adnan to the river?" I asked as I was trying to catch my breath.

"I don't know. He has not come home yet," she answered with a quiet voice.

I stood there waiting for more words, ones that would assure me that Hamid and Adnan had not sailed in the *Titanic* without me, depriving me of the most exciting fishing adventure yet, but she just stood there, looking at me with her big black eyes, waiting for me to say something. I looked at her without saying a word.

"Do you want yogurt. Are you thirsty?" she asked.

At that moment I felt her offer was kind and timely, because I was extremely thirsty from running, and I felt that only cold yogurt would heal my hellish thirst.

"Yes," I begged.

"OK, you can come in if you want."

Not thinking about the ramifications of Hamid coming home and finding me in his house alone with his sister, I hoped to see her mother there, but I saw no signs of her. The only thing I knew for sure was that I was thirsty, and I was not going to stay there for long. I would drink the yogurt and leave. Amel went inside the smaller room in the house, which they used as a kitchen. I stayed outside in the sun.

"You can come inside if you want the yogurt," she said from inside the room.

At that moment, for some reason, I remembered Khawla when she held the oranges behind her back and said, "If you want them you can come and get them."

I shivered with shame. This was not the same. I loved Khawla, and I did not even like Amel. Besides, she was my friend's sister, and I only wanted yogurt. After gathering myself, I entered the mud room.

2

To this day, I still remember the smell of that room. It smelled like prehistoric plants. The sun pierced through tiny holes in the walls and sent streams of light with millions of small particles flying in them. For no apparent reason, I sat with my back to the mud wall as Amel poured the yogurt into a tin bowl and handed it to me. I drank the yogurt, and suddenly I felt millions of ants creeping through my veins. I don't know if it was the numbing heat or the shade. I just sat there, waiting for Amel to say something. Maybe it was the yogurt. It was strange that she offered yogurt, just as Barrya did all the time after our soccer matches. The yogurt also tasted like Barrya's yogurt that quenched both our physical and emotional thirsts. Barrya always liked Amel. The Gypsy considered her a daughter, and she always referred to her as her devoted daughter. Once I heard Barrya telling Hamid to be kind to his sister and to make sure she that she was always taken care of.

"She has no one in this world but you," Barrya told Hamid, and another time she said, "My poor girl, Amel, she has all of my sadness."

I did not understand how this Gypsy woman, who seemed happy all the time, had any sadness and why she thought that Amel had all of her sadness. To me, Amel was naturally sad. She was also annoying, because whenever I asked her to deliver my love letters and quick notes to Adawya, she always replied with one answer, "OK, I will take your message, but it will be the last one, and don't ask me to do so again." She never told this to any of the other boys who asked her to deliver their important favors of love, so after that, I did not talk to Amel, and I tried to avoid her for the last half of the school year.

Among all the girls in our school, Amel was the only one who never talked about who she loved. She never told the other girls, and I was not aware that Amel had written love letters to any boy. As for us boys, we did not care, because Amel was not one of the girls who could be the beloved of any of us. Hamid's sister, she was not as pretty as Hanan, who loved Hamid, Basima, who loved Abdullah, Su'ad, who loved Hisham, Maha, who loved Ashraf, Raghda, who loved Salah, or to the Hillaly girl Bushra, who seemed to enjoy tormenting Haleem with her silence and Adawya, who supposedly loved me, and I loved her. We all thought that Amel loved Adnan, but we were quick to realize that those two had no emotional connection whatsoever. With just one look into Amel's eyes, a person could see that she was too sad to love anyone, and no one could tell what the look in Adnan's eyes meant, because of his thick glasses, like two tiny telescopes. Furthermore, Amel did not dress or act like any of the other girls. To us, she was just a boring and gloomy girl who stared at me all the time.

Sitting with my back to the wall and waiting, I did not want to go back to the house, because I knew that my father would be angry. Besides, the only way I would escape punishment was to come back with a good-sized fish that my mother could cook. Moreover, that day, there was no way I could leave without knowing if Hamid, Adnan, and I would sail the *Titanic*. With nowhere to go, I decided to wait until Hamid came home. I looked at Amel as she stood there gazing at me and smiling. I was about to ask again about Hamid when she surprised me with a question,

"What grade did you get on your Arabic poetry test?"

"What?" I answered.

"Hamid said that you got 95 out of 100. Is that true? You must be a shatter," she said.

"Yes, it was 95, and I could have scored higher, but I did not study," I said bragging, when I knew that I studied so hard for that test.

"Do you like poetry? Is that why you scored so high? I like poetry too," she said, with apparent excitement.

"Not really," I said. "I mean, not a lot, but I have to score high, because I..."

"I like poetry a lot," she interrupted me. "I always read poetry."

Suddenly her eyes, her big black eyes, turned sadder, as if she wanted to cry. I had no idea where the conversation was going or how it was going to end. I already knew that Amel liked poetry, because all the girls would ask her to write a line or two of poetry in their love letters. I also knew for sure that Haleem had asked her to write a poem in one of his love letters to Bushra, the older Hillay girl, and I knew that she wrote poetry that no one understood. Once, when her brother, Hamid, and I tried to untangle and retie the many pieces of the fishing net that Hamid had found floating in the river, Amel sat by the door of the room they used as the kitchen and said to us, "I just read a poem by Pablo Neruda. Do you want to hear it?"

Hamid and I looked at her and then went back to our task. Many other times, when she would bring vegetables and bread to us for lunch, as I hopelessly tried to help Hamid with his homework that he never did, she would sit next to us, look at me, and say. "Do you know what Al-Sayyab said about the fishermen in the Gulf?" And without waiting for my reply, she recited the poem and looked at me as though she wanted me to feel it.

> *I scream to the Gulf,*
> *Oh, Gulf, oh the giver of the fish, oysters and death,*
> *My voice echoes and returns,*
> *Like a cry without the tears,*
> *All the water of the Gulf is a tear,*
> *Empty, the nets returned,*
> *Empty, from the fish and oysters,*
> *And in it, only death remains.*

Whenever Hamid was there, she could not read poetry for long, but this time I was alone with her, and inside I felt as if I wanted to hear her reading them. I was anxious to join my two friends on the promised afternoon adventure, but for a reason that I still do not fully understand, I wanted to listen to her. Maybe it was pity, maybe politeness, or maybe compassion. I felt that I owed her something; I could spare an hour of my time. She delivered my love letter to Adawya, so I could return the favor and just spend one hour listening to her poetry. I wanted to tell her that I like poetry too and that I love Badr Shaker Al-Sayyab, that I have read all of his work, but at the same time, I did not want to tell her, because I did not want her to start the same conversation again and again every time I came to their house. I was afraid that Hamid would get upset if he saw her talking to me. Yet, I was alone with her and I thought that one hour would be enough for her to read all the poetry that she wanted to read to me, and after that I wouldn't owe her a thing. So I sat there and listened for the first time to the scratchy voice of this girl, who I started to see in a different light. The clip of hair still crossed her tanned face when she looked at me and said, "I like Badr Shaker Al-Sayyab. He is my favorite poet. I also like to read old Arabic poetry, but I feel like Badr Shaker Al-Sayyab speaks to me. I feel like he knows how I feel and knows me."

"Who?" I asked foolishly.

"Badr... Badr Shaker."

"You mean the poet?" I asked foolishly again.

"Yes. I think I will live a life similar to his life of constant pain and loneliness," she said with a strange sad voice.

I was still imagining the afternoon that I had planned with her brother and our friend Adnan and where I was at this moment was not close to what I had envisioned. I started to doubt my decision to remain here and listen to her, but I hoped that Hamid would appear, so I stayed. But Hamid did not come, and only God knew when he would return. Suddenly, I heard her voice like I'd never heard it before. Amel recited a poem I had read before, but I had never heard it recited with the feeling she expressed. I had never heard how true and meaningful the words sounded until I listened to Amel with her soft and sincerely sad voice reciting the words.

> *Your eyes are two palm forests,*
> *As the moon light moves with its shadows,*
> *Your eyes are two balconies in the early hours of dawn,*
> *When your eyes smile,*
> *The grape vines will blossom,*
> *And the moons light will dance like a thousand moons in the river,*
> *As they shake it weakly in the early hours of dawn,*
> *Your eyes hid the stars in the blackness,*
> *And drowned in a fog of sweet despair,*
> *Like the ocean covered with the shade of the evening,*
> *Warmth of the winter in it,*
> *And the shiver of the fall,*
> *Death and birth are like darkness and light,*
> *It awakens the massive desire to a cry,*
> *That overwhelms my sole,*
> *A wild joy that hugs the skies,*
> *Like the joy of the child when he is scared of the moon,*
> *Like the arches of the clouds drinks itself and leaves to the unknown,*
> *And drop by drop melts in the rain,*

The children laughed in the grapevines,
And tickled the silence of the birds on the trees,
Rain, Rain, Rain,
The evening yawns and the clouds are still,
Sheds and sheds its heavy tears,
Like a child who started mumbling before he sleeps,
About his mother who he did not find,
A year ago when he woke up,
He kept asking and they told him,
Tomorrow she will come and he thought,
She must come back,
As the peers whispered that she was there,
Sleeping forever on the side of the hill in a grave,
Breathing the sand and drinking the rain,
Like a sad fisherman who gathers his net,
Cursing the waters and the fate,
As he sang and sang again,
As the moon goes down on the grapevine,
Rain, Rain, Rain,
Do you know what sadness the rain brings
Do you know how lost the lonely feels in the rain?

Amel looked at me as though she were asking me the question, and I noticed that she had tears in her eyes as though she felt the rain. She looked at me as if I were the only human with her in this world and that she needed me to answer that question. She continued.

Do you know what sadness the rain brings to the soul?
And how the gutters cry as the water falls,
And how lost the lonely feels,
As they are drenched in the rain,
Endless is the rain,
Just like the pain,
To the poor,
Rain is like the tears,
Like the blood that has been shed,
Like the hunger,
Like love, like children, like the dead,
Rain, Rain, Rain,
And your eyes fly with the rain,
And cross the waves of the Gulf,
It wipes the lightening,
Fills the shores of Iraq with stars and shells,

Like it wants to shine,
But night covers it with a blanket made of blood,
I scream, "Oh gulf,"
Oh the giver of pearls, sand shells and death,
The echo comes back like a cry,
"Oh gulf... oh the giver of pearls, death and despair,"
I could hear Iraq,
Bloodied with men,
And let out its fierce lightening it stored in the mountains,
I could hear the palm trees as they drank the rain,
I could hear the villages of the poor cry from the pain,
As they struggle with pain,
Rain, Rain, Rain,
In Iraq there is hunger that never leaves,
And the fear flourished and blossomed are the graves,
Crows and locust eats its harvest,
The stone mill turns on the longing,
Crushing the fields and the people with hunger,
Rain, Rain, Rain,
Oh the many tears we shed in the departing night,
And then we stopped so no one will blame us,
But we blamed the rain,
Rain, Rain, Rain.

That was the first time I realized that Amel read poems, because she wanted to escape from everything around her. Her voice took me in and locked the doors on us and our surroundings. I felt like I was in a place where no one else could hear us. I felt her voice echoing within me, and I wanted to recite the poetry with her.

On the sand are the foam of salt and shells,
And the remains of a drowned fool,
Who believed in hope,
As all immigrants did,
And in Iraq,
A thousand snakes drink the life of it,
From a flower growing by the Euphrates,
Rain, Rain, Rain,
And since we were kids,
The sky was cloudy in winter,
And the rain comes,
Every year the rain comes and the grass grows,
And every year we are hungry,

Not a single year comes without hunger in Iraq,
Rain, Rain,
In every drop of the rain,
Is a tear from the hungry and the weak,
And a drop of blood from the slaves,
And as it is a smile waiting to be on a new mouth,
Or a pink nipple on a new baby's mouth,
Or it's the new tomorrow,
The life giver,
Tomorrow will come with life,
And with the rain,
Rain, Rain, Rain

She put the book aside and looked at me. Looking into her eyes, I wanted to leave. Her accusing glances made me feel that I needed to do one of two things: either leave or kiss her, and I knew if I kissed her, I would never leave that room, never.

"What did you think?" she asked.

"I think it was good. He seems very sad; I mean the poet."

"Yes, but at peace with himself, and his lifetime of loneliness did not bother him, because he thought it was his fate, and, therefore, he accepted it."

"When do you think Hamid will come?" I asked.

She did not answer. She wanted me to continue listening to her reading the poems, but it was about time for me to leave. I stood up and said, "I must go now." I was trying to put an end to what seemed like a gate to eternity in the dark shade.

"I know. I just wanted you to listen to that poem," she said without looking at me. Instead, she looked down at ground and added, "If you can come here again, I will read you poetry and maybe we can listen to Fairuz."

"I will try. I must go now," I said, begging her to let me leave, but I felt trapped in her dark shade. I felt that I had to gain her permission to go, to get rid of the need of being there and the feelings that she had awakened in me. I said, "I will come back again, and we will read poetry together."

"Promise," she said.

"I promise." I walked toward the door. I looked back at her, sitting there, as lonely as Balluria was, a young beautiful girl with big black eyes, sitting in the hot dark shade of the south, like millions of her peers, waiting and waiting for true love to arrive. I looked at the lock of hair dividing her face into two tanned pieces of surreal art and looked into her eyes, full of sadness, and I suddenly felt a familiarity with that sadness. I suddenly understood why she was sad, as I felt the same way.

3

Since that day, I had never looked at Amel the same way again; something about her was tying me to her, and my heart ached to go back to that dark shade in her house. In a way, I understood the sadness in her eyes. I also saw the same sadness in the eyes of many of the other girls in Balluria, in these parts and sometimes in my travels. I saw the same sadness, the Amel sadness, and I wondered many times if they all shared the loneliness that she lived; if they all had heard or read the poetry of Badr Shaker Al-Sayyab, if they all waited for true love to come. I believe now and have always believed that each and every human being must have the right to feel true love at least once in their lives. To me, love is the true purpose and meaning of life, and I dismiss every other purpose.

Days after the poetry reciting in the shade, and even months and a couple years later, whenever I saw Amel in her house, while waiting for Hamid to go on some adventure, or in the school yard delivering love letters from one student to another, love letters that she had generously added lines of poetry to, I realized that her sadness was because she had not been loved yet. I was sad because of that realization, although I did not feel that I was loved truly by Adawya but I was sadder for Amel because I thought she needed to be loved. The days went by quickly, and in my second year in Balluria I had barely had a chance to go sit with Amel to listen to her reciting poetry or telling the tale of the lost poet of Iraq who lived and died alone and sad as he traveled from city to city and country to country, yearning for Iraq, waiting for love to come and for the day he would return to find his true love. Even though the chance to listen to her presented itself, I avoided sitting with her to listen to her, maybe because I did not want to feel trapped again, or maybe it was her fate and mine. But her eyes never left me; they stayed with me long after I departed Balluria. I have seen her in the eyes of many beautiful girls, and I have seen many beautiful girls with the same sadness and the same look of constant longing. I have taught myself to keep from softening with emotions, because my lengthy stares into a woman's eyes have been misinterpreted and mistaken many times.

My first year in Balluria, I did not dedicate much time to Amel; I did so only when time or coincidence permitted, like between soccer games, at my school and at Hamid's house before the fabulous adventures I shared with him and Adnan. One time presented itself when I went looking for Hamid after school, because some party members came to the school and asked if anyone knew of his whereabouts. I was scared that he might have done something that required the party militiamen to look for him, so I went to his house to warn him. Although I knew that my warning him could be considered treason against the great party, the country and the "divine" leader, I did it because Hamid meant more to me than the "divine" leader and the country. Moreover, he meant more to me than the stupid great party. I walked toward the house hoping to find Hamid, but when I got there I saw Amel outside the door washing a teapot. It looked like she just had finished lunch and was preparing the tea.

"Maraca," I said politely.

"Hello, Marhaba. How are you?" she replied with a sudden joy that showed on her face with a simple smile from her dark lips. She had that same clip of hair dividing her tanned face, something that I did not see when she was in school, because she always put her hair in a ponytail.

"Hamid, is he here?" I asked.

"I don't know. I have not seen him since he returned from school," she replied and looked at me waiting for more words. I stood there waiting for her to say something, an invitation to an afternoon of poetry reciting, a cup of tea maybe, or just some shade from the scorching sun of the south. Finally she said, "Do you want some tea?"

"Yes," I answered, not realizing my apparent enthusiasm.

She looked at me, turned toward the house, and walked in front of me. I followed her as if I had no choice but to follow. She went to the dark shade in the room they used as the kitchen, sat on the faded rug inside the room, and put the tea kettle on the kerosene stove. I sat in the same place I had sat in almost a year before to the day. The sun was touching my right shoulder. I wanted to see and be visible to anyone who entered the house. Then I remembered that her mother might be in the house and that I needed to mind my manners.

"Is your mother here?" I asked.

"No, she could not bear the heat. She wanted to take a nap, so she went to the Hillalys' house, because they have an air-conditioner."

"Why didn't you go with her?"

"I don't take naps. Also, I was hoping that you would come here, so we could read poetry. You promised me that you would come."

"I was busy with school, you know. Besides, it's not appropriate for me to stay here without Hamid."

"I know," she replied and gazed at me with that same look, the one that meant she wanted me to say something, but she realized that I was nervous, so she suggested,

"Do you want to listen to Fairuz? She has this song... its lyrics are the poetry of Jebran Khaleel Jebran... you have to hear it."

She said this with complete confidence and control over me. Although I felt trapped in the dark shade again, I did not mind it this time. In fact, I felt a strange comfort; the smell of the mud room eased my fears, and I did not want to leave. She reached for a cardboard box filled with letters and photographs of people I'd never seen before. They looked like movie stars from another world. Also in the box were drawings that she drew of faces with big eyes, trees with tears and birds with shackles tied to their feet and their wings cut off, and there were many cassette tapes: white, gray, and sliver cassette tapes. She pulled one of them out and inserted it in the cassette player, which looked broken. It was not the first time that I'd heard Fairuz singing, but it was the first time that I'd heard her voice so closely that I felt I could hear it so vividly with all my senses. Amel was singing with Fairuz; she knew all the lyrics, and surprisingly, her voice was similar to Fairuz's voice.

> *Give me the flute and sing,*
> *Because singing is the secret of existence,*
> *And the sad sound of the flute,*
> *Will last long after existence ends,*
> *Have you ever followed the creeks and climbed the rocks,*
> *Have you ever showered with the scents of nature,*
> *Dried off in the sunlight,*
> *Or drank in the afternoon,*
> *The alcohol of the soft winds.*

And just as she had the last time, she recited the poetry of Badr Shaker Al-Sayyab. Amel, the tanned, annoying, tiny girl, had managed again to entrap me with her voice. This time as she sang the songs of Fairuz, who crooned about lost love, the fisherman who never returned from the Mediterranean, the drunk lovers, and the shiny, little bricks of the mountain houses of Lebanon, Amel carried me with her voice and the voice of Fairuz; she flew me away from Balluria to a place where she and I thought we belonged. But the dark shade was a fake sanctuary from the unbearable realities that surrounded us, Balluria, and these parts.

I listened to her as she finished her last song, and then she said, "Fairuz is my teacher. She taught me to dream and to never lose hope, but sometimes, I feel that she is so far away, and it scares me that I will never leave this place."

I did not understand why she wanted to leave Balluria. Of all the times I was at Hamid's house, three times I intentionally planned to be late enough so I would be alone with Amel, for reasons that I do not understand to this day. Every time Adnan and I had made plans to go to the river in the afternoon, I would go to the house looking for Hamid, even though I knew that I would always find him by the river in the same spot where we rebuilt the *Titanic*. It was the same spot that we fished, swam in, built small fires, or sailed the *Titanic,* and the many other small boats and rafts that Hamid always found floating on the river. I often contemplated spending more time eating my lunch, drinking tea, and even walking more slowly than usual, so I would miss Hamid. Many times, Hamid waited for me, but other times he had already left. I hoped that I would find Amel waiting for me, so she could read poetry or sing Fairuz's songs to me. I would play innocent when I knocked on the door, hoping that Hamid would not be the one opening it. Instead, I hoped that I would see the sad eyes of his tanned sister, Amel.

For many years, I did not know why, but I was tied to Amel by some invisible string that held me captive to her deep, black eyes. Was it the unquestionable stare of an early realized hopelessness, or was it the bond with loneliness and waiting that she prepared herself for? I did not know then, and I don't know now, but as I walked through the orchard of palm trees in the merciless sun of the south, I was driven by compassion, remorse, solidarity, friendship, and, moreover, the feeling of belonging. I felt that the dark shade of the mud walls of Hamid's house was the safest place for my troubled heart, and the voice of Amel's poetry and songs was a lullaby for my soul. Many times, I pretended that I was not listening, and other times, I pretended that I did not care, and I acted in the manner of a capital city snob, by showing that I was agitated with the heat or by complaining about the dirt floor or the smell of the okra stew. But deep in my heart, I was melted in solidarity with this tanned-faced, dark-lipped girl, who showed me that even though a human being can live in the most forgotten corners of this world, even though the world can run around and around and not notice the existence of many soft hearts, these hearts will find a way to connect to the world and to other humans who have managed to touch their hearts and souls with a song, a line of poetry, or a painting. They will touch hearts just by existing at the same time, because in the mind of the forgotten, that will be enough, as they have never asked for more than that. All they ever wanted was just to have valid lives that meant something, to be loved, or, maybe, to be remembered.

Amel had noticed that I was showing up late, too late for her energetic brother to wait for me, so she always prepared the cassette tape player with all the songs of Fairuz and stacked all the books of Badr Shaker Al-Sayyab, Hussein Merdan, Abdul Wahab Al-Baiaty, Pablo Neruda, and Adonis, and she would wait for me to arrive. When I did, she would not ask me to do anything except to listen, and I did. Once when she finished a song she asked me, "Do you know the story of the jinni girl, who kidnapped Sabah by the seven palm trees, because she loved him very much?"

"I've heard the story. Adnan says it is not true, but Fathil the Liar says it is true."

"I think it's true. I wish it's true," Amel said with a sad voice.

"Why?" I said, with an annoying, careless tone.

"Because it's so romantic," she said with a dreamy look in her eyes.

"It was scary... I was scared when we went to the seven palm trees and I am considered a brave boy."

"I would not be scared, because I wish I could slip into the other side, the side of jinn."

Amel looked at me, looking for approval of her romantic dream.

"Why would you want to do that?" I asked.

"Because I feel that it would be better than the life we live here, and I would kidnap my true love, and he would be mine forever." She said this with such a strange conviction, looking at me with her big black eyes and the hair clip crossing her right eyebrow and down her tanned cheek.

"I think it would be more romantic, easier, and less painful. And in the jinn world, a girl could love a boy, and no one would care; they would be left alone." Amel's eyes filled with tears that looked like sparking pearls.

"You can do that here. I mean on this side," I said, without realizing the stupidity of my comment, because I knew it would be impossible for a girl to love a boy and be left alone.

"I don't think I can do that. I am so afraid that I will grow old and love will have never found me."

At that moment, I lost all the words. I did not know what to say or how to finish the conversation, so I resorted to the solution I knew best.

"I must go now. Hamid and Adnan may be waiting for me by the river."

"Wait! Can I read you the song of the jinni girls who love humans? It's by Bader Shaker Al-Sayyab."

I did not want to stay, but she started reading, and I stood by the door motionless, while my back was being burnt by the merciless sun.

The rain had wet our hair,
And lit the moon,
In the lights of our hair there are candles,
So all of you Gypsy caravans,
Let our hair be your guiding lights,
Through the endless paths of the desert,
Walk till dusk,
Walk to tomorrow,
We the jinni girls don't sleep,
We stroll in the dark,
On the top of the sandy hills or the grave yards,
We love all passersby,
We sing to them the song of love and devotion,
And when a young human girl comes to the underworld,
She feels lonely in the grave,
Sacred is the darkness of her ground hole,
Our song will pierce through the dirt,
Telling her,
If you get naked the spider will spin you a new dress,
And each thread will ring like a string,
Sleep until fate calls,
When all the dead walk to the judgment bench,
Your lover has a smile on his lips,

Because he saw someone else,
He saw you in her tall appearance,
Her eyes and her eye lashes burned his heart,
He wishes he had waited,
We show the child butterflies,
Made from the sun's rays,
Flying by the trees,
Lovers see the good-byes in our eyes,
We are the feeling when the poet feels,
We are what made Sinbad sail to an island,
Where he fell in love with a myth,
With a mirage,
As he tells of a queen,
Loved by the moon,
But illusion was his love,
We are the jinni girls,
The rain drips from our hair,
The Moon drinks the water from our hair,
We run through the grave yard,
Chasing the poets and all the passersby,
Showing them the path to a dream world,
Where there is no return.

Half of me was in the shade, and the other was toasting in the sun. Although I knew that I was missing out on a priceless adventure with Hamid and Adnan, an afternoon of swimming or a walk with Haleem by the Hillaly girls' house, as Haleem waited for a reply to his love letters, I did not want Amel to stop reading. Her voice grew deeper and sadder, as if she tasted the pain and joy of the jinni girls. At that moment, I looked into her eyes to make sure they were not upside down like the jinni. Instead, I saw the mysterious deep, darkness surrounded by a green halo, just like the glow the Wolves and I saw by the seven palm trees.

4

The news about us leaving town was quick to spread among my friends and the townspeople. I tried to spend as much time as possible with Hamid, Adnan and the rest of the Wolves. During my last year in Balluria, Amel and I shared many hours of poetry reading; she reciting and I listening. Many times, I planned my visits to Hamid's house during the hours that I knew that neither Hamid nor his mother would be there. Amel would be waiting for me with a new poem from Badr Shaker Al-Sayyab, Pablo Neruda, Hussian Merdan, T. S. Elliot, and Omar Al-Khayyam, but mostly she read the poetry of Badr Shaker

Al-Sayyab. She became so absorbed in the poems that tears often rolled from her beautiful eyes. She learned that my love for Adawya, the younger of the Hillaly girls, was a youthful myth, and she in a way, also knew that I would leave Balluria with no memory of true love, or, at least, that's what I thought she knew. I, on the other hand, knew that neither of us had found true love in Balluria, at least not at that time.

A month before my family and I left Balluria, Hamid told me that when the two party militiamen came looking for him—which I failed to warn him about, because I had spent the afternoon listing to his sister singing—he was hiding for two days in the marshes alone. He had found a dead body floating in the river, and he buried it by himself, but someone saw him doing it, and they must have reported him. He told me that the body was riddled with so many bullets that it looked like a fishnet from all the holes in it. He thought that the body might have been that of an army deserter, who tried to escape from the party militiamen, who hunted army deserters and shot them immediately, no questions asked. He also said that he saw the group of militiamen approaching the river, so he sailed on the *Titanic* and spent two days and nights living in the marshes, eating what he fished and hunted. He said that while he was sailing in the marshes he felt free in a way that he'd never felt before, and he said that he could live in the marshes his whole life, but he was worried about his mother and his sister, Amel. He also told me that the Wolves were preparing for an entire day after school of swimming and fishing by the river, because Hisham wanted to put the team back together, as he still thought that we could defeat the Wild Lions, especially since their captain, Mazen, had been in a car accident and would not be able to play soccer for a long time. He told me that the meeting place would be in the same spot where Adnan, he, and I had worked long hours fixing the *Titanic* Thursday after school.

After the school day was over, I spent a few minutes waiting for my father, who usually worked only half a day on Thursdays, so he could take a daily nap. I walked slowly through the dusty walkway toward the river, and for no apparent reason, I thought I would stop by Hamid's house first. I hoped to find Amel by herself, maybe for one last chance to hear her sing or to listen to her reciting the poetry of Badr Shaker Al-Sayyab. I knocked and she opened the door,

"Is Hamid here?" I asked.

"No, he went to the river, do you want to come in?" she asked.

"Is your mother here?"

"No, she went to the Hillalys'."

Great, the two answers that I was hoping for. Hamid's mom spent so much time at the Hillaly house that I thought she was related to them. Hamid never told me that she had a severe case of asthma and she had trouble breathing during the hot summers of the south, and the hellish heat of Hamid's house did not help matters. And since the only three houses in Balluria with air-conditioning were our house, the Hillalys', and the large guesthouse of Sheikh

Jawad, Hamid's mom would spend the hours between eleven in the morning and five in the afternoon at the Hillalys', who generously let her sleep near the loud, tin air-conditioner, which sounded like a tiny train running though the town. To me it was a convenience that I did not plan for, but that I certainly was thankful for.

I entered the house walking behind Amel, who I noticed had grown into a young woman, but I tried to suppress my impure thoughts, because she was my best friend's sister. I entered the house without fear of being caught off guard by Hamid, who I thought was somewhere on the Euphrates sailing the *Titanic* or escaping another raid by the party militia, who at the time were gathering both young and old men, who were not students or who lacked any valid reason for not being in the army. If they were strong enough or not too old to fight, the militia would round them up for a speedy one-week training session, and then would send them to the war front that never seemed satisfied with the thousands of lives that it consumed. I entered the house knowing that I would spend at least two or three hours listening to her voice either singing with Fairuz or reciting poetry. She sat in the shade, and I sat in my spot, where half of my back baked in the sun. She looked at me with the same old look of sadness and said with a voice that sounded older and more mature than the sweet, quiet voice that I remembered, "Do you know what sadness the rain brings?"

"What? What do you mean?" I asked in my usual manner to steer the conversation toward questions that I could answer.

"It's a line from Al-Sayyab's poem," she said.

"Yes, I know. We read the poem together, right here, long ago," I answered.

"Yes, but do you know how sad and lonely it feels when it rains?"

"Yes, yes, I do," I said.

"No, you don't," Amel looked at me and said, "I heard that you and your family are leaving town. Is that true?"

"I don't know. My father said something like that."

"Well, if you know how sad and lonely it feels in the rain, then you will not leave," she said and looked at me. I felt trapped as I looked for a painless answer, but she just looked at me and said with a siren voice that brought me some ease. "I hope you don't leave. Many people have left already.

"I want you to listen to this song; it's one of Fairuz's songs. It's my song. She sang it for me." As strange as that sounded, I believed her. She turned the cassette player on. The piano music was amazing. The song echoed between the walls of the mud house on the bank of the Euphrates while Amel, with her sweet and quiet voice, sang the words of the amazing Lebanese goddess of love and broken hearts.

I remember so many people,
Waiting for their loved ones,
The rain came and they carried their umbrellas,
They kept waiting,
But no one was waiting for me,
Even when the skies are clear,
I have been here for a hundred years

I have written many letters,
To people with no addresses,
The walls are getting tired of me waiting,
But I will continue to wait,
Although I know, no one will be waiting for me.

She looked at me, looking for answers that I did not have.

"Do you want to kiss me?" Amel said in a voice that sounded more like a confession than a question.

"What?" I swallowed my saliva as I tried to make sure that I heard her correctly.

"What did you say?"

"Like the way you kissed Adawya, the Hillaly girl."

"No, I can't. You are Hamid's sister. He is my friend, I don't…"

That was what I said before I lost my ability to talk and think. Amel and I sat there for the longest half hour of my life. I did not want to leave, but we both just sat there silently looking at the ground in the dark shade and then at each other. Amel lifted up her head, and I could see the tears coming down on her beautiful, tanned face, right next to the black clip of hair that went down to her chin.

She said, "I hope that you don't leave. I hope that you will stay. I hope that you and my brother, Hamid, will always be friends, so that you can come to our house all the time. I hope that you will be my friend, and you and I can sit here when no one is around. We can read poetry and listen to Fairuz's songs all the time. I hope we can do these things forever."

She looked at the ground. A tear fell off of her tanned cheek, leaving a clean trace and dropped to the ground, on the floor of the dark shade, and she stopped talking.

"If we stay here…" I said.

She looked at me as I searched for words.

"If we stay here, I will always come here and we can read poetry," I said as I stood up and dusted off my clothes. "I am going to look for Hamid."

"I will always be waiting for…" She stopped and looked at me. "I will always be waiting for you, waiting to read poetry to you, and waiting to sing Fairuz's songs to you."

I walked to the river, looking for any sign of Hamid, Adnan, or any of the Wolves. I never thought that that afternoon would be the last time in my life that I would listen to Fairuz's songs sung by the voice of the young, tanned, southern girl from Balluria, who dreamt of leaving to another world, where girls could love boys with no fear of what others might say or do and who waited for true love. But it was the last time I listened to her reading poetry in the dark shade of the mud house.

The Book of the Gypsy Witches

The Dance of the Last Gypsy Witch

1

"So, you are the one who chose the name Hanan?" Salam asked.

"He never told me if I was part of his family, but that night Sheikh Jawad asked me to name his daughter, but he told me not to pick a Gypsy name.

"I wanted to name her Gazala so she could be like a gazelle running in the desert, but I figured that what the sheikh needed the most was affection, Hanan. That's why I gave her that name, although Sabrya claims that she picked it. She is a liar. May Allah bless her soul." Sadness rolled off her words. "I dreamed for a long time that he would take me as a second wife so I could be near him and Hanan, but I knew that he would never agree. He would rather kill me than have the Gypsy whore he owned as his wife. But there was one thing he never deprived me of."

"What was it?"

"Sheikh Jawad never deprived me from seeing Hanan, nor did he ever prevent her from coming to my mud hut."

"Did she come here a lot?" the man asked

"Since she learned how to walk, she came here. And before that I was at the sheikh's house every day watching her grow. She grew beautiful and brought joy to the stone-hard heart of the sheikh.

"I watched her grow every day of her life and watched how Sheikh Jawad had to endure the looks of his men and Irar as the sheikh sat in the guesthouse with his daughter Hanan sitting in his lap. He was paying more attention to her than to what I was saying."

"Then I heard Khanger, the coffee server, saying that there would be a draft. Khanger said this as he poured a coffee for the many men who shouted about how the Israelis had seized the West Bank and Gaza and had advanced into the Sinai desert.

"'All the Arab rulers are traitors,' said a man with a red yeshmagh, and a large mole on his nose.

"It was not normal or accepted for the sheikh to sit in the middle of a guesthouse with a child in his lap, especially a female child, but Sheikh Jawad did not care. He would let Hanan sit in his lap as he ate dinner with sheikhs and as he drank his tea.

"I remember seeing Hanan sitting in her father's lap. She had the eyes of an angel as she touched her father's rugged face. I think it's the baby smell that entered Jawad's heart and softened it. It was the soft touch of Hanan's hand that washed the harsh surface of Jawad's soul. She always touched her father's face, and he kissed her hands and kissed her belly as she giggled. Many times, I have looked at Jawad's eyes. I always saw the blood and hate until I saw him looking at his firstborn child, Hanan. Then I saw the color of human in them," the Gypsy woman said, and she wiped her tears. "Hanan was seven when I needed yogurt from his house. I walked to Sheikh Jawad's house and saw Sheikh Jawad sitting in front of his guesthouse, and she was showing him how to write his name. I sat next to him. I did not care if the people saw me sitting next to the sheikh. I sat next to the man I loved and my only child. I was consumed by the love for both," she said, and she looked in the space in front of the mud hut and reached out with her hand, imitating what she remembered.

"I saw Hanan holding her father's hand and tracing the pencil on a piece of paper and giggling with him when he wrote his name wrong.

"J-A-W-A-D. not J-A-W-E-D. It's J-A-W-A-D., Baba."

"That morning Sheikh Jawad looked at me with the most beautiful smile I ever saw on a man's face. He said, 'Barrya, I wish I could spend my entire life just playing and smelling my little girl. Barrya, I could not live one moment without her love and without knowing that she is alive. Allah, the people, and the world can take anything from me now, my guesthouse and my land and my herd, but they must spare this child. I breathe her breath and feel that I have lost the will to look at any other humans.'

"That morning I cried and said to Sheikh Jawad, 'May Allah keep her for you, Sheikh, and keep you for me.'

"Sheikh Jawad did not look at me when I said that. He looked at Hanan and said, 'My little jewel, I will marry you to a sheikh and you will make your father proud.'

"I could not forget the color I saw in his eyes with a human glow. The only time that he was a human was when he looked at Hanan or when he touched her beautiful, little face or kissed her tiny, delicate hands. He sat in his guesthouse and she sat in his lap. He walked the streets of Balluria, flanked by armed men, but he held her hand as she walked slowly. He and his entire retinue had to walk slowly to accommodate her short steps.

"Even when he went to the mosque, Hanan was there, climbing her father's back as he prayed. Even when Sayed Habeeb protested, 'This child better be clean because this place is pure.'

"Sheikh Jawad simply looked at him and said, 'Her urine is more holy to me than your mosque, Sayed.'

"Sayed Habeeb smiled tightly and did not say a word. After that, Sheikh Jawad stopped going to the mosque.

"I even heard Irar said to Sheikh Jawad, 'You love this girl too much, Jawad, and she is not even a boy. Why don't you love your son, Ahmed, the same way? He is your son, and he will carry your name. Females are bound to bring shame to their fathers, Jawad.'

"Jawad looked at Irar with a look that I had never seen him use with his mentor before and with his fearsome voice said, 'No one dares to shame me. My daughter will not shame me. Her love has been injected into my heart.'"

"When was Ahmed born?"

"He was born one year after Hanan."

"Was he your son too? I mean, did you have anything to do with his birth?"

"No, Gypsy dancers only give birth to female babies. No, my son Ahmed was Sabrya's son."

"It was one year after Hanan's birth when I was told that Sabrya gave a birth to a baby boy. I did not know at the time that she was pregnant. It was during those days that news came from the capital city that the sleeping general president was awakened by a mortar shell and the new era of blood had started. That's they when Ahmed was born, one year after Hanan."

"The sleeping general?"

"Yes, my son. They said he was a good man who was too good and too naïve to understand conspiracies. But no one in Balluria or in these parts cared because they did not know what the future was holding for them.

"That same year Adnan's family moved to Balluria, and they settled in the mud hut near the main road near the puddle of water infested with mosquitoes; its water changed colors as the season changed.

"Sheikh Jawad was not in Balluria when Ahmed was born. Sheikh Jawad and Irar were on a trip that no one except me knew about."

"Where were they?"

"Ahmed was born alone," the woman said, ignoring the man's question. "Poor Ahmed was a weak child from his birth. Sabrya was sick again with child labor and did not want to hold her newborn child, and a month later Sabrya died."

"She died one month after Ahmed's birth?"

"Yes, my son. That's why Ahmed was weak and shy and gentle, because he never had a real mother. Ahmed was cared for by the many women who wore black robes and lived in the sheikh's house."

"Tell me more about Hanan."

"What do you want to know? Hanan was not supposed to be born in these parts."

"Why?"

"Hanan was different. She had the Gypsy blood in her. She loved life; she loved when others did not know how to love, and she loved what others did not care to love. She loved animals and had a cat, and she laughed and smiled all the time. Years went quickly and Hanan blossomed and grew as beautiful as no other woman in these parts. She had no mother, but she had me and she had many women who lived at the sheikh's house and wore black robes, and they all treated her like a daughter, as they were all childless and hopeless. But she knew that I was her real mother."

"But you were not her mother," Salam said with unexpected surliness.

"My heart told me that you would say that. Yes, my son. I was her mother. I watched her grow every day and loved her like a mother every day. A mother is the one who gives the love, not the one who gives birth."

Salam felt sorry for his comment and mumbled, "I guess you were her mother. Please tell me more."

"Hanan grew fast, and when she turned nine, there were no women in these parts who would dare to say that she was more beautiful than Hanan. She became the light of joy in Sheikh Jawad's house and in his heart. He wanted to see her every day and sat with her every day and never prevented her from entering the guesthouse when she wanted to, even when it was filled with men. He said once to Irar that when they sat in my mud hut, 'My daughter's feet are more honorable than all the sheikhs' heads in these parts.'

"I was happy to hear Sheikh Jawad saying that, and I saw Irar smiling for the first time in his life, and I laughed when Irar replied.

"'Just don't say that in front of any man in these parts. We don't want to have war because of your little daughter.'

"My beautiful little girl made a half-man and half-wolf like Irar smile."

The Gypsy woman paused as she tried to pour tea for him and spoke with a weak voice that showed weariness.

"That was when Kamal and his mother came to live in the sheikh's house."

"So Kamal was not the sheikh's real nephew?"

"No, my son. Kamal was eleven years old when he and his mother came to live in the sheikh's house. His father was killed in the war in the north with the Kurds, and his mother was related to Sabrya, the dead wife of the sheikh."

"When I first saw Kamal, I noticed his big eyes and his fears."

"His fears? I never thought Kamal had any fear."

"Yes he did, my son. The poor boy was living in a constant fear."

"From what?"

"From not being loved. He was scared of not being loved, and I think that's why he was the way he was."

"I never liked Kamal. He was a very mean kid."

"I know, my son. None of you boys liked Kamal. He was a mean child and mean youngster and grew up to be a very mean man, mean enough to kill Hanan, the woman he loved."

"Did he love Hanan?"

"Oh, my dear Allah, yes. He loved her. He loved her very much, but just like all the men in these parts, he did not know how nor did he allow her to love another man. Kamal knew that Hanan loved Hamid. He knew about them long before he wanted to marry her, but he was not able to let go of her, because he was cursed with love for Hanan, just as Hamid was and just like her father

Sheikh Jawad was. For years, Kamal tried to make Hanan love him. He tried to do anything and everything so Hanan would look at him the same way she looked at Hamid and feel about him the same way she felt about Hamid, but all of his attempts turned to dust."

"Why not? I mean why did Hanan never like Kamal? He was a handsome kid, as I remember."

"Yes he was handsome," the Gypsy woman said with the same old laugh that chased the shadows of the mud walls, "but Hanan never liked Kamal, because cats cannot swim. It was fate."

"Fate?" Salam asked without knowing what she meant, but he had grown used to her ways of saying things that usually meant something else.

"Yes, my son. That was when Hamid and Kamal became enemies. It was fate, as I said."

"Fate? Everything is fate?" His tense question barely covered his frustration.

"Yes, my son, and you will see that everything was fate. You see it was only few months after Kamal came to the sheikh's house when his mother disappeared and no one knew where she went, and it was during those days when Hanan's cat birthed seven kittens, and they filled the house with noise and left their mess on the carpet in the guesthouse of Sheikh Jawad. That was the one thing that Sheikh Jawad did not forgive his beloved daughter for, because no one dares to disgrace the guesthouse of the sheikh. Sheikh Jawad was very angry, and he beat with his whip all the women who wore black robes. He thought that one of them was trying to put a curse on him, but another told the sheikh that it was the kittens of his daughter, Hanan, that disgraced the guesthouse.

"The sheikh was blinded with anger, and he shouted, 'Hanan's kittens disgraced my guesthouse. What will I tell the sheikhs if they ask me about the smell in the guesthouse?'

"But I thought he loved her more than he would care about what other sheikhs thought about him?" Salam asked.

"See, my son, when I say it was fate, I mean it. He was angry for a reason; it was fate. It was all written in the prophecy that Sheikh Jawad to be there that evening, because it was meant for Hanan to meet Hamid that evening."

"I don't understand."

"You will, my son. It was when Sheikh Jawad called Kamal to come to the guesthouse and asked him if there were kittens there.

"'Yes, Uncle Sheikh,' Kamal said.

"'Are they yours?' the fearsome sheikh asked the frightened orphan.

"'No, Uncle Sheikh. They are Hanan's. Hanan's cat birthed six or seven little kittens.'

"'I want you to put all the kittens in a sack and throw them in the river. You hear me?' Sheikh Jawad ordered the frightened orphan with a voice that left grown men cowering.

"'Yes, Uncle Sheikh, I will," Kamal answered with total obedience and absolute fear of the punishment he might face for refusing. Kamal snatched the little kittens one by one from Hanan's hands as she tried to hide them in the many rooms of the sheikh's house, and she cried for each one of her kittens. She begged her father not to let Kamal take the kittens from her.

"'Baba, please, they are so small and so soft,' Hanan begged her father.

"I was there in the house looking to get some yogurt, but Sheikh Jawad did not pity the tears of his beloved daughter, who cried for hours as she saw Kamal put all the seven kittens in the empty rice sack and tie its end with a twist," the Gypsy woman said.

"'Take these dirty things and drown them in the river!' Sheikh Jawad shouted at Kamal.

"Kamal ran with the sack followed by Hanan and Ahmed, and soon the three children were joined by the Hillaly children, Adnan, Hisham, Haleem, and all the other little boys and girls of Balluria. They all followed Kamal to the river.

"Hanan cried all the way to the river, begging Kamal to let the kittens out.

"'Kamal, can't you hear them crying? They can't breathe. Let them free, Kamal, please.'

"Kamal was too afraid of her father to heed her tearful pleas. 'I can't. Your father told me to throw them in the river,' he said, fighting the writhing bag of kittens on his back.

"At that time, young Hamid was throwing his net into the Euphrates to fish for dinner for his mother and his younger sister.

"When Hamid heard the cries of Hanan, he thought it was his sister, Amel, who was crying. He left his fishing net in the water and ran toward where Kamal was swinging the sack to throw it into the Euphrates.

"'Stop, don't, or I will beat you up,' Hamid ordered Kamal.

"'It's none of your concern. Sheikh Jawad told me to throw these kittens in the river.'

"'But they will die. They will drown.'

"'Yes. That's why I have to throw them in the river,' Kamal said as he swung one more time and threw the sack full of kittens into the dark water of the Euphrates.

"Hanan cried out, 'Ahhhh! My kittens! My poor kittens!'

"Without even making sure of what he saw and heard, Hamid glanced at Hanan's face and said, "I will save them." He stripped off his shirt and dove like a harpoon into Euphrates with his top half naked and muddy, and he swam like a fish toward the sack.

"The crowd of children and I were silent as Hamid grabbed the sack and swam back to the bank. That day Hanan saw the tanned face of Hamid when he dove into the Euphrates and swam to save the kittens. She saw his half-naked body leaping in and out of the Euphrates and pulling the sack of her screaming kittens.

"When Kamal saw that Hamid was trying to save kittens, he ran back to the sheikh's house shouting at Ahmed and Hanan, 'I will tell my uncle the sheikh about this. By Allah, he will be very angry and will beat both of you.' Kamal was actually too afraid to tell the sheikh and waited for the moment when the sheikh would call him and ask him about the kittens, but the sheikh never did.

"Through trying to destroy what Hanan held dear, Kamal lost the most precious thing that he desired; he lost the chance to have Hanan's love. That evening Hamid pulled the kittens out of the water, dried them with his shirt, and gave them one by one back to Hanan, who held the wet, frightened kittens to her chest, saying, 'Oh, my Allah, they are so cold and scared. I can't take them back to our house. My father will be angry at me.'

"'That's all right. I will take them to my house. I have many other animals, pigeons and dogs.'

"Hamid saw how Hanan looked at him, mesmerized by his wet, naked body and his intoxicating animal stench. Hamid put the kittens in his shirt and took them to his house, and Hanan went with him, followed by her younger brother, Ahmed. Hamid told Hanan that he would keep them in his house until they grew and she could come to his house and they would feed the kittens together.

"That first time that Hanan went to Hamid's house, she left her heart there when she left that small house full of hunger and love and animals. That's when I knew that the prophecy was coming true, when I saw the look in Hanan's eyes when she gazed at Hamid. For many years she went to Hamid's house to see her kittens, and for many years her love for Hamid grew as they both cared for the seven kittens and the other animals in the house. I watched them grow together in love." She paused briefly and then continued.

"In my heart, I knew that Kamal wanted to be the one saving the kittens, not the one who drowned them, but he was afraid of the sheikh. Kamal did not know that cats could not swim. He was twelve, and he wanted the approval of the mean sheikh who was like a father to him. Kamal was an unfortunate soul who was never loved, so he replaced love with anger and hate, two things he knew well.

"I've always thought that Kamal was mean and secretive."

"It's not his fault, my son. Kamal's mother came to live in Sheikh Jawad's house when his father was killed in the mountains and he had no other place or another family to go to. Soon after arriving, his mother left the sheikh's house one night and left him behind."

"Where did she go?"

"No one knew at the time, but I knew."

"How did you know?"

"Because Kamal's mother and her lover spent many afternoons here in my hut, and one afternoon they left, never to be seen again in Balluria or these parts."

"What happened to Kamal after that?"

"Kamal became the sheikh's adopted son. The sheikh never loved Kamal, but he liked Kamal more than his own son, Ahmed. Kamal was mean and strong like Sheikh Jawad himself, and Ahmed was weak and gentle. Never liking Ahmed, the sheikh always depended completely on Kamal, but always treated Kamal like a slave. He made Kamal do all the guesthouse chores and made him shepherd the herds, and one thing he never stopped doing."

"What was it?"

"He never stopped calling Kamal the son of a betrayer whore. Never. He used to always call him the son of betrayer whore and every time I heard him calling Kamal with those words, I looked at Kamal's face and saw the poor kid's face filled with pain."

The Gypsy woman put out her cigarette in the flaky gray ashes in front of her. And her face suddenly lit with joy as she said, "When I saw Hamid's face, I knew that he would be the one stealing Hanan's heart."

"How did you know?" Salam asked.

"Because I could feel the spirit of an Arabian horseman in him, a lonesome knight who roams the desert on the back of his horse looking for love, looking for a Gypsy witch. That's why."

Salam again felt the frustration building up with the convoluted responses to his questions, so he tried to be more direct as he asked with a quiet voice, "When did you learn about Hanan and Hamid's affair?"

"It was not an affair, my son. It was love, pure love with no boundaries and no limits and no shame and no fear; it was love not meant for these parts or this earth. It was love that was stolen from time. Pure, Arabian Sahara love that made rocky-faced rugged Arabian horsemen and knights with curvy swords melt as they saw the hips of a Gypsy dancer move. It was the love that no one in these parts knew how to show to their women.

"Hanan was eleven when she came to me, crying from a pain that was not curable. I asked where the pain was, and she pointed to her heart. She said that she couldn't sleep because she smelled the scent of man and she could not forget the smell." The blind Gypsy woman's voice became deeper as though she were revealing a secret that she had kept for years. "I knew then, without a doubt, that the prophecy of my Gypsy grandmothers was true."

2

"It was her fate to be a lover and to be the beautiful sinner. What else do you think she would have done? Be like all the other women in these parts?" she inquired with a touch of anger. Then she took a drag on her cigarette and exhaled a massive amount of smoke that seemed to calm her down so that she could speak with quieter voice, "I asked Hanan where the pain was, and she pointed to her heart."

She said that she can't sleep because she smelled the scent of a man and she could not forget the smell. I knew then the prophecy of my Gypsy grandmothers was true," the Gypsy woman said.

"Hanan came to me many times over the years saying such things as, 'Mother Barrya, every time I see Hamid, I feel like I am drunk with his stench.'

"'Mother Barrya, I feel like I want him wrap me in his arms and never let go.'

"'Mother Barrya, when I go to sleep, I sleep with his face in my mind and close my eyes imagining his big black beautiful eyes looking at me.'

"'Mother Barrya, I wish I could leave the world behind and go to the desert with him.'

"'Mother Barrya, I wish the word would disappear, and only Hamid and I would be here. Mother Barrya, I can't see anyone or anything else when I am looking at him.'

"Mother Barrya, I am afraid that my family will kill me, but I feel I want to be with Hamid even if they kill me."

"'Mother Barrya, I feel that the time is short when I see him, and I feel the time is endless when I can't see him.'

"'Mother Barrya, I look at the birds and ask them if they saw Hamid. I look at the sky and ask it if it covered Hamid.'

"'Mother Barrya, I love the night in his eyes and love the way he smiles, and I melt when hear his voice.'

"'Mother Barrya, I want to kiss the ground that he walks on.'

"'Mother Barrya, I feel if will touch me. He will make me a woman, and I wanted him to touch me whenever I smelled him.'

"'Oh, my poor child, it is the way Gypsy women would love a man.' That's what I said to Hanan, and I knew then the prophecy of my Gypsy grandmothers was true."

"The prophecy?" the man asked

"Yes, the prophecy of the Gypsy witch, who would be born in these parts and be cursed with the love of a man who is so free and so unchained, the last Gypsy witch who will die because she dared to love, and she will be the last Gypsy witch to ever live in these lands. Hanan was cursed with love for Hamid. It was her fate it be a lover and to be beautiful sinner. What else do you think she could have been? She could not be like her dead mother, and she could not be like me even as much as she wanted to. She was in between, and that is a difficult place to be in for woman in these parts. She could not be decent, she was an Arab woman who wanted to love and had the blood of a Gypsy dancer and the boiling blood of a self-made sheikh. She was half-woman and half-wolf, beautiful and wild and free as the Arabian Sahara, and silky and slithery as its snakes. She could not be decent the way they wanted her to be. She was bound for the forbidden love, and she was bound for sin from the moment she was born. And that's why she died the way she did, because she followed her destiny. Unlike the women in these parts, Hanan was the only one who chose to live," the Gypsy woman said, as she wiped her eyes.

"Since that first day when Hanan came to me complaining of the pains of love, she had no time to waste on the things other people in Balluria had wasted their lifetime for, just like their ancestors did. Hanan was consumed with love; her soul and her body were consumed with love.

"Once I heard her telling Hamid in the many afternoons they spent lying next to each other in my bed, I heard her telling him, 'Sometimes I feel like I am deaf and blind whenever I smell your sweat. Other times, I feel like I want to cry because I feel that I am so thirsty for you, Hamid.'" The Gypsy woman's blind eyes sparkled with mere joy of telling the love tales of the dead daughter of Sheikh Jawad.

"Oh, my poor girl. She should have been born a full-blooded Gypsy.

"I have never blamed myself for teaching Hanan the things I did, because when I think about life in these parts I know that Hanan did not want to live like them. She wanted to live the way she lived, and I know she wanted to love the way she did."

"What did you teach her?" the man asked

"I taught Hanan how to dance and how to hold a man's head in her hands and lure him into the tasty spiral of lust and love with a kiss. I taught her how to steal the senses of a man with the moves of the hips and the moves of the neck and the moves of the shoulders; the moves that made kings and princes and sheikhs lose their poise and act like little kittens."

"I knew that the girls from our school used to come to your house," Salam said, trying to keep the innocence of the memory they both shared.

"Hanan and Amel and Basima and the Hillaly girls—they all came here in the afternoons, and we all danced and painted our hands with henna and talked about you boys," she said. She let out a shy laugh and looked at him flirtatiously. "And I remember whenever Adawya, the younger of the Hillaly girls, talked about how groomed and neat you looked, Amel got upset and said to Adawya, 'You don't know anything about him. He likes poetry.'

"The two girls were fighting for you."

"What about my sister, Yusra? Did she ever come with the girls? And did she ever learn how to dance the Gypsy dances?"

"No, my son. Your sister never left your house. I wonder if she ever lived one day in her life the way she wanted to. Your family did not belong in these parts, my son. Your father hated me, and your mother thought that I was not decent enough to enter her house."

"Tell me more about Hanan," he said, trying to avoid the uncomfortable stream of accusations that could not be denied.

"I loved Hanan. She was my only daughter. She stole money from her house and brought it to me. She stole clothes and food so I didn't go hungry. For years, Sheikh Jawad did not give me any money or food, but Hanan did. She and I used to sit here as I painted her hair and hands with Henna, and she liked to dance and sing the Gypsy songs of love like the natural Gypsy girl she was meant to be. When she told me that she loved Hamid after she saw him when he saved her kittens, I told her that she needed to touch him and let him touch her."

"So, you were the one who..." Salam interrupted.

"Don't say a word, my son." The Gypsy woman spoke with her authoritative voice that he had not heard since the day of the soccer battle with the Wild Lions. "Hanan lived a life that was different than that all of the people in these parts. She lived inside a crystal shell that prevented her from knowing and noticing other people. She did not recognize anyone except her lover. No one else mattered to her. Her father and her brother and her dead mother did not matter. The people of the town did not matter. Time and place did not matter. Even the heat of the sun and the suffocating dust did not matter to her, as she was consumed with her love for Hamid. You will never understand that because you are like all the men in these parts who are prevented from true love. I taught Hanan how to love and how to dance, only because she was the last princess of the Gypsies, and what others thought about her or whatever Kamal and her brother Ahmed did to her was not her choice.

"When I taught her how to dance, she said she wanted to dance with Hamid and feel his eyes looking at her body as she danced, just like me when I wanted the eyes of Sheikh Jawad looking at me in that fateful night at the wedding of Sheikh Waitan's son. When Arab women dance, they feel the sting of the eyes looking at them, a tasty sting that will make any woman lose her pretentious decency and turn into a Gypsy." The Gypsy woman spoke with such clear conviction that he retreated from giving any argument, and he just sat and listened to the tales of love.

"One afternoon as the people of Balluria napped in the heat of summer, Hanan danced once for Hamid as he sat in the same place you are sitting now. He cried as he saw her dancing. She danced with moves so violent and protesting and so revealing." She said all this with the pride of a teacher about an overachieving student. "I saw Hamid's eyes tearing as looked at the most beautiful woman in these parts dancing, and when she saw him crying, she did not stop dancing. She danced more as she started to cry with him but she did not stop dancing. She said to him as she danced as the song of a woman they called the Algerian flower played in the radio singing about love,

They filled the ground with thorns and made me walk on it
Because I dared to love
They opened all the wounds of my heart
Because I dared to love
All of this because I loved
Or because I said I want to love

"And when she saw him crying, she leaned on his face and kissed him, and then she continued dancing and she cried as she said to Hamid, 'This is all I want to do, Hamid; I want to dance for you all my life, until I die between your arms. I want to dance for you until I have no breath left in me. I want to dance for you until my feet can't carry me anymore. I want to dance for you because I know that you will love me when I dance. I want to dance for you, my man, because I know that's the only way you can keep loving me. Allow me, my love, to dance for you because you will not love me another way. You will love me as I weave and as I move my body and my hips and my shoulders, because this is how you want me always, my love. Allow me, as I tempt you with my body. Seeking your true love. Allow me to show my love through my body. When I dance, my love, I laugh and cry at the same time. I scream and smile at the same time. I live and die at the same time. I accept and protest at the same time, my love. When I dance for you, my love, I am a complete woman, and I feel you are a complete man because the look in your eyes tells me that you don't want me to do anything else but dance. Let me dance, my love, because when I dance for you, my love, time does not matter. People do not matter. Possessions do not matter. When I dance for you, my love, Heaven and Hell do not matter, because I am in the Heavens of your love. Because when I dance, my love, I give you Heaven, as I am in Heaven because I love you. When I dance, my love, men and religions and tribes and places and history do not matter, because I am one soul being and this is my history and this is my region and this is my tribe and you are my man.'

"I have never seen a woman talk like that before. I think she was taught that poetry by Amel, Hamid's sister. It made me cry when Hanan said that to Hamid with tears on her cheeks, and the thick, black eyeliner that I put on her eyes made two straight lines that went down all the way to her breasts. At that moment, I wished that I could take the two lovers and run away to the desert and live like the Gypsies we were meant to be, but instead I told them to give themselves to each other."

"You mean?" Salam asked, revoking his earlier decision to just listen.

"That was when I told the two lovers that they must touch each other and that they must taste each other's flesh. They spent the afternoon kissing each other and touching each other's bodies. My son, in that hellish afternoon, heavens had opened all the doors in my mud hut and whatever was behind these walls that you see did not matter, not Balluria, not the sheikhs, not the people, and not the tribes. The only thing that mattered then were the hours that the two lovers spent in my bed away from all the eyes of the world," the Gypsy woman said, shutting all the doors of reasoning. She seemed undeterred by the man's grimness and inadequacy of the realities that he knew and lived by, but he managed to let out a question that he was too shy to ask.

"Had they mated?" he asked with his inherited pretentious Arab shyness.

"No, son. Your friend Hamid was honorable, and he never wanted to deflower his woman before they wed. He knew if he did that, he would lose her. He knew she would be killed. He also knew that her father, Sheikh Jawad, would never approve of him as a suitor for his only daughter. But the two lovers would not deprive themselves of each other's love. I was there, when the two lovers kissed and hugged and touched each other for hours. I was there because I had to see true love manifesting itself in my mud hut. I saw them crying on each other's shoulders, and I saw them looking in each other's eyes for hours, and I saw them undressing each other and lying next to each other. I could feel the blood in their veins boiling as they caressed each other's bodies. I could feel the fire in their breaths as they inhaled each other." Suddenly, her voice became more serene, and she lifted her hand and touched her lips. She wiped her tears and smeared the thick eyeliner on her own face. She talked in the spirit of a person that felt every word she was saying. The man felt that the Gypsy woman felt each letter of her own words, as she told of the events of the forbidden love that she witnessed in her mud hut years ago.

"I was there watching, the Gypsy woman said again. "As Hamid's tanned, sweaty fingers moved over the terrain of Hanan's untouched virgin body, touching the surface of her slightly tanned skin that smelled like fresh bread, the body that ached to be touched for ages.

"I saw Hanan's face as she felt the millions of ants creeping underneath her skin wherever his fingers moved. Hanan choked with desire and wanted his fingers to pierce her body and squeeze the forbidden needs and free the insatiable mouths of lust screaming to be freed." The man couldn't help but be impressed by her vivid accounts of the distant afternoon.

"Hanan did not stop Hamid's hands as they moved toward the forbidden places that were long guarded with traditions of honor, and she did not stop him from invading her last castle of decency. Instead, she not only allowed him to do, but she was secretly wishing that he would not stop there and he knew."

That afternoon, Hanan wished that Hamid would satisfy the intense ravenousness of every millimeter of virginity and claim her unclaimed physical territory. She had forgotten in that moment of numbing lust the place and the time and the people, and she was no longer willing to adhere to any logical presence of her surroundings. Even when she saw the flickering approving eyes of Barrya peeping from the slightly open door, she looked back at Barrya. She looked back at the eyes of the complicit Gypsy woman, who set the stage for the ultimate love to be manifested in these parts and the stage for the most unforgivable sin a sheikh's daughter could ever commit. Hanan looked back at Barrya and smiled and closed her eyes while Hamid's lips kissed the divinely tanned breasts and kissed the valley of the electrifying pleasure between the two mountains of her breasts. Hanan breathed heavily with fiery breath and felt the coldness of the her lover's saliva dripping on her brown nipples as a stream of chilling stings moved from her breasts all the way down to the end of her toes and all the way up the ends of her beautiful black hair.

"That night I walked Hanan to her house. I had to hold Hanan's hand as we walked, because she was spent with love," the Gypsy woman said to Salam. The image of strange innocence of the dead sheikh's daughter started to wither from his memory, and for what he did not know. Neither did the Gypsy woman who claimed to know all the secrets of the town. That night was the same night Kamal climbed the back wall of the house and made a small hole in the roof made from palm tree leaves and he looked inside the dark bathroom. That night Kamal could not breathe as he saw the most beautiful girl in these parts bathing. Kamal's heart overflowed with love and almost killed him when he saw the light of the kerosene lamp dancing in waves on the holy curves of Hanan's back and her breasts as she covered them with soap. Kamal was in tears as he realized the true magnitude of his loneliness while watching Hanan washing her body. That night, Kamal made a promise to himself that she would be his, his alone. No man in these parts and no man on earth would have Hanan. She would be his wife. He would do the impossible; he would climb mountains and cross desert after desert. And he would go to the end of the world to have her. That night, Kamal made a promise to himself that Hanan would be his and he would have her even if he had to kill all the men on this earth, even if he had to kill her.

What the Gypsy woman did not know and she could not claim she knew was that it was the same night Kamal was choked with an unbearable desire to cry as he saw the majestic nakedness of Hanan's body for the first time in his life. He was brought to silent tears as he realized the distance between himself and the eternal happiness that Hanan possessed and was depriving him of. His eyes stood still and his breath stopped as he looked at the light of the kerosene lamp painting wavy shadows of orange and black on Hanan's body, sparkling with drips of water Hanan poured on her hair that trailed down on her back to the curve of her hip. As she was bathing, she sang the song of the lonely secretive lovers.

Don't tell about us when you are asked
Keep our love secret way from people
Your eyes are my world
If you're a wound I don't want you healed

I hold the world when I hold you in my arms
You are my air and without you I can't breathe
I am all for you from my toes to the ends of my hair

"Kamal wished that she had been singing about him. He told me that in the many drunken nights that he spent here alone, long years after he killed her. The poor boy was blinded with her love, after he saw her naked and he realized the window of life that she could bring to his frightened soul, so he pursued her," the Gypsy woman said, saving the man from trying to figure out what happened after what she said

"What did he do?" the man asked, trying to keep the Gypsy woman from derailing her thoughts.

"What did he not do? He dressed nicely, wore cologne, and combed his hair. One day he even asked me if I had a love elixir so he could put it in Hanan's yogurt so she could fall in love with him."

"Did you? I mean did you have a love elixir?"

"No, son. There is no Gypsy love elixir that could change the love Hanan had for Hamid, because it was fate; it was a Gypsy prophecy. It was fate for Kamal also when late one afternoon he saw Hanan walking to my house, and he thought he could talk to her privately. He did not know that she was coming to meet Hamid, who had waited all afternoon for her. Because of his conniving nature, Kamal did not stop her before she entered my house; instead he sat outside putting his ear to the walls of my mud hut listening, but what he heard was like a dagger that went through his heart and ripped out the last thread of hope. Kamal heard Hanan and Hamid as they were lost in the heat of their forbidden love."

"That is sad," Salam said as he searched for better words, feeling a slight comfort in knowing that Kamal was hurt. "What did Kamal do then?" he asked

"Kamal was not able to let go. He was not willing to let Hamid have her. He wanted to do what Sheikh Jawad did long years ago. He wanted to marry a sheikh's daughter so he could be a sheikh too, but he chose the wrong woman. He was mistaken because Hanan was not a full sheikh's daughter. She was half Gypsy."

"What did Kamal do?" the man insisted.

"Kamal came to my hut one night. He was drunk and angry. He sat in the same place you are sitting in now and told me that he knew about Hanan and Hamid. Kamal said that he knew that Hanan was giving herself and her body to Hamid, and he knew that I was complicit with them." The Gypsy's voice became suddenly fearful. "Kamal was angry, and I was afraid that he would have killed me then. He had a pistol that was given to him by the party, and he carried it all the time. Kamal said that he would not tell Sheikh Jawad about his daughter's unforgivable betrayal. He said he would keep the secret if I helped him marry Hanan. He said he would forgive her for her ultimate sin, but she must marry him, and he said that I had to help him do that. Kamal said if I didn't help him marry Hanan, he would not only tell the sheikh, but he would kill me and kill Hanan and Hamid. Kamal waved his pistol in my face and said, 'I will be happy to empty my pistol in your filthy body, you Gypsy whore.'

"That's what Kamal said to me." The Gypsy woman spoke with disappointed sadness. "The young man who I had always treated like my son called me Gypsy whore; me, the only mother he had in his lonely life, but I forgave him because he was cursed with Hanan's love. Two weeks later he asked Sheikh Jawad for her hand in marriage, and to everyone's surprise, the sheikh agreed.

"He asked in the same way that Sheikh Jawad asked for his late wife's Sabrya's hand long years ago. Kamal had to convince the sheikh that he would kill any man who would dare to marry Hanan. That's why the sheikh agreed to Kamal's proposal."

"Were they wed?"

The Gypsy woman let out a loud laugh that chased away the eerie late shadows of the mud walls and said, "No, my son. That would never happen. You did not believe me when I said it was a prophecy."

"What happened, then?" Salam asked with festering anxiousness.

"They ran away. Hanan and Hamid ran away with their love," the Gypsy woman replied calmly.

"How?"

"Hanan came to me the day after her father agreed to marry her to Kamal and said, 'Mother Barrya, I will kill myself. I will throw myself in the Euphrates and go to the end of the marshes before I let any man touch me, other than Hamid.' When Hanan said that, I looked in her eyes, and I knew that she would kill herself. Her love for Hamid had consumed her. So I asked her if she was ready to fulfill the prophecy.

"Hanan listened to me as I told her about her prophecy and the reason she met Hamid. She believed me, and she said she was willing to fulfill the prophecy if it would make her belong to Hamid. Hanan said to me that she was willing to be Hamid's wife. She said she was willing to be his Gypsy whore. She said she was willing to be that last Gypsy dancer if that was what the prophecy was saying and she would do anything to be with Hamid.

"That's when I asked Hanan, 'Even blood?'

"'Even blood,' Hanan said to me and I told her, 'Then, my daughter, I will bring Hamid to my hut and you have to lie with him until he draws the blood of your virginity, and that way you will belong only to him, and he will always belong to you.'

"That was what I said to Hanan," the Gypsy woman said with the calmness of a wise philosopher. "She believed me, unlike all the others."

"What did Hamid do?" the man asked, as he was thrilled to learn about his boyhood best friend's love adventure, feeling a strange connection knowing that he would have been involved in it if he was living in Balluria at that time.

"When I sent for Hamid to come to my hut, he listened to me as he sat in my hut. He did not want to take Hanan's virginity. He was afraid the she would be killed. He was afraid for her, but he knew that the sheikh would never reject Kamal and approve him instead. Hanan cried for hours on his shoulder, and when evening came he looked at me and asked, 'Mother Barrya, what does your prophecy says about my death?'

"I told Hamid that the prophecy said that he would live a very long life.

"'Well, if I am alive, then Hanan will be too. Mother Barrya, you know if do this I will have to leave Balluria. Who will care for my mother and my sister, Amel?' Hamid asked.

"Hamid always cared for and loved his mother and his sister. So I told him, 'If you leave Balluria with Hanan, I will wait until they stop searching for you and Hanan. I will wait for you to send me a message telling me where you are, and then I will bring them to you,'" the Gypsy woman said to the man who stared at her with wide eyes and unwavering attention. He wondered if she believed in what she told his boyhood best friend about his own death.

"That afternoon as the people of Balluria waited and prepared to celebrate the wedding of Hanan the next day, Hamid and Hanan made love for the first time in my bed, and she became his woman forever. She became his Gypsy whore and his Gypsy dancer as I cleaned the blood of her virginity with my own hands and hid the bloody cloth in my own box of secrets."

"Box of secrets?"

"Yes, my son. It's a box that keeps all the secrets of Balluria; it is hidden here under the covers. Would you like to see it, the bloody cloths of Hanan's virginity?" Her secretive smile showed that she could be feel her guest's discomfort and was taking unholy pleasure in it.

"No. I mean it's not necessary," Salam replied quickly, fearing for his innocence and not wanting to experience the ravages of the brutal forthcomings of the Gypsy woman and the gruesome evidence of true memories that she hid.

"That night Hamid asked me to go with Hanan, so she could bring her belongings, and when I asked where he was planning to go, he told me he did not know, but he would send a message one day. He could not let Hanan face death when Kamal discovered she was not a virgin," the Gypsy woman said with a proud smile of devoted mother.

"Hamid said to me that Hanan was his wife in front of Allah and me, and then he went to see his mother and his sister, Amel, for the last time. He insisted that I bring Hanan back to my hut in an hour or she would be killed. Then he would have to kill Kamal and Sheikh Jawad, and he had no desire to kill either of them."

The Gypsy woman paused as she put her cigarette out in the pile of ashes in front of her and coughed violently as a lifetime of smoke swirled in her lungs.

"What happened after that?"

"I went with Hanan to the sheikh's house, and after she gathered her belongings, we were afraid because we could not escape the suspicious looks of the many women who lived there and wore black robes; their eyes were everywhere. I was afraid that one of them would smell the virgin blood on Hanan, so I told Hanan to enter the bathroom and stay there until I returned. Hanan was scared, and she asked me where I was going, and I told her that I would bring one of her friends to walk her out of the house because the many women who wore black robes would be very suspicious if they saw her walking with me. In these parts, a decent woman should not be walking with Gypsy woman in the early evening."

"Who did you bring? I mean who was the friend?"

"I walked in the streets of Balluria, looking for any girl that could keep the secret. I wanted to bring one of the Hillaly girls, but I know that the old man Hillaly would chase me away from their doorstep. I wanted to bring Amel, because Hamid's sister was like me, full of secrets. But the thought of her being complicit in her brother's deed made me feel remorseful since she would be left behind and alone soon, so I went to Basima's house because she was one of the Sharify tribe, and Kamal would not dare to kill her when he discovered that she helped Hanan to escape."

"Did Basima come with you?" the man asked.

"Yes, but only after I told Basima that Hanan was sick with women's illness, and she needed her help. Basima walked with me to the sheikh's house, and she went to the bathroom and told Hanan that she was there to help her."

"And what happened after?" he asked.

"I brought Hanan back, holding her hand, and Basima held the other. Poor Basima did not know what Hanan and Hamid were planning. She thought that Hanan was sick and that she needed a Gypsy woman's medicine in my mud hut. We stopped in the middle of the road, as I saw Hanan crying, and when I asked why she was crying, she said, 'I will miss my father. I know he will kill me for what I did and what I am about to do, but I miss him dearly already, and I wish I could just hug him and smell the safety of his presence, because I know that today will be the last time I will ever see him and my brother, Ahmed, ever.'

"I looked at Basima's face when I heard Hanan saying this, but I saw that she was the poor innocent and decent girl she was always. Basima thought Hanan was sick and emotional about her wedding the next day. I remember Basima saying to Hanan, 'What kind of talk is this for a bride? You will be well and will dance in your wedding tomorrow.'

"Basima was surprised to see that Hamid was waiting. When she walked with Hanan and me into the mud hut, she did not know what was happening. She was scared, but Hamid said to her as he and Hanan gathered their belongings and were ready to leave Balluria, 'Basima, swear to me that you will keep our secret for tonight only, and tomorrow, you can tell your husband, Abdullah, because he will need to know. But you must promise that you will give me and Hanan the chance and the time to save our lives, and we only need tonight.'

"That's what Hamid said to Basima, and she did not say a word, and that was the night Hamid and Hanan escaped from Balluria carrying a small bag of belongings, running with the southern wind to the unknown. That was when the last Gypsy witch decided to fulfill the prophecy and take her fate into her own hands, not fearing the reprisals of history and the wrath of rugged men with thick moustaches. That was the night when the two lovers escaped the treacherous and unpredictable tomorrows of Balluria and these parts, and that was the night I saw Hanan alive for the last time."

The Gypsy woman paused as she lit up her last cigarette from the pack that Salam offered her, and she leaned back and smoked quietly as the man looked at her and realized the calmness of her beliefs and the amazing strength of her weak and flimsy body as she told the story.

3

He tried to remember Hanan's face. It was strange to him that his silent schoolmate the pale, quiet friend of his sister's could hide all of the wildness of the world behind the sleepy eyes and the calm demeanor, but he remembered the looks on Hanan's face whenever she saw Hamid. He remembered the stare that made other girls wonder if Hanan had a stomachache. The man remembered asking Adnan about Hanan many times, and for some strange reason, Adnan did not say his usual belittling words that he said about other girls in the school. Instead, Adnan would say after a thoughtful pause, "Something about her makes me think she is not what she is or she is pretending to be something in her stare when she looks at Hamid."

The man would ask his thin friend with thick glasses what he meant, and Adnan would shrug, saying he didn't know, but she seemed to be living in a parallel world.

The man remembered what Adnan said about Hanan, and he also remembered that he tried to look in Hanan's face, looking for the stare that Adnan mentioned, but he had not seen it. He now leaned back on the mud wall and looked at the blind Gypsy woman, who seemed to be tiring of telling the story. He let his curiosity direct his actions and politely asked her to continue.

"My son, it pains me to remember that, because it was never meant to happen that way. I don't think the prophecy was wrong. I don't believe that my Gypsy grandmother was lying to me. I believe that Balluria is the place where prophecies may not come true, regardless of how mystical and secretive these parts are. I think everything that happens here is a prophecy of a crazy Gypsy dancer."

The man was surprised as he heard the Gypsy woman lose her faith in her own words, but it became clear to him that she was not delusional.

"What happened to Hanan and Hamid?" he asked.

"Two months after they escaped, two months after Kamal and Ahmed searched all the southern provinces, they found Hanan and Hamid living in a small mud hut like mine and killed Hanan in the middle of the wheat fields as many doves flew off frightened."

"What happened to Hamid? Did they kill him too?" Salam asked fearing that his trip would be pointless if Hamid, his childhood best friend whom he came searching for, was dead, but the Gypsy woman eliminated that concern.

"No, men like Hamid die of old age, like desert wolves licking the many wounds they have endured from a life of freedom in a land that was never free. Hamid is still alive, roaming the desert on his horse, my son. You may see him if you stay in Balluria for long while."

"Did you see Hanan's body?" the man asked, regretting the words as they left his lips, realizing the shameless rudeness of his question.

"I was there near Sheikh Jawad's guesthouse, waiting for Ahmed and Kamal. I went there because the night before that in my dream I heard the chants of all the Gypsy dancers of all centuries mourning the death of Hanan. They mourned the death as that of the last Gypsy witch, and they mourned the death of love in these parts. In my dreams, all the Gypsy dancers who lived for love and sin and pleasure danced as they cried and wept. They danced to the music of the Gypsy fathers and the drums of the Gypsy mothers and all the noise the Gypsies have ever created and sung in all the Arabian Sahara was mourning the death of Hanan."

"That night I woke up scared of what I saw in my dream and could not sleep again, and when morning broke, I made my tea and waited for the news, but there was none. I waited until the afternoon, and that's when I felt a sharp pain in my heart." The Gypsy woman suddenly stuttered with a lump in her throat. "That's when I knew that Hanan was dead, and I went to Sheikh Jawad's house, looked from the door, and saw the sheikh sitting alone in his guesthouse. Only he and Irar were in the guesthouse, alone waiting for Kamal and Ahmed to come back with Hanan. The sheikh looked at me, and I could see the tears in his eyes, but he said nothing and turned his face away." Tears formed in the Gypsy's eyes. "If you should ever want to see the true sadness itself, you should have seen Sheikh Jawad's face that night. I thought he would die the next morning. His heart was burned by sadness.

"He lost the only love in his life. He lost his daughter. He ordered her killed, the only woman he truly loved. He never loved me. He never loved his wife, Sabrya. He never loved his son, Ahmed. He never loved anyone. Hanan was the only human he loved, and he had to kill her to preserve his honor." She wiped her tears.

"I could not stay near him. I felt that he was willing to kill that night, so I went outside and waited where no one could see me. It was almost night when I saw the car approaching the guesthouse. My heart was melting with sadness, and I could not walk."

The blind Gypsy woman inhaled the last part of her cigarette and let out a dark cloud of smoke. The man looked at her and realized that she had been mourning the death of Hanan all these years. She had lived with the pain of losing a daughter, the only human being that she ever came close to being a mother to.

"I saw Kamal exiting the car with the grim face, and I saw Ahmed crying. When the sheikh approached the car, he asked them with his tears on his face. The sheikh said, 'Did you bring my daughter?'"

The Gypsy woman could not finish her words, as she sobbed and started to chant the Gypsy chants of mourning. Salam felt the heaviness of death setting its irremovable presence around the mud hut and looked at the Gypsy woman, who dried her tears with her head cover and revealed long, black hair laced with silvery-gray. The Gypsy woman finished her tale while she choked with tears.

"I heard Kamal saying to Sheikh Jawad, 'Uncle Sheikh, we brought the betrayer. She is in trunk of the car.'"

"Sheikh Jawad's face turned dark as he realized that Hanan was really gone. The love of his life was dead. He could not walk. He looked at Kamal's face and then looked at Ahmed, maybe waiting to tell him otherwise, but Kamal was fast to assure him of the inevitable truth that they would have to live with for the rest for his days. 'I killed her with the dagger you gave me, Uncle Sheikh, and I have severed her palm so we can nail it in the front of the guesthouse, so everyone will know that I have cleansed our honor from the shame that she brought on us.'

"Kamal was looking for praise from Sheikh Jawad, not knowing that he had just had extinguished the only candle of love in the sheikh's heart.

"The sheikh looked at Kamal, and I could swear that I saw the sheikh's eyes turning blood-red when Kamal said that. I thought that he wanted to sever Kamal's head. When he said that about Hanan, Sheikh Jawad turned to Ahmed and asked if she was dead.

"When he heard this he insisted on seeing her, 'I want to see her. I want to see my daughter.'

"The ever-present Irar was quick to say, 'No, no. What will the people say about you, Sheikh?'

"At that moment I saw the face of Sheikh Jawad in the dim lights that came from inside the guesthouse, and at that at that moment, I sensed that he wanted to kill Kamal and Irar both. I wished that he did, but instead, he wiped his tears, turned to Ahmed, and told him to bury his sister.

"When I heard the sheikh say that, the earth moved underneath my feet. I could not stay. When Kamal and Ahmed took the dead body of Hanan, I looked for Sheikh Jawad and saw him sitting by himself behind the guesthouse crying. For the first time since the night I saw him at the wedding of the son of Sheikh Waitan, I saw him crying alone. When he saw me, he said, 'Do not say a word, Barrya. Go to your mud hut. I have no heart left for you or anyone in these parts. I don't ever want to see you again, and if I ever see you again, I will kill you.'

"And that was the last time I saw Sheikh Jawad and the last time I talked to him. The only tie that was between he and I was Hanan, and when she was killed there was nothing left."

"You did not see Sheikh Jawad when he died?"

"By the time he died, people had long forgotten about him. Only Sayed Habeeb saw him and buried him.

"You knew Hanan."

"Yes, she was a classmate and a friend of my sister's, and she came to our house many times when we lived in Balluria."

"Wasn't she the most beautiful woman you ever saw?"

"She was beautiful in a special way." Salam was trying to hide his true opinion about Hanan's beauty and trying to be truthful and polite at the same time, as he never thought Hanan was the most beautiful woman on earth, only somewhat attractive.

"She was my only daughter in this life, and she was the last Gypsy witch to ever walk these parts, and now let the men of these parts drink her everlasting blood to satisfy their honor. Hanan is dead now, and her palm was nailed to the entrance of the guesthouse as a sign of clear and cleansed honor, but her curse will live forever as all the men in these parts will all be forever prevented from knowing true love." She spoke with a weak satisfaction of revenge and added, "What happened to Hanan was not her fault. It was the fault of her being born in these parts. And just like me, she was loved by many men.

"Only in these parts does a princess full of love have no chance to live or to love. Only in these parts do mean, rugged men cut off the beautiful henna-painted, delicate hands of the sinner beauty to preserve honor."

"Do you know where she is buried?"

"I know now, but that night, I did not have the heart to see the beautiful face of my child covered with blood and dirt. I wanted to follow Ahmed and Kamal as they carried the dead body of Hanan, but I didn't have the heart to see her under the ground. She was too beautiful for this Earth."

The Gypsy woman looked thoughtful as she stared with her blind eyes into to the space in front of the mud hut and said, "She could not be ordinary and loveless like her mother, and she could not be Gypsy with a free heart like me, even as much as she wanted to. She was something in between, and that's a difficult place to be in for a woman in this land."

Her voice turned deeper. "She could not be decent. She was an Arab woman from these parts, and in her veins, she had the lustful blood of a Gypsy dancer and the boiling blood of self-made sheikh.

"Hanan was half-woman and half-wolf, beautiful as the prairie and as slithery as its snakes. She could not be decent the way they wanted her to be. She was bound for love and lust, and definitely she was bound for sin, and that's why she died the way she did," the blind Gypsy woman concluded as the man looked at her and realized the pain she was feeling. She told the story of the only woman on this earth who could have been her daughter.

As she wiped her tears, she said, "What happened to Hanan was not my fault either, because men in these parts had chained their lives with boundaries that made them miserable and constantly thirsty for love. They have created emotional prisons that have prevented them from tasting the fruits of physical pleasures. Even in other parts of this earth, men have created rules that make them long for the one thing that they need the most."

"What is that thing?"

"True love, my son, the true love of a beautiful woman."

"Do you know where they buried Hanan?" Salam asked again.

"The same place many love children were buried, the same place where many unfortunate lovers were killed and buried in the middle of the night to preserve honor. She is buried where the prophecy of the Gypsy grandmothers said she would be buried, the place where angels and jinni girls dance every night by her grave." The Gypsy woman wiped the pearl-like tears mixed with black eyeliner from her blind eyes.

"By the seven palm trees."

The Book of the Man

The Unknown Triumph of the Weak Angel

Mr. Mohamed Tabra was our math teacher. Besides being a self-proclaimed math genius, there were several facts about him that everyone in the town knew. His wife had left him a long time ago and moved to the capital city, and he had no children. He had been a math teacher for a long time and a devoted party man who loved to talk about the "divine" leader. Mr. Mohamed Tabra was balding and had a thick moustache and a smaller belly compared to that of other party members. At that time, he was the acting principal, since the original principal, Mr. Abdul Ameer, was sent to the war front for not being sympathetic with the governing party and never came back. Mr. Mohamed Tabra was known as the meanest teacher, and for all I knew, he was the meanest person on the face of the earth. He always reeked with of smell of areq and other alcoholic smells all day. He always brought his socks with him in his pocket and wore them in the classroom while sitting on his desk and telling us to be quiet as he tried to recover from a bad hangover from his previous night. Besides that, he was the senior party official, and many said that he had been in the national guard militia in the sixties and seventies and was one of the group of "The Masked" who roamed the streets of the big city dragging communists and Islamists from their homes to kill them in the streets.

Many said that he was one of the group of the masked men who dragged out Qahtan, Adnan's older brother, and killed him in the main square of Balluria. He usually dressed in the dark green party uniform but sometimes wore an old gray suit. Mr. Mohamed spoke with an annoying sharp voice, and he had a saliva spot on his lower lip that kept attaching to his upper lip and made us want to vomit. He was a mean and merciless man, and he had created with a diabolically innovative mind a long list of methods for punishments that he enjoyed dishing out to the students.

One winter day, he made us all hold our hands upward as he struck us with his half meter stick almost fifty times. The entire class was in tears except for me since I was spared, because my father was the mayor and I got away with only three strikes from the fearsome stick. Ahmed and Kamal also escaped the punishment because they were Sheikh Jawad's kids. It was not only painful, but it was also shameful because the girls were watching us getting whipped by this mean and stinky beast. He would wait until the end of the class and then remember who was absent the day before or who did not prepare his homework. Every day, he would keep us hoping that he would not remember to punish us, but he never forgot. He would tell the girls to leave the room. Then he lined up the students whom he wanted to punish and hit each with his fearsome stick that he carried all the time. He was the reason that Hamid quit attending school. He and Hisham were Mr. Mohamed's favorite students to try new methods of punishment out on. As careless and fearless and extremely bad a student as Hamid was, he was the most punished person I ever saw in my life. He would be punished in three classes out of five, and when Hisham was trying to behave better and not to incur the wrath of Mr. Mohamed, Hamid did not care. He did not care about how many rounds of the painful stick he would get. He even taunted Mr. Mohamed when he was receiving the scary blows of the stick.

"Hit me. I don't feel the pain. Hit me. I am not scared."

These kinds of comments made Mr. Mohamed furious as he saw that his stick did not inflict pain on Hamid's hands so he started beating Hamid on his face, chest, and back. At one time, Hamid, as usual, had no homework ready, and on top of that he did not bring his math book or any other text to school. Mr. Mohamed stood Hamid up in front of the class and started saying painful and mean things about Hamid and addressed the class, "If you want to see a smelly animal, it's right here in front of you. Hamid is a person who will end up a garbage collector because he is garbage. His entire family and ancestors are garbage."

Hamid looked defeated and the worst thing is that on that particular day we had a joint math class with class B, and that meant that Hanan was there too, Hanan the beautiful daughter of Sheikh Jawad, whom Hamid adored.

"Open your hands, you idiot!" sneered Mr. Mohamed.

Hamid silently looked at Hanan and spread his arms with open palms as we started hearing the sound the stick made as it landed on Hamid's palms. Hamid did not flinch, nor did he look like he was feeling any pain. Instead, he kept looking at Hanan, and she kept looking at him with the same empty stare that she always had in her eyes whenever she looked at Hamid. I could see, as I sat closer to the front of the class, that a tear was going down his cheek as he tried to resist it. We hoped that Mr. Mohamed would stop after he struck Hamid twenty times with the stick, but he kept going and kept shouting insults.

"Dirty garbage, like all of your family."

Suddenly, Hamid did not resist his natural urges that we all knew he possessed. He grabbed the stick from the hand of Mr. Mohamed, who was stunned by Hamid's reaction. He hit the blackboard with Mr. Mohamed's stick, and fragmented it to pieces. Then he threw the little piece that was still in his hand out of the window. Mr. Mohamed was furious, and he wanted to choke Hamid with his hands, but Hamid was faster in getting out of the class and to the school gate and out of the school; he never returned. That day, Mr. Mohamed was so angry that he did not complete the class. I guess he never saw it coming, that a student would challenge his authority. Mr. Mohamed sent Kamal to fetch the remaining part of his stick, and we all wished that Kamal would come back empty-handed. Yet, Kamal returned with what was left of the stick. Then, we saw that the stick had blood stains, blood from Hamid's face.

That day we all hated Mr. Mohamed and wished that he would die. That day, we all wanted to run away, just like Hamid did, but we knew we could not run away. Hamid could do that because the school could not ask Hamid's father to come to school since Hamid had no father, and his mother would not come. I wished that Mr. Mohamed did not know my father. Unfortunately, Mr. Mohamed knew my father personally and knew all of the other kids' fathers too. At recess Hamid's sister, Amel, asked me and Adnan about what happened and I told her. She did not seem to care that Hamid might be expelled. She was more interested in knowing if he cried.

"Yes," said Adnan.

"I saw one tear," I added.

Then, she started crying. "He never cried before," Amel said as she walked away from us.

After the day when Hamid broke his stick, Mr. Mohamed became meaner and angrier, and he started punishing us for any reason or for no reason. We could not believe that the school or our parents would condone his reign of terror with no objections, but we had no choice but to accept and endure his sadistic punishments. Mr. Mohamed punished everyone in our class, boys and girls alike, but he spared three students from our class and one student from room B. Mr. Mohamed never punished me, nor did he punish Ahmed or Kamal from our room, and from room B he never punished Hanan. He never punished me, or he always would line me up with the students and then tell me to sit down or tell Ahmed not to forget his homework again while hitting the others with his evil stick.

I always believed it was because I was never late with my homework, but later I learned that he never punished me because my father was the mayor and the magistrate of the town, and he and my father met regularly once a week so the party could tell my father how to run the town. Mr. Mohamed did not dare to send me home with two swelled-up palms. He never dared to punish Ahmed because his father was Sheikh Jawad, and Mr. Mohamed knew that if Sheikh Jawad saw his only son Ahmed with bruised hands he might end up with a dagger in his back, or he might see the school burned to the ground by Sheikh Jawad's men. That was the same reason he never punished Hanan, because, God forbid, she would go home crying to her father, telling him that Mr. Mohamed had insulted her. That would have meant certain death to Mr. Mohamed. She was never punished while other girls, like Hamid's sister or the Hillaly girls or even Basima, who was never late on her homework, also endured some humiliating moments in front of the boys. Hanan was never even asked to stand up in the line of punishment, but to her credit, she always gave a hug or a handkerchief to crying victims of Mr. Mohamed's wrath, and she was not a bad student. She barely talked to anyone.

He never punished Kamal because he was also a relative of Sheikh Jawad, although none of the townspeople knew what kind of relative he was.

Nevertheless, he was related to Sheikh Jawad and lived in his house, and that meant that he was untouchable. There was another reason that Kamal was not punishable. Kamal, as we all knew, was Mr. Mohamed's favorite student. He was Mr. Mohamed's pet and the snitch who told Mr. Mohamed about everything that happened in the class. Kamal told him about what the students were saying about him. He told him about who cheated on the tests. He told Mr. Mohamed everything. He told Mr. Mohamed about who was writing love letters to whom, and during classes Mr. Mohamed would look at Kamal and say things like, "Kamal! Go to the principal's office and bring me my notebook." Or, "Kamal, go to my car and bring me my brown bag!"

We also knew that Kamal was a member of the party's shadow cell in the school. Being a member of the shadow cell meant that Kamal existed as a fully-fledged favorite student of the party in the school, and that also meant that Kamal was writing reports about other students, reports that could lead to prison or death of any of us.

During the days that followed, all the eighth-grade students in classroom A and the eighth graders in room B wished that Mr. Mohamed would be run over by a large truck on its way from the capital city of the province, be poisoned by a venomous snake, or be struck by lightning. I am sure that all the students in the school wanted him dead or at least gone. We all wanted to see him punished with a thousand hits by the same stick that he used on the soft hands of students, but we never got that wish. We wished that we would see him beaten by a group of angry students or humiliated by Sheikh Jawad or other powerful men in Balluria. We wished that he would just drop dead or be sent to the eastern front to fight the Iranians in the many popular army brigades that he organized and sent to the front. We wished that he would be sent with it to a place where he would be killed, where he would die, or get captured, and never return to torture us and the rest of the school students with his devilish methods and humiliating punishments. Yet, he was the vice principal, who could get away with anything he did, and at the same time, he was a party official who could mix school affairs with patriotic duties.

We hated Kamal for being Mr. Mohamed's pet and unofficial assistant, but we did not say anything because we knew Kamal would snitch on us. We wanted Hamid to come back to school because he was the only student who stood up to Mr. Mohamed. We wished for a miracle, but we never thought that it would be Adnan who would bring Mr. Mohamed to his knees. Who would have thought that this weak and extremely smart angel with big ears and thick glasses that looked like two small telescopes, that tiny Wolf of ours that no one paid attention to, would humiliate Mr. Mohamed and make a mockery of Mr. Mohamed's reputation as a math genius? We certainly hoped that Mr. Mohamed would make the mistake of punishing Ahmed or hitting or insulting Hanan and then end up being dead in the street or the main square of town with a bullet from one of Sheikh Jawad's scary men, but poetic justice made Adnan speak on that fateful February day when Mr. Mohamed had gathered the students of three rooms together. It was us, room A, the students from room B, and room G who had the laziest and the stupidest students. Mr. Mohamed referred to them as the group of tube kids from Tawsheeha, who were attending our school because the six-room school they attended was flooded from the massive rain that winter. Mr. Mohamed gathered the three rooms so he did not have to teach more than one class a day because he was busy with his duties as a party official, and he spent most of his time at the party's headquarters. The sixty-plus students all crammed into one room and listened and wrote notes as Mr. Mohamed with his alcoholic breath talked algebra between comments and insults that he spread around like gifts he did not pay for.

"And just like I said—you group of donkeys— 'A minus C equals the total of B and D.' Did you understand that, you idiots?" Mr. Mohamed would shriek.

Submissively, we would say, "Yes, sir."

That day, Mr. Mohamed assigned the entire class a math problem handed down from the high school in the big city where he lived. It appeared that one of his drinking mates was another mean math teacher who taught in the big city's high school. The problem was not part of the school's curriculum, and we had no idea how to solve it.

"Anyone who solves the problem will pass the final exams without testing," he said with a conceited gleam in his eyes. "I am the only person in these parts who can solve this problem, or maybe I am the only one in the country who can solve this problem. Maybe scientists in Europe or America are able to solve it, but in this country and in the Arab countries, I and only I can solve this problem. So write it down, you imbeciles, and show me if you can even solve the first line of it."

Most of us did not even write it down. We could not and would not even try. I wrote it down because I figured that the day would come when Mr. Mohamed would want to see if we wrote it down, and that way I would save myself from punishment. I saw that Hisham did not write anything. Ashraf, Haleem, and Salah pretended that they were writing something, but I noticed that Adnan wrote the entire problem and started working on it as Mr. Mohamed was speaking. For the following week, and as we played soccer, Adnan was on the ground on his hands and knees writing numbers and crossing out numbers and crawling for meters and meters. We did not bother him even when he left the goal unattended and even when he did not pay attention in the other classes. He looked as if he had just found the secret gate to a pyramid full of treasures. He was working on the math problem during reading class and during history class and during all the other classes. He was working on the problem when we hung out at Barrya's house drinking yogurt and tea.

The day finally arrived, and we were visited by the high school teacher and his students, who looked at us as if we were a group of tube kids. There were five high school students who were only interested in our female classmates and talked about how the school looked and smelled like a prison. The high school students sat in the front row and kept turning back to look at the girls. The high school teacher stood next to Mr. Mohamed, who looked at the blackboard, where he wrote the problem again, and then he turned and asked in his superior voice if any of us had solved the problem.

Not a single reply was heard. The room was so quiet we could hear each other breathing.

We never realized what Mr. Mohamed's intention was to invite his friend and drinking mate. Moreover, we did not know why they brought the five annoying high school students with them. Was it just for the mere satisfaction of humiliating us more, or was it for the mere satisfaction of these two sadistic math teachers to assure our inferiority to their mathematical superiority? After waiting for ten seconds, Mr. Mohamed and Mr. Khalid asked again.

"Did any of you try to solve the problem?"

No answer was heard as we tried to not look at them, and that's when Mr. Mohamed spoke. "All right then, I will show you morons and show Mr. Khalid and his morons how it is solved."

Then he started by saying, "We will suppose that A equals that... and B equals..."

I felt dizzy from the start, trying to keep up with what equals what, and I was sure that everyone else felt the same way while Mr. Mohamed kept going and going as he filled the blackboard with numbers and math signs and symbols that we had not even seen before as he looked as if he was unveiling the relativity theory. When he was done, he turned to the class with a strange, joyful look in his eyes and said from below his thick moustache, which looked like the moustaches of republican fish, "And that's the solution..." He threw the chalk from his hand into the air and waited for cheers. Kamal started clapping, and other students joined him with shy, weak clapping, and that's when we heard a soft yet firm voice.

"But that's wrong."

The entire class stood still. No, actually, the entire world stood still. The clapping stopped. The noise of joy and cheering for Mr. Mohamed from his pet Kamal and other weasels had diminished as the entire room turned to the source of the voice. Sure enough, from behind his thick glasses and weak appearance, Adnan looked like a rat who had just come out of the water to find himself in a room full of hungry, angry cats. He looked at almost one hundred and twenty pairs of eyes that were glaring at him and then at Mr. Mohamed, who looked as if he was boiling.

"What?" Mr. Mohamed asked, in a strained whisper. "What did you say?" he asked again, challenging or daring Adnan to just speak.

Again Adnan said, with a growing confidence as he sat slightly taller in his chair, squaring his shoulders, "You are wrong, sir."

Mr. Khalid, who was supposed to be Mr. Mohamed's friend and drinking mate, looked at Adnan with interest and said, "How is he wrong?"

Mr. Mohamed, who could not conceive of the idea that he would be faced with a situation like that, turned to assure his friend, "Don't listen to that blind donkey."

Since the day I met Adnan on the soccer field, and from what everyone else had told me, he had never spoken of, nor did he tell any stories, about the night that his older brother Qahtan was dragged in the middle of the night by a group of masked men who smelled of alcohol. He never said that he saw who dragged his smart, talented, and handsome brother Qahtan, who recited the poetry of Garcia Lorca and Pablo Neruda and talked about people like Karl Marx, Charles Angles, Fidel Castro, Che Guevara, and Walt Whitman, but he always looked at Mr. Mohamed with an accusing stare from behind his thick glasses. He said, one time, that he hated the smell of areq, the smell that Mr. Mohamed was notorious for. We all hated the way Mr. Mohamed smelled of areq, but it seemed like Adnan hated the smell the most. I guess it reminded him of the same smell of the night when his only bother was killed by a group of masked men who reeked with the distinctive smell of Iraqi areq.

In her moments of telling us Gypsy wisdom, Barrya said things like, "Those who knit webs to trap others get trapped in their own webs."

I don't think any of us kids gave much thought to what she said at the time, but her words started to come to me as a solid truth as I saw the saliva on Mr. Mohamed's lips coming down on the side of his chin as he walked toward Adnan in a clear move of intimidation and terrorizing. Nevertheless, Adnan, and just like Hamid before him, did not flinch. In fact, he stood up and said, "You are wrong. The problem is not solved that way."

We prayed that Mr. Mohamed would not kill Adnan. We prayed that Mr. Mohamed would not choke Adnan to death. We prayed that Adnan would kneel and ask for forgiveness, but Adnan kept the same stare of accusation as he looked at Mr. Mohamed straight in the eyes and said again, "You are wrong, and I can prove it."

For the sixty students in the joint math class, we all knew that if it was not for Mr. Khalid, who looked and seemed a little more human than Mr. Mohamed, Adnan would have been receiving the beating of a lifetime with Mr. Mohamed's new stick. Mr. Khalid, who we thought was secretly enjoying the humiliation of his friend, said, "Can you come to the blackboard and show us?"

Adnan walked past Mr. Mohamed, who looked at him like a hungry lion looking at baby deer without being able to eat him. Adnan walked to the blackboard and erased all of what Mr. Mohamed had written and wrote numbers and math symbols that were more complicated and more dizzying than what Mr. Mohamed had written. After almost twenty minutes, which seemed like an eternity, Adnan wrote down at the bottom of the blackboard, "Twelve. That's the result."

I almost clapped, but I did not because it would have meant a death sentence from Mr. Mohamed. He and Mr. Khalid were speechless as they stared at the blackboard for ten minutes, and then Mr. Khalid announced, "It's right. The kid is right."

Hisham was the first one to clap, and doing so cost him dearly, and then the entire room lit up with claps for Adnan, who stood there looking at Mr. Mohamed with the same stare, the accusing stare, but this time, it was mixed with a superior look. Adnan was looking at Mr. Mohammad's humiliation and defeat. He was looking at Mr. Mohamed's inferiority as a human and as a math genius.

We could not wait for the class to end as all the students from the three classrooms and the boys from the high school surrounded Adnan, who did not know how to deal with this sudden celebrity, which lasted only for an hour. After that, the high school boys left with their teacher, Mr. Khalid, who came to Adnan and said, "You are a smart kid. I will see you in my high school."

They went back to the big city, and Mr. Mohamed came to the classroom and asked Mrs. Khadija, the Arabic literature teacher, if he could borrow Adnan for five minutes. Five minutes! We looked at Adnan knowing, that he might not come back alive. Adnan looked at us, hoping that a student revolution would start right then and right there to save him from being alone with Mr. Mohamed in the principal's office for five minutes.

Ten minutes later Adnan returned to the classroom with his palms under his armpits as he tried to feel the warmth of his body to heal the pain of his palms. Later, we learned that Mr. Mohamed had struck Adnan a hundred times. Adnan could not hold the pencil to write for days with his palms so swollen. The only thing he said after coming back from Mr. Mohamed's office, he said it to me as he tried to fight the tears from his red eyes, "I hate the smell of areq. I hate the smell of that man."

He was on the edge of tears as we looked at his hands and saw red lines ready to burst blood. Hisham and Ashraf tried to put water on Adnan's hand to cool down the fire of pain, but he refused and kept his hands tucked underneath his armpits. We saw his hands as they looked like the inside a watermelon with red and black spots from the beating. If that would have been me, my father would have used all of his power and all of his contacts in the government to get Mr. Mohamed transferred to the most mosquito-infested school in the marshes that would require him to rise at four o'clock in the morning. If that was Ahmed or Hanan or even Kamal, then Mr. Mohamed would have ended up with a dagger or many daggers or even several bullets in his body. But it was Adnan.

Adnan had no father or older brother to go to.

Adnan could not write with his hands for days, and he did not participate in the math class at all after that. In fact, he seemed to have lost his interest in math once and for all. He did not even look at Mr. Mohamed with his usual, accusing stare. He tried to avoid looking at him. Instead he looked to the outside from the classroom window, to the outside where he knew that Hamid must be swimming or fishing. He looked to the outside where the sun was glorious and free. I was not sure what he was thinking or who he was thinking about in his long stares to the sunny outside. I did not know who he missed more at that moment. Was it his dead brother, Qahtan, or was it Hamid? I am sure now that he missed Hamid.

The Book of Balluria

Kamal's Inauguration to Manhood

1

To Comrade Uraiby, Kamal was the perfect candidate for the newly drafted list of party supporters. Comrade Uraiby had a thick moustache and a large belly that he could hardly fit his belt around. A long, red leather sheath, which contained the party-issued Tokarev Russian pistol, dangled from his belt. When Comrade Uraiby visited the school to talk to the teenaged students about the party, Kamal jumped every other second with answers to his questions, which none of the other students knew how to answer.

Comrade Uraiby asked, and Kamal answered, "When was our great party founded?"

"In 1947," Kamal answered.

"Where?"

"In Damascus, Syria," Kamal answered without giving any other student a chance to think of a reply. He shouted the answers from the desk where he was sitting and then looked around with a strange joy of supremacy in his eyes. He looked at us, waiting for some kind of cheering, which never came, from the bored and hungry students who were just waiting for the hellish boredom of that subject to end.

Kamal was the first to sign the list of newly formed supporters' cells in the class. He also was the first and only student to sign up for what no other student had ever heard of: a shadow cell, a new secret cell that Comrade Uraiby was instructed to form in the school. Members of the shadow cell were chosen by Comrade Uraiby himself; they were called one by one to the principal's office to sign the list after school. The formation of the cell came as an urgent directive from the party leadership, because during those days a forbidden party had started recruiting young men to distribute leaflets and flyers in the elementary and secondary schools across the marshlands and in the provincial capital. The ruling party realized the danger of young minds being raised on the philosophy of the forbidden party and the call to rise up against the government for the imprisonment of the outspoken Ayatollah, who unknown to almost everybody, had been shot and killed with one bullet. So the divine leader of the country conceived his new plan to combat that strategy by forming shadow cells in each school formed by a group of students willing to snitch on their peers and even their teachers. Moreover, they were charged with watching their neighborhoods and towns in order to report any people who did not support the party.

Kamal, strangely dedicated to writing the reports, was never late for the weekly meetings. Moreover, he started appearing in the party headquarters regularly and began doing chores, cleaning the yellow and gray building. He was very happy when Comrade Falih, the one-eyed party man who seemed to never leave the party's building, sent him to the market to buy tea and sugar. While his friends Hisham, Haleem, and Adnan played soccer, attended prayers in the mosque, and chatted with the graceful clergyman, Sayed Habeeb, Kamal spent most of his days after school at the party's building, waiting for any assignment or duty the comrades would honor him with. He wrote reports about people who visited the town for a day or two, and he was pulling guard shifts three nights a week at the headquarters. He also attended all the meetings in the school and wrote reports about his schoolmates. When Comrade Uraiby noticed how dedicated the lonesome Kamal was, he informed Kamal that he would be advanced from a sympathizer's rank to an ally of the party's rank. That promotion meant that he would have to go to the main party headquarters in the big city to train for his new duties. Kamal neglected his duties at Sheikh Jawad's guesthouse, which included cleaning the rugs and preparing coffee with Khanger, the old coffee man who could barely walk, and serving dinners and lunches the sheikh provided to his guests. Instead, Kamal paid more attention and dedicated more time to reading the Central Cultural Report of the party that Comrade Uraiby gave him to peruse and ask any questions about when he had when he finished reading it. Kamal completed the four-hundred-page report in just one week. Then he went directly to Comrade Uraiby and asked, "Comrade, would you like to test me on the report?"

"What?" the surprised Comrade Uraiby replied and added, "Have you finished reading it, already?"

"Yes, Comrade, and you can ask me any question about it," Kamal said with pride.

"When was our great party founded?" Comrade Uraiby asked.

"April 7, 1947, at 5 p.m. in Damascus, Syria," Kamal answered.

Comrade Uraiby asked Kamal ten questions about the great party: who founded it when the party claimed power of the military coup, which the party members referred to as the great revolution. Kamal answered all the questions in detail with specific dates and names. Comrade Uraiby was very impressed; he saw in Kamal what he wanted to see in his own spoiled son, Mazen, who was more interested in playing soccer and searching for pictures of naked woman in the magazines that the Turkish drivers brought with them as they passed through Balluria on their way to the oil-rich countries in the south.

Comrade Uraiby asked Kamal, "What's your current party rank?"

"I am in training for ally rank, sir," Kamal said.

"We need to advance you further; I will put your name on the list for training and seminars for the next round, so you can advance to the next rank. You will be a party first ally."

282

Kamal could not stand still from the excitement; he thanked Comrade Uraiby for his trust and confidence and promised him that he would do anything the party asked of him. He would be a ready soldier to defend the "divine" leader and the "Great Revolution." Comrade Uraiby seized that opportunity to test the young kid who seemed willing to perform more serious duties.

Comrade Uraiby said, "I have something to ask of you. It's an official duty of the party."

"You can ask me anything, Rafeeq," Kamal said as he stood at attention, waiting for his first official party duty.

Comrade Uraiby said, "Close the door behind you and come here next to me."

Kamal closed the heavy metal door and stood up next to the metal desk where Comrade Uraiby sat, below a picture of the divine leader.

"What I am about to tell you must be kept a secret; no one should know about it, not your friends in school, not your father..."

"I don't have a father," Kamal interrupted.

"I know. I meant Sheikh Jawad. You should not speak of it to anyone. Understood?"

"Understood, Rafeeq, Comrade."

Kamal anxiously waited to hear his secret assignment, and with a quieter and more conspiratorial like voice, the thick-moustached comrade started telling Kamal about his secret assignment.

"There are two people that I want you to watch and report on for me. I want you to see whom they are talking to and what they are talking about. You need to listen carefully to them, because sometimes they say things that may mean something entirely different. It's crucially important that you pay attention to see if they talk about our divine leader and our Great Revolution, and it's even more important to see if they start talking about politics and the war with our enemy. Listen to what they say about our enemy. Do you understand what I asking of you?" Comrade Uraiby asked Kamal while looking directly in the kid's eyes as they widened.

"Yes, Rafeeq," Kamal answered, lowering his voice.

"Do you go to the mosque?" Comrade Uraiby asked.

"Sometimes I go with my friends, and during the ten days of mourning in the holy month," Kamal answered.

"Well I want you to go there more often, and I want you to watch Sayed Habeeb, the clergyman. I want to know what he is saying and who of the townspeople stays in the mosque after prayers. You think you can do that?" Comrade Uraiby asked.

"Yes, Rafeeq," Kamal answered.

Comrade Uraiby paused for a moment, giving Kamal a second to gather himself, and then then he asked, "Do you remember the student who did not want to join the party and said that he was independent?"

Kamal knew exactly who that was, his friend Adnan, but he tried to avoid mentioning his name. He waited for Comrade Uraiby to tell him more. It was his last and only attempt to save his conscience. It was too late for him, but he tried one last time.

"I don't remember, Comrade," he said, hoping that Comrade Uraiby would not detect his lie.

"It was the thin kid with the thick glasses," Comrade Uraiby said.

Kamal felt that he was cornered, but he had done his friendship duty and it was the time to be faithful to the party.

"Yes, Comrade, his name is Adnan," Kamal said with complete surrender and a comforting sense of submission that made him feel at ease as he started his journey down this unknown road. "Yes... Adnan, he said that he was independent."

"Well in this great country, we do not have independents, you are either with us or against us. There are no independents," Comrade Uraiby said.

"Yes, Rafeeq," Kamal agreed.

"Kamal, I want you to get very close to Adnan and listen to everything he says, and I need you to report to me in writing, every week, and bring it to me. You think you can do that?" Comrade Uraiby asked.

Kamal did not think twice. He believed in what he was about to do, and he replied with confidence, "Yes, Rafeeq."

From that day on, Kamal's face carried an expression of seriousness and responsibility. He was always going somewhere and always carried a small notebook and pen. Kamal begged Comrade Uraiby to enroll him in the two-week training to learn how to shoot the Kalashnikov and the nine-millimeter Tariq pistol issued only to the party membership rank trainees. Comrade Uraiby agreed and lobbied on his behalf. When he graduated, Kamal was named to be the head of the three-member squad that wore the dark green uniform of the party militia that shot three rounds from the Kalashnikov during the Thursday flag-raising ceremony in the school. He started skipping classes and did not have to come up with excuses like Hamid did all the time. Instead, he was called out of classes by Mr. Mohammed, the math teacher, and was sent to the party headquarters two or three times a day and whenever a celebration of the many official holidays that the divine leader had created. Kamal headed the planning committee. Sometimes he even interrupted the rehearsals of the theater group and forced Salam, who wrote, directed, and acted in all of the plays, to change a line and/or a scene in the play to make it more patriotic and more in line with what the party and the great revolution intended.

Sheikh Jawad had never paid any attention to this kid, who arrived one day with his mother and lived in his house, because his mother was related to the late wife of the sheikh. But, when Kamal started wearing the dark olive green uniform, even Sheikh Jawad, who never paid him any compliments or attention, said to him one day after seeing him in his uniform, "Did you join the party?"

"Yes, Uncle Sheikh," Kamal answered.

"Good thing," the sheikh said. "I need you to tell that moron, Comrade Uraiby, not to enlist some of my men in the militia's battalion being sent to the front next month. You think you can do that?"

"Yes, Uncle," Kamal replied and did not believe his newly acquired power and respect. Comrade Uraiby was very satisfied with the two or three weekly reports that Kamal submitted about the activities of the graceful mosque clergyman, Sayed Habeeb, and the one about what Adnan had said or talked about that week and the many reports about others. However, aside from getting the approval of Comrade Uraiby and getting all of the attention and all of the responsibilities he had, Kamal wanted two things the most. He wanted a nine-millimeter pistol that he could carry around in order to show his friends and peers, especially Hamid, that he was a person to be reckoned with. And what he wanted the most were the approval, acceptance, and maybe just a smile from the person he loved. Deep inside he wanted to impress Hanan with everything he did and everything he would do. He wanted her to see him wearing the ironed dark green uniform and whenever he shot the three rounds during the flag-raising ceremony. The first thing he did, before ordering his two squad mates to fire, was to find where she was to see if she was looking at him, but she never was. He always saw her looking at Hamid, smiling at him and paying attention only to him, despite the loud sound of the bullets that Kamal fired and all the noise he made ordering his two squad mates" "To the right, turn... to the left, turn... halt... long live the leader, long live our party, and long the live the people... bang... bang... bang."

But none of it made Hanan look in his direction once, and that tormented him and made him work harder in entrenching his power and his position. He even tried to convince Hanan to join the shadow cell, so she could sit in a meeting that he co-chaired. Hanan, who listened to him for a brief second, shattered his hopes and his soul when she said with her magical voice, "You are crazy. If my father knew that you wanted me to be in the shady cell..."

"The shadow cell," Kamal corrected her.

"My father would beat you," she said as she walked away and left him to his worries that she might tell her father, the sheikh, who could likely beat him up and kick him out of the house. However, Hanan never told her father, and she even forgot about Kamal and his strange request seconds after she walked away from him.

During those days, Hamid stopped coming to school, after he broke the fearsome punishment stick of Mr. Muhammad. This was a relief to Kamal, who never liked Hamid, because Hamid tried to stop him from drowning the kittens. Hamid kept busy by chasing horses, swimming, fishing, hunting, and finding lost items floating in the river. Hamid's absence gave Kamal the opportunity to pursue his love for Hanan throughout the ninth and the tenth grades.

The ninth and tenth grades were added to the middle school, because none of the students in Balluria could afford the bus fare that would transport them to the big city, where the secondary school was. In fact, the tenth grade would never have been opened if it had not been for the dedicated lobbying of Ms. Majida, the English teacher, who never married and who was the subject of many wet dreams experienced by all the older male students. Ms. Majida lobbied the Directorate of Education in the province to open a second class for the ninth grade and one classroom for the tenth grade, so the students who could barely afford a set of decent clothes could attend secondary school grades until she could lobby the ministry to open a secondary school in Balluria.

The tenth grade was opened, and all the boys and girls attended; the Hillaly girls and Hisham, along with his team of Wolves, Abdullah, Haleem, and Adnan, who started growing his extremely scattered beard, also attended. Salam and Hamid were the only two students from the group of boys and girls who did not attend the tenth grade in Balluria. Salam, the son of the mayor, did not attend, because his family moved back to the capital when his father finished the third year of his four-year assignment as the mayor of Balluria. And Hamid never returned to school after the stick breaking incident.

2

Kamal was very keen on writing his reports. He always paid attention to the details of dates and places and wrote the exact lines of the conversations he heard from Sayed Habeeb and Adnan. He always began his report with a greeting, which he had chosen from several used by party informants and their superiors. He chose only greetings that showed devotion and submission:

A comradely greeting,

One Arab nation, with an everlasting mission,

Today, I was at the mosque, and it came to my attention that the clergyman, Sayed Habeeb, was talking to a student from our school, Adnan. They were talking about a book they called Our Philosophy *that was written by the condemned enemy of our country, the ayatollah, who was executed by our party and the divine leadership of our revolution. I heard them debating the difference between the communists and the capitalists and talking about the Islamic philosophy.*

To your comradely attention,

And forward with the glorious march of our nation.

Kamal was absorbed in his many new duties that required him to be out of the sheikh's house most of the time. He would go to trainings, seminars, and meetings with Comrade Uraiby and the other comrades. Sometimes, he would spend three or four nights a week guarding the party headquarters, even though he was only required to do that once a week. Volunteering to take the night shifts of other comrades and guards, he wanted to stay out of the sheikh's house as much as possible. He only went to the house to shower and to eat, and if possible to see Hanan, who never noticed his constant absence from the house. At one time, he was sent to the capital for training; he told no one about the training and came back with a clearly visible dark moustache on his upper lip. He was so anxious to see Hanan, but when she saw him, she did not even stop to greet him. She had just returned from Barrya's house, where she spent most of her afternoons without the knowledge of her father and the many relatives living in the sheikh's house. Hanan looked tired and peacefully spaced out. Kamal was saddened; he thought that Hanan would like his new look with the moustache and the dark green uniform, but she did not notice or say anything to him. He endured his solitude and his fears and tried to bury his loneliness with more duties and more of the endless guard shifts at the party headquarters. He spent almost half of his tenth-grade session on party assignments and attending to his party duties. At one time, Comrade Uraiby asked him a very strange question: "How far will you go to prove your loyalty to the party and to the leader?"

"I will do anything in the service of the party, my leader, and my country," Kamal said without hesitation.

Comrade Uraiby looked at this young tall man, who became the youngest trusted comrade in Balluria and these parts within two years, and he realized that Kamal would have a promising future within the party ranks. Comrade Uraiby knew that one day Kamal would be a high-ranking party official, and Uraiby wanted him to be completely involved, in such a way that he could never leave the party. He wanted to baptize his membership with blood, and that was when he asked the young comrade, "Do you think you can be part of a firing squad?"

"What?" Kamal asked with his jaw dropping. He expected that he would be sent to the front with a militia battalion forming during that time, and he expected that he would chase army deserters who filled the marshland. But to be a member of a firing squad, that was the ultimate test. Was he ready to kill? Was he ready to aim his rifle, knowing that the bullets would end someone's life? He saw dead bodies of soldiers brought back from the front with their faces shredded. He saw some dead soldiers with no arms and no legs, and he saw what a bullet could do to a human face, but was he ready to be the one who fired that bullet?

"I am ready, Comrade, to do anything the party asks of me, but can I think about it for two or three days?"

"Yes, naturally, Comrade Kamal. We all asked for time to think. In my case, I asked for a week. But after that, I did it. And since then I have realized it's my duty to my country and to my leader to execute those who betray the leader and the Great Revolution. Take your time and think about it, and when you are ready, let me know," Comrade Uraiby said to Kamal, patting him on his broad shoulders.

That night Kamal walked home, thinking of his path in life. For the first time, he started thinking about his choice to be a full-fledged member of the party. He had heard from many people that party membership was for life; once a person became a member of the party, the only way to get out was to be killed by the enemies of the party or, most likely, to be killed by the party itself. It was just like what happened to a group of high-ranking party members when they were executed by their comrades for treason and conspiracy four years before that night because of a charge never proven. He walked to the sheikh's house, the only place in the world that he could call home. On his way there, Kamal looked for his friends, hoping to find them by the public garden near the main road in Balluria where they used to spend their evenings listening to many stories by Fathil the Lair, but the garden was deserted. He walked toward the guesthouse, and he did not find anyone there either. He knew it was because Sheikh Jawad had left Balluria for a short trip to the southern province to collect a debt that was past due. He took his trusted aide, Khanger, who could barely walk, with him. In the empty guesthouse he laid on the carpet listening to the sounds of the many women, who wore black robes, inside the sheikh's house. Kamal lay there with his eyes open, staring at the ceiling, hoping to hear Hanan's voice. He knew that only her voice would bring him comfort during this agonizing inner conflict. Suddenly a fresh and warm feeling of peace entered his senses when he heard her magical voice speaking to another woman. She told the woman to bring her a lamp, so she could see her way to the bathroom to take a bath.

Kamal sat up.

"Hanan is taking a bath," he told himself. The image of her peeling her clothes off was a frontier that he had never even dreamed of crossing. Hanan, the ultimate jinni of the Sahara, the woman he had loved since the first time he had seen her standing in the courtyard of her father's house, holding what looked like a doll made of dirty cotton, the day a strange man brought him and his mother, who left one year later.

He remembered the strange man saying to the sheikh, "I am sure the son is his, but he is dead and we cannot ask him, and they have nowhere to go."

Later, Kamal realized that the strange man was talking about his father, who died in the war fighting the Kurds in the north, and that his mother was accused of bearing an illegitimate child, him. His mother would disappear and never return, but at that time none of that ever bothered him, because when he was standing there holding his mother's hand, all he could see was the girl with the dirty cotton doll; he saw her eyes, the color of which made him want to snatch the doll from her, so he could hear her cry and see the tears coming down on her rosy cheeks. Since that day, Hanan was like a thorn in his foot, poking him with the sting of little pains that left him tormented. He always tried to get close to her; he made dolls of clay and painted them with crayons that he stole from the other kids and gave them to her, but she was only interested in the real, live bird that another kid named Hamid gave to her younger brother, Ahmed. She named the bird Balbool and fed it wheat and dragonflies that she caught in the garden that her mother planted before she died. Kamal wanted her to be his friend; he felt an ache in his heart whenever she passed by him and when he smelled her skin. Her smell reminded him of his mother's smell when he used to sleep near her on the cold nights of the marsh winters as she slept naked next to a man he thought was his father. Kamal always missed that smell.

The saddest day in his life was when Sheikh Jawad told him to take the seven kittens that Hanan's cat had birthed and drown them in the river. He did not want to do it, but he knew that the sheikh would be angry with him if he didn't, so he drowned them. He wanted to dive in the river and bring the kittens back to life, so Hanan would stop crying, but then another kid named Hamid dove after the kittens and saved them. Ever since that day, Hanan never talked to him. Even after she grew up and went to school together with her brother Ahmed, she would not speak to him. She talked to everyone else, but not to him.

Kamal had noticed that Hanan had become a woman when she finished the eighth grade. He saw how her chest was ripening and took on the shape of two little hills and how she started to wear a little make up and the thick eyeliner that she brought from Barrya, the Gypsy woman who taught the town's girls how to put eyeliner on. He noticed that Hanan was no longer the little girl that he knew when he saw her one day without her abbaya cover and wearing a dark red dress. She looked ripe and full of femininity, but he could never reach her. He had never seen her before without her abbaya, because he lived in a room next to where Khanger the coffee man lived. The two rooms were behind the guesthouse, where he could not see inside.

That night when he heard her talking to the other woman about the bath, his heart started pumping blood to his brain to the point that he felt blind and deaf. He walked outside the guesthouse and entered from the door where his room and Khanger's room were. He opened the door of Khanger's room to make sure the old coffee man was not there. He climbed on the mud wall that separated the guesthouse from the rest of the sheikh's house, jumped over the roof, and crawled over so he could see the courtyard of the sheikh's house. On top of the bathroom, he lay on the roof and looked to see if he could see inside the bathroom. With his hand, he pulled the dried mud and pulled off the tiny branches of the palm tree trunk that made a supporting spike for the roof, and from the tiny hole that he made he could see the inside the dark bathroom. He lay there and waited. Minutes later, he saw the bathroom door open, and then one of the many women in the sheikh's house brought a large pot of water. Hanan walked behind her carrying the kerosene lamp. The woman poured the hot water into a larger pot of water and stirred the water to make it cooler. Then the woman left after telling Hanan to watch out for scorpions. Hanan was singing the famous song of Abdul Haleem Hafith, the dead singer who only sang about love,

Tell my lover, who has daring eyes,
Tell him the truth,
Tell him I loved him,
From the first moment I saw him.

Hanan did not pay attention to what the woman said. She set the kerosene lamp on the small wooden shelf in the bathroom. The light from the kerosene lamp made many dancing shadows on the wall of the dark bathroom, but Kamal could see Hanan clearly as she stood in the middle of the room. Kamal could not breathe as he watched Hanan take off her dress. He choked on his own breath as she peeled off her dress and then her flimsy undergarment. She stood there, looking for a bowl from which to pour water onto her silky body. She peeled off her underpants and was completely nude. Kamal thought that he was dreaming or that he had died and entered the heavenly forbidden city of the women's world. He looked at Hanan and saw the most beautiful image he'd ever viewed and would ever see in his entire life. As she poured warm water that slipped from her long hair down to her amazingly curved back and down onto her legs, she sang the famous love song. Kamal could hardly keep from screaming with love and desire. He wanted to leap inside the bathroom and wash Hanan's body with his hands and worship her angelic body with endless kisses. He wanted to wash her feet. He wanted to lock the bathroom door and never let her out. He wanted to keep the entire world locked behind the bathroom doors forever and live the rest of his life under the droplets of water from her body. He did not realize that his fingers were bleeding from pulling the leaves of the palm tree trunk. He was numb and lost while he was looking at her wet body. She had the curves of the most beautiful female in the world he would ever see, and he could not believe that no one was there to share the spectacular view with him. It was his, only his, the way it should be and must be. Hanan must be his. Hanan should be his, and Hanan would be his. When she finished her bath and put her clothes back on, he turned and lay on his back looking at the stars. When she left he stayed there, fighting back his tears. Emotionally exhausted, he waited until he made sure that no one would see him. He jumped onto the mud wall and down to the walkway behind the guesthouse and entered his room. That night, he could not sleep.

3

Needing to be at the party headquarters in the morning, he had to turn in the money he had collected from all the supporters and ally students, in the cell in the town. One of his duties was to go door-to-door asking the students for the monthly membership fee for the party. He made sure to count the money three times and waited for all of those students who were delinquent on their membership payments. After that he had to be in the school for an algebra test. He dropped off the bag full of coins at the party headquarters and raced to school, so he could see Hanan before she went home. Her naked image did not escape his mind for a single second. Kamal finished his test, to which he did not know any of the answers. Yet he was sure that he would pass, because the math teacher, Mr. Mohamed Tabra, a party member, would help him pass since the instructor knew that all the cell duties kept Kamal from studying.

He saw Hanan walking in the school's courtyard, looking fresh and happy, and that made Kamal happy. Desiring to be alone with her, so he could tell her that he loved her, he wanted to confess his love to her and to tell her that he would ask her father for her hand in marriage. He waited for the first class period to end, but he did not get the chance to talk to her, because she talked to the Hillaly girls. He walked past her and looked at her. She turned her face away and walked to her class. Waiting for the second and third class to end, he was not able to talk to her. He saw her talking to Hamid's sister, Amel. Becoming worried and upset, he did not want to tell Hanan about his feelings in front of Amel, because he thought that Amel might tell her brother Hamid. *Hamid, the dirty son of a whore that everyone knew Hanan liked and may even be in love with*, he thought to himself. Kamal planned to wait until she left the school; he would walk with her and her brother, Ahmed, to the house, and then he would tell her in front of her brother. When the school day ended, he waited outside with Ahmed, but Hanan was not there. He asked Ahmed, "Where is Hanan?"

"She left early after the fourth class. She said she was sick," Ahmed answered.

Kamal walked back to the guesthouse and asked Ahmed if he could talk to Hanan. He asked them to meet him behind the sheikh's house, because he had something important to tell her. Ahmed went inside the house and came back with a reply that made Kamal more upset. "Hanan went to Barrya's house. She went there with the Hillaly girls to do something."

Kamal did not want to go to Barrya's house, because he knew that he would not get the chance to be alone with Hanan, and he had to be at the party headquarters to meet with Comrade Uraiby, who was waiting for Kamal's answer, about becoming a member of the firing squad to execute a group of unfortunate army deserters captured in the marshes and being held at the party headquarters. Kamal put on his dark green party militia uniform and went to the party headquarters.

The meeting with Comrade Uraiby did not happen, because his son, Mazen, was hurt in a car accident in the new Volkswagen Passat that he bought for his spoiled young son. It was almost dark when Kamal walked back to the sheikh's house, and he was glad the meeting did not happen; he still was unsure of what to tell Comrade Uraiby about the firing squad proposal.

Kamal walked past the soccer field and looked to where Barrya's mud hut was. He thought of the Gypsy woman and how close she was to Hanan, and suddenly he thought that the Gypsy woman could help him greatly in his pursuit of Hanan's heart. He knew how Hanan, who never had a mother figure, always said that Barrya was like her mother. So he thought it would help his love cause if he enlisted the help of the Gypsy woman, who knew all the secrets of the town, to help him win Hanan's love once and forever. He walked toward the mud hut, and as he got closer, he saw that the mud hut door was closed; something that he'd never seen before, because Barrya never closed her door. He wanted to knock, but he heard a familiar voice, the same one that he heard the night before, as it sang the famous love song. His legs could not carry him. Hanan giggled.

"Oh, my Allah, it's her voice. What is she doing out of the house at this hour?" Kamal asked himself.

He thought it was the doing of the merciful angels of love; Hanan was here at Barrya's house. Finally, he would have the chance he was looking for to tell Hanan that he would do the impossible to make her a happy wife. He would tell her that he had loved her since that cloudy February day, when he saw her carrying her dirty cotton doll. He would tell her that everything he did would do was because of her and for her...

"Hanan, it's getting late. You must go home," said the male voice from inside the mud hut. It pulled Kamal's heart from his chest, crushing it under a giant rock, a surprise that he was not able to bear.

He walked around the mud wall so he could hear the man's voice more clearly. He walked around the mud hut to the round window where the curtain with unidentifiable shapes blocked the view of the inside Barrya's room. Kamal listened quietly to the sounds of kissing and passionate moans that Hanan let out as she surrendered her magical body to Hamid's electrifying touches. The two lovers had arranged to meet at Barrya's house every afternoon of that week, because Hanan's father was on a short trip out of town. Hanan had told Hamid's sister, Amel, to tell Hamid to meet her at Barrya's house every day after the school's fourth period, the same time Kamal had wanted to confess his undying love.

That night Kamal felt the weakness in his knees and leaned against the mud wall listening to moaning of Hanan as she received Hamid's melting kisses. He listened as the two lovers giggled, hugged, and kissed, and he listened to Hanan telling Hamid, "I swear to Allah, that I will love you and go with you to any place you want to go. Even if we have to live on fishing and in a small hut by the river, I will be happy."

Oh, how long had Kamal waited to hear these words from Hanan, almost his whole life. Kamal cried silently and did not leave his place when he heard

Hamid telling Hanan that she must go home, because it was getting late. He asked Barrya to escort her, and the three of them left the mud hut.

Kamal cried, and tears of blood came from his heart. He waited behind the mud hut for Barrya to return. He could not go home to the sheikh's house, and he could not go looking for Hamid in order to kill him. He waited for the Gypsy woman, who knew all the secrets of the town to tell her a secret that she must know, that no one else should know. Minutes later, Barrya entered her mud hut and was surprised to see Kamal standing in the middle of her room, the same room that she let Hamid and Hanan use for their secretive love sessions and rendezvous for the past two years, whenever the eyes of Hanan's father and the many women who lived in the sheikh's house were not watching. Kamal stood there knowing what he wanted to say.

She saw him and knew that the lovers' secret was exposed.

"How could you do that to Sheikh Jawad?" Kamal asked the Gypsy woman.

"Kamal, when did you get here?" Barrya asked.

"I saw everything. I heard everything. You filthy whore. How could you let this happen? You know that I could kill you and that son of a whore; you have both dishonored the sheikh," Kamal shouted. He raised his hand and struck Barrya on her face, knocking her to the ground. Barrya did not reply. She looked at him as he fought back his tears. Knowing that he was heartbroken, she also knew that her love for him would not stop him from what he was about to say or to do, and she was right. Kamal swung his right arm and landed a screaming slap on the tanned Gypsy woman's face.

"You hit me! I am like your mother," she said.

"You are not my mother, you filthy Gypsy, daughter of Gypsy whore! You are not my mother, and my mother was a whore like you! All of you are whores, and you've made Hanan a whore! You pile of filth, I swear to Allah I will make Sheikh Jawad cut off your head and your hands! I will burn your house down, and I will kill that son of whore, Hamid!" Kamal shouted as he kicked her with his Bulgarian-made party militia boots.

"Akhhh," she cried from pain.

Kamal walked away wiping his tears. She sat in the corner crying. He looked at her and said, "Listen to me. If Sheikh Jawad knew, he would kill Hanan, you, and Hamid. He may ask me to kill all of you. I can kill you and that son of a whore, but I don't want Hanan to be harmed, because I love her. I want to marry her," Kamal said.

"She will not marry you, Kamal," Barrya interrupted him with the insight of a Gypsy woman.

"Keep your silence, or I will cut out your tongue. You will tell Hanan that I know everything and I have seen everything. You will convince her to accept my proposal when I ask her father for her hand in marriage. And if I learn that she has stepped a foot in your house of filth again, I will kill you. As for that son of whore, Hamid, he will not talk to Hanan anymore. He will not see her, and he will not send her messages through his stupid sister, Amel. As Allah is my witness, if I hear that Hanan has stepped a foot in this house of whores that you've created here, you will see the stars in daylight. And I swear to Allah that I will kill you myself. Do you hear me?" he screamed with all of the air in his lungs.

"Yes," Barrya replied with a weak voice.

"I curse you and your father and all the Gypsy whores that you descended from!" he said as he spat on her and walked out.

Barrya sat alone and cried in the dark corner of her mud hut, thinking of what could happen to Hanan and Hamid. That night, Kamal walked to the party headquarters and asked if Comrade Uraiby was there. Comrade Falih, the one-eyed comrade who seemed never to leave the party building, told him that Comrade Uraiby was there earlier, but he went home. Kamal walked to the end of town, where the nicer, newer homes were recently built for the party officials and the house of Captain Naeem, the only high-ranking army officer in these parts. He asked a group of young kids, who looked healthier and cleaner than the kids from the side of town that he lived in, if they knew where Comrade Uraiby's house was. They pointed to a big house with a large metal gate. He rang the bell and waited. Comrade Uraiby opened the gate wearing his white night dress. Comrade Uraiby looked tired, and he could not believe that Kamal would visit him at his house.

"Ha, Kamal, is everything alright?"

"Yes, Rafeeq (comrade), I came here to tell you that I am sorry about what happened to your son, Mazen," Kamal said, looking for the right words.

"He is all right, only a fractured leg. I should have never bought him a car," Comrade Uraiby said and scratched his big belly.

"Thank God that he is OK," Kamal said, then added with a firm and clear voice,

"I came to tell you, Comrade, that I want to be on the firing squad team and I am ready to participate in the executions of all the deserters and all those who cause us harm. I mean all of those who cause the divine leader, our great party, and our country any harm," Kamal said and looked at Comrade Uraiby with the gaze of a soulless man.

Comrade Uraiby looked at him, saw the strange color in Kamal's eyes, and asked,

"Have you had enough time to think about it?"

"Yes, I have, and I want to be a member of the firing squad," Kamal replied.

The Book of Balluria

Doves in the Wheat Fields

1

Kamal wasted no time. The morning after the engagement night, he woke up early and went to the party headquarters, where he received the congratulations of his comrades and subordinates. He could not stop thinking of how beautiful Hanan looked in her white engagement dress as he put the ring around the remarkably delicate third finger on her right hand as she sat silently covering her face with white burka. They heard the distinctive, ear-piercing cheering of the many women who wore black robes from inside the sheikh's house. He could not believe that Hanan would be his wife finally. And when he went back to the guesthouse, where the men were sitting and waiting for him, and received the congratulations and words of blessing from the well-wishers, he was pleased to see that Abdullah and Haleem were there too. Kamal wished that Hamid was also there so he could see the defeat in his eyes, but at the same time he thought that Hamid would be too filthy and too dishonorable to be allowed to disgrace the guesthouse and the engagement celebration with his presence. For the first time in his life, Kamal was happy.

The men cheered him and wished him well as he entered the guesthouse flanked by Khanger and another man. Kamal wore his dark green party uniform and dangled his pistol in the bright orange holster, imitating the divine leader. He walked with impeccable pride, looking in the men's eyes knowing that soon he would be the son in law of the most powerful sheikh in these parts. He smiled, shook hands with all the men, and chatted with his friends, asking Abdullah about Hisham and Ashraf and Salah and why they were not there. Haleem informed him that Hisham was on the war front and that Ashraf and Salah were out of town. Haleem and Abdullah noticed how cheerful and happy Kamal was. He seemed sincere in asking about his friends.

On their way out after the engagement dinner and with his author-like sense of humor, Abdullah commented on the way Kamal acted at the engagement party.

"It must be the feeling of victory or the feeling of love."

Haleem did not understand. "What do you mean?"

"Kamal is happy for one of two reasons; either he feels victorious over Hamid or he is truly in love with Hanan."

"I know that he was happy, but I still don't understand. Why would he feel victorious over Hamid?" Haleem replied.

"You will," Abdullah said as they walked down the main street of Balluria. The town square was filled with the wreckage of two cars that had collided in the accident that had killed both drivers.

Spending most of the night awake and barely sleeping for an hour, Kamal woke up at seven in the morning, and after a short stop at the party headquarters, he took a taxi and spent the day in the capital of the province, styling his hair and shaving his face and removing all his facial hair with a thread by a soft, gentle, and very skillful barber who spoke with a womanly voice. Kamal was uncomfortable because he thought the barber was a man lover so he was careful not to have any physical contact with him while he was on the barber chair and when the barber asked him, "Where are you from, brother?"

"Balluria," Kamal answered without looking at the barber.

"Oh, Balluria, what a name. I have heard of that town, because my father was sent to Balluria a long time ago, when the country became a republic, to establish a police force," the barber said with his soft voice.

"That's interesting," Kamal said without showing any interest in continuing the conversation.

For his wedding Kamal bought two pairs of shoes: one black and one brown, as well as a sky-blue suit. He did not ask any of his friends to go with him; instead, he went alone to the capital of the province. It saddened him to feel so alone, his wedding day just a week away, the happiest day of every man's life in these parts and the happiest day of his life, and there was no one there from his family. The father that he never knew and the mother that left him in the sheikh's house years before did not know that he was getting married to the most beautiful woman in Balluria and maybe the most beautiful woman in these parts, as far as he knew. Yet no one was there with him to help him choose a suit for the wedding or suggest another color for the shoes. He was alone, but he did not care. He knew that he had gotten what he wanted: Hanan. She would be his, and even though he knew that her heart did not belong to him, he was sure that he would win her heart slowly and day by day and that when they started having children and a family she would be sure to love him. He heard many times that for elders a woman always love the man who takes her virginity. He was sure that one day Hanan would love him.

He wanted to buy something for Hanan, something for his fiancé, who was within days of being his bride. Wanting to buy her something that no other girl in town had, he spent hours looking in the many shops at the tin-covered market that filled with shoppers. They grabbed merchandise with their hands to feel the materials and make sure it was not secondhand product, even though they had no way to judge the genuineness of products. As long as it was from Japan or the Americas, and as long as there was English writing on it, they wanted it. While other shoppers listened to loud music and waited as the cassette tape vendors made a copy of the original copy, he walked back and forth looking for the perfect gift for Hanan, who seemed sad when he saw her at the engagement night festivities. She seemed sadder, and he may have seen her crying as he put the ring on the angelic third finger of her right hand; he could not escape the silkiness of her touch and the clear sadness in her eyes.

He wanted to buy all the jewelry in the world and put it on all of her fingers so he could keep feeling the silkiness of her soft hands. His heart was overflowing with impatience as he realized that very soon, only a week, and she would be all his. But that was not soon enough for him. Nevertheless, he was happy with the thought that soon she would be with him in one room with no one else, and he would have all the time in the world to look at her and touch her and feel her angelic body, centimeter by centimeter. Kamal wanted to rush back to Balluria and just wait for the moment when he would have Hanan all for himself. She would be his wife, not anyone else's. He smiled with confidence and grabbed a golden necklace that he saw in the glass display of one the many goldsmiths' shops owned by the Subbay Goldsmith, who looked like an ancient prophet with his white clothes and white beard. He inquired about the cost and looked at the graceful old Subbay Goldsmith, who was poised, ready to haggle and lie about the price. When the goldsmith offered the necklace, at an obviously inflated price of three hundred dinars, Kamal simply said that he would take it, thinking only that it would look good on Hanan's chest when he would slowly undress her on their wedding night.

It was getting dark, and Kamal was supposed to spend the night at the party headquarters as he was assigned the duty of the head of the night guards, a routine installed one month before that day, since news and rumors of looming invasion of the oil rich southern country and numerous directives by the party command demanded that all the party militia must be on alert. Kamal figured that he would have enough time to eat dinner with his future father-in-law, Sheikh Jawad. Then he would have the chance to see Hanan and give her the necklace himself, and then ask the sheikh if they could have the wedding the coming Thursday instead of waiting for the next Thursday.

Kamal anxiously awaited aboard the minibus that would take him back to Balluria at the public garage in the capital of the province, where the people from the small towns and villages near the marshes and all the people from the small city south of Balluria waited with all the soldiers who were on a short leave from the death carnivals of the eastern fronts. They all waited for the raggedy minibuses to take them back to the safety of the mud huts. Looking worried from the news of another death carnival just about to start on the southern borders, they were all waiting for the small buses to take them home, but there were never enough buses to accommodate the increasing numbers of passengers, and people kept chasing after busses that drove slowly in order to avoid the human stampede of restless and frustrated passengers. Kamal did not want to wait and jumped in a taxi. He did not care about the steep price of the taxi ride. He wanted to be near Hanan.

Kamal smiled as he thought that Hanan was on the other end waiting for him. It was the first time that he felt needed and wanted and loved. She had never waited for him before, not since the first day he saw her had she ever waited for him. She never did and she never wanted to, even when he told her that he was trying to find a cat for her after he drowned her kittens. She did not say anything back to him. He wanted to tell her that it was her father, the sheikh, who told him to drown the kittens, but she never wanted to listen, and when Hamid struck him and threw him to the ground the day he tried to drown the kittens, he was not upset about being humiliated in front of his male friends. Kamal was more hurt that he was humiliated in front of her, and he wished that he had killed Hamid that day,

Hamid, that son of a whore, his archenemy, his nemesis. Hamid, who Hanan loved. Over the intervening years Kamal watched as Hanan sent the looks of love toward Hamid in the school and on the way to school, and when the boys waited by the green fence of the public garden, he was hurting inside because he noticed how Hanan looked at Hamid, and he wished that she was looking at him. Choked with jealousy and anger, Kamal tried to do anything to impress Hanan and turn her attention to him. He obeyed the dictates of her father like a slave just to get her to turn her eyes toward him. He joined the party and advanced in the ranks so he could gain her admiration and even grew his moustache before the others boys did theirs so he could look more manly and mature, but she never cared.

She was infatuated with Hamid, that dirty son of a whore. Kamal cried when he found all the lover letters that Hanan wrote to Hamid and wished that she was writing to him. He was on the edge of killing himself when he saw her and Hamid kissing each other in Barrya's mud hut, and he could never forget the giggling, and the sounds of kissing and intimate hissings never escaped him. He could have told Sheikh Jawad about her, and Sheikh Jawad might have killed her, but Kamal loved Hanan, and he wanted her for himself. As he looked at the shimmering lights of Balluria while the taxi drove quietly toward the town, Kamal smiled and realized that Hanan was his finally; she was his fiancée and Hamid could no longer touch her. The car stopped about ten meters from where the portrait of the divine leader stood at the town's entrance, and Kamal jumped from the front seat, paid the fare, and walked with jumpy steps. He felt that he wanted to dance all the way to the guesthouse. He was racing his own feet toward the guest house of Sheikh Jawad, where Hanan was.

Kamal was so absorbed in his thoughts that he did not notice the three men standing about thirty meters from the guesthouse looking at him and shaking their heads strangely. He walked until he could see the inside the guesthouse, and to his surprise it was almost full of men. He wondered if something had happened. Perhaps one of the old men in Balluria had just died, or a car accident had claimed the life of an unfortunate street crosser. He walked slowly in respect to the poor unknown unfortunate and then because he realized that the men in the guesthouse looked at him as though they were waiting for him.

Two men—one of them was Jelwi, the notorious retired police sergeant who had killed almost seventy people during his police career—and the other was a younger man Kamal did not know. His most prominent thought was that Sheikh Jawad had died. As that idea entered his mind, he felt a devilish ease and strange comfort, but the words from the two men told another story.

"Pray for the prophet and his holy family," the men said in unison.

"Praise be for the prophet and his family," Kamal replied.

"Curse the devil and all of his work," the two men said again together.

"Shakoo? What happened?" Kamal asked.

"Come with us, Kamal. You need to sit down," the older man said.

As he entered the guesthouse, he prepared himself to hear anything and believed he had the heart to withstand the worst. But not a single nerve in his body had the ability to hear what the men were saying as he noticed that Sheikh Jawad sat at the end of the guesthouse with his head covered with the kuffia head cover. His iqal was in front him, a sign that his honor was disgraced. What honor? Kamal wondered which of the many women who lived in the house committed the ultimate sin of adultery. Who was the one? Who could be the one that he might be asked to kill that night? He wondered as he sat next to Sheikh Jawad, who looked disgraced, ashamed, and weakened, Khanger, the old coffee pourer, leaned toward him and told him the soul-crushing news.

"The sheikh's daughter, Hanan, has escaped with Hamid the son of Farhan the peasant," Khanger said.

Kamal did not understand what Khanger was telling him. He wanted to shove his pistol in Khanger's mouth and unload the nine bullets. How dare he say such words? How dare he claim that Hanan, his beloved fiancé and his bride-to-be, had escaped the town with her peasant lover? How dare he say such things in front of the sheikh and the men of Balluria? The noise from the men in the guesthouse started to sound like thousands of mosquitoes entering his ears. The earth and the entire universe spun in Kamal's head. He wanted to scream, not from anger but from the painful and overwhelming feeling of abandonment and the cry of love lost forever as the truth of the claim began to sink into his mind even as the denial held by tiny threads.

No, not Hanan. She did not leave. She is still here in the house waiting for him to give her the gift that he bought her from the city. They are lying to him. She did not leave him. She did not escape town with Hamid, Kamal thought, and he continued to stare out at the fuzzy faces of men in the guesthouse. She wouldn't dare. He did not hear what Khanger said to him at that moment. He looked at Khanger, whose words seemed to come from a deep cavern and be spoken in a foreign tongue.

Suddenly the fog cleared, and Kamal heard him all too clearly.

"She escaped the town and she disgraced the sheikh."

Kamal's face turned pale while he turned his eyes aimlessly over the faces of the men in the guesthouse.

All the men thought that he was silenced by anger and the unbearable feeling of dishonor and shame none of them could see the signs of a heart broken once and forever.

She could not leave him. She could not leave him. Voices echoed hollowly in his head. He felt nauseous and disgusted by the gathering of every man in town with their degrading looks and thick moustaches and smell of burnt tobacco and sweat celebrating his ultimate defeat and unmatchable humiliation. He wanted to run and breathe fresher air as he looked around the guesthouse, searching for a friendly face, one that would tell him that it was not true.

He stood up as he felt that could no longer bear the shame and disgrace, but ultimately he could not bear the feeling of a truly broken heart. He felt a sharp dagger ripping his heart out over and over, destroying every vein and artery in his body. He walked outside, and two men followed him. He turned toward them and calmly spoke, "I will shoot and kill any man who comes close to me."

As he grabbed the handle of his pistol, the two men stopped and turned back toward the guesthouse. Kamal stood by himself looking at the space beyond the houses where the soccer field and Barrya's house stood. He knew what he had to do. He wanted to drink areq until he was drunk. At that moment he did not want to feel anything. He did not want to hear anything, and he did not want to do anything, not for honor not for reputation and not for the sheikh. He just did not want to do anything. He wanted to sleep for a long time and wake up in a different morning with different realities. Slowly, he walked toward the Gypsy woman's mud hut and hoped that he would find Hisham or Haleem or Ashraf. He hoped to see Abdullah because he and Basima might know where Hanan and Hamid had escaped to. He wanted to find Hanan and talk to her and so she would return to him, before the night was over because when the night was over, he would have no choice but to kill her to preserve his honor and the honor of her father, the sheikh. He did not want to kill her. He wanted to forgive her and tell her that he loved her and wanted to keep her. He felt thousands of ants creeping between his skin and bones as he remembered the kissing noise he heard long time before. The noises were clear and vivid in his ears He walked toward the Gypsy woman's mud hut, wishing that the ground would open and swallow him. He wished for the end of the world, but he found himself standing in front of the mud hut with its door slightly ajar. He pushed the door, slamming it against the wall and shouted, "Barrya!"

A silhouette of a woman dressed in black appeared from the room speaking quietly in a voice meek with fear, "I am here, Kamal. I am here."

"Where is Hanan?"

"I don't know," Barrya answered.

Kamal realized that Barrya's answer was the confirmation of all of his fears. If Hanan was not at her father's house and she was not in Barrya's house, then she was gone; she had escaped with Hamid.

"Where is Hamid?" Kamal asked, his eyes ragged with redness in the light of the kerosene lamp.

"I don't know," Barrya whispered.

"Shut the door and don't let anybody in. Bring me the bottle of areq and don't you dare talk to me!" Kamal ordered Barrya as he took off his pistol and set it on the floor of the dark room and looked toward the open space where the soccer field appeared strangely peaceful in the sliver rays of the moonlight.

2

Kamal did not know that Barrya had lied to him about the whereabouts of Hamid and Hanan. He did not know that she had lied to him about knowing everything about their plan to escape and commit the ultimate sin. She lied to him about the night when he was at his peak of happiness as he put the ring on Hanan's finger, thinking that he owned her forever. In reality, she had been untying all of the shackles of a lifelong commitment to misery with a secret plan she had hatched with her lover Hamid and their Gypsy godmother of love, Barrya. Kamal did not know that Hanan had left the house of her father the same night she had become engaged to him and went to Barrya's house where Hamid was waiting for her, shivering with love and desire for the misleading guidance of the ultimate goddess of sinful lust herself. The two lovers willingly submitted themselves to the forbidden love rituals of the lost Gypsy dancer, who showed them the way to the exciting paths of indecency and the ever-festive worlds of sexual fulfillment in the wrong place and the wrong time and the deadliest inherited traditions and among the wrong people who blindly willing to honor such traditions, but the two lovers did not care, nor were they were afraid. They kissed each other with self-gratification that would make the hair of the thickest moustaches in these ruggedly conservative lands stand up and fly as though hit by gale force winds. The two lovers mated with intense passion after Hanan took off her engagement ring and tossed it into the fire while she let herself be enslaved by the massive hands of her tanned and tall peasant lover. That night he found her, his ultimate woman, the woman that every sheikh in these parts would have paid blood to own. She offered herself and her body and her honor and the reputation that took many lives and many years to build, and she threw them against the shadowy walls of the Gypsy woman's mud hut. The two lovers, sheltered by Barrya's flimsy mud hut walls, broke the commandment of all commandments, one not written in all of God's books, nor preached by his prophets or messengers. They broke a commandment written in the blood of all the beautiful virgins who longed for the electrifying touch of a man and the desire-driven widows who wanted to extinguish the fire of their bodies, burning since their husbands had gone to the endless death campaigns of divine leaders and all the wars and religious jihad adventures. The desires of the war-driven men never comprehended the needs of Arab women's loneliness and emotional solitude. The two lovers committed themselves to each other and to a fate they did not choose but was mysteriously chosen for them. They decided they would not be apart.

Hanan asked Hamid as they lay next to each other, "What will happen now, Hamid?" she asked, looking for the right answer, because she knew that that night she might have conceived a child, one that no woman wants to bare in that part of the world, the love child. She also knew that she could not be a bride for Kamal, not without her virginity.

"You will go home now," Hamid said with his deep voice, and just before she protested his answer, he corrected it with the conviction of a man who sees his destiny before him. "You will gather the things you want to bring with you and meet me here tomorrow when darkness falls, and we will leave this town."

He said the right words. Deep inside her, Hanan knew that Kamal had no chance of owning her as a wife because she had belonged to Hamid a long time ago. She had belonged to Hamid since the morning he struck Kamal by the river and saved her kittens from drowning. She had belonged to Hamid since the time she read his love letter delivered by his sister, Amel. Hamid was her man, her lover, and her husband. Hamid was her nomadic knight running his horse through the wilderness of her being, alone.

In her heart and her mind there was no chance, not in this life, not even in ten lifetimes over, that Kamal would lay a finger on her, but she would need help leaving her house when darkness fell, so she asked Barrya to help her. Barrya knew that she would be committing the ultimate betrayal of her protector, Sheikh Jawad, and the ultimate deception of two of her other children, Kamal and Ahmed, but Barrya had no choice because she was following the unholy secrets of the code of Gypsy witches and because she knew that the two lovers would have committed their final sin with her help or without it. Barrya told Hanan that she would arrive the next day at her father's house, and they would smuggle her and her small bag of belongings with them when darkness fell.

The next day, as Hamid waited by her mud hut, Barrya went to pick up Hanan, her small, unnoticeable amount of luggage and, two hundred dinars that Hanan had stolen from the house for the journey. Realizing that it would be conspicuous for a Gypsy to escort a young maiden so late in the day, she hurried around town looking for a young female friend to help; that is how the very innocent Basima became involved in such a scandal. Hamid waited impatiently in Barrya's hut.

Amel never got the chance to ask her only brother, who was about to condemn himself to the unknown, what she and her mother would do without him, what would they do when Sheikh Jawad discovered his daughter's escape and unleashed his wrath on everyone around him and all of those he might have thought contributed to his ultimate disgrace. Amel did not want to sabotage her brother's romantic fall into the abyss of the unknown fate along with his majestic, sinful bride. She kept silent as she watched from her window the shadows of Basima and Barrya hurrying to the sheikh's house. She walked behind them and reached the mud hut. To the surprise of Hamid, Amel did not say a word. She just looked at her brother, who had nothing to say to his only sister. She felt a sharp pain when she could not embrace her brother and Hanan when Hanan arrived at Barrya's mud hut. The two lovers embraced each other and waved good-bye to Amel and Barrya and Basima and Balluria as they lovers walked toward the space behind the mud hut and waited for the freight train that passed by Balluria when night falls. On time, the train stopped briefly, just long enough for the two frightened lovers to board. The shriek of the train whistle made Amel start sobbing as she realized how lonely she had just become without her brother and her friend Hanan. Barrya heard her and drew her close. Amel put her head in Barrya's lap and started to weep as the Gypsy woman comforted her with Gypsy songs of loved ones leaving.

> *Oh water of the river*
> *If you just know or feel my pains and sorrows*
> *You will change your colors if you feel my sorrows*
> *Oh they're gone. And they never returned*
> *All my loved ones had gone without saying good-bye.*

Barrya sat there soothing Amel and thinking of the ramifications of the scandal she just orchestrated as Basima, who did not know the plan of the two lovers, kept silent out of fear of the scandal she just implicated herself in.

3

When Basima entered her house a few minutes later she was not surprised to see her husband Abdullah waiting for her, and many questions lurked in his eyes. She hoped that he would avoid asking those and just let things be, at least until morning or at least until Hamid and Hanan had enough time to reach the big city, where they could disappear. But Abdullah had other thoughts in his mind, thoughts of his wife being unfaithful. He wanted to know that Basima was as honorable as he always believed, and he wanted to know why she was late coming home, knowing that no decent woman comes home after darkness falls.

"Where were you, Basima?"

Basima, who had never lied in her life, not to her parents, nor to her brothers, and never to her husband, said with a trembling voice and downcast eyes, "Can you not ask me this? I promise I will tell you in the morning."

Abdullah did not understand the answer and he knew that manhood was at stake as he heard the cryptic reply from the woman whom he loved and trusted.

He calmly said, "If I wait until the morning, you will not be my wife. I will divorce you. I looked for you everywhere. I went to your parents' house, and they told me that you were not there. I went to Hamid's house, and his mother told me that Amel was supposed to be at our house with you." Abdullah walked toward his wife with an angry look.

"You know that I am a reasonable man who does not suspect bad things before knowing the truth, but many people saw me looking for you, even the Hillaly family, when I went there asking about you, Basima. You have been gone from the house since late afternoon, and you came back after dark, so don't ask me to wait until the morning because I don't think I can sleep the night without knowing the truth."

Basima was shocked, but she had expected the reply, and she knew her husband was as serious as the scandal about to unfold on the town, so she sat down and told him. She said that she did not know what Barrya and Hanan had planned when Barrya showed up earlier in the day and asked her if she could go with her to see Hanan and visit her after the engagement night. Basima said that she was surprised when she saw Hanan putting her clothes and jewelry in a small bag, and she was surprised when the Gypsy woman said to Hanan that Hamid was waiting for her at her house.

Basima told her husband, Abdullah, that she wanted to tell Hanan not to escape because she knew how devastated her father would be. She said that she wanted to tell Hanan that if she escaped the town one week before the wedding, she would not be able to return to her father and she would never see her brother, Ahmed, again. She wanted to say those things but did not say them to Hanan because she was not able to hear anything as the ringing of the thrill of being with Hamid had blocked her ears and prevented her from hearing any other voice besides Hamid's.

"So you are telling me that Hamid and Hanan have escaped town?" Abdullah gently asked his frightened wife.

"Yes."

"Where did they go?"

"I don't know. They went to the railroad station, to catch the freight train."

"Oh, my merciful Allah," Abdullah gasped. "What about Kamal?"

"He does not know yet. He is in the big city buying a wedding gift for Hanan."

Abdullah stood up and said with his hands raised to his head, "You stupid woman! How could you do this to me and you? Do you know what will happen now?"

Basima was afraid as she heard her husband call her stupid. Abdullah, who never said one bad word to the people who wronged him, was calling her stupid, but the expression on his face were telling of looming disaster so she kept from protesting and did not reply as Abdullah started walking back and forth in the room holding his head between his hands muttering.

"Oh, my Allah, be merciful, how could you do that, Basima?"

Basima managed to say the one thing that she knew was true, "I did not know that they were escaping."

Abdullah looked at her and paused for long moments. Then he said, "I am going to see Sheikh Jawad tonight, and I will tell him about his daughter. I don't want you to say anything to any soul in this town." He put his clothes on.

Basima did not reply.

"You will stay in the house and not leave it. I will know how to handle this. If people start talking, you will say that you did not go to see Hanan tonight, nor did you see her since last night at the engagement party."

"Yes," she replied with her tears rolling down cheeks.

"And you will never go to see Amel again, and you will never set a foot in Barrya's house again. Do you understand me?

"Yes," she replied.

"I thought you had better common sense than to get involved in a matter such as this. Do you have any idea how many people could die because of what happened? Do you know that a war between the tribes may happen because of what you just did?" he said with a firm voice.

"I swear to Allah, I did not know what they had planned!" she cried out.

"I believe you. Pray for me and pray for Hamid and Hanan, because they may be found and killed before the night is over."

"I will. I will pray that you will be safe and you will come back to me soon, and I will pray for Kamal as well," Basima said as she held her husband and tried to kiss him.

He pushed her gently and said, "Kamal? I don't think Kamal needs your prayers now."

When Abdullah walked toward the guesthouse, his thought was of the possible disaster he was just about to unveil unwillingly. Many times he wanted to turn way and go back to his house and tell his wife to gather her belongings and escape town just as Hamid and Hanan had done, but he hadn't the heart to abandon his family. He must do this. He must be the bearer of bad news to the fearsome sheikh It would be the only way he could protect himself and his wife from a vengeful retaliation if he kept it a secret and let Balluria's women chew the fat and create a web of lies and rumors that would implicate his wife in the escape and then spin the vague facts to make it into a doctrine for a tribal feud that would never end. He was at the end of his rope when he approached the guesthouse and saw Sheikh Jawad sitting in the middle of it, as Khanger, the coffee server, was barely able to carry the coffee jar and place it on the fire. Abdullah entered the guesthouse, greeted the sheikh, and then sat next to him and said with clear voice, "Sheikh, I demand the oath of the grace of all the dead so I can speak."

The sheikh looked at him with his gruesome red eyes and replied, "You have my oath of the grace of all the dead. Now speak."

Abdullah said with same clear voice and calm demeanor, "Sheikh, you can tell your men to leave the guesthouse, or you can walk me with outside, as I am asking your protection from your anger, because I bare the news that you don't want to hear."

At that exact time Kamal was looking at the necklace, which he had bought for Hanan from the goldsmith.

4

When Kamal woke up, he did not know that Sheikh Jawad had sent two of his trusted men to inform his only son, Ahmed, about his sister's scandal. Ahmed was serving as a second lieutenant on the eastern front as an artillery officer at that time.

Kamal awoke with a hangover from drinking the entire bottle of areq the night before. Silent, he did not speak to Barrya. He quietly dressed in his dark green uniform and put in his loaded pistol in the holster. Barrya brought him some yogurt and tea. He smoked a cigarette for the first time in his life and walked toward the open door of the mud house. Barrya knew that he had reached the point of no return in his hate against everyone he had ever known, when she attempted to reach out to him asking him to wait.

"Kamal," she said.

Kamal stopped and looked at her with a glare that could shatter ice, saying, "Don't say a word, Barrya. The only reason I did not kill you is because I have always thought of you as my mother."

"I am like your mother, Kamal," said Barrya and paused as she looked at the color red filling Kamal's eyes.

"I don't have a mother. I never did and never will. I know that you are nothing but a Gypsy whore. You have always been a Gypsy whore, and you will always be," Kamal said, and then added with the same quiet anger, "I know that you have shared your bed with many men in this town and you have no shred of honor in your bones."

Barrya looked at him and realized that he had lost the last string of humanity that could make him love again.

"Moreover, I know that you had something to do with Hanan's escape with that son of a whore Hamid. You always loved Hamid more than you loved any of us—more than you loved me—but has it ever occurred to you that I loved Hanan? Has it ever occurred to you that I might have loved her more than Hamid did? Has it ever occurred to you that my only purpose for living was my love for Hanan?"

"Kamal, I loved the same way."

306

"Don't speak," He put his index finger on his lips and reached for his pistol. Barrya backed away as he looked at her and said, "I knew that Hanan and Hamid spent many afternoons here in your bed, and you let them. I could have killed them and you then. Do you know why I did not?"

"Why?" Barrya asked with fearful tears, as he saw how angry and hurt he was.

"Because I loved her and forgave her and always wanted to honor her with marriage; when I was about to reach that, you and Hamid and Hanan robbed me of my only chance of happiness."

Kamal..." she tried to speak but, he interrupted.

"Before you say anything, let me tell you of what's to come. I will never tell Sheikh Jawad that you have assisted in dishonoring him, so he does not kill you. But from this day forward you will mean nothing to me other than the Gypsy whore that you are, and you will never know when I will be here to empty my pistol into your sinful body. When I find Hanan and Hamid, and I will find them even if takes my all my lifetime, I will kill both of them, and I will rip Hanan's heart from her chest, and then I will come back for you, so don't say a word if you want to live past this morning."

At that he walked out.

The Gypsy woman was speechless when she heard what Kamal said. She kept her silence and realized how angry Kamal was; moreover, she was saddened by how brokenhearted he was.

Ahmed had not had been home on a leave since the war stopped on the eastern front. He was tired and dirty as he received the news of his sister committing the ultimate mistake a female could make here. He smoked a cigarette and went to ask his captain if he could go on a short leave. The captain asked for the reason to leave and Ahmed said calmly that his sister was dead.

The captain issued him a ten-day leave, gave his condolences, and asked him if he needed money for transportation. He declined the offer of money and went back to his bunker where he gathered all of his belonging in a small bag and walked toward where the two men his father had sent were waiting for him to take him to Balluria.

Sheikh Jawad appeared as though he had aged fifty years in a matter of days; his face wrinkled with despair and weakness. His frightening appearance turned softer and less threatening to the people around him as he sat in his spot wearing the kuffya with no iqal. His face lit up when he saw his son, Ahmed, exiting the car that stopped in front of the guesthouse. Ahmed had traveled with his father's two trusted men all night from the eastern front.

During the six-hour drive, Ahmed had many thoughts as the car passed the deserted highway between the death fronts of the east and passed by the all the towns of eternal solitude and boredom and the stretch of villages sleeping on the shores of the marshes. He thought of Adnan, who had left life and Balluria with a glorious celebration of the fisherman's boats that he freed. He thought of his sister and her lover Hamid as they were fearfully running from the wrath that his father and Kamal were about to unleash on them. He thought of Barrya and the possibility of her knowing all the secrets of the town as she always seemed to. She must know something about his sister and her lover; she must know what the two lovers had contemplated. He thought about himself and the upcoming duty he was about to carry out in order to preserve the family's honor.

"What honor?" he asked himself. "What family?"

His mother had died from loneliness and boredom, or so he had been led to believe. His father was unable to love and unable to feel pain. Kamal, who had almost become his new brother-in-law, was a hate-consumed beast who had been wounded. Kamal's wound would fester and increase his hate toward everything and everybody. Kamal would be like a wounded wolf, the most dangerous of all wolves. They had been told when they were young in the warm winter nights in his father's guesthouse never to trust or go anywhere near a wounded wolf. Kamal was now a wounded wolf.

What family and what honor? Why him? Why did he have to preserve that honor?

In the process of preserving that questionable entity, he must kill two of the most beautiful people in the world: his sister, the most beautiful girl he ever saw, and his friend Hamid, the most decent and honorable man he had ever known. Ahmed wished that he had been dead long before that day. He wished that he had joined Adnan in his final journey to the gates of heaven in the marshes. In the year and a half he had spent on the fronts he awaited death to come to him with a fifty-pound artillery round that would wipe him off the face of the earth, but it never did. He saw many of his soldiers and other officers die from a single piece of shrapnel, but none came to him. He thought of the task that awaited him and did not truly believe that he would be forced to do it regardless of whether he wanted to or not. Many times he wanted to tell the driver of the car to stop and let him out so he would never have to return to Balluria. He wanted to tell the two men who escorted him that they could tell his father that he was too weak to kill his sister and her lover. He wanted to tell the two men that he did not care if the townspeople said he was the most cowardly and the most dishonored man in these parts. He had already seen too much death on the war fronts, and he was not willing to see the deaths of the people he loved the most, but as always, Ahmed was not able to stand up for his beliefs, so he kept silent until the car reached the outskirts of Balluria. It was then that he became what he was before: submissive and tormented. His heart pinched him with pain as he saw his father more broken and defeated than he had never seen him before. His thoughts did not stop as he leaned and kissed his father's hand and said, "Father, the person who makes you take your iqal down has not been born yet and will never live."

Shouts rang from the several men who sat in the guesthouse.

"Well said... well said. You are your father's son!" At that exact moment, Kamal entered the guesthouse with his sudden overbearing presence. All the men felt it. It seemed as though he had inherited Sheikh Jawad's fearsomeness.

The two young men flanked the disgraced Sheikh, and Kamal was the first to address the crowd.

"Let it be known that those who dishonor the sheikh will be dead. Their blood will be shed."

Shouts again rang out.

"You are saying the truth!"

"Your tongue is righteous."

Later that day Sheikh Jawad asked his trusted confidant and mentor Irar to walk with the two young men and teach them how to wash the shame and restore the honor of the family. Irar, who had killed many people, was very generous with advice and instructions, and in the end he told them, "After you kill her, you must cut off her hand, her right hand, from the wrist and bring her palm so you can nail it to the front of the guesthouse and people will see that you washed the shame and restored you honor."

Ahmed was shocked to hear that and wanted to run away. He wanted to be as far as he could from that world of hatred and violence, but it was too late because Sheikh Jawad, despite his crippling despair, was able to put together the last death posse he would ever dispatch. He instructed one of his trusted men to prepare a car, fill it with gasoline, and pull a stack of two thousand dinars, dark clothes, and the black dagger. The same black dagger Sheikh Jawad and Irar used to kill Shershab the shepherd and many others. The sheikh did not speak a word to the two young men as they saluted him on their way to restore his honor and theirs. No one in the guesthouse saw that Sheikh Jawad was crying silently because no one, even the sheikh's son, Ahmed, knew that his father, the man who made his bones with blood and the tears of the others, the man who walked out of the river one cold night and became the master of the land—knew that he did not want to kill Hanan. She was his first child, the love of his life, the only human who was able to touch his rock-hard heart. He wanted her back next to him so he could smell her baby-like body. He wanted to sniff the unquestionable love he extracted from her breath when she was an infant. He wanted her to teach him how to read and write as she tried diligently. He wanted to hear her sweet voice. Sheikh Jawad cried because for the first time in his life he felt the coldness of being lonely and old. He cried because he was afraid for the first time in his life, because he knew that he would never see his daughter alive again.

5

For twenty-eight days Ahmed and Kamal did not speak about Hanan and Hamid and to each other as they searched the capital city of the province and the big city south of Balluira and all the cities between the Gulf and the capital, and as they asked people if they ever saw two people running with fear. They asked if anyone had seen the most beautiful girl with a man who looked like a wolf and had the energy and the smell of an Arabian horse. Kamal, who had friends in the big city's intelligence office, requested a favor from one of his officer's friends by submitting the names of Hanan and Hamid and their description to the all the military and secret police check points between the Gulf and the capital. The officer assured him that sooner or later they would find the runaway lovers, and when the officers asked who the girl was, Kamal asked them if her identity really mattered. It was a matter of honor, and her brother needed to kill her.

Kamal and Ahmed tracked the two lovers for almost a month. Many times Ahmed asked if they could go back to Balluria and stop the pursuit because they might never find the two lovers, and in all of the times that he said that Kamal assured him coldly, "I'd rather kill you and continue looking for them by myself than to go back to the town and face your father and the looks in people's eyes."

Ahmed had hoped that they would never find the two lovers, and every morning he tried to wake up later than usual and take a longer time eating his breakfast hoping that if, God forbid, Hanan and Hamid were hiding in the same town they would have enough time to escape. Ahmed had hoped that Kamal would tire of searching and give up, but he was wrong.

One night Ahmed told Kamal, "I have to go back to my unit. I am considered a deserter now, and I may be executed if I am caught."

That was enough to scare Kamal. He knew that he would lose his party rank if he was caught aiding a deserter and that none of his friends would be able to save his life or his career if he was found guilty by the revolutionary court so, he told Ahmed that they would go back soon to fix that problem with his unit, arrange for a long leave, and continue the search.

Ahmed agreed to the arrangement, hoping that more time would help Hanan and Hamid find a hiding place that no one could find them in, and as for him, he would leave Balluria and never return. He would go to the capital and live there, and never again would he set a foot in Balluria. He would spend his nights in the many bars and teahouses of the capital and forget about Balluria. He was relieved to finally realize that he would not have to kill Hamid or Hanan, and for the first time he slept peacefully, as he felt the heaviness of the rock of tradition lifted off his chest, and the burden of honor was no longer his to claim.

The next morning, as Ahmed slept in the dodgy hotel room they rented, Kamal woke up early and walked to the teahouse near the hotel. He sat there and ordered a glass of tea mixed with yogurt, as Barrya had always served him, when he overheard two men talking. He listened closely to the two men who appeared to be out-of-towners. One of the men, who looked and sounded like he had tuberculosis, coughed violently and said to his much younger-looking mate, "They must be from the south. But God bless, I have never seen such a beautiful woman in my life."

Kamal's heart almost stopped as he felt with his sharp senses of the wolf he was that the two men must be talking about Hanan.

"Does the man have a scar on his forehead?" he asked the two men, who were stunned by that inappropriate intrusion and disrespectful comment.

"Pardon, and who are you?" the young man asked.

"My name is Comrade Kamal. I am with the secret political police, and we are looking for the two people you have just described. They are wanted by the secret political police, and it's your duty to let me know where they are, or else I will inform the security office that you are aiding the enemy of the president and the country,"

Kamal said with an authoritative voice, knowing that he could say that to men who get easily scared by the hearing the name of the secret political police

The two men mumbled their words and tried to avoid giving an outright answer.

"Does the man who is with the beautiful woman have a scar on his forehead?" Kamal asked again.

The young man looked to his older partner then back to Kamal, "Yes, he does."

"Is he tall and dark skinned?"

"Yes he is," the frightened young man answered.

"Can you describe the woman?" Kamal asked, with a deepening voice and commanding gesture.

"She is very beautiful," the young man said with complete submission to Kamal's presence.

"Where are they right now?" Kamal asked, as he felt a strange weakness, the same weakness he felt when Hamid struck him the day he went to drown the kittens.

"They rented a small mud hut in our village a week ago."

"I will ask you to tell me where your village is and where that mud hut is, because soon the secret police personnel will be here so you can escort them to the mud hut."

The young man started to swallow hard to create saliva in his dry mouth. "Sir, we have nothing to do with it. We did not even know that they were wanted."

Kamal used the full extent of his authority and said, "Just describe to me where the mud hut is, and I will let you go."

The young man started to tell Kamal how to find the mud hut. At the same time Hamid woke up. He kissed Hanan as she lay next to him, and he walked outside looking for any suspicious signs as he had for the past month while he and Hanan moved from town to town and from village to village.

Finally they decided that they would stop running and settle in this village that resembled a young Balluria. The village sat approximately five kilometers from the small town, and the Euphrates ran close to it.

When Hanan asked how they would live, Hamid answered, "The Euphrates is near. I will fish and can find many things floating in the Euphrates. Soon I will find a boat floating in the Euphrates," he concluded with a smile.

"What If they find us here?" she asked with a worried look in her eyes.

Hamid paused and said after a while, "Then someone will die, but it will not be me or you, Hanan. I promise you."

The two lovers slept on the roof of the mud hut the first night as they feared someone, perhaps Kamal or Ahmed, or one of Sheikh Jawad's many trusted men would enter their hut and butcher them. Hanan held her husband, Hamid, all night and said, "If I will die, I want to die like this, holding you."

Hamid smiled and said, "You will not die, Hanan. You will not die."

The two lovers loved the wheat field that surrounded the mud hut. The field looked like an endless sea of gold as it danced in waves to the gentle rhythm of the wind of the Euphrates valley. Hamid told Hanan that he would work day and night and catch many fish, and he would save enough money to buy a small piece of land close to the river. They would raise a family, and he would secretly send a message back to Balluria to bring his sister, Amel, and his mother and Barrya to live with them. That was the same night Kamal told Ahmed that they would go back to Balluria in the morning.

Hamid walked outside and felt the May breeze gently touching his face and drawing shapes of unknown abstracts on the endless, golden wheat fields. As he stood looking at the bending wheat, he thought of his sister and how much she would love this place. A flock of doves flew suddenly from the field as he turned back to the inside the mud hut and went to wake up Hanan and ask her to make breakfast and some tea. He noticed the car that was parked on the main road to the town approximately five hundred meters from his mud hut. He looked and saw that it was not one of Sheikh Jawad's. He knew that Kamal drove a Volkswagen Passat and that the sheikh had three cars. Two of them were Toyota sedans, and other was a pickup truck, but he had never seen that light green Mitsubishi Gallant. He figured it was for one of villagers who must be a highly decorated soldier. In those days, many soldiers with lifetime injuries from the war fronts had received a Mitsubishi Gallant as an award for valor from the divine leader. Hamid walked inside and saw that Hanan was already awake that and she had started preparing breakfast and tea.

He smiled at her and said, "Sabah Al-Kahir... good morning."

She smiled back at him, and before she answered, her face turned to terror as she could see the outside the mud hut. Hamid did not understand the look on her face as she pointed to someone behind him. Hamid turned around to see what she was looking at and saw Kamal running toward the hut with the black dagger in his hand and Ahmed running after him with a pistol.

An hour before that, Kamal had rushed to the small hotel room that he and Ahmed had rented for one night and shook Ahmed out of bed, shouting, "Wake up! Wake up!"

"What is the matter?"

"I found them!" Kamal said with strange energy that seemed beastly.

"Found who?" Ahmed asked, still not completely awake.

"Get dressed and come with me," Kamal ordered Ahmed, who slowly understood the importance of Kamal's claim and could not find the energy or the courage to defend the previous night's arrangement he had struck with Kamal. The two men hastily drove the metallic green Mitsubishi Gallant that Sheikh Jawad had provided to where the young man in the teahouse had told Kamal about. On their way, Ahmed tried to talk Kamal out of what he feared.

"Kamal, maybe the two men who told you were mistaken," Ahmed protested, hoping for a last chance to save his sister and her lover from imminent death and to save his own soul from the burden of their blood, but Kamal did not let him. Kamal surrounded Ahmed's soul with the unlimited anger and hatred he had harbored for the past month.

"Stop your rubbish, and when we see them you will kill Hamid. You understand me? Take my pistol, and let me have the dagger."

Ahmed was numb. He was not ready for the blood festival that was about to take place in the glorious wheat field, and he did not know why suddenly he missed Adnan. When the two men reached the mud hut, Ahmed could see his sister inside, and he saw her as she disappeared in its dark recesses. He could see Hamid running inside too, and suddenly he saw his sister exiting the mud hut from the back and running in the open wheat field.

Kamal suddenly screamed, "Kill that son of a whore!" as he chased Hanan with his dagger in his hand.

Hamid exited the mud hut and looked at Ahmed, who stood there with Kamal's pistol in his hand. Hamid did not stop and chased after Kamal, trying to catch up to him before he could hurt Hanan.

Hamid screamed, "Hanan... Hanan!" Suddenly a shot rang out. Hamid fell to the ground. He felt a sting of fire in his right leg. As he tried to stand up, his leg went numb. He crawled on the grassy ground painting the golden wheat plants with the bright red color of his oozing blood and still screaming, "Hanan... Hanan!"

Ahmed walked toward him, shaking and crying, pointing his pistol at Hamid's back as he crawled helplessly to reach Hanan.

Hamid fell prostrate and looked at Ahmed, pleading for Ahmed to do what he wanted to do.

"Ahmed... save Hanan... Ahmed, please go save Hanan from Kamal."

Ahmed could not say a word as he choked on his tears. Hamid's voice started to fade as he bled in the wheat field.

Kamal heard the first shot as he was losing his breath chasing Hanan in the wheat field. Many flocks of doves that nested and laid their eggs in the bottoms of the wheat plants fled, terrified by the shots and screams and the cries of Hamid as he tried to save Hanan. The flocks of doves flew away from the nests and the immaculate and peaceful wavy golden wheat plants as they heard the screams and painful shouting of the four humans in their festive and bloody demonstration of love and honor. Hanan left her black abbya cover as she tried to flee and followed her tracks as she spoiled the impeccable lining of the wheat field. Kamal saw her running no more than ten meters ahead of him and could not help noticing how beautiful she looked in that light blue dress in the middle of the golden oceans of the wheat field. He struck her on her head with the bottom of his dagger. Hanan fell to the ground. He leaned down over her as she crawled, trying to escape the hands of fate that were written with the blood of all virgins who dared to dream in these heartless lands. Kamal grabbed her by her beautiful, long black hair, the same hair that he saw her washing in the dark bathroom when he first viewed her naked. He grabbed her by hair and turned her around to see her face. She closed her eyes and seemed serene as he stabbed her in her chest. His tears fell on her face. She called out with a very weak voice, "Hamid... Hamid."

Kamal stabbed her in her chest again. She cried out gently.

"Akhhhhhh... Hamid, come to me. Hamid, he is killing me," Hanan said with every blow that Kamal landed on her soft body.

Kamal stabbed her twenty times as he ranted between his tears, "This is for breaking my heart. And this is for leaving me. This is for your son of a whore lover. Here is for dishonoring me."

Never once with a single one of his thrusts of the dagger did Kamal say, "And here is for dishonoring your father."

He seemed to have forgotten about Sheikh Jawad

The doves flew away and did not return. Hamid lay there in a pool of blood. As his voice quieted down, Kamal had heard the second of four shots from the pistol while he was delivering the painful death from the old, rusted, black dagger to Hanan's body.

Hanan lay in the middle of a perfect circle of wheat in her light blue dress, drenched with red blood. Her beautiful face was covered with blood as she gasped for air through a mouth filled with bloody bubbles. Kamal sat next to Hanan's body as she lay dying, and he wept. He watched her dying and heard the third and the fourth shots that Ahmed fired at that moment. Kamal did not care to see Ahmed killing Hamid. He wanted to be alone with the body of the woman he had loved for as long as he could remember, but he realized that soon the people of the nearby village would come looking for the source of the pistols shots. After gathering himself, he grabbed Hanan's lifeless right arm and severed the hand at the wrist with the fearsome bloody, black dagger.

Ahmed came looking for him and saw him drenched with Hanan's blood. When he saw his sister's body lying motionless and painted with red and maroon spots, Ahmed broke down and kneeled next to her and cried out, "Oh, Hanan. Oh, Hanan, look at you... oh, Hanan. Oh, my sister!"

Kamal stood up and ordered Ahmed, "Yeallah! We have to leave now!"

Ahmed looked at him and cried, "You son of a dog. Look what you did to my sister."

"We have to leave now, Ahmed, before the villagers come, and God knows how they will see this." Kamal's voice had a nervous edge as he looked around to see if any of the villagers were coming toward them.

"I am not leaving my sister here... I want to take her home." Ahmed cried like a child.

"She is dead, and I have her right hand. Let's go."

"I am not leaving my sister here," Ahmed said in the same tone as he leaned on his sister's body and caressed her hair. "Oh, Hanan, forgive me."

Kamal was out of patience. He gave Ahmed a vicious look and shouted, "All right, you are a child, a weak little boy who cries like a woman. Grab her arms and help me carry her to the car."

After carrying Hanan's body slowly toward the car, they loaded it in the trunk and threw a blanket over it. Kamal threw Hanan's right palm in the trunk, and the two drove off.

On their way to Balluria, the two men stopped by a deserted bank of the Euphrates so Kamal could wash the blood from his face and hands and change into different clothes, but he did not clean the black dagger. Then he drove back to Balluria in complete silence for hours. Ahmed leaned his head on the window and looked to outside. They reached the outskirts of Balluria and saw the shimmering lights of the house. Kamal finally broke the silence.

"Did you kill Hamid?"

Ahmed did not answer.

"Did you hear me? I have asked you if you killed Hamid."

"Yes," Ahmed said without looking at Kamal.

"Did you kill him? Is he dead?" Kamal insisted.

"Yes," Ahmed answered with a sad and beaten voice.

"I heard four shots. That should have killed the son of a whore!" Kamal said with sadistic pleasure.

The car stopped in front of the guesthouse that looked devoid of life. Khanger hobbled inside and called to Sheikh Jawad, who walked outside using a cane. He looked like he had aged ten years. Sheikh Jawad looked at his son. The two men looked at each other, devoid of emotions, as they had just lost the only string of humanity that tied a father and son together.

"Where is she?"

Kamal answered, "She is in the trunk."

"Is she dead?"

"Yes. I killed her myself. Do you want to see her?" Kamal answered as he walked to the back of the car and opened the trunk, looking for approval from the old man.

"No." Sheikh Jawad fought back his tears and said to his son, "Ahmed, take your sister and bury her..." Sheikh Jawad looked at the corpse of his beloved daughter, which was covered with a dirty blanket and bloodstains.

"I have severed her right palm, so we can nail it on the guesthouse entrance, and now the people will know that we have cleansed our honor," Kamal said with enthusiasm, as he searched for the blessing and approval of the sheikh.

The sheikh looked at him with glowing, red eyes filled with tears and anger. Kamal knew that look. It was the look that had scared him most of his life. Kamal stopped talking as the sheikh turned his face to Ahmed.

"Ahmed, take your sister and bury her."

Then the sheikh, who looked and moved like a beaten old man, walked inside the guesthouse wiping his tears with his kuffia head cover as he put his iqal on his head after having not worn it since the night Hanan escaped.

"Where should we bury her? We cannot take her to the holy city," Kamal said, as he felt that he was about to bury his last chance of happiness in life without remorse.

Ahmed was not able to feel the heated looks of Kamal; he was completely numb, but he had a moment of perfect clarity in the otherwise absolute fog of despair when he looked toward the wilderness, where Barrya's mud hut with its weakened dimmed light glowed vividly. Ahmed looked farther down where Balluria ends and the desert starts and spoke between his silent tears and without looking at Kamal: "I know the only appropriate place where we can bury my sister."

The Book of the Gypsy Witches

The Gates of Heaven in the Marshes

1

The old woman sat and smoked almost half of her cigarette at once; she did not say a word for a while. Salam sat in the doorway, looking at her; he felt that he had reopened many wounds that she was trying to heal, by blocking them from her memory. But he needed to hear the stories because they were his wounds and memories, too. By cultivating the mere opportunity for her to tell these stories, he was hoping to redeem both of them. As they sat alone in the mud hut, secluded from the effects of their entirely different worlds, he allowed himself to be selfish and needy, because he knew her abilities and willingness to use them and use them some more. He had never shed a sorrowful tear in his life, but she did not stop crying. His biggest fear was that she would be able to make him cry for the others, for their pain, and their memories.

When he received the news about his father's death, he cried briefly and then went on living, and when his mother died, he did the same thing. His need to cry was one he never fulfilled or avoided fulfilling, in fear of entering unknown frontiers of emotions that he was not used to. Whenever his wife cried, he negotiated his clemency of being coldhearted with lies, compromises, and promises that he never intended to keep. Not once did he truly provide warmth for the tears of others. He always asked himself the logic of tears being warm, "Why weren't they cold?" At least to ease the pain of the crying person, tears should be cold, he told himself.

He wondered if the Gypsy woman's tears were cold, because he remembered Kamal saying, "Gypsies are cold-blooded, like desert lizards. That's why Gypsies had no honor and felt no shame for going around dancing and offering their bodies to everyone."

"They can't be," he said to himself as he saw that the Gypsy woman's tanned face turned red from the tears. She stopped crying for a moment, and he thought it would be the right time to ask her about one more person, one more friend of his that would add to the many wounds that she had.

So, he bluntly asked, "Do you remember Ahmed, the son of Sheikh Jawad?"

"How could I forget Ahmed?" she replied, and she started crying again.

The man waited until she dried her tears with her black scarf and then he asked,

"Can you tell me what happened to Ahmed?"

"Oh, my heart, my poor boy, no one knew what Ahmed was," she said.

"What do you mean?" the man asked.

317

"His father, the sheikh, never loved Ahmed like he should have. He wanted a son who was mean and tough like him, a son that would kill others. But Ahmed was gentle and kind and was not born to be the sheikh's son. As much as Ahmed tried to please his father, he could not, because he inherited his mother's, Sabrya's, weak body and tortured soul. And for that, his father despised him, gave all of his love to Hanan, and devoted all of his attention to his distant nephew Kamal, who had no problem with killing others."

The Gypsy woman lit up another cigarette, and she said, "Fate has a strange way of putting people in the wrong place. They think that fate has done them wrong, but it's the way things must be, and Ahmed's fate was to be the way it was."

The man did not understand what she meant, but he continued listening to what she was saying.

"Once, I heard the sheikh tell Ahmed that he wished his mother had died before she gave birth to him, because he was an embarrassment. All of his hatred was directed toward Ahmed, because he did not want to learn how to shoot a rifle, because he was scared of the loud sound," the Gypsy woman said. "The sheikh did not want Ahmed for a son, and I know that Ahmed did not want the sheikh for a father either. If he could have, he would have chosen to be born to some other father, in another place, or he would have chosen not to have been born at all."

Salam remembered Ahmed as being as gentle as she was saying. He was gentle to the point that he was called "half of a man" many times by his cousin Kamal. He was thin and fragile. He was not a good soccer player, but he tried to compete with Kamal to win the approval of his father. Salam remembered that Ahmed knew that Hamid and Hanan had exchanged love letters, and he knew that other students knew about it. Other boys or men in these parts would have confronted Hamid and initiated a fight or even stabbed him, but Ahmed did not care. On the contrary, Ahmed told his sister, Hanan, to be careful and discreet, so their father would not know about her and Hamid. Even Kamal was furious with Ahmed and tried to push him to tell his father about Hanan and Hamid, but Ahmed said, "They're only rumors; people can say whatever they want. I know how decent my sister is, and I know that Hamid is also decent."

And that's when Kamal called Ahmed "half of a man." Although it did not make Ahmed angry, he looked at Kamal and said, "You are a hateful person. Why don't you confront Hamid?" That was enough to stop Kamal, who never feared anyone except Hamid.

The man remembered that in the three years he spent in school in Balluria, Ahmed was like a shadow of a human. He was never angry or upset, but he was sad all the time, as he lived in a house that was empty of love, love that he dearly needed.

"There were only two times that Ahmed came to my house alone," the Gypsy woman said. "The first time was when his father, the sheikh, had slapped him in front of a gathering of many sheikhs who were at the guesthouse, because he mistakenly poured the coffee for one of the sheikhs with his left hand and not the right."

"And why was that a reason?" the man asked.

"Oh, my son, you don't serve coffee to a sheikh with your left hand. It's an insult." The man remembered his father telling him something about that, about how sheikhs in these parts were very keen on the coffee-pouring protocols; he did not pay much attention to it, though, because he always considered it traditional rubbish.

"Ahmed came here and sat where you are sitting now. He cried for many hours and told me that he hated his father, Kamal, and Balluria, and then he asked me if I knew his mother. Ahmed asked me about his mother, how she looked, how she smelled, and if she held him when he was a baby. He asked me if I remembered the color of her eyes—what the scent of her hair was."

"Do you remember Ahmed's mother?" the man asked.

"My son, I am the Gypsy who prepares all of the women in these parts for their wedding night. I remember everything about her. I remember the color of her eyes, the smell of her hair, and the way she looked on her wedding night. I even danced that evening," the Gypsy woman said and smiled with pride. "I was the best dancer these parts have ever known."

"Did you tell Ahmed about his mother?" the man asked.

"No, my son, I did not; I wanted him to forget about her, because she was gone. I wanted him to think that I was the only mother he had. I wanted him to be my son, just as I wanted his sister, Hanan, to be my daughter," the Gypsy woman said, and added with sincere despair, "What a foolish woman I was."

Salam almost smiled because of that logical comment, but he did not want to allow his smile to appear shyly on his face, fearing that he might hurt the Gypsy woman's feelings. He was more interested in the story than in the sudden self-realization of the Gypsy woman.

"When was the second time? I mean when Ahmed came to your house?" the man asked, as he felt restless and impatient.

"It was about ten years after the first time, when all my children had grown and left the town. Many of them had gotten married, and Ahmed had gone to the war front. It was about one month after Hanan and Hamid escaped town, one week before the wedding."

"What wedding?"

"The wedding that never happened and wasn't meant to be; the wedding of Kamal and Hanan, but she and Hamid escaped Balluria with their love one week before she was to wed Kamal. He and Ahmed were sent to search for them, to kill them, to cleanse the honor of Sheikh Jawad," the Gypsy woman said, with clear sarcasm when she mumbled the word honor. She paused for a moment and continued, "Ahmed came here to my house, two weeks after he and Kamal had returned with Hanan's lifeless body and her severed right hand."

319

Shades of sadness and painful memories had crept on the tanned terrain of her face. "He sat right where you are sitting now. He was never the same after the night that he and Kamal returned with the dead body of his sister, Hanan. People said they saw him sitting by the river all day, and I would see him walking to the seven palm trees each night. Many people said that he had gone mad. Ahmed did not go back to the war front and did not stay at his father's house; he barely ate, and he slept at the mosque, where Sayed Habeeb, the clergyman, had sheltered him and tried to rid him of the evil spirits that haunted him."

"Was he crazy? I mean, did he go crazy?" the man asked.

"No, my son. He was broken. His spirit was broken forever, and one night he just left."

"What happened then?"

"That night Ahmed came here asking me if I would get him some areq. He said that he wanted to drink until he felt no pain. He said that he had not slept for two weeks and that he saw Hanan's face everywhere. He said he missed her and that he wished that he were dead, so that he could be with her in the afterlife, in a world where there was no pain, no Kamal, and no Sheikh Jawad. My poor boy, I have never seen a sadder man. He was not able to cry, because he had expended all of his tears." The Gypsy woman started sobbing again and continued.

"But I knew that even with my Gypsy methods of healing pain, it was too late for Ahmed to be healed; he was broken beyond the ability of any Gypsy witches to heal his heart." The Gypsy woman dried her tears with her black scarf and continued, "So, I wanted to give him what he never had before; I wanted to give him a moment of a mother's love. I took him by his hands and let him lay his head on my lap; I caressed his hair and sang the Gypsy lullabies to him."

The man sat silently and listened as the woman started singing the Gypsy lullaby:

Dilelooool,
My baby,
Dilelooool,
Your enemy is farway and you are safe,
Sleep, my little baby, sleep,
And in the morning you will find your princess,
Dilelooool.

"I touched his face and wiped his tears, but I saw that he was not one with this earth. He was tormented by other powers, ones that Gypsy medicine cannot cure, powers that belonged to the other side, not the side of the living."

"What do you mean?" the man asked.

"He was slowly dying inside. Some people are not meant to be in the time or place they are in. Gentle and kind, they have missed their train. They are of another life and from another world, lost spirits that have found a place to exist while waiting for their ride to the place in which they really belong." The Gypsy woman paused, and then continued, "Just like his sister, Hanan, and Adnan, they were all spirits not meant to be here in Balluria. They weren't meant to be the children of Sheikh Jawad, and they were not meant to be living at the same time as Kamal and the divine leader and all of his wars. They had been traveling for a long time, and this was just one stop on their journey," the Gypsy woman said with a clear voice and doubtless conviction.

Salam looked at her and remembered his Jewish friend and his theory about traveling souls and reincarnation. He wanted to say something about his own beliefs about the theory of traveling souls, but it seemed pointless at that moment, and he wanted to listen to the old woman's stories. "Tell me more, please."

The Gypsy woman looked at him with her big black eyes as if she could see him clearly and said, "While he was sleeping on my lap, Ahmed asked me if I knew where Hamid was."

"But I thought that he killed Hamid in the wheat field with Hanan," the man said.

"That's what everyone in the town believed; it's even what Kamal and Sheikh Jawad believed, but I did not think he was dead."

"Why didn't you believe this?" the man asked.

"I did not believe that Ahmed could kill, and I did not believe that Hamid would die so easily," The Gypsy woman said.

"But, how did you know that?" the man asked again.

"Because I was there when Ahmad and Kamal returned with Hanan's dead body, and I looked in Ahmed's eyes and saw that he was not a killer. His eyes were not like his father's. They still had the human water in them that night. Unlike his father's eyes, I looked in Sheikh Jawad's eyes when he killed men and spent the night in my bed, his eyes lost the water of life and turned stale."

The man remembered Sheikh Jawad's eyes, and he understood what the Gypsy woman was saying. He remembered when he was twelve and Sheikh Jawad had come to visit his father, the mayor of Balluria, that the sheikh's eyes were red and full of anger, restlessness, and grudges. The eyes were fearsome, threatening, and unsettling. His eyes were just like what the Gypsy woman had said, without human water. Salam wanted to tell the old woman that he understood what she was saying about Sheikh Jawad's eyes, but she interrupted him with her voice, which sounded more serene and sad. She swept the raggedy carpet underneath her with her hand and collected the small particles of dried grass and said, "When the people of Balluria started talking about how Kamal and Ahmed had killed Hamid and Hanan, I knew in my heart and I saw in my visions that the wolf was still howling. I knew that Hamid was alive, because I did not feel the coldness in my heart. I knew that he was not dead and the only other person was Ahmed, because he did not kill Hamid in the wheat field."

"How do you know that?" the man asked.

"Ahmed told me that Kamal said he had to kill Hanan, because he was her fiancé, so Kamal chased Hanan in the wheat field, and he told Ahmed to kill Hamid with his pistol. But Ahmed could not do it; he could not kill his friend."

"Why not?"

Although the Gypsy woman was blind, she looked at him like she could see him and said, "Ahmed told me that he shot Hamid once in his leg." The Gypsy started to cry again and continued, "But, he said when he heard his sister Hanan crying and begging, he was ready to forgive her and Hamid, and he was ready to leave Kamal and run away with Hamid and Hanan. Ahmed told me that at that moment, when he saw Hamid lying in the wheat field bleeding and when he heard his sister's screams, he wanted to leave that field and never return to his father and Balluria."

"Why didn't he do it?"

The Gypsy woman did not hear him. She was still sweeping the carpet with her hand and said, "He told me that he wanted to run away with Hamid and Hanan somewhere far away in order to never have to face the choice of killing his only sister, because she wanted to be with the one she loved. He said he was ready to be called a coward, dishonorable, and half of a man."

"So, why didn't he do that, then?" the man asked again.

"Because, as he lay in my lap crying, he said he was weak and scared and that he let that beast, Kamal, butcher Hanan and that her voice would never leave him."

The woman stopped talking and the man looked toward the space in front of the mud hut; the haze of the soft rain made Balluria look like a mystical town. He waited for her to continue. She lit another cigarette and asked, "Would you like more tea, my son?"

"No thank you, ma'am." He could not wait any longer; it seemed she had no sense of the time, so he asked quietly, "What did you tell Ahmed about Hamid?"

"I did not tell him anything. Ahmed knew that Hamid was alive."

"How did he know?"

"Ahmed told me that he did not kill Hamid in the wheat field that day. He said he could not kill anyone, that he shot the three bullets in the air." The Gypsy woman poured tea from the pot that was mysteriously always full.

Salam felt the heaviness in the memories of his friends, as their spirits had never left the Gypsy woman's mud hut. He wished that he could leave, but the voice of the Gypsy woman tied him down again when she said, "Ahmed told me that when he heard Hanan begging Kamal not to kill her, he wanted to cover his ears. He wanted to go back and kill Kamal, but it was too late. He said that her voice and the cries of pain had diminished when he found Hamid lying on the ground screaming Hanan's name."

The woman's eyes were filled with tears as she continued, "Ahmed said that Hamid asked him. 'Where is Hanan?' He told him she was dead and Hamid said, 'Then you can kill me too, Ahmed.'"

"But, he did not kill him?" the man asked.

"Ahmed told me that he pointed his pistol at Hamid and cried... he did not want to kill him... he shot three rounds in the air and went back to where Kamal had vented his hatred into Hanan's body with his dagger. He watched Kamal as he severed Hanan's right hand, so they could nail it on the front door of her father's guesthouse."

"Why?" the man asked.

"So they could show the people of town that they had washed the shame that she brought upon the family. The shame that Hanan brought upon the family, ha, what shame? Hanan was the only one who really lived in that family; the rest of them were dead. They were dead before they were even born."

"What happened to Ahmed?" the man asked.

He deserted the army and did not go back to the front. The people in the party headquarters knew about him, but left him alone, because Kamal asked them to. Ahmed was not seen for a month. He only came here at night to ask me for areq, so he could get drunk to forget his pain. Then he would go to the mosque to sleep, and he spent much of his time in the orchard by the river. Ahmed asked me about Adnan, and that's when I knew he was thinking of leaving."

"He asked about Adnan?" the man asked.

"Yes, I knew why. I just could not believe it."

"Believe what?"

"Ahmed wanted to follow Adnan."

"He wanted to follow Adnan where?"

"He wanted to follow him to the gates of Heaven in the marshes."

Oh, my God, not that story, the man thought to himself. He wondered why everyone in these parts believed that myth. He remembered Hamid telling him that the gates of Heaven were in the marshes of the south. But it was just a myth, and he wanted to declare his beliefs, but he was too afraid to discredit the woman's emotions, as they seemed so true, so he listened.

"When gentle souls finally see what this world can do, they start searching for other souls and the path to go to where there is no pain," the Gypsy woman said with the voice of a Greek philosopher.

"Ahmed told me, as he lay in my lap, that soon he will go somewhere. To a place where there is no Kamal, a place where his father will not feel ashamed of him, a place where people like Hanan and Adnan can live in peace. He told me that Hamid was alive and that he would be coming here, to this mud hut. He sat there and looked at me and said, 'When Hamid comes here, he will be looking for Hanan's grave. Tell him that I buried her by the seven palm trees, where we saw the wolves dreaming.'

Salam's heart jumped with feelings of familiarity when he heard the name of the place. The woman cried while she poured tea for the two of them and looked at him and said, "He also wanted me to tell Hamid one more thing."

"What was it? What did he tell you?"

"He said when you see him, tell him that I will always be his friend and give him this," the Gypsy woman said. "Ahmed pulled out a dagger, and he gave me the long black dagger that looked so familiar. I had seen that dagger many times before; I knew that dagger with its chipped blade and the bloodstains. He gave me that black dagger and told me, 'Give the dagger to Hamid and tell him that Kamal used this dagger to kill Hanan. Tell him that he sliced Hanan's throat, drove it into her heart, and cut off her palm with it. Just tell Hamid what I've told you, and he will know what to do with the dagger.'

"Ahmed choked on his tears, and then he said to me..." The Gypsy could not continue, as she choked on her tears while touching the dagger. After several minutes she continued, "I took the dagger and hid it until I saw Hamid."

"Did you give the dagger to Hamid?"

"Yes, my son. I gave the dagger to Hamid."

"What did Ahmed do after that? Where did he go?"

"He was ready to leave. His face was that of a tortured angel. His guilt had left him that night, and I think I saw him smiling," she said as she wept. "He went to the river looking for Adnan."

"He went to the river?"

"Yes, after he gave me the dagger and told me where they buried Hanan, I held him in my arms and tried put him to sleep. Ahmed pushed my hands away gently and said to me, 'You have always been the only mother I've known. You have been a mother to me, to Hanan, and to all of us kids. Tonight I will leave, and I will never come back. Please don't cry for me, and don't try to stop me, because it's time for me to go to where Adnan and Hanan are.'"

"I knew that no matter what I would have done or said, Ahmed would not have changed his mind, so I let him go." She was crying again and said, "He kissed my hands and left. That night Ahmed went to the river and stood there for hours waiting for Adnan, and when Adnan did not arrive, Ahmed jumped into the river and never came back."

"He killed himself?" Salam asked.

"No, people like him don't kill themselves. They free their souls. He went to the place where Adnan and Hanan were. He went to where gentle souls like his should be, to the place where there is no pain."

"To the gates of Heaven in the marshes?" the man asked.

"Yes, my son, to the place where fearful people believe they can feel safe forever."

The woman stopped talking, and the man leaned forward and dropped his head deeper into his chest. He caressed his hair, trying to find the logic in the story she just told him about his friends. He did not want to hear her voice anymore; he wanted her to keep silent for a moment or two, so that he could recover his heart, and that's when she said with a soft voice full of sadness and complete submission to her beliefs, "I've lived through many painful deaths; my life started with pain, and it will end with pain. I was never sad, because I knew the pain would go away, and it was better to smile, laugh, drink, and dance. But do you know what makes me sad in Balluria?"

"What?" Salam asked.

"That none of my children had the option to choose their path."

"Why not?" he asked.

He did not lift his head, but her voice entered his ears and his senses when she said, "I saw that none of my boys and girls chose their path in life; it was imposed on them, forced on them; all the pain was forced on them."

How true, the man thought to himself as he recalled his own journey in life.

"My children were beautiful of heart; they were too gentle and kind to deal with the pain that others had imposed upon them. Others, who never loved my boys and girls, others who would not leave my children alone; and when they could no longer bear the pain, they went to the river that has flowed since the beginning of time. They went to the river, where they thought the gates of heaven were; where they thought there would be no more pain. But I don't know if they found the gates of heaven in the marshes." The Gypsy woman paused, and then she concluded, "I am so afraid that they only found the gates of death."

ARMAND NASSERY

The Book of the Man

Sweaty Hearts

1

I remember the time when I knew I was not in love; or the time, at least, that I knew I was not in love with Adawya, the younger of the Hillaly girls. Haleem and I would wait around for the Hillaly girls to appear in their windows. I would look for Adawya's shadow to pass behind the burgundy curtain, and Haleem would look for Bushra, the older of the two sisters. We would pass their home several times and had to do the same thing over and over: go past the market, pretending that we were going to the river or to Abdullah's house. Then we would turn back and pass by the unfinished concrete skeleton of the six shops that Ashraf's father had built, before he ran out of funds, after his bulldozer had broken down. He called it the "jinx of envy" that he felt the other contractors put on him from the day he bought that bulldozer. Haleem and I would walk past the Hillaly girls' house, which stood in the middle of the block between two unfinished homes, and then we would turn around at the corner of the street and walk back along the same route we came down several times, hoping that Bushra or her sister Adawya would open the burgundy curtains and see us. I always thought that I was in love with Adawya. She was prettier than her older sister. Actually, she was prettier than most of the girls in the school, even prettier than Hanan, the daughter of Sheikh Jawad, whom everyone thought the most beautiful girl in or near Balluria. To me, Adawya was prettier, because in a way she looked like Anouk Aimee, the French actress that I had been in love with since I was ten years old. Adawya was white-skinned and had very deep, sleepy black eyes and long hair just as her sister Bushra had.

When everyone on our soccer team claimed a girl in school as the object of their affection, I was asked who I loved, and my answer was that of a young boy eager to repel the depressing stings of being the only one without a girl. Even Adnan had a girl; he called her his queen of Greek mythology. We never knew who she was, and he never told anyone her name. He said that she was beautiful and that she wrote him love letters all the time, but we never saw any of the letters that he claimed to receive from his queen of Greek mythology. However, with my status as the son of the mayor and with the common chatter that Adawya was in love with me, I had a strange realization that I only pretended to be in love with Adawya. I did not think it was real love; I did not feel anything in my stomach whenever I saw Adawya. In fact, every time she passed by me and gave me that look of interest, I was overwhelmed with the feeling that I missed sitting in the dark shadows of Hamid's house listening to Amel reading her poetry. But for some reason, I was invaded by the overwhelming feeling of being left out on a blossomy and strangely exciting world whenever I heard

326

Haleem talking about the Hillaly girls, especially the older one, Bushra, whom he was interested in. When he spoke about their hair, how long, black and silky it was, how white their faces were and how wide and dark their eyes were, I felt that it was the right time for me to start loving someone, as all of my friends did.

All the boys in my group had girlfriends, or they thought they did. Abdullah for sure loved Basima, and she loved him. We knew this because he told Hamid, the whole soccer team, and me about it. The entire school knew that Basima and Abdullah had loved each other since they had been in elementary school. In fact, their own families had blessed and accepted that love. Even the teachers in our school treated them as if they were already married. Abdullah also told me that he was going to marry Basima as soon as he graduated from the teachers' institute. He wanted to be a teacher in the elementary school in Balluria, and he was thinking of attending the teachers' training institute in the province's capital, so he that could stay close to Basima. She had no plan to attend college, and they had no intentions of leaving Balluria. He showed me the love letters that he and Basima had exchanged. The messenger between the two lovers, Amel, would deliver the love letters from Basima to me, and I would give them to Abdullah, who sat next to me in the classroom. This process was not necessary, because Basima could give the letters to Abdullah anytime she wanted. However, they felt it was more romantic for the love letters to go through the chain of hands. It made it more exciting, especially for Amel who seemed to enjoy being the love messenger. The strange thing was that Amel delivered the love letters for almost all the young lovers in the school, even though she never received or wrote any letters herself.

All the boys in school had their eyes on Hanan. Everyone tried to impress her by walking past her classroom and acting funny or cool. Hanan seemed distant from everything; she was distant from the school. She was distant from the boys' many attempts to impress her, especially Kamal, who would drop to the ground and do thirty pushups in front of her. She was distant from the little world of young lovers that blossomed during that beautiful spring of 1984. She was so distant that she was lost in her own world. She never talked to anyone about it, not even to her closest friends Basima and Amel. To me, Hanan was estranged and weird. She would walk away without even looking at us when Haleem and I approached the Hillaly girls standing in the schoolyard talking to Amel and Basima during recess.

Hanan would come to our house accompanied by one or two women who wore black robes and lived in the sheikh's house. She came over several times, talked to my sister, although my sister Yusra was one class behind us, and did her homework with her. My sister was known as the smartest girl in the school. Hanan would also visit the Hillaly girls' house and Basima's house. Hardly talked to any of us boys in school, she would walk with Amel, in the school courtyard, holding hands with her. And from what I heard, she liked going to Barrya's house all the time. She risked severe punishment from her father and maybe a possible snitching by her brother, Ahmed, who never really told on her, or by Kamal, who was like a cousin to her and mentioned many times that he might marry Hanan. None of us really paid much attention to Kamal's comments, because we all knew that Hanan was in love with someone. We just did not know who.

At that time, Kamal seemed more interested in the government and its activities than in love, more interested in the activities than in even the soccer team or school. He spent many school days hanging up banners and posters of the divine leader on the school walls and on the light green, metal fence of the public garden. Kamal started wearing the dark green uniform every Thursday and was one of the three students who shot three rounds at the flag-raising ceremony every week. He was also the first to grow a dark thin-lined moustache. Although he was still one of us, he rarely talked about love and when he did, he did not discuss any of the girls in school. He would always stare at Hanan during the five-minute recess as we stood in a group talking about soccer and the European Cup or how a popular Egyptian television soap opera series was going to end.

On the other hand, Haleem was completely in love with Bushra, the older of the Hillaly girls. He announced this fact to me, Hamid, Abdullah, and basically everyone in the school. If he had had his way, he would have announced it to the entire town and to the world. Bushra knew that Haleem had announced his intentions toward her, but for some reason that no one understood, she never responded with a clear message of acceptance or rejection. She never looked at Haleem with the same love that he had, which was basically a long stare and wink with the left eye. She never smiled at him when she passed us, flanked by her sister, Adawya, and Amel, Basima, and Hanan. She would not even look at him when we waited after school by the public garden for her. We would wait there for her every day until the last student had left the school.

Instead, Bushra would send Haleem signs, looks, and sometimes, verbal messages that were so confusing and incomprehensible. They were messages with a special meaning, as Haleem put it; meaningful looks that Haleem struggled to understand and to explain. Haleem asked all of us about the looks that Bushra gave him and the verbal messages that Amel delivered to him during recess. He would come to us and say, "What does it mean when a girl looks at you and then she looks at the ground and then looks at you again?"

"That means that she dropped a quarter of a dinar and is looking for it," Adnan would answer jokingly, only confusing Haleem more.

"No, seriously, does that mean she is mad at me, or she is in love with me, or what?" Or he would ask Abdullah or me, "What does it mean when a girl says that lovebirds don't fly alone?"

"It means they don't fly alone," Abdullah would say, and then he asked Haleem,

"Who said that?"

"Amel told me that Bushra said to give me that message."

"She is just messing with your head," Abdullah said.

We did not know what Bushra's real intentions were with Haleem, and I did not think Haleem or Bushra really knew either. To me, it was just two young hearts playing love games with each other.

2

Three months before the end of the school year, Hamid was expelled for his tardiness and unexplainable absences. I was asked by the principal to deliver the message myself to him and to collect his textbooks. I found him by the river, naked from the waist up, as he painted a fresh coat of tar on the boat that he said he found floating in the river. He did not even react to the news of his expulsion from school. He asked me one question: "Did you see Hanan today?"

"Yes," I said, wondering in my mind why he asked about Hanan.

"Did she look happy or sad?" he asked again.

"I saw her talking to Bushra and your sister, Amel. I think she looked happy, because she was laughing," I said.

Hamid smiled and said with strange enthusiasm, "When I am done fixing this boat, we will give it a good name, and you, Adnan, and I will go all the way to the marshes, and we will sleep there for nights. I heard that there is an enormous snake. They call it affa, and they say it can eat a full-grown man in one bite. We should go catch it."

"All right," I replied.

After that, Hamid never returned to school, but he and I and sometimes Adnan kept our afternoon ritual of swimming and fishing with the new boat and a net that Hamid also found floating in the river. Possessing all the fishing equipment and gear, we had the chance to throw nets and fishhooks like fishermen do. Hamid even brought a long, thick stick, so that he could beat the enormous snake on its head when we caught it, but we never went to the marshes.

That spring the flowers blossomed before their time and so did my love, or what I thought was my love, for Adawya. Haleem kept telling me that he knew about Adawya's interest in me, because someone told him that she liked me, and she wanted to send me a love letter. Not objecting, I did not Ask Haleem who told him. I was anxious to receive a love letter since it was my time to find a girl and to love; but the awaited love letter never arrived. I waited and waited for the letter and would give Adawya the look of love, which I myself did not know how to give or what it meant, but Haleem told me that the look of love was very important in order for a girl to know that a boy was interested in her.

"But, I thought you said that she was the one who was in love with me?" I protested.

"That's what I was told," Haleem said.

"Who told you?" I asked.

"Someone who was told by another person; it doesn't matter. Just give her the look of love, and she will send you the letter," Haleem said.

I waited three weeks for my love letter, and Haleem waited for a letter from Bushra; just one line or one word that said she loved him. He had sent many looks of love and love letters to her with Amel, but there was no hope. After we reached the point of desperation, Haleem and I decided to take the initiative, and we discussed what it would take to make the Hillaly girls send us the love letters that we had been waiting. So, we came up with a plan. We figured that the reason the Hillaly girls were shy was because we were in the school among many other students and that maybe that made it difficult and inappropriate for the two of them to express their love and interest to us. Everyone knew how conservative and protective old man Hillaly was and how mean and ruthless their older brothers, who were both in the Special Forces fighting on the eastern front, were. So it was too hard for the Hillaly girls to act on their feelings toward us. We thought that if we were to see them or meet them outside the school they might be willing and courageous enough to exchange looks or words of love and that they might give us love letters. Haleem and I decided that after school we would walk by the Hillaly girls' house, and specifically, below the second floor window of the house where Bushra and Adawya's room was. So we pretended that we were walking toward Abdullah's house, which was two houses behind the Hillaly girls' house, and just before we reached Abdullah's we would turn around and go back again and again and again. I remember walking back and forth six or seven times in the hellish afternoon heat of the south that would make a full-grown donkey beg for shade and water. But the power of love and the possibility of a love letter from the Hillaly girls made it all worthwhile. Haleem and I contemplated our alibi, just in case we were confronted by the Hillaly boys or old man Hillaly. If we were caught and asked why we were walking by their house, we agreed that our answer would be, "We are going to Abdullah's house to do our homework together."

"Besides, your father is the mayor. Old man Hillaly and the Hillaly boys will not dare to confront us," Haleem said, assuring me. Our exhausting walks turned fruitless and proved pointless when we saw the curtains open, and both of the Hillaly girls looked at us, and then Bushra slowly shut the window and the curtains. After a week of scorching afternoon walks, I gave up the effort despite Haleem's repeated attempts to convince me otherwise. I was afraid of getting sunstroke, and I was afraid that one day old man Hillaly or the boys would discover the real purpose of our afternoon walks. Moreover, I did not want to continue the pursuit of love and the love letters, because I felt that my feelings toward Adawya were not those of true love.

Six weeks before school ended, the principal told me that he would allow Hamid to return if he were willing to do so. Hamid decided not to return to school, and I had to tell him that he would need to return his textbooks.

"Amel will return them. I curse the school and their books," he said as he tried to untangle yet another fish net he found floating in the river.

School was ending. Only six weeks left until the summer holiday. We were almost done with all the pretesting and were waiting for the test results that would show who would be exempt from taking the finals. Both my sister and my younger brother were among the students who were exempt from taking the final tests, because they both had perfect scores in the pretesting in all subjects. Adnan was exempt too. I was exempt from testing for literature, art, and history, but none of the other Wolves or any member of the group of girls was exempt, and they had to take all of the finals.

Nevertheless, that did not matter because all of us boys were busy with something else. We were all busy with love. Even Adnan had revealed the identity of his queen of Greek mythology. She did not look like a Greek goddess, nor did she look like a normal girl. She was a thin girl who looked like the female version of him, with thick glasses and a tiny physique. Her name Asmaa, and she was sending him love letters and her devotion even though they hardly spoke to each other. Salah and Ashraf had something to show too, love letters and dried flowers or a handkerchief. Even Kamal claimed that he got something from Hanan, but he would not show it to us. And Hisham, who was by far the ugliest member of our group, had claimed the heart of a girl who transferred to our school two months before the end of school. Except for me and Haleem, all of the wolves had love stories to talk about. Haleem had a better excuse than I had, because everyone knew, even the girls in the school, that he was spoken for by Bushra and that he and Bushra were bound to love each other in a secret, and very romantic, but strange way.

But I was feeling a little insecure, and during those days, I received love letters from a secret admirer. I just found the letters in my notebook, when I was not in the classroom, and the letters were signed with the letter L. Even Amel, who delivered all the love letters in the school, told me that she was not the one who put the letters in my notebook and that she did not know the identity of my secret admirer. Two years later, shortly before I left Balluria, I discovered my admirer's identity. A girl who never attended my school, she was the daughter of a vegetable vendor in the town's market. Her name was Lamia, and she looked as if she had not bathed in ages. I remember when walking home after school or when the Wolves and I would walk home, we would stop briefly in the town's market and pass by the shack where Lamia and her mother sold vegetables, and I always tried not to look at her.

That April was beautiful. The southern breeze filled the lungs with more than desert air; it filled our lungs with love. I noticed that Adawya was as frustrated as I was. She started to give me looks of love every day and went out of her way to stare longer than usual and longer than what common decency allowed a girl to look at a boy in these parts. That late spring was the spring of love. All the boys dressed better and acted softer than usual. Even Hisham, who was an extremely bad dresser and had no stylish clothes other than his usual track suit and soccer jerseys, managed to have a neat appearance started to comb his hair, and he wore cologne once in a while. I was always the neatest and the most well-dressed among the boys. Haleem was also a good dresser and kept a decent appearance. Though we were the two neatest boys, we still had no real results in the pursuit of love.

Abdullah, who was the only one who seemed to have the only true and mature relationship among all of us, approached me one day with something I was hearing for the first time. I remember that we were rehearsing the school play that I wrote for the celebration of the birthday of the divine president, which was mandatory to celebrate, when Abdullah came to me and said, "I have a message for you from Basima."

"Who?" I asked with a surprised look. I was expecting the message to be from Adawya, not from Basima, who everyone knew was Abdullah's perfect match.

But my imaginative suspicions withered when he added, "Basima told me that Adawya told her to tell you that you are a stuck-up and conceited person and she will never write you a love letter again."

"Why does she say that?" I asked innocently and wondered why Adawya told Basima instead of Amel, the trusted love messenger, to relay such a message.

"I don't know," Abdullah said.

"Maybe we need to ask Basima."

It was all a delusion of a fake warm feeling that I needed to have in order for me to feel loved. I was standing with Abdullah during recess when Basima came and stood next to us. She told me that Adawya had written me almost fifty love letters, that I did not get, and she bashfully said, "I was with Adawya, at her house, when she wrote all the letters."

I did not believe her, but I asked, "Why didn't she ever give me the letters?"

"She gave them to Amel, Hamid's sister, to give them to you. Adawya waited the entire school year to get a response from you, but you did not send her any."

I was speechless. After all the waiting and all the walks back and forth past her window, risking being caught by her father or brothers, that Haleem and I did, I discovered that the trusted messenger of love letters, Amel, kept all the letters that Adawya wrote me; she did not deliver any of them. She delivered love letters from all the girls to all the boys and from all the boys to all the girls, but she kept my long-awaited letters. I remember that I felt betrayed by Amel, but at the same time, I was sad to realize that I was not really in love with Adawya. I was so upset and so angry with that little tan-faced, wide-eyed, poetry-reading weirdo. I was furious with her, but I did not say or do anything, because she was Hamid's sister. With Haleem present, Abdullah, Basima, and I confronted Amel one week before school ended that year, but she would not reply. She waited until I was alone during the last recess period. She walked over to me and said that she forgot to deliver Adawya's love letters to me, and that she was afraid that Hamid would get angry with her if he knew that she delivered love letters from Adawya to me, because I was his friend. I knew that was a lie, and I knew that she kept the letters for some reason that I did not understand. She stood there with a look that could have meant many things; she looked as if she would do anything for me to forgive her. She looked like she never wanted to upset me, and she said she would give me the letters if I wanted them.

"Yes, I would like them," I said with clear frustration in my voice.

She looked at me with angry eyes, as if she did not expect me to want and ask for the letters. "I will bring them tomorrow."

At that moment, the bell rang, and everyone ran to the class. But Amel stood there staring at me. I stared back at her and did not understand her look. It was one of those meaningful looks that Haleem was talking about, but I was not sure what it was.

"Are you sure you want Adawya's letters? They have no poetry in them," Amel asked me with what looked like a little tear in her eyes.

"Yes, I am sure," I said as I walked to the classroom, leaving her in the little storm of dust that swirled in the school courtyard.

Reading the letters of love and devotion from Adawya did not give me the feeling I long awaited, the breathless gasp, the curling toes, the feeling of what Abdullah described as pure and consistent joy. In fact, I was upset that she did not write any poetry, nor did she write anything romantic. She wrote short paragraphs in which she described how she felt toward me, the way she felt when I looked at her, what the girls were saying about me, how stuck-up I was—what they call in these parts a dry-nosed person who looks down at others—how she liked my hair long, that I should not cut it, and her plans for us to get married and have three kids and move out of Balluria. She wrote that her sister, Bushra, thought that Haleem was immature, but she still liked him. I did not like that, especially knowing how my friend Haleem was tormented by her sister. The next day, after I read all the letters, I hoped that I would not run into Adawya in the school yard. I was hoping that she would not come to school. To me, she seemed boring and ordinary. Even with her crazy black hair that, when she let it down, almost reached the lower end of her back, I was more upset with Amel because she hid the letters from me, but I could not say anything to her, because I felt obligated to protect her from any more hardship and sadness.

Since Hamid had left school and was busy with his new boat and his plans to catch the biggest snake in the world, I felt responsible for Amel, as Hamid was when he was still in school. Moreover, I felt that she and I were bound by our secretive afternoons of poetry readings. In fact, I felt that she did well by keeping the love letters from me. I wasted a lot of time chasing the mirage of love, and I blamed Haleem for the exhausting walks in the heat of Balluria's ungodly afternoons.

The next day, in school, I saw Abdullah, and he told me that Basima told him that Adawya and Amel had stopped talking to each other, because Adawya accused Amel of not being a true friend, and I asked, "Why does she think that?"

"Because Adawya thinks Amel hid the letters from you, because someone else likes you. And Basima told me that she heard Amel telling Adawya that she would never understand you, because she did not like poetry and you do."

Not really catching much of what he said, I just focused on the part about someone else liking me. All I wanted to know was if there was someone else who liked me, because that would give me a last chance for love before the school year was over.

"Who does? Who likes me?" I asked.

"Basima said it's a girl that I knew very well, but she did not tell me her name," Abdullah said.

I did not reply, and we did not talk about the subject again, since we got extremely busy with our final exams.

Although I was supposed to reply to Adawya, I felt that doing so was a waste of time, and I could not bring myself to write anything not truly felt. I knew that I would see Adawya in school next year, and maybe by that time I would know my true feelings toward her. I did not see Adawya during the last week of school, but I saw Amel many times; she still had the same sad look in her eyes. I had the feeling that she was the one who liked me, the one whose name Abdullah would not tell me. It was not important to me. School was almost over, and it was just about time for another three months of adventures with Hamid and Adnan and many soccer games with the Wolves. But it was still a sad feeling knowing that I was not in love and a sad feeling knowing that I was not loved. I was sad, because for the first time I felt that maybe I did not know how to love or maybe I was unable to love. I felt as though I was prevented from love, despite the many beautiful eyes that surrounded me and the long black clips of teenage girls' hair that longed for a touch. I felt like I was sailing alone in my own ocean of imagination, trying to reach the shores of my senses and the sweaty hearts that carried the eagerness of the Gypsy dancers. It scared me to feel that I was in a protective shell, a haze of misconception of being better than others, better than being capable of being loved. I think that was why I was eternally sad.

The Book of the Gypsy Witches

The Many Journeys of the Weak Angel:

The First Journey

1

"What about Adnan?" Salam asked as he pulled his hair back and looked at the blind Gypsy woman. Adnan was the second of two friends that he remembered the most. The first one was Hamid. He remembered that the three of them had spent much time by the river, and they had rebuilt a boat and named it the *Titanic*. "What happened to him?" he asked again. "He was my friend."

The Gypsy woman looked at him through her glassy, smoke-filled eyes. She paused a moment and then started telling him about his unfortunate childhood friend.

"Oh, my poor son. Among all of you, Adnan was the only one who chose his own death. He was the only one who found the secret gate of Heaven in the marshes; he went there alone. One bright, glorious morning, Adnan freed all the boats and left."

Salam looked at her, searching for the meaning of her words, and as much as the words "boats" and "gate of heaven" sounded familiar, they did not make sense to him. He asked again, "What happened to Adnan?"

"Do you remember Adnan?" the Gypsy woman asked.

He was caught off guard. He was afraid that the Gypsy woman would reach inside him and find the emptiness of a soul without memories, a soul without a past. He looked at her as he searched the dusty corners of his memory for the thin face of his friend and said, "Yes, I remember Adnan. He was always with us, I mean with Hamid and me. We went fishing and swimming together many times. Adnan always used to lie on the front of the boat. He would put his hands in the cold river water and say that he could feel the spirits of all of those who drowned in the Euphrates. I remember he was the smartest of all of us in school; he was very good at mathematics," the man replied.

The Gypsy woman smiled when she heard what the man said about Adnan. She realized that he was hiding behind a compassionate voice and a familiar politeness. He seemed to remember the one person they had a mutual knowledge of. She felt she could tell him the story of the "thin, weak angel." So she told him.

"It was long ago, but I still remember the day when Adnan and his family came to Balluria, when the invisible thieves of the southern marshes stole all the kerosene lamps and Balluria fell into seven days of darkness."

"A thief stole all the kerosene lamps?" Salam asked.

"Yes, my son. And on the seventh night, I saw an emaciated horse pulling a carriage. It was stopped by the old mud hut once belonging to Sheikh Badr Al-Gathban; the hut has since been abandoned. It was when Kamal and his mother came to live with Sheikh Jawad. I was at the sheikh's house, and I heard that Kamal's father was killed in the mountains fighting Barzany and the Kurds. When I was on my way home from Sheikh Jawad's house, I noticed the poor family who had just moved to Balluria: Adnan's. I saw them taking their belongings, which did not amount to much, into the mud hut. I stopped to help the poor family."

Suddenly, the Gypsy woman frowned as she remembered the grim realities of that night. "Adnan's father was coughing, and he could barely walk, so I helped them. Adnan's mother was a thin, sweet woman who never spoke. I thought she was mute, but later I learned that she was mourning the death of her younger brother, Sabah, who never returned from the fighting in the mountains of the north."

The woman took a drag on her cigarette and let out many rings of gray smoke and continued. "Adnan's sister, Fatima, was like her mother. She was quiet and well mannered. Adnan's older brother, Qahtan, was a delight; tall and dark, he looked like Hamid. He was full of wild energy, and he carried all of the family's belongings to the mud hut by himself. He smiled all the time. He either had Gypsy blood or the spirit of a wolf in him. Adnan was little, thin, and scared."

The Gypsy woman continued, "When I first saw Adnan, he was a scared little boy holding onto his mother's abaya as she tried to prepare their first dinner in their new mud hut. I saw the little boy, and I felt his fears. I knew then that he needed me, he needed my warmth and love."

The man looked at the blind woman and asked, "How did you know?"

"It's a Gypsy mother's instinct; we sense the need of love in people," the Gypsy woman replied. "Just as I knew that you would never be a good son and just as I knew that Kamal would be an ungrateful and mean son, I knew that Adnan needed my love, so I gave it to him. I gave him all of my love." She made her comments with a firm yet soft voice. "Do you remember the afternoon when you and the boys had a fight with the soccer team from the neighboring town?" the Gypsy woman asked.

"Yes, I never forgot that," the man replied.

He remembered that it was the same afternoon that Hisham thought it would be a great idea to take a photograph of the soccer team, the day they played against the Wild Lions. It was the game of all games. Hisham prepared himself and the team for three weeks. The man remembered that Hisham brought a rusty trophy and on it was written "The middle school cross country championship" But Hisham and Haleem made a label with a piece of paper and covered the rusty trophy with "Champions of soccer."

"It will put our team in the pages of history," Salam remembered Hisham saying. He also remembered that for days Hisham begged Fathil the Liar, who owned the only camera in Balluria and who claimed that it was given to him as gift from the Yugoslavian dictator Joseph Bruz Tito, to show up for the long-awaited match against the Wild Lions. Hisham also begged Fathil the Liar to take just one photograph of the team with six of the boys standing up and six kneeling in the front row, with Adnan holding the ball. He wanted the picture to be like the ones of all the goalies in all the pictures they clipped from magazines and newspapers of teams in Europe like Liverpool, Byrne Munich, Juvantus, Barcelona and the ultimate American soccer team, Cosmos. It was that afternoon when the only existing photograph of the Wolves was taken by Fathil the Lair, who left the field before the soccer match ended. He left with the camera, and he did not witness the fight that broke out later that afternoon, nor did he tell anyone where he was going. He disappeared for two months, and as usual, he returned to Balluria claiming that he was on a secret mission for the president. But he kept his word and processed the film in a European country, or so he claimed, and two months from that afternoon Fathil the Lair gave the photo to Hisham. He showed it to all the team members and said, "See I told you. Now we need to send it to the newspaper."

Hisham framed the team photo with a plastic frame that he found in a garbage pile near the party headquarters building, which was being renovated on the occasion of the celebration of the divine leader's fiftieth birthday. He kept it in his home, hanging in his room until that fateful, gray morning when four of the Wolves were executed by a squad of soldiers and a group of party militiamen in the town's main square. Later the military commander ordered the bombing of all of the homes of those who participated in the rebellion. Hisham's house was destroyed by a stack of mortar shells that were tied together by a yellow wire that reduced the house to a pile of rubble. A group of hungry children and looters showed up to Balluria and ransacked the houses and looted everything, even the wood from the ceilings. It was the team's photograph that Barrya salvaged from Hisham's house after it was scorched and burned to the ground by the angered soldiers of the divine leader as retaliation for the rebellion of the marshland. It was the only item Barrya took from the rubble of Hisham's family home. His family had fled Balluria after the rebellion and never returned. Two years later, Barrya gave the photograph to Amel, Hamid's sister, who at the time lived and survived on poetry and the memories of all of those who had left Balluria. Amel kept the photograph in a cardboard box for two years, along with all of the love letters she wrote but never sent to Salam. She did, however, send the photograph to him. She sent him the photo along with a letter asking him for money, so she could help Basima, who at that time was stranded and alone in Jordan with a newborn baby girl, a sin that prevented her from coming back to Balluria.

He remembered that he did not open the letter, nor did he see the photograph of the Wolves. He did what he did with all the letters he received from the homeland; he stashed them in the red shoe box. At the time, he was always busy with his school and his life in the West. When he finally opened the letter, it was too late to salvage the remains of his conscience, so he resolved to travel across the world, to this mud hut, to listen to this blind Gypsy woman. It was the same photograph the man found when he and his wife, Emily, renovated his studio gallery in the cold city of the West, the same photograph that sent him on this journey searching for the long-lost warmth. "Of course I remember!" he said, defending his entitlement to this memory, the memory of his thin, weak friend, Adnan.

He remembered the afternoon when he and the Wolves, his old soccer team, played against the neighboring town's team. A team that had brand-new red jerseys and shoes; they called themselves the Wild Lions. He remembered that when they scored a goal they became truly wild and started attacking his teammates. He remembered that Adnan was attacked by two of the Wild Lions boys and remembered that he tried to save his weak friend. He also recalled how sad and angry the Gypsy woman was when she saw Adnan's face covered with blood. She dipped her dirty piece of cloth in a bucket of water and wiped Adnan's bloody face. He remembered the Gypsy women holding Adnan's face between her tattooed arms and her mystic cleavage was revealed as she sobbed.

"All of you were there, and you could not protect him. All of you were there, and you let those boys beat Adnan like that. Why is it always my weak angel? Why is it always the weakest Wolf?"

He remembered that the Gypsy woman screamed at Hamid, Kamal, and Hisham for letting the Wild Lions beat up Adnan.

He also remembered that that afternoon Hamid was very angry, and he stood by the door of the Gypsy woman's mud hut looking at the soccer field and mumbled, "I swear to Allah, I will beat every one of them. I will break their teeth and their backs and I will steal all of their families' boats."

He remembered that while the others were attending to their injuries, he was mesmerized by the tanned, majestic breasts of the Gypsy woman. He remembered thinking at that moment that maybe all the stories he had heard about the Gypsy woman's earlier days of wild nights with all the men in these parts might have been true. Since then he did not feel the motherhood in her; he felt that she was distant, and he felt that she was different than him. He felt that she was of a class that he and his father looked down upon. And he felt that way when she started calling him the son of the mayor, or the clean kid from capital city. The man escaped his inappropriate thoughts as he looked at the deteriorating being of the Gypsy woman.

He asked her, "Tell me more about Adnan. I mean tell me more about his family. I remember that he always talked about his brother Qahtan. Did you know Qahtan? What did Adnan say about Qahtan?"

The Gypsy woman replied, "Adnan always seemed sad when he talked about his brother. He always said that he missed him and that Qahtan was the smartest man in these parts."

"Adnan was telling the truth," the Gypsy woman said. "Qahtan was a joy; he always smiled and read books incessantly. He was my first wolf, long before you boys. He was handsome and fearless; all the girls in town loved him, and I knew this because they all confided this to me, and they all wanted me to give Qahtan their love letters and trinkets. But Qahtan did not care about women at that time. He cared more about books."

"Books? What books?" Salam asked.

"Books that he got from his friends in the big city, friends who told him that there is no God, no Allah, and he believed them," the Gypsy woman replied. "No one ever understood what Qahtan was talking about. It seemed as though he was speaking a different language. They called him a sheioey."

"You mean a shieuie, a communist?" the man asked.

"I don't remember exactly, but I do remember that he would meet with some men down by the river, and they would spend all night talking. He once met them at my house, and I heard them talking about the leader, about Allah, and about another person. I knew then that they were walking along the path of death."

"What do you mean?" the man asked.

"Oh, my dear son, I've lived a long life in these parts and have seen many good men die, and the two things that lead men to their deaths in these parts are women and when they start talking about the government. Whenever I saw or heard a man talk about the government, I knew that his life was coming to an end," the woman said as she lit another cigarette.

"What happened to Qahtan?" the man rephrased his question.

"I remember that night clearly. I was visiting Sabrya, Sheikh Jawad's wife, because she wanted me to see if her daughter, Hanan, had an evil spirit cast on her."

"Did she? I mean, did Hanan have evil spirit in her?" the man asked.

"No, my dear son. Hanan had the spirit of all the Gypsy dancers in her. I knew that she was bound for love. She was a sinner from the moment she was born, but I did not tell her mother that."

"Tell me about Qahtan," the man said.

"I was walking to my house. The moon was hidden behind black clouds, and the night smelled of death. I heard that many of the communists were killed in the big city, but I never thought that they would kill Qahtan. I saw them. I saw the men with their big bellies, thick moustaches, and red eyes. Their eyes flared with hatred and their breath smelled of areq," the Gypsy woman continued. Her voice became deeper with sadness. "I saw them walking toward the small, secluded house of the poor family. They were hiding their rifles

340

underneath their robes; I could see death walking with them. I followed them from a distance."

The Gypsy woman paused, and a sparkling tear washed her remarkably clear cheeks.

"Please continue," the man begged.

"They walked from the main road to the narrow road by the soccer field and surrounded the house. They did not knock on the door; they kicked it down and stormed inside the house. They dragged Qahtan by his hands and hair."

The Gypsy woman paused as she started sobbing.

The man paused, but waited with relentless curiosity for her to continue.

"I saw the seven men dragging Qahtan by his hair and hands, and when he resisted they shot him once and beat him with their rifle butts. He resisted and screamed while his mother and his brother Adnan watched without saying a word. They watched silently as the scary men dragged away the only hope in life that family had." She started crying again, but she continued talking between her tears. She kept reaching out with her hands as though she was reaching out to save Qahtan.

"I followed them for a distance; they dragged Qahtan to the town's main square and they shot him many times. I don't remember how many times but when they left, I walked to where Qahtan lay in a pool of blood. Oh, my dear son, they shot his beautiful face. Have you ever seen what a bullet can do to a beautiful face?" the old woman asked. The man had no answer, but she wasn't waiting for one. She asked, "Did you ever see that beautiful face being shattered with bullets? My dear son, Qahtan, was dead. The most beautiful man in these parts was lying in blood and mud."

For several minutes the Gypsy woman's face was clouded with an angry sadness, a look that the man had never seen before. He waited for her to regain her ability to tell the story, and then he remembered how he and all the other kids were mesmerized by the magic of her stories. Whenever she talked about the dead and the long-gone knights of the Arabian Sahara or the Gypsy dancers, he wondered if she really felt the pain that she seemed to express while talking.

He was surprised when she suddenly calmed and said with a clear voice, the same echoing voice that chased the shadows from the walls of the mud hut, "And they left a piece of cardboard with a message written on it on his body."

"What was written on the cardboard?' the man asked.

"At the time, I did not know what it said, because I could not read. Amel read it to me many years later. It was written: 'this will be the fate of all the communist traitors and all the agents of the foreign enemies.'"

"What did you do with the cardboard? Salam asked.

"I have it right here. I've kept it all these years."

And without warning or asking if he wanted to see the piece of cardboard, the Gypsy woman reached behind herself blindly, with strangely guided hands, and pulled it from an old box hidden under a sheet of cloth with unrecognizable shapes and designs on it. She pulled out a faded, dusty cardboard stained with darkened blood. The man looked at it, and a shiver ran through his spine.

"Did you show it to Adnan?" he asked.

"No, my son. You should know that my heart is too soft to do such a thing. The only person who has seen this was Amel, and now you."

"What happened after that?" he asked, trying not to look at the blood-stained cardboard.

"That night all of the people in Balluria and Tawsheeha stayed in their homes. The seven men with big bellies and thick moustaches walked through the streets and death walked beside them. Darkness covered the town, and Qahtan's body lay still in the street. I went to Adnan's house and stayed with the family. They cried silently in fear that the men would return. Adnan's mother stopped crying," the Gypsy woman said and inhaled what was left of her cigarette. "I knew that the only way she would be able to recover the body of her eldest son was to ask Sheikh Jawad to go with her and myself to the party headquarters to ask them if she could bury her son's corpse. Qahtan's poor father was unable to walk, and his poor mother was too frightened to ask the sheikh."

"So what happened after?" the man asked

"I went to the sheikh's house on behalf of the family, and I stood outside at the guesthouse door until I was acknowledged. Sheikh Jawad knew what I had come for, so he sent two of his men in his place. The two men carried the Qahtan's body to the poor family's house. There was no funeral and, therefore, no one knew where or when they buried Qahtan.

"But I knew," the Gypsy woman said.

"Knew what?" the man asked.

"I knew where Qahtan was buried, because I buried him myself."

"Where did they... you bury him?"

"I buried him where all of my children were buried. They would have buried him where the poor are buried, because they had no money to bury him in the holy city."

"Where did you bury him?" the man repeated.

"Qahtan's mother and I took his body and buried it in the only place I knew we could bury him."

"Where is that?" he asked again.

"By the seven palm trees," the Gypsy woman replied, and then lit another cigarette. She inhaled the unfiltered smoke deep in to her weak lungs.

The man looked outside and saw that it had started to rain again on the empty soccer field. He stared at the field, trying to reclaim what he thought was rightful entitlement to the memories of his weak and thin childhood friend, and the Gypsy woman poured two steamy cups of chai for the two of them.

The Book of Balluria

The Many Journeys of the Weak Angel:

The Second Journey

1

To Sayed Habeeb, talking to the young men about Allah was a risk that he was willing to take. He knew it was a risk, because he learned long ago not to trust others who were willing to talk about religion or politics. He knew for sure that he was healing his body and soul from the deeply embedded scars caused during days spent in secret police chambers. Instead of talking about politics, he wanted to plant the seed of belief in Allah and the practice of good Muslim values into the lives of the many lost souls in Balluria. He was especially interested in the group of young men willing to listen to his speeches. The older men in Balluria preferred the eternal guilty crying and purification rituals of chest beating, and tear shedding inflicted on themselves during certain times of the year in response to the stories of the tragedy of the prophet and his holy family. The elders did not want to listen to a true and intelligent discussion of the faith.

Sayed Habeeb struggled with his own identity and his mission as a clergyman. But as he grew older, he learned to accept this struggle along with many other events that he knew he could never change. However, for the group of teenagers soon to be young men, he wanted to try to save their souls. So he began by asking them if they wanted to learn more about the relationship between men and women according to Islam. The subject sparked the curiosity of the young men, and they began staying later in the mosque. Long after the teary-eyed elders left the mosque after listening to the overly-detailed battle of the grandson of the prophet, the young men gathered around the fire to keep the winter chill away. Sayed Habeeb was cuddled in his furry abaya robe. He talked about the ways a Muslim man should treat his wife, but he was very stingy with the precious details the young men were looking for. Most of the young men were disappointed as he steered away from the sexual aspects of the relationship between a man and a woman and focused more on human bonding and mutual respect they should have toward each other. He emphasized that the ultimate aim of a man's life was a unique relationship with God, because He is the only one we will have to answer to on judgment day. Although the teenagers were disappointed with the path of the discussion, they were still willing to stay and listen to the graceful clergyman speak.

He said, "When you have Allah in front of your eyes, the final destination of your life journey will never be misdirected. When you are looking at Allah, you are looking ahead to the end of your path, and Allah will look down at you and will help to carry you through the many hurdles of your life's journey."

To his surprise, as he seized on the level of interest in the group of the young teenagers, he noticed two extreme people among them that he had not expected. He noticed that Kamal was a careful and dedicated listener and that Adnan listened and responded with preemptive rejections and ready arguments.

Sayed Habeeb did not realize that Kamal was such an intense listener, because he was attending the meetings of the party and he was tasked with reporting everything that Sayed Habeeb said and did to them. But since Sayed Habeeb steered clear of politics and concentrated only on religion, the graceful clergyman was able to neutralize the reports Kamal was writing about him to his party superiors.

Sayed Habeeb would say things like, "Having a good relationship with Allah will make you a better man as well as a better citizen."

But Sayed Habeeb was more interested in knowing the state of ultimate dismissal he saw upon Adnan's face. He searched deep within the colors of the thin-faced boy's eyes as they sheltered his feelings behind old, thick, brown plastic framed glasses. Relentlessly Sayed Habeeb tried to insert the love of Allah into the young men's brains, and one night the clergyman said, "Allah is merciful. He sheds His mercy over the poor, because He loves them. He casts His mercy over the hungry, because He loves them. But they have to help themselves, because Allah will not change the fate of any people unless they change what's within them and become better people; for if they do, Allah will surely be there for them."

And suddenly a burst of outrage that none of the group of young men had ever heard before came from Adnan who shouted, "Who and what is Allah? And where was Allah when they dragged my brother and shot him in the street?"

Sayed Habeeb had heard the story of Qahtan before. He had heard it from Barrya, but he never thought that Adnan would bring the memory of his slain brother in the form of a question or in the context of questioning the wisdom of Allah and the divine will of the Almighty. Moreover, he was worried that Kamal was there listening to report to the party. The clergyman and the group of young men looked around searching for Kamal, the relentless snitch. Luckily, he was not there that evening as he was tasked the duty of guarding the party headquarters. Sayed Habeeb felt the pain in the young man's voice and knew it would be a heavy and difficult task to bring Adnan to Allah and put Allah back into the young man's heart and mind.

Sayed Habeeb heard from the other kids how Adnan was a math genius and how he defeated the mean math teacher, who always smelled of alcohol in school, and how some of the older kids from the secondary school in the big city had challenged the thin kid with the thick glasses to a math contest. He heard how Adnan solved the math problem after writing it out on a stretch of twenty-five meters in the dirt, using a tree branch, on the road between the main town square and the school. Sayed Habeeb had heard all of the stories about Adnan, and maybe that was the reason he felt it was his duty to Allah, to the religion, and to all of his former forbidden party comrades who died on the gallows, in the acid tanks, or in the torture dungeons of the divine leader. He felt it was his duty to save Adnan's soul and to convince him to study the teachings of the outspoken Ayatollahm who was executed by the divine leader not long before. But Sayed Habeeb wanted to be very careful with his words, because he knew that his old bones would not endure one night at the secret police chambers in the big city. So he always chose his words wisely and answered Adnan's questions with a soft voice while looking directly in his eyes. So he answered Adnan's outburst, "Allah was there watching," and concluded, "and He will always be there watching the suffering of the meek."

From that night on, Sayed Habeeb tried to talk to Adnan privately. He told Hisham, Haleem, and Ashraf whenever they showed up without Adnan, "Make sure to bring your friend Adnan next time." He asked Hamid to bring Adnan with him, alone, in the afternoons when no worshippers were around. But Hamid was busy most of the time with his boats, fishing, fish nets, and the many treasures he found floating in the river. After many relentless requests by the clergyman, Adnan started showing up when there were fewer worshippers around or when everyone in Balluria stayed at home during the lazy hours of afternoon.

At first Sayed Habeeb tried to understand why Adnan was angry with Allah.

"Because He is not fair, because neither our history nor the present makes sense, and I don't feel that the future looks very promising, either," Adnan said, "because there is no Allah."

"Do you say this because you know this or because you are angry that your brother was killed?" the clergyman asked.

Adnan was quick to reply, "I am saying this because all the scientific evidence suggests that there is no Allah and that religions are the people's opiate, just as Karl Marx said."

Sayed Habeeb realized that the anger behind the sparkling of the weak eyes, behind the thick plastic frames of the kid's glasses ran very deep. He also understood the anger and wanted to assure the kid that he was not to be blamed for the ignorant attack against names he learned thirty-five years ago, names that Adnan used to sound knowledgeable and informed.

"In my days, when I was your age, it was Fahd," the clergyman commented.

"Who?" Adnan asked.

"Comrade Fahd, the red banner, the leader of all of those who wanted to believe that the only way to bring freedom to this land was to lose their faith in Allah. Have you heard of Comrade Fahd?" the clergyman asked the boy.

"I did not hear about comrade Fahd, but I have read about him," Adnan answered.

"Where did you read about him?" Sayed Habeeb asked as his eyes widened.

"I found some books that my brother had buried before he was killed," Adnan answered.

"What types of books?" the clergyman asked with keen curiosity and undivided attention.

Adnan sensed the kindness of the clergy diminishing and his seriousness increasing. "There were hundreds of books—novels, history, books that talked about the validity and the existence of Allah and Islam, and books that stated otherwise," Adnan said with standoffish pride.

Sayed Habeeb thoughtfully grabbed his beard and groomed it gently with his hand. He realized that before embarking on the task of saving Adnan's soul, he needed first to spare his body and to save him from the possibility of torture in the chambers of the secret police. He looked at Adnan with piercing eyes and said in a very serious voice, leaving no room for him to doubt his seriousness, "Adnan, here is what you will do. You will tell me the titles of all of the books you found and you will hear two things: keep it, or burn it." Then the clergyman gave this explanation. "I tell you these two things, not because these books are telling you not to believe in Allah, but because if the party officials ever heard or knew that you possessed these books, you would bring more pain and grief to your poor mother and to your family. Do you understand me? And if you don't do as I say and burn the books that I tell you to burn, I will inform the party officials myself."

The clergyman realized that by threatening the thin kid, he was close to selling his own soul to the devil by affirming his will on the thin kid. But he knew there was no time to waste on empty discussions and that he must make Adnan realize the seriousness behind the gentle voice of his ultimatum. It worked, because after he paused for a moment, Adnan looked at Sayed Habeeb and started telling him the titles of all of the books. With a strange submission and the obedience of a good son, he stated the titles of the books and the clergyman replied.

"*Wuthering Heights*," Adnan said.

"Keep it," the clergyman replied.

"*The Old Man and the Sea*."

"Keep it."

"*The Collection of Short Poems of Garcia Lorca*."

"Keep it, and read that one more than once."

"*The Collection of Poems of Muthaffar Al-Nawab*."

"Burn it."

"*The Collection of Poems of Badr Shaker Al-Sayyab*."

"Oh, you must keep it. You must keep it and read it all the time."

"*The Communist Manifesto.*"

"Burn it, burn it tonight."

"*War and Peace.*"

"Keep it."

"*The Material Meaning of History.*"

"Burn it, burn it."

"*Our Economy.*"

The clergyman paused for a moment as he heard the title, it was written by the outspoken ayatollah, who was killed by the tyrant not long ago. Sayed Habeeb had read the book many times, and furthermore it was the book that landed the clergyman in the secret police cell for many long months.

"Did you read it?" the clergyman asked.

"Yes, many times," the thin kid replied.

"Did you read his other two books, *Our Philosophy* and *Our Society?*" the clergyman asked.

"Yes, the outspoken Ayatollah Muhammad Al-Sad..." Adnan started to answer.

"Shhhhhh! Don't say his name here. Saying his name will cost you dearly. Believe me, son," the clergyman frantically said, as he looked around making sure that no one was there listening. "If you have already read his books then burn them all now. Tonight you will take the books I have told you to burn to Barrya's house," the clergyman said. "Then burn them all and don't come back here until you have."

For the first time in a long while, Adnan felt that he had found something he lost a long time before, something he yearned for and searched for in all the people he knew, but never could find. He thought he found it in Hamid, when he had protected him from the mean bullies in school, but he was still looking for that feeling that left long ago, the feeling that he missed ever since his older and able brother was killed. It was the feeling of being a young boy who could make mistakes and bad choices and having someone around who could tell him and guide him about what was right and what wrong. He never saw the logic in asking for answers to the questions that he never understood. The simplest one of them all carried the risk of eternal damnation or the endurance of a lifetime of painful torture by the men at party headquarters. He was tired of having to search for the answers by himself.

Some of his questions were "Where is God?" "Who is God?" "And why is God?" The "Why is God" had tormented him the most because everything and everyone carried the liability "why?" God, the universe, life, religion, Balluria, the country, the war, the divine leader, the outside world, women, girls, boys, men, the school, mathematics, politics, the beginning, the end, and especially the pain, the pain, the pain. All of these things ran through his mind with a big and clear "why?" attached to them, and he was just too young and too tired to care anymore. Adnan did not have the answers, he never did. He only knew that the graceful clergyman was telling him what to burn and what to keep from his slain brother's treasure troth of books.

For the first time since he started questioning his existence and his surroundings, Adnan felt the burden of finding answers was being lifted from his shoulders and he was willing to let Sayed Habeeb lead the way to the new knowledge he was looking for. He wanted Sayed Habeeb to liberate his racing mind from the shackles and the constant struggle, by adding logic to the existence of all of his surroundings. Due to his mathematical knowledge, he was looking for the equation that would bring him to the correct results of the lives that thrust on him and his family. After witnessing his older brother being dragged by the seven men, who looked like the dark keepers of hell, he wanted to understand why; why was he was so thin and weak, why was his father unable to walk or talk? He wanted answers; he wanted to know how a family of four could live on the mere retirement pension that his father received, which Adnan's mother had to travel miles on foot to collect.

Adnan felt at peace that night as he followed the instructions of Sayed Habeeb. That night he quietly put all of the books that Sayed Habeeb told him to burn in a sack and took them to Barrya's house; he lit her fireplace with them.

He said to Barrya when she asked him what he was doing, "Sayed Habeeb told me to burn these books."

"Then you do what Sayed Habeeb told you to do," Barrya replied. She looked at his thin frame and said with a melancholy tone, "I wish there had been a man like Sayed Habeeb around to guide your brother, Qahtan, when he was reading these books."

The thin boy and the Gypsy woman watched the hypnotic flames as they consumed the historically misleading texts that made their way to the many troubled minds of unfortunate dreamers in these parts. The thin boy and the Gypsy woman cried silently as they watched the flames eating the pages of Qahtan's treasure trove.

Kamal was sent on his first military mission, with the party militia, to hunt for the many army deserters hiding in the marshes. Later that summer, Adnan spent many afternoons listening to Sayed Habeeb talk about the unbreakable bond between a Muslim man and Allah. Adnan was intrigued by the simple way the clergyman explained the remarkable love of Allah for humans and how a man would not be complete unless he had some sort of relationship with Allah.

"It does not matter what kind of relationship—love, hate, misunderstanding—but you must have and keep that relationship. You must talk to Allah and ask Him; you may question His ways, but never His existence, and most important you must believe that He loves you," the clergyman said. And time and time again he talked about that relationship and summed it all up in one word, "love." The clergyman would say, "Allah is love; the only thing you must learn from your relationship with Allah is how to love and how to find love in every situation you face in your life. When you feel the need to ask why, your answer should always be, because Allah loves mankind."

One day Adnan confessed to the clergyman that he began to feel the connection to the Almighty and he felt that he was getting closer to Allah more than ever before. The clergyman looked at him and said, "Do you remember the question that you asked that night?"

"What question?" Adnan replied.

"The one when you asked where was Allah when they dragged your brother through the street and killed him?"

"Yes," the thin boy replied.

"I can answer that now. Allah was there. Allah was in your mothers' eyes as they filled with tears for not being able to hold her eldest son one last time before the men killed him. Allah was in your father's heart, knowing that his first child was being murdered a few hundred meters away and he could not do anything about it. Allah was in the bullets of the seven evil men who shot your brother. Allah was there holding your hand as you watched your brother being dragged to his death. Allah now is walking with you and giving you the strength and ability to live through each day. Allah will be with you to help you to think and dream again," the clergyman commented.

"I have never thought of it this way," Adnan said with an apologetic tone.

"You should never ask where Allah is, when Allah is, or who Allah is; you should only ask why did this happen this way, because when you know why, then you will know the when, where, who, and the how," The clergyman said and added. "Everything happens for a reason and when you know the why, you will know the reason, which will clarify the who, the how, the where and the when."

Adnan felt defeated; his arrogant pride diminished as he looked at the graceful clergyman and then toward the ground behind the mosque. He and the clergyman rolled out the long carpet and dusted it off in preparation of the dusk prayers that would be held at the mosque.

"How can I find the answers to the why?" Adnan asked calmly.

"That's for you to decide. You must search during your lifetime to find the answers to the why," the clergyman replied, and then poured water onto his arms, performing the ablution ritual in preparation for his prayers.

2

Adnan had spent his last summer in Balluria preparing for his trip to the capital city to attend medical school. When Adnan boarded the train after summer ended there was no one at the station to bid him good-bye. Adnan barely had enough money for the train fare; he carried a small gray bag containing one pair of gray pants and a white shirt. He bought a dark blue jacket from the flea market in the capital city of the province to complete his college uniform. He was hoping that he would have enough money to buy a tie, but he was short on cash. He knew that he could not ask his father for the money for the tie, so he planned to find work in the capital city. Maybe he could find a job as a waiter in a restaurant, shining shoes or selling fried foods in one of the many public transportation hubs to afford the new tie.

He had scored a 96.2 on the general test in the province. This was the highest score in the region for secondary school and he was accepted into the medical school. The entire town of Balluria knew about the thin kid who wanted to become a doctor one day; some of townspeople were proud, and some were envious. Some did not know much about him, but they all knew that he was the son of the stricken poor family that lived in the mud hut on the outskirts of Balluria. Adnan was a wizard in math. Everyone knew that, but no one ever thought that he would become a doctor one day. When he attended the secondary school in the big city of the province, all of the other students came to him for help with math. Even students from the main secondary school came to him for help. When he was in the eleventh grade he was helping students in the twelfth grade with their math studies. No one in Balluria realized the exceptional abilities of the weak wolf who knew math so well, not even Hamid, who learned about the educational achievement of his thin friend from his sister, Amel.

Hamid shook Adnan's hand, congratulated him on his success, and said to him, "If you need money, I will find a boat floating on the river, and I will sell it to get you the money. And if anyone bothers you in the capital city, let me know and will come over there and beat them up, you've got my word."

Barrya was the proudest of them all. She spread candy that she bought from Abdullah's father's store around to the townspeople who looked at her with suspicious stares, not knowing why she was so happy for the success of the thin kid who was not even related. Some thought she was paid by Adnan's mother to do so, but it was all Barrya's doing. She knew that Adnan's mother had no money nor the heart or courage to spread the candy in the same streets that Adnan's older brother, Qahtan, was shot dead in and dragged through by the seven mean militiamen years before.

Hisham, who did not pass high school, was drafted into the army. He said to Adnan, "Congratulations, you will make us proud, and don't fail, because they will draft you into the army and you may not come back alive. I am sure that the medical school will have a very good soccer team."

Haleem, Ashraf, Salah, and Abdullah all graduated that same year. They had all scored much lower than Adnan, and they all attended colleges and institutes that led to less-promising futures, but it offered a legitimate excuse to keep them from being drafted into the army and being sent to the death machines on the eastern front.

Since Adnan had scored a 96.2 on his test, he was slated to go on a trip to meet the divine leader. This was the reward for all the students in the country who got high scores during their last year of secondary school. However, Adnan did not go on the trip, not because he had no money for the trip, but because he did not want to face the possibility of shaking the divine leader's hand, the same hand that may have signed the order to murder of his brother, and the same hand that pulled the trigger on the outspoken ayatollah. Instead Adnan spent that summer reading the books that Sayed Habeeb told him to read and burn. He hid the books near the river, in the same spot where he, Hamid, and Salam spent their middle school summers fishing, swimming, and sailing the raggedy boat they named the *Titanic*. That entire last summer that he spent in Balluria, Adnan would leave his house in the morning and spend the whole day by the river reading the three forbidden books of the outspoken Ayatollah.

Our Economy was a book that showed Adnan that there was a way between communism and capitalism. *Our Philosophy* explained that there is a life philosophy that does not require a lifetime of slavery to the state nor slavery to the exhausting pursuit of making a living. To Adnan, the book presented the case of Balluria itself.

To Adnan, Balluria was the society of nothingness with no logical direction. The society of lost souls, greed, blood and hunger, the society that had the heart to kill the grandson of the prophet and weep for him at the same time for centuries later. It was the society that crucified Christ and held the cross for blessings, the society that lived on the generosity of the two heavenly rivers, yet died of thirst in the hellish desert. The society that maintained its innocence while sliding on the all the blood of the poets and innocent sinners of history since the beginning of time; our society, with all of its unforgivable shames and dishonors, the society of historical mishaps and grotesque acclaims, the society of unplanned births of humans, rivers, orchards, deserts, tyrants, wars, towns, cities, and villages that lasted for centuries without a reason for their existence. Balluria, the society of ultimate deceptions. In his young and brilliant mind, Adnan thought it would be possible for him to correct all the wrongs of his surroundings. He would dream and plan to make a better tomorrow. He thought to make the water of the Euphrates clearer and bluer to increase its riches, so the poor fishermen would not starve during the harsh seasons. He dreamed that he could make the Euphrates reach the thirsty land behind the abandoned train station in order to grow flowers and vegetables, if only he could find a way to make the water of the Euphrates reach the dried roots of the eternal palm trees of the prairie and the Arabian Sahara to inject its blue life into them so that the faded color of the palm trees could be greener.

"There is a way to make the Euphrates more shiny and sparkling and the color of the seven palm trees more vivid," he said to himself. *I just have to believe in Allah*, he thought, willingly misleading himself and falling into the ultimate deception of the words of the book he was reading. He was mesmerized by the many reflections of tiny mirages that reflected from the shiny lights of the faded green leaves of the seven palm trees.

"I just have to find that remarkable bond with the almighty and when I go to the capital city, I will find others who dream and think like me," he said to himself as he lay on the grass near the spot where he, Hamid and Barrya prepared lunch and a farewell party for Salam, the mayor's son, who had left the town with his family years before. Adnan laid there calculating the enormous possibilities the capital city would offer—the many beautiful women, the possible adventures, people who could talk about the arts, paintings, poetry, and politics, away from the dust capital of the world, as he called Balluria. He felt Balluria should have been a town for the departed, not for the living.

Adnan waited by the river to see Hamid. No one knew when or where he might show as he loved sailing his boat on the Euphrates or riding his horse that he found lost in the prairie. Adnan was amazed at how much Hamid found floating in the river or lost in the prairie. He noticed that Hamid's boat was there, but Hamid was nowhere to be found. He waited for him Hamid his boat, the same boat that he, Hamid, and the mayor's son, Salam, thought would take them to the gates of heaven in the marshes, the same vessel that the three friends thought they could take to the Atlantic Ocean where they could sail to the Mississippi River to follow the same water path that Tom Sawyer and Huckleberry Finn sailed. Adnan lay in the front of the boat and put his hands in the water as he always did, feeling the cold wetness of the Euphrates as it ran an eternity to the marshes and then to the Gulf where endless seas and oceans collided and other worlds began.

3

One month later he was in the capital city, hoping to find a cheap meal that would stop the pangs of hunger in his weak body. He exited the train, in the main station built by the British decades before. Many travelers looked like they were resurrected from a long death as they walked toward the gates that led to the main public transportation garage. Adnan felt alone and scared as he remembered the last words of Sayed Habeeb, the clergyman, "The capital city can eat a human's soul."

He stayed in the train station for hours looking at the people coming and going he thought of boarding the train back to the province and then to Balluria. It was too much of everything for him. The buildings were bigger than he had ever seen, and there were more people in the train station than there were in Balluria. No one seemed to notice his presence, except for several men who stood in the corners watching the travelers. They wore the dark green uniforms of the party militiamen.

"Pardon me, sir. How can I get to the medical school in the medical city center?" Adnan asked the policeman whose uniform smelled of smoke and sweat.

"You go out of this station and take bus number 17, it will take you there," the policeman said and pointed toward the exit toward the bus depot. At the same time the officer turned to observe the young men and women exiting the train.

"Shukran, thank you," Adnan said and walked away not knowing where to find the number 17 bus. Adnan walked out of the station and saw the red canopy that was the bus stop; seeing the metal plate with bus number 17 on it, he only waited for several minutes before boarding the double-decker bus that smelled of burnt diesel. After asking several people to let him know when the bus reached the medical school compound, he finally reached his destination.

When he arrived, he searched for the piece of paper that Sayed Habeeb gave him, to find the name of the person that was written on the paper. It was the only thing that Sayed Habeeb gave him, as he had no money to give him when he bade him farewell. He remembered how Barrya cried and kissed him on his cheeks and said, "Don't be long. Try to come back soon, before your heart starts to harden." She wiped her eyes and the black, thick eyeliner with her head cover.

The graceful clergyman just looked at Adnan's face and said, "The capital city and its people can make a decent man lose his faith in Allah and his faith in his life. Be sure to save both your faith and your life and make sure you contact the person on this paper. He will keep you safe. He is a good man, and he is like my nephew. He is my best friend's son—a student in the capital city; he has a nice place to live. He will shelter you until you find a place to live."

Sadiq Yousif, College of Liberal Arts, History Department.

Adnan read the name on the piece of paper the clergyman gave him. He had no time to waste and he had no money to pay for a hotel room. He walked from the iron bridge where he exited the bus near the Ministry of Defense, which looked old and had the stench of blood and military coups. It was years ago that the mean general who killed the gentle, young king, and later became a beloved dictator, was himself dragged to his death by crazed mobs of militiamen and conspiring officers on these same steps. The benevolent dictator was shot to death in the radio station as said he was gravely disappointed by the support he was receiving from his communist supporters.

"Those were dark days for the country, only the faithful survived that period through prayer and patience." Adnan remembered Sayed Habeeb saying one day, telling the story of death and unrest in the capital city.

Adnan walked toward the complexes of the college and the institute that were on the six-cornered streets and saw something he'd never seen before. An ocean of young students, men and women, including many female students. He was breathless, both from walking the long distance with a heavy bag and from the waves of beautiful young females wearing gray skirts and white shirts. Some wore the hijab in accordance with the college uniform, a gray long robe and a blue or white head cover. But this did not matter, because all the beautiful female students' sultry black eyes were revealed, and that was enough for him. He reached the College of Liberal Arts and went through the gate where three men stood. They looked like the seven, mean men who dragged his brother into the street and shot him. One of the three men said, "What are you here for?"

"I am looking for a person, a student." Adnan felt the same old fear he felt years ago when he saw those men.

"What is the name of this person, the student?" the man with the thick moustache and big belly asked with clear sarcasm.

"His name is Sadiq Yousif. He is in the History Department," Adnan answered.

"Are you a new student here?" asked the second man, who wore black glasses and appeared to have lost an eye.

"Yes. I mean, not in this college. I am a new student at the medical school," Adnan replied with a clear, fearful voice.

"Then what are you doing here?" asked the man with thick, black glasses who appeared to be in charge.

"I have just arrived in the capital city, and I need to find this person. I have not been assigned to a dormitory yet, so I am going to live with him," Adnan said with the submissive tone of a potential prisoner.

"Where are you from?" asked the man with glasses.

"I am from the south, from Balluria," Adnan replied.

"The south, ha, Balluria, is that a real name of a real town?" asked the man with thick, black glasses.

"Yes, it's real," Adnan replied.

"It sounds like a place for ghosts," the one-eyed man said.

Adnan did not notice that the third man with the thick moustache and big belly was looking at a list of names, but when he saw him point to a name then showed it to the one-eyed man, Adnan noticed a certain change in the one-eyed man's demeanor. This chased away the minimal kindness that he presented, specifically the comment about Balluria being a town for ghosts, which Adnan agreed with. The one-eyed man who wore the thick black glasses looked at Adnan and said, "You cannot enter the college. You can wait here and I will send someone to fetch your friend."

"He is not my friend. He is the relative of a man in our town, and I am supposed to live with him until I get a room in the dormitory," Adnan said with an apologetic and submissive tone.

"Whatever the case may be, you are not allowed to enter until you have an identification card from the medical school that you claim you will be attending.

Just wait here," the one-eyed man concluded, and then he said to the guard with the list of names, "Go get this Sadiq Yousif. He is in the History Department."

Minutes later a thin, tall, and tanned student, who looked like he was marching to his death, walked through the gate with the guard who was sent to fetch him.

"Al Salamu Alaykum," the tall thin student said.

"Alaykum Al-Salam," Adnan replied.

"Are you Sadiq Yousif?" asked the man with thick, black glasses.

"Yes, yes I am," Sadiq answered.

"This boy here claims to have some matter with you," the man with the glasses said and pointed at Adnan who sat in the chair by the door looking at the many students who walked through the gate.

"What is that I can help you with?" Sadiq asked.

"Al Salamu Alaykum, I am Adnan, I am from Balluria and Sayed Habeeb said..."

"Would you like to go eat lunch?" Sadiq interrupted, giving Adnan a sharp look of his wide black eyes.

"Yes, Wallah, I am starving," Adnan replied.

"Let's go eat some falafel, here by the Bab Al-Muadham bridge," Sadiq answered.

"That will be great," Adnan replied.

The two students left through the college gate. Sadiq tried to walk meters in front of Adnan to avoid being seen as his acquaintance. He wanted to seek the truth behind the appearance of this thin, young student who looked more like a lost, sick poet than a freshman.

"Listen, I don't know you, and I apologize for the way I am saying this, but do not mention Sayed Habeeb's name again, especially in front of those men at the college's gate," Sadiq said.

"Why?"

"Don't ask why."

Sadiq did not sound like the kind and courteous man that Sayed Habeeb had told Adnan about. He seemed to be more serious and tense, but his first impression of Sadiq made Adnan think that he would be one those people who would ask why, just like him. It was a strange feeling that Adnan got when he heard Sadiq say, "Don't ask why" and not when or where or who. For a moment Adnan thought that it would have been better if he had not found Sadiq at the Liberal Arts College, and maybe he should not have searched for Sadiq at all. At that point, Adnan promised himself that he would look for a cheap hotel for the night.

"I apologize to have burdened you with my presence. However, Sayed Habeeb said that you would have a place for me to stay until I was assigned a dormitory room, but I think I will look for hotel tonight," Adnan said with a broken, yet clear, voice full of disappointment.

"Don't be silly," Sadiq said, and then asked, "How is Sayed Habeeb?"

"He is well. He is the clergyman in our town."

"What is the town's name again?"

"Balluria."

"Is that the real name of a real town?"

"Yes it is, why?"

"It sounds magical," Sadiq said as the two students arrived at the dirty falafel stand that sent an irresistible aroma of fried chickpeas into the air. It was Adnan's first meal since he boarded the train almost twenty hours before. He ate the falafel sandwich and felt the thickness of the frying oil sooth his hardened intestines. His initial fears of the capital city were eased, but he still needed assurance that he would not spend his first night in the streets, as he watched the many homeless men and women laying on the streets in filth.

"I am sorry to have burdened you with my presence, Sadiq."

"Don't—don't apologize twice for the same thing," Sadiq said with a firm voice.

"Do you see that teahouse? It is called Um Kalthum," Sadiq said as he pointed toward the door of a teahouse, which looked like the gate to a secret dungeon. "You go there, and wait for me. I will take you to the apartment that I am staying in. I have to go back to class now, but just wait for me, and don't go anywhere. By the way, I have two other roommates," Sadiq said, and then paid the falafel vendor and smiled at Adnan and added, "Now, I have officially acknowledged my traditional hospitality obligation."

Adnan was relieved of his fears when Sadiq relaxed and seemed more like someone from Balluria. He felt lost in this large city that felt and looked like it was capable of devouring a human mercilessly with its large buildings, black pavement, and thousands and thousands of people. In this jungle, he found a person who knew him, or at least a person who was related to a person who knew him, and that was enough familiarity for him to feel some comfort. He walked to the teahouse and sat down on one of many wooden benches. Adnan waited for Sadiq for three hours, listening to the crying voice of the old female singer that sang about lost love.

Sadiq appeared at the teahouse with two other students, and he introduced them to Adnan. "This is Luay, and this Wathiq."

"Ahlan wa Sahlan, welcome and Honored," Adnan said.

The two shook hands with Adnan, grabbed the backgammon board, and sat down and started playing with loud screams.

"That was not a double four," Wathiq protested.

"Yes it was," Luay insisted.

"My roommates, the morons, they will play backgammon for hours," said Sadiq, who seemed extremely interested in reading the newspaper, with the large title on it...

"Our Courageous Armed Forces Have Liberated the Small Peninsula in the South from the Persians, Enemy of Our Nation. Victory Is Ours."

4

The four students shared a one-bedroom apartment in the neighborhood near the medical college. The compound housed the medical school and the large hospital, among other medical colleges and institutes, in addition to several dormitories. The small apartment was on the third floor of a three-flat building. The second-floor apartment was occupied by almost twenty Egyptian laborers who worked in a bag manufacturing plant and smelled of fried eggplants all the time. The ground-level apartment was occupied by a family of four women, who seemed to never stop fighting, and countless children, who seemed to never stop screaming. All four of the women's husbands were soldiers fighting on the eastern front. The building next door, which looked fairly new, was not occupied at all. Wathiq and Luay were very excited that the building was unoccupied, and when Adnan asked them why they were happy, Luay said with breathless excitement, "Because I heard that this building was rented to the college for a girls' dormitory. In two months this building will be full college girls, right next to us."

"I hope it will be rented sooner than that; otherwise, I will die from masturbation," commented Wathiq, and Luay concurred.

In the small apartment a mattress lay unclaimed; Sadiq asked Adnan if he needed a blanket.

"No, I don't need one, it's still warm," Adnan answered. He knew that he would never be able to afford a blanket, but he would have to manage somehow to get a warm blanket by the winter.

"Don't be too proud about something like that. I will give you one of mine. I have an extra."

After that exchange, Adnan found a new friend in Sadiq; he started to see the truth in Sayed Habeeb's words. "He is a good young man. He is like my nephew." That was only half the truth; Sadiq was a good man and a good student too. He was serious and polite all the time; even in the teahouse he never played dominos or backgammon. He would rather listen to the radio or read the newspaper or a book. But Adnan noticed something very familiar in Sadiq. He noticed a deep sadness and a pained soul, like many of the people he knew in Balluria. It was as though Sadiq had grown up in Balluria or its sister village of Tawsheeha. Adnan was closer to Sadiq than he was to the other two roommates, who were always busy searching for the place that sold the cheapest alcohol, and they loved getting into endless conversations about politics.

The refreshing breeze of September brought the feeling of a new life for Adnan; it was the first month of school, and it went by fast. Adnan had acclimated and grown accustomed to the new and exciting surroundings of his new school. He would walk every morning with hundreds of students who walked to their schools and colleges among the scent of magnolias carried through the capital city by autumn's morning breeze. He looked at the faces of the people and the students; everyone was older and bigger than him. It was exciting and different, yet not as glorious and full of light, like the sunny mornings in Balluria.

Adnan had been assigned all of his classes and obtained an identification card. He was tempted to go visit Sadiq in the Liberal Arts College just to show the one-eyed, fearsome guard that he was a real student in the medical school, but the beastly images of the three guards convinced him otherwise. He spent most of his time catching up on classes that he had missed, because he was one week late in arriving at the school. He barely had enough money to buy the required medical instruments and a used white robe. He definitely had no time for politics, nor did he have enough time for questions about the logic or existence of things he did not understand. He accepted his new life in the capital city, regardless of the extreme loneliness and the unbearable and preemptive rejection by the women. In college there were many beautiful female students, young and rich, who lived in the capital city. They had never heard of Balluria or of the most skilled and inhumanly beautiful Gypsy dancer named Barrya. These girls had never heard of people like Sheikh Jawad or Sheikh Nasser the Blond. They had never heard of the gates of heaven in the marshes. The girls in college were from different towns and provinces. Some were from towns or provinces like his, but none of them had ever heard of Balluria. The most common response that Adnan heard, when he told the other students where he was from, was the usual question, "Is it a real town?"

Most of the students in the medical school were from the capital city. All of the female students in the school talked to and socialized with other students, but never with him or the group of bookworms in his class. It was the same case with his two roommates Luay and Wathiq, who hoped college would be the ultimate place for love. Adnan, Luay, and Wathiq started calling themselves the "thorny union." As Luay explained the logic behind the naming; the three of them must have invisible thorns sticking out of their bodies that prevented females from getting closer to them. Or, as Wathiq stated, "It seems like all the females in the capital city have signed a secret pact to stay away and not to talk to us."

Luay and Wathiq were from a small town like Balluria, no one had heard of before. Sadiq was from the holy city in the Euphrates valley. Sadiq, Luay, and Wathiq came from middle-class families and had money to spend on clothes, alcohol, and the occasional prostitute that Luay would bring to the apartment. Other than attending their classes, the four students would meet in the apartment in the early afternoon, nap for an hour, and then spend their afternoons in a teahouse, Um Kalthum, named after the famous Egyptian female singer who had sung of lost love for the past five decades. The teahouse was filled with old people and lost souls, who spent the afternoons there hoping that their lives would pass more quickly. The teahouse was on the same street where many years before the divine leader, when he was a young, ruthless underground assassin along with his group of fellow assassins tried, but failed to kill the good dictator, who killed the gentle, young king and declared the country a republic. The street was filled with historical memories of a nation's struggle for identity, self-realization, and hope in a future that never seems to come, the street was filled with street hustlers who tried to sell unsalable merchandise of used clothes, old magazines, and flowers. It was filled with drunks who slept on the concrete pavement, and many street vendors who sold everything. The four students sat there and sipped tea, watched others, read poetry, and talked politics. They talked about the politics of other countries, such as America, Russia, Nicaragua, and Cuba, but never about their homeland, because they knew that among the many lost souls of the sleepy teahouse there would be several informants whose ears were never at rest. They knew that these secret informants were aching to end a young man's life with a few words on white single-page report.

The four students drenched their despair and lack of a women's love with poetry and lazy afternoons listening to the dead, seventy year old Egyptian woman singer, singing about the lover who forgot about her. Adnan was carful when it came to talking about politics; the memory of the night when a group of men dragged his older brother and shot him in the street was still fresh in his mind and never seemed to wither. He was fearful of facing a similar fate. He knew that in college, his name was on the list of the "must be watched" students, along with two other male students and one female student. He knew this, because Kamal, who had became the party's second-in-command in Balluria, had sent a report to the medical school security cell and the security cell chief had summoned Adnan and asked him if he knew a person by the name of Comrade Kamal.

"Yes, I know Kamal," Adnan answered.

"Well, son, he sent a report saying that you are not a member of the party, that you are independent. Is this true?" asked the gentle and well-mannered doctor, who wore the party's dark green uniform and taught immunology.

"Yes, this is correct," Adnan replied.

"There are no independents here in the capital city, and especially in the medical school. We cannot have doctors who are not loyal to the divine leader or to the party. You will join the party and attend their weekly meetings with your classmates. Is that understood?"

Adnan sensed that the doctor was saying something that he himself did not believe in.

"Yes, Doctor," Adnan answered.

"Comrade, you must call me comrade. I am a doctor in the class only; anywhere else I am to be addressed as Comrade," the well-mannered man stated.

After that day, Adnan started attending the long and boring weekly meetings along with the other two male and the female students, who were on the "must be watched" list. Adnan would curse Kamal every time he attended the long and pointless meeting, but it was a remedy for the suspicion that tarnished his image and an excuse to sit close to the female students who wore the head scarf and had thick glasses like him. The meeting was chaired by a creepy-looking senior student, who resembled the party official with the big belly, thick moustache, and red eyes. Adnan never spoke about his brother Qahtan to anyone. He wished that time would move quickly so he would one day live without the pain of that memory. He wanted to live life again.

One day he asked Luay if he knew what the fastest method to forget someone was, and Luay was quick to answer, "You are asking the expert on this subject. It's areq, alcohol, my friend. It's the homemade alcohol made by the finest Christian families in the north. Not only will alcohol make your forget a loved one, but it will make you dumber by the day. Every time you drink you lose a percentage of your brain, so by the time you are forty, nothing and nobody will mean anything to you; that's happiness. You see all those wasted people in the bars. They are all trying to forget something or someone."

So, Adnan asked Luay and Wathiq if they could take him drinking one day, and they did. The three went to a dingy bar near the theater that showed only American movies, and they drank areq all night. Adnan was completely drunk after the first glass and fell asleep on the table; his two roommates had to carry him to the taxi and up the stairs to his mattress, where he slept all night and then missed all of his classes the next day. Since then and whenever opportunity came, he went with his two roommates, who were generous enough to buy him the cheap moonshine with the money they saved for meals. While Luay and Wathiq looked for hookers who they thought would be easy to find on the main commercial street to bring back with them to the apartment, Adnan looked for the ghost of Badr Shaker Al-Sayyab, the lost poet, who suffered the same pain of being deprived of a woman's love.

Adnan looked for him in the faces of the drunks in the dark corners of the many bars filled with sad men who passed the age of expectation and arrived at the unavoidable end of lost hope and lost dreams while they drank the bitter, locally-made alcohol. He also looked for Hussain Merdan, the poet who dreamed of leaving the homeland and traveling to Europe, Holland, or Denmark, where all the beautiful, blond women were. He looked in the street corners where Hussian wrote the unforgettable lines of his poems. With every fiery drink of areq burning down his throat and lighting up his stomach, Adnan realize that all the poets had gone long before him.

He walked the streets of the capital, asking the ghosts about his beautiful brother, the able, Qahtan, the smartest young man the marshland had ever known, who knew of people that no one knew. But it seemed that the capital city had forgotten all the poets who once loved it. Instead he found himself alone in the many corners of the capital, corners that knew many weak souls like his, vomiting his insides out and looking aimlessly for the dead poets. The corners which were stained with the blood of people who dared to have a dream that was different than that of the divine leader. Adnan did not know if it was the areq, or that he could not find the spirits of dead poets, or the constant and unannounced rejection by the many women in the capital city. Maybe all of these reasons made him feel that the capital was cold and cruel; he was beginning to feel the emptiness of his life again. Adnan yearned for Balluria. He wanted to keep his soul intact and untouched. He wanted to be with Hamid by the river. He wanted to sit in the warm corners of the mosque and listen to Sayed Habeeb read the tragic history of the holy family to the teary-eyed old men and enthusiastic young boys who loved to beat on their chests in search of redemption for a sin their ancestors had committed centuries ago. But it all made sense now. Home, Balluria, was where the thin, intelligent student wanted to be. He wanted to get away from the capital city. Feelings of loneliness and unfamiliarity started to replace the feelings of joy and the dream of a new life that he felt in the beginning of the year.

Adnan wanted to go back to where things made sense. Even though they presented the clear meaning of nonsense, he was too innocent for the capital city. He was poor, smart, and a dreamer, but he knew that his new roommates would not be the kind of people that he could share his past with. He could not share his pain and disappointment with them, so he stopped going to the bar with them and stayed alone in the apartment most evenings.

Winter cast its gray clouds on the capital, and Adnan was keener on staying in the apartment. Sadiq was there reading books and writing many papers that seemed long and unrelated to his school work. Adnan did not interrupt him, nor did he participate in the discussions between Luay and Wathiq, who seemed to have run out of money for alcohol and prostitutes, as they stayed in the apartment most of the time too. Adnan laid on his mattress listening to the radio. The other two students engaged in heated political discussions and endless arguments that ended in anger and them not talking to each other for hours. Adnan noticed that Sadiq was silent all the time and never got into any discussions with anyone. Even in the teahouse he was always silent, while the other two always argued about everything. Adnan usually did not ask Sadiq about anything, not about his family or his school, but one day when they were alone in the apartment Adnan asked Sadiq:

"Did you know Sayed Habeeb?"

"Yes, he was my father's cellmate."

"Cellmate, what do you mean?"

"They were in prison together," Sadiq said, without lifting his eyes from his book.

Adnan thought to stop asking, because Sadiq's face turned serious with dark shades of sadness, similar to the sadness that Adnan carried with him all of these years, but he wanted to make sure that Sadiq was willing to tell the story.

He did not know how to ask the question, but it was Sadiq who was quick to assure him of one thing.

"Promise me that you will never tell another soul that I told this. I am only telling you, because if Sayed Habeeb sent you to me, then I know it's OK to tell you about my father."

"Tell me what?"

"Well, if you want to know what happened to my father, he was executed along with four others, the five men were called the 'Fist of Faith.'"

"Oh! My Allah! Your father was one of the 'Fist of Faith' members?" Adnan asked.

"Yes, he was. So now you can plan to move to another place to live, because of our two other roommates. They are not really just roommates."

"What do you mean?" Adnan asked with the known curiosity of the southern people.

"I suspect they may be informants for the party intelligence agency, or they may be members of the shadow cell here in college. So, be careful, and watch what you say in front of them."

Adnan was filled with fear; he looked at Sadiq and asked, "Are you saying that Wathiq and Luay are informants? They seem to be harmless."

"I know. That's why I said they may be, because I'm not sure," Sadiq replied.

"I will never say anything anymore. I swear to Allah," Adnan said quietly.

After that discussion, Adnan realized that he was not ready for the mission of changing the world. He was barely able to handle the life of the capital. He stopped accompanying Wathiq and Luay when they frequented the smoky bars or the teahouse and made sure to never start or participate in any conversation that was remotely close to politics or religion. Life in the apartment became boring and frustrating, but the female students who started to occupy the building next door brought with them fresh and endless possibilities of love, and filled the neighborhood with a stream of feminine perfumes in the narrow streets.

Male students from all the surrounding dormitories swarmed the streets. They walked up and down the street hoping for a spontaneous encounter with one of the girls. However, the four roommates had what every male student in the neighborhood and possibly in the capital city wished for and wanted. They occupied the top-floor apartment right across from the girls' dormitory, which enjoyed a perfect view of all the rooms. This view made it possible for them to watch the female students while they cooked food, studied, and slept. It was a dream come true for Luay and Wathiq and even Adnan, but Sadiq never seemed to care much. About two hundred young and beautiful female students lived next door. Many of them would strike up a conversation with Wathiq, who was also the first to start a relationship with Hibba. She was overweight and attended the education college. Luay started talking to Mayada, another female student, who attended the college. None of the girls seemed to be interested in Adnan; even Sadiq, who never paid attention to the building full of females, started receiving notes thrown through the window, wrapped with a stone, written by a female student who signed her name as, "Your Secret Admirer." Sadiq was not at all interested in discovering who his secret admirer was.

Adnan was the only one who had not received any possible sign of love on the horizon from any of the girls. Nevertheless, the female dormitory was a blessing that came to Adnan and the other three students who shared the apartment. It was a blessing because the voices, the laughter, and the closeness of their presence were much nicer than Adnan's female classmates in the medical school, who acted like they were men in women's clothing. The female students who occupied the third floor of dormitory would smile and talk to him from across the window; they would ask him questions about medicine and medical school, but none of them seemed interested in initiating anything more than that.

Wathq and Luay competed for the attention of the female students and stayed up late at night, hoping to get a glimpse of one of them getting undressed. One girl would forget to close the bathroom window, and they were lucky many times to see Shatha or Nahla undressing. Shatha wore jeans, something that only a few female students did. They would get excited and talk about how white Nahla's breasts were and discuss the color of Hibba's underpants. Adnan's head would turn as he felt close to entering the forbidden kingdom of the women's world. Sadiq never once replied to Shatha's notes that she sent through the half-open window of the apartment wrapped around small stones.

It was to the point where a joke was made by Wathq, who said, "Sadiq, I am afraid to pass by that window from fear of losing an eye by one of your love letters."

Luay once suggested that they put a sign near the window saying, "Watch out for flying love letters."

Sadiq wouldn't even talk to her when she whistled several times by the window. That was a sign that Wathiq and Hibba used to call each other from across the window to chat. Adnan never understood the cold shoulder that he sensed from his friend Sadiq; it was like Sadiq was upset with him. So one afternoon when he saw Sadiq standing on the roof outside the apartment, staring at the empty elementary school yard next to the building, he went out of the door to the roof and asked him casually, "So, what the new on the love front?" He tried to make his tone as friendly as possible.

'What do you mean?" Sadiq asked.

"Have you talked to Shatha yet?"

"Adnan, I thought you were smarter than to ask me that."

"I am, I just wanted to..."

"No, you don't," Sadiq said with a strangely firm tone that sounded like he was reprimanding a younger brother. He looked Adnan in the eyes and continued. "I did not lecture you about the alcohol drinking. I know you are not my brother, but I feel responsible for you, and it seems like you have no interest in anything in this life except women and alcohol. You drink alcohol to forget about life instead of trying to create a better one, and it seems like you are looking for a mere sexual encounter with one of the many emotionally deprived girls in the dormitory."

"I am attending the medical school to make my life better," Adnan replied defensively.

"I know, but you seem like the others who never pay attention to their world, and the way things are. So I decided to leave you alone since our interests are different," Sadiq concluded.

Adnan stood next to Sadiq and did not say anything more. He wanted to say many things, but he did not how and where to start. He knew that Sadiq was different than anyone he'd ever met before; he was a serious and intelligent young man who never said anything without knowing the logic behind his words or knowing the purpose of the conversation.

"I thought that Sayed Habeeb had taught you something or maybe he thought that you were someone different," Sadiq said as he turned and walked toward the door that led to the apartment from the rooftop. At that moment, Adnan sensed something new. He felt like he was talking to his older brother, Qahtan. Even the voices were similar. Sadiq looked back at Adnan and waited for a reply.

Adnan walked over to where Sadiq was standing and said, "Sadiq, I am nineteen years old and poor. I attend medical school. My family in Balluria has no money, and they have not eaten in two days. Never did I see myself in the middle of a big city filled with so many beautiful women, and none of them seem to care or even know that I exist. I am sad, needy, tired, hungry, and horny, and I don't foresee a change anytime soon. How much more can a nineteen-year-old handle?"

"That's the case of almost the entire population of young men, except for the ones who have to sleep in the trenches, while leprosy, artillery shells, and bullets feast on their bodies and their souls on the eastern fronts."

"What do you want me to do? I want the war to end," Adnan said

"Wanting is not enough, but working to stop it and the many other tragedies is the way."

"The way for what?" Adnan asked.

"The way for a better life, unless you prefer to forget about life and let me and others like me try to change it for you, so you don't feel so hungry all the time," Sadiq said and smiled at Adnan.

"What do you want to do?" Adnan asked, knowing that he would never win the argument, because deep down inside he agreed with every word Sadiq said.

"I want you to meet someone," Sadiq said with a look that could be interpreted in many ways. He was afraid of discovering Adnan's weakness.

"Who do you want me to meet?" Adnan asked.

"You will know when the time comes, but don't worry. No one will know, not even Sayed Habeeb. I just want to know if you are willing to meet this person in prison with my father and Sayed Habeeb. I believe that you may be interested in what he has to say," Sadiq assured him.

"Yes, I would like that," Adnan replied without second-guessing his serious friend.

"The school year will be over in three months, and I want you to meet him before school ends."

"I will, but you have to promise me something."

"What is that?" Sadiq asked.

"Before the school year ends, you have to promise me that you will talk to Shatha, the girl who sends you love messages all the time. You're not being fair to yourself, because love is a good thing in a young man's life. And it's not fair to her either, because she has expressed her interest in many ways."

Sadiq looked at him, smiled, and said, "I have other things that are more important right now than love, and believe me it would not be fair to her to love me or to be in a relationship with someone like me."

Sadiq walked back inside the apartment leaving Adnan behind to wonder about the many comments he just heard. Trying to understand his friend's comments was confusing, because he knew that Sadiq was hiding something. He had known ever since Sayad Habeeb's comment about Sadiq, before he left Balluria. "He is a good man; he is the son of a good man, and one day he may be in a position of power. He will help you in the capital city."

Adnan's commitment to work on changing the world did not disappear from his conscience nor did his resentment toward the government and the divine leader ever diminish. But he never found a way to utilize the anger he felt. Before the afternoon talks with Sayed Habeeb, he directed his anger toward God and creation itself, but exploring that direction did not bring him any satisfaction. He felt helpless with that fact, because he could not face God when he wanted to. He wanted more, so he started reading all the books that his dead brother, Qahtan, had hidden in the small box by the clay oven in the backyard of their family's mud hut. However, the books only added to his confusion. He excelled in school and was a math genius, but even solving all the math problems in the world did not help rid him of the feelings of emptiness. The day Sadiq did not go to class he told Adnan that he would be waiting for him in the apartment. Adnan did not think that it would be anything out of ordinary, so he attended all his classes that day and then spent some time with the only two female students in his class. They were nicknamed Gandhi, because of heavy hijab dresses they wore and the glasses identical to Gandhi's. They needed his help with an upcoming test, and he generously offered his assistance. After all, he felt that any type of female companionship would help him to dismantle the borders of the forbidden world of women around him. Adnan walked back to the apartment in the middle of the day when the sun was at its peak; he was hot and tired, and when he reached the apartment, he found Sadiq waiting for him impatiently.

"Are you ready?" Sadiq asked with strange enthusiasm and apparent excitement.

"Ready for what?" Adnan asked with sincere innocence.

"Are you ready to meet the person I told you about?" Sadiq said without changing his demeanor.

"Now?" Adnan asked.

"Yes, now, he is only in the capital city for one day and he wanted to meet you."

"He wants to meet me?"

"Yes, I have been telling him about you. And he is now ready to meet you."

"Where is he?"

"Come with me. I will take you to see him. Today will be a great day in your life," Sadiq said as he tapped on Adnan's shoulder and smiled sincerely.

The two students walked out of the apartment and boarded the bus heading to the old part of the capital near the shrine of one of the prophet's grandsons, who also died a tragic death nearly sixteen hundred years ago and was buried in place that was named after him, a place called Kadhimya.

They walked through the alleys and past the small shops emitting the inviting aromas of paper mixed with scented oils and dried flower leaves that brought back the feeling of history and ancient tragedies into the senses of the shoppers and passersby. Sadiq kept looking behind him to make sure they were not being followed by a secret informant and he and Adnan stopped and sat in several teahouses along the way. This was Sadiq's way of ensuring that no one was trailing them when they entered the small alley with two or four houses that looked like they were about to collapse. He told Adnan to be ready and to listen closely before he asked any questions. Sadiq looked around to make sure there was no one in the alley, and then he knocked four times on the first door, painted light blue. Moments later, a man opened the door and said, "Al Salamu Alykum."

"Wa Alaykum Al-Salam," replied the man, whose coloring was strangely white, and he was neater than most people in the area.

"Is Abu Karrar here?" Sadiq asked.

"Who may I say is looking for him?" the man asked.

"Can you tell him that Sadiq and my friend are here to see him?"

"I sure will. He told me you were coming; please come in," the neat man said, opening the door to let the two anxious students in.

The inside of the house reminded him of the homes described in the ancient tales that Barrya used to relate to the wide-eyed kids. The house was wide open with sunlight pouring into the middle of the room from the ceiling, and there was a small fountain, which was dry, the middle of the house. The house seemed deserted of women and children. The two stood in the middle of house, and soon a middle-aged man who appeared tired and restless came in from one of the rooms and extended his hand to Sadiq.

"Welcome, welcome, to you, the good son of good people. How are you, and how is your family doing?" the man asked.

"They are well, all thanks to Allah," Sadiq replied, and he looked at Adnan, who was mesmerized by the man's appearance. The man looked very kind, confident, calm, and naturally graceful, like Sayed Habeeb.

"Abu Karrar, this is my friend Adnan," Sadiq said, urging Adnan with his eyes to step forward.

"Al Salamu Alaykum," Adnan said quietly.

"Wa Alaykum Al-Salam," the man replied, and then asked, "Are you the future doctor?"

"Yes, Inshalla, God willing."

"Welcome, let us sit in my room."

Abu Karrar led Sadiq and Adnan to his room, which was cold and dark. The fan in the room made the environment even colder and wetter than normal. There was a single bed and a clothes hanger with one shirt and a jacket on it. There was a clean carpet and an immaculately clean prayer rug with a forehead stone, a Qur'an and long black prayer beads curled up next to the forehead stone.

Sadiq and Abu Karrar engaged in a conversation about Sadiq's family and their welfare, and then Sadiq said, "Adnan has met Sayed Habeeb and learned from him."

"Yes, you've told me. How is our brother, the Sayed? Is he well, in health and his spirit?"

"Yes, he is well. He is the clergyman of our masque in Balluria."

"Balluria, is that a real name of a real town?"

"Yes, it's a real name of a real town."

"It sounds mysteriously ancient "

"Well, they say that Balluria has been there since the beginning of time," Adnan answered with a smile.

"Only Allah has been here since the beginning of time," Abu Karrar replied with a counter smile.

That's for sure," Adnan said in an agreeing tone.

"The worst character of our people is that they like to waste time," the man said while he looked directly in Adnan's eyes. "I don't like to waste time, especially the time of a medical student."

"I agree," Sadiq stated.

Adnan looked at Sadiq, waiting for him to say something to ease the seriousness of the meeting, but Sadiq said nothing.

"Do you know why you are here?" asked the man, who looked at Adnan.

"Sadiq said that you wanted to meet me."

"Yes, I do, but do you know why I wanted to meet you?"

"No, I do not."

"I wanted to meet you to see if you are willing or if you are able to join 'Our Movement,' but before you say anything, let me tell you what you need to know."

"I am listening."

"First, 'Our Movement' is the forbidden organization that everyone is scared to talk about. This means you stand the risk of imprisonment or death, God forbid, if you join."

Adnan was so overwhelmed by both the frankness of Abu Karrar and that even after hearing about the future possibilities he wanted to hear more, so he kept listening.

"I am sure that you heard of the Da'wa Party, you know that our party follows the teachings of the outspoken martyred ayatollah. Many of our leaders served prison time, and some have been executed. Many of our young members are and will be facing the same fate. Our goals are known, and our mission is known, so go back to your home."

"My apartment?" Adnan asked, as he could not find any other words to say to the graceful-looking man, who talked with a diligent, soft, and firm voice without stuttering or pausing.

The man smiled and continued. "Go back to your apartment and Sadiq will be the link between us. Go with Allah's peace and protection."

The two students stood up and shook hands with the man and then left the house without saying a word. Walking back the same way they came, they drank tea in several teahouses before they boarded the bus back to the apartment. While on the bus, Adnan could not keep from asking: "Who was that man?"

"What did you think of him? Sadiq asked.

"I felt like he knew exactly what he was talking about and he was not afraid," Adnan said what he was really thinking.

"He is one of my late father's close confidants, and he was one of the few who were not executed during the mass arrests of 1979. He has been at large for all these years, and he is now the most wanted political opposition leader. All four of his brothers were executed, and his wife was raped, tortured, burned with cigarettes, and then the secret police tied both of her legs to moving trucks, and she was torn in half. His name is... well, we will always call him Abu Karrar," Sadiq said as he looked at Adnan, who was trying to regain his composure after what he just heard about Abu Karrar. Sadiq held Adnan by his arm as the two exited the bus.

"Adnan, you don't have to worry. There is no way I will tell anyone about this afternoon, and there is no way Abu Karrar will tell anyone. So the logical thing to do is for you not to talk about it to anyone and take your time to think about what Abu Karrar said, and then you let me know when you are ready."

Adnan was not satisfied with what Sadiq said, and he wanted to know more about the man. Moreover, he wanted to know why Sadiq waited all this time to introduce him to the Abu Karrar and why he did not choose to introduce him sooner. When the two reached the apartment, they discovered that Wathiq and Luay had gone home for the Thursday and Friday break. The female dormitory also seemed very empty of the tempting noises and activity. Sadiq prayed, and Adnan washed up and laid down on the mattress for a late afternoon nap.

"Why me?" Adnan asked. "Why not Wathiq or Luay?"

"Because you are poor and smart and, because I think that Wathiq and Luay may be informants in their college to the security cell."

"There are millions who are smart and poor."

"Yes, I know, but you are the one I know," Sadiq said with a sleepy voice.

"I am a man of logic, and that does not sound like logical reasoning to me," Adnan replied.

"I know. I just wanted to spare you the answers that you don't want to hear."

"Well, that's not fair, because that tells me that I am mature enough to join a forbidden party, but I am not mature enough to know why I am joining," Adnan said with discomfort.

Sadiq sat up and asked Adnan to sit next to him and to listen.

Adnan, our people have been suffering for years under the regime of that tyrant, and only smart and brave people can bring about change. Unfortunately, that carries the risk of death and imprisonment, so we have to be extremely careful and accurate about how to approach others to join the movement. We have no time to spare. The average life-span of our members is three to five years, and only the smart ones keep themselves out of jail. As long as we have enough people who are out of jail for a certain time period, we will be able to ensure the awaited inevitable changes. It's not the will or the faith that matters now; it is the hard and dedicated work of good people that will amount to something," Sadiq said.

"Do you know why I am always serious and have no time for Shatha and her love?" Sadiq asked. "I would love to be able to walk with her on a peaceful afternoon along the river and just talk about silly things, but I have no time, because it's only a matter of time until the secret police catch up with me. I have been watched for the last three years already," Sadiq said to the wide-eyed Adnan, who was trying to grasp the many facts that he had learned that afternoon.

"I know that the movement could use a person like you. The country and the people will need a person like you. It is the path that my father and many others gave their lives for; it's my contribution to my country and to the people of my country," Sadiq said, and then covered his face with the blanket.

"Are you going to sleep?" Adnan said with apparent discomfort.

"Yes, I will dream too, and you should do the same."

Sadiq fell into a deep sleep, with not a single worry on his mind. The two never spoke about the subject again, nor did Adnan make any attempts to ask any more questions. He kept himself busy by studying for the final exams of his first year in medical school. He thought this would be the year that he would prove himself to the other students. But, he also started examining his relationship with Allah. He searched for answers to all the questions he had asked for many years, but he never asked about the where, the when and the how. Instead, all of his questions were about the why.

Why did Allah create people like the tyrant?

Why does Allah allow tyrants to be in charge of people's lives and fates?

Why are people too weak to rise up against the tyranny?

Why did Allah create many religions?

Why did Allah allow the war in the eastern front to happen, since it has no purpose and no foreseeable end?

Why did Allah make him so smart so he would ask why?

Why did he have to meet Sadiq?

Why could he never find a woman to love?

Why are the females avoiding him, although he is kind, smart, harmless, and full of love?

Why did Allah allow the mean seven men to squeeze the life out of his beautiful and good brother?

Why, why, and why. There were more whys than becauses, and he had to discover the becauses to learn the whys.

As he walked the streets of the capital searching for the spirits of the dead poets and looking for the many spirits becauses to his whys, he stopped drinking alcohol and started praying regularly. This change pleased Sadiq and displeased their other two roommates, who noticed the change in their thin roommate's behavior. He was taking his first steps on the long journey to change this world for the better.

The Book of Balluria

The Many Journeys of the Weak Angel

The Third Journey

1

"We have a cure for people like you; remedies that we have perfected, throughout the years, to rid you from a disease that could harm our country. We will treat you to make sure that you cannot harm the country or the revolution," the colonel who wore civilian clothes said, as he looked at Adnan's bloodied face. It was Adnan's third day in the dark and smelly dungeon.

"But before we start the treatment, I need to know the answers to three questions. Did you meet with a man named Abu Karrar? What did he tell you? And where is he now? These questions must and will be answered, or you will wish that whore mother of yours never birthed you. Do you understand me, you little piece of filth?" The colonel looked at Adnan with blood-red eyes that seemed to rake his body like nails. The colonel reeked of alcohol. The smell reminded Adnan of his middle school math teacher, Mr. Muhamed Tabra. For the first two days, Adnan maintained his innocence and told the truth.

"Yes, I met a man named Abu Karrar, but he did not tell me anything of importance, and I don't know where he is."

The previous night's torture session made Adnan think that he would not be able to withstand another night of torture, so he applied his mind to finding a way out of this hellish chamber. He wished that Sadiq was present, so he could tell these monsters that he was innocent. He wanted him to be present, so that he could support his statement of clemency and confirm that Adnan had never joined the forbidden party. Membership was offered but never accepted. What Adnan did not know was that Sadiq was in a cell darker than his and only fifty meters from where he was. What Adnan did not know was that at that same exact moment, Sadiq was begging for mercy as he endured torture too brutal even for an animal and what Adnan did not know was that on the day that Sadiq disappeared from the apartment and from the Liberal Arts College, he was arrested and driven to the hellish chamber by the three men who looked, smelled, and sounded like the three mean men who arrested Adnan on that beautiful, yet fateful Wednesday that seemed like it was ages ago.

It had been an exceptionally beautiful day, the kind of a day that could show a human how precious the gift of life and freedom was, even if it was fake and only temporary. That Wednesday had seemed promising, and even though Adnan was not completely ready for the test, he had spent the previous night studying in the apartment and talking to Shatha, one of the girls in the dormitory. She told him that she and another girl would be leaving in the morning to their hometowns, because they had finished their final exams. She also told him something that made Adnan lose his concentration on his studies.

"You know Nahla, my roommate. I think she likes you. She said that you are a serious and well-mannered man."

Shatha asked him, "Where is Sadiq? I have not seen him for two days." Adnan did not answer; he was keener on knowing more about this possible future love. He asked her if Nahla was still in the dormitory. "No, she is taking her final exam today, and then she will be leaving right after that to her hometown in the Euphrates valley, but she will be back next September."

Next year was too far away for love, Adnan thought to himself, but he was willing to wait. Finally, a female talked to him, a female with the sweet scent of a woman. He could not concentrate on the anatomy text book that he started reading and the many disorganized notes that he had put together, but he knew that he would pass the test easily.

He performed his morning prayers and then put on his only gray trousers with a white shirt and necktie that he borrowed from Sadiq. He thought that Sadiq had gone home for three days to visit his mother and many siblings. Adnan asked Wathiq and Luay about him, and they also thought that Sadiq had gone home to his family.

He walked to the medical school smiling. He saw many students walking to their colleges, studying their notes in preparation for their final exams. The narrow streets smelled of jasmine perfume and the natural smell of freshly washed and dried women's hair. It was a hopeful day. He entered the building with strange joy and fresh confidence, because finally he was on his way to the world that he'd always dreamt of being a part of, the world of love and lovers. Planning to finish his test quickly, he walked around the campus looking for Nahla in hopes of seeing her before she went home. He wanted to ensure a future rendezvous of love, and maybe he would get a farewell kiss. He was already planning on staying in the capital for the summer in order to find work and to save as much money as he possibly could to buy new clothes, so he would be ready for Nahla when she came back in September. He felt that it was going to be a very beautiful year, full of love.

Adnan spent half an hour reading the questions and was filling out the easy answers on the test sheet when a man he had never seen before approached the supervising professor and whispered something in his ear. Adnan did not pay much attention to them, but then the professor approached the desk where Adnan was finishing his test and asked "Are you done with your exam?"

"No, I am almost finished," Adnan said, wondering why the professor was asking only him.

"Well, let me have your paper. They need you at the registration office."

"Can I finish the test?" Adnan asked with fear in his eyes.

"No, you can come back, after you finish this matter at the registration office."

The professor took the test papers from Adnan's hand and asked him to follow him to the registration office.

Walking behind the professor, thinking that the matter had nothing to do with registration, Adnan asked, "Why I am needed at the registration office?"

"You will know soon," the professor answered, without looking at Adnan.

When Adnan entered the registration office, there was only one female clerk, Laheeb, who made many students dizzy with her larger than average hips. Adnan went to her desk and asked with sincere innocence. "You've requested me?"

"What, who are you?" Laheeb asked, clearly confused.

"Don't move!" A harsh male voice rang out behind Adnan. "And don't turn round!"

He could not keep himself from turning around to see who these orders were coming from, but when he did, he felt the heat of a painful slap turn his face back to its original position. Laheeb looked at him and realized that the thin kid was being arrested by the political secret police. It was Ibrahim, the older student in the medical college. Older than the other students, he had never graduated from the school.

With Ibrahim was another man with a thick moustache and the beginnings of a round belly. He held both of Adnan's arms and told him, "We will exit this office and go the white Toyota in the parking lot. You will not say a word, and you will not talk to any students on the way there. You will keep your mouth shut." Doing what the fat man with the thick moustache told him to, he walked silently toward the door of the registration office, followed by the frightened look of the female clerk, who many of the male students had wet dreams about. Her tempting walk and the way she moved her sumptuous hips caused the young men to swoon after her. She knew that this was going to be the last time she would ever see this thin student, who wore thick reading glasses.

The car sped through the streets of the capital city. Adnan sat between the two secret police officers, who handcuffed him and sat very close to him.

"When I tell you to put your head down, do so or I will break your neck," the fat secret police officer said, looking at Adnan.

"I will," Adnan replied, realizing the dark fate that awaited him.

"Do you know me?" said the officer who wore a student uniform and who seemed to be older than other students and never seemed to graduate.

"Yes, I know of you," Adnan replied.

"What's my name?" the officer asked Adnan.

"Mohamed," Adnan answered and received the first of many slaps on the way to the compound of many houses that formed the political secret police headquarters.

"If you are going to be smart with me, I will rape your mother and sister while you watch."

Adnan looked at him and felt extreme remorse as the faces of his hopelessly weak mother and sister jumped into his mind.

"So, what's my name now?" the secret police officer asked him again.

"Mohamed or Ibrahim," Adnan said, trying to save his dignity and maintain his ignorance of knowing anything that these three beastly men might be interested in.

"You son of a whore; it took me a year to figure you out, you and that son of a whore, Sadiq Yousif. Put your head down now, or I will break it with my shoe!"

Adnan put his head down, and the fat officer hit him on the back of his head and repeated, "Keep it down, keep it down!"

The car stopped; one of the officers blindfolded Adnan and told him to move.

"How? I can't see," Adnan said.

"So, you are blind now, you shroogy son of a shit," a voice said.

The two officers walked him up a few steps and guided him toward a room. He heard the voices of the other people. Some were laughing, and others were screaming.

"Oh, for Allah's sake. Oh, for Allah's sake, I did not do anything."

Adnan blocked out the voices and sounds, as he knew that he would need more than his civilized intuition to comprehend his strange surroundings.

"We've brought him in, sir," Adnan heard the fat officer say as he clicked his feet together. The fat officer pushed him down to sit in a chair and kept the blindfold on his eyes.

"So you are a friend of Sadiq Yousif, ha."

Adnan did not answer.

A harsh blow to his face made him bleed from the side of his mouth. A deep voice, like a bull's, said, "Answer the colonel!"

"What colonel? I can't see," Adnan protested.

A punch to his stomach and another slap immediately followed. Dizzy, he wanted to vomit from pain. He said, "He is not my friend; he is my roommate." Adnan began to cry.

"Don't cry... you are a man... men don't cry... only women cry, so you are now a woman to me. It is all right; you will wish that you were a woman, a woman like your whore mother. Take him away and teach him what he needs to learn."

After he was forced to sign a paper that he did not and could not read, because he was blindfolded, Adnan was tied by his legs and left to hang upside down from the ceiling for over four hours. Two men with masks took turns hitting him with wire cables and sticks. He lost consciousness and his sense of time. Later that evening, they untied him, woke him up with a cold bucket of water, and escorted him through a narrow walkway. Blindfolded, he was led toward a room that he could smell long before he entered. They took off the blindfold, opened a thick, metal door that made an unwelcoming, evil, screeching sound, and pushed Adnan into the darkness of the dungeon.

2

The dungeon smelled of death and human waste. The heat was unbearable and the air did not find its way to the needy lungs of the prisoners who laid silently in the darkness of the corners. Stains of dried blood of the prisoners there before him covered the walls. Adnan tried to remember what happened that afternoon, but he had lost track of time, because his head was so heavy and full of blood from hanging upside down. He remembered the voice of the man they called the colonel asking him about his roommate Sadiq Yousif, who went to school one day and never came back. Adnan had noticed that Sadiq was missing, because the two had made arrangements to start the first lesson of getting to known Allah, as the faithful did. He had asked his other two roommates, who attended the same school as Sadiq, if they had seen him, and their answer was that they had not seen him in class that day. Two days later, Sadiq still had not returned to the apartment, and he was nowhere to be found. Adnan was worried about his friend, but he did not want go to the liberal arts school to ask about Sadiq, because he was scared of the three men with thick moustaches at the school's gate, and he knew that with what Sadiq had told him about the past it would be troublesome to keep asking about him. So he resolved himself to wait, and he focused on the final exam that arrived sooner than he expected. He did not know that Sadiq had been arrested just three days before he was. Sadiq was just fifty meters from Adnan in cell A, which meant that he would soon join the march of the many people who entered the place and vanished.

After Adnan's eyes adjusted to the darkness, and he saw that he was not alone. Two or three men slept in the far corner, and he wanted to get closer to them, because he was overwhelmed with absolute loneliness and fear. But he was afraid that they were dead. Another prisoner sat near the door just staring at it, and two other prisoners slept next to each other in the other corner. Remaining close to the wall, he tried to sleep, but the wounds and bruises on his back and legs burned and prevented him from sleeping. He leaned against the wall and saw a small round hole leading to the outside, where the world was: everything beyond these walls of torture and death and villainy. The outside—it was amazingly close, yet unforeseeably impossible to reach. From the tiny hole in the wall, he saw the moon and the clouds pass by in this cold summer. He stared at the silver glow of the moon, which looked so far away and so free. It shone down on a world that it did not know—it looked strangely peaceful. Observing his surroundings, he noticed the inescapable presence of death and oppression that pounded on the hearts and souls of all the prisoners who once passed through the dark smelly dungeon. He steered his mind to focus on the pleasant rays of the moon and wished that time would move faster and faster. He wished that the rugged men with thick moustaches and blood-red eyes, who had brought him to the famous fearsome buildings of Al-Amin, the secret political police, who were drinking and shouting just two rooms down from him, would have a late-night session of horror and decide his fate and finish his life with a bullet to the head or a rope around his thin neck. He wanted that to be the end of his journey, but he knew it would be a long time before he would have the privilege of dying. There was no possibility of sleeping, and it made no sense to talk to the other prisoners, who looked like they had slipped into a peaceful coma. Adnan just sat in the corner, where he was seeing the moon and dreamt of the river and Hamid. He wondered what Hamid was doing at that moment, and he wondered if he was sailing his boat on the Euphrates while the moon cast its light on the broken waves by the banks of the millions of palm trees. He wanted so desperately to lay on the front of the boat and touch the cold water of the Euphrates with his hand. He wanted so much to look at the water and see the many lights the moon cast on the Euphrates and to recite Bader Shaker Al-Sayyab's poem...

> *And the lights will dance,*
> *Like thousands of little moons on a river.*

Oh, Bader Shaker Al-Sayyab, the lost poet who loved two things: the river and women. Women, whom he never had enough time to love, nor did they have time to love him: women who smelled of sweet soaps and cheap perfumes that left millions of little ravines of unfulfilled desire streaming through his thirsty veins. Women whom he never touched and never would, women whom he never kissed nor would he ever kiss, women who hadn't yet filled his lungs with their smells as he walked the streets of the capital city looking for the forgotten corners, consuming the lives of many poets and many dreamers before him; the capital city peacefully asleep while he lay in the dark cell waiting for the unavoidable fate of the many before him: death, execution by hanging or a firing squad.

"But I am innocent," Adnan said to himself. "I have committed no crime and never joined any forbidden party."

It did not matter that he was innocent. He remembered the stories he'd heard; it did not matter, because he was already in the prison. It only mattered that people stay away from these tall walls of the secret police directorate, because once a man gets in, he will not leave alive or normal. He heard the stories of the nitric acid tanks, the snakes, and the endless torture.

"But I am innocent. Surely, they will find no evidence against me," he thought to himself as he tried to sleep.

It was four o'clock in the morning when a bulldog-looking guard woke up all the prisoners with the banging sound of a large empty tin can. He shouted,

"Get up, get up you brothers of whores, traitors. Get up, so you can eat your breakfast!"

Adnan woke up and thought, breakfast, this place was different than he thought it would be. The other prisoners woke up, and Adnan saw that the bodies that he thought might have been corpses were not. They were alive, but they looked and smelled like death. There were more prisoners in the cell with him than he thought; he counted about nine people in total.

One of the guards lined up the prisoners and marched them to the outside, where three guards wearing masks held what looked like rubber hoses. As soon as the prisoners reached a chalk line painted on the hard pavement, the three guards started a rampage of beating; they beat the prisoners with no distinction or discrimination. They struck them on their faces, their backs, their legs, and their heads. The beating lasted for what seemed to be a half hour, until the voices of the prisoners quieted down, and then there was no more screaming. Adnan fell to the ground after a blow to his head by the overweight guards who viciously attacked him and beat him with the rubber hose. He felt the first two blows, but he did not feel the rest, as he was unconscious within half a minute. With a weak body that could not withstand the steely strength of the rubber hose and cables, he fell to the ground and later was carried by another prisoner who had been in the cell for months. He woke up when he felt something like sand pushed down his throat.

"Here you go. You must eat."

Adnan opened his eyes and looked at the man who was trying to feed him. It was one of the prisoners, bruised from the morning session, yet he still had the energy to treat and feed the others.

"You must eat... don't think. You have to eat, so you don't die," the prisoner said as he pushed a piece of bread soaked in a stew tasting like pure salt into Adnan's mouth. "I don't know what will happen to you tonight, but if they put you in the room with snake, just throw your shirt on it, it will go to sleep."

The prisoner said this quietly, stood up, walked to the door, and called the guards:

"My darling, Abu Jassim, it's time to take out the waste."

"Wait," a voice came from the outside, and then the door opened. It was the same vicious, dog-like guard who had attacked Adnan that morning. He looked around and said, "Let this new son of a whore take it out."

"As you wish, Abu Jassim."

The prisoner, who seemed to have been in the cell for a long time, brought a bucket filled with human waste to Adnan and said, "You must take this to the outside latrine and do as the guard tells you."

Adnan stood up and wanted to protest, but he was too weak to do so and uncertain of how his day would end if he did not, so he carried the bucket and walked toward the door. The mean guard looked at him and said, "How does the bucket smell? Does it smell like your mother?"

Adnan did not reply. He walked outside and felt the sun's warmth on his bloodied face. It was noon or a little after. Adnan felt a glimmer of hope as he looked at the sun and thought of how it was different and less glorious than the sun in Balluria. But it was a world of difference from the dark, cold cell. He thought of how he had never appreciated the sun while he emptied the bucket of human waste in a hole in the middle of the yard.

"This is the Sheraton," the guard said, pointing to the hole.

"Its main residents are giant rats, and you will have the pleasure of spending some nights here too."

The mean guard laughed.

Adnan realized that behind the tall walls of the many buildings of this compound, there was a city, the capital, where people lived, ate, drank, and worked; the capital city where beautiful women and young girls who smelled of jasmine, walked through the streets freely while men walked behind, looking at them. Insanity was behind the walls of the many buildings that made up the fearsome directorate of the secret police, where people had entered and mysteriously vanished for decades. Their families would never hear from them, and they would never dare to ask about them. He knew that outside these high walls was the world where Nahla would be waiting for him next year, so they could walk to school together in the morning. Outside the walls there was Balluria, and his only goal was to concentrate on how to get back to that world. None of the books that he read or the talks that he had with Sadiq before he disappeared, or the advice given him by Sayed Habeeb, mattered. None of that gibberish mattered as he started to comprehend the intensity of the nonsense he was witnessing and living. He heard many times that it would be better to die than to enter the cells of the secret police. He thought, *but there must be logic, I mean the men who run the secret police, they must have families or loved ones. They must have mothers, wives, or children to go to at night, and that makes them humans, right?*

Was he delusional to think that he would be able to reason his way out of this hellish place that seemed invisible to the city, which existed normally, without feeling the rivers of pain that flowed underneath its foundation. He was delusional to think that he would be able to convince his captors that he had done nothing wrong. Maybe he talked badly, a little, about the divine leader, just a few words, but he meant no harm to the revolution and to the country. In fact, he would tell them that he would become a devoted member of the party and he would do whatever it took to prove his love and allegiance to the divine leader. If they let him go, he would be just like Kamal, maybe not like Kamal, but in his mind he would find a way to convince his captors to free him. He would tell them that he had made a mistake, that he met with some people whom he did not know had a past or a red circle around their names, wherever their names were written in all the official records, but he had done nothing. He never met with the forbidden party members, and he never joined the party, so he would be cleared. He would swear that when and if he left this compound of fear, he would never talk politics again. He would not study religion, and never again would he try to find his bond with Allah or ask "why" on his own terms, on his own time, and on his conditions, away from the capital. He wanted to go back to Balluria. He was ready to sell his God, his friends, his beliefs, his principles, and the memory of his dead brother to get out of this place. Because he could no longer breathe in the hellishly nauseating smell of blood, human waste, and burned flesh, he realized that he no longer needed to know the answers to all of the whys he had and all of the whys of the world, because places like the cell he was in existed... and that's why.

"Tonight, try not to sleep next to the door," the prisoner who seemed to have been in the cell for a long time said. He brought Adnan a small cup of water.

"Why?" Adnan said with a weak voice.

"Don't ask. Just try to hide yourself in one of the corners around eight o'clock at night," the prisoner who had not lost his mind or his sense of time told Adnan.

"What time is it now?" Adnan asked.

"It's almost eight," replied the prisoner who seemed to have attended to all the new prisoners in the cell.

"Can I ask you something with your permission?" Adnan asked, searching for familiarities in the others.

"There are two things you don't ask about in this place. Don't ask the names of prisoners or the reason they are here, because those two things don't matter anymore. No one cares to know your name, and there is no reason good enough to get you out of here. So don't ask," answered the prisoner who still had his wits and his sense of humor.

Adnan thought for second before he knew what he wanted to ask the man about.

"Do you know of the town called Balluria?"

"Is that the real name of a real town?" asked the prisoner who seemed to have regained his madness.

"Yes, it is, at least for me. That's where I am from, Balluria, and I wanted to say... just in case I die... if I die here, I want my body to be sent to Balluria."

"My dear little man... in here... in this place, we are all from Balluria, and we all wish that we will die soon, so we can go to this town of yours that sounds like a good place for crazy people like me and you," the crazy man said, and then he put his finger to his lips signaling Adnan to stop talking. The two heard the sound of heavy footsteps waking by the door.

"He is here. May Allah have mercy on the chosen one tonight."

The man who said this was very scared at that moment; suddenly the door was opened, and a tall man who wore an olive-green dark uniform entered the cell and looked around. Adnan recognized the man from the newspapers and posters. It was the cousin of the divine leader, the notorious cousin who massacred women and children in the north and killed people while he ate his dinner. It was him: the heavy and merciless arm of the tyrant that spared no one and had no mercy. The most feared man in the land stood in the doorway of that dark, smelly cell, and before Adnan could think of a reason that might have brought this beast of man to this place, the tall man pulled out his pistol and asked the guard standing next to him, "Who do you think it will be tonight?"

"Sir, that son of a whore over there—he thinks he is brave and strong."

He pointed to a young prisoner, beaten and bloodied, but still with amazingly bright, black eyes that sparked through the dimmed light of the cell.

"Is this the son of a whore?" the tall cousin of the divine leader asked.

"Yes, sir," the guard replied.

Four shots rang through the cell, and the young prisoner made a weak sound of "akkhhhhhh." He slumped over and bled from his abdomen and chest; he would be dead within minutes.

"Son of shit," the tall man said, and then left, followed by the guard.

Not knowing what to think or say, Adnan was frozen by the scene and wanted to see if the young prisoner, who twitched, was still alive. He went to the young prisoner, checked his pulse, and said, "He is still alive; we need to take get to the hospital."

"How do you know?" another prisoner asked.

"I am a medical student," Adnan replied.

None of the prisoners said or did anything; they just sat at their places and watched Adnan try to stop the young prisoner from bleeding to death.

"Can you call one of the guards?" Adnan asked the crazy prisoner, who did not seem to care about the tragedy that just happened.

"Leave him alone. He will die, and they will take him out in the morning," the crazy prisoner told Adnan, who could not comprehend the actions of the people with him in the cell, and he did not want to waste any time arguing, because he needed to use his energy to save the young prisoner's life, but he stood up anyway and screamed, "What's wrong with all of you? Are you all crazy? The man is dying; they shot him, just like they shot my brother!" He screamed and shouted, and tears streamed down his cheeks. Not wanting the prisoner to die like Qahtan, Adnan walked to the door and banged on the heavy metal door with his fists and was shouting, "You... please, you... guards, please open the door! This poor man is bleeding, and he needs help! Please, help us... please, help me... may Allah protect you... please, open the door, brother, please!" Adnan backed away when he heard the sound of footsteps and the screeching sound of the door opening.

"What is all the noise, you son of a whore! I am trying to watch a soccer game," said the tall, dark guard, who Adnan had never seen before.

"The man, the man is dying, please, brother!" Adnan cried.

"And what if he is... you son of shit; are you new here? Bring this son of a whore outside," the dark guard said to the two guards behind him, who charged Adnan and hauled him out of the cell as they beat him on his face, chest, and back. "You will honor us at the Sheraton," the tall, dark guard told Adnan.

The other two guards dragged Adnan, who could not walk, down to the hole in the middle of the yard. They threw him in and closed the metal cover of the hole they called the "Sheraton" and walked away. After the two guards threw him into the hole filled with human waste and garbage, he started to feel the pain in his head and his back from the beating. For hours Adnan tried to stay awake, but could not keep his eyes open. The dried blood sealed his eyelids; he leaned against the wall and passed out.

Adnan dreamt of his brother, Qahtan. In his dream, Adnan was walking down a beautiful pathway filled with palms and other trees. The smell of jasmine filled the air. On his walk, Adnan saw his brother, Qahtan, sitting by himself and staring off into the horizon. For some reason his brother looked sad. He did know why his brother was sad, but Adnan was happy to see his older brother. Qahtan did not look like he did the night the seven mean men dragged him to his death. He looked clean, and although many years had passed, he still looked as young as Adnan remembered him. Adnan walked over to his brother and stood next to him. His brother lifted his head up and looked at Adnan and said, "Why do you miss me? Is it because I am dead?"

"I miss being with you and miss being your little brother."

"You are not little anymore, Adnan. You are a man now. Don't let anyone make you feel or tell you otherwise. You are a man, and you must act like a man," Qahtan said to his little brother and placed his hand on Adnan's worried head and continued, "I have something to tell you, Adnan. The hearts of your mother and sisters are melting for you. Your father is crying silently; no one can hear him, and he has no tears left. They are the ones you need to miss and yearn for, because they are alive, and they need you, not me. Also, the same men who killed me will kill you too, but never let your murderers have satisfaction."

"What do you mean, Qahtan?"

"Don't let them kill your dreams and your faith; they killed me for mine, and they will kill you for yours. Our family is crying over our blood, because of what we believed in."

And just as he had appeared, Qahtan disappeared from the dream. Adnan called for his brother to come back. He wanted Qahtan to stay with him, but Qahtan walked away without turning back. Adnan wanted to run after him, but it felt like his feet were chained with invisible shackles that dug into his ankles and toes and prevented him from moving. Adnan woke up and found a giant black rat chewing on his bloodied toes. Adnan did not move. He watched as the black rat licked the dried blood from appendages. The rat looked him in the eyes and then ran away; it was as though it realized the audacity of its actions. Adnan smiled at the rat's behavior. The cover of the hole was opened, and a stocky-looking guard shouted, "Goom yellah. Hurry, get up, you son of dog. Your stay at the Sheraton is over."

When Adnan entered the cell, breakfast time had passed, and his cell mates were treating each other from the breakfast beating session. He walked to the spot where he had been sitting and sleeping from the time he had first arrived to the cell and crashed on the floor. The crazy man, who knew what a man would experience in the Sheraton, crawled to him and said, "I just want to let you know that the young prisoner is dead."

Adnan did not reply.

"You know he would have died anyway, and there was nothing we could have done."

Adnan still had no reply.

"You know that the man who shot him is the president's cousin. He comes here every Wednesday night and shoots one of the prisoners from cell A or cell B," added the mad prisoner, who seemed saner than the rest.

Adnan remained silent.

"Every Wednesday he comes in to kill a random prisoner, just before he goes to have a party with alcohol and many female Gypsy dancers."

Adnan did not say a word.

"Last week he shot a young man in cell A. I had to carry the body the morning after out to the yard. The dead prisoner was very young and so handsome; I think his name was Sadiq. That's what the guards told me."

"You know that I have been here for four months, and he has never chosen to shoot me. I wish that he would choose me the next time."

Adnan did not say a word.

"You know why I want him to shoot me? Because of what you did last night, I think he will shoot you next week. So I pray that he will choose me instead of you, because I am so tired of carrying out the dead men every Thursday morning... I am so tired of it."

The crazy prisoner crawled back to his corner. Adnan thought of his friend Sadiq lying on the cold, cell floor bleeding to death for an entire night. He would not cry. He knew that his day was soon to arrive, and he would be dead. He knew that if they killed Sadiq, then they would kill him too, and that thought comforted him. Later that day, Adnan was escorted to meet the colonel, who appeared to be in a bad mood. Before he left the cell, the mad prisoner said, "Just remember, if you see the snake, just throw your shirt on it, and it will go to sleep." Not understanding the crazy prisoner's remark, Adnan walked behind the guard, who escorted him to the colonel's office. The colonel wore a two-piece, gray safari suit, the known uniform of the secret police. As Adnan entered, the colonel asked him if he wanted some tea.

"Yes, I do," Adnan replied, determined to face his death like a man just like his brother Qahtan had told him to do in his dream.

The colonel ordered a young thin guard to bring a glass of tea for Adnan, who reached for the glass and remembered the many times he and the Wolves drank tea in Barrya's mud hut and the many times Sayed Habeeb prepared tea in the mosque on warm nights.

"Before you drink the tea, I need some answers from you," the colonel said while combing his thick moustache.

"What answers?"

"You know what answers. Did you meet a man named Abu Karrar? Where is he now?"

The colonel's eyes were bloody and had the look of death in them.

"My answers are the same; I met him once, and I don't know where he is. I am telling you the truth."

"The truth, ha!" the colonel exclaimed and the redness in his eyes darkened.

"You will tire us and tire yourself," the colonel added. "I told you that we have a cure for people like you, people who think they are smarter than us. Take him to meet Salima," the colonel concluded.

Adnan thought that Salima was a female torturer and felt that she might be a little easier on his bones. The guards snatched him from the chair and pushed him to a room at the end of the courtyard. After throwing him in, they locked the door. Adnan stood up in the dimly lit room and tried to prepare his mind, body, and soul for the torture he was about to endure. After waiting for several minutes, he saw the door open, and the guard emptied a bucket in the room. Adnan saw what looked like a rope that moved... a tan-and-black spotted rope that moved like a snake... it was a tan-and-black spotted snake that moved around in the small room. Only he and the snake existed in this very small space. Appearing calm and lazy, the snake moved closer to Adnan, who froze in his place, fearing that the snake would sense any movement. Then he noticed that the snake looked at him and moved its fearsome head back and forth; it moved closer and closer. Adnan remembered that in Balluria many men were not afraid of snakes. Hamid had caught many of them, and he remembered that he wanted to take him and Salam to search for the biggest snake in the world that lived in the marshes. In fact, some people used to say that Sayed Habeeb was immune to snake venom, and he had a snake friend that swam with him in the river. Some people suggested that Irar, the man who raised Sheikh Jawad, was a son of snake, and some men claimed to have eaten snake as they starved in the desert while smuggling sheep. But this snake seemed different; it was as though it knew that he was a prisoner, as though it knew that his life didn't matter, and he sensed that it had ended the lives of many other prisoners. The snake was getting closer and closer; it knew what to do and how to inject chilling fear into its victims. At that moment, Adnan remembered two faces, his mother's, with her eternal sadness, because of the loss of her eldest son, and the

384

crazy prisoner's, as he said, "Just throw your shirt on the snake, and it will go to sleep."

Adnan slowly and quietly removed his shirt and waited. The snake moved closer, and when it was about half a meter away from him, he threw his shirt on it. It moved just a little bit farther. Then it quieted down and stopped moving. Adnan stood there watching the slithery creature all night, hoping that it would sleep and not wake up. He spent the whole night watching that little creature and thought about the logic of the situation. A small room, a snake, and a bloody white shirt; he thought of asking why, but he knew there was no because that would justify what he was experiencing. Considering taking the shirt off the snake to watch it sleep, he wanted to see if snakes dreamt and if they did, he wanted to see if maybe they smiled during their dreaming. He also wondered if it was a real snake or if it was just a battery operated rubber snake. He was sure that these men who tortured others for a living could have some sense of humor and play games with their captives.

He thought that if the snake was not real and if he was the only prisoner who knew the secret of snakes and their dreams, that maybe he could convince the colonel with the thick moustache, who smelled of alcohol all the time, that he had an exceptional mind, a genius mind, and maybe the colonel would think twice about letting him go. He could go back outside to the big city, where the women smelled of jasmine and coated their eyes with thick, black eyeliner. Maybe he would go back to Balluria, where he could drink all the tea in the world and sit with Sayed Habeeb listening to the tragic history of the holy family of the prophet. Perhaps he would be leaving this massive madness behind him soon. He smiled and almost laughed as he looked at the bloody, white shirt that began to move. Or perhaps he was starting to lose his beautiful mind.

The door swung open, and a stocky guard looked at Adnan and said, "You're still alive, ha?" The guard laughed and ordered Adnan, "Come with me."

Adnan did not move; he did not understand what the guard, who spoke in a dialect Adnan did not comprehend, was saying.

"You shit your pants, ha," the guard said with a joyful smile. "The colonel wants to see you."

Adnan was still looking at the snake; it still had not moved since the night before. The snake was asleep and dreaming, Adnan thought. He had stared at it for nine hours without realizing the time.

"Move, you son of a whore!" the guard shouted.

"Don't wake the snake," Adnan said.

"Snake, oh, is it here? Shallan, come and get the snake," the guard called to another guard.

Adnan stood there and watched the short guard scoop the snake up with a shovel. He put it in the same bucket it was brought in the night before. The stocky guard then entered the room and said, "You are losing your mind, ha... you're going crazy... just like the others... the colonel wants you, so don't make me beat you. Come with me."

The guard grabbed Adnan's arm and pulled him toward the colonel's office. Adnan entered the office and stood there, not realizing the insult he was committing toward the man who wore civilian clothes, massaged his thick moustache, and smelled of alcohol all the time. The colonel looked at him and said, "How was Salima?"

Adnan looked at the colonel, trying to comprehend what he was saying.

"That was nothing. It was just one night. You will see her again and again," the colonel said. "Sit down. I think you are just beginning to understand the extent of what we can do to you. You know we can kill you fast and butcher your family one by one. Or, we can force you to watch the rape of your mother and watch us put lit cigarettes into your sister's vagina. Then we can put your sister on your chest and rape her. We can also rape your father and all of your cousins. But first we need you to tell us what we need to know, and you will do that, because right now your body, your mind, and your soul are in my hands," the colonel said as he squeezed his fist.

"I can do whatever I please with you," the colonel continued. "I can shoot you. I can hang you, or I can just keep beating you and pull out your teeth and nails one by one. I've realized that you are smart, and because of that I will treat you with the method we have designed for smart people like you, so we don't waste our time." Then he asked, "Do you want some chai? Would you like to drink some tea?"

Adnan looked at the colonel, whose voice and smell were becoming more and more familiar. The colonel had the same stench of alcohol he smelled on his middle school math teacher, Mr. Mohamed Tabra, when he was getting the punishment that no other student ever received: sixty whacks from a hardened eucalyptus stick, because he was smart, in a society and time not meant for smart kids like him.

The colonel kept talking and saying things like, "I can order the guards to shoot you in your legs, and they will do it. If I tell them to shoot you, you will be crippled just like your father. See, we know everything; we've received the report from the party headquarters, which was sent by Comrade Kamal, telling us that your father is a cripple and that your brother Qahtan was a traitor, just like you. A communist traitor, unlike you. You believe in Allah, who will not save you from me."

The colonel glared at Adnan with a fearsome bloody look in his eyes. Adnan was listening to the colonel's voice; it seemed he recognized his voice from a distant memory. The colonel's voice scared him; sounding familiar, it brought back the childish fears that he had lived with ever since the night he saw the seven mean men, who looked like this mean colonel. He wore civilian clothes but was not civil in any way. The colonel was as calm as death itself was inevitable, as true as the pain of torture was, and as clear as the insanity of the idea of putting a man and a snake in a small room together for an entire night.

Adnan listened to the colonel, who kept telling him how he was going to torture and kill his entire family. He remembered his family and felt a lost ray of sun on his face and in his heart that appeared from the invisible window in the portal-less room that made its way to his lifeless senses and injected energy back into them. His poor, weak family never had had three meals on any given day, and the meals they did have consisted of mainly bread and tomato stew for dinner and bread and tea for breakfast. He remembered that his brother Qahtan was always smiling and joking about the breakfast, which he called "the warm your stomach" breakfast.

"It's plenty," Qahtan would say. "Some people don't have food or water for days. Warm your stomach is enough for me and you; it's enough until we can create a better tomorrow and a better world for all the poor starving people in the world."

Oh, Qahtan, Qahtan, the strong, beautiful and able; Qahtan who was shouting,

"Don't hurt my brother, you bastards. You will never enslave me, you bastards. You do not scare me, you bastards!" He shouted all this as he was dragged to his death by the seven mean men who looked and sounded just like the colonel, who wore civilian clothes and smelled of alcohol all the time. They all looked the same; they all wanted to enslave him, just like they wanted to enslave his brother before him. They wanted to enslave Sadiq, Sayed Habeeb, and the mad prisoner, who had gone crazy because he had been forced to carry all the dead bodies of the young,- beautiful men who refused to be enslaved and had dared to dream. That small sting of the sun's rays cleared the cold shell of fear from his heart, and he said with a clear voice, "You do not scare me."

"Shino, what?" the colonel, whose face exploded with anger, asked.

"Even though you've killed my brother, you do not scare me. Even though you've killed Sadiq, you do not scare me. You are a slave to a beast of a ruler. I hate your smell. Your stench disgusts me."

"What did you say, you son of a whore?" the colonel said and spit on Adnan.

Adnan looked at him and said with same clear and calm voice, "You are ugly, and you will always be ugly. Your life is worthless, because you will always be a slave to the tyrant, who will never recognize you as his equal. You are as ugly, stinky, and worthless as an old shoe. The dirt on my mother's feet is more honorable than you or your family that you feed by spilling the blood of the innocent people you torture and kill," Adnan said, and then spit in the colonel's face and looked the colonel directly in his eyes.

The colonel, who was shocked by what the thin, bloodied man said, reached to his side and grabbed a rubber hose and beat Adnan mercilessly.

Then the colonel screamed for his aides. "Take this son of a whore and put him in the sack!"

Seven guards appeared from all corners and started beating Adnan with their hands and feet and dragged him the same way the seven mean men had dragged his older brother, years ago. The guards took the near-dead, thin young man to a room next to the colonel's office and shoved his small body into a sack that smelled of animal feces. He did not know what the seven guards were going to do to him. He thought they would tie the sack and throw him in the river, just as Kamal did with Hanan's kittens many years ago.

He was confused when he heard one guard order another, "Sa'ad, bring the cats."

Adnan sensed that there were about three cats, three large cats, which were put into the sack with him. Trying to protect his face from the sharp claws of this new enemy, he rolled around the room in the sack, screaming and yelling. This made the cats crazier and more vicious. The laughter of the guards echoed between the walls of the room. Adnan was in the sack with these three, mad cats that had been used many times to torture prisoners. He tried to cover his face and started to lose consciousness. Having lost his breath from trying to push the cats away from his face and neck, he kicked and screamed and cried; he quieted down as he lost his sense of reality and wailed like a baby. He was happier where he was at that moment, because suddenly it seemed like things were going to be all right. His mind started to slip into a spiral of black and white oblivion, and he still felt the burning sensation of the cats' claws on his face and his chest, but this was not hurting him anymore. He started to laugh as he realized how easy it was to die and how easy to just lie there and do nothing. He no longer heard the voices of the guards, and he could not remember why he had been brought there in the first place. Moreover, he stopped feeling the heat of the sack and the cold sweat on his back, which was mixed with blood. He felt and tasted water; the taste was similar to that of the Euphrates' water. He no longer felt hungry, and he did not smell anything, not even the distinctive smell of the cat feces filling the sack. It was as though he had experienced the much-needed shutting down of his senses, for the first time since he been brought to the multi-housed compound, where people had entered and vanished. He felt free, free of his fears and his needs; altogether, he felt that his mind and his soul had become spotless.

Adnan woke up in the cell; he looked around, but he saw no one that he recognized. There were many faces he did not recognize, faces of people he'd never seen before, faces that moved slowly toward him. They appeared to be swimming through thin gray air; they were coming closer and closer to him and started. Their voices, unrecognizable to him, sounded similar to the noise the mad cats made in the sack. He heard them saying something, but it was totally gibberish to him. He could not comprehend it.

"Oh, you poor kid; look what they have done to you," the crazy prisoner said, knowing what had happened to Adnan.

"Look what they have done to you," he repeated and seemed to have suddenly regained his sanity.

Adnan stayed in the same spot, where he laid, for three days and three nights, without moving, eating, drinking water, or even going to use the bucket serving as the latrine. He simply did not need to do any of that. He lost his sense of time and his sense of living. Looking like a bloodied statue, the only thing he wanted to do was to sit in that dark, cold corner.

One of the guards called his name three times, and Adnan did not respond. The guard entered the cell shouting, "Don't you hear me calling you, you son of a whore!"

The guard kicked Adnan in his face. Adnan, who only seemed to notice the guard then, gave the guard a questioning look. Seeing only a faded image, he did not know what the image said to him. He only heard a loud noise when the guard said, "The colonel wants to see you. Come with me! You filthy son of dog. You have been sitting in your own urine for days."

Adnan did not move; it took two guards to lift and carry him to the colonel's office. Adnan looked at the colonel and saw a new face, one he'd never seen before, but it was the same colonel who wore civilian clothes and smelled of alcohol. He looked at Adnan and smiled as he said, "You did not believe me when I told you we have a cure for people like you. It appears that you have been cured. Take him away," the colonel ordered.

The Book of Balluria

The Many Journeys of the Weak Angel

The Last Journey

1

The gray car that quickly passed through Balluria dumped Adnan near the main road of town, leaving him in a mist of dust. The two officers took off very fast after they threw his clothes out next to him. His clothes were wrapped in a cloth bag stained with blood and human and animal feces. For hours, Adnan sat there; he had no sense or memory left in him of this place. He sat there all day until nightfall. When he felt tired, he lay down, and hours later he was asleep in the middle of the road. Khanger, the coffee server, who could barely walk at that time, found the thin kid with glasses, who was once the smartest young man in those parts. Finding him sleeping in the middle of road, Khanger thought that the man was dead, so he kicked him with his foot. Adnan woke up, and Khanger asked him, "Son, are you well?"

Adnan did not answer.

"Who is your family? Where is your family's home, so I can take you there?"

Khanger asked Adnan, but he still did not answer. He stared at the old man, talking to him, and thought it was one of the officers who came to torture him. He curled himself up in fear of being beaten by the rubber hose and started to cry.

Khanger quickly realized the state of mind the young man was in and he said, "In the name of Allah; we come from Allah and to Allah we return." Instead of taking Adnan to Sheikh Jawad's guesthouse, Khanger knew that it would be better to take the young man, who looked like he hadn't eaten a meal in months, to the mosque. When Sayed Habeeb saw the young man being aided by Khanger, he realized that he had failed to save the man's mind and body from the wrath of the secret police dungeons. The clergyman had also failed to save his soul, because without a mind, the soul just becomes a worthless corpse. He received the sick young man in his mosque, and he thanked Khanger for bringing the young man to him.

After Khanger left, Sayed Habeeb sat Adnan down and tried to help him to remember who he was. Adnan seemed to have gone to a place where names and faces were taken up into an evaporating state of matter and ever fading shapes that kept moving like an endless spiral in his brain. Sayed Habeeb knew that what Adnan had seen and endured in the dark dungeons of the secret police had destroyed Adnan's most precious asset, the only thing he had going for him in this world. They had destroyed his mind, his genius mind.

"Oh, my Allah. They knew exactly what to do with you," Sayed Habeeb said as he realized that the smart, thin, young man had lost both his exceptional mind and his innocent memories.

Barrya knew of Adnan's mysterious arrival back in Balluria. She brought with her a fresh jar of yogurt and fed it to the young man, who did not remember her. Sitting a vigil next to him, she washed his face with a wet, dirty cloth and cried for long hours. She asked Amel and the Hillaly girls to visit him; Adnan did not remember any of them.

He preferred to spend his days walking through the streets, and when his mother, who wept constantly, tried to keep him in the house by tying him to a wooden pole in the middle of the courtyard in the shaded area near the kitchen, he cried and shouted the names of his dead brother, Qahtan, and his departed friends. He tried to bite through the rope to free himself. All he wanted was to walk all the time. So, after two days of constant crying and shouting for the long departed, his mother decided to let him loose. After he was freed, he walked all day. He would walk for hours, talking to himself and shouting out animal-like sounds.

The entire town knew of the state of mind of the young man who was once going to be the first doctor that came out of Balluria, but instead he became the town's madman. Barrya always carried a jar full of fresh, cold yogurt and looked for the young madman as he slept under the leaves of the palm trees. He walked through the orchards in search of the ghosts of his brother, Qahtan, and his friends Ahmed and Hanan. He did not believe his friends when they told him about the tragic death of the daughter of the sheikh and her gentle brother.

He said to Amel, Hamid's sister, who tried to convince him that Ahmed and Hanan were dead, "I see them every day by the river where Kamal drowned the kittens."

Although Kamal believed that Adnan was crazy, he kept sending party militiamen to watch the young man. He would send them on a surveillance mission to watch Adnan to make sure that he was not just pretending to be crazy. And when he heard what Adnan was saying he mumbled, "He'd better be crazy, so we can write that in a report to the capital city about him." In spite of Kamal's belief that Adnan was truly crazy, he would always say, "I think he is faking his insanity to escape punishment."

Kamal leaned back in his chair, in the newly painted yellow and gray party headquarters building. He spent all of his time at the headquarters chasing any leads that suggested that Hamid was still alive and leading a group of bandits that roamed the shores of the marshlands and the prairies. Hamid was wanted by all of the local governments of the marshlands and the party militia, yet they did not know whether he was dead or alive.

Barrya told Amel, Hamid's sister, that she should tell Hamid about Adnan. So one night, when Hamid came home, as he did from time to time, secretly in the middle of the night accompanied by one or two of his bandits, who stood guard by the door with their rifles charged, Amel told her brother about his friend. Hamid did not believe Amel when she told him that Adnan had gone crazy and that he roamed the streets of Balluria chased by children who threw rocks and garbage at him.

"Are you sure it is Adnan?" Hamid asked his sister.

"Yes. If you doubt me, ask Barrya."

"Well, if Barrya believes it's Adnan, then it is Adnan," Hamid said after a long period of thoughtful silence.

"It is all because of that bastard Kamal!" Hamid said, as he put his Kalashnikov on his shoulder and mounted his horse together with his two trusted bandits. They took off and disappeared into the darkness of the orchards.

2

Many of his old friends tried to shelter and feed him. Abdullah and Basima tried to convince the crazy young man to come to their house for lunch and made it a habit to leave a plate full of food and a cup of water by the door, just in case he passed by their home and he was hungry or thirsty. Basima also asked Bushra and Adawya, the two Hillaly girls, if they could do the same. They left him food and drink in front of their home; once when they saw Adnan being chased by a group of vicious young children who threw small rocks at him, the two Hillaly girls, who had just returned from the town's market carrying a small watermelon, shouted at the children and chased them away. They wiped the sweat and blood from Adnan's face, and Adnan snatched the small watermelon and ran away disappearing into the palm trees. Adnan had officially become the towns' madman.

Sheikh Jawad walked home from his meeting with the mayor and was intercepted by Adnan, who stood in the middle of the towns' main street and shouted, "I do not fear you, and you are worthless!"

Sheikh Jawad, who was grieving the loss of his son Ahmed and his daughter Hanan, smiled briefly and prevented his armed men from killing Adnan.

"Leave him alone," Sheikh Jawad said. "And tell everyone in town that this crazy kid is under my protection."

That was the only and the last act of kindness that Sheikh Jawad performed before he went into obscurity; he did not leave his home again after that day.

Kamal stopped sending his party militiamen to watch Adnan. Even Fathil the Liar, who showed up in town one day after claiming that he had been on a secret mission in China, said to Adnan, "See, I told you that you were like a donkey who wore glasses. But, please don't tell Sheikh Jawad that I said that."

His former Wolves' teammates made it their duty to make sure that Adnan was fed and cared for. With the help of Sayed Habeeb and Barrya, they would take Adnan every Friday with them to the prayers. After the prayers they would bathe him in the river and comb his hair. Barrya would bring clothes from Abdullah and Basima's house to clothe the crazy young man. Hisham, who was in a wheelchair, after losing both of his legs when a landmine exploded, killing half of the young men in his platoon, during the last days of the war on the eastern front, sat with Adnan and talked to him, trying to push back some of the memories that had permanently escaped from Adnan's mind.

"Hanan is dead, Kamal killed her," Hisham would say. "You remember Hanan, the daughter of Sheikh Jawad; she was the most beautiful girl in these parts. And Ahmed is dead too. Hamid, your best friend, no one knows if he is dead or alive. Many people say that he is dead, because Ahmed said that he killed him, but others say that they have seen Hamid riding a black horse in the desert. As you can see, I can't play soccer anymore."

As much as Hisham, Haleem, Saleh, and Ashraf tried to bring their weak friend back to reality, he seemed to have reached a place of no return.

"It is all because of Kamal, that son of a... one day, one day I will know how to repay him," Haleem would always say as he and the other Wolves bathed their weak friend in the Euphrates. Touching the river's waters seemed to help Adnan temporarily regain some of his sanity.

Sayed Habeeb did not mind keeping the young madman in the mosque. After all, he felt it was he who sent him down that dangerous road. It was the clergyman who wanted to help the smart young man to be able to dream. On many occasions when Adnan seemed to have regained some of his sanity, he would say, "Shukran Sayedna, thank you our clergyman."

One time, Adnan looked at the clergyman with the same look he had years ago when he asked him. "Where was God when they killed my brother?" He looked at the clergyman and told him that he was close to seeing Allah and that he was very close to understanding why Allah was doing what he was doing.

Adnan said to Sayed Habeeb, "It's all right, Sayed Habeeb, I've accepted what has happened to me. It was what Allah wanted, not what I wanted, but I know why. I know now why Allah allowed the death of my brother, Qahtan, and made me the town's crazy man. I understand it and I accept it." Adnan said the words with complete sanity and in a very clear voice. The clergyman looked at him, and Adnan smiled and said, "I forgive you, Sayed Habeeb. I know you tried to show me the way. I am telling you that I am feeling the bond with the almighty; I feel him in my blood, calling me. I forgive all the people who were in my life. I even forgive my torturers. I forgive all of my friends who left and all of those who died. I forgive all who will be born. I forgive the reason the world was created, and soon I will be going to where I belong."

Adnan turned and walked away from the clergyman, who realized that Adnan had reached a point of clear sanity that was far beyond madness. He had crossed the boundaries of humans and their earthly logic of why. Adnan spent most of his years on earth asking why, and finally, he had found his why. He disappeared for two days; no one had seen him or knew where he had gone to. Barrya looked for him in all the places she thought he might have gone. Abdullah and Sayed Habeeb looked for him in the orchards, behind the mosque, and by the river. Amel went to the Hillaly girls' house, but they had not seen the young crazy man since he'd stolen the watermelon from them when they had come back from the market. Haleem and Ashraf looked for him by the train station and by the other bank of the river, and along with Hisham, the three searched the entire town, house by house, checking the mud huts on the banks of the Euphrates and asking everyone they passed, "Have you seen a thin young man wearing thick glasses who acts like he is crazy, but he really is not?"

Haleem started to wonder, "Maybe Kamal, that son of a whore, killed him and threw his body in the river."

The four friends walked all the way to the village of Tawsheeha, searching all the palm tree orchards and all the small rivers. They searched for the crazy young man, but no one thought to look for him by the seven palm trees, where Adnan spent two days and two nights crying over the faded unidentified graves of his brother, Qahtan, and Hanan and all the thieves and beloved children who were buried there in a hurry, during the many rainy or dusty nights in these parts. That night Adnan walked all the way from the seven palm trees to the river. When he saw the Euphrates, he remembered the time when he, Hamid, and Salam had sailed the boat they named the *Titantic*, which Hamid found floating on the river. Kneeling, Adnan touched the cool water of the Euphrates and washed his face after two days of constant crying. Suddenly, he remembered the poem of Bader Shaker Al-Sayyab asking the Euphrates...

> *A Forest of tears*
> *You are*
> *Or, just a river?*

Adnan screamed, "Qahtan! Ahmed! Hamid! Hanan! Salam!"

His voice did not echo, and his shouts were swallowed by the stream of the Euphrates as it ran forever toward the gates of heaven in the marshes. He wanted to hear the voices that he loved, the voices of those who loved him, but he heard one voice, a voice he had never heard before coming out of the thousands of lights that danced like moons on the Euphrates. It was the voice of the dead poet, who lived his entire life yearning for two things: the true love of a beautiful woman and the day when he could return to the Euphrates. He heard the poet saying:

The Bells of death in my veins,
Shakes the ringing,
And tears go down,
Like thousands of rivers,
As I sail my final journey

It was almost dawn. A light rain fell and washed the tops of the palm trees, painting them a glorious sparkling green, the same color Adnan wanted to paint them years before when he dared to dream of the possible beauty he could add to the orchards, while lying on the wet and tiny grass with his hand dangling in the cold water of the Euphrates. At that moment, Barrya woke up frightened; she was visited by her departed Gypsy ancestors. She awoke from her sleep, because she knew it was time; it was the day that the Gypsy witches of her ancestors had told her about many dreams ago, the day of the departure of the weak angel, who had never kissed a woman. She put on her only dress and started walking toward the river. She made her way toward the mosque to wake Sayed Habeeb; she wanted him to witness the departure of Adnan. She found the clergyman boiling his coffee on an open fire outside the mosque. He spent his entire night wondering about the two angels who had not visited him in his dreams for a while. He looked at her and saw the sadness and the tears; he knew it has something about one of the kids.

"Who is it today?" the clergyman asked, trying to sound calm.

"It's Adnan, my weakest wolf," the Gypsy woman said with strange and complete submission and acceptance to the inevitable near fate of Adnan.

3

The sun had not fully come out yet. Adnan, who spent the night screaming and calling for his friends, looked out at the horizon and realized how beautiful that morning was. It was glorious, like all the mornings in Balluria and in these parts. He gathered what was left of his sanity and started reciting the poem of Badr Shaker Al-Sayyab:

The sun is prettier in my country
Prettier than in other countries,
Even the darkness is prettier,
Because it hugs Iraq.

Adnan saw a boat floating on the river and thought that Hamid had sent him one of the many boats that he always found. The boat sailed calmly toward Adnan, who waited by the river bank The shy, first light of morning broke the deep sleep of the town, and the sun started washing the face of the river with its golden rays. He touched the sides of the boat and felt the coldness of the water on the black tar. He moved his hand, touching the sides of the boat, as though he was touching the neck of a beautiful Arabian horse. "It is time, my friend."

He untied the ropes that were tied to the boat and looked at the other boats, which were all tied together by many ropes, on the bank waiting for the poor fishermen of Balluria to start another disappointing day in the relentless pursuit of their daily meal. He felt that all the boats were tied with shackles, similar to those he wore in the dark dungeons. He felt that the boats wanted to be freed after years and years of witnessing the agony of living in these parts. After years of silently witnessing the struggles of the poor, as they sailed the small boats looking for fresh fish to feed the many hungry, young mouths and the frail bodies of the women, who made magical fish stews that tasted like the Euphrates itself, Adnan sensed that all the boats had always dreamt of being elsewhere, where they no longer had to be a part of this endless cycle of misery. In his innocent, incapable mind, Adnan heard all the boats asking him to free them, so they could go with him to the marshes, where the gates of heaven were and into the beginning of endless oceans. Adnan felt that the boats had contributed enough to the ungodly tragedy of life in these parts and that they deserved to be freed, so he freed them. He untied all the town's boats and pushed them into the middle of the river, as the sun started to rise with its golden rays ushering the start of a new day.

4

The town woke up that morning to the noise that came from the river. Many of the young children told their stories, as they breathed heavily.

"The crazy man stole all the boats," a sweaty kid said.

Three men ran toward the river and several others followed. The police lieutenant sent three of his men in a truck to see why all the townspeople were walking toward the river. Many storekeepers left their shops unmanned and walked to river to see why the crazy man of the town, who was once a very shy and very intelligent young kid, stole all the boats.

Hamid and his band of bandits had spent that night close to Balluria, because he wanted to visit his mother and his sister. He noticed the crowd gathering in the same spot that he, Salam, and Adnan used to fish and swim in all summer long. He watched from a distance and saw the strangest thing he'd ever seen: an armada of small boats, flanking a single craft with one man in it. It seemed that all the boats were following the man in the small boat without any guidance toward the southern end of the Euphrates. He looked at the man in the small boat and realized who he was and mumbled, "Adnan... Oh, Adnan."

The rain did not stop. All of the people screamed and shouted, begging him to return their boats, but Adnan was unable to hear them over the roar of the rain and the flow of the river. He sat in the boat, flanked by all the other boats that ever sailed the Euphrates, that were forever drenched with the sweat of the struggles of the poor as they tried to feed their hungry families with what the Euphrates was willing to give. All the boats that had witnessed the blood that oozed from the shiny gills of the silver fish, as they jumped around on the wide wooden boards of the boats nearing their death and the imposed circle of unbearable life that Adnan and many others in these parts had to endure the divine decision to make them a part of it. Adnan did not steer the boats or stroke with the oars; he just looked forward, with both of his hands submerged in the cold water of the Euphrates. He then looked to the sky and shouted animal-like shouts. He again looked forward, directed by his vivid senses and the remarkable clarity of his madness, as he aimed for the gates of heaven and death. He knew he would find the gates of death at the beginning of the marshes and heaven would be there to greet him. So would all of his friends, who chose the Euphrates to be their final passage to freedom. Adnan knew that soon he would be in the painless heavens of Allah. He raised his hands toward the sky and shouted with his weak angelic voice, reciting the poetry of Bader Shaker Al-Sayyab.

Floored on your doorsteps,
Oh lord
Waiting for your majestic touch
As I long yearned for your Glorious presence.

The boats calmly sailed toward the south end of the Euphrates to where the marshes began and to where, long ago, the Gypsy woman had told a story to the many infatuated wide-eyed young kids, mesmerized by her words. She told them that the invisible mysterious gates of heaven and death were where the Euphrates ended and the marshes began. The group of infatuated children, who had just finished playing soccer, would sit around the Gypsy woman they called Mother Barrya, in the late afternoon, as the sun of the Arabian Sahara dusked these parts, listening to this inhumanly beautiful Gypsy woman, who knew all the secrets of the world, tell the story of the beast, while they drank cold, fresh yogurt and tea.

"Kan Yama Kan, many years ago, in these parts we call our homeland," the Gypsy woman began. "Once upon a time, in the land of everlasting sunshine, lived a beast. The beast was created in hell and came down to earth to feed on the souls and the hearts of the innocent and the poor. The beast was hungry all the time, and no matter how many lives and souls he devoured, he was never satisfied. He, the beast, was never satisfied with the many lives he destroyed; never satisfied with all the tears shed by the mothers, as he stole the lives out of their children's bodies; never satisfied with the pain he caused the fathers, as they searched for their missing sons who disappeared in the middle of the night. The beast created death machines that fed on the bodies of the young men and women. He hated dreams and hated all of those who dared to dream. He, the beast, knew that if people started to dream, it could mean his end. So, he made sure that no one dared to dream by seeking the help of other beasts from other lands, beasts that spoke different languages and had different-colored eyes and hair, beasts who gave him the advice to feast on the youth, because they were the ones who would forever dream."

The children were frightened, but the beautiful Gypsy woman continued, "And for a long time the beast feasted on the youth. He devoured their minds, bodies and their big, beautiful, black eyes. The pain was unbearable. No one on this earth could live with such pain, especially the people in these parts, because their pain was everlasting. So they chose death. They chose to leave. People left the kingdom in their boats in order to flee the madness of the beast and his pack of hungry cubs, which could not and would not let the poor people of the land of eternal sunshine live peacefully. The beast and his hungry pack survived and flourished on the youthful lives that were cut short. They survived by harvesting and destroying the dreams of the beautiful young men and women. They survived on the sorrows and tears of the widows who wept for their husbands and on the tears of the everlasting pains of the mothers who would never see their children grow up, the children that were fed to the beast and his pack, on their tables of merciless greed. The people freed themselves, on the awaiting boats, by sailing to the marshes that opened their gates of death to the passage on the other side of the world, where everything was different, where all the lies became truth and all the truth that we knew became myth, the other side, where Gypsies were loved and lived life like all the others.

"Do not be wary of the gates of death," the Gypsy woman said, "as they are the gates to the impeccable freedom of the mind, body, and soul from the beast and his pack of beasts who once tried to block the flow of the Euphrates River to the marshes. No matter how much the beast and his pack tried to stop the Euphrates, they could not. The joyful armada of the poor continued to sail their wood and tar boats to the gates of death in the marshes, where the heaven of eternal happiness was and where there would be no pain, no suffering, no hunger, and no needy people. No one would ever again need to sell their bodies or souls so they could live. Everyone would be equal; they would all wear the same clothing, smell of jasmine, and eat fresh bread. They would all smile at each other sincerely and sing songs of love. And the music of all the Gypsy singers would bring constant joy. Everyone would dance, and they would all know how to dance. Everyone there would love you, and they would be your friend. They would all smile at you when you arrived, and the best thing is that they would all be beautiful people: handsome men and beautiful women, who would wait for you; handsome men and beautiful woman with many different colors of skin, hair and eyes. They would all be very skilled dancers, better than all the Gypsy dancers, and they will all be waiting to receive you, because it will not be your death. It will be your wedding."

The townspeople stopped shouting as they realized that they could not stop the armada of boats that carried Adnan to the marshes. Sayed Habeeb walked along the riverbank and recited the prayers of the traveler.

Barrya, the Gypsy woman, walked next to him and said with a quiet voice, so no one would hear her, "So long, Adnan. So long, my dear son; tell Ahmed and Hanan that we will be following you soon. So long, my son. You are free now. There will be many beautiful Gypsy women waiting for you to celebrate your glorious wedding."

She bit on her dark lower lip, and her crystal tears moved the thick, black eyeliner downward on her tanned beautiful face. She watched the armada of boats disappear into the horizon, where the river ended and the marshes began.

ARMAND NASSERY

The Book of Balluria

Soldiers of Eternal Deception

1

That winter was hard. It was hard on the souls, and it was hard on the hearts and the faces that were covered with a dark, glazed shed of need. That winter was hard on the hands which became rougher as they tried to keep up with life's bare necessities and it was hard on the stomachs as they hardened and withered due to the many nights of hunger. Balluria had never starved before in history, but it did that winter. Even the Euphrates was stingy with its fish, and the palm tree orchards had stopped loving their people. That winter a dark cloud started rising in the sky from the southern borders. Many people thought it was the beginning of the end, and many thought it was the awaited return of the savior, who promised to return and save the meek and the poor when earth is filled with the tyranny of evil men. It was not because of what the long stream of barefooted soldiers who filled the highways and the streets that led to the capital city of the provinces, as they deserted their trenches and fox holes in the desert and walked miles and miles to reach the towns and villages near the marshes and asked for food and water and shelter for a night or two until they could regain their strength to walk again. It was the boyish-looking soldier who sold his rifle for a meal and told Hisham and the other boys that the black cloud was because of all the burned bodies of dead soldiers and the smoke from the bombed bunkers and oil fields in the south. Hisham and the other boys gladly bought his Kalashnikov rifle for a pair of shoes and enough rice and bread for two days.

Other boyish-looking soldiers who appeared as though they had not eaten, slept, or shaved for a month told the people that the dark cloud was because all the oil fields in the south were set on fire as an act of defiance by the divine leader whose army of the millions of starving and ill-armed soldiers was defeated and destroyed within one week after the beginning of the great, thirty nations war, and his troops were humiliated and massacred by the hundreds of thousands on the highways and remote desert posts.

The sky rained black drops, and Sayed Habeeb had asked the people to pray the fear prayer because the end was near as the world had gone mad. The people in Balluria did not believe him, nor did they take him seriously; they had not taken the graceful clergyman seriously since the time he was taken to the secret police headquarters in the capital city of the province. The people in Balluria learned of what happened to the smart, young man Adnan who had gone mad after he was released from the secret police dungeon headquarters. People knew that anyone who went to the secret police dungeons came out mad, no matter how strong and smart or faithful he or she might be, so they considered the gentle clergyman crazy, especially when he isolated himself from the people for six months after he was released. Only the young men who used to call themselves the Wolves—Hisham in his wheelchair, Salah, Ashraf, and Haleem—kept going to his mosque even when no one was there. They went to his house, started the fire, cleaned the mosque, and called for prayers. They took these actions out of devotion to the graceful clergyman and to keep him from going delusional like Adnan did.

As Haleem put it, "We cannot lose him. When towns like ours lose people like Sayed Habeeb, the sole purpose of the town's existence disappears."

In the last days of the thirty nations war, the group of young men had spent most all of their evenings at the mosque for two reasons: first, the fire that Saayed Habeeb lit every night at the fire pit in the mosque's corner was too delicious and too tempting to pass; second, many deserting soldiers spent their nights lying on the mosque's raggedy carpets and eating the dried bread or cold rice. In the night, the young men sat and listened to soldiers telling of the shameful defeat of the army and how many soldiers were blinded with anger and rage and how they wished the rebels in the marshes would spark a rebellion. The soldiers said that they witnessed group of disgruntled soldiers defacing one of the divine leader's many portraits near the desert highway.

Others who were not soldiers, merely strangers and passersby who spent a night at the mosque, told the news from the marshes, suggesting that the rabble had started coming out of the endless marshes and ambushing and killing the party militiamen. The rebels told of the near end of the divine leader, or the tyrant, as they started calling the divine leader. That topic on everyone's tongue was a rebellion that seemed inevitable. Even people who stopped briefly in the small market in Balluria looking for wheat and flour and rice and any items of food that seemed to vanish from the markets in the whole country, all said that something big would happen soon: a revolution or a rebellion. Most of them concluded that the barrier of fear had been broken.

Haleem and Hisham and the other young men were exceptionally excited about such news. They looked all day for deserters and people who brought news from the capital of the province, and the men who had never been seen before in Balluria talked about groups of bandits attacking police stations and party headquarters in the villages near the marshes. They also told of news of army deserters and rebel gathering in the marshland and seizing towns and villages near the marshes and the disappearing of the party militia leaving the towns practically out of control. In the last ten days of the war and as the people slept in Balluria waiting for a morning that would bring about other news, the group of young men sat in the mosque, near the front, and watched the horizon, where they could see and hear the loud noise of the fighter planes getting closer and closer to Balluria.

Hisham, who was the only one in Balluria who had served in the eastern fronts and lived, said, "They are bombing the ammunition storage near the highway. It's logical to destroy the ammunition supplies before they enter a lawless country."

2

For a month, bombs dropped by invisible airplanes had shattered the capital city, making it impossible to live there, so people moved elsewhere. Some had moved all to way to the eastern borders where the smell of the recent war that ended not long before were still fresh in their minds and in the noses, but the border area was safe and away from the ruthless bombardment of the invisible planes. People in the capital had gathered whatever they could carry and loaded it in their small cars and left their homes unattended just to survive the relentless rain of bombs that destroyed everything: buildings, bridges, offices, military camps, houses, chicken coops, and even cars that traveled any highway. People were watched from their rearview mirrors as they drove, and when they heard a noise from the sky they stopped their cars and trucks and ran to the safest hole in the ground. All the major cities were completely destroyed, and the exodus of families roamed the country looking for shelter with other families. The capital city of the province, only forty miles to the north of Balluria, was hit very hard. In one bombing raid, people said the pilot flew very close to the main bridge but did not bomb it. The people who were crossing the bridge thought he had gone away. Then they say he returned for the second time. When almost two thousand people were crossing the bridge, he blew it up with two missiles. The shredded corpses of seven hundred people flew all over the river. Bodies in varying degrees of completion floated all the way to the big city in the south, and some stayed by the riverbanks bloated and rotting as women fetched water in the morning. They turned away with their pots and buckets empty, and their noses covered from the unbearable stench of decaying flesh.

Hisham and the small group of young men had heard many stories, stories that told of looming uprising and how men in other towns had defaced the portrait of the tyrant and other stories about how small groups of young men are starting to show disrespect to the party officials, they heard many other stories about how army deserters who have been hiding in the marshes for years are starting to come out and walk the streets of the villages with their guns visible, Hisham and the others heard all of the rumors and stories but they did not share them with other people; they just listened. At night they went to Barrya's house and asked her to close the door; they asked her not to tell anyone, especially Kamal, who was at the time pulling twenty-four-hour guard shifts on the entrances of the town with only ten members of his party militia at that time.

In the mud room of the Gypsy woman's house, gathered around the dancing dim light of the kerosene bottle, Haleem, Hisham and the rest of the young men debated for hours and talked about many things. Barrya listened, and she knew what they were talking about; she knew that the young men were talking about the thing they must not talk about, the thing that she did not want to hear them talking about. She knew the end of the road they were about to take, and she was afraid because the young men who she loved like her own children were all grown up now and they were talking about revolution.

Haleem said, "They did it. They did it in the big city, and I saw it myself. The picture was smeared with shit and red paint. And if you don't want to help me, I will do it alone."

Hisham was sitting in his wheelchair smoking his cigarettes when Ashraf and Salah silently sat down on the dirty piece of carpet. Ashraf looked at Hisham and said, "Someone must break the barrier of fear, and people will rise and revolt when someone takes the lead."

"And who will be that one?" Salah asked.

"Me and you with me," Haleem answered. The four young men looked at each other and then looked at Hisham for guidance just as they always had on the soccer field.

Hisham looked at them and said, "All right, we will do it. Here is what we will do. I want all of your identification cards. All of them. We will leave them here with Barrya," Hisham said with the firm voice of a leader. "Salah, you will go and bring your father's old revolver that you showed me the other day. I will take the pistol and position myself in a spot about fifty meters across from the party's headquarters so if anyone notices you and wants to shoot you, I will kill them. You and you will carry the black paint and hide it within your clothes," Hisham ordered Ashraf and Haleem. "Salah, you will walk a hundred meters behind them to make sure that no one sees them deface the tyrant's portrait."

"What will defacing the tyrant's mural will do?" Ashraf asked. He seemed thoughtful and quiet. "I mean, the entire country is going up in flames in a week or so, and we will risk our lives by defacing a giant portrait that means nothing. Shouldn't we wait?"

"You said someone needs to break the fear barrier," Haleem replied.

"I meant someone else."

"This is the way to break the fear barrier," Hisham replied as he looked at Ashraf, seeking agreement. Ashraf did not reply, and Haleem took the initiative, knowing that he had to lead. "We will do it. We will deface the president's portrait. So, are you with us or not?"

Ashraf paused for a moment and then said, "Do I have a choice? I know that you will do it with me or without me. I have a Kalashnikov in my house. It's my father's. I will bring it."

They looked at each other and looked at Barrya who entered the room at that moment and said with a sad, knowing look, "You boys are on your way to die."

"Well, if we are going to die, we will die together like men," said Haleem, and waited for response for the others. Haleem, who had initiated the idea of defacing the giant portrait of the divine leader and was the most enthusiastic among the young men, insisted that because he was the one who suggested that action, he would smear the portrait with black paint and human feces himself. Ashraf said he would do it with him. Haleem was in no mood to debate political ideas or to back away from his offer to take the lead and responsibility because he knew that he must do it. He trusted the Wolves, and he would always do so, and he knew that they would never tell any other soul about his idea and his role in defacing the president's mural. Nevertheless, he knew that if his initiative did not break the barrier of fear and spark the revolution in Balluria, the party militia would hunt and kill him and the other three, so he embraced his fate wholeheartedly and was ready to die at that moment, although he was not clear about what purpose he was willing to die for. He just knew that he had taken his first steps on a one-way road with no chance to return. He was the one who told Hisham about his idea of defacing the giant mural of the divine leader, which stood up in the northern entrance of Balluria, and he knew that what the mural meant to the party militia and the party members. He also knew that that the mural was the symbol of the fear that the tyrant imposed on the people. The mural meant the absolute authority and unchallengeable dominance of the tyrant over the lives and fates of the people. The mural meant that as long as the people were afraid of the mural, the tyrant would stay in power. Haleem was angry as he saw that his friends did not have the same level of anger that he had. He announced that he would do it with them or without them even if it meant he would be shot in the town square by a firing squad. He would smear this dictator's face with the feces of the poor.

The three realized that he was not backing down, so they decided to share the fate with him, not knowing what that fate was or how short it would be. It was raining outside as they asked Barrya if there was anyone she could see coming toward the house. Fearing that Kamal would show up for his drinking routine, they were visibly relieved when she answered that no one was coming up the path. As they exited the room, she stopped them and asked them to wait. She went inside the room, searched in her many cans and boxes, and came out with her hand closed on a powder that looked like black pepper and smelled like it. She showered them all with it, and Salah complained that it smelled.

"Shut up," said Barrya, barely able to fight back her tears. "So, all of you want to leave me now. All of you want to be killed. Why do all of my men like to die young?" she said, continuing to shower them with the dark powder. "This powder will keep the bullets away from you, so I can see you again. I will smell this powder and will know if you are coming back or not." She was crying, but the four young men did not see her tears in the dark as they went to commit the act that led their muddy feet to the firing squad.

3

Little by little, news from the marshes started reaching Balluria, and news from the radio stations that were not affected by the radio wave interceptor brought some grim realities of the fighting on the southwestern fronts. It seemed like the first announcement by the military command was all lies. The national army was defeated, and the national forces were scattered all over the desert. The invading armies had advanced into the country through many axes, the long column of military convoys were moving fast with no one to stop them, and it seemed as if it was only a matter of one or two days before the invading armies would reach the towns near the southern desert. That night four young men, one of them in a wheelchair, made their way to take their position. Salah pushed Hisham's wheelchair right in front of the party headquarters with the Kalashnikov that Ashraf stole from his father, who got the rifle from the party headquarters to be ready just in case the invading enemy's paratroopers parachuted into Balluria. He managed to sneak into his father's room and steal it with one full magazine, which was more than what Hisham wanted. Ashraf and Haleem filled the inner pockets of their winter jackets with small plastic bags that were filled with feces and black asphalt paint. They walked twice by the overbearing mural of the divine leader's portrait facing the incoming travelers from the north passing by Balluria while Salah walked one hundred meters behind them with his fist frozen on the old revolver pistol. He was shivering with cold and shaken by the fear of the unimaginable act he had committed himself to. He froze in his shoes when he saw a pickup truck stop fifty meters from the mural. He did not take another step because the pickup truck looked similar to the kind the party militiamen used. He calmly pulled his pistol and hid it behind his back, ready to shoot. He walked toward where his two friends were just about to deface the offensive portrait. He wanted to shout for them not to start because he thought that their plan had been foiled, but he was relieved as he saw the pickup truck unloading many women in black robes and took off in the opposite direction. There was one man walking with women as they passed by him, and the man looked at him.

"Asalamu Alykum, brother. Can you tell me where one can find the house of Sheikh Jawad?"

"It's at the end of this road. It's the biggest house in the town," Salah answered as he kept looking toward the portrait, trying to see what his two friends were doing in the middle of the darkness. At that moment Hisham was pointing his Kalashnikov toward the party headquarters door and wishing that he would not have to shoot anyone. Hisham wished that his two friends would hurry up and finish defacing the mural and that he would not have to shoot any other human being, not after what he had seen and done during his years of service on the eastern fronts. He had seen what a bullet could do to the flesh, and he did not want to inflict that on any human. He knew that Kamal had been in charge of security and that he was leading guard shifts and patrols of party militiamen throughout Balluria and Tawsheeha, and he knew that Kamal would be in the headquarters that night.

Hisham prayed under his breath, "Please, Allah, don't let him come out."

Of all the Wolves, Hisham was the only one who stayed on good terms with Kamal. Kamal kept a good relationship with Hisham because he had lost both of his legs in the war on the eastern front and was crippled and there was nothing that he could do to hurt Kamal or to compete with him. At that moment as much as Hisham wished that Kamal would not step out of the headquarters building, he knew that he would have no choice but shoot. He charged his rifle and waited as he glanced at where the mural of the divine leader stood, and he could see the silhouette of two men throwing black paint and human feces on it. Hisham was not conflicted. He knew that if Kamal or any of his men noticed that someone was defacing the portrait and they came out of the buildings with their guns, he would shoot them to protect his other three friends. He just hoped that no one would leave the building and force his hand in the matter. It was as if he was bracing himself for the unwanted act when he noticed that there was no one by the mural. He heard quiet voices behind him. Hisham turned around and saw Salah, Ashraf, and Haleem. They did not say a thing; they just grabbed his wheelchair and started pushing it toward Barrya's house. The four young men did not say a word all the way there, and Haleem and Ashraf stopped by the many water puddles on the way to wash their hands from the black asphalt and human feces.

They did not think it would be that easy. After an hour and a half, which seemed like an eternity, the four young men went back to Barrya's house and sat in the same place and asked Barrya to make them some tea. They started telling nervous jokes about how the first bag of feces did not explode on the dictator's face and how Haleem had to smear the feces on the dictator's moustache by hand and how they hid under the portrait when they saw the white pickup truck. They made fun of Salah, who told them that he almost pissed on himself when the many women in black robes with the masked man approached him. That night the four young men had committed the deadliest grievance in the country when they defaced the dictator's portrait. It was a crime that could land them in front of a firing squad, but they just sat there, laughing to overcome the fear and the nervousness they felt. At this moment they felt the same exhilaration they had felt when they had returned from the seven palm trees after they saw the young wolves dreaming. It was the feeling of the pure joy of victory and the feeling of true courage of manhood.

They did what millions of people in the country wanted to do but never had the courage for. They challenged the secret informants that no one knew. They challenged the police. They challenged the party militiamen who roamed the streets with white pickup trucks and red kuffias. They challenged the existence of the tyrant and his multiple security organizations and injected the town's heart with an adrenalin shot of courage. Tomorrow the town would wake up knowing that the rule of tyrants was almost over as long as there were men who did not fear the tyrant, men like them.

The four men stayed in Barrya's house for almost three hours after their infamous act. They wanted to stay there all night. They wanted to stay together. For some reason they felt that they must stay together and never be apart. They feared that if they separated they would never meet again. Barrya, who served them yogurt and tea and cigarettes was standing outside fearing that someone was coming to her house. She stormed into the room and said with her frantic voice, "Hide the weapons. Kamal is approaching!"

The four young men froze as many questions raced into their heads. *Kamal? Is he alone? Is the party militia with him? Had they been discovered? Is it time to face the firing squad?* They scrambled as they tried to hide any evidence or any sign that he might notice as Kamal entered with a grim look.

"There you are. I was looking for you," he said with a tone that brought a sense of comfort as the four men noticed that he was alone. Salah, who made a secret pact with himself that he would never be taken alive if they were discovered, reached into his pocket and touched the revolver as they all greeted Kamal. Kamal's body had become heavier, as though the extra weight and big belly represented a natural evolution for party members. He laid half way on the old carpet and grabbed a pillow, saying, "You know why I am here?"

They did not open their mouths, and he did not notice the looks on their faces in the dimmed light of the kerosene lamp. Kamal continued, "Someone or some people have committed the ultimate crime against the country and against His Excellency the president. They defaced the president's face. You know, the portrait."

"What?" asked Hisham, as he tried to act shocked.

"Yes, Hisham. Some traitors have defaced the mural of the divine leader. May Allah protect him," Kamal said with unmistakable anger. "And I am responsible for the security of this area. I wish I knew who did it," Kamal said as he looked at Salah, who smiled back at him and answered, trying to derail the conversation.

"Do you know who did it?"

Clutching his hands on the grip of his own pistol, Kamal answered, "No. Not yet, but I will know soon," Kamal said, fixing his eyes on Haleem, who did not look back at Kamal. Caressing his pistol, he said, "This is bad for me and my position in the party." He looked at Barrya, who entered the room at that moment bringing him a cup of tea.

"I swear on my honor I will shoot the person who did this myself, after I rip his heart out. This coward traitor."

"Calm down, Kamal," Hisham said.

"I am calm. I just gave orders to two patrols to go search the town, but I am tired and I need to relax tonight," said Kamal, stretching his legs on the dirty carpet. "That's why I am here, because I am upset and depressed so I came here to drink, and I am glad that you, my friends, are here too so we can drink together."

Haleem knew how violent and rude and unpredictable Kamal could be when he drank. Haleem did not want to stay in the room with Kamal, but he stayed calm as he was thinking of an excuse for leaving, knowing the possibility of a confrontation with Kamal and the possibility that one of the other three might lose control of his tongue and say something. He was afraid that Salah or Ashraf might say something that would land them all in the town's square facing the rifles of the party militia, so he suggested that he and Salah should go because they had something to take to Salah's house.

"Salah and I will go to Salah's house because we need to fix the water pump," Haleem said. Without waiting for an answer, he got up, trying to avoid looking at Kamal who looked him with anger.

"What water pump?" Kamal asked.

"Yes, our water pump. It's broken," Salah said as he stood up and tried not to reveal his left hand that was in his pocket holding the revolver. The two stood up and left the room hastily, leaving Hisham and Ashraf to come up with an excuse to leave. Haleem and Salah got up and left the room, looking at Barrya who stood up in the doorway, waiting for a sign from any of the four men because she was ready to do anything to protect them even if she had to kill Kamal. Hisham, with the calmness of a person who is willing to lose anything because he has nothing to lose, laughed and said to Kamal, "Yes, sure I will drink with you, but I am hungry and Barrya has nothing but yogurt and tea."

"Yes," Kamal said and added, "I wish I could eat some grilled tikka."

Hisham capitalized on that comment and thought that he found a way to get Ashraf out of that room. Hisham was willing to stay alone with Kamal. "Ashraf, why don't you go to your house and see if you have anything to eat there and bring it to us."

Ashraf smiled and said, "Yes, I am sure I can find something." He stood up and walked toward the door, and when he passed Hisham, he whispered in his ear, "Don't come back, Ashraf. I will take care of him."

Ashraf was relived. He went outside and quickly walked back to his house, where he stayed awake, waiting all night for something, a sign or a knock on the door from the party militia or from the secret police, anything that would signal the beginning of the end, but there was no knock. The night was quietly passing as the rain washed the town from its everlasting fear. Only Hisham stayed all night entertaining the rage-filled Kamal in the secluded mud hut of the Gypsy woman.

4

Hisham and Kamal stayed drinking as Barrya served them areq, the Iraqi moonshine. They talked about many things—about the war and what would happen soon. Kamal assured Hisham that the divine leader would have a plan to defeat the invading enemies.

"The president and his troops will be victorious, and he will punish all of those who will not stand with their country and their president," Kamal said and downed the milk-like alcohol in his mouth. "It's simple. This is the war of all wars, and after this war we will be the kings of all Arabs."

Hisham tried not to drink as much as he liked and tried to agree with what Kamal was saying and steer the subject away from the defacing of the portrait, but Kamal mentioned that he was upset about how disrespectful Haleem and the other two were toward him and how they did not want to stay to drink with him.

"I know they don't like me. One day I will show them who the true Kamal is," he said with a grim look from his eyes.

Hisham tried to calm him down by saying. "Don't you wish that we could have some music?"

"We don't need music," Kamal said as he looked at Barrya. "This old Gypsy can dance for us," he said as he pointed his pistol toward Barrya.

Hisham asked him to be polite because she was older now. Kamal turned his pistol and pointed to Hisham, staring him in the eyes.

"Do not say things that you are not willing to risk your life for. That's what I learned," Kamal shouted. Then in a quieter yet more menacing tone, he said, "If I say she will dance, then this old Gypsy whore, this Gypsy witch, she will dance, or I will shoot her."

Hisham braced himself against Kamal's volatile temper and looked at him, speaking with a firm voice, "This Gypsy whore? She is like our mother, you know."

Kamal was enraged by Hisham's comment. He threw the bottle of areq and what was left in it on Barrya, who dodged the bottle and tried to diffuse the situation.

"Don't worry, Kamal, I have another bottle."

As she stood up and went to fetch the other bottle, Hisham knew that Kamal was drunk already and that he might harm Barrya so he changed his mind about leaving and decided to stay to protect Barrya even without his legs, and even though he himself might be harmed or killed. Kamal was looking at the dancing flames of the fireplace as he started to weep quietly.

"They are all whores. They are all whores. Just like my mother and just like Hanan."

Hisham was saddened to hear Hanan's name, but he knew that even with tears flowing unchecked down his face, Kamal was beyond rage. Hisham lit up a cigarette and listened to Kamal as he kept weeping and saying, "Do you know that I know all the whores in this province? I am telling you. Many women of status, they are all whores. If you knew half of what I knew about this society, you would vomit. You would vomit blood," Kamal said as he spat in disgust and looked at Barrya with eyes full of rage. "They are all whores, and this Gypsy whore is the queen of all whores. I swear to you, my friend, my only friend, many women who act like they are saints from heaven and pray and do all that crap are in reality all whores. They love the pennies and they love intercourse. Ask me. I know if you just could see the reports I get from the informants, it makes me want kill all the people in the town and all the people in this province. Where is this bitch with the bottle?" Kamal screamed as he pushed his feet toward the fire and then waved his pistol and pointed it Hisham, who could see in the dim light of the kerosene lamp that Kamal was crying.

"Ohh, if you just knew how much I loved Hanan, and that son of a whore Hamid stole her from me."

"Kamal, you must calm down," Hisham said as started to worry about every word he would say in fear of angering Kamal, who kept waving his pistol.

"You know what I think. I think he is the one who defaced the president's portrait. So I will be executed because of that," Kamal said after a brief, thoughtful pause.

Hisham was silent all that time, but when he heard the subject of the portrait he tried to look for a good answer, an answer that would spare him the agony of convincing this mad drunk not to point his pistol at him and shoot him. He regretted not keeping Salah's revolver with him.

"Do you mean Hamid?"

"Yes. That son of a whore, brother of a whore, Hamid," Kamal said and fixed his steel gray eyes on Hisham, who lost the tail of the correct course of this flying argument that would end up in family honor disgraced if Kamal kept it on this level.

"But Hamid has been dead since, well, you know, since you and Ahmed killed him, may Allah have mercy on the soul of the dead. You are just tired and you need to rest."

"No!" Kamal shouted angrily and looked at Barrya as she entered the room with a full bottle of areq. "I think that this whore right here knows some things and she doesn't tell me. I think Hamid is not dead. I have some informants telling me that they saw someone who looks like him riding a horse in the prairie with the nomads." He glared at the silent Barrya with eyes glazed with the haze of alcohol and blood. "Why don't you tell me, my Gypsy whore... mother... hahaha, you love him, don't you, you love Hamid. That's why you let him dishonor Hanan on your bed, because you are the same. Gypsies with no honor. Is he still alive? I need to know!" He screamed with his hand firmly on the pistol grip. "Answer me. Is he the one who defaced the portrait of the president?" He pointed the gun to where Barrya sat mixing areq with water, turning it into a milky colored liquid and she handed one glass to Hisham and one to Kamal.

"I have not seen Hamid since that night." She paused and looked at Kamal as she prepared herself for the worst because of what she was about to say. "When he and Hanan ran away I never saw him again," Barrya calmly said and went back to the other room, leaving Kamal and Hisham alone in the room full of smoke, anger, and memories.

Kamal lowered his pistol and looked at Hisham, "You know I have never hurt any of you," Kamal said with a suddenly serene voice. "I mean the people that I know. I mean the Wolves, my friends. I have only hurt the ones that deserved it, like that idiot Adnan who joined a forbidden political party of traitors, and it was my duty to report him. He was not man enough to endure what he had set himself up for," Kamal added and looked at Hisham with eyes again full of tears. "But other than that, I always tried to not hurt any of the Wolves, for the sake of the old days."

"I know that, Kamal."

"But this time, if I knew who defaced the portrait and if it was Hamid, and if I knew that you knew who did it and you did not tell me, then you would wish that your mother never bore you."

Hisham tried to defuse the tension that electrified the dark room with one suggestion: "Why don't you wait until this war is over? I mean many things could change," Hisham said, fearful that that was something Kamal did not want to hear; that something could change the government and his position, his authority over these miserable souls.

"What could change, Hisham? I want you tell me what you mean," he insisted with the intention to drive Hisham into a trap in which he would have to ask for mercy. But Hisham was too smart and not drunk enough to walk into that trap, so he smiled.

"I don't know. I mean the morning will tell, and you will know who defaced the portrait, I am sure, and then you won't need to be angry."

That was not enough for Kamal, who was looking for prey. He wanted more. "I know what you mean, Hisham. You mean the thirty country aggression on our nation will result in the removal of our beloved president from power. And we, the party loyalists, will run way. Is that what you meant?"

"No... I mean, no... Wallah, I did not mean that."

Kamal smiled, realizing that Hisham had just entered his den and that he was the only one who could let him out. He had the power to simply arrest him for even thinking like that, and he could write up a statement back at the party headquarters, and no one would question it, and he could have Hisham facing a firing squad the next morning. The beast in Kamal was not in the mood for hunting that night. He suddenly wanted to rest to get ready for tomorrow's fight. He smiled at Hisham with a superior look from his squinty eyes, enjoying his absolute power over his only friend and said, "Don't worry, Hisham. No one will know about what you said." Kamal put his pistol back in the holster. "But here is something you need to know. The country will prevail forever through the thirty countries aggression, and the divine president, may Allah protect him, will stay in power forever, and I will stay in charge of these parts. Forever. I will make sure of that, and anyone who tries to change that will face death. I will always be in charge, and if anyone dares disrespect that fact with any act, I will slice his throat and drink his blood even if it was one of you, my Wolf friends, even if it was Hanan, and even if it was my dead mother."

Kamal turned to the door where Barrya had entered the room. "And as for you, my Gypsy whore... if you see Hamid, tell him that I will be waiting for him."

He got up and left, leaving Hisham and Barrya alone, wondering whether the night would ever be over. Hisham saw no sense in going home, and it would be difficult for him to push his wheelchair through the mud, so he asked Barrya if he could spend the night at her house. She silently pulled a mattress from the pile of old mattresses she had stacked in the room's corner and laid it next to the fire. He slid from his chair onto the mattress and stayed awake all night like the other three young men who stayed awake awaiting the promised day of revolution and an unknown fate when Balluria woke up to the shock of the incident. Kamal was supervising some of the party members as they covered the mural with white sheets to keep the people from seeing the divine leader's face smeared with feces and black asphalt, and a group of the party militiamen with their dark green uniforms and red hats had set up a checkpoint at the north entrance of the main road, asking everyone who passed if they knew who committed the crime and asking all the people if they ever saw a man riding a horse the night before.

Hisham drank the tea Barrya made with no food or bread. Barrya pushed his wheelchair all the way to Salah's house, and then she returned to her mud hut and consulted the Gypsy stones that her grandmother, the great Gypsy witch, had left her. What she saw scared her as she threw the stones on the ground; she saw four of the stones were on the path to the other world. Knowing that death was coming to people she loved, she wept and prepared herself for lasting mourning. Preparing herself the Gypsy way, she painted both of her palms with brown Henna lines that were shaped like tears, and she lined her eyes with black, thick eyeliner, she looked at the town that was awakened by the shouts of the party militiamen rushing to the site of the defaced mural, and she knew the unavoidable was coming soon.

Barrya looked from the door at Balluria and mumbled, "How many of my children will satisfy you... you whore?"

5

Hisham knocked on the door. Salah cautiously opened it and let him in. Salah, who had not closed his eyes the night before, was exhausted and worried and wanted to hear what had happened after he left the hut. He wanted to know if Kamal suspected anything. Hisham assured him otherwise and told Salah that it was too late to worry; they had to prepare themselves for the worst. The two sat in tense silence as they drank some tea. Soon enough Haleem joined them with his Kalashnikov, and they all waited for Ashraf, who came late with another young man who they knew from the town; his name was Hamza, and he claimed that he spent the night before in the big city in the south and he had news.

"The rebels have descended from the marshes and now they control all the routes in and out of the big city, and the Americans are about fifty miles from Balluria. The end of the dictator is near" he said as he smoked his cigarette and looked at them waiting for a reply.

Haleem, who was the most enthusiastic for a revolution, said with confidence, "Last night I heard on the radio that the American president had promised support if the people revolted against the tyrant. We must do it now."

The ever-cautious Salah was not so eager to jump to arms. "Wait, Haleem, we are only four." Then he looked at Hamza, the new member of the group and said, "Five men with weapons, and the Americans are not here."

Hisham, who was still in shock from his night talk with Kamal looked at him and said, "That's right, and we don't know how many party militiamen are in the headquarters."

"That's right," Ashraf agreed.

"However, there will be no other time. It's now, or we will always be afraid of Kamal," Hisham said with growing conviction. "For all of our lives," Hisham added. The four others looked at him and waited for a sign or an order. The five young men sat and waited for one of them to say the ultimate word, the ultimate statement what would energize all of them with the intent to revolt, and it would mean that they would have to face the consequences they were most familiar with; the fate of all the people who rebelled against the tyrant.

It was Haleem with his fiery personality who everyone in that room was waiting for. Although he was in his last year of engineering college and had a decent future ahead of him, he hated the tyrant very much and he had the personality of a brave warrior and an unstable daredevil who did not care about where the next step would be. In his mind he wanted to declare a revolution for Balluria, lead a desperate army of five young, starving rebels, invade and liberate the capital of the country, and defeat the tyrant. As absurd of an idea as it was and as much as he knew that Hisham must be the leader of that revolution, just as he had been the leader in the soccer field before, Haleem knew that it was his destiny to lead the little revolution. At that moment he was the leader of the five rebels. At least for that day. But he was hopeful that soon enough hundreds, thousands, and maybe millions of starving, young rebels would follow him to the capital and shake the grounds underneath the tyrant's feet, so after a short moments of silence, he spoke firmly as he gave his first order as a revolutionary leader,

"Let's go to the main square and let's take our weapons with us, but hide them under our coats."

"Why should we hide them? Everyone is carrying a gun," Hisham queried, his impotence from the previous night turning into anger.

Haleem did not pay attention to him. He insisted, "Hide your weapons until you see me shoot. God is with us today."

Haleem pushed Hisham in his wheelchair as he hid the Kalashnikov under his fur coat. The five young men walked toward the town's main square. Almost all of the townspeople had gathered. As they arrived, they heard some exciting and encouraging news. The rebels had taken over the stretch of villages and small towns along the marshes and banks, and the army troops were heading back to the capital city defeated and hungry. Some people had said that the soldiers were selling their weapons for food and shelter. Another person, who worked as a minibus driver, drove to the main square with a white flag tied to his windshield wipers. The townspeople bombarded him with questions.

He told them with a convincing voice that the Americans were in Khameesia near the big city to the south. It was over. They would be in Balluria by night fall. It was a lie, but that was all that Haleem needed. It was the moment that millions of people had been waiting for twenty years. It had become a reality. The tyrant's days were numbered, and out of the confusion and mumbling of the crowd, a shout rang in their ears and shocked all of the people who were in the town's square.

It was Haleem, without a real sense of his surroundings, shouting, "Down with the tyrant! Death to the enemy of the people!" Then he clapped his hands, thinking that the crowd would follow him. His four friends looked around at the people who looked at the five young men like they were from a different planet. No one clapped or chanted... a long moment of extremely tense silence.

Then Hisham grew wary of the consequences, and he did not know what he would do, so he gathered himself, and from his wheelchair, he shouted, "Oh, to hell with it! A man only dies once!"

He grabbed the Kalashnikov hidden under the blanket that covered his waist and fired in the air. A burst of bullets, and suddenly almost half of the people in the square left their sandals behind them as they fled, not knowing who was shooting. The six young men presented their weapons and waved them as they circled Hisham and Haleem, who stood up in the middle of a circle of people. Some were admirers and potential followers, and some were informants who wanted to see who these men were who dared to break the barrier of fear; the barrier of silence. They wanted to know who these men were who provoked the irrevocable and crossed the uncrossable lines.

Many young men in the crowd looked at them with admiration and many wanted to do exactly what they did, but it was too early because the town square was exactly in the middle of the town and was exactly an equal distance from the town's two symbols of the tyrant's authority: the party headquarters near the defaced portrait in the north end of town and the police station in the south end. There was no time for planning and definitely no time and no way to retreat. It was Haleem again who instigated what happened afterward as he, Salah, Ashraf, Hamza, and Hisham and several other young men looked at the remaining people, waiting for a reaction.

The crowd seemed more intent on waiting for the young men's next action. Hisham, in his wheelchair, started moving toward the police station, and the others walked slowly behind him first, then a little faster, and then they charged at the police station with their two weapons.

"There must be weapons." The five young men charged the police station followed by hundreds of spectators who were buoyed by the unfolding events. The station was deserted, and no policemen were there. They found a dark green, wooden box with Russian writing on it and in it there were ten Kalashnikovs. They also found three metal boxes of ammunition. Haleem broke into the case of ammunition and addressed the crowd, which gathered in the doors of the police station.

"Brothers, it's time for revolution. It's time to rise against tyranny and oppression and its time to bring freedom to the people!"

No one joined him in his poetic status of people's hero as he always thought he would be. The minimal support of his chanting was not an issue at all as he started walking toward the party headquarters where they heard that the party militiamen had fortified the building and prepared to resist. Haleem walked toward the building. He was followed first by Ashraf who put his revolver in his belt and carried a Kalashnikov. Then Salah, then Hamza and another young man who took one of the Kalashnikovs and joined them; his name was Murtada, and he had a very large head for a boy his age. The six men walked, following Haleem, and they were followed by Hisham with his wheelchair, then by more than three hundred people from the town and the neighboring towns. The march became smaller as the seven men got closer to the party headquarters building and as people hid in the side streets fearing stray bullets that might fly from the battle that was just about to begin. As the seven followed Haleem they became anxious and started to feel the fear they always felt whenever they looked at the party headquarters. The people of the town fell back and waited for the six young men to attack, and before they could gather or plan for the attack, they heard a shout.

"I am the son of my father!"

It was Haleem alone who ran with his Kalashnikov in one hand as he charged the street in front of the yellow and gray building and started shooting the windows and the posters of the tyrant. He entered the building alone. There was only one guard, who surrendered immediately and was spared because Haleem knew who he was; he was the father of the Hillaly girls, Haleem's neighbors. The old man worked cleaning the building and serving tea. Haleem asked him if there were any militiamen, and the old man said that they all had left when they heard the shooting in the town's square. They all vanished. The other five young men followed Haleem inside, and soon after that all the townspeople where inside the building looting everything inside. They waited for a sign from the inside that told them it was safe. Soon they saw Haleem appearing from the roof waving his Kalashnikov and chanting.

"Down! Down with tyrant! The enemy of the people!"

They did not join him in his victorious chant, but they joined him and his small group of young rebels in jubilant looting and vandalism of the party headquarters. The six young men sat in the main room where comrade Uraiby and Comrade Kamal used to sit. The six young men sat there and wished they could have some water and tea, as they had just victoriously won the first battle in the doomed revolution of Balluria.

6

No one knew where Kamal had disappeared to. The young men and their followers hoped that he would be found hiding somewhere in town, yet no one knew what they would do with him if they captured him. Almost all the comrades in the party headquarters had disappeared. Many of them hid in Sheikh Jawad's house and asked for the tribal right of protection; it was a time of jubilation in the town. The people felt that the unbearable weight of tyranny was lifted from their chests, and the new rebels tried to look as utopian as possible as news started to arrive of liberation of all the towns and provinces. The provincial capital was taken over by rebels and revolutionaries within twenty-four hours after Balluria fell. A smaller city to the south was liberated before Balluria. Almost all the southern and northern provinces were in the hands of the rebels, who took over the streets and burned and destroyed all the tyrant's symbols, portraits, and murals, but no news came from the capital, and no one had confirmed that the tyrant himself was dead, nor was there any suggestion that he had stepped down. Rumors suggested that he sought asylum in Russia or Algeria or some other country. Other rumors said that he fled to Cuba because he was offered asylum by Fidel Castro.

Nevertheless, after appointing Haleem as the new town leader, the small group of rebels wanted to show the people the benefits of the new era of freedom and the human face of the new government; no one knew who was really in charge but it was clear that the small group of young rebels followed Haleem. The rebels with their misdirected actions wanted to show the people that they were in a different time and that the suffering and oppression were over. They started thinking of distributing food to the people and forcing the only tanker truck driver to provide water from the river to all the houses. Many of the townspeople and people from neighboring towns had joined the rebel forces and started security patrols around Balluria and Tawsheeha and near the Euphrates.

They lacked a vital connection with the outside world. There was no communication with any other towns and no contact with the leadership of the revolution, which no one knew about and some had never heard of. The first ten days of the revolution were quiet and there were no major events except when a young rebel accidentally discharged his weapon and shot another young rebel in the stomach. Haleem had to find a vehicle to transport the wounded, young rebel to where the Americans were; he heard that they treated wounded people.

Bad news began to arrive, news they did not want to hear. Government forces were marching down to the south, scorching every town that rebelled against the tyrant and killing all of those who participated in the uprising, although many young rebels had abandoned the headquarters and stopped showing up for guard duties that Haleem and Hisham had put together. A week before the government forces reached the outskirts of the province's capital there was no one to guard the checkpoint that Hisham had set up near the defaced portrait of the tyrant.

Haleem told his friends that all the experienced and ready followers of the exiled ayatollah were on their way. In three days to a week the streets of the capital would be swamped with exiled rebels who had been waiting for long time. All the army deserters would return from the country to the east and emerge from the deep waterways of the marshes, and the tyrant would face his deserved fate very soon.

It was Hisham who suggested that they go and meet whoever was in charge of the revolution in the province's capital. He argued, "We need ammunition and a place to run to when everything is over."

They were disappointed by their first contact with Americans, who stayed beyond the desert highway. The meeting was short and turned fruitless when the American captain told them that he had no knowledge of the rebellion; moreover, the captain rejected their request for support and ammunition, and he had no orders to support it. Ashraf wanted to ask the Americans if they knew a man named Salam, who left Balluria and went to America but the American solders said they had to leave the checkpoint and go away.

They felt isolated from the world, and in a way they liked this isolation. Their town was small and forgotten. When they returned from meeting the Americans, relentless Haleem with his two-vehicle entourage of six rebels drove to the capital of the province and met with the revolutionary leadership. There the meeting was short and disappointing Also, the leader of the rebels was a young, tall man with a face of a lost saint, who sat in the chair where the slain governor of the province was shot dead two weeks earlier. The young leader was calm and soft spoken. He talked about how important it was that all the rebels must act as one and get ready for the future, and he gave vague directions and instructions about how to run their towns.

He simply told them, "Stay in your towns, and keep the peace and be nice to the people until our leadership decides the next step." The meeting had taken place in the bombed provincial government's headquarters. There was no electricity; a weak and dimmed kerosene lamp provided the only source of light, casting its many shadows on the worried faces of the young rebels, sitting drinking their tea and clenching their Kalashnikovs and their hopes. The heavy feeling of uncertainty weighed on all of the men in that meeting. The young leader, who looked like a lost saint, talked about the possibility of rebel forces entering from the neighboring country to the east, where the exiled ayatollah had been preparing to return to the homeland for twelve years. The meeting was interrupted by a panicking rebel who drove all the way from the province's border towns. Without giving a greeting, he quickly informed the leader and his guests of the bad news they feared to hear, the news they were not expecting.

He shouted, "The tyrant's elite guard units have entered the border towns and are marching toward the province's capital. They will reach it within three days. We need to get ready for a battle!"

Suddenly all the hopeful rebels felt all of their courage had vanished and all of their dreams had been crushed. Haleem was looking at the dimming lights of the kerosene lamp, and he missed Barrya and her mud hut and wished that he was there, safe and warm and worry free. If the tyrant's elite guard units were marching toward the south, then the tyranny was not dead, and the tyrant was not out of the country. He was alive, and he was coming, coming to punish all of those who dared to revolt against him. One thing Haleem was sure of was that his fate awaited him, and he accepted it, but at the same time he was not sure of the capability of the young leader in the big city, and he was not confident that there would be any assistance from the groups of rebels in neighboring countries. He was not sure of the loyalty and the willingness to fight on the part of his rebel followers and the many young men back in Balluria, but he was sure of one thing. He would fight to the end, whatever that end might be, and as they drove back to Balluria, realizing the unavoidable fate that awaited them within a week's time or so, the six young men were silent and weary.

When they reached Balluria, Hisham declared, "Drop me off by my house. Or drop me by Barrya's hut. I am done with this revolution."

Salah tried to argue about the noble purpose of the revolution and the hopes of victory that awaited them and the news about the opposition leaders who promised to send their many rebels across the marshland to aid the revolution.

"First, that promise is a mirage," Hisham said. "Second, I did not revolt so an ayatollah could be the new tyrant."

"But we must fight for our lives and our right to live freely," Haleem said.

"Haleem, I served in the military, and I know how vicious, merciless, and disciplined the elite units are. We have no chance of winning one single battle against them."

Haleem was ready to talk all night to convince Hisham, with talks about the heroic endeavor they were about to embark on but when he saw that Hisham was determined to leave their ranks, he tried to change his argument, saying, "I don't think the Americans will allow the tyrant's units to enter the cities. I mean, after all, they believe in human rights, and they have promised us they will help us, and to them a promise is a big thing; it is a commitment. I have seen that in many movies when they make a promise, they always keep it."

Neither Salah's arguments nor Haleem's begging eyes stopped Hisham from insisting that he was done.

"I am a crippled man in a wheelchair. I have done my duty for the revolution. I don't think I will be helpful in a battle. I have been in many battles in my life and would like to sit this one out. If you need me, I will be drinking areq at Barrya's house."

It had been three weeks and two days since the start of the revolution, when the small number of rebels who decided to stay and fight saw the first sign of the nearing human catastrophe. Flocks upon flocks of families and injured people escaping the province's capital and passing through Balluria on their way to where the Americans are people told that they had left because the fighting had reached the outskirts of the big city, and the relentless bombardment of the town had left it in ruins. Many civilians were killed by mortar shelling, and many of them told the weary, young rebels of the atrocities committed by the elite guard units.

"They executed the young men and hanged them from the barrels of the tanks and set many of the rebels' dead bodies on fire. They spared no one," a hairy, frantic, skinny man said. The man then asked if they had any fuel for his truck, which was loaded with stacks of boxes filled with tomatoes and other vegetables, along with children and women covered with black robes.

"I saw them setting one young man on fire alive. He was screaming," another man with a red kuffia head cover said as he, too, asked around for a gallon of gasoline for his truck. When Ashraf told them that there was no gasoline and asked if they would stay and fight, the two men quickly drove away, leaving the town as if they were escaping famine.

Although Haleem and a small number of his followers had joined the big city's rebels in defending the northern outskirts of the province for the past three days, he never thought that mass numbers of rebel forces would disappear so quickly. Nor did he anticipate all the volunteers who were roaming the streets of the province's capital when he witnessed thousands of young rebels storm the government center and kill the governor. Just two weeks before, he saw thousands and thousands of people, and he through that all of them would forever defend the city—the revolution, the uprising, or whatever they wanted to call it—or at least defend themselves and their lives because they all knew the tyrant and his forces would not forgive anyone. Haleem was part of the very small minority who believed in the revolution and believed in all the promises by the leaders of the opposition and the promises of the American president.

Haleem wished that he could have five hundred young rebels who would be loyal to him. Then he might be able to stop the advancing elite guard units and defeat them. Then they would march all the way to the capital and free the people from decades of tyranny. He hoped that the rebels would defend their right to live and their children's right to live, even if doing so meant that the tyrant would govern a land full of dead people. This would be all worthwhile as long as they would be free and as long as they fought and fought forever until the tyranny was dead, until the tyrant was dead, until there was no fear. No fear, once and for all. Haleem hoped that Allah would stand beside the poor and the oppressed as it said in the Qur'an. Haleem hoped that the Americans would change their mind, keep their promise, join the fight, support the revolution, and stand with the people. Haleem hoped for many things as he tried to maintain the small force of rebels that began to dwindle with every passing hour and with every time someone from the big city told stories of horror.

Haleem tried to maintain order, and he dispatched two patrols. He and Ashraf led and manned two checkpoints guarding the town's entrances. Looking for anyone willing to join the fight in the big city, he left Ashraf in charge with only three young men and went to join the last battle to defend the big city on the province. He was hopeful and full of true courage, but out there in the battlefield, Haleem and his three young companions escaped death many times as the tyrant's well-fed and well-trained troops with armored vehicles, tanks, and helicopters hammered the starving, ill-trained, and extremely disorganized rebel forces and shattered the hopes and the poetic and immaculate heroism that many young men showed in the muddy battlefields.

Haleem finally realized that he and the rest of the true believers in the revolution had no chance of winning. And as he returned to Balluria with Hamza and Hayder and Murtada, the fearless young man from a village near the marshes, who was not even a Wolf, had heard Haleem begging the people to go to the front lines and he felt a sting of bravery. After that moment, he stayed with Haleem and the small of group of rebels throughout the battles in the outskirts and then in the alleys and small streets of the big city and then near the bridge. During the final battle, a force of one hundred starving and short-supplied young men stopped the offensive of four brigades of the tyrant's elite guards who tried to cross the Euphrates for days. If they had been successful they would have taken Balluria within two days and would have allowed the tyrant's forces to reach the open road to the great city. In the south, that would have been the end of the revolution, but the fierce fighting in that battle had cost the rebels their best fighters and had eaten all of their ammunition supplies.

When Haleem returned to Balluria, he asked Rahman, the only young man in Balluria who could speak English, to go with him to the American checkpoint. He wanted to ask for help, for support and ammunition, and to allow the thousands of injured people to be treated in the American military hospital. Haleem tried to reason with the slender, American lieutenant colonel and tried to remember what he read about Abraham Lincoln and the right of the people to govern themselves but the American commander had neither the desire nor the interest to hear about the atrocities the tyrant's forces were committing against the people. He also told Haleem that he had no ammunition to give to the rebels. The only thing he offered was, "If you have any wounded, bring them to the hospital, but we are not authorized to give you weapons, and we are not authorized to fight; a peace agreement was signed."

Haleem did not believe what he heard and asked Rahman to ask the American lieutenant colonel, "What about the promise by your American president?"

"I don't know what you are talking about. I have no orders to help you," the American commander said as he started to drink his coffee in a strangely shaped, gray tin cup. "That's all that I can do."

The disheartened Haleem and his small group of young rebels left the American checkpoint. As they returned to Balluria, Ashraf noticed that Haleem's spirit appeared broken, and the torch-like amber light in Haleem's eyes had diminished. It seemed as though the revolution was a baby that no one wanted and everyone was willing to abort. He put his hand on Haleem's shoulders and said, "Haleem, in the big dark world of politics, oil traders, and weapons merchants, small people's lives like yours and mine do not matter."

Haleem, who was leaning on the car's windows staring at the black ducks in the water puddles along the road back to Balluria, where miles and miles of empty fields were filled with water from the constant rain of that winter, Haleem felt tired. He had had no sleep for almost two weeks, and he had been in almost ten battles in one week. He could not remember the last time he ate. Even though Ashraf, Salah, Murtada, Hayder, and Hamza were with him all the time, he was the only one who had fought in all the battles since the start of the revolution. Haleem missed Barrya so much, and at that moment he wished that he was in her mud hut drinking tea and listening to her stories about beautiful Gypsy women and young Arab men who searched for true love. He leaned on the window and slept, dreaming of Bushra, the older of the Hillaly girls, the girl who never answered any of his hundreds of love letters, and wondered if she was still in the old house with the big wide windows.

7

When Haleem and his small group of rebels arrived back in Balluria, they dropped Rahman near the mosque as they stopped to see if Sayed Habeeb, the graceful clergyman, was still there, but the mosque was deserted. Only a flock of pigeons once belonging to Hamid filled the sanctuary. Amel, Hamid's sister, had brought the pigeons to the mosque and given them to the clergyman because she said that she and her mother did not have enough food to feed the pigeons, which had nested inside the mosque and looked in dire need of the warmth of the spirits of worshippers. Haleem looked at the empty mosque and said to Ashraf, "I need to pray."

"But you never really prayed before," Ashraf replied.

"I know. I really need to pray, at least once," Haleem said as he washed his hands and face with rain water and started praying. Ashraf did the same. The two friends prayed next to each other silently in the empty mosque. Then they went back to the car without saying a word to each other and drove to the party headquarters, where they had set up their command, but they found that the yellow and gray building was almost deserted and that all the young rebels had disappeared. The only ones there were Hamza, Hayder, Salah, and the fearless fat kid Murtada. That was when Haleem knew that Kamal had been hiding at Sheikh Jawad's house during the first two days of the uprising. The fat kid Murtada told Haleem about Kamal, and he also told him that after two days of hiding at the sheikh's house Kamal, disguised in women's clothes, made his way toward the big city and then to the outskirts and waited in a deserted orchard for the government troops to arrive. Little did they know that Kamal walked all night, to the outskirts of the provinces, wearing a woman's black robe and later he surrendered to the government's troops led by the tyrant's cousin. He joined them and provided them with a long list of all of those who participated in the rebellion and provided the elite units with valuable information about the size of the rebel force and how many machine guns they had. He gave the government troops all the information they needed about the locations, numbers, and weaponry of the rebels. The general in charge of the government force was the cousin of divine leader himself and was notorious for his ruthlessness. Rumors circulated about him shooting political prisoners every Thursday when he drank. He asked Kamal if he was loyal to the divine leader.

"Sir, if you want me to, I will execute all the people from my town who revolted against our divine leader. I will execute them with my own hands."

The general smiled and said, "That is what you will do," and gave Kamal a Kalashnikov and ordered him to join the troops and be their guide. At that moment, people in Balluria and Tawsheeha and the surrounding villages started to evacuate their homes, as no one was willing to stay and fight. People loaded their belongings and valuables into cars, carriages, and wheelbarrows. They started walking toward the south and the west, where the Americans were. Even Abdullah and his wife, Basima, left the town. Haleem was not angry with them. He was sad about the fate of the revolution, the beautiful revolution was not meant to be. Haleem sat on the chair outside the party headquarters building enjoying the feeling of the afternoon's sun touching his face and asked Murtada to make some tea. He sat there thinking of what would happen in the next twenty-four hours while the force of five rebels manned the only checkpoint left on the road between Balluria and the capital of the province. They stood there waiting for any vehicle and any information. The six men stayed awake all night. None of them could sleep. They stayed all night waiting for any news, but no vehicle had passed by them that night. In the morning Ashraf made some tea and looked around the party headquarters for food, but there was none. He and Hamza walked to the market, but none of the stores were open. They headed back to the headquarters. Haleem was resting his head on his chair. Hayder was loading the PKC machine gun, the only one they had, and counting the grenades.

"One, two, three. Four and five. We have five grenades."

Haleem opened his eyes and asked if there was any tea left and asked again if there was any news from the big city. No one said anything.

"There is tea, if you want."

Looking at his group, Haleem knew they had no chance of defending Balluria from the unavoidable attack, and even if they defended it for one day, what would happen the next day, and the day after, and the day after that? Even though he wanted to stay because there was nowhere to go and no place to hide, he hoped that that some miracle would occur to stir up the hellish waiting for the end, whatever it might be. It would be better than the waiting. "If it's going to be death, then let it come soon." Haleem started thinking about his mother and his little brothers, who left town without saying good-bye to him. They went to a village near the marshes to stay with relatives because he had no time to look for food for them. Too busy with his little revolution, he started thinking about Ashraf and Salah, Hamza, Hayder, and Murtada the young men who followed him and believed in what he was preaching. He started believing he would be responsible for their deaths too. He knew that the government troops were only a few hours away from Balluria, and he knew that he would not leave the town. He knew that he would die defending his town and his home and his dream and his revolution. With these thoughts in his head, Haleem called the five young men to gather so he could address them.

"A man could never ask for better friends and better companions. I am honored to have been with you at this time of our lives. If any one of you wants to leave, now is the time," he told his small group, but the five men did not respond. They were distracted by the gathering of many families who had not left Balluria yet. A number of women, children, and older men gathered by the checkpoint, hoping that Haleem and the five young rebels could stop a bus or any vehicle that could carry the many women who wore black robes and many noisy children who cried continuously.

Balluria was deserted. Almost all the people had left the intersection where the roads led to the great city in the south, but they were told that the great city was controlled by the government forces. All the people of Balluria and people from Tawsheeha and other villages stayed near a small American force distributing canned food and thin blankets. Some of the people who thought they would not be punished stayed in Balluria, locked their doors and waited, but when they heard sounds of artillery on the horizon, they all rushed to the checkpoint and waited for any passersby who might have news.

It was a beautiful April day. The glamorous sun rose; its rays washed the streets with a fresh and energetic breath. Haleem ordered his comrades to man the checkpoint in front of the headquarters and to stop all vehicles and ask for three things: how far the tyrant's troops were from Balluria, if they had any ammunition, and if they could take the women and children with them to the Americans. The five men stood at the checkpoint and waited for people who might have any answers or for a vehicle that might have enough gasoline or space to take the many women and children to where the Americans were.

When the news came, it was in a different form than what Haleem had hoped for. It came in the form of an artillery shell that landed on the northern outskirts of Balluria. It hit a palm grove about a mile away from the headquarters. The women and children and older men flew into a panic as they realized how close the government's elite guard unit was. If they could hit Balluria with an artillery shell, then they would enter the town before sundown. The artillery shell was a confirmation for all of those who had not left Balluria that the heavy hand of the divine leader was about to crush Balluria. Many people opened their locked doors, carried their essentials, and made it to the headquarters to ask for any available transportation. They found Haleem standing in the front of the building with Hamza, Hayder, and Ashraf, while Salah and Murtada walked to where they saw rising smoke to see where the artillery shell had landed and if there were any casualties. All the people still in Balluria went to the checkpoint, asking for help to go to where the Americans were, where they would be safe. Haleem did not waste the opportunity to try one last time to boost his rebel forces with new volunteers and to convince the people to stay and fight for their town and defend their right to life and freedom. He read a fiery speech to the shivering crowd as he stood on the metal desk left in front of the building because it was too heavy to be looted.

Haleem shouted at them from his perch. "Where are you going?"

The crowd turned their heads and eyes to Haleem.

"Do you want to go to hunger and humiliation? Why are leaving your houses and your belongings? Did you read the Qur'an, where it says that those who die defending their homes are martyrs? Stay with me, and let us defend our homes!"

Silence ran through the crowd, and, for a moment, Haleem thought that he had reached the hearts of the people.

"The tyrant's troops are heading to your town and they will not leave anyone alone. They will punish you—they will kill you. Listen to me, people. A man's life is a noble stand, and here we should make our stand defending our hometowns and our homes."

There was no response from the crowd as they all looked at him without replying. Haleem again thought that his words were having the right effect, and he thought that he might be able to convince enough people to defend Balluria, and maybe others would join him later when they heard about his heroic battle, and God only knew that the fate of the entire revolution might depend on him and his stand in Balluria.

"Let history remember us as the town that stood up to the tyrant and defeated him here in Balluria." He spoke his words and looked to see if any of the people standing like statues were affected by his heartfelt speech. He looked into the crowd, and something grabbed his attention. One face in the crowd made him forget about the nearing battle. He saw the Bushra the older of the Hillaly girls standing in the crowd with her sister, Adawya, father, mother, and younger siblings. He stopped talking.

It was a beautiful April day, and the sun had washed the town with a fresh ray of near realities that no one was ready for, but for Haleem, his realities had disappeared when he saw the sun casting its glorious light on the faces of the two Hillaly girls. His eyes were fixated on the scene in front of him, the scene of the beautiful face of Bushra and the massive darkness of a her hair. Haleem wished that everyone and everything could disappear for him so that he could have a few moments alone with the woman he had loved for many years. He wished that he could reach her and touch her hair as she stood in the end of the crowd. He looked at Bushra and realized that she looked older, and she tried to cover her head with a black veil, but her hair could still be seen from underneath the veil. She looked at him and he looked at her like they were both seeing each other for the first and last time.

She had never seen him as she saw him that day; he was grown. She no longer saw the desperate teenager who had been in love with her and had tried to win her heart for long years. She did not see him as the sweaty kid who spent many afternoons walking by her window with Salam, the son of the mayor who left Balluria years ago. She did not see him as the student who sent her ten love letters a day, letters that she never replied to because deep in her heart she knew that he would always love her forever, and he did. She looked at him as he stood there talking like a leader preparing to lead his small army into a desperate battle like all the movie stars she always dreamed of meeting. She looked at him and remembered that in one of his hundreds of love letters to her that she never answered he asked her for a lock of her hair so he could keep it with him for the rest of his life. She not only did not send the hair, but she also told Barrya to ask him to stop sending love letters. She stood there looking at the man who had loved her for years just as he was about to face his sad fate. At that moment, she wanted to cut all of her hair and give it to him. He looked like a beaten commander betrayed by all of his army. His deep eyes looked deeper and wider as fatigue and hunger dripped from them onto his bony cheeks as he was in tears asking the people of the town to stay and fight, but no one did.

He begged, "Stay not for me but for your sons and daughters. Stay with me so we can defend the people we love."

His speech was interrupted with another artillery shell that hit about six hundred meters from where the crowd had grown tired of Haleem's speech. That was the sign for everyone to flee. People ran toward the south end of the town and disappeared between the houses and the orchards. Haleem stopped talking as no one was there to listen. The five men gathered outside the headquarters and looked for direction or orders from Haleem, who appeared lost. A family consisting of a man with an injured arm, his pregnant wife, and two small children came running from where the shell just landed and passed by the five men.

"Did the shell hit your house?" Salah asked.

"No, it hit a house near mine," the frantic man replied.

"Is anyone hurt?" Ashraf asked.

"Yes. Lamia, the grocery vender. Um Qadoury's daughter, she is dead. The bomb landed next to her and tore her into many pieces," the man said, and then he asked if there were any vehicles to take him and his family to the Americans.

Haleem looked at his friends. They all knew Lamia, a girl who did not attend school with them, but she sold vegetables with her mother, Um Qadoury, in the town's market. In fact, she was, for a brief period, an unknown admirer who sent many letters to their friend Salam.

"Poor girl," Haleem said. He looked at his men. "The tyrant's troops are very near," Haleem said as he grabbed his Kalashnikov and walked to the checkpoint where his small rebel force of five men looked at the horizon, where the smoke of the artillery shell still rose. They waited for him to say something. He looked at them and said, "If any of you want to leave, the troops will be here in one hour, and no one is left in the town. If you want to leave, you'd better hurry up."

Hayder, Hamza, and Murtada had followed Haleem in all the battles, they had followed him since the start of the revolution and then in the big uprising in the capital of the province. Once on the outskirts of the province's capital, they followed him like they were his staff officers in his imaginary army, but seeing the smoke coming from the distance as the government troops scorched everything they passed by made the three young men think twice about facing certain death. It was Hayder who looked to Haleem and said, "If you want me, I will stay, but if you allow me to go, I will go."

"You can go, Hayder. You are a brave kid."

"Can I go too?" Hamza asked.

"Yes, you can. Just leave your Kalashnikovs and the bullets. Here, you can take my pistol." Haleem turned to Murtada. "You can go too."

"But I don't want to go. I want to stay with you."

"No, you will go, and if you really want to fight, you can come back again when there will be another revolution."

"When will that be?"

"You never know. Surely there will be others like us," Haleem said in a disappointed voice.

Murtada gave him his Kalashnikov and two magazines and began to walk away with Hayder and Hamza. Haleem reached into his coat and said, "There is something else I want to give you boys." The three boys turned to him, and he handed Hayder all the money he had in his pocket and said, "You will need it. I don't have any use for it now. Divide it among you, and if you see my mother and my little brothers, please give them some."

The fat kid Murtada started to cry, and so did Salah and Ashraf, who looked at Haleem and realized that he was preparing himself to die.

"Go with God's peace," Haleem said. The three boys took the money and hurried away on the main road that led out toward the intersection to the great city in the south. That's where everyone was saying that the Americans were offering canned food and blankets and safety. Haleem went back inside and sat on the chair where Kamal used to sit. He could not escape the image of Bushra and her dark, beautiful hair.

Ashraf entered the room. "Why don't we just leave? I mean we cannot defend the town. The three of us."

"You can go if you want."

"But I can't. Where is Salah?"

"He is outside looking for anyone that brings him some news," Ashraf said.

"Let us go and be with him," Haleem said.

The two went outside and joined Salah at the checkpoint in the street looking toward the northern outskirts of the town. They looked in the direction in which where the smoke of the artillery shell was still rising and waited for the troops to arrive. Hearing the screeching noise of the metal behind them. They turned around, and to their surprise, they saw Barrya pushing Hisham in his wheelchair toward them. Haleem knew that she would never leave, and she would never leave Hisham behind. He felt safe for the moment.

"That is Namsawi artillery. An Austrian-made artillery shell," Hisham shouted from a distance. "I recognize the smell from my days on the eastern front," Hisham added as he pointed to the smoke of the artillery shell. "Ten more shells will be enough to destroy this miserable town," he said as he reached his three friends standing at the checkpoint near the defaced portrait of the tyrant.

"What in the hell are you still doing here?" Hisham screamed in his loud voice that reminded them of his screams on the soccer field.

427

"Yes, what are you still doing here?" Barrya asked. Ashraf and Salah did not reply; instead, they waited for Haleem to answer, and he did with an argumentative tone.

"Hisham, why are you still here? Barrya, please go and take him with you to the intersection where the Americans are."

Hisham looked at them and said, "Don't worry about me. Just tell me what you are planning to do."

"What do you think we will do? We will stay and fight," Haleem said.

"I don't think that's a good idea," Hisham said. "I don't see anyone digging trenches and fortifying barricades. You want to fight four armored brigades with three men? What's wrong with you, Haleem? You know you will die."

"There is nothing wrong with me, Hisham," Haleem replied. "But I will not leave Balluria to the tyrant's troops"

"What is in Balluria that is so sacred and worth dying for?" Hisham asked sarcastically.

"Home. To me dying is better than living with people who cannot or will not defend their right to life," Haleem replied with a calm voice.

"Home could be anywhere," Hisham rebutted

"No matter what you will say, Hisham, I am not leaving. Even if I stayed alone, Allah would be with me. Don't you believe in Allah?"

"No, I don't." Hisham answered. "But I believe that you and these two morons will be dead soon. You can stay and die, but for what?" Hisham said as he looked at Haleem and realized that he was wasting his breath since Haleem had no intention of leaving. Hisham turned to Ashraf and Salah. "What about you two?"

"They can leave if they want," Haleem said.

"I am not leaving; I will not leave him to die by himself," Ashraf said.

"I am not leaving either," Salah answered. Barrya could not keep herself from crying. She started wiping her tears as she heard the words of the three young men. Hisham paused for a moment, and he tuned his voice down and exhaled his cigarette's smoke.

"Wallah. You are a group of idiots, and all of you will be dead within two hours. Tell me. What weapons do you have?"

"We have five Kalashnikovs and five grenades and a PKC with one strip of bullets," Ashraf answered.

"Where is the PKC?" Hisham asked

"We mounted it behind the tyrant's portrait."

Hisham put his hand on his face and started acting like he was the leader again just like when they were Wolves on the soccer field. "Ashraf, you and Salah. Take the PKC machine gun and mount it on top of the old mayor's house. You know, where Salam used to live. It's the best place for it. It will give you cover fire as you fight the troops, because they can only enter from this road unless they decide to take the riverbank. As for you, Haleem, you take two Kalashnikovs and two grenades and stay at the headquarters. You two." He pointed to Salah and Ashraf. "You see that house across the street? It's attached to another house and to several other houses. You shoot only once from each house. So when they attack us, we will fire from three points."

"What do you mean us?" Haleem asked with some surprise and slowly growing confidence.

"Well, my friend, you win. I am not leaving either, and from the way you lead this small revolution I believe that you could have been the captain of our soccer team," Hisham said with smile.

"You will always be a better captain, Hisham," Haleem replied with a smile.

"If any of us stay alive, we will meet at Barrya's house when darkness falls," Hisham said as he turned his wheelchair backward toward the town's main square where the deserted old mayor's house was.

"What will you do?" Halem asked.

"Barrya will take me to the mayor's house. I will be on the PKC machine gun. Don't shoot unless I shoot first, you hear, and don't say good-bye to me or to each other. The last thing I need in this situation is a soft moment with tears," Hisham said and turned his face away, trying to hide his own tears.

"Yellah, Barrya, push me and don't look at them because soon you will be looking at all of us lying here with thousands of bullets in each of our bodies. Just push me."

Barrya pushed Hisham toward the deserted mayor's house, when he turned around and shouted, "Hey, Haleem!"

Haleem and the others stopped and looked back at Hisham.

"What, Hisham?" Haleem replied.

"You were right."

"About what?"

"Dying is better than living with people who can't defend their right to life," Hisham said as he looked at his friends, who walked toward the north entrance of the town waiting for the tyrant's army and the party militia to arrive in massive force. Barrya pushed Hisham in his wheelchair back to the deserted mayor's house, where he and Barrya struggled very hard to push the wheelchair up the stairs. When they realized that it would be impossible to do that, Hisham jumped out of the wheelchair and crawled up the stairs, saying, "I will not need this royal carriage anymore." He used his hands to crawl to the roof, while Barrya carried up the PKC machine gun and the strip of bullets. Breathless, he laid next to the machine gun, lit up a cigarette, and told the teary-eyed Gypsy woman to leave.

"You must go to your house now, Mother Barrya, and don't come out until you stop hearing the sounds of battle."

Barrya stood there, cried for a minute, and asked him, "Will I ever see you boys alive again?"

Hisham looked at her and said with a smile, "You will see us alive at least one last time. You will see all of us. I promise."

The Book of Balluria

The Last Three Standing

1

The government's special troops entered Balluria on a beautiful April day. After saying their farewells, they agreed to meet at the Gypsy woman's house if they stayed alive. Haleem did not say anything, nor did he try to ramp up the morale of his tiny force. Ashraf smiled at Haleem and said, "At least we will be remembered in the folk poetry recited in guesthouses in these parts."

Salah agreed with a nod. After they watched Barrya pushing Hisham's wheelchair to the old mayor's house, the two friends shook Haleem's hand and searched for a suitable battle position, where they could hold on and resist the attacking regiment. They walked toward the strip of deserted houses facing the party's headquarters building. The houses had a complete and open view of the road that led to the province's capital, and the only paved road that Hisham thought capable of allowing the passage of armored vehicles and government troops. The armored vehicles and the government's troops would be coming through the strip of houses attached to several other houses, which would make it easy for them to escape if they ran out of ammunition, and while Ashraf took a position in the house that directly faced the north entrance of Balluria, Salah took a position in the second story of the house that once belonged to Comrade Uraiby, the party's chief who never returned from the war with the Americans on the southern borders. The house was one of the biggest in Balluria, and it was painted gray and yellow, similar to the building of the party's headquarters, and its walls were built with hardened concrete. Salah pointed his Kalashnikov from one of the windows and waited for a sign of the government troops. Three miles north of Balluria, a sizable force of the presidential guard elite units led by a stocky colonel with a thick moustache and big belly prepared to attack Balluria. The colonel ordered his artillery battery to shell the town in order to spread fear and intimidation among the rebels. The military regiment was joined by almost one hundred of the party's irregular militia led by Kamal, who acted as a guide for them, riding in the first armored vehicle. Before the battle, the commander asked Kamal how many rebels he thought would be in Balluria.

"No more than twenty men with Kalashnikovs. Maybe fewer," Kamal answered, but the colonel was not about to take a risk of losing more men since he had lost almost three hundred of his best men in the battle for the capital of the province in which a small rebel force of fifty determined young men put up a fierce resistance and prevented the government troops from entering the city for two weeks. He had been forced to bombard the city with a thousand rounds of artillery, which cost more casualties among women and children and forced the rebels to leave the city. The colonel wanted to do the same with Balluria.

The commander then ordered a battalion of his force to attack Balluria after he shattered the town with fifty rounds of artillery that landed on the outskirts of the town and near the main square, except for one that directly hit the middle school because Kamal had urged the commander to do so. He advised that the school might be where the rebels would set up their headquarters.

The battle was short and fierce. The government troops simply drove up the main road dividing Balluria into two. Haleem positioned himself by the door of the old party headquarters, Ashraf and Salah stayed in the empty houses facing the main road, the same position Hisham told them to be in. Haleem, Ashraf, and Salah waited for Hisham to fire first. Hisham, who had smoked almost all of his cigarettes, was the only one of the four friends who had formal military training and had been in several battles on the eastern front. He realized that he and his three inexperienced rebel friends had only half an hour to put up a fight. So he waited for the troops to enter the town so they could be in his firing range and waited for the government vehicles to be in the narrow streets and between the houses so that they would lose the advantage of maneuvering and for the gunners to lose the advantage of using their machine guns.

It was about two in the afternoon when the first armored military vehicle could be seen in the distance. The young men's hearts pounded with fear and anxiety. The first military truck carried twenty masked solders wearing their dark green uniforms. They quickly dismounted from their vehicle. Other trucks carrying soldiers and party militiamen with their weapons drove into the main road and dismounted. Soldiers took positions and ran to take cover by the walls of the town's houses. Several other trucks followed as hundreds soldiers and party militiamen kept dismounting and entering the narrow roads. Spreading out in groups of two and three, they fired at each of the houses they entered. The colonel and Kamal, with the rest of the force, entered Balluria riding in the armored vehicle. They dismounted about four hundred meters from the party headquarters and looked for any movement. A squad of soldiers then walked toward the yellow and gray party building with their weapons pointed ahead. Haleem, alone in the building, waited for the signal from Hisham, who patiently watched and waited for the soldiers to get closer. The short colonel thought that the town was empty. He ordered the soldiers to shoot anything that moved, and he ordered his soldiers to bring him anyone they found alive in the town as they walked slowly. The soldiers fired on the windows and doors of the nearby houses, and there was no response. He asked Kamal what he thought.

"They must be hiding somewhere, sir, like the rats they are," Kamal answered.

"Nonsense," the commander said. "They must have gotten scared and left." He ordered a full sweep of the town. Groups of soldiers walked toward the main square and closer to the party headquarters. Kamal looked at the building, with ashes and smoke still rising from it. The walls were painted with graffiti that condemned the tyrant. The words freedom and equality were spelled out in a red paint on the main entrance and on the walls. He breathed with relief as he realized that he would be back in the headquarters and sitting in his chair by the day's end. As he walked toward the building with a group of soldiers and party militia, when suddenly a scream of pain ripped through the unrecognizable noises of the soldiers. A spray of bullets took down three of the soldiers, who walked in front of the column. Hisham opened fire.

2

The soldiers had no idea where the precise and accurate fire was coming from as they scrambled for cover, but they were too close and too exposed. Haleem opened fire, spraying the truck closest to the party headquarters with his first magazine. He did not see how many soldiers, if any, he hit. He just reloaded and threw his first grenade. Then he leapt over the back fence of the building and ran toward the nearest house. He quickly ran to the roof and looked at the street as the government troops ran for cover from the experienced firing that Hisham laid down on the main street. Almost thirty soldiers fell to the ground, and some started to crawl and scream with pain. Blood painted red shapes on the perfect black pavement of the main road. Salah and Ashraf had perfect shots at the armored vehicles carrying the colonel and Kamal, and they unloaded all of their ammunition on it. Bullets hit and ricocheted off the vehicles, whizzing by Kamal's face. The battalion of soldiers looked like a herd of sheep penetrated by a pack of hungry young wolves as they ran for cover into the houses on the side of the road.

The commander screamed, "You cowards! I want to launch an attack now." He pulled out his side arm and started shooting at his retreating soldiers. "Mortars, mortars. Bomb them with mortars."

Hisham kept firing until his strip of bullets was empty, and that's when the first mortar round hit the house next to him, and soon after, three rocket-propelled grenades hit the mayor's house. As he regained his senses, Hisham was covered with dust, pieces of wood, and stones from the blast, and he searched for his pack of cigarettes. He was out of ammunition. Haleem had only one magazine and one grenade left, and Ashraf and Salah had half of a magazine each. Salah and Ashraf jumped from house to house and kept shooting in the direction of the government troops, who did not know how many rebels were actually in the town.

When the first ten mortar rounds hit Balluria, Haleem looked at the town and saw the smoke coming from the burnt houses, and he realized that all the rounds had landed in the old section and that one of the rounds had hit the deserted and deteriorating house of Adnan's family. After realizing that he was running out of bullets, Haleem stopped shooting and retreated walking to where Salah and Ashraf were positioned, hoping that he would find them. He had only six bullets left. He walked past the school and entered the old section by the corner where Abdullah's house was. He leaned against the wall exhausted and thirsty, wishing he could have a sip of Barrya's fresh, cold yogurt. He checked his weapon to see if it was still functional, and then he heard voices coming from a house nearby. He pointed his Kalashnikov and looked toward where voices came from. He saw Ashraf and Salah pulling a dead woman's body from the street where a mortar round had landed minutes before. He saw his two friends trying to pull the shattered dead woman's body from the wreckage while two of her children still held the dead woman's hands. Bullets whizzed by them as they finally were able to pull the dead woman's body off the road and into the open door of one of the deserted houses. Ashraf carried the two young boys inside and told them not to leave the house.

Haleem waved to Salah, and he smiled back and said, "Here, we are here." He leaned against the wall and looked toward the main road to see if the soldiers were heading in their direction. Haleem was so happy to see his friends still alive that he forgot for a brief moment the situation they were in and walked toward the house. Bullets shattered a brief quietness and Salah fell to the ground for cover.

Haleem did not feel the pain, but he walked toward Salah and asked him to get up. Haleem felt his right leg as it grown heavy and numb. He grabbed Salah by his hand and helped him get up. He asked, "What happened to Hisham?"

"He is probably dead," said Salah, who looked at Haleem's leg and added, "You are wounded in your leg."

Haleem looked at his leg and said, "I am all right. I don't feel any pain. We must find Hisham now."

"We can't," Ashraf said as he looked from the window to where many soldiers had set up checkpoints in the town square and concluded, "The soldiers are in the town square. We must stay here until dark. We can't go anywhere now."

Haleem looked at his two friends and at the two young boys and said, "These boys must be hungry. I will stand guard. You need to rest but look first for some food in the kitchen "

"You are bleeding," Ashraf replied as he pointed to Haleem's jeans drenched with blood.

"Let us wait until dark, and then we will go to Barrya's house. We may find Hisham there and maybe some yogurt and food for these two boys."

The three young men stayed in the house with the dead woman's body and her two children. The government troops drove their armored vehicles and walked on the main road as the sounds of battle fire wound down and darkness fell on Balluria. The government troops searched many houses looking for the three rebels, and finally they reported to the commander that the rebels must have run away. The three men stayed quietly in the house and tried to comfort the two little boys who were strangely silent as they stared at the dead body of their mother.

Haleem stayed by the window and did not sit down despite his wounded leg, and he could not hear any more noise outside; there was no shooting.

Just an hour before that, the short colonel, who had a thick moustache and big belly, ordered a group of twenty-five soldiers to storm the old mayor's house where Hisham was positioned. The soldiers moved toward the house as they walked close to the walls for cover, and they entered the mayor's house and kicked the door open. The soldiers were amazed about how neat and well-groomed the house and garden were. They entered the house.

As he ran out ammunition, Hisham could not move away from his machine gun; he laid there waiting for the soldiers to arrive. He searched the pocket of his old military jacket that he wore over his traditional Arab dishdasha dress for his pack of cigarettes and found two cigarettes. He smoked the first one and leaned against the wall waiting for the soldiers to enter. He knew that he would be dead soon. He did not say any prayers; instead, he wondered if heavens or the afterworld would have soccer fields and if he would be able to play there. The soldiers smashed all the doors and shot the glass windows out. They fired on the furniture and the kitchen as they cleared the rooms in the house. Cautiously, they climbed the stairs, and then threw a grenade and looked out on the roof. They saw Hisham lying next to the PKC machinegun and smoking his last cigarette waiting for them. He was out of bullets, and had no legs to run with. So, he just waited for them to show up and spray him with bullets. They did not; instead, they clubbed him with rifles butts and beat him with their boots. Some of them were screaming and shouting.

"You crippled bastard. Do you know how many soldiers you killed?"

They had orders not to kill him. The commander needed one rebel alive for interrogation. The soldiers dragged Hisham with his bloodied face and neck down the stairs and outside the house, put him in his wheelchair, and pushed him to where the colonel and Kamal had set up their command post in the party headquarter as the yellow and gray building started to regain its fearsome and grim impression of unquestionable authority and fear. Soldiers and party militiamen in dark olive-green uniforms stood next to the entrance and others stayed in military vehicles with mounted machine guns, Kamal was surprised to see Hisham entering the headquarters in his wheelchair. He did not believe what the soldiers were saying about Hisham being the gunman.

"Sir, we got him. This crippled bastard was the one shooting at us with the PKC."

"Are you sure?" the commander asked.

"Yes, sir, we found him on top of the house with this machine gun," the sergeant said.

Kamal was so angry. He asked the sergeant again, "You found this man, this crippled man?"

"Yes, Comrade. He was waiting for us," the thin, tanned sergeant answered.

Kamal stood up and grabbed what looked like a thick, black rubber hose. "You son of a whore. You son of a whore. He started to beat Hisham with the rubber hose that he carried around as new symbol of the way he would deal with those who revolted against the divine leader."

He screamed to his comrades, "Put this dog in jail until the commander interrogates him. Then we will know when to execute him." The comrades and soldiers pushed the bloodied Hisham in his wheelchair into the back of the building, where a dark cell filled with empty boxes of ammunition was. Hisham asked one the soldiers if he had any cigarettes, and the soldier said no.

When darkness started dressing the town with its shadows of death and destruction, it also brought with it a feeling of calmness and easiness. Many families who did not fear any punishment and only hid in the nearby palm orchards and waited for the battle to end, returned to the town that night. The graceful clergyman Sayed Habeeb was one of these returners; he went directly to the headquarters and asked to see Kamal. Sayed Habeeb asked Kamal for permission to collect the dead bodies from the streets and bury them. Kamal granted this permission and told the clergyman that if he needed help, he could send some soldiers and militiamen to aid him, but Sayed Habeeb said no; he would seek help if he needed it. Other families who did not reach the Americans that day started to return to the town. The Hillaly family had returned as well that night. Abdullah and Basima also returned as did Iman; Salah had asked for her hand in marriage only weeks before the uprising. They all shared a ride in one old truck back to Balluria. It seemed like they all knew that the battle would not last long, and they had all decided to come back at the same time.

The short colonel was ready to advance to the south with his troops. So he left Kamal and his party militiamen in charge of Balluria, and with him he left a platoon of soldiers under the command of a young arrogant lieutenant. Before he left, the short colonel with a thick moustache and big belly gave Kamal strict orders. "If you arrest any of the traitors, execute them. These are the orders of His Excellency, the divine leader."

"I will do that gladly," Kamal replied.

When Kamal sat in his chair, there was one person that he wanted to see the most: Haleem, who he knew, had something to do with defacing the president's portrait. Kamal thought that Haleem was hiding somewhere by the river or in the prairie near the train station. But Kamal also knew that Haleem was not the kind of a person who would run away.

At that same moment, Haleem, Ashraf, and Salah waited until dark had completely covered the town and took the two children with them and walked past the many water puddles where Adnan's house was still smoking from the early mortar round. Ashraf had his Kalashnikov hidden under his robe, and Haleem had one grenade. Without discussing anything or thinking, planning, or even looking at each other, the three carried the two orphans and walked the road they knew by heart as though a mysterious magical hand had guided them to the place where they would feel safe in, at least for that last night before the fearful unknown. They went to the end of the town, passed the soccer field where the secluded mud hut stood alone, as though it was built standing on a chicken leg from the folk tales that had sacred children in these parts for ages.

The three young men entered the house carrying the two boys. Barrya was waiting for them as she lit up a small fire and prepared the teakettle and did not say a word. They sat near the fire. They were tired and hungry, and the two little children were silent, as they did not comprehend what had happened that day and what that day would mean to them as they lived their lives in Balluria.

"I know one thing I can do," Barrya said, and she disappeared for twenty minutes and came back with a big pot of fresh yogurt.

3

Deep in his heart Kamal knew that his three friends who betrayed him and betrayed the divine leader had not left Balluria. He also knew that he would spare nothing and no one to find them before the night was over. He knew that he was willing to kill all of them. Kamal knew that if they managed to escape, he would lose all of his power in these parts. He also knew that if they managed to escape, they might join Hamid with his group of bandits, and soon they would come to kill him. Kamal knew that Hisham would be executed in the morning and that there was nothing he could do about it, nor did he want to do anything about it. That would be something that the Wolves would never forgive him for. Hisham's death would be enough reason for the Wolves to hunt him for the rest for their lives. Kamal thought of the many places they could be hiding in. He sat watching the young lieutenant, who proved to be a torture expert. Kamal watched as the young lieutenant was strangely cheerful as he made Hisham cry from pain as they put metal wire into his wounds and sprayed salt on his opened flesh and squeezed it in. Hisham's tears mixed with the blood on his face, making it unrecognizable. Kamal sat there watching as the two of the elite guards, directed by the neat-looking lieutenant, squeezed Hisham's fingers with a vise grip. Kamal heard the distinctive cracking noise of Hisham's bones.

The lieutenant, who seemed to be enjoying his task, said, "You know, we have a cure for people like you, people who think they will not talk. Just to let you know, in the end you will talk. I have many other methods, and we have all night."

But it did not take a long time and more innovative torture techniques to make Hisham talk. He was thankful that they waited until the night was over before they started to interrogate him. Hisham thought that one night was enough for his three friends to escape from Balluria. He thought that his three rebel friends would be enjoying a hot meal near where the Americans had set up many checkpoints on the main highway of the southern provinces, a checkpoint that became the gateway between hellish fear and warm safety near the desert highway. The young lieutenant with a neatly groomed moustache wanted the answers for two questions: "Who was with you? And where are they?"

And Kamal wanted the answer for one question: "Who defaced the tyrant's portrait?"

Hisham tried to say that he was alone, but the pain was too severe. He confessed, realizing that he would be executed no matter what answers gave. But he knew it would be the end of his pain.

"It was me, Haleem, Ashraf, Salah, and three other kids. I don't know their names."

"Where are they now?" the lieutenant asked.

"They may be dead or fled the town," Hisham answered.

"Who defaced the portrait?" Kamal asked him.

"I don't know," Hisham said as he choked with blood.

Kamal was not convinced. When they searched the dead bodies scattered in the streets, the soldiers did not find any bodies that looked like those of the three men. The bodies were mainly those of women and children. After the search parties of soldiers and party militia came back empty handed to the headquarters, Kamal was furious and angry. Kamal knew that Haleem was the one who had instigated the uprising, and he knew that he would not flee Balluria. Kamal looked outside, to where Balluria's houses ended and the prairie began and said, "I know where they are hiding." He looked to the end of town beyond where the soccer field was.

Hastily that night, Kamal formed a mixed force of thirty men. Some were elite guard soldiers, and some were party militiamen. Quietly, they walked through the narrow streets of the town toward Barrya's mud hut. The force surrounded the hut and Kamal shouted, "Surrender yourselves, or I will burn you alive in the house."

Barrya and the other two men looked at Haleem, waiting for a response. Ashraf and Salah grabbed the Kalashnikovs and readied themselves, to fight, but Haleem signaled them not to. He pointed to the two little boys sleeping and said to Ashraf:

"Wake them up gently." Then he added, "If we fight, they will kill all of us, and they will burn Barrya's house."

Haleem looked at Barrya and said, "Go out there and tell them there are children in the house, and tell them that we will surrender."

Barrya walked out cautiously and said, "Kamal, it's me, Barrya. I am coming out."

"Do not shoot," Kamal ordered his troops.

"There are children in the house, and Haleem said they will surrender," Barrya said with a fear-rattled voice.

Kamal looked at her and asked, "Haleem is here? Who are the children?"

"Two orphans. Their mother was killed in the bombings. They have no one and nowhere to go," Barrya answered.

Kamal took a deep breath and said, "You keep the children with you inside until someone claims them. And tell the Wolves to come out with their hands on their heads. It's over. He charged his Kalashnikov and put his finger on the trigger and then added,

"Tell Haleem to come out first with his hands on his head."

Haleem and the others were listening to the conversation. Haleem shouted, "We are coming out"

The three young rebels walked out one by one to where Kamal and the force were waiting. Slowly and quietly, they were handcuffed, thrown to the ground, and then beaten by the soldiers of the elite guards aided by the party militiamen.

"Traitors."

"Sons of dogs."

"Sons of whores."

Shouts rose from the group of soldiers, as they kicked and clubbed the three young men.

Kamal stood silently and watched without interfering, and when Barrya begged him to order the soldiers to stop, she cried, "They are your brothers. They are your friends."

He pushed her away and shouted, "Not anymore."

The soldiers beat the three men with their rifles butts and their boots, and one of the soldiers kicked Haleem in his wounded right knee.

"Son of shit," the solder said.

After twenty minutes of merciless beating, Kamal ordered the soldiers to stop beating the three men and said: "It does not matter now. They will be dead within a day or so."

The force of thirty men walked all the way to the headquarters with Kamal in front, with his black rubber hose in his right hand and his Kalashnikov in his left. People gathered in the streets after hearing the noise of the soldiers to see the three men being paraded toward the headquarters. Some people who had returned to town after the sounds of the battle had quieted down looked at the three men who looked like historical prisoners from a mythological war. Mud and blood covered their faces, their hair, and their bodies. Some of spectators spat at the three men to show the soldiers that they were loyal to the divine president. Some called the men traitors. Others just looked in disbelief at the scene. The three men walked with their heads high and eyes looking at the people, who were speechless. There were no chants, as many people walked behind the group of soldiers and party militiamen leading the men to the yellow and gray buildings. The cell inside the headquarters was dark, which made the men somewhat comfortable after the long and extremely stressful day. The three men were pushed inside, with kicks from the guards.

A familiar voice greeted them with, "Ahlan washalan. Welcome." The three men did not believe their ears. They all jumped with joy to see the silhouette of the man who was sitting in the dark corner of the cell.

"Hisham?" screamed Ashraf.

"Ya-Allah. Hisham, are you alive?" Haleem screamed with tears.

"Yes," Hisham said. The three young men surrounded Hisham and hugged and kissed him. For a moment, the four young men forgot the time and the place they were in.

"Oh, my Allah, look what they have done to you," Ashraf said to Hisham.

"Look what they have done to you," Hisham replied, and then he smiled and asked, "How is Barrya? Did the soldiers harm her?"

"No, she is fine."

A moment of silence ran through the room and, and the reality started to sink into their minds and the conscience.

"Hisham, what do you think they will do to us?" Salah asked.

"We will be executed, my friend. All of us will be executed tomorrow. I suggest you either pray or sleep," Hisham said with acceptance of his fate, but they all stayed awake.

The four friends did not talk about events of the battle, nor did they talk about the certain death awaiting them. Instead, they talked about soccer. The four men spent the night laughing about the time Hisham was angry with Lateef for three months because he wasted a perfect chance to score a goal against the Wild Lions. They also talked about how Hayat, the town's whore, destroyed their goals and tore their nets, and they spoke of the seven palm trees and the pack of wolves who were dreaming in that glorious Arabian desert night. The four men wondered where Hamid was that night and if he was dead or alive. They also wondered whether Salam was really in America. Or was he still in Baghdad? They also talked about Abdullah and the other Wolves and the girls. Haleem was wondering about what happened to the Hillaly girls, especially Bushra. The sting of pain and deprivation slashed his heart as he realized he would die without touching the hair of the older Hillaly girl. Salah thought of Iman, his bride who would become a widow before she would be a wife. And he wondered what would life have been like if he had married her. He wondered if she was thinking about him that moment, and that's when Hisham asked, "Do you think Barrya will be all right? I mean after we are dead?"

The four men cried as they remembered Barrya, the mother of Wolves, being alone in her mud hut crying about her cubs.

Kamal walked by the cell and saw them crying. He ordered the guard to give them cigarettes, and later he opened the cell and sat with them after he made sure they were all handcuffed.

"I heard you laughing," Kamal said. "What were you laughing about?"

"We laughed because we remembered when Hisham beat up Lateef for missing scoring the goal against the Wild Lions, and the game had to stop because he chased after Lateef for ten minutes," Ashraf said.

"Oh, yes. That was some time ago," Kamal said, with a slight smile, and he looked to Haleem and his wounded leg and said, "You are not going to die from that. It's a flesh wound. Haleem looked at him with a grim look without answering.

"Kamal, what will happen to us?" Salah asked.

"You will be executed. It is the commander's orders," Kamal answered without any apparent emotion on his face.

"Can I ask you for one last thing, Kamal?"

"What is it?" Kamal replied

"Can you make sure that the two young boys we left at Barrya's house are cared for?" Haleem said.

He was interrupted by Kamal's firm voice. "Don't ask me anything, you traitors. Just answer me one thing. Who defaced the president's portrait? It was you Haleem?"

The four young men looked at Kamal, and then looked at Haleem, who stood up and said, "Yes, I did. They did not. It was my idea, mine alone, and I will do it again. If I leave this cell alive, I will do it again, time and time again, and I will use shit to deface the tyrant's face, only shit," Haleem screamed from the dark end of the cell.

Kamal looked at him without anger. He stared at all of them and then said with a calm and clear voice, "You will all be executed in the town square tomorrow. If you are lucky, you will live until noon tomorrow, but you will all be shot, and I will make sure to be there to see you die, Haleem." Kamal exited the corridor where the four men fell into the darkness of the cell and the thoughts of their last night on earth.

That night the rain did not stop. It rained the entire night. It seemed as though the sky was crying for them. Rain water was drowning the town, and small twisted endless rivers had washed the blood off the streets of the town as it waited for the morning slaughter of the four condemned men who everyone had known and talked to or heard about. That night the rain did not stop Barrya from walking to the Hillaly house at the other end of the town. She went there to see the Hillaly girls, who returned to the town along with many other people, after amnesty had been given to all those who did not bear arms against the divine president. Barrya went to the Hillaly girls' house looking for Bushra, the older of the Hillaly girls. She was there for few minutes.

At first, the Hillaly mother did not want the Gypsy woman entering her house because she said that the Gypsy woman carried three liabilities, each one more dangerous than the other. The Hillaly mother said that Barrya brought with her a dishonorable reputation that would infect any woman she talked to.

441

And bad luck and evil spirits that would enter any house she entered. And the third liability, and the worst of all, she heard people saying that the Gypsy woman was a danger for being a collaborator with the rebels, because she harbored the three rebels in her house before they were captured.

But the Hillaly girls begged their mother to let her in. They took Barrya to the kitchen in the back of the house and asked her about the three men and what had happened in the house and what would happen tomorrow and who was killed in the battle and who came back to town. They talked about the four young men who would die the next day, and the two girls cried on Barrya's shoulder, and soon they were joined by all the women in the Hillalys' house who couldn't help feeling remorse for the Gypsy woman, who sounded like a mother about to lose all of her children in one night.

Before she left the house, Barrya took Bushra aside and told her that she had something very special for her, but she would not give it to her unless Bushra gave her something in return. "It's from Haleem," she claimed.

"Oh, my Allah," Bushra said as the Gypsy woman handed her a small notebook with flowers on the cover. It was the notebook Haleem used to write poetry and collected love notes in. He had sent it to Bushra many times before but every time she had sent it back with Amel, Hamid's sister, who finally gave it to Barrya. It had all the poems of Nazar Qabany and Qais and Layla.

"Haleem wrote me all of these poems when we were in school," Bushra said between her tears as she started to read the through the pages of the notebook and remembered the times when Haleem and his friend Salam, the son of the mayor, spent many hot afternoons walking back and forth by her window trying to give her the notebook, but she never opened the window.

"Yes, and he wrote more for you, throughout the years," the Gypsy woman replied.

"Haleem sent it to me many times with Amel, but I did not accept it and sent it back to him with Amel," Bushra said as a sharp thrust of regret ripped through her heart.

"I know, but Amel did not take it back to Haleem. She brought it to me because she thought it would break his heart," the Gypsy woman said as she wiped her tears. "I kept the note book all of these years in my house. Haleem thinks that you have it and you have read it," the Gypsy woman said. "I think he wants you to have it now, but I want you to give me something that he will want to see and touch before he dies."

Years later, when Bushra left town to marry a man who was twenty years her senior, she gave the notebook back to the Gypsy woman and said to her that her husband was much older than she, and she was afraid he would find the notebook and beat her or divorce her. Years afterward, the Gypsy woman sat in her mud hut talking to a stranger who had long hair, she showed him the notebook. The man who traveled to Balluria from a faraway country touched the book and almost cried. He remembered that notebook. He had written some of the poems in that notebook.

4

That night, as Balluria slept in the rain, the Gypsy woman left the Hillalys' house and walked alone in the mud toward the party headquarters, where the soldiers of the elite guards and the party militiamen were holding the prisoners. She wanted to see her Wolves for the last time.

She knew that somehow she must see them and give Haleem what Bushra had given her, even if she would be humiliated, beaten, or killed that night. The Gypsy woman had the instinct of a mother wolf who wanted to see her cubs for the last time.

The guards at the front door did not know what the old Gypsy woman wanted at two o'clock in the morning as she begged them to see the prisoners for the last time. One of the guards tried to explain to her that he had orders not to let anyone to see the condemned men, but he was not successful, as she insisted on seeing them. He kept telling her to get lost or he would hit her or put her in jail, when finally she said, "I want to see Comrade Kamal. I am related to him."

The guard paused for a minute and then said, "You wait here, I will let him know," and he turned and walked toward the inside office, where men in dark green uniforms with Kalashnikovs and cigarettes were loudly speaking and laughing. She did not wait. She followed the guard inside the main hall, where the command room was and saw Kamal sitting in his chair leaning backward half asleep with his Kalashnikov on the desk. The guard said, "Rafeeq, Comrade, there is a woman who insists on talking to you. She claims that she is the mother of the prisoners and that she is related to you, but I think she is lying."

Kamal opened his sleepy red eyes and looked at the guard, then looked behind him and saw Barrya who screamed from behind the guard, "I want to see them for the last time; you know I am their mother."

Kamal looked at her and waited for three seconds before he said, "She is not lying. She is their mother. Let her see them. Search her first and make sure she does not have any weapons on her," Kamal said as he looked at her and knew that she would not leave unless she saw them, even if he tried to scare her. She had the mother wolf in her, and he knew that look. After the guard searched her and found no concealed weapons on her person, Barrya was led to the dark cell. She quietly entered the cell and found Hisham smoking a cigarette and talking to Haleem while Salah and Ashraf sat across the cell in the corner with their eyes closed. She sat across from the iron bars, leaned on them, and wept.

Hisham was surprised to see her. "Don't cry, Barrya. Seeing you crying is harder on us than death," Hisham said.

Haleem moved closer to where she sat and asked, "How are the two little kids?" She was surprised that Haleem did not ask about his mother or his little brothers. He was more worried about the two orphans. She looked at him and answered, "They are fine. I left them at Hamid's house. Amel is taking care of them until we find their relatives."

Salah and Ashraf opened their eyes and moved closely to Haleem and Hisham. The four condemned men were happy to see Barrya. They touched her hand and begged her to stop crying.

She looked at the dark cell, and looked at four men trying to recognize the features behind the blood and mud that covered their faces and said, "I know you. You are my boys. My Wolves. Death is not a bad thing, it's not a bad thing for you and for anyone who did what you did. You are beautiful Arabian princes and always will be, and many beautiful women will be waiting for you in the afterlife," the Gypsy woman said to them. The four did not respond then she looked at Haleem, who looked at her as he tried to fight back his tears.

"Haleem, I have brought you something." She pushed her hand into her blouse, where she hid a long black clip of shiny silk like beautiful black hair and said with a quiet voice, "This is from Bushra. It's her hair. She sent it to you, and she says that she always loved you and she always will love you, and she will wait for another time and another place to be with you forever."

Haleem reached and touched the clip of hair. He felt that he was free, free once and for all. He felt that the walls of the dark cell could not contain his true love that he felt. He wanted ask the Gypsy woman about Bushra but he refrained when the guard shouted.

"Come on, old woman. You need to leave."

She looked at them with her eyes drowning in tears mixed with thick, black, Gypsy eyeliner and stood up and said with the calm, soft, yet firm voice of a devoted mother, "May my miserable soul and may my life be the sacrifice for your beautiful faces, and ransom for these beautiful black eyes," the Gypsy woman said.

The three men cried, but Hisham smiled at her with one tear coming down his bloodied rugged face and said, "See, Mother Barrya. I told you that would see us alive again."

5

The rain did not stop that night as many people in Balluria stayed up all night waiting to see what the fate would be of the four men who would be executed in the early dawn. Sayed Habeeb stayed up all night praying for mercy and comfort for the souls of condemned four men. All the girls in town stayed up talking about them. Hamid spent the night in the wilderness by the seven palm trees near Hanan's grave staring at the flames of the little fire he built from the falling leaves of the seven palm trees. He remembered the time when they first saw the wolf cubs dreaming in that faraway summer night. When morning came, it seemed like nothing was happening. But the rain stopped briefly and the sun peeked from behind the weak gray and white clouds. It was a glorious Balluria morning similar to the one on which Adnan stole all the boats. The sun rose up between promising clouds full of rain More people had arrived in Balluria and small groups of people walked to the main square, which started filling up with spectators.

Bushra stayed up all night reading the poems in the little notebook with flowers on its cover and waiting next to her window with no tears left in her eyes. She fell asleep by the early dawn, while her sister Adawya slept all night. Adawya was early to rise and she sat drinking her tea by the window, watching the main road to the town's square, where they said they would execute the four men. She opened the window slightly so she could see better. Bushra, who waited to see Haleem for the last time, was awakened by her sister, Adawya, when she saw a group of soldiers and party militia forming in front of the party headquarters.

"Oh, they are bringing them out," Adawya said

Bushra woke up and opened her window wide. She looked to where her sister pointed. Basima and Abdullah made sure to open their window. Abdullah started to recite verses from the Qur'an so he could help the souls of his friends who were just about to reach the other side.

"And from the faithful there are those who fulfills their promise to Allah, some had died and some are still waiting but they will never change their commitment to the lord."

He looked at the soldiers starting to check their weapons and smoke cigarettes. Almost all the houses that oversaw the main road dividing Balluria into two sections had their windows open to see the four men executed and to let the sun in. It had been a long time since a fresh breeze of clean air had gone through Balluria. The windows had been closed and for a long time. Bushra ran to the bathroom where she made herself up. She combed her long black hair, and put the thick, black eyeliner on her big, black eyes; she asked her younger sister to do the same. When Adawya asked why, she said, "Because this is how Arab women mourn their men, I want Heleem to see it before he dies," she answered.

"But he is not your husband, and you never talked to him or replied to his letters."

"Shut up. This is not the time," Bushra told her sister. As tears started running down her beautiful face, she said, "He would have been my husband, if we had been born in a different time, in a different place, but it's Balluria, where true love dies early."

Suddenly a voice from a loudspeaker shattered the majestic silence of that morning. The voice of the young arrogant lieutenant echoed between the sleepy walls of the town. "Citizens of Balluria, it's the end of the betrayal and treason page in the history of our country and it's the ultimate victory for our divine leadership of our president. May Allah grant him a long life and protect him."

The two Hillaly girls ran to the window as the soldiers and the militiamen formed two columns.

Abdullah was praying next to his window, when Basima told him, "Hurry up, Abdullah. They are bringing them out."

Barrya stood next to Amel and Hamid's mother by the doors of Hamid's house. Amel held Barrya's hand and cried on her shoulders. They could see the town's square. But they could not see the four men, and Sheikh Jawad was sitting on his porch silently with his cane in his hand looking down at the square. Sayed Habeeb was in his mosque praying and asking Allah to forgive and receive the souls of four young men into his splendid hands and open paradise and eternal painless life for them. On the outskirts of the town, a black Arabian horse stood with its rider on it back. The horse screamed. Hamid sat on his horse, looking at the town and the crowd of people.

At that same moment, Kamal loaded his weapon and went to the cell. He shouted, "Well, Wolves. It is time."

The guards tied all four men's hands in front of them and asked if they wanted blindfolds. The four men said no, and Haleem said to Kamal, "We want to see Balluria before we die."

"Let's go, then. Why the delay?" Kamal said.

The guards led the four men outside. Haleem walked in front. Ashraf was behind him, and Salah followed last. Hisham's wheelchair was pushed by two guards in the back of the formation, and as they passed the defaced portrait of the tyrant, Hisham smiled and said to Kamal, "What a memory. It's for you to keep, Comrade Kamal."

Kamal looked at him, ignored the comment, and ordered the platoon of soldiers and militiamen, "To the right turn..."

Adawya looked at the men from her window and said, "Oh, my Allah. There they are. They are so beautiful. Can you see them?" she asked her older sister, Bushra, whose face was drenched with pearly tears mixed with black eyeliner.

"Yes, they are so handsome," Bushra said to her sister, who also started to cry when she suddenly remembered Salam, the son of the mayor, who left Balluria long years before. She wished that he was present. She wished that he was with four men so she could mourn him like her sister was mourning Haleem.

The two columns of soldiers walked toward the main square escorting the four men, leading them to where Kamal ordered the execution to take place, by the wall of the old school, near the town's square. The four men looked into the faces of all the spectators standing along the way to the town's square, the four men looked around and noticed that at all the windows had been opened for the first time. Haleem walked in front with the posture of a young king being led to his death by a group of conspiring vagabonds, Ashraf looked to see if his father was in the crowd; he hoped to get his final forgiveness, Salah looked that ground trying to hide his fear. Two soldiers pushed Hisham in his wheelchair in the back as he kept asking them for a last cigarette.

The weak yet persistent sun cleansed the town from its inner grudges. Kamal stood up near the town's main square with his pistol in his hand and waited for the soldiers to line up the four young men against the wall as the young lieutenant read the sentence of death. Haleem touched the clip of Bushra's hair in his hand and smelled it. He had been right all of these years; it smelled like heaven.

At the same moment, Abdullah looked from his window and could not keep himself from crying. He wanted so much to be with them. Abdulla's tears made him feel ashamed that he was not with them, but Basima tried to comfort him, saying that the four men would be with Allah very soon. Abdullah looked again at his four friends being led to their death and mumbled, "So long, my friends, my friends. My fellow Wolves. You are the real wolves," and he buried his face in Basima's chest as they wept together.

At that same moment, Sayed Habeeb, who stayed awake all night praying for the souls of the four men, looked from the roof of his mosque to where the four young men were being lined up against the wall and started reciting his favorite verse of the Qur'an.

"Oh, blessed meek souls return to me the lord, your creator, as I accept you, cherish you and bless you, enter my heavens and enter among my herd as I am your shepherd."

At that same moment, Hamid spurred his horse to where the he could see the town square and looked at the formation and wondered if he could storm the crowd alone and save his friends but he knew he could not and, for the first time in his life, he felt weak and helpless. He sat on his horse and he mumbled an old poem:

> *Let the time cry as the brave men marched*
> *To their deaths*
> *As no one was left to protect the meek.*

It was his favorite poem from an old Arabian tale of the heroic deaths of brave knights. And that was the only poem Hamid had memorized from his time in school.

6

For as long as Balluria existed, all the windows were forbidden from being opened, because many parents feared that doing so it would invite all the lusty intentions of the young boys and would encourage the love-filled hearts of deprived young boys to look at their daughters and then to start walking back and forth underneath the windows, trying to send letters and looks of love. But that morning all the girls in Balluria had stayed awake all night waiting for the four young men to face death. Many girls who had cried with pearl-like tears mixed with black eyeliner had painted their rosy cheeks with black shadows of sadness. That morning all the girls in Balluria could not resist the urge to open their windows, the near fate of the four young men was the reason all the girls decided to challenge all the restrictions their parents had imposed.

It was when first light of dawn uncovered Balluria from its heavyhearted night, and when the first ray of sunlight peeked from the horizon of the Sahara, all the girls in Balluria opened their windows. All the beautiful young girls of Balluria opened their windows for the sun to enter the rooms filing them with a promising breeze. Hundreds of windows opened and many girls let their hair fly free out of their windows as the platoon of soldiers lined the four men against the wall.

The seven-man firing squad, whose members had their faces half covered with checkered kuffias, took position with their Kalashnikovs on their shoulders. The young lieutenant tried to read again the execution decree. His voice was weak and was hardly heard as many of the townspeople wept. Girls in their windows started to cry and said silent prayers for the four young men, who were about to depart. Kamal looked at the firing squad and signaled to the lieutenant to stop reading and lifted up his hand for the firing squad to get ready. Haleem looked at his friends and smiled. Ashraf was praying silently and Salah looked sacred. Haleem wanted to hold Salah. It was the moment when Hisham from his wheelchair screamed, "Death to the tyrant. Long live the poor people."

It seemed like Hisham wanted to say what Haleem was saying and chanting all this time. He looked at Haleem, who smiled at him, and it was in that moment exactly when Haleem felt the silky touch of the lock of hair he had in his hand and looked at the window where he and his old friend Salam, the son of the former mayor, had spent many afternoons together walking back and forth, waiting for the Hillaly girls to open their windows for a reply to one of his many love letters. He looked at the window for the last time in his earthly life, and there she was: Bushra, with her beautiful face and big black eyes and the hair that travels beyond the senses of men, her long, black, silky hair, that she let down and combed and oiled. Haleem looked at the window where Bushra stood letting her hair fly free from the window. Her hair moved like thousands of black waves and rivers and rivers of black pearls. She waved at him while she held in her hand the notebook of his poems and love notes. She smiled at him. He smiled back at her while his friends Salah and Ashraf joined Hisham and they were all chanting the chant with which he had started the uprising. Haleem looked at the window where Bushra was standing, smiling at him. That was all he had wanted and hoped for and dreamed of; it was what he needed that moment. He smiled back at her and listened to his friends as they chanted, "Death to the tyrant, freedom to the people."

It was at that moment when Kamal ordered, "Fire..."

Shots rang out in long bursts. Dust and pieces of small stones flew from the wall behind them. Hisham was the first to fall, out his wheelchair. Ashraf fall backward, and Salah leaned to the side and then lay down. Haleem fell to his knees as he tried to stay standing. He looked at the window where Bushra let her hair fly in the refreshing dry wind of the southern desert. He could not see her anymore. And then there was silence.

Kamal ordered the firing squad to cease fire, and he walked toward the four dead bodies of his friends. White flimsy lines of smoke still rose from where the bullets entered the bodies of the four young men and from the wall behind them. Their bodies were riddled with bullets. Blood oozed, rapidly draining the life away. Hisham's eyes were still open. Kamal thought that he was alive. Kamal walked to where the bodies were, pulled his pistol, and emptied his clip into their heads one by one. Then he emptied his pistol into Haleem's head, reloaded again, and emptied it one more time. He wanted to make sure that Haleem was dead.

The platoon of soldiers and the party militiamen did not allow any relatives to take the bodies.

As his body and the bodies for his three friends lay lifeless, Haleem still had the clip of Bushra's hair in his hand, there in the mud. Rain started to fall, again while the sun was still out. That day in Balluria was a glorious day, although the white and gray clouds cast their sad shadows on the walls of Balluria. But the glorious rays of the sun managed to emerge and send their warmth into the streets of the small town and into the heavy hearts of its people as they all wept. All the windows of all the beautiful young girls who had no tears left in their eyes and no black eyeliner left to rejuvenate it, all the windows of young beautiful girls were wide open in Balluria since the beginning of time.

ARMAND NASSERY

The Book of Balluria

The Devious Road To the Snowy Hills of Denmark

1

The road to Jordan would take at least nine hours and maybe longer if the border police delayed the bus, and it would be a disaster if they found out that Basima's passport had some forged information. Abdullah braced himself for the worst, but he knew that he had no other choice. He had made up his mind to leave Balluria a long time ago when he learned that his wife, Basima, had unintentionally aided her friend Hanan, the daughter of Sheikh Jawad, in her scandalous escape from Balluria with her lover, Hamid. The two lovers escaped Balluria one week before the Thursday that Hanan was to be wed to Kamal and only one night after Kamal had invited Abdullah to attend his engagement dinner. Abdullah was angry with his wife, who he had thought would have more common sense than to get involved in something that might cost him his life and maybe cost her reputation as a decent woman. He knew that even though he belonged to a decent family with an impeccable reputation and even though they belonged to the Sharify tribe, the largest in Balluria, he could not face the consequences of the scandalous escape. He also knew his friend Kamal very well. Moreover, he knew the powerful Sheikh Jawad and his unpredictable actions and violent reactions to those who disrespect him.

Years ago when Abdullah heard the details of the escape from his frightened wife, Basima, he told his wife to be prepared for the worst when he walked that night to tell the sheikh about his daughter's escape. He used what he knew of the tribal customs to secure his own safe return to his house and family. That night, he walked the main street of Balluria hoping to see any of his friends who would be willing to walk with him to the sheikh's guesthouse, but none of them were there. As he got closer he saw that the sheikh's guesthouse was empty of its usual crowd of men, and only Khanger, the old coffee server, was nursing the coffee fire. He saw that fearsome sheikh was sitting in his usual spot, the spot that only Irar, the mysterious man with wolf's eyes, was allowed to sit in when the sheikh traveled. Abdullah entered the guesthouse and saluted the sheikh. "Al Salamu Alaykum Shaikhna."

"Alykum Al-Salam," the sheikh replied as he looked with his bulging, red eyes at this young man who appeared to be troubled.

"I am Abdullah, the son of Mohan the Sharify," Abdullah said with a shaky voice.

"Welcome to you," the sheikh said with his deep voice and a stare that sliced through his young guest's courage and self-confidence.

Abdullah sat and stared, wondering if he had just made the mistake of being the bad news bearer to the fearsome sheikh who killed many people in his life for various reasons, but Abdullah knew that was the only way he could protect himself and the only way he could protect his wife, Basima, his distant cousin, the woman he had loved since they were in elementary school. This was the only way to protect her reputation because no matter what the sheikh would say or do after he learned about his daughter's escape, no one would dare to challenge his judgment; after all, he is a sheikh and he was bound by tribal customs and an honor code.

"I demand your oath on the grace of the dead and your permission to speak," Abdullah said, wondering if he said the tribal code phrase right.

"I give you my oath on the grace of the dead. Now speak and say what you want to say."

Abdullah fought the urge to run from the guesthouse with each word he uttered as he saw the colors changing on the sheikh's face while he spoke of the terrible news.

"Sheikh, my wife told me that she saw your daughter Hanan running away with a man, other than her fiancé, Kamal. She saw them running away from Balluria. They have escaped."

Abdullah had not completed his words by the time the sheikh stood up and loudly exclaimed, "I am the son of my father," and ran inside the house, followed by Khangar the coffee server, who could barely walk due to age and infirmity. He followed his master after hearing his angry reaction to what Abdullah had said.

For a moment, Abdullah sat alone and waited. Then he realized that it would be better if he left. He started doubting himself; he was afraid that what his wife, Basima, had told him was not true or that it was true but that Hanan had returned. Maybe she had changed her mind or maybe Hamid had returned her to her father's house. Abdullah hoped that the two lovers had escaped, not for their own sake but for his sake because he did not want to be the one who brought false news of such magnitude to Sheikh Jawad, He was sitting alone in the guesthouse without knowing what he would face next. Would it be Sheikh Jawad with a loaded rifle? Would it be Kamal with a pistol, or Khanger or any of the other sheikh's men with daggers and knives? He realized that he must leave at least to be in the land of his tribe and family on the other side of Balluria. Perhaps they could protect him if what his wife, Basima, had told him about the escape was either true or not true but he must leave the guesthouse. He stood up walked out of the guesthouse, and never returned.

When he reached his house, he found that his wife, Basima, had prepared dinner and waited for him, He did not eat. Instead he lay on the floor of the bedroom and stared at the ceiling. Basima did not speak a word. She looked at him, undressed, and lay next to him. He did not touch her. She lay there knowing that he was not asleep. They lay there for hours, and then she asked, "Why are you still awake?"

"I am waiting to see if Kamal or the sheikh's men will come to our doorstep with their rifles to kill me and you because of what you did," Abdullah said with the submission of a man waiting for the inevitable.

Basima realized what her unintentional actions had brought upon her and her husband, but she was powerless to do anything else except to be with Abdullah to the end, whatever that end might be. She cried and wrapped her hands around him. He buried his face between her breasts and breathed in her scent. She felt the warm exhalation he let out and knew how deep his worries were and how scared he was.

"I will be here with you and protect you with my life, Habeeby."

"I know. And that's what's keeping me awake. They may kill us both, and they may even harm my father," he answered, and, with his face still between her breasts and with his eyes closed, he said, "Basima, do you remember when we were in elementary school?"

"Yes, Habeeby, I remember," she answered as she caressed his hair.

"Everyone thought that we were crazy. Everyone thought we were two immature kids making promises about marriage when we were eleven or twelve," Abdullah said.

"I know."

"And then when we were in middle school, when Hamid and Hanan started their love, and Haleem was in love with Bushra, and Salam was in love with Adawya, and when Amel used to give you my love letters, do you remember that?"

"Yes, Habeeby," Basima replied.

"Through the years and whenever all of my friends asked me if I really loved you and if I truly wanted to marry you, I said yes, and when I was in teachers' training institute, many of my classmates asked me the same thing, and my answer was always the same: my answer was always that I loved you and wanted to marry you, and I was sure of it since I was twelve. I was sure as I am now that the only thing I want in my life is to be with you and to be your husband and for you to be my wife forever and for us to have our own small family," Abdullah said, as he turned his face to the ceiling.

"And that's all of what I want too, Abdullah," Basima said as her eyes shone with tears.

Without looking at her, Abdullah continued with his eyes fixed on the ceiling, "In my life, I have faced many situations where I had to choose between many paths, and I have always chosen that path that leads back to you. In many situations I felt cowardly and weak, with my choice but I was happy and content with my choices as long as by the end of my day I would be with you."

"I know, Habeeby."

"Let me remind you, then," Abdullah said, "to be cautious and to stay alive and away from danger, is not what men in these parts do. But I did it and it was not something I wanted for myself nor did I do it for me only. I did it for both of us. See, when you and I talked about Denmark and us moving to Scandinavia, I was very serious about it, and still to this day I am very serious about it. It was because one day I saw a magazine that Adnan brought with him to school, and in that magazine there was this beautiful house built from wood, and it was in the middle of the a field of endless white snow. I looked at that picture, and I realized that had I found my dream home, the place where I wanted to be with my wife and my children, away from Balluria and these parts."

"I remember, Habeeby. You showed me the picture."

Abdullah lifted his head slightly and looked at his wife before continuing. "Many of our friends and family have joked about my dream to go to Denmark, and they said that I live in an imaginary world and that I could never reach Denmark. They laughed at me whenever I talked about it, but today I realized that in this town and in this country it will only take a good-hearted woman like you committing one unintentional mistake, for her and her husband to be threatened with certain death and the end of all their dreams."

"I understand, Habeeby."

Abdullah sat and wrapped his hands around his knees and said, "I was very afraid today when I went to the sheikh's guesthouse. I was very afraid when I talked to him, and I thought of you. I thought that I might not be coming back to you alive, and as I sit here scared for you and myself, I am thinking now that although my dreams to take you to Scandinavia may sound silly and stupid to others, they are as valid as my fear, I realize now that it may be extremely difficult and it may take years of our lives and require a lot of money that we don't have, but I know if I manage to keep us alive for a while, things will come out in our favor. I mean, I figured that life doesn't have to be this difficult. I knew that the way only way to do it is to keep you and me safe and alive until we have the chance and the money to travel. When I saw my best friends lined up facing a firing squad in the main square, I wanted to be with them..."

"Oh, my Allah forbids."

"Don't cry, and let me finish. When I saw my friends lined up to be executed, I wanted to be with them, but I wanted to stay alive for you and be with you, so the only thing I did was to watch them die. I chose to be a coward because I love you and chose to be weak because I am saving my strength and my courage for the road that we have to travel in order to reach our dream, I was saving my courage to build our family and to love my family, to love you and our children."

"Habeeby, I know, wa'Allah, I know," said Basima as she kissed his forehead and cheeks and tried to kiss him on his lips, but he pushed her away gently with tears coming down his cheeks. He turned to her and held her face between his palms and said, "Look at me."

Basima met his eyes with tears as he looked in her eyes and said, "I watched my best friends fight and stayed home like a woman. Then I watched them imprisoned and stayed home like a woman. Then I watched them lined up and shot to pieces and stayed home and cried like a woman, and I did all of that because I love you and wanted to spend every moment of my life with you, alone with two or three children, girls if God will bless us with girls so they will look as beautiful as you are. I chose you and our future life over the basic meaning of my manhood, and today I truly feel all that I have waited for and my life with you could end at any time, and this thought scared me."

"Inshalla. Nothing will happen to us, and we will stay together until you bury me," Basima said, begging her husband to stop, but Abdullah continued.

"It seems to me that the time has come for us to leave Balluria and these parts because it seems like the pain here will never end. Every day there is something and every year there is a war and suffering and people who are willing to kill others, and I know it will be difficult for us, but we will have to start somewhere. We will have to try to get there and live in that wooden house in the middle of snowy hills of Denmark and have two daughters and maybe a boy and name them Nimma, Rehma, and Salam, a blessing and mercy and peace. My dream of leaving this town is more valid then the reality that I am living now and more suitable for me as a man. At least this is the way I see it, and I want you to see it the same way."

"I know, Habeeby, my love. I will go with you to the end of the world. I will go with you to Siberia, if you want," Basima said as she kissed him on his neck.

"Denmark is as cold as Siberia, but it's more beautiful."

Abdullah looked at his wife and said with the clear instructional voice he used with his students, "I want you to do something for me."

"I will do anything for you."

"Tonight I will stay up and wait to see if God will save us from Kamal's and Sheikh Jawad's wrath. I will keep my pistol with me and defend you and me from their unpredictable anger. They will have to kill me first before they will lay a hand on you."

"Don't say that, Habeeby."

"Don't cry. Just listen to me," Abdullah said again as he pulled his wife's hands away from her face as she wept. "Listen to me, Basima. For the next week, I don't want you to go anywhere, and I don't want you to visit any of your friends, especially Hamid's sister, Amel, and never set a foot in Barrya's hut and never let her in our house."

"Yes," she confirmed.

"What I want you to do is start gathering all the money you can. If some of your friends owe you money, I want you to collect it from them immediately, and if you have to sell your wedding jewelry, then do so," Abdullah said.

"Yes," Basima replied with complete agreement.

"We will need as much money as possible for the trip to Denmark. As for me, I will work to get us passports and make the necessary arrangements for our travel. We should be ready within a month to leave these parts. I have heard that there is a way to reach Denmark if we go to Jordan. I heard some people have already made it to Scandinavia."

"All right, Habeeby." She nodded.

Abdullah looked at her and said, "That's what we will do for me and you and our children to reach the wooden house in the middle of snowy hills, where I can be sure that nothing will harm you and our children. There will be no wars, no starvation, no food embargos, no Kamal, and no Sheikh Jawad."

"Yes, Habeeby. We will leave these parts, and we will go to Scandinavia and live in that wooden house with our daughters, Blessings and Mercy," Basima said as she kissed him on his face and kissed his hands and neck and chest. Abdullah reached out and touched her hair and her neck and kissed her. He caressed her body, looking for the hidden sanctuary in her body, while his ears were vigilant for any sound that he might hear by his door. That night, Basima conceived their first child.

2

That night Kamal did not show up at Abdullah's house with his pistol, nor did the sheikh's men with their rifles, daggers, or knives, but Abdullah and Basima did not leave the house for almost a week. They waited until they finally heard the news from Amel, who came to their house crying and told them that two nights earlier people saw Kamal and Hanan's brother, Ahmed returning from the honor chase that had lasted almost fifty-seven days, when Kamal and Ahmed had searched for Hanan and Hamid in the big city of the province and in all the cities and towns along the Euphrates valley. The next day people saw Hanan's right palm nailed to the guesthouse entrance. She told them that no one knew where they buried Hanan, and no one knew what had happened to Hamid, but Ahmed had told his father and the other men that he killed Hamid.

"Did they bring his body?" asked Abdullah

"No," cried the overwrought Amel. "They left my brother's body in the wheat field of a faraway town. They left my brother lying there alone." Amel wept, slapped her face, and asked if Abdullah could travel with her and Barrya to recover her brother's body and bury it.

Abdullah had no desire to be part of this scandal anymore, and he did not want to reinitiate the wrath of Kamal and Sheikh Jawad, but at the same time, he could not let Amel and Barrya travel alone to recover Hamid's body, because no other man would be willing to do so. Abdullah believed that if he helped Amel recover Hamid's body, he would have some self-redemption, a redemption that he had been searching for since he saw his four friends being shattered by the firing squad's bullets, a redemption that would allow him to leave Balluria with no regrets and no emotional debts, so he agreed with one condition.

"Amel," he said, "I will go with you and look for Hamid's body, but we must not bring the body back to Balluria. We must bury him in the holy city and not tell anyone in the town that we did that. It's better that way."

Two days after that, he was on his way with the two women, searching for the dead body of his friend, Hamid. Abdullah, Amel, and Barrya traveled to the village where Ahmed had told Barrya that they found Hamid and Hanan hiding. Ahmed had told Barrya that Kamal and he found Hamid and Hanan hiding in a small village by the Euphrates where an amazing golden wheat fields stretched for many kilometers. The two women and Abdullah reached the town with the endless wheat field and asked if anyone had found the dead body of a tall and tanned young man lying in the wheat field with three bullets in his body. None of the villagers had heard that story, and none of the villagers had seen the body. Abdullah then asked if they had seen a wounded, tall, tanned man roaming these parts, but the answers were of disbelief, strange reactions, and suspicious looks.

"Maybe it was another village?" one villager suggested.

"Is there any other village that has endless golden wheat fields in these parts?"

"No, this is the only one."

After three days of searching and asking almost a thousand people who all claimed they had never heard of the story and they had never seen a tall, tanned man walking around bleeding from his three bullet wounds and screaming the name of Hanan, the two women and Abdullah returned to Balluria and never told anyone of their trip. Barrya was smiling as she told Amel when they reached Balluria, "I can feel it in my heart and see it in my vision. My boy Hamid is not dead."

Abdullah asked Amel politely to stop visiting his wife, Basima, for a while because he was afraid of what people might say, and Amel agreed. After that, Abdullah, who had just finished his mandatory year as an elementary school teacher in a village near the marshes had started teaching in the elementary school in Balluria, the same school in which he had seen Basima long years before, and he thought that she was the most beautiful girl he had ever seen.

Abdullah was exempt from serving in the army because he had a heart condition, and to prove it, he had visited almost all the doctors in the capital city in order to gain the necessary documents of exemption. Most of the doctors did not have the right instruments to perform the needed tests on his heart, and he was almost drafted into the army, but luck smiled at him when a tiny doctor who charged him a lot of money was able to do all the needed tests that confirmed the weakness of his heart due to a valve malfunctioning. The malfunction meant that he could die at any time. He told Basima when they got engaged.

She replied with a meaningful smile on her innocent pretty face, "As long as you will be able to give me babies."

Abdullah and Basima were related by their seventh or eighth grandfather. They both belonged to the Sharify tribe. Their grandfathers were part of the tribe forced to leave the marshland after the feud between the Sharifys and the tribe of Sheikh Nasser the Blond, and they were related to the late Sheikh Badr Al-Ghathban, whose guesthouse was inherited by his son-in-law Sheikh Jawad. Abdullah and Basima never paid much attention to that relationship. In fact, they never paid any attention to their family connections and the tribal ancestry, unlike most of the people in these parts. Abdullah saw Basima when she was permitted to enter the fourth grade in the town's only elementary school, and after that day they had been inseparable. They played in the mud in front of her house together and fought many times, but they had been always together. Their families and all their relatives and all the people in Balluria just accepted that the two belonged together, even Barrya the Gypsy woman had told them that their bond was written by a Gypsy queen, and they would always be together. Even when mixing of the boys and girls was not allowed in the primary schools, it was normal for the teachers in Balluria's primary school to see Abdullah and Basima sitting or walking together.

They entered middle school together, and in the seventh grade they sat in one class, and if it had been allowed, they would have sat next to each other. Everyone in the school knew about them and how they had been promised to each other. It was normal for Basima's family to have Abdullah coming for lunch every day after school. Even her brothers did not mind or try to prevent him from walking her from school to the house every day—something that might cost another man his life. Abdullah's family did the same with Basima; she stayed at his house for lunches and dinners and helped his mother with cooking and cleaning since Abdullah had no sisters. He only had younger brothers. Abdullah's mother told Abdullah that if he did not marry Basima, she would never forgive him and she would die without giving him her blessing, something that every Muslim man wanted: the blessing of the parents before they die. Abdullah's mother had nothing to worry about, nor did his father; Abdullah was different from the other kids in Balluria. Although he was not a high-achieving student, like his friends Adnan or Salam, the son of the mayor, and he was not as athletic as his friend Hisham nor was he daring and brave as his friend Hamid, Abdullah was well-mannered and neatly dressed with his always combed hair and ironed clothes.

He was never a main member of the Wolves soccer team because of his heart condition, and he barely played half of the time and did not show up to most of the games, which drove Hisham crazy, but he participated in the big fight with the Wild Lions, although he did not fight much. After that he stopped playing and barely showed up to soccer games. When the Wolves became the official members of the secondary school soccer teams, he was more interested in attending to his father's needs and to the tiny store they owned in the town's main square when they sold candy and gum and other sugary colorful things.

He did not want to leave Balluria and Basima when he graduated for secondary school. Moreover, he knew that his family could not afford his education in the capital city, although he scored high enough to be eligible to enter the teaching academy. Instead, he attended the elementary teachers' institute in the big city in the province. He finished the institute in three years and was exempt from the military service because of his heart condition. Abdullah never wanted to leave Balluria; he wanted to stay with Basima and his parents. That was all what he wanted.

3

When Abdullah was in the seventh grade, his friend Adnan, who wore thick glasses and talked about countries far away, brought a colorful foreign magazine with pictures of many blond people on its pages. Adnan brought the magazine to show Hisham and the others and to prove his story about an airplane called the Concorde, which was built in France. The pointed cockpit of the airplane opened from the front, something the kids did not believe. So he brought his precious magazine to school to show them. Hisham, Haleem, Salam, and Ashraf lost their interest in the airplane and opened the magazine to the pages with many blond women posing with bottles of alcohol and on top of cars. When Adnan flipped through the pages, Abdullah stopped him when he saw an amazing photograph. It was a photo of a wooden cabin in the middle of snowy hills with pine trees. Colorful lights decorated the porch of the wooden cabin, and the word Christmas was written on top of the round picture. Abdullah asked Adnan if he knew where the wooden house was and in what country. Adnan had explained that from the snowy hills it looked like it was either in Alaska or one of the Scandinavian countries. That was not enough of an answer for Abdullah because he wanted to know the name of the country, so he showed the picture to Fathil the Liar, who was in town resting from a secret mission that the president had sent him on in China, or so he claimed.

Fathil the Liar took one look at the photograph in the magazine and said with no hesitation, "This is Denmark. I know it because I was there many times, and I have spent many nights with the top actress of Denmark. Her picture is in this magazine too."

As he was looking at the picture of wooden cabin Abdullah felt that it was the most beautiful place on earth. Since then, he always asked, read, and dreamed of Denmark. He told Basima and showed her the magazine after depositing one dinar as collateral with Adnan and an oath on the Qur'an that he would return the magazine after showing Basima the picture. Basima did not think much about the picture but was just ready to go anywhere with Abdullah, even to Siberia, a place she learned about that day in geography class.

To Abdullah, not being part of the Wolves did not bother him, and not being with the adventurous trio of Hamid and Adnan and the new kid Salam, the son of the mayor, did not bother him either. Not being with them as they swam and fished did not bother him because he enjoyed being with Basima, as he cherished his new dream of the snowy hills of Denmark. He rejected all the offers that the three friends made to him to join them in their adventures in the river, even when Hamid found the unmanned boat floating on the river, and everyone participated in painting and reconstructing the raggedy boat and named it the *Titanic*, Abdullah contributed least to the project by donating a half-empty can of hardened red paint. He preferred to stay at Basima's house and help her brothers with building a new brick fence, which was destroyed in later years by the mortar rounds fired by the military force that retook Balluria from the small rebel force of the four friends.

Abdullah and Basima were married in the night when the moon was shyly hidden behind a strange red cloud that covered the skies. They were married there in Balluria when the infernos of death on the eastern fronts had finally burned out and after it became known that there was no more youth to feed its beastly appetite. The wedding night was joyful and quiet. Barrya, the Gypsy woman who was the best dancer these parts had ever seen, danced with joy, but she did not dance to the men. She danced in the room where the women gathered around Basima. She was dressed in a long and beautiful white dress and, with Barrya, danced with the Hillaly girls, Bushra and Adawya, who let their hair down and danced. And she danced with Amel, Hamid's sister, who stood next to Basima and danced briefly. Even Hanan, the sheikh's daughter, clapped and kissed Basima on the cheek and gave her a small necklace as a wedding gift. Sayed Habeeb, the clergyman, performed the wedding rituals. He sat between Abdullah and Basima and started with a verse from the Qur'an.

"Good women are for good men," he said, and then he asked Abdullah if he was willing to accept Basima as his wife.

Abdullah said, "I accept."

Then the clergyman asked Basima if she was willing to accept Abdullah as her husband, and she said, "I accept."

The new couple stayed with Abdullah's family, and Basima had promised Abdullah's mother that she would give birth to her first grandchild. That was three months before Hanan and Hamid escaped from Balluria and almost two years before the four friends were executed in the town's main square and a year after Adnan had freed all the boats and led them in his final journey to the gates of heaven and three years before starvation bit the tiny stomachs of the people in these parts with its merciless fangs. For Abdullah, the divine duty of keeping his family fed and safe was all he cared about. He did not participate in the rebellion. Instead, he packed up his father and his mother and his wife, Basima, who was ill at the time, from her second miscarriage, and escaped Balluria when a battalion of mean soldiers attacked Balluria to reclaim it from the small rebel force consisting of four of his friends and three teenagers. Abdullah took his family to where the Americans were camping on the outskirts of the province. The Americans had offered safety and many brown bags of canned food for the thousands of refugees who escaped the hellish mortar rounds of the army that sacked the capital city of the province, executed, and then hanged the dead bodies of the young rebels by the neck and left them dangling from the barrels of the tanks.

One night before the army attacked Balluria, Abdullah gathered his family and walked all night to where the Americans were and stayed there overnight. He was the only one who could read English and was able to tell the starving people if any of the Meal Ready To Eat brown bags had pork, and as he sat among the people who asked if their brown bags had pork meat in them, his thoughts were with his four friends, who were at that time spending their last night on earth as they waited to face the firing squad the next morning. Abdullah returned to the town at three o'clock in the morning when the battle had stopped and the sounds of booms had quieted and a messenger from the military force commander came and told the fleeing families to return to the town. Abdullah brought his family back to their house. They found that the outside fence of Basima's family house was destroyed. Abdullah spent the night praying and thinking about his four friends, who at the time were being visited by the only person who stayed in Balluria and did not escape. They were visited briefly by Barrya, the Gypsy woman.

4

The two years that followed that night were exceptionally harsh on the souls and the bodies of the people in Balluria. The town and the country slipped into the devilish madness of starvation and massive neediness as the people stopped smiling, and their bodies started to get thinner and thinner, and their hearts became more rigid and merciless. Abdullah barely managed to keep his family and his wife's family alive with his meager teacher's salary and the money from his father's store. He shared this money with Hamid's mother and Hamid's sister, Amel, who had no real way to stay alive. So he offered them the option of selling candy to the children in the morning, and he manned the store in the evenings after school. Through all of those years, Abdullah was afraid of Kamal. He was afraid that Kamal did not forget that Basima was one of three women who helped Hanan escape, and although Kamal was distracted with the war and the executions of his friends and many others through the years, and even though Abdullah's effort to save as much money as possible within a short period of time was not promising any tangible results, he knew that Kamal would come back for him one day.

Abdullah was not afraid of the sheikh anymore since he learned that the sheikh had not been the same since the death of his son, Ahmed, but Abdullah was afraid of Kamal because he knew Kamal well. He knew that Kamal would never forget, and one day or one night, Kamal would be at his doorstep demanding retribution, retribution for his forever broken heart, retribution for a reputation that would never be regained, and retribution for a life that would never be. Abdullah knew that Kamal was not the kind of man who would forget. He was just waiting for the right time.

For years, Abdullah lived with that fear every day after he informed Sheikh Jawad of his daughter Hanan's escape, but also he lived with the hope that one day he would have enough money to leave Balluria and set sail to Scandinavia, to Denmark, where his dream home sat in the middle of the snowy hills. Three years from the day when almost seven hundred people were killed when the great nation's pilots bombed the bridge of the big city in the province just thirty miles north of Balluria and after four years of the beginning of the starvation, Abdullah finally reached the point where he could not stay in Balluria anymore. He realized that his plan to leave Balluria had not worked because he could never save enough money, even if he stayed in Balluria for a thousand years. It was the day when Comrade Kamal and the party's delegation came to visit the elementary school to ask about the preparation for the divine leader's birthday celebration. Abdullah was in the teacher's office when Kamal entered the office and greeted him.

"Alsalmu Alykum Abdullah," said Kamal, who entered the office and sat in a chair looking at Abdullah.

"Alykum Al-Salam Rafeeq, Comrade Kamal," Abdullah replied with concealed fear in his eyes.

"How are you, and how is your wife, Basima?" Kamal asked in his clear, authoritative voice.

"She is well, Rafeeq. Comrade Kamal, how are you? And how is the sheikh?" Abdullah asked politely.

Kamal ignored Abdullah's well-mannered gesture, and instead looked at Abdullah and said in a deep and calm voice, "I meant to ask you something."

"Comrade, if you want to ask about the preparations for the birthday of the divine leader..."

"No, I have another thing to ask you about. It is a question that I have wanted to ask you for years." Abdullah's weak heart started to beat with fear. "I heard from the women in our house that your wife, Basima, was with Hanan on that shameful day. I did not ask you because Sheikh Jawad had prohibited me from bringing up this subject again since that shameful day. Now the sheikh is not in a state of mind to remember what happened, but I have not forgotten, so I am asking you if your wife, Basima, was with Hanan when she escaped." Kamal looked at Abdullah directly in his eyes searching for the fear the prey shows before an attack.

"Kamal, whoever told you that was mistaken. What Basima said is that she saw Hanan. May God bless her soul, running away with Hamid."

461

"Running away?" Kamal frowned. "How did she know that they were running away?"

"I don't know, but I assure you that Basima was..." Abdullah mumbled as Kamal stood up and turned around and walked toward the door.

He mumbled, "I will know the truth, Abdullah. I will know the truth."

That afternoon, Abdullah came to the house and asked Basima to go and ask Hamid's sister to come to the house for an urgent matter. Amel came to the house, fearing that something had happened to Hamid, but she was surprised when she learned that Abdullah only wanted to sell her and her mother the candy store that he owned. The store was almost empty of everything, except the relentless flies.

"But we have no money," Amel said.

"I will accept anything you have and you can give me, maybe you can borrow the money from Barrya," Abdullah suggested. "Barrya has money, and you know that."

Finally, Abdullah agreed to let Amel and her mother, who had no way of making a living, take over the tiny store that sold candy and other colorful shiny items that made children stare for a long time before deciding which candy bar they wanted. The store had nothing left in it except for three boxes of Nestle's and two boxes of gum. Abdullah asked Amel if she could pay him with anything of value that she could offer as a compensation for the store, and when Amel said that the only thing of value that she could think of was her poetry books, Abdullah let out a pained smile and said, "I don't think your poetry books will help me, not where I am going."

He stared at his wife, who listened to the entire sad business proposition, and said to Amel, "All I wanted to do was leave Balluria and make sure that you and your mother and Barrya were cared for. So I am leaving you the candy store. There is not much left in it, and I cannot afford to buy any new candy. If you can send me money whenever, I will be grateful for any money that you can spare that does not make you go hungry. Please do. Basima and I are leaving soon," Abdullah said to Amel, who again was visited by the same anxiety of her loved ones leaving the town.

"Where will you be going?" asked Amel with tears sparkling in her big, black, beautiful eyes with a green halo.

"I don't know yet, but we are going to Jordan first. That's where everyone is going to get away from hunger."

Basima fought back her tears as she realized how scared her husband was, and when Amel left, she asked him, "Are we going to Jordan?"

"Yes," he answered, looking at the receding figure of Amel, walking alone in the scorching afternoon of Balluria.

"When?"

"I don't know exactly, but soon, very soon. I know it should be before Kamal shows up at our doorstep with his pistol."

Basima did not want to bother her husband with questions that she already knew the answers to. She looked in her husband's eyes for confirmation of her fears, and she received it in the same look that she had seen in his eyes the night he went to inform Sheikh Jawad about Hanan's escape. She asked her husband, "What do you want me to do?"

"Sell your jewelry and sell our wedding furniture. Maybe one of the Hillaly girls will buy them. And ask your parents or your brothers if they can loan us any money. I have a friend who promised to get us passports; they may be forged, but it's the only way that we can travel soon."

"I am a pregnant woman, Abdullah. I am afraid that I will have another miscarriage from traveling, and I don't want to go to jail if we get caught on the borders," Basima said.

"We are not going to be caught," Abdullah assured her. "Allah will protect us." He lay down, staring at the ceiling. Basima lay next to him with her head on his arm. "I don't want my children to be born in Balluria. The pain and fear in this place is unbearable for humans," Abdullah said as he thought about all of their departed friends and how much he missed them. Mostly, he missed Adnan and missed the chilling feeling of freshness of senses when Adnan showed him the magnificent wooden cabin in the middle of snowy hills as they looked at Adnan's special magazine and how they did not pay attention to Salam, the mayor's son, who claimed that it must be a picture from America. Abdullah had decided that it had to be Scandinavia because Scandinavian countries looked like that all year round. They had all believed him.

"If it is Denmark, then we will go to Denmark," Abdullah mumbled as he tried to nap.

5

Traveling the road to Jordan would take at least nine hours and might be longer if the border police delayed the bus for any reason, and it would be a complete disaster if they found out that Basima's passport was forged and had incorrect information that did not match her civilian identification card. Abdullah braced himself for the worst, but he knew that he had no other choice. He could not return to Balluria, and he had no other place to go. Two days before that day, Abdullah and his pregnant wife loaded their two suitcases and boarded a bus heading to Jordan. Two nights before that, he said his good-byes to Sayed Habeeb in the mosque. He went there looking for the clergyman, who seemed to be the only one in Balluria to have the sanity and coherence to offer advice and guidance, since there was no one left in Balluria that Abdullah could trust. Abdullah sat and listened to the graceful clergyman, who seemed to have lost his motivation and willingness to give advice to people. Abdullah sat and listened to the graceful clergyman as he calmly said, "Do what you heart tells you, because you cannot lose with your heart. Don't listen to your mind because minds are easy to corrupt and make evil, but the heart is always right and righteous."

While his wife, Basima, went to the mud hut of the Gypsy woman, Barrya, to say her good-byes and ask for forgiveness for any wrongs she might have committed, Barrya cried, and so did Amel, Hamid's sister, who was saddened to see the last two of her friends leaving Balluria. Amel said with sadness, "It looks like I will be the only one left here. I have nowhere to go."

The three women cried as Barrya tried to cheer them up and save them from entrenching themselves in the sickening thoughts of loneliness.

"If I still have the same hips you do, I will dance until I fall to the ground," Barrya said to console her young friends who hugged each other as they started to see what life could do to innocent souls.

When he decided to leave Balluria with his wife, Abdullah counted his savings. It was four thousand dinars, barely enough to get them to Jordan. When he paid one thousand dinars to his friend, who helped him get two passports, he protested the price and the quality of his wife, Basima's, obviously forged passport and the wrong information about her father's name and her birthdate, but his friend assured him that no one at the borders would notice. The next day Abdullah and Basima packed two sky-blue leather suitcases with everything they owned and all the things they thought were necessary for their journey and waited for the evening. Abdullah had invited his wife's family to come for dinner and gathered his father, who had completely lost his ability to walk, and his younger brothers, who had grown and become young men. He also invited Hamid's sister, Amel, and her mother. He invited the Gypsy woman, Barrya, and Sayed Habeeb, the clergyman.

When the guests finished dinner Abdullah said, "Basima and I are going to Jordan tomorrow. I don't want any of you to tell anyone else about this until we leave. It's better that way. I have prepared this dinner for you because you are the only people in Balluria who would care if we leave. The others have more serious things to worry about like feeding their children."

Sayed Habeeb started to cry, and so did Amel, but Abdullah kept smiling and continued, "I don't want you to feel sad, because Basima and I are going to a place that we have wished to go to for a long time. I don't want you to cry or to worry about us. I wish for you to keep praying for us and to wish us good luck and ask Allah to keep us in his mercy."

Abdullah's father, who was confined to a wheelchair, could not help but cry. He covered his eyes with his old handkerchief and wept. He was joined by Basima's brothers, who became emotional and asked Abdullah to reconsider. While the men argued for Abdullah to stay in Balluria, the women in the other room wept as well. The only one who did not cry was Amel, who had already cried enough tears to fill a small pond.

She asked Basima, "Do you think you can travel to America from Jordan?"

"I don't know, but Abdullah said he wants to go to Denmark."

"I wish I could go to America," said Amel with a hopeless look.

Basima looked sadly at her friend and said, "I will miss you so much, Amel. I will miss you and Barrya so much, and if you see Hamid, please extend my respect and my deepest true emotions. He has always been a good friend of Abdullah, and he has been like a brother to me."

Barrya wept inside, when she heard Basima saying what she said and thought about the whereabouts of Hamid, who had not been seen in Balluria for months. At that exact time Hamid was being chased by a patrol of government irregulars, called the Feda'ayen, or those who sacrifice themselves for the president. The patrol was tasked with capturing Hamid and his group of bandits dead or alive for various charges, ranging from smuggling to stealing boats to freeing a group of prisoners who were on their way to be executed in the big city. Late that night, Hamid and his bandits reached the outskirts of Balluria, but could not enter it. Barrya had no time to look for anything that she could give to Basima and Abdullah for their journey, but she knew that if there was one thing that she could give, it would be one of her grandmother's lucky stones, which her family of Gypsy dancers had inherited and passed down from generation to generation of Gypsy witches who could tell the future. Barrya knew that Basima was never coming back. She knew that in her heart, and she had seen it in her dreams. She had no power to stop the future, not with all the powers of all her ancestors of Gypsy dancers, who turned into witches when they got old. She gave Basima a blue stone that had many black spots and said with a loving grandmotherly voice, "My dear Basima, you will be protected. You will be protected by the love and care and the watchful eyes of all the dead Gypsy women of my tribe. You will be protected by all the women who followed men because they loved them and all the women who followed men because they had no other choice." Basima listened to what Barrya said and had no thoughts about what the Gypsy woman was saying. Basima simply liked what she was hearing.

"You will be protected by the spirits of my mother and my grandmother Lolowa, the one who made the ameer of the Rabeey tribes fight the Turks and defeat them only because the Turks had kidnapped her. You will be protected by my love, the love of a childless woman who was cheated out of her natural destiny of being a mother and saved all of that love for the children of other women. You will go with your husband, and when you feel lonely and you see him sad or weak or lost, you must dance for him and sing and dress up in a very tempting dress and make love to him until he tires and sleeps. And when he wakes up, rest assured that he will do anything to live one more day," Barrya said as she gave Basima the stone and closed her hands on it. "Keep it close to you, and don't lose it." Basima looked at her, not understanding the importance of what the Gypsy woman was saying. She stared at her and kissed the Gypsy woman on her forehead. Barrya stood and asked if she could talk to Abdullah.

Abdullah came out of the room where the men were sitting. He looked at Barrya and said, "Mother Barrya, I could bear seeing the tears in the eyes of the others, but I cannot bear to see you crying."

"I will not cry, Abdullah. I always knew of all of you kids, my sons and daughters, I could always depend on you to be the responsible one, the one who could provide, but now you are leaving, and I fear that we will all starve—your family, Basima's family, Amel, and her mother. As for me, don't worry about me. I cry for the others and not for me; besides, I will always know where to find yogurt." She smiled.

He smiled back and said, "I know that no one is left to care for you and the rest of my loved ones, but I leave them in Allah's hands and your hands, and if you see Hamid, let him know that he must take care of you and his sister. She has no one left."

The Gypsy woman could not help letting a tear fall as she replied, "I will. I promise I will."

Abdullah held her hands and paused for moments as he thought of the words that he was about to say, "I am so afraid, Barrya. I am so afraid of this journey. I don't know what will happen, but I cannot stay here. Kamal came to the school the other day, and I could see the intent of harm in his eyes."

Barrya squeezed his hands gently and said, "You should not fear your journey. Your wife, Basima, has enough fear in her, but you are right about Kamal. He has not harmed anyone in a while, so he will be coming to you. You listen to me. You take your wife and leave Balluria, and don't look back, even if you see me dying on the streets, even if you see me crying blood from my eyes to keep you. You go where you promised Basima you would take her, and we will wait for your letters." Then she kissed his forehead.

The next day, in the early hours of dawn, and like Hanan and Hamid had run away with their love from Balluria years ago, Abdullah and his wife, Basima, loaded their two sky-blue leather suitcases on top of a Volkswagen Passat and left Balluria as Barrya stood up on the dirt road that led to the river watching and waving to them. Within brief seconds Balluria disappeared in the dust behind the car. Abdullah pressed on his wife's hand as she cried the entire way to the capital city. He also pressed on the four thousand dinars that he had wrapped in an envelope and hidden in an inside pocket of his jacket for extra security. He heard that many travelers had fallen victim to the many decent people who turned into desperate muggers, robbers, highwaymen, and petty thieves who robbed travelers of everything with value, even their shoes and socks. When they arrived in the capital city, it was too late to travel to Jordan, so they spent the night sitting by their two sky-blue leather suitcases in the main public transportation bus terminal, where many thieves, soldiers, and prostitutes slept in the corners in the inhumanly harsh nights of sin and crime in the merciless capital city, which had lost its innocence since the war of the thirty nations.

Abdullah stayed up all night as Basima tried to sleep. All night Abdullah thought of the people in Balluria. He thought of Sayed Habeeb and the cozy corners of the mosque filled with the warmth of faith and humility. He thought of Barrya and her secluded mud hut full of unconditional love of life and children and her Gypsy wit and wisdom as she sat by the little fire that she made every night from the fallen palm tree leaves and wild prairie thorns, but mostly he thought of his friends. He thought of Adnan and wondered if he had reached the gates of death and heaven in the marshes. And he thought of Ahmed, who followed Adnan in his escape from the life imposed on him. Abdullah thought of Hamid and his endless struggle against everything. He thought of Amel and her mother and wondered if they could survive the starvation by selling hardened old candy to children who have no money.

For a brief moment, he thought of Salam, the mayor's son, who left Balluria a long time before and wondered if he and Basima could contact Salam. The last they heard was that Salam was in America, and he might be able to help them. Abdullah thought that as soon as they arrive in Jordan, he would try to contact Salam. Abdullah never thought of Kamal. Or he tried not to. As the sun peeked from behind a marvelously shaped gray and orange cloud, Abdullah woke Basima for breakfast.

The young couple ate egg sandwiches and drank two small cups of tea that they bought from a young boy who looked like he had smeared himself in all the dirt of the deteriorating pavement of the capital city. Later, they boarded a bus heading to Jordan. The bus looked like it was filled with people who were running away from something or someone just like him and Basima. Abdullah knew that all the people on the bus were all running away from all the Ballurias and from all the Kamals that filled the country, but mainly they fled the starvation that turned the humans in this land into hungry animals in the endless cycle of bare survival that left innocence in shambles and made crossing the lines of shame and indecency as easy as it has never been. He also knew that all the travelers on that bus were heading somewhere in the world that might be willing to open its doors and let them rest for a while, and he wondered of any of the travelers were going to Denmark or if any of them were going to the snowy hills in the pictures that he saw many years ago.

He thought to himself that it would be good to have familiar neighbors who could speak his language and share meals within the snowy hills of Denmark. At the same time, Abdullah noticed that all the travelers on that bus shared something they tried to hide behind jokes and tears as they started to realize that they were leaving their homeland and that they might never be able to return. Abdullah noticed that all the travelers shared the same look in their eyes: that of fear and the clear anxiety of the near unknown. As the bus approached the border checkpoint, Abdullah pressed harder on Basima's hand, fearing the unthinkable possibility of degradation and torture if the border police with the thick moustaches and bright red berets discovered the forged passports He recited the verse from the Qur'an that Sayed Habeeb told him to read at the border: "*And we have blinded the unfaithful from the front and the back, and they will never see.*"

He recited the verse a hundred times as the bus pulled in the large parking lot of the border checkpoint, where many other buses, incoming and outgoing, had stopped to be searched. It was the same place where years later Salam spent one night on his way back to Balluria. Basima was awake, and she was more worried than her husband. Two border police patrolman boarded the bus and instructed the men to go to one building and the women to another building closer to the bus. The travelers obeyed the orders in complete silence. In the building where the men entered, there were several desks and many border policemen with their thick moustaches and bright red berets. The men were instructed to present their passports and the amount of money they possessed. Abdullah presented his passport and his wife's passport and the three thousands dinars hiding one thousand dinar with his wife, he waited in line.

When he got to the desk, the overbearing policeman questioned him, "Why are you leaving the country?"

Abdullah could think of a thousand answers for that question, but he answered with the only one he knew that could prevent the ramifications of misunderstandings and preemptive threats in the question. "I have no choice. My wife is ill, and she needs medical help."

The border policeman looked at him skeptically, having heard many such answers. "What is she suffering from?"

"Women's illness."

The border policeman asked with calm, authoritative voice, "Did you serve in the military?"

"I am exempt. It's posted in my passport," Abdullah answered with clear submissiveness.

"Exempt, huh?" the policeman mumbled. He flipped through the passport's pages and said, "Where is our good-bye gift?"

"What? I mean where do you want me to put it?" Abdullah asked with fake innocence.

"I will give you back your passport, and you will put our good-bye gift in it then you will give me the passport," the border policeman said in a quieter voice.

"All right."

The border policeman handed Abdullah back his passport and Basima's passport. Abdullah put a one hundred-dinar bill between the pages and gave it back to the border policeman, but he made sure not to put it in Basima's passport, fearing the policeman might be extra vigilant and notice the unmistakable forgery in Basima's document.

The policeman took the passport and said, "There are two passports. So we need two gifts." He handed the passports back to Abdullah, who looked at the policeman and smiled.

"All right, you are right."

Abdullah inserted another one hundred dinars in the passport and gave it back to the border policeman, who stamped the passports and gave them back to Abdullah, telling him to go to the other building, collect his wife, and board the bus. Abdullah thanked him, and as he was walking away, the border policeman called him back and whispered, "When you get to the Jordanian side, look for a man by the name of Ibrahim, and give him a hundred dinars. He will help you pass through with these two forged passports."

Abdullah froze as he heard that, but he looked at the border policeman with humble and sincere gratitude for sparing him and his wife the fate of being detained and sent back to the capital city prison, where many people mysteriously disappeared. The border policeman signaled for him to leave as he called, "Next in line!"

As the bus crossed the border, Abdullah looked back at his homeland that he was leaving behind. He fought his tears and tried to console Basima as she wept. "It's all right, Basima. One day we will be back when things are better and safer. It's all right, Habeeby."

He felt that that it might be the last time he would see his country, and suddenly he felt the massive yearning to go back to Balluria with all of its fears and harshness and its forgotten raggedy existence. He missed Balluria. When the bus reached the Jordanian side with its similar building and similar border personnel with thick moustaches and red hats, Abdullah asked about Ibrahim, who was standing nearby smoking a cigarette, and without introductions Abdullah handed him the two passports with a hundred dinars between the pages and said, "Your gift is inside."

"Wait here," replied Ibrahim.

After processing the necessary paperwork to enter Jordan and paying yet another two welcome gifts to the Jordanian border police, Abdullah and Basima were in the middle of Amman that evening looking for an address that Abdullah obtained from his friend, the same one who provided the forged passports. The address was that of a person who knew another person who knew the people who could smuggle people to Europe. Abdullah did not want to waste time in Jordan because he knew that his and his wife's visas were only good for six months and that he must leave before the visa expired.

After spending the first night in a hotel in the downtown district of Amman where all the poor exiles lived, Abdullah started to realize the grim realities of his new situation as he heard stories from others who sat in a well-known teahouse all day exchanging stories of despair and waiting and death while Basima stayed in the one-bedroom apartment they rented for a month. In Amman, Abdullah started spending all of his days at the teahouse waiting for

Jabbar, the name of a man he had on a small piece of paper that he smuggled with him across the border. With the name there was a phone number. Abdullah called the number several times, and after the seventh time a voice answered the phone.

"Allo, who is calling?" the voice asked

"Al Salamu Alykum. You don't know me. My name is Abdullah. I got your number from a friend of ours; his name is Sameer."

"Sameer. Who is Sameer? I don't know Sameer," the voice pretentiously claimed.

"He said to call you when I got to Jordan," Abdullah insisted with a bit of tension in his voice.

"I told you that I don't know Sameer," the voice said, "but you can go to the Sharq teahouse and wait there." A click and then silence filled his ear.

Abdullah did not understand why the man on the other end of the line was acting that way. He tried calling again, but no one answered the phone. So he started spending all day at the Sharq teahouse, where he heard the many stories that made him wonder if his dream of the wooden cabin in the snowy hill would be a hellish nightmare. He sat listening to the songs that told of how much the patrons missed their homeland. He overheard a hard-looking, tanned man telling his story.

"All of my life," the man said, "I have readied myself to face any situation possible. Everything. Death, prison, being a refugee or being homeless, but to be sitting on top of tree and a lion is waiting at the bottom of the tree waiting to eat me—that was not on my mind."

"How did that happen?" asked another thin, tanned man who chain-smoked a cheap brand of cigarette that smelled of burning wood.

"Well, an African smuggler in Yemen told me than he could get me to France if I was willing to go through Africa, so I traveled to Sudan, and from Sudan we were smuggled to Chad, and from there we had to go to Nigeria, but on our way there we had to cross the borders on foot. It was nighttime, when twenty other people and I walked to Nigeria, and suddenly we were ambushed by the border patrol. Everyone ran in a different direction. I ran by myself. I ran for half an hour and found myself alone. I walked in the jungle. Then I heard some noises behind me. I looked, and my Allah. I saw a large lion that was running to eat me. I climbed the nearest tree, and the lion came to the tree and circled it several times, and then it sat at the bottom of the tree waiting for me to come down so he could eat me. I stayed like that until the morning, when the lion heard the border patrol trucks and ran away. I climbed down the tree and surrendered myself to them. Just like I said, I was ready for anything, but I was not ready for that." He laughed.

Abdullah listened to several stories, and he told Basima about them at night. Abdullah waited for ten days, sitting in that teahouse, listening to more stories of how thousands of people were cheated out of their money and fell prey to con artists who posed as smugglers and robbed poor hopeful exiles of their life's savings and their dreams. He listened as one man told the story of the hundreds of people lost in small boats in the Mediterranean as they tried to reach the shores of Italy and the thousands who drowned as they tried to reach the shores of Australia, but he never heard anything about the road to the snowy hills of Denmark. So he kept waiting in the teahouse until one afternoon, he noticed that a man was staring at him continually. He looked back at the man, who nodded once as a greeting, and Abdullah nodded back. The man approached him and said, "Where is the brother from?"

"From a small town in the south. It's called Balluria."

"Balluria. Is that a real town?" the man asked, and then said, "I am looking for my cousin. His name is Sameer. Do you know a good man named Sameer?" the man asked.

Abdullah almost jumped with joy. Finally, someone who knew him. "Yes, I do," Abdullah said with a wide smile and hopeful eyes.

"All right. He is a good man, and he is my cousin," the man said.

"Mashaallah," Abdullah replied politely.

"You must be Abdullah," Jabbar said.

"I am Abdullah," he replied.

"I am Jabbar... Let's walk outside."

Abdullah and Jabbar walked in the streets of Amman as Jabbar explained the process of being smuggled to the west.

"First, we have to send you to Turkey. From there you will be transported to Greece. From there you will board the train to Holland, and from Holland you will be smuggled to Denmark. The trip will cost you six thousand dinars for two people. You and your wife."

Abdulla's heart sank to his toes. "But I only have approximately three thousand and five hundred dinars," Abdullah pleaded.

"Well, that is a problem," Jabbar said, "because the people will not accept less than six thousand dinars, so please do not waste my time. When you have six thousand dinars, call me."

Jabbar left Abdullah in the middle of the noise of the downtown district and walked away. Abdullah walked home to Basima with a grim look on his face. He could not eat his dinner of fried tomatoes and bread that she prepared. She asked him why he was upset, and he told her. She suggested that they send a letter to Balluria, asking Amel or Barrya to gather the money somehow. She also suggested that they send a letter to Salam, the mayor's son, who left Balluria a long time before and went to America.

"Where will we get his address from? And will he remember us?"

"We have to try. I have his address from Amel. She told me that she sends him letters all the time," Basima assured him.

"All right, I will write the letter tonight and, Inshallah, good things will happen."

Three weeks later, they had not received any reply from the two letters they had sent, and Abdullah figured that even if they waited another year, they would not receive any reply. At night, he lay next to Basima and touched her belly, which was getting bigger, and said, "I am the only Arab man who wants to have a girl as his firstborn child. If she will be a girl, I will name her Rahma, Mercy, because the one thing that we need and many people need is mercy from Allah and mercy among themselves."

"As long as we are together, Abdullah... we have the mercy of Alallah," Basima said as she put her head on his shoulders.

"We need mercy because I am thinking tomorrow to tell Jabbar that I will go alone to Denmark. We only have money for one traveler, and you cannot travel like this. I am afraid you will have a miscarriage."

Basima did not answer. She turned her face toward the wall and cried all night. Abdullah did not say a word; he knew that any words he might say would make her sadder. So he waited, and when the dawn's calls to prayers started to break the peaceful sleep of the white stone buildings of Amman, Basima turned toward her husband and said, "All right, you can go alone but don't leave me alone here. Please find me a family or someone you know that I could stay with and I will wait for you with your daughter who will be here, in a month or six weeks."

"Is that what the doctor says?" asked Abdullah.

"Yes."

"It will only be few months, Basima. As soon as I get to Denmark, they will reunite us, as they did with many other families. This is what everyone is telling me. I am doing this for me and you and our daughter."

The days went by quickly as Abdullah prepared for his journey. Basima stayed with a family that Jabbar introduced to Abdullah and Basima. The husband of that family was going on the same trip, and he was leaving his wife behind as well, with two children, so Abdullah and Jabbar arranged for Basima to stay with the wife and the two children. It was Friday when Jabbar arrived in a small car and rang the bell of the apartment. The night before, Abdullah and Basima could not sleep as they spent their last night together. She stayed up all night, crying and kissing his hands and his forehead and his face. He tried to calm her down and assured her that he would come back for her no matter what stood before him.

"As soon as I feel I am settled, I will come back for you. or I will bring you to me," he said, but deep inside, he felt that was the first time he had made a promise to Basima that he was not sure of keeping.

In between her tears, Basima pleaded, "Promise me that you will return to me and if you find it's too harsh or too dangerous, you will return. If you think it's difficult and you can complete the trip, you will return to me and we will go back to Balluria. I could live with fear and hunger, but I could not live without you. We are simple and poor people, Abdullah, and we may be simple and poor forever, but we have each other, Abdullah. Promise me that you will stay alive for me and for our children."

"I promise," Abdullah said quietly to Basima with all the love in the world in his eyes as he walked down the stony stairs on his first steps on the journey to the wooden cabin in the middle of the snowy hills of Denmark.

6

That morning a group of twenty-two people gathered in the teahouse waiting for the two guides, who were supposed to take them to their dream destinations. Abdullah looked at his journey mates, who did not talk to each other. They all looked frightened of the unknown things of the journey they were about to start. There were young and older men, young and older women, and some children who played and laughed. None of them knew that the journey they were about to take might be the most decisive one of their lives. It was the journey between fear and safety, between hunger and gluttony. This journey might afford them the ability of choosing their meal and dessert and the drink for each day, a privilege few people in the world have. It was the journey between certainty and uncertainty, and mostly it was the journey between an identity threatened to be lost and revoked all the time and a new identity that might last a lifetime and mean protection and respect as a human. The twenty-two people thought, as Abdullah did, that time would pass by quickly. They also hoped that the world would close its eyes for a little while until they reached their destinations safely. He asked the husband of the woman who was Basima's new housemate, "Do you think something may happen on the way?"

"No, Inshalla, nothing will happen."

"Inshallah. Do you think the women will be all right by themselves in Amman?"

"Inshallah, there is nothing to fear... it's an Arab country and it's safe. People here have manners and traditions like ours."

They loaded the bus, and Abdullah sat next to his new journey mate. The two guides acted like they did not trust anyone and talked only to one man in the group who seemed to be one of the smugglers. The man told everyone to sit quietly and not to move until they were told do so. After four hours the bus reached the Aqaba harbor. The guides ordered the twenty-two people to unload their bags and follow him. He walked into a small alley that led to the harbor, where they saw a black-bellied ship and were told to wait for a minute. Then they saw a man waving from the ship with a white cloth that looked like a flag. The guides walked to the ship and came back and told the group of people to board the large ship, which looked like an oil tanker. It was almost two o'clock in the afternoon, and the harbor looked deserted. Abdullah noticed the vehicle that looked like a police vehicle, and he also noticed that after they boarded the oil tanker, one of the guides who stayed on land had walked toward the police vehicle and handed an envelope to one of the policemen who stood outside the car.

"Everyone gets a gift," said the man, standing next to Abdullah.

After an hour of waiting that seemed like eternity, a shipmate guided the group of people along with another group of men and women and children, who were waiting on the ship. The shipmate guided them to a cell that looked like it had been used by hundreds of other smuggled people. Pieces of clothes and blankets and empty small boxes of chocolate and the remains of opened canned food were scattered on the floor. The place smelled of utter despair.

The guide said with his clearly broken Arabic and in a harsh voice, "You will stay here and sleep here, and if you want to use the bathroom, there is only one, so men and women have to share it. I suggest that you stay quiet until I come back, and don't you ever try to go up to the deck or to the other rooms. Do you understand me?"

The group of frightened people nodded and scattered in the cell, looking for a place to rest. One man said, "Brothers, let us let the women and children use the bathroom first."

All the men agreed as women and children started to walk toward the metal door of the one bathroom. The group divided itself into smaller groups as families gathered and ate the canned food they brought with them. Some men smoked and talked. Abdullah sat with his back to the metal inner wall of the ship, put his small duffel bag behind his head, and tried to rest. He was thinking of Basima and feeling more alone than he ever had before. Moments later, the ship let out a sad siren call, the sign of departure, and sailed into the unknown. One man started to recite the verse from the Qur'an that tells of the arch on Noah: *"In the name of Allah the way it sails and when it anchors."*

The swinging movements of the ship rocked Abdullah to sleep, and others lay on the hard metal floor and tried to sleep. Abdullah woke up when he heard noises of the other people in the cell. He opened his eyes and saw the others gathering their belongings. He asked the man next to him for the reason.

"We have arrived in Antakya... we are in Turkey," the man replied.

Abdullah quickly gathered his belongings and frantically pushed them inside the duffle bag, and rushed to the cell door as the others waited, when suddenly he heard the steps of someone coming down the metal stairs of the cell. The group of people moved back as the door was opened, slowly, making an ominous screeching sound.

"Are you ready?" said the bearded man with a soft voice. "All right, follow me."

The group followed the bearded man, who limped to the deck. The fresh air from the sea hit their faces and injected a breeze of hope into their lungs and a feeling of freedom into their hearts as they followed the bearded man to the partially lit deck. The Mediterranean moon was complete. The town's lights were very far away and so unfamiliar. Three lifeboats were dropped to the surface, and the people were ordered to board them. The men, women, and children boarded the lifeboats and slowly went down to the dark waters of the Mediterranean. Gentle waters of the shores of Antakya carried the worried and frightened people to a new destiny. The moon looked like the one in Balluria, Abdullah thought, and wondered if Basima was looking at the same moon that moment as the three lifeboats reached the sandy shores of Antakya. The people realized that they were considered illegal and unwanted, and yet wanted by the authorities at the same time. The man who guided the boats asked who was going to Greece. Some people raised their hands. Others said with quiet voices of uncertainty, "We are."

"All right, the people who are going to Greece, stay here and don't move. The rest of you stay with Hamash. The group of people looked at Hamash and did not speak a word. "The rest of you who are going to Turkey, follow me," the bearded man said.

Abdullah followed the bearded man, who led them single file to a bus waiting with its lights turned off. Abdullah looked back and saw that all the families with women and children had stayed with Hamash, who seemed to be deaf and mute because he hadn't said a word the entire time. Abdullah felt better for them because he was wondering about the difficulties they might face by crossing the mountains.

Abdullah and the others boarded the bus with two men who were waiting inside and watched as the bearded man gave the bus driver an envelope with what was likely money. The driver set off with the lights of the bus off until they reached the entrance of a deserted highway, and then he turned the lights on. There was music of a Turkish singer, who cried about lost love. Abdullah knew the singer's voice. His name was Tatlises, and Basima liked his songs. Abdullah leaned on the window and thought of what Basima was doing at that moment. He fell asleep for hours, and when he woke up, it was dawn. The bus was still moving northward as the sun tried to appear from behind a strip of majestic mountains.

"Oh, my Allah, how beautiful," Abdullah said to the man next to him, who did not comment. Abdullah felt that the journey had truly started. It was a good sign to see the mountains covered with snow, something that he had never seen before in his life. The mountains were covered with white snow and green trees, just like the ones he saw years ago in the magazine that Adnan brought to the school. Those mountains were the gates to freedom. They were the doors to Europe, beautiful Europe, Europe the civilization, Europe the history, and Europe of the free humans. Abdullah wished that Basima was with him to see the view. Two hours later, the bus arrived in a small village of a few stone houses and almost deserted of people.

The two men who took turns driving the bus told the group of hopeful and fearful smuggled people to stay inside, and they got out and entered a house. A few minutes later, they came out accompanied by a scruffy and extremely rugged-looking man, who seemed to be in his middle fifties but had the strength of ten men. Speaking in Turkish, the men pointed to the bus and then signaled to Abdullah and the others to exit the bus and bring their bags. The group of men exited the bus and entered the rugged man's stony house.

Before dark the two men, who spent the time outside the house drinking tea and talking to the rugged man in Turkish, told the group that they needed to dress warmly because the mountains were merciless, and it would take them three days to cross to another village, where a bus would wait for them to take them to Istanbul, but they had to make it through the mountains first. One of the men asked why they separated the people who were going to Turkey and then Greece from those left behind with Hamash, who never spoke a word.

One of the two men said, "They have paid more money, and they will be traveling to Cypress by boat. They are Christians, and someone is waiting for them." The answer was suspicious but there was no time to argue about logic and fairness, as it seemed that the parallel worlds of reason and madness were twins in the diabolical game of the pursuit of dreams. This was especially true for people like Abdullah and the group of unfortunate dreamers with him. Abdullah tried to think of Basima as he heard the two men who drove the bus give the final instructions.

"Wrap your feet with warm socks, and cover your neck and face because it's cold in the mountains. Make sure to stay quiet and not make any noises because the border patrols will hear you. And don't get lost. Never ever stop walking because you are tired. No one will wait for you, and you will be left alone in the mountains," the two men said in broken Arabic, and they walked away toward the bus, taking with them the last glimpse of familiarity.

7

Thirty-eight hours before Abdullah fell to the snowy ground gasping for his breath, the rugged man who was supposed to take the men through fifty-two kilometers of ferocious, cold, and treacherous terrain, where only wolves and mountain lions could survive—the extremely rugged-looking man—gave his marching instructions very clearly when he told the men in broken Arabic, "You will follow me. When we walk we don't stop. If you stop, you will be left behind and when you are left behind, you will die. We will walk at night and hide during the day. It will take us four days to reach the village, where someone will wait for you to take you to Istanbul. We will leave when night falls."

The men prepared for the trip of their lives. Some of them prayed, and some wrapped their extra socks and clothes around their bodies, and others wrote their wills, and when darkness started to cover the mountainous horizon, the rugged man looked outside and signaled to the eighteen men.

"Yellaa, let's go."

The men followed the rugged man who walked in wide steps and did not talk to any of the men. The rugged man did not turn to check on the men behind him, who followed silently as they walked through a long valley and were guided by each other's dark ghosts. They avoided a small village that looked abandoned on the side of the mountain. The group of frightened and scared men rested as the sun rose from the top of the mountains. They looked around and saw they were in the middle of a valley that belonged to another dimension of existence.

The rugged man signaled for them to sit and said in his broken Arabic, "Hide here and don't move all day. Sleep until the night." As he spoke, he looked for a hole between the rocks and wrapped his body with his dirty robe-like jacket and slept.

Crawling between rocks and bushes, the men tried to keep themselves from freezing to death. Abdullah was exhausted, and he realized that his weak body had started to give out on him. The men had walked for almost sixteen hours. Abdullah wrapped the only clean shirt in his bag around his bleeding left foot and tried to sleep. He had difficulty breathing and wondered if he could continue the journey, but he did not tell anyone in fear that they might leave him. He prayed that by nightfall he would be able to walk again.

He was awoken by one of the men, who said, "Brother, wake up. It's time to walk." Abdullah stood up and walked slowly. He ended up at the tail of the line of dark ghosts, and he thought that he had started losing his vision, because of the lack of oxygen. He walked slowly and wobbled as he stepped on the sharp-ended rocks. His heart started beating irregularly; he began to have difficulty breathing. Flakes of snow danced, warning of a coming storm that could bring the journey of the misguided men to a tragic end. Abdullah fell behind, as he could not walk as quickly as the others and not nearly as quickly as the rugged man, who guided the unfortunate dreamers in their journey to unwelcoming and uncertain destinations in Europe. Abdullah stopped and shouted to the eighteen men, "Brothers. Please wait for me. Please don't leave me behind."

"Bring your strength together, my brother. You have to, because no one will wait with you," the last man in the column said to Abdullah as he passed him by. Abdullah walked the next three kilometers and felt his heart weaken and his breath shorten. The storm pushed its wind against his body and slowed his steps to a crawl. He fell farther back, and the gap between him and the last of the men widened. He fell to his knees and thought that he must stand up and catch up with the line of the ghost men or he would face a certain death. He tried to stand, but he could not. He could not breathe. He tried to shout.

"May Allah protect you... wait for me. Don't leave me here."

The storm howled through the treacherous terrain of the mountains, carrying the sounds of all those lost through the centuries as they tried to overcome the mountains. The sounds of the storm played a symphony of extraordinary dreams requiring a sacrifice of life. The storm ran across the hands and faces of the destitute men like thousands of swords. Abdullah fell to the ground the first time when the eighteen men, led by their rugged middle-aged guide, crossed an elevated walkway between two mountains. As he felt his heart, his weak heart that had prevented him from playing soccer, the same weak heart that had saved him from certain death in the many wars of the tyrant and the same heart that started beating with love when he first saw Basima holding her books in the elementary school, that same heart that had chosen this ungodly setting to give out, that same heart had decided to stop while Abdullah was on his way to the most beautiful place on earth, a wooden cabin in the snowy hills of Denmark.

"Help me... help me. Please. I have a wife and a baby daughter. Please help me. Don't leave me here to die."

There was no echo, as the storm would not allow his plea to reach the men who could have witnessed his death. He lay down in the snow gasping for breath. He tried shouting again and again with a voice no more than the faintest of whispers, but no one responded.

"Please, my brothers. Come back to me. Don't leave me here to die. Please... Please." His tears froze on his cheeks. The weakness moved quickly from his heart to his legs as he felt the stony heaviness swallowing his feet and his hands. He felt the dizziness of a spiral free fall into the darkness of his inner pains and remembered the day when Kamal took Hanan's kittens to drown them in the Euphrates. He remembered the time when his soccer team, the Wolves, scored the goal against the Wild Lions. He remembered his wedding night and how beautiful his wife, Basima, looked in her white wedding dress, he remembered the morning when the firing squad shattered the bodies of his remarkable friends, but mostly he remembered Basima. He remembered Basima and all the dried flowers she put in his notebooks as she borrowed them when they were in school together.

As he felt the touch of death creeping with its frozen claws, claiming his body inch by inch, Abdullah tried to cry, but his tears were frozen. He tried to scream, but his throat was dry like a stone, and his tongue became heavy as the line of men disappeared in the abyss of snow and darkness that wrapped the mountains. He tried to move, but the heaviness of his body became unbearable. He wanted to pray. He cried inside and prayed to Allah to save Basima from sadness.

"Oh, my lord, Allah. Not like this I die. Not here. Oh, Allah. I beg your mercy. I beg your forgiveness for what I have brought on myself and my wife and my child, my child that I will never see and who will never know her father. Oh, Allah! If you choose for me this death, please choose a better life for

Basima. Oh, Allah, the God of heavens and earth, I beg your forgiveness for my poor soul and accept me into your heaven. Oh, my lord, please wrap your merciful hands around my wife, Basima, and spare her the sadness and grief and protect her with your ever watchful eyes that never sleep."

He looked to the horizon as the sun emerged from the majestic stretch of white and gray mountains, and he wondered if that was how it felt when a person dies. But he suddenly felt tasty warmth in his body and soul, he felt lifted from the freezing hole where he laid and flew over the Euphrates, searching for Basima, and looking at Balluria. The snow storm calmed down and the sun appeared from the top of the mountains. It shined on a miniature snowy hill covering a lonesome dead body.

8

Six weeks before she wrote the letter to Amel, Basima gave birth to a baby daughter. She knew what to name her. Abdullah wanted to name his two daughters Rahma (mercy), and Niema (blessings). He had stated that if any human would have the mercy and the blessings of Allah, then life would be easy and joyful, but Basima realized that they needed mercy more than blessings, so she named her firstborn child Rahma. Basima did not hear anything from Abdullah for two weeks after he left with smugglers that Jabbar brought to the teahouse. Basima had no doubt in her mind that Abdullah was on his way to the snowy hills in Denmark and that he would call her or write to her as soon as he had access to a telephone or a place where he could write a letter. She waited for the first week of her daughter's birth to pass, and she made lunch and invited Jabbar over. She called him and told him that she gave a birth to a baby girl and she wanted to do the necessary traditional baby blessing lunch to rid the child of the influence of the evil eye and bring the blessing of Allah to the life of the newborn. Thus, she invited him and his wife to a lunch that she could barely afford. Basima wanted to hear of any updates about her husband, who had not sent any news for almost a month. Jabbar arrived to the lunch alone, and when Basima asked about his wife, he said that she was ill, and she sent her best wishes to the baby and her mother.

Basima was reluctant to let Jabbar into the apartment where she lived with the other woman, but she had no choice because the other woman had received good news from her husband, telling her that he had reached Italy, and he would be in Holland in a few days and that she should prepare herself to follow him soon, so she wanted to travel to Syria and stay with her sister, which would leave Basima in dire need of money for food and rent. Jabbar was not interested in the other woman's plans, and he told her that she could leave anytime, but he did not say a word when Basima asked, "Brother, did you hear anything from my husband?"

Instead, he started talking about how the immigration police were chasing all those with expired visas and throwing them back to the borders. Basima waited until he finished his lunch and drank his tea before asking again, "Brother Jabbar, my heart is telling me that something is not right, and I have run out of money, so I beg you to tell me the truth about my husband."

Jabbar reached into his pocket, pulled out a red Dunhill cigarette pack, and started smoking as he looked at Basima. "Listen, sister. I am not sure of what happened, but I think you should prepare yourself to hear the worst news, because I have seen this happen many times before, and the only thing I can advise you is that you should ask your family to send you money soon, because I think you will need it."

Basima started to cry, and she held her newborn daughter close to her heart, saying, "Oh, my Allah is merciful."

"Don't cry," Jabbar said. "We don't know anything for sure yet, and he may call you today or tomorrow, but you should be prepared, and you need to pay the rent this month."

Two weeks later, Abdullah still had not called and Basima had not heard the worst news yet, but she had not heard any good news either. Jabbar had visited her several times in her apartment, which she had not paid rent on in a month. Basima noticed that Jabbar was looking at her differently. Something was in his eyes as he looked at her as she sat and when she stood up to bring him the tea. In his last visit Jabbar told her that she must leave the apartment and find another place to live. That night she wrote the letter to Amel. Realizing that some people's dreams could easily turn into nightmares, she wrote the letter that night and gave it to a man who was returning to the homeland after giving up on his dreams of reaching France. He was returning after he was almost eaten by a lion in the jungle of Nigeria.

Amel could not believe the man who knocked on the house's half-tin and half-wood door and told her that he had a letter for her. She hastily washed her hands of the dough and took the letter from the man after asking him how he had arrived with the letter from her friend. He said that his name was Sameer and someone who was in Jordan had brought the letter with him after coming back to the homeland after many failed attempts to reach Europe. Amel did not understand the man's explanation of the letter's origin and hoped that she finally got a response from Salam, the mayor's son who left Balluria a long time before and went to America. But her joy vanished as she saw the name of the sender. It was Basima. Amel sat in the dark shade of the mud wall, where she used to read poetry with Salam and opened the letter. Her disappointment turned into sadness as she read.

Dear Amel:

May Allah's peace and blessings be upon you.

I ask Allah that this letter reaches you and that you and your mother and Barrya are well.

I don't know how to start and what to write. Abdullah left to go to Denmark four months ago and I haven't heard anything from him yet. I have asked everyone who traveled with the same people that took him, and they all say they have not seen him. In my heart I know that a terrible thing has happened to my husband. I have given birth to a baby girl, and I named her Mercy, as Abdullah and I had agreed to name her. She is beautiful and has Abdullah's eyes. I am writing this letter because I have no one else to write to, but I am truly in need of help. All the money that Abdullah left me has been spent long ago, I have borrowed money from people I don't know, and they don't know me. I am in need of money. My visa will expire in two months, and after that I have to leave Jordan, or else I will be chased by the immigration police. Rahma now is two months old, and we are on the verge of starvation. It seems like starvation does not want to leave us alone. I have done things that... I have committed the unthinkable, and some people here have known what I have done, and I am afraid that I will face the same fate as that of Hanan, but you will understand. It was the only choice I had. It was a choice between my dignity or being in the street with my newborn baby. Abdullah would never leave me like this, but I know that he is going through something preventing him from coming to my aid. I am afraid that he is in a bad situation... Allah forbids. I pray every night that he is safe and that he will return to me.

Dear Amel, I trust that you will keep my secret, and please try to help me with any money that you can send me. I don't know what the days ahead will have for me and my daughter, but I have to tell someone, and you are the only one left who knows me. I did not want to tell my brothers because I am sure they will not help me, and they will tell me to go back to Balluria, and I cannot go back until I know what happened to my husband If you can help me with any money from the candy store or any money that you may have, I will be able to save my soul before it will be too late.

Dear Amel, this world is a cruel world, and it crushes people like me and you, and the saddest part is no one will understand our shortcomings because the world has set the stage for us to fail as people. Do not be sad and don't think of me a lot. Just pray for me and take care of your mother, Barrya, and tell her that I miss her dearly. And pass my respect to your brother Hamid and tell him about what happened to me and Abdullah and tell him that it was all because we were afraid of Kamal.

The ever devoted,

Basima

Amel put the letter aside and washed her hands and face, fetched her black abbaya, and walked out of the door walking toward Barrya's mud hut. She was thinking of asking Barrya for whatever money she might have to send to Basima. She had only six dinars from selling candy to the children since she took over the candy store that was almost empty. She thought she might be able to gather twenty dinars, and maybe she could send it to Basima.

Earlier that day and before Basima felt that she had started losing her soul slowly, and before she wrote the letter in an attempt to grab the last threads of her dignity, Jabbar had shown up at the apartment, asking if he could come in for a cup of tea and to talk about her situation. Basima agreed, hoping that he had news about Abdullah.

"I cannot let you stay in the apartment anymore. You have not paid the rent, and the building's owner," he stopped and pulled out a red pack of Dunhill cigarettes, "the man wants his money, and you have none," he said as he calmly smoked his cigarette.

"Where should I go? I have nowhere to go and no one to stay with," Basima said as she fought back her tears and held her newborn close to her breasts. "I could work. Anything. I could clean houses and care for other people's babies."

"You cannot work because your visa is temporary, and they will not let you work. Do you know how many women are willing to do these jobs? There are thousands of women from all countries who willing to do everything. And I mean everything."

"Oh, my Allah. What should I do, brother? Can you help me?" she begged.

Jabbar looked at Basima and realized for the first time how beautiful she was.

"I have a stone, a precious stone that you may sell and use the money for the rent," Basima said as she walked inside her bedroom and fetched the stone that Barrya gave her.

She brought it to Jabbar, who looked at the stone and examined it carefully before he said, "This is just a stone, a worthless stone." He threw the stone back to Basima, who did not know if she was sad because of the bad news of her husband or because of what Jabbar said about Barrya's stone.

"I don't know what to tell you. I mean your husband did not leave me any money to take care of you, and I have many other women just like you who need a lot of help. I used to care for and help these women, but it became like a bag with a large hole in it. I put money in it, and the money is gone. I am sorry, but you have to figure something out. Ask your family for help."

"I have no family," Basima said as she wept.

Jabbar looked at her as he waited for the right moment to propose the unthinkable. "The only choice is that... and I am only saying this because... well, the only choice is that there is a woman who will take care of you. Do you understand?" He searched her features looking for the glimpse of any indecency that she might possess.

"What do you mean?" Basima asked with sincere innocence.

"I mean there is a woman who knows a lot of men, men who have money, and they attend parties, and you will go to these parties," Jabbar said as he started to show the true colors of his intentions in his face.

"I don't know what you mean, brother," Basima said with a dry voice that showed a dawning of understanding.

"All right, listen to me," Jabbar explained. "I am sure you know what I mean, and you are not the only woman who cried before me. This woman will sponsor you and she will teach you and protect you even from immigration police. You have what it takes. I mean, you are young and beautiful and well dressed. She will show you the way, and you will start earning money and when you have earned enough money, maybe you can follow your husband to Norway."

"Denmark," Basima interrupted.

"Denmark or Sweden or Germany. The point is that you have no money, but you are young and beautiful, and you will earn twenty times the money if you accept what I am offering you. I am saying this only because I have no other offer," Jabbar said as he smoked his Dunhill cigarette and turned his face toward the window.

"How could you talk to me like that? Do you know who I am?" Basima said with a clear anger.

Jabbar looked at her again and said, "I don't care if you are the daughter of the president. Without money, you are nobody, and unless you have the rent money for me tonight, I will be forced to tell the building's owner to throw you to the streets."

Basima again cried and held her daughter closer to her heart. "If my husband only knew of what you said."

"Your husband? Yes. If he was here, I wouldn't tell you this. I have been in this country for many years, and I have seen everything. I've seen honorable women from prominent families who have been forced to sell their bodies because they needed to eat, and I've seen Gypsies treated like royalty because they know that honor is just a word we used back in the homeland."

"Please, Brother Jabbar, I don't expect this kind of talk."

"That does not matter. You have to give me your answer by tomorrow. And about the rent?"

"I don't have money. I only have thirty-five dinars," Basima said, feeling defeated and weak.

Jabbar paused for a moment as he looked at her and then he said, "I could arrange for something, and you can stay here for the rest of the month..."

"How?" Basima's naive spirits lifted slightly.

"Well," he said with an oily grin, "you and I can go to bed right now."

"I swear to my Allah that that will never happen, even if I die from starvation," Basima said as she raised her hand to slap Jabbar.

Jabbar grabbed her hand, squeezed it hard, and put his other hand on her mouth. "If you dare to slap me, I will put you in a car and send you to the borders tonight—where you will lose your honor in the homeland to the many border police who will beat you and rape you—you whore. You have no honor and when you live in the street you will be willing to sell your honor for two dinars."

That afternoon, Jabbar raped Basima twice as she laid there without moving and without resisting. She cried hopelessly, thinking of her husband, Abdullah, whose body was still frozen in the Turkish mountains. Basima stayed in the rented apartment for the remainder of the month as per the settlement with Jabbar, who later brought another woman to live with her in the small one-bedroom apartment. She shared the small room, the lifestyle, and the fate of another unfortunate wife of another unfortunate dreamer who thought he could reach the shores of the Pacific and live in a fisherman's village in Seattle.

"A beautiful town in America, where it never stops raining," said the wife of the other misguided soul who, once back in his homeland, had watched a movie that told the story of a vengeful killer whale in Seattle.

"It was Richard Harris, the man who killed the killer whale's mate in the movie," the woman said.

Basima knew in her heart that something terrible had happened to Abdullah, but she did not want to believe it. She roamed the streets of Amman alone carrying her newborn daughter Rahma during the day and attended parties at night. Basima danced as Barrya had taught her. She danced alone at parties arranged by Jabbar and his female friend, who knew many men who had the money. They were all from the rich Gulf countries, men who were generous with their money and strange in their sexual requests. Basima had no doubt that news about her infidelity and her new life had reached Balluria, and, more specifically, her brothers, who properly prepared their weapons and waited for her return to cut off the rotten part that tarnished the name of the family and dishonored them forever. She was also sure that they had prepared their daggers to sever her right palm.

Deep in her heart, Basima knew that she would never go back to Balluria just as she knew that Abdullah would never return from his journey. She knew that she would never have the chance to live in a cozy wooden cabin in the snowy hills of Denmark with Abdullah and their children. Basima knew for sure that her life would be short, because sooner or later the Jordanian immigration police would catch up with her and send her back to her homeland, where she would face an unspeakable fate, but she knew for a fact that the world would not allow her to live peacefully with her husband and two daughters named Mercy and Blessing, but this world or God would not allow it. All the kings and divine leaders and all the human smugglers and all the sheikhs conspired so that she and her weak-hearted husband would never reach their dreams.

Basima remembered that afternoon when Barrya told the mesmerized children the story of the beast who lives on human pain, the beast who was never - and will never be- satisfied, the beast who enjoys eating the hearts and souls of the unfortunate and the poor. She remembered the afternoon when she and all the boys and girls in Balluria sat and listened to the Gypsy woman telling that story and realized that it was her time to be feasted on.

Basima realized all this as she walked to the hotel, where Jabbar and his female friend were waiting with many men with money who were willing to pay for her body and to watch her dance the way Barrya had taught her long years ago. Basima let one tear roll down her cheek as she felt that she had neither remorse nor shame about offering her body to the many beasts awaiting it, her body only, as she had no soul left in her.

The Book of Balluria

Daggers in the Dust

1

Kamal's body was found in the late morning. The man who found the body was frightened by the disfigurement of the face and neck of Kamal's corpse and said, as he kneeled to make sure that Kamal was dead, "Your killer must have hated you so much."

The man ran to the police station and told the only awake police guard who was drinking his tea while sitting on the bench outside the station about the dead body. The police officer said to go away and come back later because the sergeant was not in. Many people gathered around Kamal's dead body, looking at it with pity and relief as he was lying there defenseless and calm. Some of them discreetly spat on the corpse when no one was looking. Kamal's body was deeply cut by a dagger, and his face was cut in many places. Both of his palms had been severed. His dark olive green uniform was completely drenched with blood, a dry, dark brown blood. Scratches from claws or nails drew reddish black lines on his face, neck and chest, as well as on other parts of his body. Some people who stood looking at the dead body thought that Kamal's body was ravaged by a wolf or a pack of angry wolves, but the deep cuts of the dagger dismissed that theory.

Quickly, the news about his death spread in the town. Many people talked about his death in the town's market and small shops. Groups of men and young boys stood looking at his body as the sun rose higher in the sky and the heat moved in between the walls of Balluria. There was a feeling of discreet easiness after they learned about his death. Three men placed the shredded body in a dirty, old green and white army blanket and carried it to the police station, because no one knew where else to take it. Kamal had not endeared himself to anyone in the town, and the old fearsome sheikh, who people thought that Kamal was related to, and who had once been such a commanding presence, had been conspicuously absent for so long that many thought he had died and been spirited off by the jinnies.

Kamal's body stayed in front of the police station until noon and started to stink. The police sergeant did not know what to do with it, and he asked his men if they knew whether Comrade Kamal had any family. None were sure, but one of them suggested that there was the Gypsy woman that he knew.

"No, I heard she is evil and she can put a curse on us," said the police sergeant, who had transferred to Balluria a few months earlier.

"We can take it to the mosque," said a young policeman.

"Yes, the mosque. I am sure that mad clergyman can still perform Islamic funerals," said the sergeant, and he ordered his men to fetch the clergyman.

Two young policemen went to the mosque looking for Sayed Habeeb, who spent most of his time in the deteriorating mosque reading the history of the holy family. When they found him, they asked him to help prepare Kamal's body for his eternal journey. Sayed Habeeb, who did not recognize the young policemen, refused to perform the death rituals. Without comprehending his surroundings and the ramification of his words, he started screaming at the two young policemen, who realized that the old, white-haired clergy was not sane. He said that he would never do that because of what Kamal did to the people of Balluria and because of how Kamal was the reason for his arrest for preaching the history of the holy family. The clergyman especially remembered the time where he was beaten nearly to death by the secret political police because he was spreading the word of the holy family. In his delusional outrage, Sayed Habeeb started shouting, "He killed everyone. He killed Hanan and Ahmed and Adnan. Kamal killed them all."

The two young policemen, who were not from the area, did not understand why the clergyman was angry. They stood there and looked at the feisty old man who had not performed any prayers in the last few years and lived alone in his deserted mosque. They didn't understand what he was saying, nor did they recognize any of the names he mentioned, and they went back to notify the sergeant, who told them to inform the party headquarters.

The two young policemen went to the headquarters, where they found a group of party officials talking about the death of Comrade Kamal and forming a search party to go hunt for his killer. The party officials had learned about the death early in the day, but they were afraid it was in retaliation for the executions of the two bandits the day before, and many men in dark green uniforms gathered in the main room where Kamal used to sit. A young comrade asked the two policemen where the body was.

"It's at the police station, Comrade," said one of the young policemen. The young comrade looked at two of the big-bellied party officials with thick moustaches sitting on the tan cloth couch and ordered them into action.

"Go to Sayed Habeeb, the clergy, and tell him that he must perform the death preparation for Comrade Kamal. Tell him it's my order, the order of Comrade Mazen, the son of Comrade Uraiby, and tell him that I am in charge of Balluria now, and I still have a file on him."

The two men had big bellies and thick moustaches, dark olive-green party uniforms, and two party-issued Tariq pistols on their waists. They went to see Sayed Habeeb, who had temporarily regained his sanity when he saw the two men, and was quick to deny what he said to the two young policemen about Comrade Kamal. Instead, he claimed that what he had said was that he wanted Comrade Kamal to be buried the way he was murdered because he was a martyr of the country, and martyrs were traditionally buried wearing the clothes they were killed in. The bloodstains should be left in, without any washing or final preparation so that the martyr could face Allah in the manner in which he died.

The party officials with thick moustaches and big bellies accepted his lies and ordered him to wash Kamal anyway because of the disfigurement that was inflicted on his body and face. Sayed Habeeb agreed reluctantly.

Kamal's murder caused a round of investigations by the party headquarters. They wanted to know who did it and why, although some of his comrades and subordinates were relieved when they learned of his death because Kamal had dirt on all of them. He knew many secrets about them that would end with them facing a firing squad. He knew who stole what and who killed who and who wrote a report about whom. He had secrets that could instigate a small war between the tribes if he wanted. He used all of that information to his advantage. He used it to manipulate his comrades and his subordinates and to advance himself through the ranks of the party. He never hesitated to end the life or career of his comrades with a report that he wrote to the party leadership whenever he felt threatened in his position or whenever he noticed competition by one of his comrades. He was the fastest to climb the ladder of the ranks as a junior comrade in the history of the party in the south.

He was only thirty-three years old, but he was two steps away from making the national command, which he never tried to achieve because he liked being in control of small towns and provinces in the south. He knew each and every corner and orchard and river bend, every secluded mud hut and every alley and narrow dirt road in each village. He had what he wanted; he was the boss of fearful and simple people. Simple and fearful people who only wished to be left alone and to be spared the grim fates of trenches of the eastern fronts. Besides that, Kamal was the unquestioned party official in these parts and never attempted to take a shot at the national command position, he knew that it had been known by the high-ranking party members that staying away from the close circle of the divine leader was a good way to stay alive longer.

He was asked once if he wanted to take the leadership of the entire party's southern secret intelligence organization, but he apologized, saying that he was the devoted son of the party, and he thought other comrades were more deserving than he. It was his way of pushing Comrade Muhsin Ajlan out the provincial position of authority that he enjoyed. Within two weeks of the invitation, he sat in the same chair that Muhsin Ajlan had occupied just six months before. Later, Comrade Muhsin Ajlan was executed for treason. Kamal stayed alive by remaining away from the divine leader's way and sight, he stayed alive longer because he was quicker than other comrades when it came to protecting his position and his power. He knew everything about all the other comrades, their secret wives and mistresses, their shady deals, and their scandalous intimate secrets of homosexuality and murder. He also knew about their roles in the executions of army deserters and members of the forbidden parties. Although he wanted to live in the capital city and be an important figure in the country, he knew he would be stomped on by the feet of his superior comrades, who loved the divine leader more than he did—men who had served the party longer than he had and had executed and tortured more people than he had.

Kamal never left Balluria. He never accepted a bribe; he never even bought a car, jewelry, or expensive clothes. He did not want to get married after Hanan and spent some of his nights with some of the local women, whose secret less-than-honorable profession was known to the top party members only. All of the women worked as secret informants for the party, and Comrade Kamal knew all of them and slept with all of them. He worked fourteen hours a day, and he drank every night. Drinking heavily was his only way to go to sleep and the only way to stop thinking about Hanan. Many nights he went to Barrya's house and talked to her for hours about things that no one else would hear him talk about, and when he finished talking, he issued his usual threat.

"If anyone heard what I have just told you, I will burn this house with you in it, you Gypsy whore!"

She believed him as she always did, but she listened to him as she always did. She knew that he was lonely, and she hoped for him to die so he would be with Hanan, because she knew that was the only way he would rest.

Kamal came to Barrya's one or two nights every week. The rest of the weeknights he spent at Atta's carpenter shop, where they drank areq with nothing but green narang lemons. Atta's shop was close to the main square in the town, where many years before Kamal executed four of his friends. Every night after Kamal walked from the party headquarters to Atta's shop, and after they drank a full bottle of the white moonshine, Kamal walked alone from shop, taking the main road that divided Balluria into the old and new section built in recent years. Then he would turn in the small street near the deserted mud and reed house, where Adnan's family used to live. The house was next to the eternal color-changing puddle with millions of mosquitoes. Then he would turn left by the Hillalys' house, where Salam and Haleem walked many years before, hoping to catch a glimpse of the Hillaly girls with their long hair in the window of the second floor. Then he would turn left and make his way on the graveled street that was supposed to have been paved twelve years before. It never was paved, and there he would decide if he would go to his secluded room full of Hanan's clothes and memories behind the guesthouse of Sheikh Jawad or walk another half mile toward the desert and spend the night at Barrya's house, talking to her. Most nights when he came to Barrya's house and asked her to go and knock on the door of a certain woman in town who was his bedmate sometimes, and sometimes he just sat in the doorway and talked to Barrya all night. Kamal told Barrya everything, even about his dark scary secrets, about his official party work. He never said anything to another soul, but he could not keep a secret from the old Gypsy woman. No one else knew anything about his personal life, but he was like an open book to Barrya because he knew that she would never reveal his secrets to another soul. He knew that she knew all the secrets of the town anyway. She was the only one left that he could trust.

He told her about the time he was selected to execute five army deserters for the first time in his life. He said that he could never forget their faces.

"They were young and scared, like I was."

He told her how he cried all night because he saw what his bullets did to the faces of the condemned army deserters. But in the morning he was ready to execute more people. He told her how when he served on the eastern war fronts he went for days without food and water and how he drank water from a puddle of rain water gathered in a hole filled with blood and decomposed bodies of dead soldiers from both sides. He told her how once he and another comrade of his had ripped apart an Iranian prisoner of war, tore him in two parts by tying him to two opposite moving vehicles, and he told her how they had captured Iranian prisoners in the marshes and how they buried them alive. He told her how in the dungeons of the secret police he tortured many people. He laughed as he told her how he tortured women by putting cigarettes in their vaginas, he told her that he enjoyed torturing women, but never talked about the day when they executed the four Wolves—Hisham, Haleem, Salah, and Ashraf—he never talked about that day. He mostly talked about Hanan and how much he loved her. He also talked about how he had hated Hamid since the day when Hamid struck him, the day he took Hanan's kittens to drown them in the river. He told her that he never wanted to kill Hanan; he wanted to kill Hamid only, but the sheikh wanted Hanan and Hamid dead. He told Barrya that he knew that she was the one who let Hanan and Hamid make love in her bed, and he would never forget it, and he would never forgive her. He told the Gypsy woman that he came to her hut every night to make sure that she was still there, and he would always come to her house and threaten to kill her. He said he would make sure that she would be tormented forever. He told her that he was waiting for Sheikh Jawad to die then he would kill her, but many nights, he let down his guard and sobbed like a child. On those nights, he talked about Hanan only.

He told Barrya that when he killed Hanan he wanted to kill himself, but his honor and the honor of Sheikh Jawad prevented him from doing so. But he wished that he had killed himself like Ahmed did, because he couldn't bear living without Hanan, and he always stated that there was no life without Hanan.

He told Barrya that since the day he killed Hanan, he looked at all the women and saw his mother in all of them. He saw that all women are bound to leave him, and they were all whores. All of the women were traitors, cheaters, and heartless. All of the women were whores who must be tortured and killed.

"Just like you," he would say to Barrya. Then he would cry and say, "I could have made Hanan very happy. We could have had a house and children, and all I wanted was a house, a woman who loved me, and children I could love, you know. But instead that whore Hanan chose that son of a whore, Hamid."

He then told her that he had enjoyed and never regretted killing Hanan because he knew that she would not be with any man after that, and he said that sometimes he could hardly wait to die so he could be with her, and that was enough for him, but he missed her terribly. He told her that many nights he went into Hanan's room and buried his head in her clothes, inhaling the smell of her body from the clothes she took with her when she ran way, and told her that he kissed the notebooks and the pencils and everything she touched. He told her he knew that she loved Hamid and that he could not accept that. He told the old woman that he wanted to kill Hamid first when he and Ahmed chased Hanan and Hamid in the golden wheat fields that stretched forever.

"That weak coward Ahmed could not kill his sister," Kamal said angrily. "I had no choice but to kill her. And after I stabbed her the first time, I don't know what happened to me. I just wanted to stab her more and more," Kamal said as he buried his head in his hands and cried.

During the last month of the long winter that seemed never to end, many times Kamal never went to his room behind the guesthouse of Sheikh Jawad, nor did he open the guesthouse. He did not even care when someone told him that there were new arrivals among the many women who wore black robes living in the house now. Women with no names and no clear relationship to the sheikh. He just said, "Tell them not to enter Hanan's room or I will kill them."

One night, a month before the three bandits were ambushed by the bridge, Kamal became insanely drunk at Atta's shop. He could hardly make his way in the darkness and the mud hut where Barrya was waiting for him. She cleaned the mud and vomit from his face and his dark olive-green uniform and put him to sleep on the thin mattress of sponge until the morning.

He was breathing heavily and announced in the middle of his scary rages of drunkenness, "I know Hamid is still alive. I can feel him. I know that he and I will meet one last time, and I know that he will come here to your house."

"What are you saying, Kamal? You are drunk. Just sleep. Hamid has been dead for years," the Gypsy woman said, fearing his wrath.

"Shut up, you filthy Gypsy whore witch. Just tell him what I will tell you. If you see Hamid, tell him that I am waiting for him," he said as he lay in the same spot where Hanan and Hamid made love years before when they escaped town.

2

Two nights later, as the townspeople started saying the name of Hamid and talked about how fearsome his Kalashnikov was after the public execution of the two bandits, Atta the carpenter poured the remainder of the clear areq moonshine in the glass and splashed some water over it turning it into a milky consistency, and put four evenly cut pieces of green narang lemon next to it and some salt on the side as he presented it to Kamal, who arrived at the shop early that night. Kamal never bought the liquor and never paid for it. He always expected Atta to have it ready, and Atta did just that because he knew that was the only way to keep Kamal off his back. Whenever there was a new army being formed or a battalion of militia being sent to an imaginary front, some people offered officials bribes, some ran away to another town, and one man was forced to let Kamal sleep with his wife so he wouldn't be sent to face death on the eastern front. For that reason, Atta the carpenter never complained about the cost of the alcohol and food that he prepared every night for Kamal, who was satisfied and scratched Atta's name from lists of draftees, and Atta always acted as though he was a true friend of Kamal's.

Sometimes he grilled some lamb meat and offered the dish to Kamal with compliments, though he spent almost his entire daily earnings on the liquor and the meat and salad, but he was spared from service with the People's Army and the Jerusalem Army and the Holy Vengeance Army or any other armies that the divine leader had dreamed of forming. Many armies and many imaginary missions became through the years Kamal's tool to send men he did not like, or the men whose wives he liked, to the wet, cold, and diseased training camps and faraway fronts for months at a time, where they faced death, captivity, and leprosy. But that night Atta was very nervous because he saw what Kamal did in the town's square to the two bodies of Rashid and Jassim, the two bandits who had been roaming these parts, killing any party member they could find. They were captured because some old man saw three men on horses crossing the bridge near Tawsheeha and informed the party headquarters. Kamal believed that Rashid and Jassim were two feared members of the group of bandits led by none other than Hamid himself. The two outlaws were captured by Kamal and a group of party militiamen that same day, and they were executed in the town's main square. Atta the carpenter was there that afternoon, and he saw how angry Kamal was and saw him emptying two magazines of his party-issued Mekaroov Russian pistol into the heads of the two outlaws and swore that he would kill more people. Atta knew that when Kamal was angry he could be very unpredictable with his pistol, just like the tyrant was with his ministers. Atta made sure to buy enough areq to last the entire night. He did not want Kamal to stop drinking that night, and he also bought two kilos of narang lemons and two kilos of tender lamb shoulder meat and started cutting the lamb as he felt the wind shake his shop. The dust blew harder. The windows of the shop slammed on the walls, as Atta lit the fire barrel inside the shop. He shut and locked all the windows and prepared for the long night. Although Kamal had treated him fairly, that night was an exception. It was about nine o'clock when a knock on the door shook Atta's senses and sent him into a scare. It was dark and windy outside. The cool wind had carried all the dust of the Sahara and topped the narrow streets of Balluria with a light layer of sand. When Atta opened the door, he saw Kamal with a look in his eyes that summed up all the tyranny in the universe and all the lust for revenge. The thirst for blood poured from his eyes as he announced, "Tonight, I want to drink areq and blood."

Feeling the ground spinning, Atta the carpenter waited for Kamal's next word.

Kamal entered the shop and sat on the chair that no one else was allowed to sit in, even when he was not there.

"Don't worry, Atta. It's not your blood I want to drink. It's the blood of a wolf," Kamal said. "But, first, bring me my glass and a narang lemon. I want to drink. I want to get drunk and be ready for what will happen tonight."

Atta did not understand what Kamal talking about. He only made sure to mention how good the areq was.

"I have sent Uday, the errand boy, to the big city, and I told him to bring the best areq for you. I told Uday that Comrade Kamal would be very upset if he did not bring the best areq. How is the narang lemon?"

Kamal looked at him with his cold, soulless eyes and said, "Did you see what happened in the town's square? Were you there?"

"No, I was here all the time," Atta frightfully replied, hoping that his lies would not be detected, and he hoped that the conversation would steer itself away from what happened that cold, late afternoon. He feared that he would inflame Kamal's anger with anything he said. Kamal was not ready to change the conversation. "I could just shoot everyone now, after all these years... he comes so close to me and he escapes. What the hell will I do with the dead bodies of Rashid and Jassim? I mean, the party leadership will be happy with it, but what about me? I wanted to see him bleeding. I wanted to kill him myself. I wanted to see him dead. I wanted to drag his corpse in the mud and dirt and then cut him to pieces, but what can I do to the twenty morons who don't know how to aim and shoot? Where is the salt? You son of a whore, where is the salt?" Kamal shouted.

Atta ran to the end of the shop and brought a metal can of salt. He gave it to Kamal and said, "Who are you talking about, Mr. Kamal?"

"That son of a whore, Hamid. You don't know him. He lived here long before you came to Balluria. Just pour me another glass," he groused as he pulled out his pistol, loaded it with bullets, and made sure that he had another magazine. "I know that he is here. I can smell him like a wolf. Like a wolf smelling another wolf."

"Who is he, Comrade Kamal?" Atta asked, trying to smile in a submissive effort to calm Kamal down. Kamal looked at him and did not answer as he looked at his pistol and started loading the bullets and wiping his weapon silently.

"Sit down," said Kamal as he drank his glass of milk-colored liquor. "Put the music of Salman Al-Mankoob in the cassette player. I want to hear something sad, something about lost love and death."

Atta put the tape in the cassette player. And the two sat drinking in silence while listening to Salman Al-Mankoob singing about his grief and sadness that he would live with forever because he had to kill his own brother because they both loved the same woman.

3

Although he wanted to sleep forever when he was at Barrya's mud hut, Hamid was no longer feeling pain from the bullet that had entered his right leg in the same spot as the bullet wound he received years before when Ahmed shot him in the endless golden wheat fields. The wound had stopped bleeding when Barrya had poured him a glass of areq and applied the Gypsy remedy. She opened a small jar of dried prairie herbs and added cooking oil to it. Then she mashed the herbs with her metal spatula and placed them on the wound. Hamid lay on the floor without letting go of his Kalashnikov that he kept pointed at the entrance of the mud hut. He was silent, angry, and sad after Barrya told him of the execution of his two loyal companions, Rashid and Jassim, who had been with him since the days he had escaped the draft and chosen the life of the constant fear of an army deserter who could be shot on sight, but he knew it would be the same if he joined the meaningless and endless march of young men to the war on the eastern fronts.

Rahsid and Jassim were army deserters too, and the three of them had been together in many daring escapes from certain death and many fearless raids on party militia and rural police outposts. He was angry because it was his idea to visit Balluria to see his sister, Amel. That decision had caused the three bandits to walk right into the ambush by the party militiamen. Something inside him had told him that it would be the last time that he would see his sister when he and his two loyal companions left the house. They walked to where they had left their horses and walked to the bridge that led to the marshes, not realizing that they were walking right into an ambush. When the shooting started, he fired his Kalashnikov in all directions and emptied three of his banana clip magazines before he felt the sting in his leg. He dove into the Euphrates and let go of his horse, which ran all the way to the other bank. He saw his two wounded, trusted companions surrender to the militiamen after being shot several times. He floated in the river like the many things he used to find on the river. He floated for almost a mile before he found his horse eating grass by the riverbank. Slowly and painfully, he mounted his horse and rode it away from Balluria. Then he waited until dark before he rode his horse around the palm orchard of Tawsheeha and near the train station by the seven palm trees, where he stayed until he could see no one walking toward the prairie. Then he made his way to the Gypsy woman's mud hut.

When Barrya saw him, she knew what had happened that day, and she was waiting for him to show up. She had prepared some food, fresh yogurt. He dismounted cautiously from his horse and walked into the mud hut, telling Barrya that he had been wounded.

"I know. I heard the shooting, and I knew it must have been you."

He crashed on the floor. She ran into the other room and brought him the refreshing yogurt. "They have killed your two companions."

"I know," he said with a weak voice.

"Kamal killed them, in the town square hours ago."

"I know. Did he torture them?"

"No. They dragged their bodies and shot them as they lay down on the ground. You are bleeding. You must drink areq, and I will stop the bleeding with the Gypsy medicine."

The Gypsy woman knew that since he had left Balluria and started roaming the desert and the prairies and the marshes, that pain was not his concern. Bleeding, hunger, and fear were not things that he ever felt, but that night she looked in his eyes and saw something different. She saw that her favorite Wolf of them all had reached the point where he could not let the promised meeting with Kamal wait any longer than that night.

Hamid had spent the last fifteen years of his life roaming these parts, and after he led groups of bandits in defiance against the most ruthless tyrant in the world and attacked many party headquarters, many army outposts in the marshes, and many remote police stations, the man who was known for his fearless raids and fearsome Kalashnikov had reached the end of the road he had started. It seemed as though, with the many battles he had been through and with the numerous wounds he had received through his life, he was waiting to heal the wound that hurt him the most—the longing to be with Hanan.

He had waited all of these years to meet Kamal. He had wanted to meet Kamal since the day when he struck Kamal and knocked him to the ground when he tried to drown Hanan's kittens. The two men had lived their lives waiting for that night. It was a secret pact baptized with blood, the blood of Hanan, the blood of Adnan, the blood of the four executed Wolves, and the blood of many bandits and party militiamen who died in the battles between the two of them. The two had waited so long because they knew that when they met, one of them would die and the one who died would meet Hanan first in the afterworld. Whether it was in hell or heaven, she would be there, but there was no reason for waiting anymore. Hamid had lost the last two of his bandits, and he had grown tired of the pointless fighting against the tyrant's troops and grew bored killing policemen and party militiamen.

Kamal was about to lose the only thing that mattered to him in his life—his authority over the people of Balluria and Tawsheeha and all the towns and villages near the marshes. It seemed as though that night the two men would fight for the only thing to fight for from the start: Hanan. They knew that all of their other fights were because of Hanan and all of the small victories and defeats were because of Hanan. They knew that their last fight would be for the true love they both wanted but never had.

When Barrya tried to stop the bleeding in Hamid's leg, she said, "Kamal was here last night."

"I know." Hamid replied.

"I know you knew. He said he would be waiting for you," the Gypsy woman said, realizing that it was time that the two friends who became enemies because of the love of a woman would meet.

"It's time for me and Kamal to meet for the last time," Hamid said as he stood, leaving his Kalashnikov on the floor

"Take your rifle," Barrya said.

"Not tonight, Mother Barrya. Tonight I only need the dagger," Hamid said as he limped, exiting the door of the mud hut where dusty wind blew making noises similar to long, quiet cries.

Hamid walked across the empty and deserted soccer field and remembered the days when he and the Wolves used to play and fight. Voices had been heard that night within the walls of Barrya's mud hut. The wind carried the voices of the past, the voice of Hisham screaming at the rest of the Wolves for not playing according to the plan he put before the game and the voice of all the other Wolves as they struggled to defend their goal from the merciless attack of the Wild Lions. Hamid stood there and listened to the wind as it brought back memories that no one was left to claim, memoires of faces and spirits that had long since fled. He stood there and wondered if fate had determined that he and his childhood friend Kamal should each seek the demise of the other that night. Could it have been different?

Hamid stood there as the dust brought back the faces of all those who departed and felt extremely lonely because he was certain that after that night he would be alone, just as all the other souls that had departed before it was time for all the Wolves to leave. All the girls had left already. Hanan had long gone, and her body had been cooled by the rainwater in her unknown grave. Basima was selling her soul and her beautiful body in the streets of Amman. The Hillaly girls had disappeared into the mist of events that made no sense to anyone, although many tales of how long, black, and beautiful their hair was were still floating around in these parts. But they were not there, and lovers had waited for them underneath their windows since all the beautiful girls had left Balluria. Raghda, tall and tanned, and Rasha and Shaima, with their wondrous beautiful brown eyes—all the beautiful girls had left Balluria.

Only his sister Amel was still there, and she would always be reading poetry and listening to Fairuz's songs and writing letters to people who had no addresses. Ahmed and Adnan went to the gates of heaven by the marshes, and Abdullah stayed frozen for years in the Turkish mountain on his way to the snowy hills of Denmark. Salam had gone to the country beyond the Atlantic Ocean and had never returned. Haleem, Ashraf, Salah, and Hisham met their deaths facing the firing squad on that beautiful April day.

He looked back at the mud hut and Barrya. As she stood in the door of her mud hut, he did not wave; she did not wave either. She just stood there, looking at him as he disappeared into the dust of Balluria as he walked to Balluria to meet Kamal for the last time.

When Barrya gave him the areq, he felt noxious from the cadmium-tasting liquor and the sandy herbs and wanted to throw up, but he knew that that night was not the night that he could feel sick. He wrapped his raggedy attire around his body and made sure to feed his horse. And as he walked in the dark, the pain in his arm and his thigh had disappeared. His senses were sharp and vigilant as he sat on a small hill made by the demolished mud house where Adnan's family once lived. He sat on the remains of house looking at the town. The dust covered the roads and the houses and made it difficult to see. The wind started to peel the flimsy house rooftops off the mud huts of the old section of Balluria, and tumbleweeds crawled in the streets of Balluria, chasing the spirits. Windows sang an endless slamming song in a synchronized symphony. The fateful preparation of death was as vivid as a shadow of a man wrapped on a dark robe clutching his dagger in his hand, waiting in the dark for the childhood friend and his arch nemesis for the final battle.

Hamid knew the night would not be over until death claimed one of them. It had been a long-awaited showdown. He felt that perhaps death would depart Balluria when one of them was dead. All the Wolves were dead, all of them except for he and Kamal, He knew that whoever died that night would be the one to see Hanan's face first, and the one who stayed alive would spend his lifetime in an endless agony of waiting. He touched his dagger, making sure of its length and sharpness. He imagined the sting and heat of the blade entering the soft heart of the woman he loved and held his tears back, and he spoke to himself.

"Tonight, fate will determine who will be the last Wolf."

Hamid had left Barrya's mud hut after telling her that if he returned alive, he would leave Balluria and go to the desert.

"What if you don't come back?" Barrya asked.

"If you can claim my body, bury me."

"Where should I bury you?" she asked.

"Next to Hanan, by the seven palm trees."

"Wolves like you don't die, Hamid. I will wait for you," she said without flinching.

It was about one o'clock in the morning when he saw a silhouette of man wobbling as he walked in the mud halls and tried to stay standing. The dust blew between the mud and brick walls of Balluria. The familiar voice reached Hamid's ear. He knew that Kamal was close. He stood up and walked to the middle of the road, wanting to give Kamal a fair last chance. He wanted to stand clear in the middle of the dusty road so Kamal could aim and shoot right. If he missed, then it would be his turn.

Kamal walked with his eyes on the ground, not able to lift his head up as he tried to avoid looking into the dust because together he and Atta had emptied an entire bottle of areq and had eaten nine narang lemons. He wanted to go home and bury his face in the smell of Hanan's clothes and sleep as he remembered the events of his entire day from the morning. The day was not right, he thought to himself. The comrades at the headquarters brought him some bad news about the possibility of being transferred to another province. Worse than that was that he was told that his replacement would be a young comrade, Mazen, the son of Comrade Uraiby, the same Comrade Mazen who was once his soccer nemesis and the son of his mentor who taught him how to kill. This was all because the party leadership in the province was growing impatient with his consistent failure in being able to eliminate the wrath of Hamid's three-man gang that had busted the myth of the iron fist of the tyrant and the fearsome reputation of the government. His own reputation as a party strong man was tarnished.

Then he was surprised to hear that the three-man gang, led by his lifelong enemy Hamid was in Balluria, and he was barely able to summon the twenty militiamen force, but he did not go with them. He was afraid, afraid of Hamid, and hoping the militiamen would capture Hamid alive or kill him. He had never been afraid of anyone or anything in his life except for two people: his adoptive father, Sheikh Jawad, and Hamid.

He had not been afraid when he served three tours on the front lines in the treacherous mountains of the north or the vicious middle plains or in the marshes of death, where bodies of soldiers from both sides floated for months. He was not afraid of fifty-pound bombs falling on his bunker for ten days. He had not been afraid when his name was on the list of those to be investigated by the party command, but whenever he knew that his time to meet Hamid was near, he felt the same childish fear he had felt when Hamid struck him when he was about to drown Hanan's kittens. That night and after he left Atta's carpenter shop, he caressed his pistol, slowly rubbing the holster, and he unbuttoned the strap, because he smelled a wolf.

He walked slowly. As he felt the breath of the wolf lurking around all the corners in Balluria, he did not see Hamid. The dust blew harder, and the howling of the desert's wolves became louder as he reached the road that led to the soccer field and then to the desert. Kamal stooped, looked into the dust, and saw the shadow of a man standing in the middle of the road. The dust was so thick that he was not sure who it was. Nevertheless, he pulled his weapon and walked slowly, taking three slow steps, and realized it was him. It was Hamid. Who else would be standing in the middle of the road that divided Balluria into the old section where the poor lived and the new section where the rich and party and government officials lived? Hamid was standing in this insanely dusty night. His hair flew in the wind, and his beard was glazed with dust as the wind blew in between his shoulders, making the rags on his head and his back fly. He was waiting.

"Hamid?" Kamal shouted in the silence of the night, staring at the ghost standing in front of him. "I have been waiting for this hour for a long time," Kamal said without moving.

"Me too," Hamid replied calmly.

"Well, my Wolf friend, you should have never stolen Hanan from me."

"It is too late for that now," Hamid replied in the same calm voice, as he pulled out the black dagger, the same dagger Irar bought from the mysterious man so long ago near the ruins of Ur, the same dagger Sheikh Jawad and Irar used to kill many of their unfortunate enemies. The same dagger that Kamal used to end Hanan's life with merciless blows to her heart and with which he severed her right palm, the same dagger that Ahmed gave to Barrya and asked her to give to Hamid.

"It's time for you to die, you son of a whore!" Kamal shouted.

"It's time for one of us to die." Hamid's composure did not waver.

Kamal aimed his pistol in the dark and fired all of the bullets in his magazine in one spray. The dust blew harder, and the sounds of the wolves filled the air with cries of love, fear, hope, and despair. He hadn't been able to load his second magazine by the time he received the first thrust to his heart as Hamid wove through the bullets, ran through the air, and leapt toward him like a mythological warrior. Hamid spiked his dagger into the fearful heart. Hamid felt the dagger going through Kamal's heart, and a gush of warm, darkened blood spurted violently from the open wound.

Kamal made an inarticulate grunt as he fell to the ground.

Hamid pulled his dagger from Kamal's heart and struck again and again and again—one for Amel and one for Hisham and one for Haleem and one for Ashraf and one for Salah and one for Ahmed and one for Adnan and one for Abdullah and Basima and many for Barrya and Balluria. But the most were for Hanan, for every moment she spent begging for her life as Kamal drove the same dagger into her soft heart and for every moment she was scared as he and she had been chased in the golden wheat field. One for the lost love and one for the lost life that could have been if it had not been for Kamal. Hamid sat on Kamal's body as it stopped moving and eased into the calm sleep of death. Hamid did not realize that he clawed Kamal's body and face with his nails and stabbed Kamal's body with the black dagger a hundred times He sat next to the dead body and waited there until he felt no movement or life heat from the body. He looked at his old childhood friend lying there lifeless and remembered the day he struck him when Kamal wanted to drown the sack of kittens in the river. He remembered how red Hanan's eyes were as she cried to save her kittens. And he realized that they both loved her, but in their own ways. He and Kamal. They both loved Hanan very much. Only then he felt that he had done

Kamal a favor by killing him because he realized that Kamal now could see Hanan in the afterlife.

He looked at his dead enemy and said, "Well, my friend. It looks like I will be the one spending a lifetime in waiting."

That night Hamid walked back to where his horse waited. Filled with all the loneliness in the world, he mounted his horse and disappeared into the dark dusty desert night.

The Book of Balluria

The Redemption of Balluria

1

Long before he faced the angels, Sayed Habeeb had not heard about what had happened to Sheikh Jawad. It seemed as though everyone in town had willingly decided to wipe the fearsome old man from their memories. It was during these days that Sheikh Jawad's hair had turned completely white and he spent most of his days sitting in the chair looking at the town's main street from his porch without speaking to anyone. His household consisted at that time of Kamal and many strange women who showed up during the many glorious mornings and stayed in the house. They did not talk much, and they all wore black robes and burkas that hid their identities and their eyes and, moreover, hid their thoughts. Sheikh Jawad was not interested in knowing anything about them and what family relation they have to him or to his dead wife, Sabrya, nor was Kamal, who never asked about the many women who showed up at the sheikh's house. Kamal was happy with finding a ready meal, a bed to sleep in, and a frequent bedmate in the younger ones of the many mysterious female houseguests. People in the town thought they were all the relatives of the sheikh's dead wife, Sabrya. All of them claimed they were widows who lost their husbands in the many wars of the tyrant's army. Sheikh Jawad did not speak to nor did he recognize the many women in his house. He had lost the ability to speak. He sat all day, looking at the same road that he had walked almost fifty years ago when he left the marshes, escaping capture by a small patrol of provincial rural police, and walked toward the big guesthouse of Sheikh Badr Al-Ghathban. Then he was young, strong, and able. Not like now. Now he could not even reply to the people who looked at him and saluted him and gave words that he could not hear. He simply kept staring at the road that led to the river; the river where his son Ahmed shot himself in the head one winter night.

He noticed new houses had been built and new people he did not recognize were walking the same road. Then one day he was not able to walk to the chair where he sat every day. He waited for Kamal to help him, but Kamal never came. He tried to shout but he made sounds that no one heard and no one answered. He tried to call his dead wife, Sabrya, forgetting that she had died so many years earlier. Yet in his delusional mind, Sheikh Jawad knew that his son, Ahmed, and his daughter, Hanan, would not come to help him, so he did not call them. Slowly, his senile mind realized that he was mute too, and for the first time in his life he felt weak, so he cried... alone in his closed guesthouse, empty of guests.

It was in those days that everyone in the town thought that Sheikh Jawad had died, when they stopped seeing the fearsome old man sitting in his wooden chair that he had made for himself, looking with his hawkish eyes at frightened pedestrians. It was in those days when the two men with big bellies and thick moustaches arrived from the big city and became in charge of the party headquarters. They were rarely seen in the market or the square; they were known only as the two men with big bellies and thick moustaches. It was during those days that Sayed Habeeb started wondering about his dreams of the angels.

2

It was a glorious late morning as always in Balluria when the two men with thick moustaches and big bellies went to see Sayed Habeeb to ask him if he could bury Comrade Kamal the proper Muslim way. When they realized that they never had a funeral for Sheikh Jawad, the two men did not think much about that matter, they blamed it on the memory of the town, as it was known that Balluria forgets its own people. That morning when Sayed Habeeb agreed to wash the body, he told the two men with big bellies and thick moustaches that they would need to open Sheikh Jawad's guesthouse so a three-day funeral could take place there. No one in the town was capable or willing to spend any money on Kamal's funeral, not even his comrades and subordinates in the party, so they buried the body quickly by the seven palm trees. They dug a half-meter grave and stashed the body in it just a few feet from where he and Ahmed had buried Hanan's body years earlier. Later that day, they went to Sheikh Jawad's house and tried to convince the mysterious black-garbed women living in the house to start the funeral. Their efforts were fruitless, as the women refused to talk to them. Nor did they have any knowledge about what to do or what had happened. Finally, Sayed Habeeb went to the sheikh's house and gently talked his way into them letting him open the old guesthouse that had been empty of its guests for years. As they entered the guesthouse, Sayed Habeeb and his two big-bellied companions started moving carpets and pillows and Arabia coffee jars, tools, and Dellas. The guesthouse was still dust free as though someone had kept it clean for all this time. To the surprise of Sayed Habeeb and the other two men, they found what looked like a skeleton of a white-bearded man lying down on his carpet half dead. He was thin and old. The two men did not want to get close to him, believing him a ghost, since everyone in the town told stories of ghosts in that house. They also considered that he was stashed there because of a contagious disease. Sayed Habeeb looked at the old man and examined his face carefully.

"Oh, my merciful Allah," he said to himself, as he recognized the hardened face behind the weedy white hair that camouflaged its features, "Sheikh Jawad. Is that you?" Sayed Habeeb said. The old man did not answer; he just looked at Sayad Habeeb, turned his eyes to the ceiling, and stared at the long palm tree trunks.

In the midst of all the dust, the town had forgotten about Sheikh Jawad when he stopped sitting in his wooden chair made from palm tree branches and slicing everyone with his piercing eyes the way he had once used his vicious dagger. They had noticed that he was not sitting in his usual spot, but they did not ask the reason. It was a silent approval of removing him from their sight and from their hearts. They did not know that Kamal had confined the old man to the guesthouse, which was long abandoned by guests from afar and all the people in the town who preferred not to see or to talk to the old man. He had lost his power, influence, and fortune. He had been under Kamal's mercy for the last five year of his life. Kamal did not want the people of Balluria to doubt his new authority, and whenever his comrades asked him about his uncle, as they still called Sheikh Jawad, he would tell them that he was sick with tuberculosis and that he didn't want to see anyone. Kamal moved the old man to the guest room and closed the main door, which opened to the street, and assigned one of the many women in dark dresses and black robes who lived in the house to serve the sheikh three meals a day, tea after each meal, and tea in the afternoon. He allowed Jawad to sit in a chair close to the closed main door of the guesthouse so he could hear people outside. The sheikh did not resist or complain about the arrangements, he only mumbled or gave signs if he needed to eat or use the bathroom. He spent most of his day lying down looking at the ceiling and the big palm tree trunks it was made of and looked like an equally divided farming field ready to plant the spring wheat. The rest of the day, the women who served him moved him near the door so he could listen to the voices outside. He never dared to open the door. He was afraid, afraid that the people of the town would see what he had become. He was afraid of Kamal, who one day found him in the courtyard and started yelling at him, and the many women who occupied the empty rooms in the house.

Kamal started screaming at the women, who did not say a word. He told them that the sheikh was not allowed to be moved around the house because of his health. In reality, Kamal was trying to coerce the sheikh to sign a paper that would allow Kamal to inherit all that the sheikh owned. He tried to convince him with sweet talk and threats, but the old man looked at him and could not say a word. Kamal consulted a friend of his who suggested that the only way to do that was to convince the sheikh that he was mad. Then they would forge some papers, but as long the sheikh could walk, Kamal was afraid that the sheikh could wander away or go to the police, so he forced the old man to stay in the house and told the women who wore black dresses all the time not to let him out. One day Kamal found him near the main door of the house and lost his temper. Kamal pushed the sheikh away from the door and onto the carpet-covered floor and told him if he ever saw him near the door, he would shoot him. Kamal then went to the women in all the rooms and beat them with a rubber hose he had inherited from Sheikh Jawad; the rubber hose was the same one Sheikh Jawad used to beat him.

Sheikh Jawad rarely cried, not even when he was told that his son Ahmed's body could not be found. The river seemed to have kept the body as an offering. He did not cry when his wife died, or when almost half of his herd had disappeared into the desert. He cried once when he looked at the formation of the Ba'athist soldiers and militiamen forming a line to execute four young men. He wept alone as he saw the boys that he knew falling down with the bullets shredding their bodies and faces. The second time he cried was when he looked at his daughter's body when Kamal and Ahmed brought the beautiful corpse of Hanan covered with blood. But when he was able to crawl near the door and could see the sunlight and hear the voices of the people, he wept silently. It was the last time he looked at the outside world.

Many nights Kamal woke up and reached for his pistol and walked through the house when he heard a noise, only to find Sheikh Jawad mumbling with unrecognizable sounds talking to the ghosts of his past. It was the only time when the sheikh could talk, he would talk to his mentor and his partner Irar. They would talk about the herd and the soldiers on the borders and about the prices of sheep and the difference in the price between Kuwait and Iraq. They talked about Balluria and Shershab. They would talk about Sheikh Badr Al-Ghathban and his son Reyhan. When Kamal tried to stop him from talking, Jawad looked at him with the same look that made men shiver in their sandals when they looked into his fiery red eyes, the same look that forced even the hardest of men to want to retract any statement they had made, so Kamal backed off and let Sheikh Jawad talk to his ghosts.

After this, however, Kamal took extra measures since he had seen that look. He moved his bed to one of the rooms, locked the door, and brought a Kalashnikov with him. He also brought one of the women who lived in the house and made her sleep outside the door. He was afraid of the old man and the look he knew so well. He never slept again. He feared that the sheikh would one night return to his former self and kill him. In his mind he saw the same look that Sheikh Jawad had given him when the sheikh had ordered him to drown the sack of kittens in the river.

One day one of the women saw the old man writing on a piece of paper as she was bringing him his lunch. She did not know where he had obtained the paper or the pen. She told Kamal about it. Kamal's face turned red, and he started screaming at the many women who lived in house wearing black robes.

"But he can't read or write!"

It was a secret Sheikh Jawad had kept during his life. It was the one thing Hanan taught her father. She taught him how to read and write. She taught him as the two of them spent much time together and while he smelled his daughter's skin and kissed her on her neck many times away from the eyes of the others. He asked her once if the shapes in her reading books were similar to words. It was then that she started teaching her father how to write his name as she sat next to him eating their favorite dish of fish stew.

"J. Yes, like that. WA. Not WE, but J, A, WA, D. She taught him slowly and with extreme patience. Sheikh Jawad enjoyed his lesson because of her. She was his only window to humanity. He never told anyone that he could read or write. He thought if others believed that he could not read or write, it would give him an advantage over many of his business partners who were illiterate. He thought he would have an edge, the longer side of the stick, something he could use against them, another weapon in his arsenal. Kamal did not believe the woman, but he did not take any chances. He thought it was just another trick the old man was using to deprive him of what he thought was rightfully his. He thought that if he really knew how to write then the old man might have written his will, and he wanted to know; he wanted to see if all of his years of submission to the tyranny and abuse of Sheikh Jawad would go unrewarded and to whom the crazy old man was giving all the riches that he had hid. He was sure that Sheikh Jawad was hiding much of his money in gold and other worthy items somewhere in the house. His only hope was to find that paper the woman in the black robes told him about. He tried many methods to gain this scrap of paper. He became nicer to the old man. He made sure to take lunch to him and made sure that tea time in the afternoon was a ritual he would not miss, even with his increased responsibility at the party headquarters. He would sit and talk to the old man, telling him about what was happening in the outside world and how the embargo was making people sell their souls to the devil in order to survive and how he and the party members were doing the impossible to make sure that order was kept in these parts. He told him about who died, who got married, and who was sent to jails that no one ever returns from. He became as close as a good and loving son could be.

He tried not to talk about the paper or the will although many times, such as when he helped the old man to the bathroom, he frantically searched the carpets, the pillows, coffee cups, and the coffee fireplace. He even searched the old man's deteriorating dishdasha dresses, but he could not find the paper. He finally asked the old man about it, but Sheikh Jawad did not say a word; he just stared at Kamal in the same way he looked at him when Kamal brought the dead body of Hanan years ago. Kamal begged the old man, stating that he needed the money so he could keep up with expenses of keeping the guesthouse open and feeding the many guests that bedded there in order to maintain the reputation and prestige of the sheikh. He had no luck; the sheikh just stared at him as though he was talking in a foreign language.

Furious, Kamal went to extreme measures to force the old man to tell him the location of the paper. He ordered the many women who wore black robes not to feed the old man for days. He sat by the old man with his pistol in his hand, waving it and telling the old man that he was really tired of his old games and refusal to reward him for years of serving with obedience and devotion as a real son. But all of his tactics turned fruitless, and one day he came home from work drunk and angry and ordered the many women who wore black robes to clean the guesthouse and turn everything upside down. He pushed the old man violently away from the carpet where he slept and searched for that piece of paper. He begged the old man to tell him where the paper was and if he wrote his will and what was in the will. He cried in front the old man, who stared at him with a lost look without saying a word. Finally Kamal gave up, but he made sure the old man would never leave the house again. Kamal ordered the many women who wore black dresses and long robes not to let anyone near the old man. That was a month before the dusty night when Kamal was killed.

3

Sayed Habeeb wasted no time in trying to salvage the old man's soul. He asked the two men with big bellies and thick moustaches to help him carry the old man outside where the sun shone. They agreed reluctantly while covering their noses and trying not to breathe. Death filled the old man's breath. Sayed Habeeb asked the many women with black dresses to prepare a bath and to get a wooden comb and wool threads. They started combing the old man's hair, removing from it lice and their many white eggs nesting in his completely white hair and beard. Later, he helped the old man into the dark room they used as a bathroom and took off his dishdasha. He sat him on the two cement bricks and started pouring warm water on the old man's body. It was true what they say about the old man, Sayed Habeeb, said to himself as he looked at the old man's skin. The scars of the wolf claws were still brown and vivid, there were many exit wounds and healed bullet holes. It was true what the people in the town said about Jawad being shot seventeen times and survived because he had a jinni protector from the ghost world, just like his mentor Irar had. The old man sat there as water dripped from the thick bush of his head and beard. Without saying a word, Sayed Habeeb dried him and asked the many women who wore black dresses to bring a clean dishdasha, kuffia, and iqal. He dressed the old man and moved him back to the guesthouse. Then he moved all the piles of carpet with the help of the two Ba'athists who were looking at Sheikh Jawad as if he was the relic they always thought he was. Sayeed Habeeb asked them to prepare the coffee and start to bring the coffee tools in order to let the people in the village know that the guesthouse of Sheikh Jawad was open for Kamal's funeral.

He opened the outside door to the guesthouse, which Kamal had locked with several locks and chains, and a breeze of fresh outside air moved life back into the guesthouse. Sayed Habeeb sat Sheikh Jawad in the middle of his guesthouse, in the same spot he used to sit during his glorious days as the absolute sheikh of Balluria, the same spot he sat in with no iqal when Hanan ran away with Hamid, the same spot where he and Irar plotted the killing of Shershab, the same spot where the people of the town told him that his son, Ahmed, had shot himself by the river and his body could not be found. He sat there with his head lifted up looking at the outside waiting for mourners who never came. Sayed Habeeb stood outside and waited for people to come to the funeral. He even stopped some of the pedestrians, told them about the funeral, and asked them to enter. Some refused, and some told him that they would come another time, and the two Ba'athists with big bellies and thick moustaches sat inside drinking coffee and smoking cigarettes as they talked about how dirty the carpet of the guesthouse was.

Later that evening, the two Ba'athists told Sayed Habeeb that they had to go back to the party headquarters, because the entire country was under a high alert since the start of the threats by the country they called the great Satan of the West. They promised to be back the next day. Sayed Habeeb asked the many women in the house who wore black dresses to prepare anything they had for dinner. One of the women told him that they had nothing to cook since the death of Kamal. No one had brought any money or groceries to the house, and they had been living on the last sack of flour and the vegetables from Hanan's garden, which miraculously never quit producing a large variety of vegetables. Some of the vegetables had not been seen or heard of ever before in Balluria or the surrounding towns. The women just liked to eat them. Sayed Habeeb asked them to bring him and the old man something to eat because he was planning to spend the night at the guesthouse waiting for mourners. He ate the bread and noticed that the vegetables had many colors: green, maroon, blue, reddish orange, and red. Red... the most distinctive color of them all was red. He felt like he could not stop tasting the vegetables. It seemed as though he had been hungry all his life, and now he had found what satisfied his starvation. He began eating the vegetables without bread. He felt ashamed and said to himself, "Decent people don't eat like this... they don't eat like this." He willingly shut down his desire to go to Hanan's garden and eat the vegetables raw without washing them or harvesting them, just like that, from the soil. He said to himself, "I beg forgiveness of the almighty Allah. I beg forgiveness of the almighty Allah."

He looked at the old man, who sat there without moving or touching his food. The old man was sitting the same way he had sat since Sayed Habeeb set him there. Sayed Habeeb was tired. He spoke to the old man and said with a caring voice, "Sheikh, tomorrow mourners for Kamal will come. You need to sleep." He put his own head on a pillow, covered himself with his robe, looked at the fire in the brick coffee oven, and tried very hard to resist the urges that opened in his skin like like a thousand holes filled with ants to go to Hanan's garden and eat all the vegetables. He calmed his urges by reciting verses from the Qur'an and reminding himself that he must get up early to do the dawn prayer and prepare for the many mourners. He woke up when the call for payers came from the lousy prayer caller in the next town, whose voice grated and whose grammar was close to an unforgivable sin. He called the names of

Allah and recited the Qu'ran: "*... and if the night diminishes as the morning breathes... a soul will know what it has committed...*"

He got up half asleep and washed for prayer, performed his two rikaa morning prayers, and sat on the carpet. It was then that he looked toward the old man, and he was surprised to see him sitting in the same spot as the night before with the same look on his face, but with one hand closed on something. He looked to the end of the guesthouse and called out to the sheikh.

"Sheikh, you should go to sleep at least for two hours. Many mourners will be here. Sheikh... Sheikh... Sheikh Jawad..."

He shook the old man gently. The old man did not move. He was dead.

The two Ba'athists kept their promise and arrived when the sun had risen to almost midsky toward the high noon hour. They found Sayed Habeeb sitting with his head resting on his hand looking for all meanings, intents, and purposes of life as though he had lost his best friend. For Sayed Habeeb, the death of Sheikh Jawad was an end to many things he knew. Most of them were bad; nevertheless, would be the man he promised himself would be, a pure man with no earthly ill feelings and grudges. He wanted to meet Allah with the clearest conscience and a clean rap sheet. So he readied himself to prepare the dead sheikh for eternity, breaking his own oath of not preparing any more dead people for their final journey.

At Sayed Habeeb's direction, the two Ba'athists prepared the white cloth and started to shred it to many pieces to wrap it around the dead body. Then the two men carried the body in a blanket and took it to the bathroom, where they stripped the dead man of his clothes. Then one of them noticed that the old sheikh's fingers held tight to something and he told Sayed Habeeb. They looked closer and saw that the he held a small slip of paper in his clenched fist. It took all three of them to get him to release his grip on the paper. It was small white paper with faded words that appeared to be written with a badly sharpened pencil. There was only one line written on it and it gave the impression that the person who wrote it was either a young school child or an illiterate adult. The faded lines on the one side only spelled one word, "J.A.W.A.D." It was the same paper Hanan used years before to teach her father how to write his name, and it was same letters Sheikh Jawad kept wrapped in a small piece of cloth next to his heart. It was the piece of paper he wrote his name on for the first time his life. Sayed Habeeb did not understand why the dead sheikh had that paper in his hand until he turned it and looked on the back of the paper, where one line was written: "Bury me next to my daughter, Hanan, by the seven palm trees."

It was the only sentence the sheikh had ever written in his life. And it was the piece of paper that Kamal had spent the last three months of his life looking for, thinking it was the sheikh's will.

Sayed Habeeb did not know what to do with the burial arrangement, he knew that none of the people in the town would be willing to pay money or contribute anything to Sheikh Jawad's funeral. The women who wore black robes had started to put their clothes and belongings in small cloth bags, and they were not in a generous mood to help the sheikh with the funeral. He knew that none of them had any idea of what to do with the body or who would pay for the funeral expenses, and he was afraid to let any mourners in because he was worried that they may discover the garden that Hanan planted long ago.

So, he decided to bury the body by the seven palm trees as the sheikh's last stated wish. He decided that was the best and the least costly solution, one that would be accepted by Muslims. Any other plan required money, money that no one in the town possessed or was willing to spend. The two men with big bellies and thick moustaches agreed to the plan and agreed to help. They stood there and admirably watched Sayad Habeeb pour water from the metal jar on the body and use the tree leaves for barriers to wash it as he recited, "*In the name of Allah... and there is no God but Allah... you are dead and all will be dead and everyone and everything will die, but the everlasting is for almighty Allah only; the creator of heaven and hell. From the dust we have been created, yea, and to the dust you will return, and from it, yea, will be resurrected again... Oh, you content soul, return to your creator...*"

The two men watched him silently as he wrapped the body carefully with the white shroud and put the kafur liquid in the ears and nose and closed the eyes gently. Then the three moved the body to the guesthouse and waited for mourners to come. Later that afternoon, the entire town knew that Sheikh Jawad had died, but none went to the mourning time at the guesthouse. Years earlier, when Sheikh Jawad learned that Sheikh Imarn Al-Haj Talib had died, he went to his funeral. It was a carnival of old rifles carried on the shoulders of the rough-looking men, and the robes of sheikhs were unrecognizable to the young man's senses. He had been impressed and jealous and wanted his own funeral to be the same way or better, but no one had come to the guesthouse. The two Ba'athists sat by the door of the guesthouse drinking coffee and smoking cigarettes. By sundown they realized that none of people of Balluria would come to the funeral. Sayad Habeeb announced that they would bury the body in the morning because Islamic teaching states the best way to treat the dead is by burying them quickly. The three slept in the guesthouse after talking about how serious the threats of invasion made by the Americans would be.

In the morning the three men woke up and drank several cups of bitter Arabian coffee. One man went to fetch someone with a car to take the body to the seven palm trees. The rain started to shower the dirt roads, palm tree trunks, the green leaves of the qasab tree in the banks of the river, and the wooden-built roofs, with their metal drains and gutters playing the sad music of a winter coming too soon to the town. The early-October-late-September warm showers prepared the town for the departure of the ruthless patriarch. The man with the big belly and thick moustache returned to the guesthouse breathing heavily and telling Sayad Habeeb that no one was willing to take the body there because of the rain. They were afraid their cars might sink in the merciless mud. Besides that, no one wanted to take the body of the man who instilled fear and resentment in every heart for miles around for so many years.

Sayed Habeeb then went to the square and begged for help, saying, "We cannot leave the sheikh like this. He will rot and this is not a good reputation for our town." No one was willing to listen to that argument; instead, they told Sayad Habeeb to dump the body in the river. He refused to do so and kept asking for someone to help him take the body to the outskirts of the town. One man, a stranger to the town who had a horse and carriage, offered his services. He did not ask much in return, but he wanted to help bury the body before discussing his fee. The two men went back to the house where the two Ba'athists were still drinking coffee and smoking cigarettes. The four men loaded the body on the carriage and walked behind it as they tried to make the last ride of the patriarch as dignified as it could be. The carriage wheels sank several times in the mud, and the horse almost broke his back when the carriage and the body fell into what looked like a shallow puddle of water and turned out to be half a meter deep. The white shroud had turned to a muddy beige. Brown spots of mud dripped with dirty water.

Sayed Habeeb carried a little mud in his beard as they reached the destination. They dug a meter-deep hole that filled up with rain water twice before they were able to place the body in it. The three bedraggled strangers stood up as Sayed Habeeb recited the death verses from the Qur'an. Rain dripped from their faces, and the thick moustaches of the two big-bellied men were wet with sweat and water.

Sayed Habeeb said, "From dirt we have created thee, and to the dirt you will return, and we will resurrect you one more time for judgment." After they filled the grave with mud, they sat for an hour resting before walking back. Sayed Habeeb walked closer to the horse and carriage owner saying, "You know, it's a sin to steal from the dead."

The man looked at him, realizing that when he slipped the ring off of Sheikh Jawad's left ring finger, he had not been as surreptitious as he had thought. Rather than deny it, he replied with the calm of someone justified in his actions, "It belongs to me. I am the only son of Shershab the shepherd, the one that this dead man killed thirty years ago. That ring was my father's."

With his calm and thoughtful voice, Sayed Habeeb said, "Then accept that ring as payment for your service."

"I don't want anything else," he replied and parted from the group to find drier ground for his horse to walk on as he left Balluria.

Sayed Habeeb asked the two men with big bellies and thick moustaches if they wanted to go back with him to the sheikh's house to close the guesthouse and collect whatever they thought belonged to the government. One man said that Kamal's weapons and his clothes and papers had to be sent to the headquarters, as they were awaiting developments about the imminent threats of invasion. Suddenly, one of them asked, "Are you Sayed Habeeb Al-Mosawi, the same one that Comrade Kamal used to write reports about, saying that you are not Ba'athist and that you don't like Ba'athists?"

Sayed Habeeb had learned not to argue with the Ba'athists. So he said, with complete submission to what would come, "Yes, the same one. Should I come with you to the headquarters?"

The two men looked at each other for a moment, and then the one with bigger belly said, "There is no need for that. Soon, things will be a lot different. The Americans will be coming soon and things will not be the same, you know. Go in God's peace." They shook his hand.

"Go in God's peace as well," he replied as they made their way to the gray and yellow party headquarters building, and he made his way back to the big guest room in the sheikh's house. He knocked on the door to alert the many women who lived in the house and wore black robes of his presence, but there was no answer. The main door was wide open. He walked into the courtyard and saw that all the doors in the house were open, and once he was in the house, he went from room to room, shouting and searching. Everything was empty.

He had the urge to go to the garden and feast on the raw vegetables, but he was scared that his soul would be unleashed. He shouted for the women, but none of them were there. He wanted to see the garden for the last time and in his mind he planned to dig up all the vegetables and burn them so would never be tempted to come back and eat from them again. He didn't want anyone to know about the garden either. He remembered that Barrya had once told him that she had some seeds she inherited from her grandmother, the best Gypsy dancer ever to roam the Arabian Sahara. The one whom kings and sheikhs had slobbered over the whiteness of her thighs and the brightness of her pearl-like teeth. She told him that the seeds were for vegetables and flowers that would bring all the urges of life into the veins of anyone who tasted them, but he did not know how the seeds ended up in Sheikh Jawad's house.

He walked behind the guesthouse and in front of the grape vines and the deserted room where Kamal climbed one night to watch Hanan from the small hole in the ceiling as she bathed. To his surprise he found the garden looking as though it had been ravaged by a stampede of starved women. It looked like the many women who lived in the house and wore black robes had waited all these years for Kamal to be killed and for the old man to die so they could eat the fruit of their wasted youth. It seemed as though they had all disappeared in the mist of the warm rain with their clothes and their mere belongings. It seemed that all the women who wore black robes and hid their identities and desires behind their black burqas were waiting for the sheikh and Kamal to die so they would be set free, Sayed Habeeb thought as he walked back to his old mosque, with its warm, familiar, and innocent look. He prepared himself for yet another funeral. He thought about the infinite waiting these women had to endure.

Then within moments they became butterflies who had just grown beautiful wings.

"It must be the vegetables," he mumbled as he tried not to slip into the many holes filled with millions of happy bubbles swimming joyfully in the muddy water on the main road of Balluria.

The Book of Balluria

The Defeated Soul of the Graceful Clergyman

1

His face was full of faith and his hands looked like white doves. He loved doing good deeds and was kind to everyone. This is what everyone who ever mentioned the name of Sayed Habeeb, or anyone who talked about him, said. Even Sheikh Jawad, who never liked or got along with the short and graceful clergyman, never said ill things about him; the sheikh just called him the short man who faked faith. The entire town talked about Sayed Habeeb with respect and endearment, from the time he had arrived in Balluria, he was naturally graceful. He was a short, stocky, yet handsome-looking clergyman. His beard was well groomed all the time. He was always clean, his white dishdasha robe was always buttoned all the way to the top. He always smelled of the Gulf AUD oil, which had a rare aroma; he used it because it had all-natural ingredients. He never used any foreign or domestic colognes, because they contained alcohol.

Sayed Habeeb was simple in his ambitions, hard with his opinions, and strong in his faith. He did not eat a lot even when he was invited to the many feasts that Sheikh Jawad's generously catered every Thursday or in the many sad commemoratives of the tragic deaths of the prophet's holy family, All the people from Balluria and all the villagers from the surrounding villages had come to him for advice and confessions, and they came to him seeking cures for diseases and snake bites. He tried to steer them toward what he knew was right: patience and prayer. He did not know how to heal sickness, pain, or broken hearts, but he was never stingy with his prayers on broken legs, difficult pregnancies, or any problem brought before him. He even tried to heal one young man, Haleem, from his love for a girl who never responded to the thousands of love letters that he wrote her. He smiled at the young man's request, but he enjoyed the company of the group of young kids who were with Haleem. Sayed Habeeb asked them if they wanted to know about the love poetry that would make a girl's heart melt, and they all showed enthusiastic interest in learning about the poems. Sayed Habeeb became an older friend and a father figure to them, especially when they agreed to start attending the prayers and helping with the mosque's chores, such as cleaning and preparing the food. Sayed Habeeb was particularly interested in two of the boys: Hamid, who never complained about doing the mosque's chores, and Adnan, who showed a keen interest and curiosity in learning the religious philosophies and was the most talkative kid among the group of youngsters whenever the discussion was about God.

When Adnan commented, "The scientists have proven that there is no God," Sayed Habeeb did not get angry nor he did not ask Adnan to leave the mosque; he simply said, "One day you will find God. You will find him yourself. You don't need me to convince you."

Before the group of kids left the mosque, Hamid whispered in Sayed Habeeb's ear that Adnan's older brother was a communist and that he was killed for it.

The clergyman replied, "That's sad; just make sure to bring him with you whenever you come to the mosque."

Sayed Habeeb talked about God all the time. He talked about the prophet and the twelve holy imams who succeeded him. He talked about the need to live life by following the examples of the holy family. When he arrived in Balluria, the mosque that was built by Sheikh Badr Al-Ghathban was falling apart, and the new sponsor, Sheikh Jawad, was more interested in claiming lands on the other side of the river and was not willing to spend any more money on renovating the mosque. Sayed Habeeb wrote many letters to his grand ayatollah, his superior, asking him for help. When the letters went unanswered, he traveled to the main holy city to lobby for funds for his mosque, but he came back two weeks later empty-handed. He was told that the government had suspended all the funding for the mosques, because of its trouble with the outspoken Ayatollah, who was now in jail.

Sayed Habeeb came back with a strange will to renovate the mosque and to care for his flock of sinful worshipers, so he sat in front of the mosque and wrote a big banner that said, "Lend God Money and He Will Reward You with a Palace in Heaven."

He did not receive one dinar on his first day of righteous begging. The people passed him by, saluting him and pretending they did not see the banner. When Sheikh Jawad heard that Sheikh Waitan—his old rival who witnessed his humiliation during the wedding of his son, Ra'ad, years ago—was planning to donate a large amount of money to renovate the mosque as a last good deed before he died, Sheikh Jawad sent one of his men to Sheikh Waitan, telling him that Balluria did not need his money. He then walked to the mosque with his men and gave Sayed Habeeb enough money to renovate the mosque.

Extremely happy, Sayed started renovating the mosque the next morning. Soon people arrived to help until the renovations were complete Sheikh Jawad also sent many volunteers to help. Sayed Habeeb was in his late forties, yet he had the energy of a twenty-year-old-man. He wanted to steer his flock, who he thought were filled with misguided truths from their old beliefs and ignorant traditional ways of worshipping. He called the people to prayer himself; he did not rely on Khalaf, who normally did the call to prayers, because Khalaf was never on time, especially for the Morning Prayer. He delivered sermons every Friday and established a Thursday night remembrance to tell his flock the many sad stories of the tragedies that beset the holy family, the martyrdom of Imam Hussain, the principles of Imam Ali, and the many tragic deaths of the descendants of the prophet. He was at his prime when Muharram, the ten days of mourning that commemorate the martyrdom of Imam Hussian, the grandson of Prophet Muhammad, was in full swing. He planned the events and activities very well and made sure to invite everyone. People were very impressed with the black outlining of the inside the mosque and the many red, green, and black flags. People in Balluria and even people from Tawsheeha and the other villages attended the events of Muharram every night and Sayed Habeeb was ecstatic. He even asked the men to bring their wives and daughters to the mosque. He started the initiative of inviting women into the mosque and divided the mosque with a large curtain of cloth, so he could listen to their stories and their concerns, but none of the men allowed their women to attend. One woman did show up one day. She sat by herself and waited. Her face was covered with a black scarf and when Sayed Habeeb said, "Al Salam Alaykum, sister," she replied, "You don't want me to be your sister," with her deep scratchy voice that chased the shadows on the walls.

Her answer surprised him; he remained silent for a moment and then asked, "The Gypsy?"

"Yes, the sinful Gypsy," she answered.

"We are all sinful, and God is forgiving," he told her with a comforting and assuring voice.

She started to cry.

"What makes you cry?"

"My heart is full with the secrets of this town, secrets that are heavy to keep, and my body is rotten with sin."

"The secrets you must keep and never reveal, because it's not a sin to keep a secret, it is better than hurting another by revealing it. As for the sins, you can ask Allah for forgiveness."

Barrya, who believed him, wanted more tangible assurance. "Can you forgive me?"

"You don't need my forgiveness. God will forgive you, and I have no ill thoughts about you. You are who you are. We will all face the same God, and He is full of mercy."

Since then Sayed Habeeb and Barrya became close friends; he was the only one who accepted her and treated her with decency, besides the group of young boys and girls who treated her like a mother. He was the only adult who never said ill things about her and her reputation. She brought him yogurt, and he taught her how to say prayers. She taught him the tricks of Gypsy fortune telling, and he told her how to ask for forgiveness after committing adultery and how to cleanse herself immediately after. The town did not understand the relationship between the clergyman and the Gypsy woman. They speculated that the mere physical loneliness of the two humans had brought them together, but everyone grew weary of what Sheikh Jawad might think of the relationship between the two. Many expected that things could turn unpleasant because in the end the Gypsy woman belonged to Sheikh Jawad.

Rumors were spread throughout the town by the dedicated women gossipers who volunteered their help in making up stories and added details, fewer facts, and more lies and made the rumors sound unbelievably believable. They said that the clergyman was the secret lover of the Gypsy woman because she put the Gypsy curse of love on him. Sayed Habeeb and Barrya laughed when they heard the story as they sat under the shadow of the palm trees in the hot afternoons behind the mosque. They talked about the townspeople and about how they had shared the same love and emotions toward the same group of youths. They also shared the same special interests, hopes, and dedication to protecting and helping the group of young boys and girls. The two talked as if they were a man and his wife who had been married for a long time. They talked about the kids like good parents did.

That prompted Barrya to say one day, "If fate was just, we could have been married, and the kids would have been ours."

He smiled to himself. He knew that he could never marry her, not because he did not desire to, but because he knew one thing that no one else knew; he had been impotent for the past ten years. His impotence was one of many things he inherited from the harsh torture in the dungeons of the secret police when he was jailed for suspicion of being a member of a forbidden rival political party, something that he never told anyone about. Extremely harsh sessions of torture almost cost him the ability to walk but he lost his ability to perform his manhood duties. It was simply by luck that he was spared the imminent fate of facing the firing squad or being dissolved in the acid tank.

In the beginning, and after he was released from the dark dungeons of the secret police, he was devastated and almost lost his faith in God. But one night he lay in a dirty hotel room in the capital, after a night of drinking and a failed attempt at adultery, he had a dream. In his dream, he was lying in the same dirty hotel room, when two magnificent-looking men woke him up and shook him. One of them asked, "When will it end with you? When will it end with you?" Sayed Habeeb did not understand what the magnificent-looking man in his dream was saying; nevertheless, he heard their voices very clearly.

The second magnificent-looking man in his dream asked, "Do you want to see hell?" He pulled a white shroud over Sayed Habeeb's face, and suddenly his eyes were open to an endless swamp. Dark and steamy swamp voices were rising from the water, voices of pain and pleading. In his dream, Sayed Habeeb could not breathe from the stench of blood and dead bodies. He begged for mercy and suddenly the shroud was lifted off his face and he saw the magnificent two men standing near his head again. He was relieved as he started to breathe.

Then the first man asked, "Would like to see heaven?" And another white shroud was pulled over Sayed Habeeb's face, and he breathed in air that he'd never inhaled before and saw endless fields of green and gold. But what intrigued him the most was the light, the peaceful bright sunlight that made him feel at ease and at home. When he woke up, he found himself in the dingy hotel room, sleeping in filth.

Although he was penniless, he traveled that same day to the holy city and started attending the religious circle of a well-known ayatollah, who was known for his outspoken personality and his many brushes with the dictator's government. After seven years of studying religion and as the secret police was tightening their grip on the spoken ayatollah and his students, Sayed Habeeb confessed his fears to the ayatollah and said, "If they take me back to the dungeons I will lose my faith in Allah."

The ayatollah asked Sayed Habeeb to choose a city or a small town where he could save the people from their misguided approach to religion and preach the word of God and the immaculate examples of the righteousness and bravery of the holy family.

Sayed Habeeb had already found that town and he told his teacher, the outspoken ayatollah, about it.

"There is town called Balluria."

"Balluria? Is that a real name for a real town?" asked the outspoken ayatollah.

"I am not sure," he replied.

Sayed Habeeb did not choose Balluria; nor did he know if it existed. He saw the name on an old book that told of a town by the ruins of Ur where mornings are glorious and the palm trees have a splendid green color. He thought it was the same color he saw in his dreams when the two magnificent-looking men showed him heaven and hell. He traveled south, along the Euphrates, looking for the town that God chose for him but none of the people he asked knew about a town that had a splendid palm trees with heavenly glowing green color, and when he said the name Balluria, they replied, "Is that a real name for a real town?"

When he was about to return to the holy city from the capital of the province and sleeping in cheap hotel filled with migrant Egyptian workers, when he was visited in his dream again by the same two magnificent-looking men, who showed him heaven and hell. The two men woke him up and one of them said, "To the south of here you will go to the town of many sinners. You will meet the last Gypsy dancer and, when the time comes, the dusty wind will destroy the house of God. We will meet you again to take you home."

He woke up scared and mumbled, "I seek refuge in the grace of Allah from the devil and his work." The next day he asked the people he knew in the big city if they knew or had heard of a Gypsy woman who was the last Gypsy dancer. He faced many accusing looks of the people who stared at this clergyman who was asking about a Gypsy dancer. Finally, he met an old police sergeant, who looked like a relic from ancient times. The police sergeant, who said that his name was Jelwi, told him that in his town lived a Gypsy woman who claimed to be the last Gypsy dancer in this world. He also told him that she claimed to know all the secrets of the world.

When Sayed Habeeb asked, "What is the name of your town?"

"Balluria," the old Sergeant Jelwi answered.

Sayed Habeeb realized this was a sign, and that same afternoon he rode in the bus and arrived in Balluria before sundown. He asked about the mosque and spent the night there alone, looking at the town, which looked plain and sinful.

"Balluria, I will stay here and cleanse you of your sins. Allah has chosen this town for me, and I will stay here until I die," he said to himself, as he crawled to the dark cold corner of the deteriorating mosque that worshipers had deserted. And he stayed there knowing that it would be the last place for him on this earth; he would not leave alive. He knew that he would die in Balluria. He was at peace, feeling that he was home at last.

2

As a man of faith, Sayed Habeeb was one of the best students of the group of clergymen who graduated from the class led by the outspoken ayatollah. But he was one of the lucky ones. He was lucky that he left the holy city a few days before the secret police arrested and jailed the outspoken ayatollah and all of his devoted religious students, his disciples. He'd heard that some of his classmates endured severe torture and some had been executed. They were executed by hanging or by being thrown into a tank full of nitric acid, which dissolved their bodies. When he heard of his classmates, Sayed Habeeb stopped talking or mentioning any reference to politics and any reference to tyranny. Instead, he talked more about the relationship between a human and his God, the logic of having religion as a doctrine to live by, the boundaries of right and wrong, and the righteous paths of living.

He also paid attention to his flock that he started to love. He used his strong faith, patience, and prayers to fight the massive despair and disappointment on a personal level, as he realized that he would never be a complete man again. He also saw the hope of establishing a religious utopia disappear with the news from the capital telling of the death of the outspoken ayatollah, his mentor, teacher, and beloved leader. He felt a great sense of weakness and personal defeat when he learned that the ayatollah was shot in the head by the tyrant himself.

Ultimately, he heard the grim news of the death trenches in the east, and he saw the many young men who went there and came back in wooden boxes wrapped in the national flag. He resorted to complete submission to his new life and gave up the desire to revolt or to try to change the world around him. He read, taught prayers, and befriended the Gypsy woman, whom he believed was divine and pure. Whenever he thought about the logic behind the events in his life, he always answered his own questions by reciting his favorite verse from the Qur'an, "*And that is the wise divine planning of the Almighty.*"

Although they loved the group of young boys and girls equally, like all good parents, Barrya and Sayed Habeeb paid special attention to five of them in particular. The first one was Adnan, because of his exceptional intelligence, troubled mind, and constant questioning of religion and existence. The second one was Hanan, because Barrya told Sayed Habeeb that behind her pale and mysterious appearance, Hanan hid the energy and characteristics of the ancient Arabian women that could turn Balluria into a sinful Atlantis. Then there was Hamid, who was unofficially adopted by both Sayed Habeeb and Barrya, because they had sensed his animal side oozing from every pore in his tanned, thin build. They cared for Amel, Hamid's sister, because of the unmistakable solitude in her eyes and the obvious future bound up with loneliness. And the last one was Kamal, because Sayed Habeeb and Barrya both saw the evil shades of color in his piercing eyes. Barrya had seen his evil in her coffee cup, and Sayed Habeeb saw it in a vision as he performed his evening prayers. Although they never shared what they had seen about Kamal, they agreed to keep watching over these five kids. Sayed Habeeb went out of his way to save their souls.

Barrya knew that Sayed Habeeb had no interest in her body and that he was only interested in her soul. He was never stingy with his speeches of redemption and repentance. She taught him how to read one's future in coffee cups, and he taught her the tales of the life of the prophet. She taught him the secret of the Gypsy love dance, and he tried to teach her how to pray. She taught him the secrets of a woman's body, but on that he quit, because he feared his faith would be defeated by this magnificent sinner with the laugh that attracted butterflies. He loved her coffee and the tales of her ancestors, the old Gypsy witches, and their long love stories about sheikhs, knights, and jinnies. She, on the other hand, liked the grilled fish lunches that Sayed Habeeb and Hamid cooked once or twice a week on an open fire behind the mosque that they would serve to anyone who showed up after the Friday prayers. Barrya always brought her fresh, cold yogurt; no one ever knew just where she got it from. Sometimes Hamid, Amel, and his mother would show up, and the five of them would have a family lunch away from the watchful eyes of Sheikh Jawad and his informant Kamal, who reported everything that Sayed Habeeb did or said. Kamal also told Sheikh Jawad of everything that Barrya did and all the places she frequented.

For a while, the relationship between the clergyman and the Gypsy woman was the talk of the town. People thought that that was the reason Sheikh Jawad never liked Sayed Habeeb, but they were mistaken. The hate between the two men started when Sayed Habeeb first arrived in Balluria and after the fearsome sheikh donated his gift of money to renovate the mosque. The sheikh always felt that he owned the clergyman as he owned everything and everyone else. He thought that Sayed should religiously validate his actions and deeds, but this was contrary to what the clergyman believed his mission to be. The short and feisty clergyman believed that he was sent to be the spiritual mentor of the hardened marshland people who never understood their relationship with God and who used religion for two things: to marry as many women as they could afford and to carry the black, red, and green banners during the Muharram ten day-festival of mourning. Sometimes, they used their religion to stop major tribal bloodshed, like the one between the Sharifys and Nasser the Blond's tribe. That was when a well-known Sayed walked into the middle of a huge battle in the marshland carrying the flag of the martyred Imam Al-Abbas and stood up between the two fighting tribes as they were shooting at each other. Although not one single bullet hit him, when they saw him standing there risking being shred by the ocean of bullets, the feud stopped after thirty men had perished. After that event, the people asked all the clergy who attempted or dared to redeem them to perform similar miraculous acts whenever there was a feud, no matter how small or large. Luckily, Sayed Habeeb never had to face such challenges in Balluria. However, he knew that Sheikh Jawad did not like him, because they were like two lions in one den. When Sayed Habeeb showed up at Sheikh Jawad's guesthouse with a cloth bag full of books and clothes that cold winter evening, he was very happy about the generosity of the sheikh. He stayed in his guesthouse until the renovation of the mosque was completed, but then he learned that the sheikh wanted to use him to pressure the Tamimi widow, who lost her husband on the eastern front, to sell her priceless orchard to the sheikh.

"Why do you need my help, Sheikh?" Sayed Habeeb asked.

"I need your help, because the widow will not sell her land to me," the sheikh answered.

"If she does not want to sell, then there is nothing I can do," Sayed Habeeb replied with faithful confidence.

"Yes, there is, there is one thing you can do," the sheikh said, looking in Sayed Habeeb's eyes for a glimpse of wickedness.

"What is that one thing that you believe I can do?"

Sheikh Jawad wanted Sayed Habeeb to tell the widow to sell her land to the sheikh, because the grand ayatollah wanted to build a large mosque that would house the poor and the needy.

"And will you build that mosque?"

"No, I have wanted to own that land since the day I arrived in Balluria, when I crossed the river," the sheikh answered.

When Sayed Habeeb found out about the sheikh's scheme, he was disgusted by it and wanted to spit in the sheikh's face. He stood up and said, "Sheikh, even if I knew that you would build that mosque, I would never allow it, because of your ill intentions. Good deeds are nothing without good intentions."

That same night, he asked about the Tamimi widow's house. He was taken there by a young, tanned boy. His name was Hamid. When he got there he told the Tamimi widow never to sell her land to the sheikh, because the grand ayatollah had sent him to tell her that. After that the two men never spoke again. Sheikh Jawad realized the threat, and even with all of his power and fearsome willingness and ability to harm others, he could never cause any harm to Sayed Habeeb, because the equation was balanced by Sayed Habeeb's status as a representative of the grand clergy and the holy prophet's ancestry that linked him to the holy family, along with his good deeds and untarnished reputation. Sheikh Jawad could not even use the clergyman's relationship with Barrya to tarnish his reputation, because Barrya belonged to him, and no man would ever dare to sleep with her. So, he just verbally expressed his anger and dissatisfaction with the clergyman. The most that he could do was to cut off the little money that he gave to Barrya for support and stop his contribution to the mosque.

Nevertheless, the sheikh never gave up on the land, and he approached the Tamimi widow another way to claim the land. He sent his trusted confidant, Irar, to ask her for her hand in marriage and supplemented his proposal with a threat that he would drown the land with irrigation water from the river if she refused his proposal. The widow accepted reluctantly, and the sheikh asked Sayed Habeeb to perform the religious marriage ritual, but Sayed Habeeb declined the request. This forced the sheikh to ask for the help of the clergyman of the neighboring village, who had no religious credentials and a bad reputation of being a part-time thief who happily agreed to perform the religious rituals of the wedding for only one hundred dinars. The sheikh was extremely angry with Sayed Habeeb, because he did not attend the wedding dinner, which was small and had no festivities. But when the Tamimi widow died suddenly, one year after the marriage, Sayed Habeeb performed the death ritual, prepared the widow for burial, and hid his suspicion of the possibility that the sheikh killed the poor widow to inherit her land.

During these days, bodies of soldiers who served on the eastern borders started becoming a common scene in the big city and in the little towns and villages along the marshland. Taxi drivers were hired by the army to deliver the soldiers' flag-wrapped dead bodies to their families. They had to endure the humiliating reception of the angry and violent family members and mourners, who sometimes smashed the taxi's windows or beat the driver, but they never did anything to the flag, because they knew that a party informant might be watching. Some drivers had to resort to measures to protect themselves by sending someone from the neighborhood to tell the dead soldier's family that they could find their son's body next to the police station or the mosque. They would drop the body off in a hurry without knocking on the door of the mosque, which left it up to Sayed Habeeb to figure out whose son was in the wooden box and what family he had to inform. It was always Sayed Habeeb who had to come and initiate the funeral and make sure the body was washed in the proper Islamic way. He would spend two nights reading parts of the history of the holy family and their ordeals with pain and sacrifice and allow the family and the mourners to do all the crying and self-beating they needed to do in the three days of the funeral and move on, maybe, to another tragedy.

Sayed Habeeb never rejected a dead body, nor was he ever late for a funeral. When the four dead bodies of the young men that he had known and loved since they were little boys were left in the main square of the town after the men were executed by the squad of military soldiers and party militia, he risked being arrested by going to the party headquarters to ask permission to wash the bodies and bury them. At that time, Kamal was the official party leader in these parts and he allowed the clergyman to wash the bodies of his childhood friends. Sayed Habeeb noticed that night when he looked in Kamal's eyes that he clearly saw the shade of evil color was still burning in Kamal's eyes. He hoped that one day he would be able to save Kamal's soul. He always wanted to save the souls of the kids he loved. He wanted to save Adnan's soul when he started teaching him about God and the logical reasoning of the existence of God and the necessary fight between good and evil. He thought that he was showing him the way to self-realization and inner peace. He missed assessing the boy's ambition and intelligence when Adnan was later found guilty of joining the forbidden political party that Sayed Habeeb once belonged to and was sentenced to four years of imprisonment and torture for his membership. He felt guilty, but he knew that Adnan was too intelligent to make a choice of belief based on others' teachings. Sayed Habeeb consoled himself whenever he remembered Adnan by saying, "He must have figured it out by himself."

It was during that time that the secret political police had visited the mosque and searched it for something Sayed Habeeb did not know about. Members of the police force asked him who stayed longer for prayers and who read more books and if there were any young men who talked about politics or the war. He was escorted to the secret police headquarters and released a few days later. No one knew what happened to him inside the secret police building, but he was more careful of who he talked to after that. Nor did he find any interest among his flock of worshipers to hear about those matters, as people cared more about what was happening on the Eastern border as dead soldiers' bodies became as common as pigeons on a mosque's minaret, which meant more work for the good clergyman. He was even requested to go to the big city to perform his religious ceremonies over dead soldiers' bodies.

When he heard another rebellion was just about to start, he knew that he would not join, because he was no longer the fighting type. He calmed his fears of being a coward forever by telling himself, "The prophet said, 'If you see wrong, try to change it with your hands. If you cannot, then try to change it with your speech and if you still cannot, then try to change it with your heart. That is the weakest of the faith."'

So, he thought to himself that he would try to change things with his preaching and in his heart only, and he accepted once and for all that he was one of the weak faithful.

3

When the devastating war with the thirty nations happened, Kamal ordered Sayed Habeeb not to allow any army deserters to take refuge at the mosque, because they were all traitors. In spite of that, Sayed Habeeb secretly allowed the many hungry and barefooted soldiers who abandoned the trenches in the desert, which was hammered by American war planes, to take refuge in his mosques. He allowed them to spend a night of much-needed rest after walking for hundreds of kilometers from the southern and western fronts and provided them with a simple meal of bread and yogurt that Barrya brought to the hundreds of soldiers who slept in his mosque. He would stay up all night guarding the tired, dirty soldiers, looking out for Kamal and his group of party militiamen who might search for deserters to be executed and made an example of.

Sayed Habeeb knew how to keep a secret just as he knew how to prepare the dead for their final journey. He did not tell Kamal about the time he saw Haleem—the kid who came to him asking to be healed from the love of the girl who never responded to his love letters—trying to buy a Kalashnikov rifle from a very hungry soldier ready to sell anything just for a meal. Sayed Habeeb did not tell Kamal that Haleem, Ashraf, and Salah had asked soldiers about how far the Americans were from Balluria and when they were expected to reach it. When the four young men started the rebellion in Balluria it was rumored that Kamal fled the town. Sayed Habeeb never told the enthusiastic rebels that Kamal had spent the first night hiding in his mosque before fleeing the next morning to the big city wearing a woman's black robe. To Sayed Habeeb, keeping a secret was an essential practice of his faith; he believed keeping secrets was a religious virtue that would help him save his own soul and the souls of many others in the town, the town of many sinners and many secrets, the town seeming to have a secret pact with death.

Sayed Habeeb was never scared of death, and he was never sad to see or touch a dead body. He believed that death was the natural end to many things and the start of many other things. He believed death was the end of earthly pains and sadness, and that people should be happy to meet the angels of death, for it was the beginning of the life in the hereafter where there would be no dark dungeons and no secret police. He waited for his own death with joy and anxiety.

The only time he felt the pain and sadness of death was when he spent the night praying for the souls of the four young men who were condemned to death, not only because he had known all of them since they were young kids, but also because he knew that they would die that next morning. And waiting for the morning was hard, because it gave him time to think about death. And he felt that he failed in saving their lives and their souls, but that night he was there praying for the four men before their deaths. Sayed Habeeb could not sleep. He spent the night in prayers, by himself, and when he tried to close his eyes, the two men from his old dream woke him, telling him to wash the bodies of the four men with water from Euphrates. Sayed Habeeb woke up and walked to the river to fill his bucket. He thought that he would never wash another dead body after the four young men. As he remembered that morning, when Kamal and his group of militiamen searched the mosque for the four young men, he remembered that the evil shade of color in Kamal's eyes was at its brightest, and he wished that he had spent more time with Kamal when he was just a young kid.

Years later, he started to see the two men in his dream more often, and he realized that his own end was near. He started to pray longer and minimized his contact with people. He spent most of his time sitting in the shades of the palm trees behind the mosque avoiding hearing the cries of people suffering from hunger and starvation, and asked him why Allah is allowing such suffering. The only person he was willing to see or talk to was Barrya, who told him many stories about Balluria and its people. She told him about what had happened to the young boys and girls they loved, but when Adnan freed all the boats and went on his final journey to the gates of heaven in the marshes, Sayed Habeeb stopped asking about the kids. He simply could not face the defeat of his soul. He felt that he failed in protecting the children he loved; moreover, he realized that he acceptance of being a weak faithful was the reason for him not being able to save the souls of the people he loved. Years went by slowly, during which he treated his lifelong fears and permanent disappointments with constant prayers and nonstop reading of the tragic history of the holy family.

He was starting to forget about Adnan's death when one day two men with thick moustaches and big bellies, who looked like they were members of the secret police, showed up at the mosque and requested that he accompany them. Although the memories of his arrest and torture in the secret police building were still painful and never left him, he was not scared. He lost his faith in the possibility of saving the soul of the town, and so he was ready for anything. As they walked next to him, the two men with thick moustaches and big bellies asked him if he knew Comrade Kamal. He answered yes. The two men said that Comrade Kamal was killed the night before and they needed someone to prepare him for burial, according to Islamic law, because comrade Kamal "died as a brave martyr," according to one of the two fat men who wore dark olive-green uniforms.

Sayed Habeeb did not want to wash the body of the man who had inflicted so much pain on the town and its people, but he knew that it was all a part of his penance and self-redemption, believing that treating his spiritual anguish by doing good deeds for people who were purely evil would save his soul. It's all part of the divine plan of the almighty Allah to purify his own defeated soul. He agreed to go with them, put his turban on, and walked with the two men who wore dark olive-green suits and smelled of sweat and okra stew.

Sayed Habeeb washed Kamal's body with water from the river, as a last attempt to save the soul of the evil man he had known since he was a kid. He walked to the river and filled a bucket of water to wash the body shredded by what appeared to be a hellish dagger. As he washed Kamal's body, he opened the corpse's eyes and looked for the fiery color of evil. He looked in Kamal's dead eyes and saw no color; it was gone. He felt comfort and thought it was a sign that Kamal found peace at last. For him, that was the end of his journey, it was the end of road. He wanted to die because his life had lost its purpose. He wanted to go to the other world because he was spent spiritually and had no energy left to save anyone's soul. He yearned for a sign from God that would tell him of his time to depart, Kamal's death was a sign that evil had its own end, but he waited for a clearer sign, one that would leave no doubt, a sign that would give him what all the faithful were searching for: the eternal acceptance of the Lord's will and complete submission, the feeling of heaven.

He thought he had that feeling when he found the forgotten, ailing figure of Sheikh Jawad, lying in his guesthouse. Later that week the sheikh died, and Sayed Habeeb performed his last Islamic washing ritual. He declared that he would no longer wash dead bodies, nor was he willing to perform Islamic rituals in funerals. He also announced that he was no longer willing to lead prayers, since no one was showing up to pray. No one in the town understood why the graceful clergyman stopped caring about his flock, or why he stopped performing his duties as the spiritual protector who must save the town's soul. The people forgot about Sheikh Jawad. He was swept from their memories by the many sandstorms that washed the town of its sins and its memory.

What no one knew was that when Sayed Habeeb and the two Ba'athist men with thick moustaches found the ghostlike figure of the forgotten Sheikh, Sayed Habeeb had his revelation of the truth he had long awaited. That truth manifested itself through color, the sign that he was waiting for, seeing the color of heaven he saw in his dream long ago when he was visited by two magnificent-looking men. It happened when Sayed Habeeb and the two Ba'athists with big bellies and thick moustaches hired the stranger who had shown up out of thin air and offered to carry Sheikh Jawad's body to the seven palm trees for burial, because this was Sheikh Jawad's last wish.

At the burial site, Sayed Habeeb looked to the tops of the palm trees and was mesmerized by the immaculate shapes of the palm trees, even though they had never been watered or cared for. He was mesmerized by the symmetrical tops of the trees. It was as though the hands of a divine gardener had shaped the leaves and trimmed the trunks of the seven palm trees. The trees looked as though they had been cared for since the beginning of time by some being other than humans. The color of the leaves was not as green as the palm trees in the surrounding orchard of his mosque, nor it was the color of the palm trees of the widow Tamimi's orchard, which was the healthiest orchard in those parts, but it was a heavenly green. It looked like the eternal dust of the Arabian Sahara that had blown since the beginning of time had passed near the seven palm trees but never touched nor tainted the pure and spectacular green of its leaves.

As the two men with thick moustaches dug the grave to bury Sheikh Jawad, Sayed Habeeb looked up and saw what the other three men did not see. He saw the two magnificent-looking men from his dream sitting on top of the palm trees looking down at the graves and looking at him. He did not believe what he was seeing, and he thought it was the effect of the vegetables that he ate earlier from the garden that Hanan had planted, before she escaped with her lover. He thought he was hallucinating; he looked up again and saw the two magnificent-looking men, who had long hair and groomed beards, sitting on the treetops looking at him. Sayed Habeeb wanted to ask the man with the horse and carriage, who had appeared from nowhere and was willing to carry the sheikh's body to his final resting place with little reward if he could see the men. He wanted to ask his three companions if they could see the two men who looked like angels sitting on the top of the palm trees, but he feared that he might be accused of being senile or mad in a town that loved accusing its people. He did not want to be treated like the town's new crazy man as Adnan had been, so he kept quiet. He kept looking up where the two magnificent-looking men looked down at him and at the many graves by the seven palm trees.

As the four men walked back from the deserted burial ground, Sayed Habeeb could not resist his urges and he wanted a confirmation of the sign so asked his three companions if they saw how beautiful the seven palm trees were and if they felt that there was someone watching them. The two Ba'athists with thick moustaches and big bellies said that the palm trees looked like any other palm trees and they felt no one watching them. The man with the horse and carriage did not answer.

That day, Sayed Habeeb realized that his days on this earth were numbered and he must prepare for his last journey. He stopped calling for prayers and depended on Khalaf, the Mu'athan to do so, he even asked Khalaf to lead the prayers if any worshipers showed up. Sayed Habeeb stopped giving sermons on Fridays and stopped preaching the tragic history of the holy family. He barely attended the prayers led by Khalaf, who often did not remember to recite the right verses from Qur'an with small number of elder faithfuls who showed up now and then to the mosque. Sayed Habeeb waited for the two men from his dreams to show up and collect his soul as they promised in his dream. He waited and waited, and sometimes he wondered if he was slipping into the murky waters of madness, but he remembered what Barrya always said, "People in these parts die from waiting and boredom."

Even when starvation and lack of medicine had devastated the town and its people and even though the party officials had sent him the two men with thick moustaches and big bellies to urge him to do his patriotic duty of washing the bodies of the men, Sayed Habeeb refused to perform the Islamic cleansing ritual for the dead men, women, and children who died of malnutrition, starvation, and shortage of medicine. The two Ba'athists men with thick moustaches and big bellies spent almost three hours trying to convince him of the importance of him participating in the national effort to defeat the enemy, and the fatter of the two said to him, "The satanic West has imposed a devilish embargo on our people to break the will of our great nation, but with the divine leadership of our divine leader, we will defeat the satanic West, and we need you to do your patriotic part and start washing the dead bodies of the many citizens who died, because it's the way you will be of service to our divine leader."

Sayed Habeeb stared at them with glassy eyes and asked, "Do you remember when we buried Sheikh Jawad by the seven palm trees?"

"Yes, Sayedna, we remember," one of the men with thick moustaches and big bellies answered.

"Did you see the two men with white robes, long black hair, and groomed beards who were sitting at the tops of the seven palm trees?" he asked again.

"No, Sayedna, we did not see two men with long hair and groomed beards sitting on the tops of the palm trees. It must have been your imagination."

Sayed Habeeb stopped asking questions and stopped talking even when one of the men with thick moustaches and big bellies insisted, "So are you ready to do your patriotic duty to our divine leader?"

He kept silent, because he knew that he would go mad if he kept asking about the two men with long beards and white robes, and he would go mad if he kept washing dead bodies and preparing the dead for their final journey. He remained silent through all the years of starvation, and death that followed. He talked only to Barrya and Amel who kept telling him that she wrote many letters to all the people who left Balluria but not one had replied. Sayed Habeeb nodded silently as he sat on the rooftop of his house of God, which was falling into permanent disrepair. He stared at the river with his glassy eyes, thinking of how green and beautiful the seven palm trees looked, and he wondered if the lost souls of all the people who were buried there kept the seven palm trees groomed, trimmed, and beautiful. He wished that he was sitting on the tops of the seven palm trees with the two magnificent-looking men looking at soft sands where the graves of all the illegitimate infants were buried by sinful virgins and unfaithful wives, who sought the help of Barrya, the Gypsy midwife, to abort their children. And where the graves of all the unfortunate sheep smugglers who dared to challenge the territorial rights of Sheikh Jawad and his mysterious partner Irar, the graves of all the lovers who made the mistake of believing that love would overcome the tribal and religious codes in these parts and the many other graves of people the world never knew existed,

He mumbled to himself, "What a way to spend eternity." Then with a complete submission to his fate and a clear acceptance of the divine plan of the almighty he pulled a pen and a piece of paper and wrote, "This is the will of the unfortunate servant of Allah, Sayed Habeeb Al-Mosawi. I bear witness that there is no god but Allah, and I wish to be buried under the seven palm trees, among all the good and unfortunate souls." And he wrote one of his favorite verses from the Qur'an:

"And they mixed a good deed with a bad deed, hoping the Almighty would forgive them and accept them as they repent."

Later, as his hair grew completely white and his ability to walk weakened, Sayed Habeeb spent most of his time sitting in the shade he made for himself outside the mosque. He looked at the river, wondering if Hamid would pass by, sailing a boat that he found floating on the river, or if Ahmed and Adnan would rise from the water of the Euphrates with no guilt and no grudges. He stared at the river, asking it many times, "Allah said that you are a river of heaven. How could you take so many lives?"

After his daring thoughts, he always repented by reciting the forgiveness prayer,

"I seek refuge in God's grace from Satan and his works."

Barrya and Amel never stopped visiting him. They brought yogurt and tea. Barrya talked about how people forgot how to smile, and Amel talked about the man she loved, who left town a long time ago and never returned her letters.

Sayed Habeeb knew that there would be no one to prepare him for his eternal journey. He wished that Adnan or Hamid or even Barrya would be there to recite the two lines of deliverance when he closes his eyes forever, but he realized that Hamid would be in the wilderness chasing the wolves, and Adnan was already in heaven, and Barrya did not know how to recite the two lines. He also did not want his last deliverance to be by a sinful Gypsy woman, although he forgave her a long time ago, but he wanted another human who led a less sinful life to deliver him to the angels. He crawled to the bathroom in his mosque and washed himself. He crawled back to his prayer rug and prayed two rikk'ats (cycles of prayer). In them, he asked for Allah's forgiveness and asked for the Lord's mercy for being a weak faithful. He asked for mercy for all the people in Balluria, for all the people in the country, and asked for forgiveness and mercy for all the people in the world. He said, "Oh, my Lord, my God, the God of heaven and earth, forgive your servants as they live this life and as they die. I seek refuge in the light of your glory. Do not leave me to my inabilities and my sinful soul. You are the Savior of the meek, and you are my Savior."

When he finished praying, he looked toward the mosque door and wondered if the angels had arrived yet. He knew it was time. He felt a cold breeze entering the deserted mosque, and he remembered the many times he led the prayers and masses and the people chanting the sad chants that mourned the death of the holy family of the prophet and wished that he could do it one more time. He felt a breeze going through his skin. He realized that the two angels from his dreams were in the mosque.

"Ahlan, wa sahlan, wa marhaba... welcome to you and welcome to the one who sent you and welcome to what you are about to do," he said, thinking that the angels were hearing him. He lay on the old worn carpet and looked toward the small fire he lit for warmth. He covered himself with a thick blanket and recited the verse,

From earth you were created, and to earth you will return, and from earth you will be resurrected again. Oh content soul, return to your Creator and enter my heavens among my worshipers. Those heavens were created for those who do not seek vanity nor do seek wickedness; and the everlasting happiness is for the meek to have.

Sayed Habeeb waited to die, but the angels did not appear. He wondered if he should ask for mercy and ask the Lord to take his soul. He asked for mercy again and again, and suddenly he saw a person sitting next to his head and another one sitting by his feet. He wondered who they were. He could not see their faces. He could only hear them talking about him. He thought they were strangers who entered the mosque, and he felt happy that someone was there to witness his departure. He listened as their voices started to become clearer and clearer. It sounded like they were talking about him when the one by his head asked the one by his feet, "What is his name?"

"Habeeb," the one by his feet answered.

"Habeeb, the son of whom?" the one by his head asked.

"Habeeb, the son of Layla," the one by his feet answered.

Sayed Habeeb was surprised to see these two strangers, who wore white robes and had beautiful long hair and groomed beards, talking about him. And he was more surprised that the one by his feet said his mother's name and not his father's.

He felt coldness in his legs and felt the coldness creeping higher and higher into his body. He calmed down as he saw a light shining by the two men who sat at his head and his feet, and he noticed that their faces were familiar, very familiar.

He felt safe and joyful, as he realized that the two men were the two angels from his dreams, and he mumbled, "In the name of Allah, my God, and for Allah my God and on the path of his messenger Muhammad, I am on Islam and on the loyalty to my Imam Ali. I bear witness that there is no god, but Allah, and I bear witness that Muhammad is his messenger."

As he saw the other side, the side that was lit with a glorious and peaceful green light and many palm trees that looked excitably like the seven palm trees, he let himself go.

The Book of the Gypsy Witches

Hope Dies Silently

1

The old woman inhaled half of her cigarette in one deep inhale. The bright, flickering blue light rising from the tip of the burning little leaves of the cigarette made her eyes glow. She looked at the man as though she could see him, and then she looked outside through the open door of the mud hut. The rain kept playing its eternal sad symphony on the tin plates covering the roof of the mud hut.

"It was like a disease," the blind Gypsy woman said. She kept a steady face and looked down at the fire as she tried rejuvenating it with her little stick.

"It was like yellow sickness, a disease, and everything was sick. I heard people saying that the tyrant grew crazy, because he could not wage any more wars, because he was paranoid that some of his own family and his close friends were trying to kill him," the old Gypsy woman said to the man who rested his head on his crossed hands as he listened. "The tyrant was willing to sell his soul to the devil, so he would not die. The witches and warlocks of the devil worshippers in the north told him that he would not die as long as he brought death upon others. I heard that one of the warlocks told him that he must be wary of youth and beauty. They told the tyrant that youth and beauty were his enemies and he must destroy them," the Gypsy woman said with complete belief in what she was saying.

"But how could he kill youth and beauty?" the man asked restlessly.

"My son, no one can kill youth and beauty. But the tyrant tried. The tyrant had his trusted followers carry out his will, those evil men who only said yes to him and did whatever he wanted, along with his aide, who was an obedient, submissive man who looked like Irar. Those evil men multiplied into thousands and thousands of men, and they all wore dark olive-green uniforms, just like the one Kamal used to wear. It was like the country was filled with men like Kamal, men who forgot about love and only wanted to inflict pain and suffering on people," the Gypsy woman said.

The man looked at the Gypsy woman. He did not know what to say or how to reply to what she said. The rain did not stop, but he was in no hurry to go anywhere. He wished that she would pour him some tea, but she did not seem to be in a gracious mood, and all the stories that she told him did not improve her hospitality. He knew she was telling him a story mixed with her own Gypsy beliefs of witches and warlocks, but as she told her tale of the crazed tyrant, her face turned darker with fear and anger and ultimately resentment as her voice grew deeper; it was like she was feeling fear whenever she said the word tyrant. She had not said the word tyrant until then. Since he had arrived at her mud hut, this was the only time she called the dead dictator a tyrant. It seemed like telling her story had liberated her from her fear, as it liberated him from his many fears.

"The tyrant must have asked the evil spirits of the north how he could kill youth and beauty and that's when he started the death holes, death rivers, and death valleys and sent the young there; all of them. He sent them to be soldiers forever in the wars that never end. He sent them to fight on many fronts, under holy banners, in an endless march toward death. He created army after army and kept sending the young boys to fight. All of the young men of Balluria and all the towns and villages were gone; they were all emptied of their youth."

The Gypsy woman started to cry again, and when she stopped, she wiped the tears, stained black after mixing with eyeliner, from her cheeks. She reached into a small can and drew a new, thick, black line around her blind eyes. She smiled at the man as though she could see him and said, "During all of these I waited for my children to come back to me. Every day I went to the soccer field with a jar full of fresh yogurt and waited for any kid who was thirsty. But my wait was long, and no children ever came to play. I started to feel the pain in my feet when I walked, but I kept going and waiting."

"Waiting for what?" the man asked.

"I waited for you and the others to come back. I waited for all my boys and my girls to come back home. But all of my children had grown and gone away." She wiped her tears again with her scarf, leaving a line of wet eyeliner mixed with tears and said, "But hunger has no mercy. For years people waited for a sign of hope, but it seemed that we were forgotten by Allah and by the people of the world. For years, people feasted on what was left of their dignity, their decency, and the beauty of their souls." The Gypsy woman extended her hand to where the teapot was. She shook the empty pot, but had no apparent desire to make another pot. She continued her tale of the devilish starvation of the bodies and souls of Balluria.

"And when people have lost their souls and when hope dies in their hearts, they will do whatever they must to survive." The Gypsy woman said like she was revealing a hiding truth.

"When hungry, a human feels nothing else but hunger."

"People sold their homes, their furniture, and their clothes for food. And when they had nothing else to sell, they sold their bodies and souls. Everyone was hungry, and you could see the pain of hunger in their faces," the blind Gypsy woman said and continued, "The river's water was reducing each day, until it dried up. All the fish had disappeared or migrated to the marshes, where the gates of heaven are. And Hamid said that there were no animals left in the wilderness. He said the wilderness was hungry too."

"Did you see him often, I mean Hamid?" the man asked.

"He came to visit me often riding on his horse. He always sat where you are sitting now and told me about the many wolves he encountered in the desert. Once, he brought me a falcon."

"A falcon?" the man asked.

"Hamid told me that he trapped falcons and sold them to rich sheikhs in the southern country for ten thousand dinars, and he gave me some money to give to his mother and his sister, Amel."

"How did you survive? How did you live?" the man asked.

"Death does not visit Gypsy women very often. I survived on waiting and yogurt."

The man wanted to ask where she got the yogurt. Since he was a young boy he heard many of his friends saying that she had a jinni partner who brought her fresh yogurt. The man restrained himself because the relevancy of the question was not valid at that moment, as the blind Gypsy woman was telling the story of the ultimate hunger imposed on the meek and helpless. Instead, he asked, "How did the people of Balluria survive?"

"My son, the really sad thing was not that the people starved but it's the people's hearts that started to change. Their faces were dressed with the most grim and most ugly expressions, expressions of need. Their eyes were glazed over with a frightening color of massive greed that overshadowed the beautiful black and brown hues of their eyes, which was replaced with the color that will never change."

"And what is that color?" Salam asked.

"It is the color of constant anger. Everyone had forgotten how to smile, and everyone wanted to hurt others," the Gypsy woman said. "Anger and greed, my son, that's what years of hunger did to the people of Balluria."

2

"Hunger is like infidelity to the soul, my son," the old Gypsy woman said, speaking with the soft tone of an Eastern philosopher.

"When humans go hungry, they lose faith in God." She lit another cigarette and continued. "Hunger will drive them to kill. It drives them to hurt others, who will in turn try to hurt them. This is how smiles disappear, and it's how beautiful faces turn ugly." The Gypsy woman concluded her statements and exhaled a mouthful of cigarette smoke.

"What happened to the town?" the man asked.

The old woman paused for a moment, and then said, "Many had packed their belongings and left. We did not hear from the people who left. Nobody sent a letter, nor did they send a reply to the letters that Amel sent, but we heard some stories about their fate. We never heard from Abdullah and Basima, and the little bit we knew about them was not enough."

"Where did they go?" the man asked.

"They went to the places where they thought there was no fear of hunger. Amel kept sending them letters; she was not sure of the address, but she insisted on sending the letters anyway. None of the letters was ever answered, but once Basima wrote back asking Amel to send her some money and clothes, because she was about to sell her soul in the streets of the city that she was in. The letter had no address on it. We did not have any money to send."

The man remembered that he received a letter from Abdullah, but he never opened it. He did not say a word to the Gypsy woman and continued with his stale and ruthless pretensions.

"Poor Amel did not have any money to send. She asked me, but I did not have any money either. Amel read the letter that Basima sent to me. She said that she could not leave Jordan, and she was being chased by the police. She was alone with her newborn daughter. She said that she was scared and she had not heard from Abdullah in a long time. My poor little girl."

"I remember Basima and Abdullah; they were very happy together," the man said.

The Gypsy woman cried, "Yes, yes, they were in love, and I hoped that I would see their children. They were the only two among all of my children that had a chance of bringing me more children. But love and children could not survive hunger and fear. My poor little girl," the Gypsy woman said and cried again.

The man smoked his Marlboro and started thinking about the time by the river when he and Abdullah had had the conversation about Basima and how she was the perfect match for Abdullah. Abdullah said he was going to marry Basima, and they had two plans. One was to stay in Balluria and raise a family, and the other plan was to go to Denmark if they ever had the chance. He remembered Abdullah saying that he wanted to stay in Balluria forever, but at the same time he showed him a photo of a wooden cabin surrounded by white snow in the middle of rolling hills. The man remembered Abdullah saying, "This is either in Alaska or Denmark. I am sure its Denmark. It will be the perfect place for Basima and me."

He also remembered Abdullah saying, "I know that I will be a teacher in the elementary school in Balluria, but my dream is to leave, and I am afraid to chase my dream, because people like us should dream simple dreams."

Salam remembered asking Abdullah, "What are your dreams, Abdullah?"

"To go to a place like the one in the photo; it's the perfect place for me to study history, and Basima will raise the children. We will settle in a country that has wooden cabins and year-round snow, white snow."

The man also remembered Abdullah saying that he would send him a postcard from every city they passed through. The man remembered that Abdullah said that he and his wife, Basima, would be teachers in a university and they would raise two beautiful children, and their names would be Niema and Rahma (blessings and mercy).

"And that's our simple dream. I don't think it's too much to ask Allah for."

The man remembered replying, "No, Abdullah, that's not too much to ask from Allah."

He never thought that he could be wrong until he sat and listened to the old Gypsy woman.

"No, it's not too much to ask God for."

It's ironic, the man thought to himself, as he realized the way Abdullah died frozen in the snow of the Turkish mountains, as greedy smugglers led the desperate men to their impossible dreams and toward an unknown fate through the borders between Arabia and Europe. I guess it was too much to ask, the man thought to himself. He saw the old Gypsy woman staring as though she saw something with her lightless eyes.

"What happened after?" the man asked.

"The river and the palm trees no longer loved their people," the blind Gypsy woman said.

"What do you mean?"

"It was a fruitless disease of despair. People lost their taste for life. They existed for the sole purpose of waiting, waiting for something, but they did know what. I know what I was waiting for, and I know what Amel was waiting for."

"What were you waiting for?"

"I was waiting for you and the rest of my children to return, and Amel was waiting for you to write back. I saw her once or twice a week. I have always been guided by the light in her eyes. It was the only torch of life that never died, but one day I looked in her eyes and saw that the light was dimming, so I asked her."

"'Why are you looking like this?' She did not answer me. So I kissed her face and sat her on my lap and sang to her.

> *Between death and hunger,*
> *Between despair and anger,*
> *Always draw your eyeliner, thick, black, and bright,*
> *Your eyeliner must be as vivid as the color of the night,*
> *Your smile as wicked as the difference between wrong and right,*
> *Because life is a cheating game,*
> *And a silly fight,*
> *And the winner is the most fake,*
> *Who keeps a smile and dances through it all.*

The man did not understand what the woman was saying, although it sounded intriguing. He wanted to ask her the meaning of what she said.

"Don't ask. I will tell you the meaning of what I said to Amel. It is what my Gypsy grandmother told me as she dressed me to dance in the wedding, where I saw Sheikh Jawad for the first time. I was young. I was afraid and started crying. I was afraid, because I knew what was going to happen to me after the wedding was over. I had heard from the other Gypsy women what happens to the youngest Gypsy dancer after she dances in a wedding in these parts. My tears smeared my black eyeliner, which made my grandmother angry. She taught me that in this life, some people do not have a choice other than to live, no matter how hard and unfair this life may be. She slapped me on the face and she said, 'We come into this world without knowing why and not knowing where we are going. The steps have been planned for our feet, and we walk in the solitude of our nights.' When she saw I was sad, my grandmother, the Gypsy queen, who danced for sheikhs and princes, set me on her lap and sang that song to me." The Gypsy woman gazed into the space in front of the mud hut and then looked at where the man sat.

"It's what my grandmother sang to me when I was sad, and that's what I sang to Amel when I saw that she was giving up on hope. I know that she gave up on her brother, Hamid, who never recovered his humanity after he lost Hanan and after being in the wilderness for too long. I know she had given up on you and the hope that one day you would return to save her, but she should not have given up on hope, because she had nothing and no one else."

"What did Amel say to you when you told her that?" the man asked.

"She told me that she would continue sending you letters, and she would continue listening to Fairuz, who sang about the little princess who could not escape from the castle with the high walls."

The man felt a steep warmth rising in his blood when he remembered the many times he sat in the dark shade and listened to that song with Amel. He remembered the look in her eyes when she asked him if he had ever heard the song about the little princess who was trapped in the castle and wanted to fly away. The princess wanted to escape from the prison of her life, but the walls were too high. And for the first time since he set sail on his journey back to Balluria, he felt the wetness of a small tear coming down his cheek. He did not want the Gypsy woman to see it, so he turned his face and looked outside as he wiped the single tear. The rain started to pour again, and he did not want the woman to keep talking about Amel. He wanted to know why the town was so dusty, why the walls were so faded, and why people did not paint their walls with lively colors to chase away despair.

"Why is the town so dusty?" he asked.

"It's our destiny and our fate," the Gypsy woman said.

"I don't understand."

"You don't have to understand, because you never belonged here. When people live in a place, they must love the place first, and then they call it home. And when they do, they share the destiny of the place itself. This is our home, the home that took everything from us, yet we still give. It took our youth, and we still give. It took our smiles, and we still give and give, and others don't understand that."

The man heard the words of the blind Gypsy woman and felt that he never really had a home or a place that he could call home. Even in his town in the West with his wife, his gallery, and his paintings, he had never felt at home. He never had the peace that he yearned for. Something was always missing. He insisted on having a fireplace in his two-story building to make it feel like home. He wanted to paint the walls with many shades of green, like the colors of the palm trees, to make his gallery look or feel like home. But no matter what he did, it never did feel like home.

"One of the hardest things on the soul is not having a home," the Gypsy woman said, as though she was reading his mind. "Even if it was as dusty and as weathered as Balluria. Do you know why Gypsies have never had a home?"

"No," the man answered.

"It's because Gypsies have loved all the places they have passed through, since the beginning of time, and they were afraid to stay in one place, because they did not want to surrender to the loose end of the memory."

Oh, what a statement, words that meant many things yet did not mean a thing at all, the man thought to himself, and waited for the blind Gypsy woman to explain, which she was quick to do after she lit another cigarette.

"That's why they will always keep walking, because they do not want to be like others who've always wanted to leave, but never did."

"Who are the others?" the man asked.

"All the people in Balluria and in the Arabian Sahara, who will always be prevented from love yet could never leave the Ballurias within them."

"Why can't they leave?" the man asked.

"Because they all have an inheritance here that they cannot abandon. It's hard to carry around the grudges of the past forever; it's hard to live on the guilt of the sins that your ancestors committed; it's hard to walk the earth with the chains of knowledge that no other wanted to bare, and it's hard to live with a special relationship with God, because others will not allow you to have that. That's why all the people in Balluria wanted to leave, because they could not withstand the burden of the secrets they kept and what they knew about themselves."

"But I left," the man said.

"And you lost both, your heart and your home," the Gypsy woman said.

The man did not condone her statement about him. Who was she to tell him what he had lost? What did she know about him and about what he had experienced on the many lonesome nights in the West? He wanted to change the direction of her thoughts, because he wanted to remain courteous, so he asked, "Who else has left town besides me, Basima, and Abdullah?"

"The Hillaly family left; I saw the Hillaly girls two weeks before they left. They were sitting in the street selling their belongings: their clothes, their books. Basically, they were selling their lives."

"Bushra and Adawya?" the man asked.

"Yes, I see you remember their names," the Gypsy woman said with a sincere smile.

"Haleem and I used to pursue their love and attention," the man replied bashfully.

"Yes, I know. Before you and your family left town, Amel brought me all the letters that Adawya wrote to you. She came here crying; she showed me the letters and asked me what she should do."

This surprised him.

"What did you tell her to do?"

"I told her to hide the letters and to bring me a lock of your hair, so I could do an old Gypsy spell that would make you fall in love with her."

"And did you do that?" he asked

"Yes, I did," The woman answered to his surprise.

"But it did not work, because the Gypsy love elixirs could not break the walls that were around your heart at that time. You were unable to love," she concluded.

The man looked at her and wondered how she knew what he already knew about himself. He knew that he never felt love like others did. He knew that when people expressed or talked about love in movies or books or when they told their own love stories, he never felt that way. He knew that he was prevented from love. Even with his wife, Emily, he often wondered why he had the urge to leave, to abandon her, to start a new life somewhere else, to meet other women, to meet other people, to see new horizons and new mornings. He wondered why wine tasted better in Italy than in Chicago; why the water of Lake Michigan was not the same as the water of the Mediterranean or not even the same as the water of the Euphrates. He wondered why he always longed for the smell of other women's hair and bodies. He felt there were breathtaking views that he needed to see. He felt like he was always thirsty, thirsty for more love, more attention, more of everything. More alcohol—the constant thirst for everything in life tormented him his entire life. When he painted, he tried to make the colors more vivid, more exuberant, and livelier, but he always felt that it was not enough, and he needed to add more colors. When he drank, he wanted to drink more and more. Even in his relationship with his wife, he always felt that there was something missing. He knew that he loved her, but there was always that feeling of something missing. He did not know what it was or what it could be; he asked himself many times. Was it because he was prevented from love as this blind old Gypsy woman was saying, or was it that he just didn't know how to love? He wondered, were other people like him? He knew that he was trying, trying to be the perfect husband to his wife, and the perfect lover, and ultimately a perfect artist and human being but there was always something missing, in the looks, in the touches, and in the feelings, something was just not there. He tried to defend his heart and protect himself from the offensiveness of the truth.

He asked bluntly, "Did Amel love me?"

"She died many times for you. She died time and time again; she died every time she looked at you, because she knew that she would never be with you. When Hanan came to me, telling me that she felt like she could not breathe every time she looked at Hamid, I knew she was in love with him, and I consulted the Gypsy stones and saw their fate. When Amel came to me and told me that she was dying slowly every time she heard your name or saw you walking, I knew that she would never have you, because I saw in the stones that you were prevented from love, and I also saw that she would always be alone, and that broke my heart."

"What did Amel say about me?"

"She told me that she wished she was the cover that you covered yourself with when you slept, and she wished that she could be next to you just so she could exist."

For some reason, beyond his comprehension, the man thought that statement was illogical, yet exceptionally romantic. He remembered the sad look in Amel's eyes whenever he looked at her and started to understand that maybe it was the true love she felt that brought that kind of sadness to her beautiful black eyes.

"Amel told me that she knew that you would never be with her and that you would never love her. I tried to make you love her with my Gypsy love elixirs," the woman said with the expression of a Gypsy witch.

"We Gypsies know that we can drive a man crazy with our dances, and we can make a man leave his wife and children and follow us to the end of the world, but we cannot make a heartless man feel true love. Gypsy love elixirs do not work on those who are prevented from love," the Gypsy woman concluded, putting the unbearable weight of massive guilt on the man's heart.

He searched for the correct words to say that would spare him.

"I was just a kid," the man protested.

"It doesn't matter now. A long time has passed," she replied.

The man looked outside again at the space in front of the mud hut. He watched the rainfall that made tiny rivers with many bubbles that spread in undirected circles like a happy group of children with no care in the world. He looked at the steam rising from the walls of the mud hut, and he thought about Amel and wondered what she was doing at that moment. He also thought about his wife, Emily, and wondered what she was doing at that moment too, but he knew he could not remove his protective shell, at least not yet.

3

"What happened to the Hillaly girls? Salam asked.

"They left. The two older Hillaly boys never returned from the war fronts. People say the two Hillaly boys were killed by the Americans on the long highway of death. Old man Hillaly died when he broke his pelvis because there was no doctor and no hospital to treat him. They kept him in the house as he was crying like a child from the pain, and after three days he died. The Hillaly girls left with their mother because they did not have food or money. They sold everything they had. The girls sold their furniture. They sold their beds and mattresses. They sold their carpets, and in the end they sold their clothes, even their undergarments. I saw them sitting in the town's square, covering their faces with shame as they tried to sell their undergarments."

"They sold their undergarments?" the man asked.

"Yes, but that was not what made me cry. I cried when they wanted to sell their hair because of hunger."

"What do you mean?" he asked.

"Bushra came to me and asked me if I knew anyone who wanted to buy her and her sister's hair."

"Their hair?" the wide-eyed man said with sincere interest as he remembered how he and basically every young man in the town, especially his friend Haleem, had talked and dreamed about the Hillaly girls' hair.

"What happened? Did you find someone to buy their hair?"

"Oh, my son, the only person who would have paid with his life for Bushra's hair had already done so." The old Gypsy woman wiped her tears. "Haleem was the only man who would pay for her hair. And that's what I told Bushra."

The Gypsy woman extended her hand to him, offering him a cigarette that she rolled. The man clearly remembered their faces, their names, and their hair, but when he looked into her eyes, he realized that she was not only telling the story of all of his friends, she was seeing the people that she was talking about like they were sitting with them in the mud hut looking out at the rain as he and the blind Gypsy woman were.

"Are you all right?" he gently asked.

"I am, always," the Gypsy woman said as she inhaled the smoke of the rolled cigarette. She offered him another rolled cigarette.

"Shookrun, thank you," he said politely and took the cigarette from her. He put it aside and pulled out one of his Marlboros.

"Don't be afraid, my son," the woman said as though she saw what he did.

"There is no Gypsy love elixir in it," she added with a smile that brought back all the innocence and all the natural beauty to her face, the same tanned face that he remembered many long years ago.

"I know. I am sorry, but it's better for my chest that I don't change brands," he replied politely.

"Smoking does not hurt the chest; it heals he heart."

He smiled at that grossly misinformed statement.

"It heals the heart by making a greater pain seem smaller," she explained.

"I agree," he said.

He looked at her to see if she was ready to talk some more. He wanted her to tell him more about his friends; about Hamid, Amel, Adnan, and about all the boys and girls who once walked these dusty streets and wrote love letters. Salam wanted her to tell him about the people who lived here in this godforsaken haven of solitude and boredom.

"What happened to Amel? Is she still alive? Is she still around?" he rephrased his question.

"Where would she go?" the old woman answered. "Women like Amel don't leave towns like Balluria."

"Why don't they? Did she get married?" he asked.

"She was and will forever be waiting for you. To her, you were not just a man; you were the life that she thought she could live," the Gypsy replied

The man felt extremely uncomfortable with the accusation of abandonment the Gypsy woman was implying. He wanted to defend himself, but the old Gypsy woman was quick to assure him.

"Don't do that to yourself. It was not your fault that she spent her life waiting."

The Gypsy woman was quick to save him from his preemptive standoffishness.

"Where is Amel now?" the man asked.

"She is selling candy, on the same corner where her mother used to sell candy. She sells candy to children, so they won't grow up and leave. She is still waiting, listening to Fairuz, and reading poetry. She is still waiting for you."

He inhaled the smoke from his cigarette and was ready to defend himself again, but the Gypsy woman assured him again.

"It was not you, my boy. Amel is doing what all of her female ancestors before her did. She is following and living the path of life written for her long before you existed; it was not you, my boy."

He felt a temporary relief from the burden, and then she added, "It was her fate. She had no chance and no hope, like all the women in these parts. They live and dream only until they are seventeen, and then they die slowly, just like their mothers and grandmothers before them."

The Gypsy woman exhaled a long stream of gray smoke that rose to the ceiling. She looked outside where the rain had started to ease, and amazingly, white clouds started to move southward. She thought about what she would say next. And just like the temporary clarity of the sky, she turned her blind, beautiful black eyes toward him and said with a clear voice, "They die slowly just like their love stories. They die slowly, like all of their dreams. They die slowly as they dream of leaving these parts and this town. They die slowly and silently just like hope itself," the Gypsy woman said and paused, leaving him drenched in his deep thoughts, looking at the thousands of happy bubbles swimming in the muddy puddles of water.

The Book of the Man

So Long to Balluria

1

The day we left Balluria was hot and cloudy, almost the same as the day we came to Balluria. My father was the happiest man in the world when he announced that morning that we were leaving in the afternoon. He never stopped shouting, "Finally, we will be out of this black hole of scum."

He had ordered my brother and I to start packing two days before that. My mother started packing almost a month before that day. It was the same day school finished, but she never told us why. Later we found out that my father had received his transfer order back to the ministry in April, but he waited until we finished school to leave. My father told me one day that he was working on something very good for me and that he was hoping that he would be able to get it. I had no idea what he meant. I thought he was thinking about marrying me to one of my many available cousins, but I hoped that was not what he was thinking.

At that time, Balluria had lost almost sixty of its finest young men on the eastern front. The last one was Hazem, Haleem's brother, who was brought home on the top of a taxi, covered by the flag, two days before we left Balluria. It was my first time seeing a dead man.

When the casket reached Haleem's house, followed by a crowd, mostly children that had gathered very quickly, they were mesmerized by the scene. Haleem's entire family burst out of the house and shook the conscience of the crowd with their screams and chants of mourning. This outburst caused everyone in the town to cry. Hazem, as I remember him, was a decent man who was quiet and educated. He barely left the house when he was on leave from the eastern front. He was engaged to Sanna, the elementary school teacher in Balluria, and he was killed just one month before the wedding. After seeing his brother's dead body, Haleem went into a rage and started tearing the flag apart. Later, I learned that Kamal had sent a summons to Haleem from the party headquarters, warning him about the ramifications of his act of ripping the flag. It was a sad day.

That evening I went to Hamid's house just before dinner. Amel was there, and she told us that she was at Haleem's house and that she saw the body of Hazem in the open casket inside where the women were mourning. She said that his face looked like he was in a deep and peaceful sleep and that his fiancée, Sanna, was hysterical. She told us that Sanna had slapped her own face and she pulled out almost all of her hair and was crying and screaming so hysterically that it made the other women pull out their hair too. She also told us that the Hillaly girls were the only ones who did not touch their hair, especially Bushra.

She said Bushra did not even take off her scarf. She told us that there was no dinner and that her mother was still at Hazem's house with his mother, because she had lost the ability to walk due to the shock. So some of the townswomen helped his mother with the dinner for the mourners who showed up.

Hamid and I went to sit on the roof of the mud and brick room because we did not trust the roofs of the other rooms to withstand our weight. From where we sat, we watched the Euphrates that night. The waves were silver, and the water's surface glittered with millions of tiny lights. We were hungry and sad. We thought about our friend Haleem, who had just lost his older brother on the eastern fronts. We were saddened because Haleem now was the only adult male member in the family with five little siblings and a paralyzed mother. We talked about school and Haleem's brother Hazem and how young he was and how sad it was that he had to die. That's when Hamid paused for a long moment and then turned to me with a clear look in his eyes and firm voice. Hamid told me that he would never serve in the army and if anyone tried to force him to do so, he would kill them.

"No man will tell me how to live or how to die, and what to die for," he said. Then he looked back at the Euphrates and added, "Not even a divine leader sent by Allah."

While I was sitting with Hamid, I saw Amel peeking from her room; she was looking at me. She was staring at me like she was mad at me for some reason. Hamid and I sat on the roof for hours before his mother came home and brought us dinner from Haleem's house.

To this day, every time I remember the coolness of that evening, the simplicity of the night's setting sun, and the ray of emotional streaks that came from people's generosity and not from the sad event of the death of our friend's brother—in spite of the sad and accusing looks from Amel—I think that that night was the closest to serenity and happiness I had ever felt. It was not the happiness of the events, but a complete happiness of all the senses synchronized together on a non-dimensional track where time and reality just did not matter. Just to feel, hear, see, and sense the exact moment of time, like it was moving through my veins. I was really happy and content with my inner feelings. They were real, no matter how sad or happy I was. The emotion was so vivid in my heart that I felt that I could trace the blood in my veins, meet the fears and uncertainties that were deep down within me, and confront them with my everlasting being, without a single doubt about the validity and purpose of my existence.

On that dark night, the moon washed the mud hut with its silver brush. To this day I wish that I would never have had to leave that night or any of the nights that I spent at Hamid's house, Haleem's house, Barrya's mud hut, or the soccer field, in the school, or just in the streets walking and getting dirt on my feet because my sandals broke off from overuse, drowning in the Euphrates, chasing mysterious fish that knew our names, our faces and our voices, drinking the rainwater that fell from the leaves of the palm trees while the heavenly sun dried the gleaming, cold, fresh, unpolluted water, and the heat of the Iraqi southern parts all slashed the boredom out of a life that would never change. That was my black hole, the black hole of innocence, wilderness, love, and hope.

But for my father, it was the right time to leave, because he had just had it with his squad of policemen, where the youngest one of them was older than the palm trees in the courtyard of the mayor's office building. None of them were willing to retire. He had had it with the party headquarters because in reality he had no authority. Even on things like the sewage system, and the time when my father assigned the only gardener that the town had to grade our soccer field, he needed the approval of the party's highest ranking comrade. To my father, Balluria was like a prison with no gates, and he just wanted to escape as soon as he could.

That evening I found out why Amel was upset with me. She had heard from Hanan, who had come to our home with one of the many women who wore black robes in the sheikh's house. They came to our house and found out that that we were leaving. My sister told Hanan, who was her classmate, that we were leaving town. That was the first time I ever saw Hanan up close; she had almost run into me when she entered our house, totally covered with a dark abaya. I was on my way out to meet Hamid, when the trail of her female scent, which would make any man follow her to the end of the world, caught up with me. The woman with her, who I thought was her mother, seemed invisible. Hanan had come to visit, because she wanted to buy some of my sister's collections of Burda fashion magazines that my sister brought with her from the capital. That's also when I found out that Amel and I had created a bond, something that she might have created in her imagination and never told me about, a world that only the two of us belonged in and where she felt that she could not live without me. I never knew about its existence, or maybe I just did not want to know about it; nonetheless, it was there. Amel did not want me to leave, and deep inside, I did not want to leave Balluria. Not because of Amel and our dark shade poetry. Rather, I did not want to leave Hamid, Adnan, Hisham, Haleem, and the Wolves. I did not want to leave our boat, the *Tetaneek*, and for some reason I did not want to leave Barrya and her crazy tales about adventurous Arab men roaming the Sahara in search of true love and fortune. I did not want to leave the seven palm trees where the secret of manhood manifested itself in the gelatinous forms of harmony of man, beast, and reality, mixed in the imagination of children with believable fairy tales. I did not want to leave my adolescent years behind, because I had just started to smell the aroma of the early April orange trees blossoming white flowers in my veins and arteries. Even though I knew that the world would exist for millions of years and never realize or feel the existence of Balluria, I just did not want to leave that day. And for some reason I remembered the line of poetry that Amel read to me many times and felt how true it was.

> *Death is a hidden world*
> *That infatuates children*
> *And its secret gate is*
> *Within you, oh... Euphrates*

I was an infatuated child who did not want to leave Balluria. Amel was right because she told me many times that she believed Balluria was the gate to death.

2

My mother made sure that the house was cleaned and spotless for the upcoming family that would replace us in the house, and their father would replace my father in his job. I learned that the new mayor had no children; it was just he and his wife. They showed up one day before we left to wish my parents good luck and to examine the new house. My mother was a gracious hostess and offered to leave several of our household items behind for them, which they thankfully accepted. My sister and my brother had neglected their packing completely and had to slave two days prior to our departure with their cleaning and duties as I successfully managed to escape it all.

I realized that I had not confronted my sister about the love letters that I had found in her book. They were from Ahmed, and she had never replied to them, so I did not say anything to her. I just looked at her and realized that she had grown; she had black, wondering eyes and a sharp memory. "She will be a doctor," I said to myself. I never told her that I knew about the love letters. I just did not want to invade her privacy and her special world that every young woman needed to create in these parts to escape the real world. I especially did not want to waste my final hours in Balluria by creating a situation where traditions and other nonsensical actions, which I would be forced to follow, would take too much time and energy.

The sound of the Qur'an being recited at Haleem's house pierced the air. My father went to the funeral to pay his respects with the new mayor, who spent the night in his office while his wife slept at our house. I did not have anything to do, so I just inhaled the last breeze of air in Balluria, and I spent as much time with Hamid as possible. At noon, Hamid and I walked through the soccer field and went to Hisham's house where we found Ahmed, Kamal, and Adnan sitting in the guest room playing chess and dominos. We stayed there for an hour watching Adnan win all the chess matches games, which were all five-minute timed. Then we went to visit Barrya; she was preparing food and yogurt.

We sat in her breezy, cold hut, which never seemed to be affected by the scorching heat. It seemed like it had a secret window to another world.

"Salam, I heard that you and your family are leaving to go to Baghdad," she commented.

"Yes, we will leave today or tomorrow," I said.

"Tell your mother I said good-bye, and don't tell your father anything." She laughed the laugh that chased the shadows off the walls. I never understood her comment about my father. I thought it was just the Gypsy people's sarcasm and their ways of talk. Later, I learned that my father the mayor tried unsuccessfully to force the Gypsy woman to leave Balluria.

Hamid and I grilled and ate the fish that he caught that morning, and we drank the yogurt. Then we laid down for a nap. I don't remember how long we had slept, but I remember my dream. I dreamed that two hands with a silky, smooth, and gentle touch had undressed me and caressed my body and my hair. I felt like a vigilant child who started to feel for the first time. I could not see the person; I could only see the hands. I did not want the dream to end, because I was afraid to lose the feeling of ultimate satisfied belonging. The hands were not those of my mother or any other woman that I knew but they were definitely a woman's hands. The feeling was similar to the serenity I felt on the roof of Hamid's mud hut, looking at the Euphrates. This was a human touch, and electricity was shooting through me deep into my flesh, blood, and bones. It tore my chest apart and took out my heart and washed it with a cold, slick, oily liquid that left nothing behind except complete spotlessness and eternal light. The hand covered my eyes, and the darkness of its palm was like velvet. In my dream, I saw many people that I knew, but I had never talked to them, nor had I ever thought that my life would cross with theirs. Yet they were close to me, and the hand kept caressing my face and my hair in way that seemed like a christening. I saw Sheikh Jawad, the fearsome ruler of these parts, my friends Ahmed and Hanan, and the caretakers of my friend Kamal. I had never sat nor talked to the sheikh, because he was scary to me, and also he never liked my father. I saw him sitting alone listening to the song of Nasser Hakeem, who sang about men's lives in these parts.

> *Be patient oh man it's only life,*
> *After hardship it will ease up,*
> *Never let go of your dignity,*
> *Always keep your pride,*
> *Step hard on the ground and build yourself from dirt,*
> *We have never seen a man,*
> *Who died before his day.*

I was not sure why he appeared in my dream, but I did not mind, because in my dream he was not as frightening as he was in real life. In fact, I felt he was as normal as my father and as friendly as many older figures I knew. He seemed so nonthreatening in my dream. I saw Jelwi, the toughest and oldest sergeant of police this world had ever seen, smoking his cigarettes and coughing his lungs out, singing Hussain Nimma's most popular love song at that time.

> *Throw your handkerchiefs, oh virgins,*
> *In sadness and look how red the lips are,*
> *When you see the wedding parade,*
> *Cry for me.*
> *Cry for my soul as it is so gentle and cannot handle all of this,*
> *As they cheered for the wedding of my love.*
> *To another man she went,*
> *Night moon and stars, my soul is crushed,*
> *As I hear the joyful noise of the wedding of my love,*
> *And my life will be spent with waiting and patience.*

For some reason Jelwi's voice was sweet and had lost its extreme scratchiness. I did not hear any songs of my own; I did not hear Fairuz, Michael Jackson, or Elton John. I only heard the tunes that the people in these parts listened to. Although they were enjoyable and real, in my dream I did not want the hands to stop touching or caressing me, but suddenly, the mysterious hands stopped. This ceasing caused me to wake up; Hamid was still napping. I looked toward the end of the room and saw Barrya looking at me with a strange examining glare, almost cursing me with her eyes. I had never paid much attention to her. Although I had been to her house a hundred times before, she always paid more attention to Hamid, Adnan, Ahmed, Hisham, and the girls. She always called me the kid from Baghdad or the magistrate's son. She never could distinguish between a mayor and the magistrate since they meant the same thing in these parts, but one day, she started calling me by my name. Once she leaned over and kissed me on the cheek, and I looked and saw the space between her breasts, which appeared to me like a tanned, secret canyon to another world, a world I was not supposed to be in or think about for the sake of the decency of social classes and terms of behavior.

From the look in her eyes, I realized that she wanted to say something to me, like she knew about the dream I had. I felt like she wanted to tell me something that would change my entire life, but I did not want to listen, and I had no time left. I did not want to hear anything. I was afraid, and I was not sure of what she wanted me to do, and her bluntness was so scary to me. I was too young, and I had all the excuses in the world not to hear what the Gypsy woman wanted to say that afternoon when she was looking at me that way. Looking at her eyes, I knew it would not be simple, normal, or harmless. She was like our mother, and I was not her favorite kid. Although I had taken advantage of her help and generosity many times, like when we built the soccer field goals and netted the nets, the time when she offered her endless fresh yogurt that quenched our thirst whenever we were defeated by the Wild Lions, or when she willingly conspired to have me have some moments alone with Adawya, the younger Hillaly girl,

However, I knew that she had something to say to me because I was about to leave Balluria, something about her or about another person, something that might tie me to Balluria forever, or maybe she felt that she was losing me too soon, and she did not claim me as her son as she did with all the others. I was just a passerby. I may be one of the Wolves, but I was not like the others to her. I knew that from the beginning. I knew that we would leave Balluria one day, so I paid no attention to the faces, eyes, or hearts around me. Barrya could not change that, not with her Gypsy magic or with that look in her eyes that could have changed a king's heart. I was an arrogant sixteen-year-old whose father had already planned his future for him, a sixteen-year-old who did not belong in these parts, and I only had twenty-four hours left in Balluria. She kept looking at me, and then she backed down, probably because she read my mind. I wanted to say something to her, anything, but I found no words. She would just have to accept that I was not like the others. I didn't need that milk from her; she could feed the others, but not me. Hamid finally woke up and asked her, "Mother Barrya, can we have some tea?"

She poured tea from the kettle that was never empty or cold from the first day I entered her house. She poured two cups, looked at me, and said, "One day, you will come back. Even if you go beyond the seven seas, cross the mountains of darkness, the plains of manhood, even if you see the blue and green eyes, you will come back to the only mother that you know. The hands will guide you. I see that in the stones of fortune, you will come back looking for love but it will be too late then."

I didn't know what she was talking about and did not know what to say, nor did I clearly remember my dream of the two hands with a silky touch. Hamid and I drank our tea in a hurry, and we left Barrya's mud hut. I did not know that it would not be the last time for me to ever be in the Gypsy woman's mud hut.

Hamid asked, "What was she talking about?"

"I don't know," I answered.

"Are you coming back, maybe one day, to Balluria?" Hamid asked.

"I don't know. Maybe one day. Or maybe I just won't leave," I said sarcastically.

"You can live with me in our house," Hamid said.

"I know I can, Hamid. We are like brothers," I replied.

"We are brothers," he confirmed, "and we always will be." Hamid was the only human being in this world that I could call my best friend. Out of the twenty kids my age that were either Wolves or just part of the group we all hung out with, I liked Adnan because we could talk about movies and books and America, things that Hamid had no interest in and no time for, but Hamid was my soul twin and the only one that I felt a real connection with. I was sad that we were leaving Balluria, but I was happy too, because I knew what my father had been planning for me once we got back to Baghdad. He was able to use some of his personal relationships with old friends to land me the approval to leave the country to study abroad, something that happens only in dreams. It could happen to only a few young students, maybe ten or twelve students in all the country.

My father did this, because he wanted me out of the country before the age of eighteen. The possibility of failure in school would land a man in a trench infested with leprosy on the eastern front. In exchange, my father had to pay bribes to the officials in the ministry of higher education and give many gifts—a watch here, a sheep there, a hundred dinars to this person, and on and on to the endless lists of beneficiaries. My father also had to travel to Baghdad several times to follow up on the paperwork to get the final approval from the intelligence agency, the national party headquarters, the passport agency, and many other agencies in order for me to be able to leave the country. I had to have a high grade point average, which I was earning anyway, and I had to sign a peace of paper that stated that I would return if the call to duty arose. My father, without telling me, sold the family home in Baghdad, where my mother had planted her garden, in order to secure payment of the bribes, for the travel expenses and for at least one year of living expenses for me. He was teaching me how to live abroad, but I did not pay much attention to his classes, as I was extremely absorbed with my life, especially the wild life I experienced with Hamid.

My father said to me that there were many things that were different from what I knew.

"Like what?" I asked.

"Well, like, some people could send their dogs to the market, and the dog would do the shopping, or there are places where people feel it's all right to take their clothes off and lie on the beaches all day."

Hearing that from my father was embarrassing and uncomfortable; I wanted to leave the room, but he insisted on telling me that when we got to the capital I would have some time before I traveled to study abroad. I wanted ask him if I could stay in Balluria for a little longer, but I did not ask, knowing what his answer would be.

My final day in Balluria had arrived, and the sun's rays were hidden behind the clouds. I skipped breakfast and went straight to Hamid's house; his mother made us fried dough and tea. Amel was noticeably sad. I did not know why she was being so dramatic, and I certainly could not figure out why she was blaming me. After we ate, Hamid and I walked along the river. He was not emotional at all. I intentionally tried to stay away from our house, because the memory of unloading the truck when we moved here was still fresh in my mind. This time, however, my father had almost twenty municipal workers loading the truck, which was being supervised by the oldest police force in the world, and

Sergeant Jelwi would make sure they did the job right, so there was no need for me to be there. I knew that my father had planned for us to leave in the afternoon, so I had plenty of time to spend with Hamid. We walked through the orchard where I saw his snake for the first time and the spot where I kissed Adawya, where Basima and Abdullah met at night in a sacred, innocent love ritual, and where Hamid started meeting Hanan. Then, we went to the river. At the river, the entire soccer team was waiting for me. It was a surprise. Hisham was already half naked and in the water. He had a bag of food, mostly tomatoes. Kamal was putting a fire together. Adnan was putting a cassette in the cassette player, and songs of Boney M's were coming.

Brown girl in the ring,
Shlalalalala,
She was a brown girl in the ring.

Hamid and the other Wolves decided to have a lunch with me by the river, and out of nowhere, Fathil the Liar appeared and was commenting about the music of Boney M.

"This band is not from Germany. They are from England, and they are communists, and they sang the song 'Rasputin.'"

I was hoping that he would stop before he made his lies extremely unbelievable, but what he said about the band was true. He was correct; nevertheless, he continued.

"I met them, and they told me this in England, when I was on a special mission," but it was Fathil the Liar, who seemed to be on an eternal secret mission from the president and would always meet musicians and movie stars.

Kamal said, "We need some fish. Ahmed is bringing bread, vegetables, and some onions, so we only need fish."

Hamid said he would get the fish, and he went to unhook the nearest boat. Adnan went with him to get away from Fathil and his stories. Minutes after that, Ashraf showed up with a huge watermelon in his hands, walking with Salah. I looked at the boat that Hamid freed and jumped on with his silliya net. Adnan was lying down in the front of the boat with his hands in the water, as he always did. His eyes were lost in the water, and soon enough Hamid and Adnan managed to catch almost thirty small to midsized fish, enough to feed all of us. The boys were dancing and swimming, and Hisham was dancing an unknown dance and screaming the whole time, while looking at me and smiling. Dancing and swimming, dancing and swimming, he was trying to dance the famous John Travolta dance on the muddy bank of the Euphrates when Hamid brought his catch back to where Kamal and Ahmed started grilling the tomatoes and onions on the open fire. Some of the boys were still in the water when Hisham looked at the end of the road where the orchard began and shouted, "Oh my God!"

We all looked toward where he was looking, and we saw Barrya and Haleem walking toward us. Barrya was carrying a metal jar full of what we all guessed to be fresh cold yogurt, and Haleem was carrying a stack of fresh bread that Hamid's mother had baked for the funeral. We felt awkward, because he was mourning his brother and here we were dancing to the music of Boney M. He gave the bread to Ahmed and put us at ease when he said, "You don't need to mind my feelings. Although the pain and sadness because of my brother that was in my heart will not disappear now, I am here because I want to be here with you," Haleem said.

That afternoon we swam, danced, ate the grilled fish, bread, and vegetables, and we drank the yogurt. Around two o'clock in the afternoon, I saw my younger brother walking toward us, and I knew that it was time to leave.

"I have to leave," I said.

Adnan stopped the music, and all of my friends lined up to bid me farewell. Kamal shook my hand and said, "I might see you in Baghdad. I may go there for training or something."

Ahmed just shook my hand, kissed me on each cheek, and said, "I will miss you." Hisham started crying and told me that he would never forget me and how he must look for new good midfielder for the soccer team now. It was sad because I was not a good midfielder.

Haleem embraced me and said, "You are adding more sadness to my heart. You are a good friend, and I wish that you could stay in Balluria." I embraced him and wished that we could spend one more afternoon walking under the windows of the Hillaly girls' house.

Ashraf and Salah told me to come back and visit. "We will be here," Ashraf said. Fathil the Liar shook my hand and looked at me like he was seeing me for the first time in his life. He told me that he was stationed in Baghdad by the Republican Palace, near where the divine leader lived, and he said that if I needed anything I could just look for him near the palace or he might run into me one day. But I knew that would never happen.

Adnan embraced me longer. He kissed me on the cheeks and said, "Never forget me, and never forget the Euphrates. If you have a chance, come back to see us." I almost cried as I felt that his words were coming from the heart.

Hamid waited until everyone else had bid their farewells and then he walked to me, shook my hand, looked me in the eyes, and said, "I know I will never see you again. I can feel it in my heart. Just remember that we are and always will be brothers, and make sure you live the life of a real man." Then he whispered in my ear, "If you have time, you could say farewell to my mother and my sister." I embraced Hamid, and I knew he would not have time to come with me to my house.

Without saying a word, Barrya just looked at me with same look she had in her eyes when I was napping in her mud hut.

I left the riverbank and all my friends and my heart behind. While I was climbing the sandy barrier, I looked back at my friends, and I saw what looked like a real family of wolves with their mother sitting in the middle of an enchanted wilderness, I had a strange feeling that I was the first Wolf to leave the pack and maybe would be the only one. That was the last time I saw the Wolves.

3

When I got to our house my father was angry because I was late. I found many people at our house saying their good-byes and good wishes and helping to load household items. A messenger from Sheikh Jawad showed up and whispered something in my father's ear. Then he left as quickly as he had arrived. Sayed Habeeb, the clergyman, came to recite a prayer over the moving truck and talked to my father briefly. I was consumed with sadness; I wanted to go back and stay with the Wolves by the riverbank. My sister was crying; almost all of her friends from school had come to say good-bye to her. Hanan was there, and so were Basima and the Hillaly girls. Their mother and many other girls that I knew by face only were there. Amel and her mother were there, and I could see that Amel was trying to leave the room where all the women were. She was looking from the door to see if I was there. She looked at me several times. I could see that she was crying. Her eyes were red, and I realized that she wanted to tell me something, so I walked to the kitchen door that led to the outside and pretended to fill up a jar with water from the outside faucet. I was hoping to see Adawya, the younger Hillaly girl. Maybe I could kiss her one last time, but there were too many people around, and she was nowhere to be seen.

I saw Amel peeking out from the kitchen door with tears and a look that begged me to come closer to her. When I did, she said, "We will miss you. I will miss you." Then she came closer to me and whispered as she tried to avoid being heard by other women in the room. "Promise me that you will always read poetry, the poetry of Al-Sayyab, and listen to Fairuz's songs. She smiled when she said that. It was as though she had waited all this time to talk to me, and that was the only thing she could think of to say.

"I promise," I said.

She choked back her tears and said, "Promise that you will never forget me and that you will write me letters."

I did not know why she wanted me to write her letters, but I replied, "I think my sister, Yusra, will write you."

I thought that was the appropriate response.

"No, I want you to write me. Promise me."

"I promise," I said, and that's when my father called for me.

Then suddenly almost thirty people emerged from our house: men, women, young girls, and children. They all walked my mother and my sister to the car. I never knew that they had made that many friends. Luckily, this time we had plenty of room in the car. My brother was the one who rode with the

553

truck driver back to Baghdad. I felt remorse for my brother, because his only two friends never made it to say good-bye to him. I jumped into the back of the car. My mother sat in the front, and my sister sat next to me. I looked for Hamid, but he was nowhere to be seen. The car started moving slowly, I looked around to see Balluria for the last time and thought to myself, *In my heart, always you will be.*

I turned to look back at the house, and Amel was looking at me and crying. I looked at her and smiled, hoping she would stop crying. She started walking beside the car when it started to move. Then she walked behind the car like she was going to chase it. She did not want us, or at least she did not want me, to leave. When the car sped up, raising a small cloud of dust, I saw Amel still walking and waving at the car.

Then my father shouted joyfully, "Finally, we are out of this miserable hole of scum."

A year and a half after we left Balluria, I was packing my bag to travel to Jordan, my first stop before traveling to Athens, then maybe Europe, and then to the United States of America. I was in my room trying to sleep, but excitement kept me up. I barely was able to close my eyes when, around four o'clock in the morning, I dreamed of Balluria again. In my dream, I felt hands creeping on me. They slipped their inescapable silky ropes around my wrists and dragged me back to the day we left Balluria. I had not kept in contact with any of my friends, but my sister gave me a letter she had received from Amel. I never opened it. Instead, I put it in a red shoe box and stashed it in the big bag that had all my belongings in it. In my dream that night I was in the car leaving Balluria and Amel was chasing the car. The car was too fast, and Amel was thirsty. She was very young and very little. I heard music. It was the music of Fairuz telling the story of the little princess who had no chance at love and no chance of leaving the castle with high walls. In my dream I was happy to leave Balluria. I looked back from the rear window of the car and saw Balluria and Amel for the last time. I saw the town and the girl. They both looked abandoned and alone. Balluria was dusty, and Amel looked like the ghost of a woman, standing there waving, disappearing in the eternal dust of Balluria.

The Book of the Gypsy Witches

Wolves Cry Alone

1

"One night after he killed Kamal and learned of the violent deaths of his two loyal companions, Hamid gave the cursed black dagger of death that ended many lives back to me to keep as a last secret to add to all of my other secrets."

"That night, when he cried the last of his tears, Hamid wore his father's bluish-black robe and mounted his horse, and into the wide-open desert he disappeared. Since then the legend of the mythical Arabian knight was born in these parts," the Gypsy woman said with a clear conviction and doubtless belief.

"People did not know that Hamid killed Kamal. No one knew Hamid by name at that time," the old woman said as she looked through the open door of the mud hut. Her voice became softer and quieter, as she remembered the last time she saw Hamid. "Many people had left Balluria by that time, many had forgotten about him, and many people have not been around for long time." The Gypsy lit a fresh cigarette and said through the smoke, "People in these parts only knew him as the wanted outlaw and the bandit who killed party officials and the tyrant's soldiers. They did not know about him and Kamal and Hanan. He had not been seen in these parts for such a long time. Sometimes I saw him riding his horse and running it to the prairie on the edge of the desert. Sometimes I heard the lonely howl of a wolf or a lonesome cry in the night and knew he was near, but he never came to my hut. Many people had talked about the ghost of a lonesome mythical knight on a majestic Arabian horse, but they all said he was always running his horse and never stopped to talk to people. No one knew who the knight was, but I knew it was him. It was Hamid, the only one of my Wolves who is still alive."

The man sat silently and waited for her to finish and did not say anything, when she mentioned that Hamid was the last of her Wolves who was still alive. Silently, he protested that she never once, since he had sat and listened to her, mentioned him as one of her Wolves. He wanted her to say that he was a Wolf too and that he was one of her children too. He was still alive as well. He wanted her so much to say that he was a Wolf. He had no idea why he desperately wanted her to say that, but she did not, and he was unable to ask, so he let her continue.

"He was the only one left, and lonesome wolves don't stay in one place because they will die. That's why he had to go to the desert. Riding his horse forever, he had to go to the desert so he could breathe, so he could be free for eternity," the Gypsy woman explained.

The man looked at her and realized what a mother of wolves she was. She knew her cubs very well. So he did not bother to assert his status as a wolf. Instead, he wanted to know about his friend, the true wolf.

"Is he still alive? Is Hamid still alive?" the man asked.

She looked at him with her blind eyes and said, "Hamid will never die. He will live forever because the spirits of all the wolves in the Arabian Sahara live through the ages within him. He was born to be a wolf."

The blind woman asked, "Would you like more tea?"

2

One night before he went into the desert forever, and three nights after miraculously escaping certain death when the tyrant's troops crushed the small rebellion of the notorious outlaw known as the prince of the marshes, Hamid and his two loyal companions, Rashid and Jassim, came riding their horses close to Balluria. Hamid looked at his house and swore that he would never leave Balluria that night unless he could see his mother. His two friends begged him not to do so because the authorities in Balluria were just waiting for them. Hamid's two companions told him that a ruthless man named Comrade Kamal, had sworn to kill Hamid on sight, but Hamid was not ready to listen because he desperately wanted to see his mother and his sister.

The three men dismounted about half a kilometer away from the only bridge in town and walked in the night toward the shimmering lights of Balluria. As they crossed the bridge, one old man kept staring at the three rugged men with their faces covered with their kuffia masks, their Kalashnikovs' muzzles peeking from the bottoms of their robes. Walking in silence, they noticed the old man had looked at them longer than usual but did not suspect anything, deciding that he was too old to do anything. He was too old to go to the town and inform the police and the party headquarters. Even then, the two men asked Hamid to be quick because they knew that the town was filled with party militiamen who were aching to kill the gang of the three bandits. When they reached the house, Hamid knocked on the door when his two loyal companions positioned themselves in the dark shadows of the orchard trees nearby, waiting for the unexpected.

When she heard the familiar knock, which she had not heard for years, Amel shouted, "Mino? Who is there?"

"Shinnaga, open the door," Hamid replied as he tried to make his voice quieter than he wished to. That was her nickname, which he had called her since she was a baby. Amel was in tears as she opened the door to see her brother with his stone like engraved features, dark tanned skin, ruggedness flowing from every shade of color in his eyes, and the unlimited manhood of a desperate Arabian outlaw. She cried, hugged him, and hung from his neck as though by doing so she could prevent him from ever leaving again. To her, he was not only an older brother. He was a brother and the father and the poetic friend that could not leave. To her, he was the love of a lifetime that would never travel beyond the borders of Balluria.

His mother stood nearby wiping her tears, looking at her son, realizing what grave danger he put himself in, just to see them briefly. At the same time, she realized that this must be the last time she would see her only son, her only man. She would smell him for the last time. She would kiss him for the last time, and she would never see him again. She realized that as he looked at her son who looked at her and said, "Mother, Ishlonik, how are you?"

She did not answer. Instead, she covered her face with her hand when she saw the shadows of Hamid's two loyal companions and said, "You have other men with you; they can come in the other room. I will prepare dinner."

There was no time for dinner. Hamid sat with his mother and his sister, Amel, who kept asking him all the questions she could think of. "How are you, brother? Where have you been? Are you leaving us again? Can you stay? Can you take me and Mother with you? Are you wounded? What happened in the marshes? Were you with the prince of the marshes?"

He smiled at her, and then he replied gently and lovingly, "Shinnaga, one day I will tell you all about it."

His two companions had barely enough time and patience to eat half a piece of bread with vegetables and drink some tea. Then they stood up, mumbling their gratitude and thanks for the hospitality.

"Sufrra Amra. May Allah bless your table and your house." They grabbed their rifles and headed toward the door.

Hamid stood up and looked at his mother. There was nothing to say. He pulled a stack of dinar bills with the tyrant's face on them from his pocket and placed them on the floor. Then he reached to his waist and pulled out a black pistol that he put on the floor. He looked at his mother, asking, "When was the last time Kamal and his men were here looking for me?"

"They were here last week and the week before that. They come here looking for you every time something happens in these parts. They say it's you who did it," Amel answered.

Hamid looked at his sister and asked, "You remember before I left, I showed you how to shoot the pistol?"

"Yes."

He gave her the pistol. "I know that Kamal and his dogs will come here again looking for me and that they will search the house. They will tear things and break things. You let them do that and don't resist, but make sure that they don't find this." He handed her the pistol. "If they ever try to humiliate you, dishonor you, or touch you then you will know what to do."

Amel fought back her tears and wrapped her arms around his neck, kissing him on the cheek. He pulled her hands down as he smiled, saying, "You are almost as tall as I am, Shinnaga. I want you to do something for me. I want you to keep reading the poetry that you are reading and always listen to Fairuz's songs and sing them with her as you listen and stay like this. Don't change, and don't worry about what the townspeople say about me or you and our mother. We are poor people. We have been poor all our lives, and we will be poor for the rest of our lives." He looked at his young sister, trying to find that hope that she always possessed in her eyes. "Our ancestors have been poor peasants since day they were born, just like the people of this town and the many towns and villages by the marshes. There are mean and bad people who think that we are not worthy of living and will try to make you believe that. Don't believe them, and don't worry, Shinnaga. You stay the way you are. Read poetry and sing, and you will always be alive and, God knows, maybe one day he will return."

"Who?"

"Salam," said Hamid, noticing the colors of life returning to his sister's eyes when she heard the name. "Maybe one day he will return and take you away from this place. Has he responded to your letters?"

"No, not yet," she replied with a shy childish voice filled with tears.

He hugged her. "He will. I am sure he will one day. You just keep sending him letters and go visit Barrya whenever you can. She is alone, and she has no one left except us, and take care of this woman here," Hamid said, as he pointed to his mother. "Our mother, because as much as I tried not to, I am sure I have disappointed her plenty, just like our father, whoever he was, did before. She is alone, and you are alone. I will always be close by. I will not die until I make sure that you and she are safe. Let go of me now, Shinnaga."

She pulled her hands down and walked to his mother saying, "I must go now, Mother."

His mother looked in his eye. He was no longer the child that she had birthed, nor the toddler who walked long before others his age. He was not the twelve-year-old boy who hunted and fished by himself to keep his family from starving in the cold nights of the southern winter when older fishermen of the town did not dare to risk the elements. He was not the young man who cried from love when he first felt the pinch of his heart, when he saw Hanan walking to school with his sister. He was not the man she envisioned a long time ago in his father's robe dancing with a sword on his wedding night, the wedding night of her son, the night that every woman in these parts waits for. To his mother, Hamid was not even a human; he was a wild wolf that would never be domesticated. His eyes had fire, a desert fire, where there was no rain to extinguish it.

So she realized that she had no choice but to let go of him without saying a word, because there was nothing that she could say that would bring her son back to her and just like her husband before, her son was leaving too. It seemed as though she must accept that fate. That all the men in her life must leave at an early age. Although they all were rugged and tanned and had the overflow of manhood in their veins, they all left even with the brightness of love pouring from their eyes and the natural unlimited goodness and courage that goes beyond the boundaries of fear itself. They all leave and go to the desert. Then they all turn into mysterious knights. They ride horses like they were built from their backs. Then they all turn to legends, legends of Arabian knights, like an inescapable destined evolution. She looked at her son's eyes for the last time.

"May Allah protect you, my son."

"He will," he answered, putting his kuffia mask back on his face again and grabbing his notorious Kalashnikov. Then he signaled to his two loyal companions to be ready.

"Oh, what a knight," his mother said, wishing to hold him forever and never let go, because in the end no matter how brave he was and no matter how rugged he looked and no matter what legend of a fearless man he became and no matter what the people in these parts said and would say about him and his gang of bandits, he was still her first child, her man, her son, her only son.

She cried, "Wait, son. There is something I want to give you." She disappeared in the back of the room and came back with what looked like a wrapped artifact. She started unwrapping the white cloth and exposed a magnificent Arabian robe with silver lining and majestic bluish black color. She unwrapped the robe and said, "It was your father's robe, and now it's yours. I have no chance of seeing you wearing it in your wedding. I am giving it to you now because I don't know if I will ever see you again."

Amel began to cry, and so did one of the two bandits. Hamid took the robe and looked at his mother. He wanted to say something, but he realized that wolves don't apologize for the way they live; they follow their natural instinct, and he knew that there would be nothing that he might say that would compensate a mother for her son. Hamid consoled himself with the thought that wolves like him only react to things and feelings imposed on them by others; they do not feel pain. They cry, and when they cry they cry alone. He took the robe and disappeared into the dark, where his two companions were waiting impatiently.

They walked back the same way they came, and that was their mistake, because the old man who spotted the three men with their horses crossing the bridge worked as the night watchman at the high school, where he had known Hamid since he was a boy. He was familiar with his face and the way he walked. He was quick to realize who the three men were. After thinking about what he must do, the old man sent his grandson to the party headquarters where Kamal had waited for months to hear news about Hamid and his bandits. Kamal hastily mobilized a force of twenty party militiamen and sent them to bridge to ambush Hamid. He told them to wait for the three men by the bridge and concluded with a strict order.

"If the skies fall on the earth, do not allow him to escape. I want him alive. Alive. You can kill the others but I want Hamid alive."

The militiamen walked through the orchards in the darkness. When they reached the bridge, they positioned themselves by its two ends, hid in the thick reeds and bushes by the riverbanks, and waited nervously for the notorious three-man gang. The militiamen were scared because they knew how fearless and skilled with rifles and knives the three men were.

They did not have to wait long with their anticipating eyes fixed on the dirt road that led from the bridge to Balluria. As Hamid and his two companions approached the river and noticed the suspicious calmness, it was Rashid who felt that something was not right. He did not see any other people crossing the bridge even though it was almost ten o'clock at night and people in Balluria usually are gathering around fires and coffee, but it was unusually quiet. Too quiet, like the calm before a storm. A bullet storm. That is what it felt like when the three approached the bridge. The three men started walking cautiously with their horses on the bridge. Hamid's horse jumped when movements from the thick reeds by the riverbanks became loud and noticeable. He had just enough time to let go of his horse and reach for his fearsome Kalashnikov. He loaded its chamber with a bullet and aimed in the darkness, when the twenty-party militia opened fire.

3

The old woman inhaled her cigarette and paused for a moment as she remembered the accounts of that bloody night.

"Many thought that Hamid was killed that night. They thought that he was shot and drowned in the Euphrates. I knew that he was alive. Just hours after the battle on the bridge, Hamid was here sitting where you are sitting now, bleeding from his leg and arm, and I was sitting where I am sitting now, burning my scarf and mixing it with the Gypsy herb remedy so I could stop the bleeding from his wounds."

"How did he survive?" the man asked.

"Wolves don't die that way. That night the town shook with the sound of rounds of fire and bullets coming from the river, and the people gathered in the streets wondering what could the fighting be, and they walked to the river. When I heard the sound of the fierce battle coming from the river, I knew it was him. I knew it was Hamid, so I put my abaya cover on and went to see. When I reached Hamid's house, I saw the people returning from the river as the party militiamen were dragging the two gravely wounded men to the town's square.

"People in Balluria gathered around Jassim and Rashid as the party militiamen dragged them with ropes and laid them in the town's square awaiting the orders of Comrade Kamal, who went to the river looking for the body of Hamid. The people in Balluria were surprised because they thought that the gang of the three bandits would never be caught. People looked at the bodies of the nearly dead men, which had been shredded by so many bullets. They also looked at the dead corpses of nine of the militiamen comrades that were laid in front of the party headquarters.

"Comrade Kamal returned from the riverbanks with the search party, and he was furious when he realized that Hamid had escaped the ambush. He started screaming and called the party militiamen cowards and morons and threatened an investigation against all those who acted in such a cowardly way in the service of the party and the country.

"As he went into a shouting frenzy of how he would find Hamid in the town and execute him in the morning, he kicked the nearly dead Jassim and Rashid with his boots and he emptied his pistol into their bodies. He ordered his men into the white Land Cruiser. They drove again to the land beyond the bridge looking for Hamid or Hamid's body. They returned that night empty-handed.

"When I saw Kamal doing what he did to the dead bodies of two bandits, I knew that he was angry enough to kill, and I knew that he would hurt Hamid's sister, Amel, and her mother, so I went to their house to warn them and protect them if I could. I also knew that if he saw me at their house, he would kill me. Then Kamal went to Hamid's home and kicked the door open and screamed at Amel and her mother and demanded that they tell him where Hamid was," the Gypsy woman said, and she started to weep again.

"I saw him as he slapped Hamid's mother and pulled Amel's hair. He put his hand in her long black hair, pinned her to the ground, and said, 'I swear to the holiest things that I believe in, if you don't tell me what where your brother is, I will burn this house and its inhabitants. I will. I know that he is not dead.'

"'Don't touch me,' Amel cried. 'I swear to you on the soul of Hanan. Don't touch me, Kamal.'

"She knew that this would bring him back to humanity. She had no other defense, not even with the pistol that Hamid gave her, which was within her reach, under her dress. She did not and could not use the pistol to shoot Kamal. She chose to use love to get herself and her mother out of an almost certain death. She chose to use the memory of her dead friend, so she could save herself and her mother. She swore on Hanan's soul and she knew that Kamal would listen to her. Kamal softened his grip on her hair, and then he let go of her hair and ordered his men out of the house and looked at Amel and spoke to her in a quiet voice that vibrated with tension.

"'Only because of Hanan.' he said.

"He walked toward the door, leaving the two women in their fearful tears, and before he exited, he turned to Amel.

"'If you see your brother again, tell him that it is time for us to meet. Tell him that I am waiting for him.'"

The old woman blew the smoke from her cigarette, letting it curl around her head like a lazy snake.

"What Kamal did not know is that I was there hiding behind the pile of palm tree trunks next to the clay wok."

"But how did Hamid survive the ambush?" the man asked again, hoping that the Gypsy woman would answer directly, for once.

"The Euphrates saved him."

"Pardon me?"

"When the shooting happened, Hamid emptied his rifle into the bodies of four of Kamal's men, and when he was shot, he dove into the river. He told me that he felt the bite of the flamed lead entering his left thigh. He also told me that he felt like he lost all of his strength when he dove into the Euphrates and was sure that he would drown so he submitted his soul to the mighty current and tried to pray. Hamid told me that he looked into the darkness of the Euphrates' depths. He knew that it was death that he saw, but he was wrong. It was not his time to leave.

"He told me that as he drifted into the soothing feeling of drowning, he felt he was pulled by four hands from his hands and shoulders, two hands from each side of him, and he felt the four hands were pushing him upward toward the surface. He felt the gentle touch of the two hands holding his form, his shoulders, and pushing him to where he breathed again. Hamid told me that the four hands were familiar in their touch and in their caring. He knew they were Ahmed's and Adnan's hands—my two gentle Wolves that never left the river where they died."

The old woman cried for a moment.

"Hamid told me that he turned around to look at his saviors and saw Ahmed and Adnan smiling at him without saying a word as they pushed him up to the surface."

The man looked at her, not wanting to interrupt. He knew that any question from him about accuracy and logic and would be extremely inappropriate.

"Bleeding from his arm and leg, my Wolf crawled to where he could look for his horse. He did not know what had happened to his two companions. He found his horse by the riverbank waiting for his master who mounted his horse and took the swamp road that leads to the outskirts of the town, close to the seven palm trees. Later that night, as the people of the town were still looking at the bullet-shredded corpses of Rashid and Jassim at the main square by the market, I came back from Hamid's house. I went there to see what Kamal had done. Hamid's mother asked me not to tell Hamid, but Amel whispered in my ear what Kamal told her. Kamal was waiting for Hamid. I came back and waited for him. Not long after that, I heard the cry of his horse. Then Hamid came into my hut, and he sat where you are sitting now and said simply, 'I am wounded.'

"He asked what happened to his two loyal companions and I told him they were dead. Then I burned my scarf and mixed it with dry herbs and filled his wounds to stop the bleeding. He did not seem to feel the pain of his wounds."

Then he asked if Kamal had gone to his house.

"I said yes and that he told Amel that he was waiting for you.

"Hamid asked if Kamal had touched his sister or mother. I said he needed to go see Kamal."

The old Gypsy woman paused as she looked at the man, as though she could see him. She pushed a gray cloud of smoke from her mouth and explained, "There was no sense in telling him what happened between Hamid and Amel," the Gypsy woman said, "because Hamid and Kamal were both waiting to meet for the last time that night. Since they were young boys, they both had evaded that last meeting, because they knew one of them must die by the other's hand. When I told him that Kamal was waiting for him that night, Hamid looked at me.

"'I will go see him tonight, and one of us must die.' he said.

"That night I knew for certain that Hamid would kill Kamal. I knew that one of my children must die, but I had no remorse, because Kamal, that evil child of mine, had to die," the old Gypsy woman said as her voice grew louder with anger. "He was the evil, damned child of mine. I searched in all the corners of my heart to find mercy for Kamal but it was not there so I resorted to grief and sadness and chose to live with pain of sending a child of mine to kill another child of mine." Her anger gave way to tears.

"Maybe I was not a good mother to him, but Kamal needed peace, and if he died he would find peace in the other side of being. I thought, when he goes to the world of the dead and sees Hanan, he will find peace."

Suddenly she stopped crying, and her face lit up with a strange color. "At that moment, I remembered the dagger—the black, rusted dagger that Ahmed brought to me the night he killed himself. The same dagger that Kamal slashed Hanan's beautiful neck with and cut off her beautiful balsamic hands."

"The same dagger?"

"Yes. I gave Hamid the dagger and told him that when he went to meet Kamal he must kill him with this dagger. This dagger had entered Hanan's heart, and Kamal used this dagger to sever Hanan's palms," the Gypsy woman said as she choked with tears. "Hamid took the dagger from me. He looked at it. He cried and kissed the dagger's blade, cried some more, and started calling her name. 'Hanan. Hanan. Oh, Hanan.' Like a child, Hamid sobbed and wept as he sat in the same place you sit right now."

"Why did you give him the dagger?"

"It's fate, my son," the Gypsy woman simply replied. "Then Hamid stood up and said to me that he was going to meet Kamal. If Kamal killed him, he should be buried by the seven palm trees next to Hanan." He walked out, and I watched him as he disappeared in the dust."

The Gypsy woman stopped talking briefly as she inhaled her cigarette and drank her tea.

"That night after he killed Kamal, Hamid came here to my hut. He was covered with blood, his and Kamal's. He again sat in the same place you are sitting now. Sad and alone, he sat in this place for hours without saying a word. It seemed that he had no reason for staying in these parts. Hamid then told me that he would go into the desert and never come back. That night Hamid gave me back the black dagger and told me that he did not need it anymore, and since then, and for all of these years, I have kept the black dagger with me right here."

She reached back to the box of secrets that she kept and pulled out a dagger that looked like it was made by the crafty demons of hell, a black dagger with rusted blade and dried blood stains on it and a thick black leather grab. She showed it to the man.

"Do you want to hold it?" the old Gypsy woman asked.

"No, ma'am, thank you," the man replied as a shiver of cold fear ran through his spine. He looked at the dagger that had entered many hearts and ended many lives. The old woman put the dagger back in the box.

She inhaled her cigarettes and said, "That night, after he killed Kamal, Hamid came back to my hut and gave me the black dagger and said to me, 'Only you and the desert, Barrya. Only you and the desert.'

"And into the desert he went," she concluded

4

On the night after the battle of the bridge, and one night after he killed his childhood friend and before Hamid rode his horse to the desert and disappeared into the dust, he made a final pilgrimage to the seven palm trees, where long years before, he and a group of young boys saw a pack of young wolves dreaming. That night he sat on the back of his horse and saluted the graves.

"Peace be upon you, the dead. You have been to the land of mercy, of no pain, and no earthly strings."

It was a salute that Sayed Habeeb taught him and the group of boys long years ago.

Then Hamid dismounted from his horse, feeling the pain in his hand and thigh. He looked at the many graves by the seven palm trees. He noticed that the palm trees were starting to die. He thought that the blood of Kamal was the final blood that would irrigate the soil of the seven palm trees. The wind started to blow harder and the leaves began to fall from the trees. As he looked at Balluria from the comfortable distance of another dimension of being, he felt the magnitude of his lonesomeness and sat by Hanan's grave, touching the dirt that covered the remains of the woman that he loved, and he wept. He wept for hours and wished that he would die that night so he could be with her. Hamid wept for himself, for the thought of how weak and helpless his sister Amel was. He had left her alone with no one to love her, no one to read poetry with her, and no one to protect her. He also wept for his mother. He knew that his sister and mother would be poor, lonely, and helpless for years to come. He wept for his friends, for Hisham, Haleem, Salah, and Ashraf. As he stared at their graves, he wept for Ahmed and Adnan, his two gentle friends, who could not survive in a world created by the hatred and ambitions of beast-like humans. Instead, they chose to live in the form of ghosts in the dark deep of the Euphrates. He wept for all the Wolves and all the beautiful girls of Balluria. He wept for Balluria and for himself as he felt alone when he looked at the endless massive Arabian Desert calling him to absolute solitude and obscurity.

He never wondered why he was unable to leave; he never wondered why he was so attached to the dirt on the ground or the wind in the leaves of the palm trees. He felt the ravenous need to chew the leaves and rub them against his face and eat the dirt. The rain sent the aroma of belonging, in this life and in the hereafter; maybe it was the feeling of true belonging to a piece of land that everyone calls home, and there it was his home.

Sayed Habeeb once said, "The lord Allah covers with his mercy the brave and tough men who cry alone in the desert when they feel abandoned and lonely."

He could not help himself from feeling weak and lonely when he remembered those words, and he could not help himself from weeping for Kamal too.

Hamid spent the entire night talking to Hanan, in her grave, and talking to Kamal in the fresh dirt grave next to hers. He sat between the two graves, that of Kamal, his childhood friend and his adulthood foe, and the grave of Hanan, the woman they both loved but in different ways. He spoke to them as though they would answer.

"Why does it have to be this way, Kamal? Why couldn't it be that we are all live now? Why does have to be me who is still alive?" he asked and realized that he could only ask and would never get any answers, so he briefly allowed the silence to surround him. He asked questions he never dared to ask when they were alive and talked to the four graves of his four Wolves friends, who were buried hastily—Hisham, Ashraf, Salah, and Haleem—in one mass shallow grave. He wept for them all and all the other lost souls of desert thieves and illegitimate love children, secretly murdered sheikhs, and dishonored women who shared one final fate of being buried next to each other in the heavenly content solitude of a majestic piece of earth of the seven palm trees. He talked to them and asked them for answers. He asked for guidance but silence was his only answer and his only companion. Whatever the questions he asked and no matter how deep his sadness was, it was not enough to bring back the spirits of the departed to comfort his tormented and utterly lonely soul.

His horse grazed on the last remaining green grass by the graves as he stood up and put his meager belongings in the tan, cloth sack. He did not have much, and he had even less after giving the black dagger back to Barrya.

He had first wanted to keep the dagger. It was his to keep, the bloodthirsty weapon from hell that he earned. He believed that he had rightfully inherited the tool of death that shaped the bloody history of his hometown, but he knew that he would be inheriting the history of Balluria itself with all the devious motives and the feelings and the will and lust for blood; the same as Kamal and the same as Sheikh Jawad in their relentless pursuits of blood and fortune as they mistakenly searched for the mirage of true love. After dancing closely with the idea of embracing the power of the blade, he chose to give up the dagger, fearing that his soul could not bear the magnitude of the guilt of blood of the innocents. He wanted no part of that history and no part in this present and no part in that future.

He chose to give away the dagger to the only human worthy of keeping a secret. The dagger that had been party to so much death since it was formed so long ago by hands long buried. Its first victims were unknown to its current owner. It was the same dagger that Sheikh Jawad and Irar had used to kill their competitor Shershab and other competitors and many rival sheikhs. It was the same dagger Kamal had used to kill Hanan and cut off the palm of her hands to wash the shame and dishonor she brought on him and on her father, Sheikh Jawad, in the one honor killing to ever happen in Balluria since the beginning of time. It was the same dagger that he had used one night before to kill Kamal, the same dagger he drove deep into Kamal's welcoming flesh a hundred times. He had driven the dagger into the dark heart of his childhood friend, who betrayed the code of the Wolves and the secret sibling ties of Balluria.

He knew that he would be sentenced to death by the tyrant for desertion of the army, avoiding the mandatory service, and for the robberies of countless supply trucks loaded with flour sacks, which were heading to the south to aid the tyrant's defeated troops running away from the vicious fire of the American war planes. Instead, he and two other men stopped them with their fearsome rifles and forced the military truck drivers to unload their cargos and distribute them to the starving outskirt villagers and nomads, who had not eaten for long days. He was wanted for freeing numerous prisoners from the prisons near the marshes with his two notorious loyal outlaws: Rashid Al-Hacham and Jassim Al-Arbeed. They roamed the marshland on horseback while half of the provincial security forces were after them with help from special security guards, who came from the capital with orders to capture and kill the gang.

As the legend of Hamid and his group of outlaws grew, the people in the marshland started to call them many names and started to make stories about them, stories that were part true and part fiction. The people told stories about how the three men stormed the outpost of party militia headquarter s in Tawsheeha with two pistols, one in each hand, and shot all the party militiamen there and how they almost killed the provincial governor, and about how the three had never been caught because they were not really humans; they were ghosts from Allah sent to avenge the poor people and save them from the hands of the tyrant and his party militiamen.

People also said that the three wanted men had joined a notorious outlaw named Abu Hatem, or the prince of the marshes, in his relentless rebellion against the tyrant and his troops. That story was close to the truth because at that time Hamid and his two companions spent two months in the marshes sleeping with snakes and being eaten alive by mosquitoes. They joined the outnumbered and ill-equipped group of the notorious outlaw who, when a sizable government force attacked the floating scattered hideout huts of the notorious outlaw known as the prince of the marshes, the three barely survived the merciless helicopter attacks on defenseless buffalo herders and marsh Arabs. Hamid and his two loyal companions had walked for five nights and hidden during the days, until they reached the outskirts of Balluria, where they recovered their horses, which they had left with Rashid's cousin, a man who lived alone by the edge of the great marsh.

After the government troops' attack on the marshes, the three men escaped the marshes; after that, they stayed near Balluria. After that, Hamid was the not the same. He was silent all the time and deep into his thoughts. Something inside him had awakened the longing to his mother's scent and his sister's peaceful eyes. He wanted peace. He had grown tired of seeing dead bodies. He had grown tired of the stench of blood, the deteriorating flesh of corpses floated in the marshes; moreover, he had grown tired of his life. He never fought battles that were unjust, but he saw no end to his road. When Hamid and his two loyal companions reached the outskirts of Balluria, he wanted to see his family and wanted to seek the blessing and the approval of his mother before disappearing into the desert forever. He did not want to be like his father, who left without a trace and without a word. He did not want to leave his mother without a final word or a hug or what every Arab and Muslim man wanted, the blessing of their parents. Deep in his heart, he felt that the end might be near, and in many ways he led himself into the trap, the trap of yearning, knowing that it might mean his death.

That night, after he killed Kamal, he did not want to kill anyone anymore. He did not want to smell blood anymore. He did not want to hear any more stories that people made up about him. He did not want to be wanted or known anymore. He did not even want to hear or see or talk to any other human being. He just wanted to be and to breathe, and the deep desert was the only place he could be. He gave the cursed dagger to the old Gypsy woman and kept one thing, the one thing that was truly his, the only beautifully crafted thing that was bought with the clean money of sweat and hardship of his father, the poor peasant of the southland, a magnificent bluish-black robe glazed with silver lining that once belonged to his father, who he never knew. It was a bluish-black Arabian robe that had survived the hands of thieves of different names and different skin and hair and eye color, a bluish-black robe that survived the ignorant, violent searches and raids of the party militiamen and the wrath of the mortar bombs of the young and ruthless soldiers who obeyed the orders of the ambitious military officers who always became divine leaders and lifelong presidents. It was the bluish-black robe that his mother had kept in a wooden box with "Indian Tea Company" written on the side of the box that they used as a closet. She kept it safe from the moths and the deteriorating hands of time. For so many years, Hamid's mother had kept the only thing that her husband left her, hoping that she could see her only son wear it at his wedding, the wedding that never would be.

A part of her had given up the dream of him coming back since he was wanted at the age of eighteen for his many crimes against the people and against the state and the divine leader. She waited for years to see her only son once more. Every time she heard news about his exploits and his daring escapes, she wished that he would come by her house and stay for while so he could take a nap, dream, eat dinner, and talk. She never asked for more than that. So she prayed. She prayed that she would see him one more time, and that was the same night he was close to Balluria and felt the pinch of yearning in his heart that felt like the painful bites of millions of ants of hunger that had ravaged the stomachs and the senses of the people in these parts during the long years of the embargo. He felt the cries of the war widows and the fatherless children, who learned the word death before they learned the word love. He felt the excruciating pain of loneliness, and the waiting of millions of beautiful young girls who only had the choice between an endless wait and the steely sting of the honor blades. Hamid knew that the end was near, so he obeyed his yearning and insisted to his companions that he must return to Balluria to see his mother and sister one last time. Against their better judgment they agreed, even though they shared their concerns that they might be ambushed or captured, but loyal to the end, they followed him to their doom.

The three men had ridden to Balluria for the last time.

One night after he killed Kamal, after he learned of the deaths of his two loyal companions, and the same night he gave the Gypsy woman the cursed dagger that ended many lives, after he cried his last tears, Hamid wore his father's bluish-black robe, mounted his horse, and into the wide open desert he disappeared.

"It was then that the legend of the mythical Arabian knight was born in these parts," the old Gypsy woman said as she inhaled the last of her cigarette. "People in these parts say they often ran across a mythical-looking Arabian knight, in the darkness, riding his horse faster than the wind. Desert nomads claimed that they saw him by the borders as he was running with a pack of wolves. Even Sayed Habeeb told me once that he saw Hamid swimming in the river where he used to find so many things floating in the Euphrates.

"His myth grew, but people never believed he really existed. Even the party officials, the new mayor, and the government troops had declared him a myth and made it illegal to talk about him, his fearsome Kalashnikov, and his group of bandits who had all died. The government claimed that he was a hoax created by the government itself, so people would stop talking about him, but from time to time I saw many militia troops coming from the desert exhausted and beaten after they had chased after him for days and weeks without capturing him.

"Many people said that he died a long time ago. Others told that he married a jinni girl, a ghost bride from the world of the dead, and he is now just a ghost roaming the Arabian Sahara. Many said that Hanan had returned to earth in the form of jinni, and she took him with her forever.

"In the few times that I saw him, he was riding his horse into the mirage; his hair was long, and his beard covered his handsome face. Many travelers on the train from Baghdad said that they saw a long-haired, bearded man chasing the trains riding a majestic black Arabian horse. He shouted with a crying sound of pain and yearning to the world of the living. Travelers on the only train that went to the south said they saw a man who looked like an Arabian knight from a long time ago. He chased the trains, trying to stop them by shouting the shouts of pain. They thought he was trying to stop the train from traveling more to the south, where the final destinations were death, hunger, and despair. Many other passersby said that they heard the unearthly sound of a man howling like a wolf, crying over the graves by the seven palm trees at night.

"They all were telling the truth," the old Gypsy woman said.

"How so?" the man asked impatiently

"They saw Hamid. They did not know what they saw, but they all saw him. He ran with wolves, and he chased the trains full of humans who were unable to change the course of their destinies," the Gypsy woman said, adding to the man's confusion, before she explained, "Hamid was the wolf. He was the horse. He was the free wind that travels in the desert; he was the desert itself, and there was no time or reason left for him to live with us humans anymore. After what happened in Balluria, it was time for him to live the way he was destined to since the day he had been born. Free forever." She paused for a moment. "The crying sound everyone heard by the seven palm trees was genuine. When wolves howl, they cry, and when wolves cry, they cry alone." The old woman said this as she poured tea for the two of them.

ARMAND NASSERY

The Book of Balluria

The Home That Never Was and Always Will Be

1

By the time the old Gypsy woman stopped talking, the man had no pride left. His well-established self-loving, superior ego and limitless pride were reduced to fragmented remains of a facade. He felt like a lost child in the middle of a bazaar, filled with voices, scents, and tales of another life and another time, a life and a time that somehow were his to feel, hear, and live. When the old, blind Gypsy woman stopped talking, the man had the feeling of an intense, ravenous, and a sudden massive need to be touched by her. He wanted to extract from her hands the human sense of familiar warmth and unconditional acceptance that she naturally possessed and he so desperately needed. He extended his hands and reached out to hold hers. He touched them, and she let him; he held her hands and kissed her inner palms and washed her hands with his tears. She felt the warmth of his tears as they dripped between her fingers. They were the tears of a beaten man; tears of man who was at the end of his journey in search of love, a man who was tired from an endless search for redemption. Redemption from guilt that he never understood, or that he was ready to admit.

She gently pulled his hands and placed them on her heart and told him, "You must put your hands here, my son. You must put your hands on your heart, my son."

She was right. In the forty something years of his time on this earth, he had never put his hands on his heart. He had waited for others to put their hands on his heart. He wanted others to feel his pain first and to understand him. He never made an attempt to listen or to understand the others. He always wanted to be loved first but never offered his love.

When he placed his hand on his own heart for the first time and felt his own heartbeat, he realized the people that he had abandoned and the people that he was willing to abandon. All the people in his past and present life were not flawless paintings; they were not pieces of art that always must be in a remarkable harmony of subject and soul and color. They were just humans. When he felt his own heartbeat, the man realized that the perfect world that he envisioned, dreamed of, and searched for since the day he left Balluria was the world that he already knew; the world he lived in.

The life that he envisioned for himself as a man, was the life he knew and lived and would live for the coming years of his life. He must learn to love the life and be part of it, like a missing and much-needed touch of a brush of abstract colors in a beautiful flawless masterpiece of a painting. As he sat in the doorway of the forgotten mud hut of the old blind Gypsy woman, he realized that both of his worlds were the same. They were the same in many ways. They contained the same pains, needs, sufferings, joys, successes, disappointments, and journeys. Whether it was on the frigid corners of Chicago streets or in the sweaty afternoons of the Iraqi south, or in the dingy corners of the taverns of north side of Chicago or the in dark shade of the palm trees, the same hopes and dreams existed, like a diptych, two panels of a painting that must not be separated.

He knew it was time for him to leave the mud hut of the old, blind Gypsy woman but he needed something from her, something that would comfort him, a touch of a blessing or an approval or a sign of forgiveness. Perhaps a touch from her hands, which he desperately needed to make up for the forever lost life of his. He searched for it in the terrain of her face where the unkind years had engraved lines of merciless aging around her eyes and her mouth. He felt somehow responsible for the guilt of prolonged abandonment and desertion that he believed that he did not commit or at least he was not willing to admit. It was a feeling that was similar to what he had toward the dreams of his father or the hopes of his mother, the abandonment of his brother and sister, or the always ready and preemptive dismissals he had for the plans and dreams of his wife, Emily, or the unspeakable carelessness he imposed on the pure feelings and promises of the eternal love and endless waiting of Amel.

At that moment he was no longer prevented from love. He was no longer afraid of willingly admitting that he had always been chasing the mirage of true love. He had missed it so many times during his lifetime. He was no longer afraid to offer love. At that moment he felt that he was no longer prevented from loving the others, even when they were not as perfect as he thought they might be or as perfect as he thought they must be.

Maybe that's why he wanted the blind Gypsy woman to say or do something that would heal him. He needed a Gypsy remedy to redeem his overwhelming feeling of unexplainable guilt, yet he felt that he needed to do something that would show his gratitude. He wanted to somehow compensate the Gypsy woman for telling the story of the life that he could have lived, the story of the true friends and true friendship and true love and true life that he never had, the many stories of lost love, the stories of the Wolves, his friends. All gone now, but the old Gypsy woman who once chased the shadows with her laugh looked like she was done telling her stories forever. The blind old Gypsy woman, who once was able to boil the blood of the rugged hot-blooded men of the Arabian Desert with her dance moves and then reduce them to mere needy children with her seductiveness, was now blind, and strangely emotionless. She looked as though she had no more free true love to offer and that she needed someone to love her for a change. He remembered how beautiful her eyes had been and how her eyes always had the inviting look of a silent hunger and screaming ravenousness of all being.

In his mind as he sat in the doorway readying himself to leave, the man searched for the appropriate thing to offer her as compensation. With the quick and practical and most effective method of thinking he had learned from his long years in the West, he barely managed to make his offer: "I can take you to the hospital, for your eyes, or I can give you money."

She laughed the same laugh that woke up all the wolves of the Arabian Sahara and sent all the jinni daughters on their nightly hunt for free love and sinful pleasure and lost young princes. It was the same laugh that chased shadows off the walls of all the mud huts of absolute despair. She looked at him as though she could see him and said, "Since the beginning of time, and since Balluria was created, passersby thought that they could compensate us for a lifetime of pain with money or good deeds when all that is needed is true love."

He could not argue.

"I can see. I can see with my heart, but I don't need to see anymore," she proclaimed. "Why do I need eyes when all my children, all my beautiful boys and girls are gone? My children have waited all their lives for a true life. They have waited for a long time for a life of their own, but others will not let them have it. Passersby never loved my children, sheikhs with no hearts, kings with no feelings, military men with no true human senses, greedy thieves without love. All of those stole the color of life from of my children's eyes. I don't want to see anymore. I don't want to see a life filled with senseless constant fears."

She put out her last cigarette, looked at him, and said with the voice of a messenger revealing the truisms of forgotten religion, "Why do I need to be able to see when all my children who have spent all of their lifetime in meaningless waiting and went in journeys on all the roads that led to nowhere? All my children. All my young Wolves, my Wolves who just wanted to be left alone, playing in the vast fields of the Sahara, running with the Wolves, hunting doves and fishing in the Euphrates, and writing love letters to girls with long, black hair and big beautiful eyes. They are all gone."

As the Gypsy woman spoke, she threw in the fire all of her numerous and mysterious jars that contained the many Gypsy herbs and remedies for battle wounds and cures for little scratches and soccer injuries and all the remedies of love and broken hearts as she protested with her pained voice, "And all my beautiful little Gypsy witches never found true love."

The small fire lit up with magical colors and dizzying aromas as the man sat mesmerized, watching.

"My girls, oh, my poor beautiful girls, with beautiful big black and brown eyes, my girls who wanted only to be loved. My girls who dyed their hair with henna. My girls who loved to dance and read poetry. None of my girls had the chance to find true love."

She started to throw all the love letters and poetry papers and love artifacts that she kept in her little box of secrets into the fire. All of the tactile memories burned with alarming speed.

"My children have all gone, and so will you. You will be gone too," the blind Gypsy woman said as she stood up and started tearing down the burgundy curtains on her little windows and tossing them into the hungry fire as the wind outside whistled and the rain persisted.

Finally, exhausted, she sat and said, "So, my stranger son, what do I need eyes for? When there will no one or nothing to look at."

The man could not say a word. He did not reply as he watched the amazing colors rising from the little fire. The Gypsy woman sat down and pulled the fearsome black dagger from the box of secrets. She looked at the dagger, touched it, smelled it and slowly dangled it over the fire, and said with a quiet and serene tone that reflected the comfort of reaching the end of a long and exhausting journey; "My weak, true fire will burn the history, the blood, the leather, and the blade, of this damned black dagger, and then, my fire will die forever."

The man was speechless as he watched the blade and the leather hilt of the bloody black dagger melt in the fire, and he could not explain, ask, or talk. He watched the little, beautiful, and peaceful fire eat away the hardened metal of the damned black dagger that had ended so many lives—those of his friends and many others in these parts over so many lifetimes. He sat in the doorway and watched as the old Gypsy woman looked at him.

"There are no more stories to tell, my son. You must go now. You are healed. You will know how to love again." She stopped talking and stared through the flimsy lines of smoke that rose from the dying fire and into the empty space between her and the rest of the world through the open door that had never been shut.

"It's time for me to shut my door, because no one will ever come through it after today," she said as she looked to the space between her mud hut and the soccer field and Balluria as though she was bidding farewell to the outside, where the drizzly drops of rain gently played the sad whining music of final and eternal despair over the muddy walls of the tin roof. She had nothing else to say.

He stood up, looked at her, and felt the warmth of the minimal, yet true, sense of belonging start creeping to his heart. He felt that he was surrounded by all the sadness of the world, yet the hope of redemption was clear and heartfelt within. He felt older, weaker, and less able to move as he walked out of the room, leaving the old woman to the smoke of the little fire that started to fade more quickly than he thought it should. He left her to the eternal shadows that cast shapes of dreamy beings on the walls of the mud hut that had forever been and always would be standing on a chicken leg, as in all the histories of the Gypsy dancers and fairy jinni girls and lustful kings in the tales she told to the mesmerized young boys and girls.

The man walked away knowing that she was the tale. She was the ultimate fairy jinni girl and the ultimate and the last Gypsy witch that would walk the earth. She was Balluria. She was all the Ballurias that stretched from the shores of the Gulf to the tips of the freezing mountains of Turkey and from the eastern fronts of death to the shores of the Atlantic Ocean, where ships had sailed to the land of dreams filled with hopeful dreamers. He looked at her again, as he wanted to say farewell. He saw her with the eyes of the boy he was years ago and felt the souls within the mud hut entering him, urging him to stay and play with them in the mud and the little puddles of water created by the remarkably generous rain of the stingy southern skies.

The souls of his departed friends invited him to stay and play in the courtyard of the house where they once played. A tasty chill separated his skin from his bones and left him weak and less emotionally guarded. He wanted to cry, but he was barely able to shed two tears, one for her and one for himself. His shattered pride prevented him from crying more tears. His made-up composite of arrogance and pride, the last remains of fakeness and pretentiousness, prevented him from achieving the spiritual self-cleansing he had hoped for. Realizing that he was now free to seek his final redemption with love, he knew that he must go. It was time. He walked toward the outside door and slowly made his way toward Balluria, feeling like he walked forever to reach the door that would soon be shut. Looking back at the mud hut, he saw its door moving away from him like in an everlasting nightmare. He felt like he had walked for a thousand years to reach the door where he leaned on the side of the wall where the door of the Gypsy woman's mud hut was open to the outside world for the last time.

The man looked back at the old Gypsy woman one more time hoping for an invitation to go back, or a forgiving look, for a hug, or for a last inhalation of the smell, the same smell, that dragged him all the way from the gray and brown spiritless buildings of Chicago to this gate, to this dimension of another existence. He looked back to the old woman for the last time, but did not see her; instead, he saw a shadow of a mythical and mysterious being weaving and moving and dancing with the last lines of smoke that rose from the dying fire and disappeared into the scented air. In the darkness of the room, a shadow moved in the same manner as the Gypsy dancer. She was dancing as she always had in this life and all the other lives. The house started to disappear in the mist of foggy rain, bit by bit. The palm tree trunks that spiked their ends from the hut's roof started to fade in the mist of rain and warm fog as mysterious hands pulled them back into the mystical unknown. He was not afraid. It seemed like he was expecting what he was imagining, because he knew that this was the end of his tale.

The wind blew harder as he walked in the empty field, and the leaves of the palm trees sounded like the harmonic clapping of thousands of sweaty hands to joyful Gypsy dances. Even the stones were carried away by the same mysterious hands. The house started disappearing in the warm fog of the Iraqi southern rain. And it was gone. He felt that he was passing out and needed to sit down. He looked around and found himself standing in the empty soccer field, where he sat down and closed his eyes, listening to the remarkably harmonized sounds of rain and wind and the voice of the past. He sat in the middle of the soccer field and closed his eyes, letting the rain soak through his clothing, the rain that he loved so much and missed so much. He drifted in the land of numbing medium between sleeping and awakening, listening to the distant sounds of thousands of young Iraqi children singing and running in the rain, reciting the poem of Badr Shaker Al-Sayyab, talking to the rain and asking why he was left alone in the rain grieving for the lost love of the most beautiful girl in the south, Assia, the daughter of Chalabi Pasha.

O Rain, Rain halaby
Let the daughters cross
The daughters of Chalaby
Oh Rain. Rain Sha-Sha
Let the girls cross.
The Beautiful girls of Chalaby pasha
And I looked as I thought
Beautiful Assia will come to my date
At the place she told me she will
But she never came and her window was shot
Dust all my dreams had become
Myths all my feeling had became
And they grew like abounded trees
Fruitless and flowerless.

2

When Salam opened his eyes, he found himself in the middle of the soccer field. His hair was wet, and his light gray suit was drenched with rainwater. He looked back where the mud hut was and saw nothing. Was it just a dream? It could not be. He must have walked far away from the mud hut. His face was washed with rainwater, and he felt energetic and able to walk. He just wanted to make sure that he was alive, so he touched the ground and felt its warm wetness. Lovely, teasing small droplets of rain ran down his face through his hair, and he felt alive. His feet were heavy, but he managed to stand up and look at the space between the soccer field and the endless prairie, where there was nothing in front of him, nothing but an open space, clear and inviting. It was a complete freedom, where he could inhale all the oxygen of the world. The sky started to clear as he felt the breeze of the cold wind washing his soul. He stood there looking at the mysterious wavy lines of the mirage, when he noticed a silhouette on the horizon of a knight on a dark Arabian horse. His robes were long, and their ends waved as the horse ran to the endless desert behind the town. He thought to himself that this must be Hamid.

He ran toward the knight on the horse and screamed his friend's name with all of air in his lungs.

The mythical-looking knight briefly and slowly turned his head, looked at Salam, who could see the face of the knight vividly. Salam could not tell for certain if it was Hamid. It was the face of an older man, older than what Hamid would be. The mythical knight looked at him with a strange stare. Salam could see the many wrinkles of his rugged face as the mythical knight turned his face away and went into the desert. He went into the desert just as the legend says about Hamid. He came from the dust and returned to the dust. Salam stood in the middle of the soccer field, hoping for the knight to return. He remembered what the old Gypsy woman said in her chanting as she mourned the death of her Wolves.

"We die when the heart and eyes start to see other things without hope. The young will be old, and the right will be wrong. The beautiful becomes ugly. It is when the heart dies. Hope dies too, silently, and what is life without hope?"

Salam started to remember the words of the forgotten Gypsy song. Suddenly, he realized the meaning of her words, and he started reciting the Gypsy chants: *"What is life without hope? What is life without hope?"* Hope. Amel!

"Oh, my God. Amel. Amel. Is she still alive?" Salam walked in the mud back to the town, hoping to see another living human. He managed to reach the first street, where the prairie faded into the dusty street and the mud huts of Balluria started. He walked for twenty minutes before he saw an old Brazilian-made Volkswagen Passat that had no distinctive color. He looked and saw the man behind the wheel. He waved to the driver, who stopped cautiously as he looked at the dust-covered Salam in his wet gray suit. He looked like he had risen from the grave.

"Ha, may Allah help you. My brother, are you all right?"

"May Allah help you too. Can you take me somewhere? To the main square of the town, where I can find the taxi driver, who brought me here? His name is Alwan."

"Yes, I will take you there, sir. Are you all right?" the driver replied politely.

"He said he would wait for me."

"All right. Then he will. Maybe he went to fill his car with benzene."

"Maybe," Salam replied as he tried to look back at the soccer field and the mud hut.

"Did you come from the train station, sir?"

"No, no. I was at visiting an old friend of mine."

"Here in Balluria?"

"No, she lives on the outskirts of Balluria. A Gypsy woman. Her name is Barrya."

"A Gypsy woman?"

"Yes, do you know her? "

"Oh, my Allah. Are you all right, sir?"

"Yes, I am all right. Why are you asking?"

"Because, I think the Gypsy witch died long years ago."

"What? No, she is alive," Salam proclaimed. "She is alive, I tell you. I just saw her."

"All right, sir. As you say. Where should I take you?" the driver asked as he looked at the man sympathetically.

Salam was confused and drained, and he wanted to go somewhere, anywhere. He just wanted to make sure that the world that he knew still existed. After what he heard from the driver, he leaned against the window and looked at the houses, the faded houses, which looked like they were painted by an artist who ran out of colors and mixed the wrong colors just to finish. The impeccable yearning for the past overwhelmed him again. He closed his eyes and asked the driver, "Do you know of any candy store in this town? I need to eat candy."

The driver looked at him. "Do you want to go the other end of the town? I thought you wanted to go to the main road to find your driver."

"No, we will look for him later. Let us go and see if there is candy. I mean, I heard that there is a woman who sells candy somewhere."

"What did you say, sir, a woman selling candy?"

"Yes, I heard there is a woman who sells candy in this town," Salam said and tried to avoid looking into the driver's eyes for fear of being assumed mad or drunk.

The driver waited several seconds before he answered, "All the shops had moved nearer to the main road that leads to the big city in the province, but there is a lonely woman who sells nothing, just some old candy. No one knows where she gets it from. She barely sells one or two a day. She has been in her small shop at the end of the town for a long time. She was there long before my family moved to this town."

"Take me there to that shop, please," Salam begged the driver.

For the first time, he felt very familiar with his surroundings, as he started to remember the houses: the corners, the twisted tiny roads, and the windows of the old part of the town. He saw the corner where Adnan's house once stood, near the puddle filled with all the mosquitoes in the world. He saw the same street where he and Haleem had walked back and forth in the scorching afternoon sun waiting for the shadows of the Hillaly girls to peek from their window. He started to recognize and remember all the roads and all the windows. There was the street on which Adnan wrote and solved the longest mathematical problem in the world, followed by students from the high school in the big city. From there he could see the Euphrates. Oh, the Euphrates where Hamid found many floating things: boats, fishnets, and dead bodies. He saw the street where he and his brother and sister used to walk to and from school every day and the spot where his younger brother, who was a chronic walker, always slacked behind and screamed.

"Wilek, Salam. Hey, Salam, wait for me."

There was the spot near the public garden, where he and the rest of the Wolves sat and listened to the amazingly crafted stories of Fathil the Liar, the same spot where he and Hamid and Adnan and Kamal and Ahmed and Abdullah stood every day after school and waited for all the beautiful girls in Balluria to walk home. The place where they waited every day after school for a love letter and for the look of love or for a wink from a big beautiful eye. Just before the girls of Balluria went to their houses where they entered the secretive and prohibited world of women in these parts. From where he was, Salam looked at the orchard and saw Hamid's house, where Hamid showed him the pigeons and the many animals for the first time. Salam saw the house where Amel used to read him poetry in dark and sweaty shades of the southern summer.

"There she is," the driver said as he pointed with his hand to the end of the street.

"Where?"

"By the end of the street in the small shop." Salam's heart started pounding with anticipation and the softly piercing pain of the yearnings of the years. He felt a stony lump in his throat and had a strange desire to scream to Amel. There she was sitting in the same place where her mother had sat before selling candy to the children of Balluria. His heart started to beat more quickly as the car stopped in front of the small shop. The dark silhouette of Amel sat at the shop of the thousand walls selling candy wrapped in colorful paper. It was cheap candy, which offered the unmistakable taste of dreams. She was wearing the same clothes her mother had worn long years before. It seemed that with the candy shop she also inherited the solitude and the eternal waiting. She was looking at the space right in front of her eyes and no farther. She had an absolute contentment with what she had become. It was Amel, as he remembered the same Amel with her black, beautiful eyes reading poetry of lost love to him years ago. She was sitting alone in her candy shop, smoking her cigarette in the same manner the Gypsy woman Barrya did, blowing the smoke slowly and gently from her dark lips, waiting for time to pass. It was the same look in her eyes, similar to the look she had when he had melted her with prohibited emotions and desires and fears in the dark sweaty shades of her house as they listened to the pain-soothing voice of Fairuz signing the tale of the little young girl, who spent a lifetime waiting for true love. The sounds of the ultimate song of love echoed in his ears as he got closer to the candy shop.

I remember seeing people
Waiting for others

And when rain falls
They carry umbrellas
But they kept waiting
But for me, no one was waiting
Even when the sky was clear
No one was waiting
I have been here for one hundred years
In this little shop
The walls had hated me
I have been writing letters
To people with addresses I made up
And waited for the all dates of the earth
And no one wrote back
And no one waited for me
And still the people waiting for their lovers and friends
But no one was waiting for me.
Even in the clear beautiful days
No one was waiting.

After crying to the driver to stop, he looked at her. Her face had invited more than wrinkles. He face was darker than he remembered and sadder. She was sitting behind a small counter that rose a little bit from the ground. She did not look at the car stopping in front of her shop as she sat, wearing dark clothes and had covered her beautiful hair with the Sheila scarf. Her cigarette hung from the left side of her beautiful mouth. She looked like Barrya.

He felt degraded

In the cavern of his mind, he cried out, *Oh, my love, my darling. Oh, Amel. Oh, Amel. I am here.* He wanted to scream out loud, but he did not. His courage failed him again, one last time. He wanted to jump out of the car and run toward her, but courage had failed him yet again, and when their eyes met, hers were just like he remembered them. Her beautiful black eyes still had the ability to contain his soul. Her eyes were filled with the same ravenous flickering, with oppressed desires needing to be freed. The colors were of multiple layers of extraordinary patience built by years of waiting and suppressed pain. He could see the same eyes he saw years before, as she read the poetry of Bader Shaker Al-Sayyab in the heat of the dark shade of the mud hut. When she was able to steal tiny moments from time, life, history, and from the realities of an unreal place that was carved into his heart and conscience forever with words of Jebran Khaleel Jebran and Bader Shaker Al-Sayyab and with Fairuz's heavenly tunes of love. No one had ever touched his soul the way she had. No one had ever loved him the way she did, because she loved him the way she did, knowing that he was prevented from love. He realized that he had willingly deprived himself of love, and he knew it, and as much as he tried to permit himself otherwise he failed, but he kept pretending. As he sat in the car looking at her, wanting to ask her for forgiveness, just like he wanted to ask the Gypsy woman for forgiveness and just as he wanted his wife, Emily, for forgiveness, she noticed him.

Suddenly she noticed him. She noticed the look in his eyes. From behind her icy, shaded eyes she looked at the forty-something-year-old man with his long, black hair, glazed with gray and eyes staring at her, almost like those of a lost child would. She looked back at him without knowing who he was. Suddenly her eyes became bigger and shinier as she started to remember him. She smiled slightly with the same noble misery and the majestic weakness and proud humility and the undoubting acceptance of the unchangeable path that was her life. It had been a life that passed without stopping in the forgotten dusty corners of Balluria and without questions or answers and without complaining. It was a lifetime that passed by on hope, nothing but hope. He wanted to say something or to do something, but he felt the heaviness of his guilt and ignorance like iron chains on his feet and hands and heart. He wanted to ask her about herself and her mother. He wanted to ask her about Hamid and Kamal and Adnan and Ahmed and Hanan and the Hillaly Girls and Abdullah and Basima, Hisham, Haleem, Ashraf, Salah, and all the boys and girls that were once there filling the dusty roads of despair with love, dreams, laughter, and life.

Looking at her, he realized that she had nothing to tell him because just like the Gypsy woman had said, "They died a long time ago. They are all gone."

From her looks he realized that she would never be back, like he wanted her to be, and he would never be back like she wanted him to be. He realized that he was late and he, if he had to do it again, he would leave her in the dust again and would not stay. When Salam looked at Amel, he saw Hamid in her eyes and knew that her brother would keep running his wild horse through the southern Iraqi desert and across the borders many times. Because to Hamid there were no borders in chasing Hanan's spirit; she followed the path of the seven daughters of the seven kings, who in their need to live and in their pursuit of love, had committed the ultimate sin and the ultimate grievance by breaking the unbearable chains of traditions. They had dishonored their fathers and turned into seven fairy jinnies who kidnapped lost princes and handsome brave young men and kept them as prisoners of love as they lived an eternity singing the jinni songs written by the lost poet and answering the calls of forbidden body lust and unchaining the secrets of women's desires.

When Salam looked at Amel, he saw Adnan in her eyes, and he knew that Adnan would always keep sailing the Euphrates with his armada of small empty boats, searching for the origin of the meanings to his solitude and the many answers that would consume all the whys and where's and who's, not in an eternal search for the truth. When Salam looked at Amel, he saw Kamal in her eyes, and he realized that Kamal would always be consumed with his hate of himself and his fate and his loneliness. Yet at the same time he would always be yearning to be just a boy with a father, a kid just like other kids, and he would always curse the Kurds for killing his father in the war that meant nothing to the world, but to him it meant living life without a father forever. When Salam looked at Amel, he saw Abdullah and Basima in her eyes, and he realized that Abdullah and Basima would always be traveling the trains of Europe searching for the cottage with the fireplace, waiting to feel safe once and forever and to have two baby girls living in a land with white snow and majestic mountains. When Salam looked at Amel, he saw Hisham in her eyes, and he knew that Hisham would always run the dusty fields of soccer with or without legs, and one day he would score a goal just like the goal scored by Steve Highway of Liverpool against Manchester United or the one Maradona of Argentina scored against England or the one Falah Hassan of Iraq scored against Austria. When Salam looked at Amel, he saw Bushra, Adwaya, and the Hillaly girls. And he knew that the Hillaly girls would grow their hair to infatuate young men in these parts, and they would keep a clip ready for unfortunate soldiers who waited for love all their lives. Yet somehow they had the time to join another unfortunate revolution in the land of eternal revolutions and everlasting rebelliousness. They would be able to make a young man's heart beat with life as it was shredded to pieces by the bullets of a firing squad.

When Salam looked at Amel, he saw himself, and he knew that he was too late because unlike lives in other places, the lives in these parts do not wait for humans. Instead, life here stomps at them and passes quickly without stopping to feel the pain. When Salam looked at Amel, he saw her. He saw Amel, and he knew that she would never leave the candy shop. He knew that she would never leave the Euphrates, and he knew that she would never leave Balluria. He knew she would always be there to document their lives with her poetry. She would always keep writing letters to people with no addresses and wait for responses that would never come, and she would be there reminding the departed that they have a home, and she would wait for them to come back. She would keep reading poetry to the exhalation of hearts and souls and witnessing the passing of her own life and the lives of others.

When Salam looked at Amel, he realized that he was too late. He did not want to interrupt the delicate balance of a life and fates and emotions that existed without him. When Salam looked at Amel, he saw in her eyes the same sadness he saw long before in the dark shade of her house, a sad look he was too afraid to question and too arrogant to understand. When Salam looked at Amel, he saw the same sadness she had in her eyes when she read the poetry of a redundant chanting of life in these parts. Salam remembered that she always cried when she read the last chapter of the poem of lost poet Badr Shaker Al-Sayyab, who spent the last years of his life on his deathbed not able to walk as he waited in Kuwait yearning for the smell of the southern Iraqi soil as the aromas of true belonging rose from it, agitated by the water of the Iraqi summer rain, when the splashes of refreshing rain cleansed the tired hearts and played the symphony of misery, boredom, and infinite waiting. When Salam looked at Amel, he remembered the words of the poem, and he remembered that Amel always had a tear in her big, black, beautiful eyes as she recited the lines with her pained voice.

> *No year had past and there was no hunger in Iraq*
> *No year had passed and there was no pain in Iraq*
> *In Iraq*
> *A thousand snakes drinks the juice of the flowers*
> *As the souls of the poor grinds in the*
> *Mills of despair*
>
> *Twenty years had passed like ages every year*
> *And now whenever. Darkness falls*
> *And as I lay in bed with no hope to sleep*
> *And listen to voice in my conscience*
> *And On my pillow*
> *I feel the coldness of your summer breeze*
> *Oh Iraq*
> *When I will sleep*
> *And when all you're lost sons in*
> *All of the world*
> *Feel at home in within you*
> *Within you is death*
> *Death is mystic place*
> *A Mysterious playground*
> *That infatuates all children*
> *And*
> *Its secret gates*
> *Are Here*
> *In you, Oh Iraq.*

He looked at Amel, and he realized that he must leave, at least for now, because no matter what he might be able to say, or no matter what his courage would allow him to tell her, he would need more than minutes or hours and days. He would need years. He would need a lifetime to prove to her that he was not barred from love anymore, and it would take a lifetime to prove to her that he would not leave again, and he would need a lifetime to prove to her that despite the eternal waiting and despite distances and oceans and borders and languages, her letters finally reached someone, and that someone was him. And he was answering and returning the letters. Salam looked at Amel's beautiful, black eyes, smiled slightly, and waved his hand. She looked at him the same way and smiled at this middle-aged man so out of place in a world he once lived in.

Her eyes were shining as they always did. She lifted her hand, saying hello and farewell at the same time, just as twenty-five years earlier Amel chased the departing car with sad eyes. Just as twenty-five years before, he left the town, leaving her and Balluria, like a ghost disappearing in the dust.

3

After waiting for an hour by the main road, Alwan sped up and waved from the windshield of his car. The driver stopped and interrupted his passenger's reverie.

"I think this is the man who drove you here, sir."

Salam looked and saw Alwan waving from his car window and said, "Yes, that is the car."

Alwan, who looked as though he had just returned from a battle, was apologetic and loud. "I had to go to the other town to find some benzene. There is no gas station anywhere in these parts."

Salam did not mind the tardiness of Alwan, and he generously paid the other driver, and said to him, "The Gypsy woman is alive. She must be alive."

"Yes, sir, whatever you say," said the other driver, smiling at the bundle of American dollars that Salam gave him. "Thank you. Thank you, sir. You are most generous."

Salam sat in the backseat of Alwan's car, thinking of the way Amel looked at him, and said to Alwan, "Take me back to Baghdad, Abu Husain."

The picture of Amel's eyes did not leave him as he leaned on the window and felt an overwhelming desire to sleep for a long time.

"Would you be willing to take me all the way to the Jordanian border? I will pay you the price you want."

"Only for you, sir. I will charge two papers."

"Two papers? What is that?"

"Yes sir. Two hundred American dollars."

"All right, take me there then," Salam said, hoping that Alwan would stop talking for the remaining part of the long trip, so he could have some sleep, something that he had not had for a long time, but he did not mind Alawn's random talking and his irrelevant questions about how easy or hard it is to meet women in the bars in the United States, because Salam knew that for now he would be able to sleep. For now the trip to Baghdad would be tiring and exhausting, and then the trip from Baghdad to the Jordanian border through the desert highway would be long and unsafe. Alwan seemed very agitated and energetic. He sounded energetic, and he looked like he had more questions about America and the West, and he also seemed to have more stories to share and to tell. He looked like he would talk for hours, but was OK. He was willing to listen this time, or at least he was planning to be polite, because for now the sun was glorious and its rays were clear and warm, shining on the cold dark little heart of his, warming it with hidden feelings he never felt or that he had long forgotten, and strange sensations pained him with the tasty pain of redemption.

For now he would leave Balluria and not look back at it with its dusty, old Gypsy witch and the house on the chicken leg, which was like it was always: a tale. For now, he would sleep and dream. No one can tell the future, not even Barrya with her Gypsy powers. This time, when his eyes closed, there would be no mysterious hands with a silky touch that would prevent him from breathing. Now he would put his arm under his heavy head and go to sleep. Perhaps he would catch a dream. Maybe he would see all the faces of his childhood friends. Maybe he would see Hamid running after a wild, Arabian horse so he could ride it into the wilderness. Or in his dream, he would see Hamid for one last time just to tell him how much he missed him and how much he wished he had taken that wild horse ride long years ago and had gone to the prairie to live like red Indians they saw on television shows. In his dream he might see Hisham score a vengeful and long-awaited goal against the Wild Lions with a double kick and humiliate them when all the girls of Balluria were looking from their windows.

His dreams might show Ahmed left alone and not forced to face the challenges of the traditions of honor and manhood in these parts, free from the burdens of an unexplainable and imposed heritage. Maybe in his dream he would see Haleem looking at the window of the Hillaly girls and maybe they would open it for a change. Or maybe he would see Adnan still thinking about math and Einstein and the theory of relativity and the theory of creation and the big bang theory and the secret books of all the religions and the basic answers for the existence of mankind, yet smiling with joy as he dipped his hand in the cold December water of the Euphrates lying in the front of the safeena boat with no fear in his eyes.

He would not have fear anymore because the divine leader's henchmen were all gone now just as all the women who wore black robes had escaped from lifetime imprisonment of Sheikh Jawad's house after he died. There would be no more dark dungeons of torture and no snakes and cats in tanned sacks and no more diabolical, mean men with thick moustaches and big bellies. For now there would be no more dark and humid underground dungeons where young, weak and flimsy bodies and beautiful minds are melted in the nitric acid tubs.

For now he would dream and maybe he would see Abdullah and Basima living quietly as they always wanted to, somewhere in a wooden house in the snowy hills of Denmark where the snow never melts. They would have no fear on their faces of freezing smuggler's routes and no fear of honor retributions as they lived in the small world they wanted to create with two beautiful little daughters named Niema and Rahma, blessing and mercy.

Now he would dream. Maybe he would see Hanan with her palms still attached to her wrists and her beautiful body intact, and her wild eyes still burning with all life's desires and her hair still smelling of the fake French perfume. Or maybe he would see Haleem, Salah, Hisham, and Ashraf as they stood facing the fiery saliva of the party death squads' rifles with their wide beautiful, black eyes and tanned, textured skin looking at the windows of the Hillaly girls as Bushra and Adawya unleashed the secrets of the darkness of the black colors of their hair. Maybe he would see the spot in her hair where she cut off the lock and the "I will love you forever" spelled by the deep black color of her eyes, and maybe he would see that he was with them in the line of death holding someone's hair clip. Maybe Amel's hair. And maybe he would be able to push Hisham away in his wheelchair and save his life and die in his place, or he would see Kamal drunk, yet serene, as he realized how simple life could be without thinking too much about things or how easy it would be to just exist without hate, and he could have a normal talk with him and maybe he could convince Kamal to live with no fear, no fear from a fearsome sheikh, the divine leader, or anyone.

If he were so fortunate, he could see Barrya as he remembered her with her tan skin covered with tattoos and the smell of biscuit-sweaty skin that lasted for centuries as she was leaning toward him, offering him the freshest yogurt in the history of mankind. And when he looked into the dark terrain of the shadows of her breasts he felt like he found a home in her dark-skinned lips and amazingly white teeth and the waves of her exuberant locks of hair hitting his dizzy head with invitations of an exciting manhood, an invitation to the mad world of women's eternal warmth and lust. Maybe he would see his brother Wisam, who grew up to be a better man than he. He grew into a man who cared about family and country, a man who cared about other humans who needed help and needed and counted on the strength of true, brave man. If he saw his younger brother, he would hug him and tell him that he always thought that he was the best brother any man could have. And if he should see his pest of a sister or his mother who offered the love of the world to him, he would kiss her hands in gratitude.

For now he would sleep because he wanted to see his father in his dream. He wanted to sit down and talk with him man-to-man, leaving all worldly worries and differences aside, and he would ask his father for forgiveness and he would be forgiven. In his dream maybe he would have a family again.

Now Salam wanted to sleep and dream because in his dream he would see Emily and tell her, "Yes." They will have a baby and name it two names, one Iraqi and one American. Maybe they would name it Hamid and Eric as he wanted or Shawn and Hussain like she wanted to. He wanted to dream because he wanted to see his wife, Emily. Oh, Emily, how much he missed her and how much he needed to hug her and tell her that he had loved her since the day he saw her and wanted to be with her forever, but he was afraid that she might be a female wolf from another continent, a continent with blond hair and blue eyes. He was afraid because he thought that she was from a pack of wolves who looked tired and busy all the time; wolves who liked the cold winters of Chicago and New York and Montreal. Wolves who lived in massive and meaningless structures of the massive forests of steel and concrete and communications wires. Wolves who hunted mercilessly even if they weren't hungry not like any other wolves, not like his pack of wolves that roamed the Arabian wilderness and lived on minimal necessities and copious amounts of poetry.

But for now he wanted to sleep, and he wanted to dream. He wanted to see Emily to tell her that he had an idea. He would ask her if she would come back with him to Balluria and start their own Wolves family, a pack of half-breeds. How they would look beautiful, with a mixture of his tanned skin and her piercing blue eyes and their curly long hair. Maybe she would agree to come here and get away from the godlessly cold winter nights of Chicago, and they could open a gallery or build the soccer field or have a pottery shop like she always wanted.

For now he lost his ability to debate, and he was willing to admit all of his guilt. For now he would sleep and dream about Emily and ask her if she wanted to come back with him to Balluria and build another gallery, a gallery of a true and meaningful harmony of colors and subjects and life.

And for sure, her father would help them just like the good American Midwesterner he was, who always was working to cure his racism and prejudices with the natural kindness of a genuine human.

As he felt the heaviness of a tasty drowsiness creeping into his head, he thought of Emily, as she was always a reasonable and loving partner. She was always there, no matter what. Oh, Emily, he would see that it did not matter now because there was still time. It did not matter because for the first time, he was not afraid and not guilty. For the first time, he was not mad or angry at anyone. He let Alwan talk about how things were getting bad in some parts of the country as people started feeling the heavy presence of the their heavily armed and extremely standoffish guests who didn't speak the language and carried weapons to kill the adults in one hand and sweet candy to give to the children in the other hand. He could barely hear Alwan's stories as his voice grew distant. He complained of the many roads that were turned by the heavy armored vehicles of the Americans and other soldiers who came from faraway country to these parts.

When Salam fell asleep for the first time since he left Chicago, when he closed his eyes, he started hearing another sound similar to the church choir recital that his wife liked to go to, and he always wanted to attend with her. In his dream, Salam looked around in the vividly visible shapes and faces of people and amazingly familiar places of his dream. He saw Amel sitting in the same shady corner of the old dark room in her house, and with her sat Emily. They both recited poetry. Salam knew that he was dreaming again. In his dream that pulled him to that world again, it was Amel's voice reciting the poetry of Bader Shaker Al-Sayyab. He started listening as he saw her sitting in her light blue dress in the dark room of Hamid's house, listening to Fairuz singing the same song of a lonely girl left behind, and none of her loved ones or her friends cared to remember her. She sang in a crying voice.

The gentle bells of tasty sleepiness started ringing gently in his ears. He tried to remember the poem that Amel was reciting and that his wife, Emily, was listening to. He remembered that it was the same poem Amel read to him just before he left Balluria forever. He had never liked the poem, but he remembered every word, but this time the poem was different in its words and different in its sounds and different in the way Amel sang it. Her eyes were shining with a pearl of tears, and her voice was deeper than all the other times she had read poetry, as she looked at him, searching for an emotion as he saw her for the first time as the woman she was or the woman she wanted him to see her as.

Twenty years have passed by
And no one returns, for they have no home
Like me, like the Euphrates, like the poor
A forest of tears you are?
Or just a river?

In his dream, Amel looked like the other people he knew. She looked like Barrya, with her eternal lust for life and her nobility and acceptance of pain and abuse like a fallen, sinful angel from the heavens of the righteous, who secretly wanted to follow her to her sinful life. Amel looked like Hanan, with her easy ability to sin and amazing courage to go beyond the imaginary borders of decency as it was set by the ignorance and shortcomings of males in these parts for thousands of years. In his dream, Amel looked like his sister with her questions and wonderings and the will to ask and discover. She looked like his mother, with her secret pact with patience and the ability to endure the constant pains and sorrows and the acceptance of disappointments as a companion for life. Amel looked like all the women in his life. She looked like all the women who loved him and never needed to. Amel looked like all the women he thought he loved. She looked like all the women he was searching for. In his dream Amel looked needy, yet standoffish, wanting but selective, pained but elegant, reserved but full of possibilities. Weak but full of hope.

As she finished her last lines of the poem that summed all the pain and dreams of generations of beautiful young boys and girls who waited for true love to come, he heard the yearning of all of those who left Balluria but whom Balluria never left.

He realized now that the poem was for him. He looked back at Amel and wished for her to start reciting poetry again.

He felt the sun's rays piercing the windshield. They pinched him gently on his cheek. His long hair moved to the center of his face as he kept looking in

Amel's face. He knew that he was dreaming and that she was not there, but he heard her voice as she read the poem, and Fairuz's voice was clear, and the colors of her hair and her eyes and the shades of the room were truly vivid and touchable. And although Alwan was talking to someone on the cell phone very loudly, the man kept dreaming and looking at Amel's face. He was looking at her eyes, deep in her eyes. And he realized that her eyes were not all black, not completely, beautifully black. He noticed she had a little green in her eyes, just a little green around the big, sad, sleepy, tired, black pupils. He thought to himself that her name was hope. As he fell into a deep sleep, he mumbled the last lines of the poem they had both liked and read many times in the dark shades of the southern Iraqi orchards. They were just like the green fields of Indiana and the Midwest in the late spring, and suddenly he heard his own voice, reciting his favorite Bader Shaker Al-Sayyab poem, and he did not see the women who were sitting to him listening. He could not tell if it was Amel and Emily. It did not matter since it was a dream, a dream that lasted a lifetime to be realized as reality, a dream that had been waiting in the hearts and minds of all the people in these parts. He started mumbling the poem with Barrya as she was running in the desert wind with her arms open. He started reciting the poetry with Hanan as she ran for Hamid, and he started reciting the poem as he ran with Hamid, riding two historical Arabian horses, and all of the wolves were there too.

In his dream, and as he slept peacefully for the first time, Salam saw Hamid running his horse, and he knew that Hamid would never be slave for any man even if he lived for thousands of years. He would always be like all the Arabian horses roaming the desert free forever, and Barrya was dancing, and he knew that Barrya was and would always be honorable and decent and as beautiful as the wilderness of Arabian Sahara itself.

In his dream Salam started reciting the poem with Emily as she spoke Arabic with no fear. He started reciting the poem with Emily and Amel together as their eyes shined with true love. They all started reciting the ultimate poem of Bader Shaker Al-Sayyab.

The sun is brighter and prettier in my country
Brighter than the sun in other places
Even the darkness is prettier
Because it hugs Iraq
Because you are there my love
In Iraq
And Your eyes
Your eyes are like two forests of palm trees
At the early hours of dawn
Or two balconies when the moon light
Moves away and leaves its half shadows
When your eyes smiles

WHERE WOLVES DREAM

The grape vines will blossom
And lights will dance like moons
At night on the Euphrates water.

In his dream, Salam looked at Amel, and he was wondering who she looked like. Because he could see that between all the people in his past and present and maybe the people that would be in his future life, she looked like that one person, that one person that knew him very well, loved him very much, and accepted him without preconditions. She looked like his wife, Emily, with her assuring commitment to love him and her comforting acceptance of him as a man and as a partner and as a husband and, ultimately, as a human.

In his dream, Salam knew that he was dreaming, and he was happy because after all of these years he felt that he could dream sweet dreams, like what Emily wished him to have before he fell asleep every night. He knew that he would be himself again. He would be able to love again, and he would not stop loving. He knew that he would have all of his life to tell Emily that he loved her and work all his life to keep that love alive because he knew that only love would make dreams come true, and he also knew that he would return to Balluria again and that he would tell Amel that he loved her too, and he would have what would be left of his lifetime to never let her lose hope.

He smiled, realizing that he could sleep again and dream again, and while the car made its way northward toward Baghdad, passing by numerous convoys of military armored vehicles, he laid his head against the car window, enjoying the touch of the tasty sunrays on his face. He smiled slightly, thinking about the names of the two women who loved him and never needed to; the two woman that he must learn to love and dedicate his lifetime to. He must live, cherish, and keep that love. He smiled in his dream as he realized that their names were the same. They were the same in different letters of different languages and even though there were thousands of miles between them, the names of the two women he loved meant the same thing. Their names were the same. The ways they loved him were the same, and the way that he must learn how to love and must love forever was the same. Amel and Emily. Amel. Hope. Emily, my hope. These were the two names that would make tomorrow better than today. The two names that he truly loved: Amel and Emily: both names meant hope.

Amel. Hope , Emily. My Hope.

Everlasting Green Hope, just like the strong, beautiful and mysterious hollows of mixed black and green colors in their beautiful eyes.

(The End)

(Personal note)

This novel was completed exactly one year after the passing of my mother, the ultimate green hope that kept me and the wolves dreaming. It was completed on March 7, 2010, the same day Iraqis went to the election polls, in the first true democratic election in Balluria, that is, Iraq.

Badr Shakir Al-Sayyab

Born in southern Iraq, Al-Sayyab's mother passed away when he was only a child. As a result, Al-Sayyab spent much of his youth a lonely boy with few friends. Out of this loneliness, Al-Sayyab discovered a joy for writing. Crafting poems detailing the sting of isolation and young love, he was able to fully express the thoughts he kept locked away from the always-prying eyes of nosy relatives and busybody neighbors.

Al-Sayyab eventually found a warm sense of camaraderie with local youth cadre of the Iraqi Communist Party. However, Iraq's brutal ruling Ba'athist regime had little patience for social or political agitators. Constantly on the run from Ba'ath Party persecution, Al-Sayyab grew tired of the chase, choosing to leave Iraq in the early 1960s. While in exile, Al-Sayyab contracted a crippling disease that left him bedridden. Essentially immobilized and wracked with pain, Al-Sayyab continued to write poem after poem. His words led readers into both Al-Sayyab's smoky and twisted Baghdad corners and dingy bars and the bright, exhilarating sunny open spaces of southern Iraq he had known as a child. For years, he yearned to return to Iraq, but he feared he would be an easy target for the Ba'athists. After his death in a quiet Kuwaiti back room, Al-Sayyab's body was smuggled back into Iraq in the back of a taxi. In an ironic twist, a thunderstorm marked the arrival of Al-Sayyab's remains into Iraq, ending months of drought.

For younger Iraqis, Al-Sayyab remains the very definition of "youthful dreamer": deep in thoughts and very much alone, yet at the same time,

591

genuinely inspired by his memories and hopes for brighter days Iraqis, Arabs, and humanity.

Fairuz

The famed Lebanese diva Fairuz has been an inspiration to millions of love-struck Arab youth for decades. She has been one of only a handful of artists capable of touching the very soul of Arab romantic culture. Beginning in the secluded valleys of eastern Lebanon some forty years ago, she continues to win devoted fans from all ages across the Arab Middle East. From Baghdad's urban sprawl to even the smallest, most insular Algerian villages, her songs can be heard echoing everywhere, from world-class sound stages to the crackly speakers of a hand-cranked radio.

Her heartfelt lyrics, delicate voice, and soulful tunes continue to offer young Arabs an escape from the region's restrictive social atmosphere, faltering economy, and stifled political space. Her albums crack open the window, letting in a fresh breath of badly needed, heavily perfumed air. And the genuine hope of true love.

www.ingramcontent.com/pod-product-compliance
Lightning Source LLC
Chambersburg PA
CBHW030740030726
47497CB00001B/68